Ten Thousand A Year

Vol. 1

By

SAMUEL WARREN

COMPLETE IN ONE VOLUME

WILDSIDE PRESS

Fortuna, sævo læte negotio, et
Ludum insolentem ludere pertinax,
   Transmutat incertos honores,
     Nunc mihi, nunc alii benigna.
Laudo manentem. Si celeres quatit
Pennas, resigno quæ dedit, et mea
   Virtute me involvo, probamque
     Pauperiem sine dote quæro.—HORACE.

Fortune, that with malicious joy
   Does man, her slave, oppress,
Proud of her office to destroy,
   Is seldom pleased to bless;
Still various, and unconstant still,
But with an inclination to be ill.
Promotes, degrades, delights in strife,
And makes a lottery of life.
I can enjoy her while she's kind;
—But when she dances in the wind,
And shakes the wings, and will not stay,
I puff the prostitute away:
The little or the much she gave, is quietly resigned;
   Content with poverty my soul I arm,
And virtue, though in rags, will keep me warm.
          HORACE—BY DRYDEN

PREFACE.

The Author of this Work begs gratefully to express his conviction that no small share of any success which it may have met with, is attributable to the circumstance of its having had the advantage of an introduction to the public through the medium of *Blackwood's Magazine*—a distinguished periodical, to which he feels it an honor to have been, for a time, a contributor.

One word, only, he ventures to offer with reference to the general character and tendency of " TEN THOUSAND A YEAR." He has occasionally observed it spoken of as merely a " comic," " an amusing and laughable " story; but he can not help thinking that no one will so characterize it, who may take the trouble of reading it throughout, and be capable of comprehending its scope and object. Whatever may be its defects of execution, it has been written in a grave and earnest spirit; with no attempt whatever to render it acceptable to *mere* novel-readers; but with a steadfast view to that development and illustration, whether humorously or otherwise, of principles, of character, and of conduct, which the author had proposed to himself from the first, in the hope that he might secure the approbation of persons of sober, independent, and experienced judgment.

Literature is not the author's profession. Having been led, by special circumstances only, to commence writing this work, he found it impossible to go on, without sacrificing to it a large portion of the time usually allotted to repose, at some little cost both of health and spirits. This was, however, indispensable, in order to prevent its interference with his professional avocations. It has been written, also, under certain other

considerable disadvantages—which may account for several im-
perfections in it during its original appearance. The periodical
interval of leisure which his profession allows him, has enabled
the author, however, to give that complete revision to the
whole which may render it worthier of the public favor. He
is greatly gratified by the reception which it has already met
with, both at home and abroad; and in taking a final and a
reluctant leave of the public, ventures to express a hope, that
this work may prove to be an addition, however small and
humble, to the stock of healthy English literature.

London, October, 1841.

NOTE.—For the beautiful verses entitled " PEACE," (at page 194),
the author is indebted to a friend.

TEN THOUSAND A YEAR.

CHAPTER I.

ABOUT ten o'clock one Sunday morning, in the month of July, 18—, the dazzling sunbeams which had for several hours irradiated a little dismal back attic in one of the closest courts adjoining Oxford Street, in London, and stimulated with their intensity the closed eyelids of a young man lying in bed, at length awoke him. He rubbed his eyes for some time, to relieve himself from the irritation occasioned by the sudden glare they encountered, and yawned and stretched his limbs with a heavy sense of weariness, as though his sleep had not refreshed him. He presently cast his eyes on the heap of clothes lying huddled together on the backless chair by the bedside, and where he had hastily flung them about an hour after midnight; at which time he had returned from a great draper's shop in Oxford Street, where he served as a shopman, and where he had nearly dropped asleep after a long day's work, in the act of putting up the shutters. He could hardly keep his eyes open while he undressed, short as was the time required to do so; and on dropping exhausted into bed, there he had continued in deep unbroken slumber, till the moment at which he is presented to the reader. He lay for several minutes, stretching, yawning, and sighing, occasionally casting an irresolute glance toward the tiny fire-place, where lay a modicum of wood and coal, with a tinder-box and a match or two placed upon the hob, so that he could easily light his fire for the purposes of shaving and breakfasting. He stepped at length lazily out of bed, and when he felt his feet, again yawned and stretched himself. Then he lighted his fire, placed his bit of a kettle on the top of it, and returned to bed, where he lay with his eye fixed on the fire, watching the crackling blaze insinuate itself through the wood and coal. Once, however, it began to fail, so he had to get up and assist it, by blowing, and bits of paper; and it seemed in so precarious a state that he determined not again to lie down, but sit on the bedside; as he did, with his arms folded, ready to resume operations if

necessary. In this posture he remained for some time, watch‐
ing his little fire, and listlessly listening to the discordant jan‐
gling of innumerable church-bells, clamorously calling the
citizens to their devotions. The current of thoughts passing
through his mind, was something like the following:—
"Heigho!—Lud, Lud!—Dull as ditch water!—This is my
own holiday, yet I don't seem to enjoy it!—for I feel knocked
up with my week's work! (A yawn.) What a life mine is, to
be sure! Here am I, in my eight-and-twentieth year, and for
four long years have been one of the shopmen at Tag-rag and
Co.'s, slaving from half past seven o'clock in the morning till
nine at night, and all for a salary of £35 a year, and my
board! And Mr. Tag-rag—eugh! what a beast!—is always
telling me how high he's raised my salary! Thirty-five pounds
a year is all I have for lodging, and appearing like a gentle‐
man! 'Pon my soul! it can't last; for sometimes I feel get‐
ting desperate—such strange thoughts come into my mind!—
Seven shillings a week do I pay for this cursed hole—(he
uttered these words with a bitter emphasis, accompanied by a
disgustful look round the little room)—that one couldn't swing
a cat in without touching the four sides!—Last winter, three
of our gents (*i. e.*, his fellow-shopmen) came to tea with me
one Sunday night; and bitter cold as it was, we four made this
cussed dog-hole so hot, we were obliged to open the window!—
And as for accommodation—I recollect I had to borrow two
nasty chairs from the people below, who on the next Sunday
borrowed my only decanter, in return, and, hang them, cracked
it!—Curse me, say I, if this life is worth having! It's all the
very vanity of vanities—as it's said somewhere in the Bible—
and no mistake! Fag, fag, fag, all one's days, and—what for?
Thirty-five pounds a year, and ' *no advance !*' (Here occurred
a pause.) Bah, bells! ring away till you're all cracked!—Now
do you think *I'm* going to be mewed up in church on this the
only day out of the seven I've got to sweeten myself in, and
sniff fresh air? A precious joke that would be! (A yawn.)
Whew!—after all, I'd almost as lief sit here; for what's the
use of my going out? Everybody I see out is happy, excepting
me, and the poor chaps that are like me!—Everybody laughs
when they see me, and know that I'm only a tallow-faced
counter-jumper—I know that's the odious name we gents go
by!—for whom it's no use to go out! Oh, Lord! what's the
use of being good-looking, as some chaps say I am?''—Here
he instinctively passed his left hand through a profusion of
sandy-colored hair, and cast an eye toward the bit of fractured
looking-glass that hung against the wall, and which, by faith-

fully representing to him a by no means ugly set of features (despite the dismal hue of his hair) whenever he chose to appeal to it, had afforded him more enjoyment than any other object in the world for years. "Ah, by Jove! many and many's the fine gal I've done my best to attract the notice of, while I was serving her in the shop—that is, when I've seen her get out of a carriage! There has been luck to many a chap like me, in the same line of speculation: look at Tom Tarnish—how did he get Miss Twang, the rich piano-forte maker's daughter?—and now he's cut the shop, and lives at Hackney, like a regular gentleman! Ah! that *was* a stroke! But somehow it hasn't answered with *me* yet: the gals don't take! How I have set my eyes, to be sure, and ogled them—all of them don't seem to dislike the thing—and sometimes they'll smile, in a sort of way that says, I'm safe—but it's been no use yet, not a bit of it!—My eyes! catch me, by the way, ever nodding again to a lady on the Sunday, that had smiled when I stared at her while serving her in the shop—after what happened to me a month or two ago in the Park! Didn't I feel like damaged goods, just then! But it's no matter, women are so different at different times!—Very likely I mismanaged the thing. By the way, what a precious puppy of a chap the fellow was that came up to her at the time she stepped out of her carriage to walk a bit! As for good looks—cut me to ribbons (another glance at the glass) no; I a'n't afraid *there*, neither—but—heigho!—I suppose he was, as they say, born with a golden spoon in his mouth, and had never so many a thousand a year, to make up to him for never so few brains! He was uncommon well-dressed, though, I must own. What trousers!—they stuck so natural to him, he might have been born in them. And his waistcoat, and satin stock—what an air! And yet, his figure was nothing *very* out of the way! His gloves, as white as snow; I've no doubt he wears a pair of them a day—my stars! that's three and sixpence a day; for don't I know what *they* cost?—Whew! if I had but the cash to carry on that sort of thing!—And when he'd seen her into her carriage—the horse he got on!—and what a tiptop groom—that chap's wages, I'll answer for it, were equal to my salary! (Here was another pause.) Now, just for the fun of the thing, only suppose luck was to befall *me!* Say that somebody was to leave me lots of cash—many thousands a year, or something in that line! My stars! wouldn't I go it with the best of them! (Another long pause.) Gad, I really should hardly know how to begin to spend it!—I think, by the way, I'd buy a title to set off with—for what won't money buy? The thing's often

done; there was a great biscuit-baker in the city, the other
day, made a baronet of, all for his money—and why shouldn't
I?" He grew a little heated with the progress of his reflections, clasping his hands with involuntary energy, as he
stretched them out to their fullest extent, to give effect to a
very hearty yawn. " Lord, only think how it would sound!—

' SIR TITTLEBAT TITMOUSE, BARONET; OR, LORD TITMOUSE.'

" The very first place I'd go to, after I'd got my title, and
was rigged out in Stulze's tiptop, should be—our cursed shop,
to buy a dozen or two pair of white kid. What a flutter there
would be among the poor pale devils as were standing, just as
ever, behind the counters, at Tag-rag and Co.'s when my carriage drew up, and I stepped, a tiptop swell, into the shop.
Tag-rag would come and attend to me himself. No, he
wouldn't—pride wouldn't let him. I don't know, though;
what wouldn't he do to turn a penny, and make two and nine-
pence into three and a penny? I shouldn't *quite* come Captain
Stiff over him, I think; but I should treat him with a kind of
an air, too, as if—hem! 'Pon my life! how delightful! (A
sigh and a pause.) Yes, I should often come to the shop.
Gad, it would be half the fun of my fortune! How they would
envy me, to be sure! How one should enjoy it! I wouldn't
think of *marrying* till—and yet I won't say either; if I got
among some of them out-and-outers—those first-rate articles
—that lady, for instance, the other day in the Park—I should
like to see her cut me as she did, with ten thousand a year in
my pocket! Why, she'd be running after *me*, or there's no
truth in novels; which I'm sure there's often a great deal in.
Oh, of course, I might marry whom I pleased. Who couldn't
be got with ten thousand a year? (Another pause.) I should
go abroad to Russia directly; for they tell me there's a man
lives there who could dye this cussed hair of mine any color I
liked—egad! I'd come home as black as a crow, and hold up
my head as high as any of them! While I was about it, I'd
have a touch at my eyebrows."—Crash went all his castle-
building, at the sound of his tea-kettle, hissing, whizzing,
sputtering in the agonies of boiling over; as if the intolerable
heat of the fire had driven desperate the poor creature placed
upon it, who instinctively tried thus to extinguish the cause of
its anguish. Having taken it off and placed it upon the hob,
and put on the fire a tiny fragment of fresh coal, he began to
make preparations for shaving, by pouring some of the hot
water into an old tea-cup, which was presently to serve for the
purposes of breakfast. Then he spread out a bit of crumpled

whity-brown paper, in which had been folded up a couple of cigars, bought overnight for the Sunday's special enjoyment —and as to which, if he supposed they had come from any place beyond the four seas, I imagine him to have been slightly mistaken. He placed this bit of paper on the little mantelpiece; drew his solitary, well-worn razor several times across the palm of his left hand; dipped his brush, worn within a third of an inch to the stump, into the hot water; presently passed it over so much of his face as he intended to shave; then rubbed on the damp surface a bit of yellow soap—and in less than five minutes Mr. Titmouse was a shaved man. But mark—don't suppose that he had performed an extensive operation. One would have thought him anxious to get rid of as much as possible of his abominable sandy-colored hair— quite the contrary. Every hair of his spreading whiskers was sacred from the touch of steel; and a bushy crop of hair stretched underneath his chin, coming curled out on each side of it, above his stock, like two little horns, or tusks. An imperial—*i. e.*, a dirt-colored tuft of hair, permitted to grow perpendicularly down the under lip of puppies—and a pair of promising mustaches, poor Mr. Titmouse had been compelled to sacrifice some time before, to the tyrannical whimsies of his vulgar employer, Mr. Tag-rag, who imagined them not to be exactly suitable appendages for counter-jumpers. So that it will be seen that the space shaved over on this occasion was somewhat circumscribed. This operation over, he took out of his trunk an old dirty-looking pomatum pot. A little of its contents, extracted on the tips of his two forefingers, he stroked carefully into his eyebrows; then spreading some on the palms of his hands, he rubbed it vigorously into his stubborn hair and whiskers for some quarter of an hour; and then combed and brushed his hair into half a dozen different dispositions—so fastidious in that matter was Mr. Titmouse. Then he dipped the end of a towel into a little water, and twisting it round his right forefinger, passed it gently over his face, carefully avoiding his eyebrows, and the hair at the top, sides, and bottom of his face, which he then wiped with a dry corner of the towel; and no further did Mr. Tittlebat Titmouse think it necessary to carry his ablutions. Had he been able to "see himself as others saw him," in respect of those neglected regions which lay somewhere behind and beneath his ears, he might not possibly have thought it superfluous to irrigate them with a little soap and water; but, after all, he knew best; it might have given him cold; and besides, his hair was very thick and long behind, and might perhaps conceal anything

that was unsightly. Then Mr. Titmouse drew from underneath the bed a bottle of Warren's "incomparable blacking,"
and a couple of brushes, with great labor and skill polishing
his boots up to a wonderful point of brilliancy. Having replaced his blacking implements under the bed and washed his
hands, he devoted a few moments to boiling about three tea-
spoonfuls of coffee (as it was styled on the paper from which
he took, and in which he had bought it—whereas it was, in
fact, *chicory*). Then he drew forth from his trunk a calico
shirt, with linen wristbands and collars, which had been worn
only twice since its last washing—*i. e.*, on the preceding two
Sundays—and put it on, taking great care not to rumple a
very showy front, containing three little rows of frills; in the
middle one of which he stuck three "studs," connected together with two little gilt chains, looking exceedingly stylish—
especially coupled with a span-new satin stock, which he next
buckled round his neck. Having put on his bright boots
(without, I am sorry to say, any stockings), he carefully in-
sinuated his legs into a pair of white trousers, for the first time
since their last washing; and what with his short straps and
high braces, they were so tight that you would have feared
their bursting if he should have sat down hastily. I am almost
afraid that I shall hardly be believed; but it is a fact that the
next thing he did was to attach a pair of spurs to his boots;
but, to be sure, it was not *impossible* that he might intend to
ride during the day. Then he put on a queer kind of under-
waistcoat, which in fact was only a roll-collar of rather faded
pea-green silk, and designed to set off a very fine, flowered,
damson-colored silk waistcoat; over which he drew a massive
mosaic-gold chain (to purchase which he had sold a serviceable
silver watch), which had been carefully wrapped up in cotton
wool; from which soft depository, also, he drew HIS RING
(those must have been sharp eyes which could tell, at a distance, and in a hurry, that it was not diamond), which he
placed on the stumpy little finger of his red and thick right
hand—and contemplated its sparkle with exquisite satisfaction. Having proceeded thus far with his toilet, he sat down
to his breakfast, spreading the shirt he had taken off upon his
lap, to preserve his white trousers from spot or stain—his
thoughts alternating between his late waking vision and his
purposes for the day. He had no butter, having used the last
on the preceding morning; so he was fain to put up with dry
bread—and very dry and teeth-trying it was, poor fellow—but
his eye lighted on his ring! Having swallowed two cups of his
quasi-coffee (eugh! such stuff!), he resumed his toilet, by

drawing out of his other trunk his blue surtout, with embossed silk buttons and velvet collar, and an outside pocket in the left breast. Having smoothed down a few creases, he put it on; —then, before the little vulgar fraction of a glass he stood twitching about the collar, and sleeves, and front, so as to make them sit well; concluding with a careful elongation of the wristbands of his shirt so as to show their whiteness gracefully beyond the cuff of his coat-sleeve—and he succeeded in producing a sort of white boundary line between the blue of his coat-sleeve and the red of his hand. At that useful member he could not help looking with a sigh, as he had often done before—for it was not a handsome hand. It was broad and red, and the fingers were thick and stumpy, with very coarse deep wrinkles at every joint. His nails also were flat and shapeless; and he used to be continually gnawing them till he had succeeded in getting them down to the quick—and they were a sight to set one's teeth on edge. Then he extracted from the first mentioned trunk a white pocket-handkerchief— an exemplary one, that had gone through four Sundays' show (not *use*, be it understood), and yet was capable of exhibition again.

A pair of sky-colored kid gloves next made their appearance; which, however, showed such barefaced marks of former service as rendered indispensable a ten minutes' rubbing with bread crumbs. His Sunday hat, carefully covered with silver paper, was next gently removed from its well-worn box—ah, how lightly and delicately did he pass his smoothing hand round its glossy surface! Lastly, he took down a thin black cane, with a gilt head and full brown tassel, from a peg behind the door—and his toilet was complete. Laying down his cane for a moment, he passed his hands again through his hair, arranging it so as to fall nicely on each side beneath his hat, which he then placed upon his head, with an elegant inclination toward the left side. He was really not bad-looking, in spite of his sandy-colored hair. His forehead, to be sure, was contracted, and his eyes were of a very light color, and a trifle too protuberant; but his mouth was rather well-formed, and being seldom closed, exhibited very beautiful teeth; and his nose was of that description which generally passes for a Roman nose. His countenance wore generally a smile, and was expressive of—self-satisfaction: and surely any expression is better than none at all. As for there being the slightest trace of *intellect* in it, I should be misleading the reader if I were to say anything of the sort. In height, he was about five feet and a quarter of an inch, *in his boots,* and he was rather

strongly set, with a little tendency to round shoulders; but his
limbs were pliant, and his motions nimble.

Here you have, then, Mr. Tittlebat Titmouse to the life—
⁀ertainly no more than an average sample of his kind; but as
he is to go through a considerable variety of situation and circumstance, I thought you would like to have him as distinctly
before your mind's eye as it was in my power to present him.
—Well—he put his hat on as I have said; buttoned the lowest
two buttons of his surtout, and stuck his white pocket handkerchief into the outside pocket in front, as already mentioned,
anxiously disposing it so as to let a little of it appear above the
edge of the pocket, with a sort of careful carelessness—a graceful contrast to the blue; drew on his gloves, took his cane in
his hand; drained the last sad remnant of infusion of chicory
in his coffee cup; and the sun shining in the full splendor of a
July noon, and promising a glorious day, forth sallied this
poor fellow, an Oxford Street Adonis, going forth conquering
and to conquer! Petty finery without, a pinched and stinted
stomach within; a case of Back *versus* Belly (as the lawyers
would say), the plaintiff winning in a canter! Forth sallied, I
say, Mr. Titmouse, as also sallied forth that day some five or
six thousand similar personages, down the narrow, creaking,
close staircase, which he had not quitted before he heard exclaimed from an opposite window, "My eyes! *a'n't* that a
swell!" He felt how true the observation was, and that at
that moment he was somewhat out of his element; so he hurried on and soon reached the great broad street, apostrophized
by the celebrated Opium-Eater, with bitter feeling, as—"Oxford Street!—stony-hearted step-mother! Thou that listenest
to the sighs of orphans, and drinkest the tears of children!"
Here, though his spirits were not just then very buoyant, our
poor little dandy breathed more freely than when he was passing through the nasty crowded court (Closet Court) which he
had just quitted. He passed and met hundreds, who, like
himself, seemed released for a precious day's interval from
miserable confinement and slavery during the week; but there
were not very many of them who could vie with him in elegance of appearance—and that was a *luxury!* Who could do
justice to the air with which he strutted along! He felt as
happy, poor soul, in his little ostentation, as his Corinthian
rival in tiptop turn-out, after twice as long, and as anxious,
and fifty times as expensive, preparations for effective public
display! Nay, *my* poor swell was in some respects greatly the
superior of such a one as I have alluded to. Mr. Titmouse
did, to a great degree, bedizen his back—at the expense of his

belly; whereas, the Corinthian exquisite, too often taking advantage of station and influence, recklessly both pampers his luxurious appetite within, and decorates his person without, at the expense of innumerable heartaching creditors. I do not mean, however, to claim any real merit for Mr. Titmouse on this score, because I am not sure how he would act if he were to become possessed of his magnificent rival's means and opportunities for the perpetration of gentlemanly frauds on a splendid scale.—But we shall perhaps see by and by.

Mr. Titmouse walked along with leisurely step; for haste and perspiration were vulgar, and he had the day before him. Observe, now, the careless glance of self-satisfaction with which he occasionally regards his bright boots, with their martial appendage, giving out a faint clinking sound as he heavily treads the broad flags; his spotless trousers, his tight surtout, and the tip of white handkerchief peeping *accidentally* out in front! A pleasant sight it was to behold him in a chance rencounter with some one genteel enough to be recognized—as he stood, resting on his left leg; his left arm stuck upon his hip; his right leg easily bent outward; his right hand lightly holding his ebon cane, with the gilt head of which he occasionally tapped his teeth; and his eyes half closed, scrutinizing the face and figure of each " *pretty gal* " as she passed, and to whom he had a delicious consciousness that he appeared an object of interest! This was indeed HAPPINESS, as far as his forlorn condition could admit of his enjoying it.—He had no particular object in view. A tiff overnight with two of his shopmates had broken off a party which they had agreed the Sunday preceding in forming, to go that day to Greenwich; and this trifling circumstance had a little soured his temper, depressed as were his spirits before. He resolved to-day to walk straight on, and dine somewhere a little way out of town, by way of passing the time till four o'clock, at which hour he intended to make his appearance in Hyde Park, " to see the swells and the fashions," which was his favorite Sunday occupation.

His condition was, indeed, forlorn in the extreme. To say nothing of his *prospects* in life—what was his present condition? A shopman, with £35 a year, out of which he had to find his clothing, washing, lodging, and all other incidental expenses —his board being found him by his employers! He was five weeks in arrear to his landlady—a corpulent old termagant, whom nothing could have induced him to risk offending but his overmastering love of finery; for I grieve to say, that this deficiency had been occasioned by his purchase of the ring he then wore with so much pride. How he had contrived to pacify her—lie upon lie he must have had recourse to—I know not. He was in debt, too, to his poor washer-woman in five or six shillings for at least a quarter's washing; and owed five times that amount to a little old tailor, who, with huge spectacles on his nose, turned up to him, out of a little cupboard which he occupied in Closet Court, and which Titmouse had to pass whenever he went to or from his lodgings, a lean, sallow, wrinkled face, imploring him to "settle his small account." All the cash in hand which he had to meet contingencies between that day and quarter-day, which was six weeks off, was about twenty-six shillings, of which he had taken one for the present day's expenses!

Revolving these somewhat disheartening matters in his mind, he passed easily and leisurely along the whole length of Oxford Street. No one could have judged from his dressy appearance, the constant smirk on his face, and his confident air, how very miserable that poor little dandy was, but three fourths of his misery were occasioned by the impossibility he felt of his ever being able to indulge in his propensities for finery and display. Nothing better had he to occupy his few thoughts. He had had only a plain mercantile education, as it is called, i. e., reading, writing, and arithmetic; beyond a very moderate acquaintance with these, he knew nothing whatever, not having read more than a few novels, and plays, and sporting newspapers. Deplorable, however, as were his circumstances—

"Hope springs eternal in the human breast."

And probably, in common with most who are miserable from straitened circumstances, he often conceived, and secretly relied upon, the possibility of some unexpected and accidental change for the better; he had heard and read of extraordinary cases of LUCK. Why might he not be one of the LUCKY? A rich girl might fall in love with him—that was, poor fellow! in his consideration, one of the least unlikely ways of luck's advent; or some one might leave him money; or he might win a prize in the lottery—all these, and other accidental modes of getting enriched, frequently occurred to the well-regulated mind of Mr. Tittlebat Titmouse; but he never once thought of one thing, viz., of determined, unwearying industry and perseverance in the way of his business, conducing to such a result.

Is his case a solitary one? Dear reader, *you* may be unlike poor Tittlebat Titmouse in every respect except *one*.

On he walked toward Bayswater, and finding it was yet early, and considering that the further he went from town the better prospect there was of his being able, with little sacrifice of appearances, to get a dinner consistent with the means he carried about with him, viz., one shilling, he pursued his way a mile or two beyond Bayswater, and, sure enough, came at length upon a nice little public-house on the road-side, called the Squaretoes Arms. Very tired, and very dusty, he first sat down in a small back room to rest himself, and took the opportunity to call for a clothes-brush and shoe-brush, to relieve his clothes and boots from the heavy dust upon them. Having thus attended to his outer man, as far as circumstances would permit, he bethought himself of his inner man, whose cravings he satisfied with a pretty substantial mutton-pie and a pint of porter. This fare, together with a penny to the little girl who waited on him, cost him tenpence, and having somewhat refreshed himself, he began to think of returning to town. Having lighted one of his two cigars, he sallied forth, puffing along with an air of quiet enjoyment. Dinner, however humble, seldom fails, especially when accompanied by a fair draught of good porter, in some considerable degree, to tranquilize the animal spirits, and that soothing effect began soon to be experienced by Mr. Titmouse. The sedative *cause* he erroneously considered to be the cigar he was smoking; whereas, in fact, the only tobacco he had imbibed was from the porter. But, however that might be, he certainly returned toward town in a far calmer and even more cheerful humor than that in which he had quitted it an hour or two before.

As he approached Cumberland Gate, it was about half past five, and the Park might be said to be at its *acme* of fashion, as far as that could be indicated by a sluggish stream of carriages, three and four abreast—coroneted panels, in abundance—noble and well known equestrians of both sexes, in troops—and some thousand pedestrians of the same description. So continuous was the throng of carriages and horsemen that Titmouse did not find it the easiest matter in the world to dart across to the footpath in the inner circle. That, however, he presently safely accomplished, encountering no more serious mischance than the muttered " D—n your eyes!" of a haughty groom, between whom and his master Mr. Titmouse had presumed to intervene. What a crowd of elegant women, many of them young and beautiful (who but such, to be sure, would become, or be allowed to become, pedestrians in the Park?) he encountered, as he slowly sauntered on, all of them obsequiously attended by brilliant beaus! Lords and

ladies were here manifestly as plentiful as plebeians in Oxford
Street. What an enchanted ground! How delicious this soft
crush and flutter of aristocracy! Poor Titmouse felt a withering consciousness of his utter insignificance. Many a sigh of
dissatisfaction and envy escaped him, yet he stepped along
with a tolerably assured air, looking everybody he met straight
in the face, and occasionally twirling about his little cane with
an air which seemed to say: "Whatever opinion *you* may
form of me, I have a very good opinion of myself." Indeed,
was he not as much a man—an Englishman—as the best of
them? What was the real difference between Count Do-'em-
all and Mr. Tittlebat Titmouse? Only that the Count had
dark hair and whiskers, and owed more money than Mr. Titmouse's creditors could be persuaded to allow *him* to owe!
Would to Heaven—thought Titmouse—that any *one* tailor
would patronize *him* as half a dozen had patronized the Count.
If pretty ladies of quality did not disdain a walking advertisement of a few first-rate tailors, like the Count, why should
they turn up their noses at an assistant in an extensive wholesale and retail establishment in Oxford Street, conversant with
the qualities and prices of the most beautiful articles of female
attire? Yet alas, they *did* so. He sighed heavily. Leaning
against the railing in a studied attitude, and eying wistfully
each gay and fashionable equipage, with its often lovely and
sometimes haughty inclosure, as it rolled slowly past him, Mr.
Titmouse became more and more convinced of a great practical
truth, viz., that the only real distinction between mankind was
that effected by money. Want of money alone had placed him
in his present abject position. Abject, indeed! By the great
folk, who were passing him on all sides, he felt, well-dressed
as he believed himself to be, that he was no more noticed than
as if he had been an ant, a blue-bottle fly, or a black beetle.
He looked and sighed—sighed and looked—looked and sighed
again, in a kind of agony of vain longing. While his only day
in the week for breathnig fresh air, and appearing like a
gentleman in the world, was rapidly drawing to a close, and
he was beginning to think of returning to the dog-hole he had
crawled out of in the morning, and to the shop for the rest of
the week, the great, and gay, and happy folk he was looking
at, were thinking of driving home to dress for their grand dinners, and to lay out every kind of fine amusemnt for the ensuing week, and that was the sort of life they led every day in
the week. He heaved a profound sigh. At that moment a
superb cab, with a gentleman in it dressed in great elegance,
ard with a very keen and striking countenance, came up with

a cab of still more exquisite structure and appointments, and at which Titmouse gazed with unutterable feelings of envy—in which sat a young man, evidently of consequence; very handsome, with splendid mustaches; perfectly well-dressed, holding the reins and whip gracefully in hands glistening in straw-colored kid gloves—and between the two gentlemen ensued the following low-toned colloquy, which it were to be wished that every such sighing simpleton (as Titmouse must, I fear, by this time, appear to the reader) could have overheard.

"Ah, Fitz!" said the former-mentioned gentleman to the latter who suddenly reddened when he perceived who had addressed him. The manner of the speaker was execrably—infernally familiar and presumptuous—but how could the embarrassed *swell* help himself? "When did you return to town?"

"Last night only—"

"Enjoyed yourself, I hope?"

"Pretty well—but—I suppose you—"

"Sorry for it," interrupted the first speaker in a lower tone, perceiving the vexation of his companion, "but can't help it, you know."

"When?"

"To-morrow at nine. Monstrous sorry for it—'pon my soul, you really much look sharp, or the thing won't go on much longer."

"Must it be, really?" inquired the other, biting his lips—at that moment kissing his hand to a very beautiful girl, who slowly passed him in a coroneted chariot—"must it really be, Joe?" he repeated, turning toward his companion a pale and bitterly chagrined countenance.

"Poz, 'pon my life. Cage clean, however, and not very full—just at present—"

"Would not *Wednesday?*" inquired the other, leaning forward toward the former speaker's cab, and whispering with an air of intense earnestness. "The fact is, I've engagements at C——'s on Monday and Tuesday nights with one or two country cousins, and I *may* be in a condition—eh? you understand?"

His companion shook his head distrustfully.

"Upon my word and honor as a gentleman, it's the fact!" said the other, in a low, vehement tone.

"Then—say Wednesday, nine o'clock, A. M. You understand? No mistake, Fitz!" replied his companion, looking him steadily in the face as he spoke.

"None—honor!" After a pause: "Who is it?"

His companion took a slip of paper out of his pocket, and in a whisper read from it—"Cabs, harness, etc., £297, 10s."

"A villain! It's been of only three years' standing," interrupted the other, in an indignant mutter.

"Between ourselves, he *is* rather a sharp hand. Then I'm sorry to say there's a detainer or two I have had a hint of—"

"D—n their souls!" exclaimed the other, with an expression of mingled disgust, vexation, and hatred, and adding: "Wednesday—nine"—drove off, a picture of tranquil enjoyment.

I need hardly say that *he* was a fashionable young spendthrift, and the other a sheriff's officer of the first water—the genteelest *beak* that ever was known or heard of—who had been on the lookout for him several days, and with whom the happy youngster was doomed to spend some considerable time at a cheerful residence in Chancery Lane, bleeding gold at every pore the while; his only chance of avoiding which was, as he had truly hinted, an honorable attempt on the purses of two hospitable country cousins, in the meanwhile, at C——'s. And if he did not succeed in that enterprise, so that he *must* go to cage, he lost the only chance he had for some time of securing an exemption for such annoyance by entering Parliament to protect the liberties of the people—an eloquent and resolute champion of freedom in trade, religion and everything else, and an abolitionist of everything, including, especially, negro slavery and imprisonment for debt—two execrable violations of the natural rights of mankind.

But I have, for several minutes, lost sight of the admiring Titmouse.

"Why," thought he, "am *I* thus spited by fortune? The only thing she's given *me* is—nothing! *D—n everything!*" exclaimed Mr. Titmouse aloud, at the same time starting off, to the infinite astonishment of an old peer, who had been for some minutes standing leaning against the railing, close beside him, who was master of a magnificent fortune, "with all appliances and means to boot," with a fine grown-up family, his eldest son and heir having just gained a Double First, and promising wonders; possessing many mansions in different parts of England; of exquisite taste and accomplishment, and the representative of one of the oldest families in England, but who at that moment loathed everything and everybody, including himself, because the minister had the day before intimated to him that he could not give him a vacant ribbon, for which he had applied, unless he could command two more votes in the Lower House, and which at present his lordship saw no earthly means of doing. Yes, the Earl of Cheviotdale and Mr. Tittlebat Titmouse were both miserable men; both had been hardly dealt with by fortune; both were greatly to be pitied, and both quitted the Park, about the same time, with a decided misanthropic tendency.

Mr. Titmouse walked along Piccadilly with a truly chopfallen and disconsolate air. He almost felt dissatisfied even with his personal appearance. Dress as he would, no one seemed to care a curse for him, and, to his momentarily jaundiced eye, he seemed equipped in only second-hand and shabby finery, and then he was really such a *poor* devil. Do not, however, let the reader suppose that this was an unusual mood with Mr. Titmouse. No such thing. Like the Irishman who "married a wife for to make him *un-aisy*," and also not unlike the moth that *will* haunt the brightness which is her destruction, so poor Titmouse, Sunday after Sunday, dressed himself out as elaborately as he had done on the present occasion, and then always betook himself to the scene he had just again witnessed, and which once again had excited only those feelings of envy, bitterness, and despair, which I have been describing, and which, on every such occasion, he experienced with, if possible, increased intensity.

What to do with himself till it was time to return to his cheerless lodgings he did not exactly know, so he loitered along at a snail's pace. He stood for some time staring at the passengers, their luggage, the coaches they were ascending and alighting from, and listening to the strange medley of coachmen's, guards', and porters' vociferations, and passengers' greetings and leave-takings—always to be observed at the White Horse Cellar. Then he passed along, till a street row, near the Haymarket, attracted his attention and interested his feelings, for it ended in a regular set-to between two watermen attached to the adjoining coach-stand. Here he conceived himself looking on with the easy air of a swell; and the ordinary penalty—paying for his footing—was attempted to be exacted from him; but he had nothing to be picked out of any of his pockets except that under his very nose, and which contained his white handkerchief. This over he struck into Leicester Square, where—he was in luck that night—hurrying up to another crowd at the further end, he found a man preaching with infinite energy. Mr. Titmouse looked on, and listened for two or three minutes with apparent interest, and then, with a countenance in which pity struggled with contempt, muttered, loud enough to be heard by all near him, "poor devil!" and walked off. He had not proceeded many steps before it occurred to him that a friend—one Robert Huckaback, much such another one as himself—lived in one of the narrow, dingy streets in the neighborhood. He determined to take the chances of his being at home, and if so, of spending the remainder of the evening with him. Huckaback's quarters were in the same ambitious proximity to Heaven as his own, the only difference being that they were a trifle cheaper and larger. He answered the door himself, having only the moment before returned from *his* Sunday's excursion, *i. e.*, the Jack Straw's Castle Tea-Gardens, at Highgate, where, in company with several of his friends, he had "spent a jolly afternoon." He ordered in a glass of negus from the adjoining public-house, after some discussion, which ended in an agreement that he should stand treat that night, and Titmouse on the ensuing Sunday night. As soon as the negus arrived, accompanied by two sea-biscuits, which looked so hard and hopeless that they would have made the nerves thrill within the teeth of him that meditated attempting to masticate them, the candle was lighted—Huckaback handed a cigar to his friend, and both began to puff away, and chatter pleasantly concerning the many events and scenes of the day.

"Anything stirring in to-day's 'Flash?'" inquired Titmouse, as his eye caught sight of a copy of that able and interesting Sunday newspaper, the "SUNDAY FLASH," which Huckaback had hired for the evening from the news-shop on the ground-floor of his lodgings.

Mr. Huckaback removed his cigar from his mouth, and holding it between the first and second fingers of his right hand, in a knowing style, with closed eyes and inflated cheeks very slowly ejected the smoke which he had last inhaled, and rose and got the paper from the top of the drawers.

"Here's a mark of a beastly porter-pot that's been set upon it, by all that's holy! It's been at the public-house! Too bad of Mrs. Coggs to send it me up in this state," said he, handling it as though its touch were contamination. He was to pay only a halfpenny for the perusal of it. "Faugh! how it stinks!"

"What a horrid beast she must be!" exclaimed Titmouse, after, in like manner as his friend, expelling his mouthful of smoke. "But, since better can't be had, let's hear what news is in it. Demmee! it's the only paper published, in my opinion, that's worth reading. Any fights a-stirring?"

"Haven't come to them yet; give a man *time*, Titty!" replied Huckaback, fixing his feet on another chair, and drawing the candle closer to the paper. "It says, by the way, that the Duke of Dunderhead is certainly making up to Mrs. Thumps, the rich cheesemonger's widow—a precious good hit that, isn't it? You know the Duke's as poor as a rat?"

"Oh! *that's* no news. It's been in the papers for I don't know how long. Egad, 'twill quite set him up, and no mistake. Seen the Duke ever?"

"Ye—es! Oh, several times!" replied Huckaback. This was a lie, and Huckaback knew that it was.

"Deuced good-looking, I suppose?"

"Why—middling; I should say middling. Know *some* that needn't fear to compare with him—eh! Tit?" and Huckaback winked archly at his friend, meaning him to consider the words as applicable to the speaker.

"Ah, ha, ha!—a pretty joke! But come, that's a good chap. You can't be reading both of those two sheets at once —give us the other sheet, and set the candle right betwixt us. Come, fair's the word."

Huckaback, thus appealed to, did as his friend requested, and the two gentlemen read and smoked for some minutes in silence.

"Well—I shall spell over the advertisements now," said Titmouse; "there's a pretty lot of them—and I've read everything else—though precious little there is *here*, besides. So here goes! One *may* hear of a prime situation, you know— and I'm quite sick of Tag-rag!"

Another interval of silence ensued. Huckaback was deep in the instructive details of a trial for murder, and Titmouse, after having glanced listlessly over the entertaining first sheet of advertisements, was on the point of laying down his half of the paper, when he suddenly started in his chair, turned very pale, and stammered:

"Halloo! halloo, Hucky! Why—"

"What's the matter, Tit—eh?" inquired Huckaback, greatly astonished.

For a moment Titmouse made no answer, but, dropping his cigar, fixed his eyes intently on the paper, which began to rustle in his trembling hands. What occasioned this outbreak, with its subsequent agitation, was the following advertisement, which appeared in the most conspicuous part of the "SUNDAY FLASH:"

"NEXT OF KIN—Important.—The next of kin, if any such there be, of GABRIEL TITTLEBAT TITMOUSE, formerly of WHITEHAVEN, cordwainer, and who died somewhere about the year 1793, in London, may hear of something of the

GREATEST POSSIBLE IMPORTANCE to himself, or herself, or themselves, by immediately communicating with Messrs. QUIRK, GAMMON and SNAP, Solicitors, Saffron Hill. No time is to be lost. 9th July, 18—. *—The third advertise-ment.*"

"By George! Here *is* a go!" exclaimed Huckaback, almost as much flustered as Titmouse, over whose shoulder he had hastily read the above paragraph.

"We aren't dreaming, Hucky—are we?" inquired Tit-mouse, faintly, his eyes still glued to the newspaper.

"No—by George! Never was either of us fellows so pre-cious wide awake in our lives before! that I'll answer for!" Titmouse sat still, and turned paler even than before.

"Read it up, Huck! Let's hear how it *sounds,* and then we shall believe it!" said he, handing the paper to his friend.

Huckaback read it aloud.

"It sounds like something, don't it?" inquired Titmouse, tremulously, his color a little returning.

"Uncommon! If this isn't *something,* then there's noth-ing in anything any more," replied Huckaback, solemnly, at the same time emphatically slapping the table.

"No! 'Pon my soul! but do you really think so?" said Titmouse, seeking still further confirmation than he had yet derived from his senses of sight and hearing.

"I do, by jingo! What a go it is! Well, my poor old mother used to say, 'depend on it, wonders never *will* cease,' and curse me if she ever said a truer word."

Titmouse again read over the advertisement, and then pick-ing up and relighting his fragment of cigar, puffed earnestly, in silence, for some moments.

"Such things never happens to such a poor devil of a chap as me!" exclaimed Huckaback, with a sigh.

"What *is* in the wind, I wonder!" muttered Titmouse. "Who knows—hem!—who knows. But now, *really*—" he paused, and once more read over the pregnant paragraph. "It can't—no, curse me, it *can't* be—" he added, looking very serious.

"What, Tit? *What* can't be?" interrupted Huckaback, eagerly.

"Why, I've been thinking—but what do *you* think, eh?—it can't be a cursed hoax of the chaps in the premises at Tag-rag's?"

"No!—Is there any of 'em flush enough of money to do the thing? And how should they think it would ever come to be seen by you? Then besides, there isn't a chap among them that could come up to the composing a piece of composition like that—no, not for all a whole year's salary—there isn't, by George! You and I couldn't do it, and, of course *they* couldn't!"

"Ah! I don't know," said Titmouse, doubtfully. "But—honor!—do you really now think there's anything in it?"

"I do—hanged if I don't, Tit!" was the sententious answer.

"Tol de rol, de rol, de rol, de rol—diddl'em daddl'em—bang!" almost shouted Titmouse, jumping up, snapping his fingers and dancing about in a wild ecstasy, which lasted for nearly a minute.

"Give me your hand, Hucky," said he presently, almost breathless. "If I *am* a made man—tol de rol, lol de rol, lol de rol, lol!—you see, Huck!—if I don't give you the hand-somest breast-pin you ever saw! No paste! real diamond! Hurrah! I will, by jingo!"

Huckaback grasped and squeezed his hand. "We've always been friends, Tit, haven't we?" said he, affectionately.

"My room won't hold me to-night!" continued Titmouse; "I'm sure it won't. I feel as if I was, as you may say, swelling all over. I'll walk the streets all night; I couldn't sleep a wink for the life of me. I'll walk about till the shop opens. Oh, faugh! how nasty! Confound the shop, and Tag-rag, and everything and everybody in it! Thirty-five pounds a year. See if I won't spend as much in cigars the first month."

"Cigars! Is that your go? Now *I* should take lessons in boxing, to begin with. It's a deuced high thing, you may depend upon it, and you can't be fit company for swells without it, Tit. You can't, by Jove!"

"Whatever you like, whatever you like, Hucky!" cried Titmouse—adding, in a sort of ecstasy, "I'm sorry to say it, but how *precious* lucky that my father and mother's dead, and that I'm an only child—too-ra-laddy, too-ra-laddy!" Here he took such a sudden leap that I am sorry to say he split his trousers very awkwardly, and that sobered him for a moment, while they made arrangements for cobbling it up as well as it might be, with a needle and thread which Huckaback always had by him.

"We're rather jumping in the dark a bit, aren't we, Tit?" inquired Huckaback, while his companion was repairing the breach. "Let's look what it all means—here it is." He read it all aloud again—"'*greatest possible importance*'—"what *can it* mean? Why the deuce couldn't they speak out plainly?"

"What! in a newspaper? Lord, Hucky! how many Tit-

mouses would start up on all sides if there isn't some already.
I wonder what ' *greatest possible importance* ' can mean, now?"
"Some one's left you an awful lot of money, of course—"
"It's too good to be true—"
"Or you may have made a *smite;* you a'n't such a bad-
looking fellow, when you're dressed as you are now—you a'n't,
indeed, Titty!" Mr. Titmouse was quite flustered with the
mere supposition, and also looked as sheepish as his features
would admit of.
"E-e-e-eh, Hucky! how ve-ry silly you are!" he simpered.
"Or you may be found out heir to some great property,
and all that kind of thing. But when do you intend to go to
Messrs. What's-their-name? I say, the sooner the better.
Come, you've stitched them trousers well enough now; they'll
hold you till you get home—you do brace up uncommon tight!
and I'd take off my straps, if I was you. Why shouldn't we
go to these gents now? Ah, here they are—Messrs. Quirk,
Gammon and Snap, solicitors."
"I wonder if they're great men? Did you ever hear of
them before?"
"Haven't I? Their names is always in this same paper;
they are every day getting people off out of all kinds of scrapes
—they're the chaps *I* should nat'rally go to if I anyhow got
wrong—ahem!"
"But, my dear fellow—*Saffron Hill!* Low that—devilish
low, 'pon my soul! Never was near it in my life."
"But they live there to be near the thieves. Lud, the
thieves couldn't do without 'em. But what's that to you?
You know ' a very dirty ugly toad has often got a jewel in his
belly,' so Shakespeare or some one says. Isn't it enough for
you, Tit, if they can make good their advertisement? Let's
off, Tit—let's off, I say; for you mayn't be able to get there
to-morrow—your employers—"
"My employers! Do you think, Hucky, I'm going back to
business after this?"
"Come, come, Titty—not so fast—suppose it all turns out
moonshine, after all "—quoth Huckaback, seriously.
"Lord, but I *won't* suppose it! It makes me sick to think
of nothing coming of it!—Let's go off at once, and see what's
to be done!"
So Huckaback put the newspaper in his pocket, blew out
the candle, and the two started on their important errand. It
was well that their means had been too limited to allow of
their indulging to a greater extent than a glass of port wine
negus (that was the name under which they drank the " *pub-*

lican's port "—*i. e.*, a decoction of oak bark, logwood shavings, and a little brandy) between them; otherwise, excited as were the feelings of each of them by the discovery of the evening, they must in all probability have been guilty of some piece of extravagance in the streets. As it was, they talked very loudly as they went along, and in a tone of conversation pitched perhaps a little too high for their present circumstances, however in unison it might be with the expected circumstances of *one* of them.

In due time they reached the residence of which they were in search. It was a large house, infinitely superior to all its dingy neighbors; and on a bright brass plate, a yard long at least, and a foot wide, stood the awe-inspiring words, " QUIRK, GAMMON & SNAP, SOLICITORS. "

" Now, Tit, " whispered Huckaback, after they had paused for a second or two—" now for it—pluck up a sperrit—ring! "

" I—I—'pon my life—I feel all of a sudden uncommon funky—I think that last cigar of yours wasn't—"

" Stuff, Tit—ring! ring away! Faint heart never wins! "

" Well, it *must* be done; so—here goes, at any rate! " he replied; and with a short nervous jerk he caused a startling clatter within, which was so distinctly audible without, that both of them instinctively *hemmed*, as if to drown the noise which was so much greater than they had expected. In a very few moments they heard some one undoing the fastenings of the door, and the gentlemen looked at one another with an expression of mingled expectation and apprehension. A little old woman at length stood before them with a candle in her hand.

" Who are you? " she exclaimed, crustily.

" Is this Messrs.—what is it, Huck?—Oh! Messrs. Quirk & Co. 's? " inquired Titmouse, tapping the end of his cane against his chin, with a desperate effort to appear at his ease.

" Why, were are you eyes? I should think you might have seen what was wrote on this here plate—it's large enough, one should have thought, to be read by them as *can* read!—What's your business? "

" We want—Give us the paper, Hucky "—he added, addressing his companion, who produced it in a moment; and Titmouse would have proceeded to possess the old woman of all his little heart, when she cut him short by saying, snappishly—" They aren't none on 'em in; nor never is on Sundays—so you'll just call to-morrow if you wants 'em. What's your names? "

"Mr. Tittlebat Titmouse," answered that gentleman, with a very particular emphasis on every syllable.

"Mr. *who?*" exclaimed the old woman, opening her eyes, and raising her hand to the back of her ear. Mr. Titmouse repeated his name more loudly and distinctly.

"Tippetitippety!—what's that?"

"No, no!" exclaimed Titmouse, peevishly; "I said, Mr. Tit-el-bat Tit-mouse!—will that suit you?"

"Tick-a-tick-a-tick?—Well, gracious! if ever I heard such a name. Oh!—I see!—you're making a fool of me! Get off, or I'll call a constable.—Get along with you, you couple of puppies! Is this the way—"

"I tell you," interposed Mr. Huckaback, angrily, "that this gentleman's name *is* Mr. Tittlebat Titmouse; and you'd better take care what you're at, old woman, for we've come on business of *wital consequence!*"

"I dare say it'll keep, then, till to-morrow," tartly added the old woman.

The friends consulted for a moment, and then Titmouse asked if he might go in and write a letter to Messrs. Quirk.

"No indeed!" said she; "how do I know who you are? There's a public-house close by, where you may write what you like, and bring it here, and they'll get it the first thing in the morning. So that's what you may take away with you!"—with which the complaisant old janitress shut the door in their faces.

"Huck, 'pon my life, I am afraid there's nothing in it," said Titmouse, despondingly, to his friend—both of them remaining rooted to the spot.

"Oudacious old toad!" muttered Huckaback, indignantly.

"Hucky—I'm *sure* there's nothing in it!" exclaimed Titmouse, after a long pause, looking earnestly at his friend, hoping to draw from him a contrary opinion.

"I—I own I don't half like the looks of it," replied Huckaback, putting his newspaper into his pocket again; "but we'll try if we can't write a letter to sound 'em, and so far take the old creature's advice. Here's the public-house she told us of. Come, let's see what's to be done."

Titmouse, greatly depressed, followed his friend; and they soon provided themselves with two glasses of stout, and after a little difficulty, with implements for writing. That they made good use of their time and materials, let the following epistle prove. It was their joint composition, and here is an exact copy of it:

" *To Messrs.* QUIRK, GAMMON *and* SNAP.

" SIR,

" Your Names being Put In an Advertisement in This present *Sunday Flash,* Newspaper of To-day's Date, Mr. T. T. Begs To inform Your respectable House I feel Uncommon anxious To speak with them On This *truly interesting subject,* seeing It mentions The Name Of Gabriel Tittlebat Titmouse, which Two last Names Of That Deceased Person *my Own Name Is,* which can *Any* Day (As soon As Possible) call and *prove* To you, By telling you The Same, *truly.* He being Engaged in Business During the week Very close (for The Present), I hope that If they Have Any thing particular To say To Him, they will write To me without The least Delay, and please address T. T. at Tag-rag and Co.'s, No. 375. Oxford Street, Post-Paid, which will ensure Its Being duly Taken In By my Employers, and am,

" Gents.

" Yours to Command,

" TITTLEBAT TITMOUSE.

" P.S. My friend, that Is With me writing This (Mr. Robert Huckaback) can prove who I am If necessitated so to do.

" N.B. Shall have on objections to do the Liberal Thing if anything suitable Turns Up Of It. T. T.

(" *Sunday Evening,* 9/7/18—.

" Forgot to Say, am The only Child of my Honored Parents, one of which (my Mother) Died; before I knew them In Lawful Wedloc, and Was 27 last Birth Day, Never having Seen your Advertisement Till This Night, wʰ, if Necessary *can Prove.*")

This perspicuous and truly elegant performance having been thrice subjected to the critical examination of the friends (the paragraph concerning Huckaback having been inserted at the instance of that gentleman, who wished to be mixed up from the beginning with so promising an affair), was then folded up, and directed to " Messrs. Quirk and Co." a great straggling wet wafer having been first put upon it. It was safely deposited, a few minutes afterward, with the old woman of the house; and then the two West-End gentlemen hastened away from that truly plebeian part of the town. Under three different gas-lights did they stop, take out the newspaper, and spell over the advertisement; by which ingenious processes they at length succeeded in satisfying themselves that there *was* some-

thing in it—a fact of which, upon the old woman shutting the
door in their faces, it may be recollected they had had grievous
misgivings. They parted, however, with a considerable abatement of the excitement with which they had set out on their
voyage of discovery.

Mr. Titmouse did not, on reaching his room, take off and
lay aside his precious Sunday apparel with his accustomed care
and deliberation. On the contrary, he peeled it off, as it were,
and threw himself on the bed as quickly as possible in order
that he might calmly revolve the immense event of the day in
his mind, which it had agitated like a stone thrown into a
stagnant pool by the road-side. Oh, how restless was he! not
more so could he have been had he lain between horse-hair
sheets. He repeatedly got up and walked about two or three
little steps, which were all that his room admitted of. At the
very first peep of daylight he started out of bed, got out of
his pocket the newspaper which Huckaback had lent him,
strove to decipher the advertisement, and then sunk into bed
again—but not to sleep, till four or five o'clock; having nevertheless to rise at half past six, to resume his detested duties at
Tag-rag and Co.'s, whose shop he assisted in opening at seven
o'clock, as usual. When he and his shopmates were sitting
together at breakfast, he could not help letting out a little,
vaguely and mysteriously, about "something that might happen in the course of the day;" and thereby succeeded in satisfying his experienced companions that he expected the visit
of a policeman, for some *row* he had been concerned in overnight.—Well, eight, nine, ten o'clock wore away heavily, and
nothing transpired, alas! to vary the monotonous duties in
which Mr. Titmouse was engaged; bale after bale, and package after package, he took down and put up again, at the bidding of pretty capricious customers; silk, satin, bombazines,
crapes, muslins, ribbons, gloves, he assisted in displaying and
disposing of as usual; but it was clear that his powerful understanding could no longer settle itself, as before, upon his
responsible and arduous duties. Every other minute he cast a
feverish furtive glance toward the door. He almost dropped
at one time, as a postman crossed from the opposite side of
the street, as if to enter their shop—then passing on immediately, however, to the next door. Not a person, in short, entered the premises, that he did not scrutinize narrowly and
anxiously, but in vain. No—buying and selling was the order
of the day, as usual!—Eleven o'clock struck, and he sighed.
"You don't seem well," said a pretty young woman, to
whom, in a somewhat absent manner, he was exhibiting and

describing the qualities of some cambric. "Oh—ye—es, uncommon!" he replied; "never better, ma'am, than when so
well employed!" accompanying the latter words with what
he conceived to be a very arch, but which was in fact, a very
impudent look at his fair customer. At that moment a voice
called out to him from the further end of the shop, near the
door—"Titmouse! Wanted!"
    "Coming!" he shouted, turning as white as the cambric he
held in his hands—which became suddenly cold, while his heart
went thump, thump, as he hastily exclaimed to the astonished
lady, ' Excuse me, ma'am, if you please—Jones," addressing
the shopman next to him, "will you attend to this lady?" and
he hastened whither he had been called, amidst a prevalent
grin and "hem!" from his companions on each side, as he
passed along the shop, till he reached the spot where stood the
stranger who had inquired for him. He was of a slight gentlemanly figure, above the average height. His countenance
was very striking; he was dressed with simplicity—somewhat
carelessly perhaps; and appeared somewhere about thirty-six
or thirty-seven years of age. He bowed slightly as Titmouse
approached him, and an air of very serious surprise came over
his expressive countenance.
    "Mr. Titmouse?" he inquired, blandly.
    "Ye-e-s, sir, at your service," replied Titmouse, trembling
involuntarily all over. The stranger again slightly inclined
toward him, and—still more slightly—touched his hat; fixing
on him at the same time an inquisitive penetrating eye that
really abashed, or rather perhaps alarmed him.
    "You left—you favored us by leaving—a note at our office
last night, addressed to Messrs. Quirk, Gammon and Snap?"
he inquired, lowering his voice to a whisper.
    "Yes, sir, hoping it was no—"
    "Pray, Mr. Titmouse, can we be alone for about five or ten
minutes?"
    "I—I—don't exactly know, here, sir; I'm afraid—against
the rules of the house—but—I'll ask. Here is Mr. Tag-rag.
—May I step into the cloak-room with this gentleman for a
few minutes, sir?" he continued, addressing his imperious employer, who, with a pen behind his right ear, his left hand in
his breeches pocket, and his right hand impatiently tweedling
about his watch seals, had followed Titmouse, on hearing him
inquired for in the manner I have described, and stood at a
yard or two's distance, eying the two with a fussy dissatisfied
look, wondering what on earth any one could want with one of
his young men.

As Mr. Tag-rag will figure a little on my canvas by and by, I may as well here give the reader a slight sketch of that gentleman. He was about fifty-two years old; a great tyrant in his little way; a compound of ignorance, selfishness, and conceit. He knew nothing on earth except the price of his goods, and how to make the most of his business. He was of middle size, with a tendency to corpulence; and almost invariably wore a black coat and waistcoat, a white neck-handkerchief very primly tied, and gray trousers. He had a dull, gray eye, with white eyelashes, and no eyebrows; a forehead that seemed ashamed of his face, it retreated so far and so abruptly back from it; his face was pretty deeply pitted with the small-pox; his nose—or rather semblance of a nose—consisted of two great nostrils looking at you—as it were, impudently—out of the middle of his face; there was a perfect level space from cheekbone to cheekbone; his whiskers, neatly and closely cut, came in points to each corner of his mouth, which was a very large, shapeless, sensual-looking affair. This may serve, for the present, to give you an idea of the man who had contrived to excite toward himself the hatred and contempt of everybody over whom he had any control.

"You know quite well, sir, we never allow anything of the sort," was his short reply, in a very disagreeable tone and manner, to the modest request of Titmouse, as above mentioned.

"May I beg the favor of a few minutes' private conversation with Mr. Titmouse," said the stranger, politely, "on a matter of the last importance to him? My name, sir, is Gammon, and I am a solicitor."

"Why, sir," answered Tag-rag, somewhat cowed by the calm and gentlemanly, but at the same time decisive manner of Mr. Gammon—"it's really very inconvenient, and decidedly against the rules of the house, for any of my young men to be absent on business of their own during *my* business hours; but—I suppose—what must be must be—I'll give him ten minutes—and he'd better not stay longer," he subjoined fiercely—looking significantly first at his watch, and then at Titmouse. "It's only for the sake of the other young men, sir. In a large establishment like ours, we're obliged, you know, sir," etc., etc., etc., he added, in a low cringing tone, deprecatory of the contemptuous air with which he *felt* that Mr. Gammon was regarding him. That gentleman, with a slight bow, and a sarcastic smile, presently quitted the shop, accompanied by Titmouse, who scarce knew whether his head or heels were uppermost.

"How far do you live from this place, Mr. Titmouse?" inquired Mr. Gammon, as soon as they had got into the street.

"Not four minutes' walk, sir; but—hem!"—he was flustered at the idea of showing so eminent a person into his wretched room—"Suppose we were to step into this tavern here, sir—I dare say they've a room at our service."

"Pray, allow me to ask, Mr. Titmouse—have you any private papers—family writings, or things of that sort, at your rooms?"

Titmouse seemed considering.

"I—I think I have, sir," he replied—"one or two—but they're of no consequence."

"Are you a *judge* on that point, Mr. Titmouse?" inquired Mr. Gammon, with a smile; "pray let us, my dear sir, at once to your room—time is very short and valuable. I should vastly like to look at these same insignificant papers of yours!"

In less than two minutes' further time, Mr. Gammon was sitting at Titmouse's little rickety round table, at his lodgings, with a sheet of paper before him, and a small pencil-case in his hand, asking him a number of questions concerning his birth and family connections, and taking down his answers very carefully. Mr. Titmouse was surprised at the gentleman's knowledge of the family history of the Titmouses. As for papers, etc., Mr. Titmouse succeeded in producing four or five old letters and memoranda from the bottom of his trunk, and one or two entries, in faded ink, on the fly-leaf of a Bible of his father's, which he did not recollect having opened before for very many years, and of which said entries, still pressed on the subject by Mr. Gammon, he had been hardly aware of even the existence. With these several documents Mr. Gammon was so much struck that he proposed to take them away with him, for better and more leisurely examination, and safer custody, at their office; but Mr. Titmouse significantly hinted at his very recent acquaintance with Mr. Gammon, who, he intimated, was at liberty to come and make exact copies of them whenever he pleased, in his (Mr. Titmouse's) presence.

"Oh, certainly—yes," replied Mr. Gammon, slightly coloring at the distrust implied by this observation; "I applaud your caution, Mr. Titmouse. By all means keep them, and most carefully; because (I do not say that they *are*), but it is quite possible that they may become rather valuable—to *you*."

"Thank you, sir; and now, hoping you'll excuse the liberty," said Titmouse, with a very anxious air, "I should

most uncommonly like to know what all this means—what is
to turn up out of it all?"

"The law, my dear sir, is proverbially uncertain—"

"Oh, Lord! but the law can give me a *hint*—"

"*The law never hints*," interrupted Mr. Gammon, impress-
ively, with a bland smile.

"Well, then, how did you come, sir, to know that there
ever was such a person as Mr. Gabriel Titmouse, my father?
And what can come from him, seeing he was only a bit of a
shoe-maker—unless he's *heir* to something?"

"Ah, yes—exactly; those are very interesting questions.
Mr. Titmouse—very!—"

"Yes, sir; and them and a great many more I was going to
ask long ago, but I saw you were—"

"Sir, I perceive that we have positively been absent from
your place of business nearly an hour—your employers will be
getting rather impatient."

"Meaning no offense, sir—bother *their* impatience! *I'm*
impatient, I assure you, to know what all this means. Come,
sir, 'pon my life I've told *you* everything! It isn't quite
fair!"

"Why certainly, you see, Mr. Titmouse," said Gammon,
with an agreeable smile—(it was that smile of his that had
been the making of Mr. Gammon)—"it is only candid in me
to acknowledge that your curiosity is perfectly reasonable, and
your frankness very obliging; and I see no difficulty in admitting at once, that *I have* had a motive—"

"Yes, sir — and all that — *I* know, sir"—hastily interrupted Titmouse, but without irritating or disturbing the
placid speaker.

"And that we waited with some anxiety for the result of
our advertisement."

"Ah, you can't escape from *that*, you know, sir!" interposed Titmouse, with a confident air.

"But it is a maxim with us, my dear sir, never to be premature in anything, especially when it may be—very prejudicial; you've really no idea, my dear Mr. Titmouse, of the
world of mischief that is often done by precipitancy in legal
matters; and in the present stage of the business—the present
stage, my dear sir—I really do see it necessary not to—do anything premature and without consulting my partners."

"Lord, sir!" exclaimed Titmouse, getting more and more
irritated and impatient as he reflected on the length of his absence from Tag-rag & Co.'s.

"I quite feel for your anxiety—so perfectly natural—"

"Oh, dear sir! if you'd only tell me the *least bit*—"

"If, my dear sir, I were to disclose just now the exact object we had in inserting that advertisement in the papers—"

"How did you come to know of it at all, sir? Come, there can't be any harm in *that* anyhow—"

"Not the least, my dear sir. It was in the course of business—in the course of business."

"Is it money that's been left me—or—anything of that sort?"

"It quite pains me, I assure you, Mr. Titmouse—I think, by the way"—added Gammon suddenly, as something occurred to him of their previous conversation, which he was not quite sure of—"you told me that that Bible was given you by your father."

"Oh, yes, sir! yes—no doubt of it; surely *that* can't signify, seeing he's dead, and I'm his only son?" asked Titmouse, quickly and eagerly.

"Oh, 'tis only a circumstance—a mere circumstance; but in business, you know, Mr. Titmouse, every little helps—and you really, by the way, have no recollection of your mother, Mr. Titmouse!"

"No, sir, I said so! And—meaning no offense, sir—I can't abide being put off in this kind of way—I must own!—See what I have told you—you've told *me* nothing at all. I hope you haven't been only making me a cat's-paw of? 'Pon my soul, I *hate* being made a cat's-paw of, sir!"

"Good heavens, Mr. Titmouse! how can you imagine it? You are at this moment the object of a considerable share of our anxiety—"

"Not meaning it rudely, sir—please to tell me at once, plainly, am I to be the better for anything you're now about?"

"That may or may not be, sir," answered Mr. Gammon, in the same imperturbable manner, drawing on his gloves, and rising from his chair. "In justice to yourself, and other parties concerned—"

"Oh! is anybody to *share* in it?" exclaimed Titmouse, alarmedly.

"I am sure," said Gammon, smiling, "that you will give us credit for consulting your best interests. We sincerely desire to advance them; and this matter occupies a good deal of our time and anxiety. It—it is *really*," looking at his watch, "upward of an hour since we quitted your place of business —I fear I shall get into disgrace with that respectable gentleman your employer. Will you favor us with a call at our

office to-morrow night, when the business of the day is over?
When do you quit at night?"

"About half past nine o'clock, sir; but really—to-morrow
night! Couldn't I come to-night, sir?"

"Not to-night, I fear, my dear sir. We have a very important engagement. Let us say to-morrow night, at a quarter past ten—shall we say that hour?"

"Well, sir, if not before—yes—I'll be with you. But I
must say—"

"Good-day, Mr. Titmouse." They were by this time in
Oxford Street again. "Good-day, my dear sir—good-day—
to-morrow night, as soon after ten as possible—eh? Good-
bye."

This was all that Mr. Titmouse could get out of Mr. Gammon, who, hailing a coach off the stand beside them, got into
it, and it was soon making its way eastward. What a miserable mixture of doubts, hopes, and fears had he left Titmouse!
He felt as if he were like a squeezed orange; he had told everything he knew about himself, and got nothing in return out
of the smooth, imperturbable, impenetrable Mr. Gammon,
but empty civilities.—"Lord, Lord!" thought Titmouse, as
Mr. Gammon's coach turned the corner; "what would I give
to know half about it that that gent knows! But Mr. Tag-
rag! by Jove! what *will* he say? It's struck twelve. I've
been more than an hour away—and he gave me ten minutes!
Sha'n't I catch it?"

And he did. Almost the very first person he met, on entering the shop, was his respected employer, Mr. Tag-rag, who
plucking his watch out of his fob, and, looking furiously at it,
motioned the trembling Titmouse to follow him to the further
end of the long shop, where there happened to be then no customers.

"Is this your ten minutes, sir, eh?"

"I am sorry—"

"Where may you have been, sir, all this while?"

"With that gentleman, sir, and I really did not know—"

"You didn't know, sir! Who cares what you know, or
don't know. You know you ought to have been back fifty-
five minutes ago, sir. You do, sir! Isn't your time my property, sir? Don't I pay for it, sir? An hour!—in the middle
of the day! I've not had such a thing happen this five years!
I'll stop it out of your salary, sir!"

Titmouse did not attempt to interrupt him.

"And pray, what have you been gossiping about, sir, in this
disgraceful manner?"

"Something that he wanted to say to me, sir."

"You low puppy!—do you suppose I don't see your impertinence? I *insist*, sir, on knowing what all this gossiping with that fellow has been about?"

"Then you *won't* know, that's flat!" replied Titmouse, doggedly; returning to his usual station behind the counter.

"I sha'n't!!"

"No, sir, you sha'n't know a single word about it."

"Sha'n't know a single word about it! Vastly good, sir!! —Do you know whom you're talking to, sir? Do you really know in whose presence you are, sir?"

"Mr. Tag-rag, I presume, of the firm of Tag-rag and Co.," replied Titmouse, looking him full in the face.—One or two of his companions near him almost turned pale at the audacity he was displaying.

"And who are *you*, sir, that dare to presume to bandy words with ME, sir?" inquired Tag-rag, his deeply pitted face having gone quite white, and his whole body quivering with rage.

"Tittlebat Titmouse, at your service," was the answer in a glib tone, and with a sufficiently saucy air.

"You heard that, I hope?" inquired Tag-rag, with forced calmness, of a pale-faced young man, the nearest to him.

"Ye—es, sir," was the meekly reluctant answer.

"This day month you leave, sir!" said Mr. Tag-rag, solemnly, as if conscious that he was passing a sort of sentence of death upon the presumptuous delinquent.

"Very well, Mr. Tag-rag—anything that pleases you pleases your humble servant. I *will* go this day month, and welcome —I've long wished—"

"Then you *sha'n't* leave, sir," said Tag-rag, furiously.

"But I will, sir. You've given me warning, and if you haven't, now I give *you* warning," replied Titmouse, turning, however, very pale, and experiencing a certain sudden sinking of the heart—for this was a serious and most unlooked-for event, and for a while put out of his head all the agitating thoughts of the last few hours. Poor Titmouse had enough to bear—what with the delicate raillery and banter of his accomplished companions for the rest of the day, and the galling tyranny of Mr. Tag-rag, who dogged him about all day, setting him about the most menial and troublesome offices he could, and constantly saying mortifying things to him before customers, and the state of miserable suspense in which Mr. Gammon had thought fit to leave him; I say that surely all this was enough for him to bear without having to encounter at night, as he did, on his return to his lodgings, his blustering landlady, who vowed that if she sold him out and out she would be put off no longer—and his pertinacious and melancholy tailor, who, with sallow unshaven face, told him of five children at home, all ill of the small-pox, and his wife in an hospital—and he *implored* a payment on account. This sufferer succeeded in squeezing out of Titmouse seven shillings on account, and his landlady extorted ten, which staved off a distress—direful word!—for some week or two longer, and so they left him in the possession of eight shillings or so, to last till next quarter-day. He sighed heavily, barred his door, and sat down opposite his little table, on which was nothing but a solitary thin candle, and on which his eyes rested unconsciously, till the stench of it, burning right down into the socket, roused him from his wretched reverie. Then he unlocked his box, and took out his Bible and the papers which had been produced to Mr. Gammon, and gazed at them with intense but useless scrutiny. Unable, however, to conjecture what bearing they could have upon himself or his fortunes, he hastily replaced them in his box, threw off his clothes, and flung himself on his bed, to pass a far more dismal night than he had known for years.

He ran the gantlet at Messrs. Tag-rag and Co.'s all Tuesday as he had done on the day preceding. One should have supposed that when his companions beheld him persecuted by their common tyrant, whom they all equally hated, they would have made common cause with their suffering companion, or at all events given no countenance to his persecution, yet it was far otherwise. Without stopping to analyze the feeling which produced it, and which the moderately reflective reader may easily analyze for himself if so disposed, I am grieved to have to say, that when all the young men saw that Tag-rag would be gratified by their *cutting* poor Titmouse, who, with all his little vanities, fooleries, and even selfishness, had never personally offended or injured any of them—they did so, and when Tag-rag observed it, his miserable mind was more gratified with them by far than it had ever been before. He spoke to all of them with unusual blandness; to the sinner, Titmouse, with augmented bitterness.

CHAPTER II.

A FEW minutes after ten o'clock that night a gentle ringing at the bell of Messrs. Quirk, Gammon and Snap's office announced the arrival of poor Titmouse. The door was quickly opened by a very fashionably dressed clerk, who seemed in the act of quitting for the night.

"Ah—Mr. Titmouse, I presume?" he inquired, with a kind of deference in his manner that Titmouse had never been accustomed to.

"The same, sir—Tittlebat Titmouse."

"Oh, allow me. sir, to show you in to Messrs. Quirk, Gammon and Snap. I know they're expecting to see you. It's not often they're here so late. Walk in, sir—" With this he led the way to an inner room, and opening a green-baize door in the further side of it, announced and showed in Mr. Titmouse, and left him—sufficiently flustered. Three gentlemen were sitting at a large table, on which he saw, by the strong but circumscribed light of two shaded candlesticks, were lying a great number of papers and parchments. The three gentlemen rose when he entered, Mr. Quirk and Mr. Snap involuntarily starting on first catching sight of the figure of Titmouse; Mr. Gammon came and shook hands with him.

"Mr. Titmouse," said he, with a very polite air, "let me introduce you to Mr. Quirk "—(this was the senior partner, a short, stout, elderly gentleman, dressed in black, with a shining bald head and white hair, and sharp black eyes, and who looked very earnestly, nay, with even a kind of dismay, at him)—"and Mr. Snap "—(this was the junior partner, having recently been promoted to be such after ten years' service in the office as managing clerk; he was about thirty, particularly well dressed, slight, active, and with a face like a terrier—*so* hard, sharp and wiry)! Of Mr. Gammon himself I have already given the reader a slight notion. He appeared altogether a different style of person from both his partners. He was of most gentlemanly person and bearing—and at once acute, cautious and insinuating—with a certain something about the eye, which had from the first made Titmouse feel uneasy on looking at him.

"A seat, sir," said Mr. Quirk, rising and placing a chair for him, on which he sat down, they resuming theirs.

"You are punctual, Mr. Titmouse!" exclaimed Mr. Gammon, with a smile; "more so than, I fear, you were yesterday, after our long interview, eh? Pray what did that worthy person, Mr. Rag-bag—or whatever his name is—say, on your return?"

"Say, gents?" he tried to clear his throat, for he spoke somewhat more thickly and his heart beat more perceptibly than usual. "Meaning no offense—I'm ruined by it, and no mistake."

"Ruined! I'm sorry to hear it," interposed Mr. Gammon, with a concerned air.

"I am, indeed, sir. Such a towering rage as he has been in ever since, and he's given me warning to go on the 10th of next month." He thought he observed a faint smile flit over the faces of all three. "He has, indeed."

"Dear me, Mr. Titmouse! Did he allege any reason for dismissing you?" keenly inquired Mr. Quirk.

"Yes, sir—"

"What might it have been?"

"Stopping out longer than I was allowed, and refusing to tell him what this gentleman and I had been talking about."

"Don't think that'll do; sure it won't!" briskly exclaimed Mr. Snap; "no just cause, that," and he jumped up, whisked down a book from the shelves behind him, and eagerly turned over the leaves.

"Never mind that now, Mr. Snap," said Mr. Quirk, rather petulantly; "surely we have other matters to talk about to-night."

"Asking pardon, sir, but I think it *does* matter to me, sir," interposed Titmouse; "for on the 10th of next month I'm a beggar—being next door to it *now*."

"Not quite, we trust," said Mr. Gammon, with a benignant smile.

"But Mr. Tag-rag said he'd make me as good as one."

"That's evidence to show malice," again eagerly interjected Mr. Snap, who was again tartly rebuffed by Mr. Quirk; even Mr. Gammon turning toward him with a surprised—"Really, Mr. Snap!"

"So Mr. Tag-rag said he'd make you a beggar?" inquired Mr. Quirk.

"He vowed he would, sir! He did, as true as the gospel, sir."

"Ha, ha, ha!" laughed Mr. Quirk and Mr. Gammon—but such a laugh!—not careless or hearty, but subdued, and with a dash of deference in it. "Well—it perhaps may not signify much by that time," said he, and laughed again, followed by the soft laugh of Mr. Gammon, and a kind of sharp, quick sound, like a bark, from Mr. Snap.

"But, gents, you'll excuse me if I say I think it *does* signify to *me*, and a'n't any laughing matter!" quoth Titmouse earnestly, and coloring with anger. "Without being rude I'd rather come to business, if there's any to be done, without so much laughing at me."

"Laughing at you! my dear sir—no, no!" exclaimed all

three in a breath—"laughing *with* you," said Mr. Quirk.
"By the time you mention you may perhaps be able to laugh
at Mr. Rag-bag, and everybody else, for—"

"[—No use mincing matters?" he whispered, in a low tone,
to Mr. Gammon, who nodded in apparently reluctant acquiescence, and fixed his eyes earnestly on Titmouse.]

"I really think we are warranted, sir, in preparing you to
expect by that time—that is, you will understand, sir, if our
efforts are successful in your behalf, and if you yield yourself
implicitly in all things to our guidance—*that is absolutely
essential*—a prospect—we say, at present, you will observe
only a prospect—of a surprising and splendid change in your
circumstances!" Titmouse began to tremble violently, his
heart beat rapidly, and his hands were bedewed with a cold
moisture.

"I hear, gents," said he, thickly, and he also heard a faint
ringing in his ears.

"It's not impossible, sir, in plain English," continued Mr.
Quirk, himself growing a little excited with the important
communication that trembled on the tip of his tongue, "that
you may at no distant time, if you turn out to be the person,
be put into possession of an estate of somewhere about Ten
Thousand a year—"

The words seemed to have struck Titmouse blind—as he saw
nothing for some moments, then everything seemed swimming
around him, and he felt a sort of faintness or sickness stealing
over him. They had hardly been prepared for their communications affecting their little visitor so powerfully. Mr. Snap
hastened out, and in with a glass of water, and the earnest
attentions of the three soon restored Mr. Titmouse to his
senses. It was a good while, however, before he could appreciate the little conversation which they now and then addressed
to him, or estimate the full importance of the astounding intelligence Mr. Quirk had just communicated, "Beg pardon—
but may I make free to ask for a little brandy and water,
gents? I feel all over in a kind of tremble," said he, some
time afterward.

"Yes—by all means, Mr. Titmouse. Mr. Snap, will you
be kind enough to order Betty to bring in a glass of cold
brandy and water from the Jolly Thieves next door?" Snap
shot out, gave the order, and returned in a trice. The old
woman in a few minutes' time followed, with a large tumbler
of dark brandy and water, quite hot, for which Mr. Gammon
apologized, but Mr. Titmouse said he preferred it so—and
soon addressed himself to the inspiring mixture. It quickly

manifested its influence, reassuring him wonderfully. As he
sat sipping it Messrs. Quirk, Gammon and Snap being engaged
in an earnest conversation, of which he could understand little
or nothing, he had leisure to look about him, and observed
that there was lying before them a large sheet of paper, of
which they all of them often and earnestly looked, filled with
marks, so:

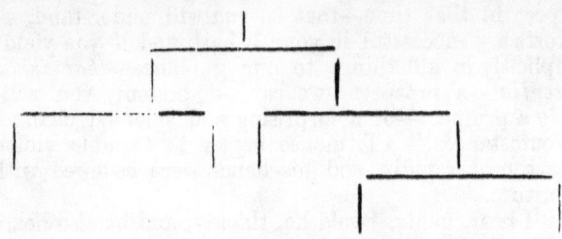

with writing at the ends of each of them, and round and
square figures. When he saw them all bending over and
scrutinizing this mysterious object, it puzzled him, and many
a better head than his has a pedigree puzzled before, sorely,
and he began to suspect it was a sort of conjuring paper.
    "I hope, gents, that paper's all right—eh?" said he, sup-
ported by the brandy, which he had nearly finished. They
turned toward him with a smile of momentary surprise, and
then:
    "We hope so—a vast deal depends on it," said Mr. Quirk,
looking over his glasses at Titmouse. Now what *he* had
hinted at, as far as he could venture to do so, was a thought
that glanced across his as yet unsettled brain, that there might
have been invoked more than *mere earthly assistance*, but he
prudently pressed the matter no further—that was all Messrs.
Quirk, Gammon and Snap's lookout; *he* had been no party to
anything of the sort, nor would he knowingly. He also observed the same sheets of paper written all over, which Mr.
Gammon had filled at his (Titmouse's) room, the night before,
and several new and old-looking papers and parchments.
Sometimes they addressed questions to him, but found it
somewhat difficult to keep his attention up to anything that
was said to him for the wild visions that were chasing one
another through his heated brain, the passage of which said
visions was not a little accelerated by the large tumbler of
brandy and water which he had just taken.
    "Then, in fact," said Mr. Quirk, as the three simultaneous-
ly sat down, after having been for some time standing poring

over the paper before Mr. Quirk, "Tittlebat's title accrued in 18—? That's the point—eh, Gammon?"

"Precisely so," said Mr. Gammon, calmly.

"To be sure," confidently added Snap, who having devoted himself exclusively all his life to the sharpest practice of the criminal law, knew about as much of real-property law as a snipe—but it would not do to appear ignorant or taking no part in the matter in the presence of the heir-at-law, and the future great client of the House.

"Well, Mr. Titmouse," at length said Mr. Quirk, laying aside his glasses—"you are likely to be one of the luckiest men of your day. We may be mistaken, but it appears to us that your right is clear, and has been clear these ten or twelve years, to the immediate enjoyment of a very fine estate in Yorkshire, worth some £10,000 or £12,000 a year at the least!"

"You don't say so. Oh, gents! I do believe we're all dreaming! Is it all true, indeed?"

"It is, Mr. Titmouse—and we are very proud and happy, indeed, to be the honored instruments of establishing your rights, my dear sir," said Mr. Gammon.

"Then all the money that's spent this ten or twelve years is my money, is it?"

"If we are right it is undoubtedly as you say," answered Mr. Quirk, giving a quick apprehensive glance at Mr. Gammon.

"There'll be a jolly reckoning for some one then shortly—eh? My stars!"

"My dear Mr. Titmouse," said Mr. Gammon, "you have a most just regard for your own interests; there *will* be a reckoning, and a very terrible one ere long, for somebody—but we've time enough before us for all that. Only let us have the unspeakable happiness of seeing you once fairly in possession of your estates, and our office shall know no rest till you have got all you are entitled to—every farthing even!"

"Oh, never fear our letting them rest!" said Mr. Quirk, judiciously accommodating himself to the taste and apprehension of his excited auditor—"Those that must give up the goose must give up the giblets also—ha, ha, ha!" Messrs. Gammon and Snap echoed the laugh, and enjoyed the joke of the head of the firm.

"Ha, ha, ha!" laughed Mr. Titmouse, immensely excited by the conjoint influence of the brandy and the news of the night; "capital! capital! hurrah! Such goings-on there will be. You're all of the right sort, gents, I see. 'Pon my life,

.aw forever. Let's all shake hands, gents. Come, if you please, all together! all friends to-night!" And the little fel- low grasped each of the three readily proffered right hands of Messrs. Quirk, Gammon and Snap, with an energy that was likely to make all the high-contracting parties to that quadruple alliance remember its ratification.

" And is it all a ready-money affair, gents—or rent, and all *that* kind of thing?"

" Why, almost entirely the latter," answered Mr. Quirk, " except the accumulations."

" Then, 'pon my soul—I'm a great landlord, am I?"

" Indeed, my dear Mr. Titmouse, you are—(that is, unless we have made a blunder such as our house is not often in the habit of making)—and have two very fine houses, one in town and the other in the country."

" Capital! delightful! I'll live in both of them—we'll have *such* goings-on. And is it, *quite* up to the mark of £10,000 a year?"

" We really entertain no doubt—"

" And such as I can spend all of it, every year?"

" Certainly—no doubt of it—not the least. The rents are paid with most exemplary punctuality—at least," added Mr. Gammon, with a captivating and irresistible smile, and taking him affectionately by the hand—" at least they *will* be, as soon as we have them fairly in our management."

" Oh, *you're* to get it all in for me, are you?" he inquired, briskly. The three partners bowed, with the most deprecat- ingly disinterested air in the world, intimating that, for *his* sake, they were ready to take upon themselves even that troublesome responsibility.

" Capital! couldn't be better! couldn't be better! Ah, ha, ha—you've hatched the goose, and must bring me its eggs. Ah, ha, ha! a touch in *your* line, old gent!"

" Ha, ha, ha! excellent! ah, ha, ha!" laughed the three partners at the wit of their new client. Mr. Titmouse joined them, and snapped his fingers in the air.

" Lord—I've just thought of Tag-rag and Company's—I seem as if I hadn't seen or heard of those gents for Lord knows how long. Only fancy old Tag-rag making me a beggar on the 10th of next month—ha, ha, ha!—I sha'n't see that in- fernal hole any more anyhow."

[" There!" whispered Mr. Gammon, apprehensively, in the ear of Mr. Quirk, " you hear that? A little wretch! We have been perfectly insane in going so far already with him. Is not this what I predicted?" " I don't care," said Mr. Quirk, stubbornly. "Who first found it out, Mr. Gammon, and who's to be at the expense and responsibility? Pshaw! I know what I'm about—*I'll* make him knuckle down—never fear me!"]

"*That*," snapping his fingers, "for Mr. Tag-rag! *That* for Mother Squallop. Ah, ha, gents. It won't do to go back to that—eugh!—eh? will it?—you know what I mean! Fancy Tittlebat Titmouse standing behind—"

The partners looked rather blank.

"We must venture to suggest, Mr. Titmouse," said Mr. Gammon, seriously, "the *absolute necessity* there is for everything on your part and our parts to go on as quietly as before, for a little time to come; to be safe and successful, my dear sir, we must be *secret*."

"Oh, I see, gents! I see; mum—mum's the word for the present. But I *must* say, if there is any one whom I want to hear of it sooner than another it's—"

"Rag-bag and Co., I suppose! ha, ha, ha!" interrupted Mr. Gammon, his partners echoing his gentle laugh.

"Ha, ha, ha! Cuss the cats—that's it—ha, ha, ha!" echoed Mr. Titmouse, who, getting up out of his chair, could not resist capering to and fro in something of the attitude of a stage-dancer, whistling and humming by turns, and indulging in various other wild antics.

"And now, gents—excuse me, but to do a bit of business—when am I to *begin* scattering the shiners, eh?" he inquired, interrupting a low-toned but somewhat vehement conversation between the two senior partners.

"Oh, of course, sir," replied Mr. Gammon, rather coldly, "some delay is unavoidable. All we have done as yet is to discover that as far as we are advised, and can judge, you will turn out to be the right owner, but very extensive and expensive operations must be immediately commenced before you can be put into possession. There are some who won't be persuaded to drop £10,000 a year out of their hands, Mr. Titmouse, for the mere asking!" added Mr. Gammon, with a bitter smile.

"The devil there are! *Who* are they that want to keep me any longer out of what's my own?—what's justly mine? Eh? I want to know. Haven't they kept me out long enough? hang 'em. Put 'em in prison directly, don't spare 'em—rascals!"

"They'll probably ere long find their way in that direction —for, however," replied Mr. Quirk, "he's to make up, poor devil, the mesne profits—"

"*Mean* profits?—is that all you call them, gents? 'Pon my life, it's rogue's money—villain's profits! So don't spare him—he's robbed the fatherless, which I am, and an orphan. Keep me out of what's mine, indeed. Curse me if we shall, though!"

"My dear Mr. Titmouse," said Gammon, gravely, "we are getting on too fast—dreadfully too fast. It will never do; matters of such immense importance as these can not be hurried on or talked of in this way—"

"I like that, sir. I do, by Jove!"

"You will really if you go on in this wild way, Mr. Titmouse, made us regret the trouble we have taken in the affair, and especially the promptness with which we have communicated to you the extent of your possible good fortune."

"Beg pardon, I'm sure, gents, but mean no offense; am monstrous obliged to you for what you've done for me—but, by Jove, it's taken me rather aback, I own, to hear that I'm to be kept so long out of it all. Why can't you offer him, whoever he is that has my property, a slapping sum to go out at once? Gents, I'll own to you I'm most uncommon low—never so low in my life—devilish low. Done up, and yet can't get what's justly mine. What am I to do in the meanwhile? Consider *that*, gents."

"You are rather excited just now, Mr. Titmouse," said Mr. Quirk, seriously; "suppose we now break up and resume our conversation to-morrow, when we are all in better and calmer trim?"

"No, sir, thanking you all the same, but I think we'd better go on with it now," replied Titmouse, impetuously. "Do you think I can stoop to go back to that nasty, beastly shop, and stand behind that counter?"

"Our *decided* opinion, Mr. Titmouse," said Mr. Quirk, emphatically—his other partners getting very grave in their looks—"that is, if our opinion is worth offering—"

"That, by Jove! remains to be seen," said Titmouse, with a pettish shake of the head.

"Well, such as it is, we offer it you, and it is, that for many reasons you continue, for a little while longer, in your present situation—"

"What! own Tag-rag for my master—and I worth £10,000 a year?"

"My dear sir, you've not got it yet," said Mr. Quirk, with a very bitter sarcastic smile.

"Do you think you'd have told me what you have if you weren't sure that I *should* though? No, no! you've gone too

far, by Jove!—I shall burst, I shall! Me to go on as before!
they use me worse and worse every day. Gents, you'll excuse
me—I hope you will, but business is business, gents—it is, and
if you won't do mine I must look out for them that will—'pon
my soul, I must, and—" If Mr. Titmouse could have seen,
or, having seen, appreciated, the looks which the three partners interchanged, on hearing this absurd, ungrateful, and
insolent speech of his—the expression that flitted across their
shrewd faces; that was, of intense contempt for him, hardly
overmastered and concealed by a vivid perception of their own
interest, which was, of course, to *manage*, to soothe, to conciliate him.

How the reptile propensities of his mean nature had thriven
beneath the sudden sunshine of unexpected prosperity. See
already his selfishness, truculence, rapacity, in full play.

"So, gents," said he, after a long and keen expostulation
with them on the same subject, "I'm really to go to-morrow
morning to Tag-rag and Co.'s, and go on with the cursed life
I led there to-day, all as if nothing had happened—ha, ha,
ha!—I like that!"

"In your present humor, Mr. Titmouse, it would be in vain
to discuss the matter," said Mr. Quirk. "Again I tell you
that the course we have recommended is, in our opinion, the
proper one; excuse me if I add that you are entirely in our
hands, and if I ask you what *can* you do but adopt our advice?"

"Why, hang me if I won't employ somebody else—that's
flat. S'elp me, Heaven, I will! So, good-night, gents: you'll
find that Tittlebat Titmouse isn't to be trifled with." So saying, Mr. Titmouse clapped his hat on his head, bounced out of
the room, and, no attempt being made to stop him, he was in
the street in a twinkling.

Mr. Gammon gazed at Mr. Quirk with a look whose significance the old gentleman thoroughly understood—'twas compounded of triumph, reproach, and apprehension.

"Did you ever see such a little beast!" exclaimed Mr. Quirk,
with an air of disgust, turning to Mr. Snap.

"Beggar on horseback!" exclaimed Snap, with a bitter
sneer.

"It won't do, however," said Mr. Quirk, with a most
chagrined and apprehensive air, "for him to go at large in his
present frame of mind—he may ruin the thing altogether—"

"As good as £500 a year out of the way of the office," said
Snap.

"It can not be helped *now*," said Mr. Gammon, with a sigh

of vexation, turning to Mr. Quirk, and seizing his hat—"he must be managed—so I'll go after him instantly, and bring him back at all hazards; and we must really try and do something for him in the meanwhile, to keep him quiet till the thing's brought a little into train." So out went after Titmouse, Mr. Gammon, from whose lips dropped persuasion sweeter than honey; and I should not be surprised if he were to be able to bring back that little stubborn piece of conceited stupidity.

As soon as Mr. Titmouse heard the street door shut after him, with a kind of bang, he snapped his fingers once or twice by way of letting off a little of the inflammable air that was in him, and muttered, "Pretty chaps those, upon my soul! I'll expose them all! I'll apply to the lord mayor—they're a pack of swindlers, they are! This is the way they treat *me*, who've got a title to £10,000 a year! To be sure"—He stood still for a moment, and another moment; and dismay came quickly over him; for it suddenly occurred to his partially obfuscated intellect—what *hold* had he got on Messrs. Quirk, Gammon and Snap?—what *could* he do?—what HAD he done?

Ah—the golden vision of the last few hours was fading away momentarily, like a dream! Each second of his deep and rapid reflection, rendered more impetuous his desire and determination to return and make his peace with Messrs. Quirk, Gammon and Snap. By submission for the present, he could get the whip-hand of them hereafter! He was in the act of turning round toward the office, when Mr. Gammon softly laid his hand upon the shoulder of his repentant client.

"Mr. Titmouse! my dear sir, what is the matter with you? How could we so misunderstand each other?"

Titmouse's small cunning was on the *qui vive*, and he saw and followed up his advantage. "I am going," said he, in a resolute tone, " to speak to some one else, in the morning."

"Ah, to be sure—I supposed as much—'tis a matter which of course, however, signifies nothing to any one but yourself. You will take any steps, my dear sir, that occur to you; and act as you may be advised."

"Monstrous kind of you, 'pon my life! to come and give me such good advice!" exclaimed Titmouse with a sneer.

"Oh, don't mention it!" said Gammon, coolly; "I came out of pure good nature, to assure you that our office, notwithstanding what has passed, entertains not the slightest personal ill feeling toward you, in thus throwing off our hands a fearfully expensive, and most harassing enterprise—which we had too rashly undertaken—"

"Hem!" exclaimed Titmouse once or twice.

"So good-night, Mr. Titmouse—good-night! God bless you! we part friends!" Mr. Gammon, in the act of returning to the door, extended his hand to Mr. Titmouse, who he instantly perceived was melting rapidly.

"Why, sir," quoth Titmouse, with a mixture of embarrassment and alarm, "if I thought you all meant the correct thing —hem! I say, the correct thing by me—I shouldn't so much mind a little disappointment for the time; but you must own, Mr. Gammon, it is very hard being kept out of one's own so long—honor, now! isn't it?"

"True, very true, Mr. Titmouse. Very hard it is, indeed, to bear, and we all felt deeply for you, and would have set everything in train—"

"Would have—"

"Yes, my dear Mr. Titmouse, we *would* have done it, and brought you through every difficulty—over every obstacle, prodigious though they are, and almost innumerable."

"Why—you—don't—hardly—quite—mean to say you've given it all up?—What, already! 'Pon my life! Oh, Lord!" exclaimed Titmouse, in evident trepidation.

Mr. Gammon had triumphed over Mr. Titmouse! whom, nothing loath, he brought back, in two minutes' time, into the room which Titmouse had just before so rudely quitted. Mr. Quirk and Mr. Snap had now *their* parts to perform in the little scene which they had determined on enacting. They were in the act of locking up desks and drawers, evidently on the move, and received Mr. Titmouse with an air of cold surprise.

"Mr. Titmouse again!" exclaimed Mr. Quirk, taking his gloves out of his hat. "Back again!—an unexpected honor."

"Leave anything behind?" inquired Mr. Snap—"don't see anything—"

"Oh, no, sir! No, sir!" exclaimed Titmouse, with eager anxiety. "This gent, Mr. Gammon, and I, have made it all up, gents! I'm not vexed any more—not the least, 'pon my soul I'm not."

"*Vexed*, Mr. Titmouse!" echoed Mr. Quirk, with an air sternly ironical. "We are under great obligations to you for your forbearance!"

"Oh, come, gents!" said Titmouse, more and more disturbed, "I *was* too warm, I dare say, and—and—I ask your pardon, all of you, gents! I won't say another word, if you'll but buckle to business again—quite exactly in your way—because you see—"

"It's growing *very* late," said Mr. Quirk, coldly, and look ing at his watch; "however, after what you have said, proba bly at some future time, when we've leisure to look into the thing—"

Poor Titmouse was ready to drop on his knees, in mingled agony and fright.

"May I be allowed to say," interposed the bland voice of Mr. Gammon, addressing himself to Mr. Quirk, "that Mr. Titmouse a few minutes ago assured me, outside there, that if you, as the head of the firm, could only be persuaded to let our house take up his case again—"

"I did—I did indeed, gents! so help me—!" interrupted Mr. Titmouse, eagerly backing with an oath the ready lie of Mr. Gammon.

Mr. Quirk drew his hand across his chin musingly, and stood silently for a few moments, evidently irresolute.

"Well," said he at length, but in a very cool way, "since that is so, probably we may be induced to resume our heavy labors in your behalf; and if you will favor us with a call to-morrow night, at the same hour, we may have, by that time, made up our minds as to the course we shall think fit to adopt."

"Lord, sir, I'll be here as the clock strikes, and as meek as a mouse; and pray, have it all your own way for the future, gents—do!"

"Good-night, sir—good-night!" exclaimed the partners, motioning toward the door.

"Good-night, gents!" said Titmouse, bowing very low, and feeling himself at the same time being bowed *out!* As he passed out of the room, he cast a lingering look at their three frigid faces, as if they were angels sternly shutting him out from Paradise. What misery was his, as he walked slowly homeward, with much the same feelings (now that the fumes of the brandy had somewhat evaporated, and the reaction of excitement was coming on, aggravated by a recollection of the desperate check he had received) as a sick and troubled man, who, suddenly roused out of a delicious dream, drops into wretched reality, as it were out of a fairy-land, which, with all its dear innumerable delights, is melting overhead into thin air—disappearing *forever.*

Closet Court had never looked so odious to him as it did on his return from this memorable interview. Dreadfully dis-tressed and harassed, he flung himself on his bed for a mo-ment, directly he had shut his door, intending presently to rise and undress; but Sleep, having got him prostrate, secured her

victory. She waved her black wand over him, and—he woke
not till eight o'clock in the morning. A second long-drawn
sigh was preparing to follow its predecessor, when he heard
the clock strike eight, and sprung off the bed in a fright; for
he ought to have been at the shop an hour before. Dashing a
little water into his face, and scarce staying to wipe it off, he
ran down-stairs, through the court, and along the street, never
stopping till he had found his way into—almost the very arms
of the dreaded Mr. Tag-rag; who, rarely making his appearance
till about half past nine, had, as the deuce would have it, happened to come down an hour earlier than usual, on the only
morning out of several hundred and a half on which Titmouse
had been more then ten minutes beyond his time.

"Yours very respectfully, Mr. Titmouse—Thomas Tag-
rag!" exclaimed that personage with mock solemnity, bowing
formally to his astounded and breathless shopman.

"I—I—beg your pardon, sir; but I wasn't very well, and
overslept myself," stammered Titmouse.

"Ne-ver mind, Mr. Titmouse! ne-ver mind!—it don't much
signify, as it happens," interrupted Mr. Tag-rag, bitterly;
"you've just got an hour and a half to take this piece of silk,
with my compliments, to Messrs. Shuttle and Weaver, in Dirt
Street, Spitalfields, and ask them if they aren't ashamed to
send it to a West-End house like mine; and bring back a better
piece instead of it! D'ye *hear*, sir?"

"Yes, sir—but—am I to go before my breakfast, sir?"

"Did I say a word about breakfast, sir? You heard my
orders, sir; you can attend to them or not, Mr. Titmouse, as
you please!"

Off trotted Titmouse *instanter*, without his breakfast; and
so Tag-rag gained one object he had had in view. Titmouse
found this rather trying; a five-mile walk before him, with no
inconsiderable load under his arm, having had nothing to eat
since the preceding evening, when he had partaken of a delicate repast of thick slices of bread, smeared slightly over with
salt butter, and moistened with a most astringent decoction of
tea-leaves sweetened with brown sugar, and discolored with
sky-blue milk. He had not even a farthing about him where-
with to buy a penny roll! As he went disconsolately along, *so*
many doubts and fears buzzed impetuously about him that
they completely darkened his little soul, and bewildered his
small understanding. *Ten Thousand a Year!*—it was never
meant for the like of him. He soon worked himself into a
conviction that the whole thing was infinitely too good to be
true; the affair was desperate; it had been all moonshine; for

some cunning purpose or another, Messrs. Quirk, Gammon
and Snap, had been—ha, here he was within a few yards of
their residence, the scene of last night's tragic transactions!
As he passed Saffron Hill, he paused, looked up toward the
blessed abode,

"Where centered all his hopes and fears,"—

uttered a profound sigh, and passed slowly on toward Spitalfields. The words, "Quirk, Gammon and Snap," seemed
to be written over every shop-window which he passed—their
images filled his mind's eye. What could they be at? They
had been all very polite and friendly—and of their own seeking; had he affronted them? How coldly and proudly they
had parted with him overnight! It was evident that they
would stand no nonsense—they were great lawyers; so he must
(if they would allow him to see them again) eat humble pie
cheerfully till he had got all that they had to give him. How
he dreaded the coming night! Perhaps they intended civilly
to tell him that they would have nothing more to do with him;
they would get the estate for themselves, or some one else that
would be more manageable! They had taken care to tell him
nothing at all about the nature of his pretensions to this grand
fortune. Oh, how crafty they were—they had it all their own
way!—But what, after all, had he really done? The estates
were his, if they were really in earnest—his, and no one's else;
and why should he be kept out of them at their will and pleasure? Suppose he were to say he would give them all he was
entitled to for £20,000 down, in cash? Oh, no; on second
thoughts, that would be only two years' income! But on the
other hand—he dared hardly even propose it to his thoughts—
still, suppose it *should* really all turn out true! Goodness gracious!—that day two months he might be riding about in his
carriage in the Parks, and poor devils looking on at him, as he
now looked on all those who now rode there. There he would
be, holding up his head with the best of them, instead of slaving about as he was that moment, carrying about that cursed
bundle, ough! how he shrunk as he changed its position, to
relieve his aching right arm! Why was his mouth to be stopped
—why might he not tell his shopmates? What would he not
give for the luxury of telling it to the odious Tag-rag? If he
were to do so, Mr. Tag-rag, he was sure, would ask him to dinner the very next Sunday, at his country house at Clapham!—
Thoughts such as these so occupied his mind, that he did not
for a long while observe that he was walking at a rapid rate
toward the Mile-end road, having left Whitechapel church

nearly half a mile behind him! The possible master of £10,000 a year felt fit to drop with fatigue, and sudden apprehension of the storm he should have to encounter when he first saw Mr. Tag-rag after so long an absence. He was detained for a cruel length of time at Messrs. Shuttle and Weaver's, who not having the required quantity of silk at that moment on their premises, had some difficulty in obtaining it, after having sent for it to one or two neighboring manufactories; by which means it came to pass that it was two o'clock before Titmouse, completely exhausted and dispirited, and reeking with perspiration, had reached Tag-rag and Company's. The gentlemen of the shop had finished their dinners.

"Go upstairs and get your dinner, sir!" exclaimed Tag-rag, imperiously, after having received Messrs. Shuttle and Weaver's message.

Titmouse having laid down his heavy bundle on the counter, went upstairs hungry enough, and found himself the sole occupant of the long close-smelling room in which his companions had been recently dining. His dinner was presently brought to him by a slatternly slipshod servant-girl. It was in an uncovered basin, which appeared to contain nothing but the leavings of his companions—a savory intermixture of cold potatoes, broken meat (chiefly bits of fat and gristle), a little hot water having been thrown over it to make it appear warm and fresh —(faugh!) His plate (with a small pinch of salt upon it) had not been cleaned after its recent use, but evidently only hastily smeared over with a greasy towel, as also seemed his knife and fork, which in their disgusting state, he was fain to put up with, the table-cloth on which he might have wiped them having been removed. A hunch of bread that seemed to have been tossing about in the pan for days, and half a pint of flat-looking and sour-smelling table-beer, completed the fare set before him; opposite which he sat for some minutes, too much occupied with his reflections to commence his repast. He was in the act of scooping out of the basin some of its inviting contents, when—"Titmouse!" exclaimed the voice of one of his shopmates, peering in at him through the half-opened door, "Mr. Tag-rag wants you! He says you've had plenty of time to finish your dinner!"

"Oh, tell him, then, I'm only just beginning my dinner— eugh! such as it is!" replied Titmouse, masticating the first mouthful with an appearance of no *particular* relish, it may be supposed.

In a few minutes' time Mr. Tag-rag himself entered the

room, stuttering—"How much longer, sir, is it your pleasure
to spend over your dinner, eh?"

"Not another moment, sir," answered Titmouse, looking
with ill-concealed disgust at the savory victuals before him;
"if you'll only allow me a few minutes to go home and buy a
penny roll instead of all this—"

"Ve—ry good, sir! Ve—ry parti—cu—larly good, Mr.
Titmouse," replied Tag-rag, with ill-subdued fury; "anything else that I can make a *leetle* memorandum of against the
day of your leaving us?"

This hint of twofold terror, *i. e.* of withholding the wretched
balance of salary that might be due to him, on the ground of
misconduct, and of also giving him a damning character, dispelled the small remains of Titmouse's appetite, and he rose
to return to the shop, involuntarily clutching his fist as he
brushed close past the tyrant Tag-rag on the stairs, whom he
would have been delighted to pitch down head-foremost; and
if he had done so, none of his fellow-slaves below, in spite of
their present sycophancy toward Tag-rag, would have shown
any particular alacrity in picking up their common oppressor.
Poor Tittlebat resumed his old situation behind the counter;
but how different his present from his former air and manner!
With his pen occasionally peeping pertly out of his bushy hair
over his right ear, and his yard measure in his hand, no one,
till Monday morning, had been more cheerful, smirking, and
nimble than Tittlebat Titmouse: alas, how crest-fallen now!
None of his companions could make him out, or guess what was
in the wind; so they very justly concluded that he had been
doing something dreadfully disgraceful, the extent of which
was known to Tag-rag and himself alone. Their jeers and
banter were giving place to cold distrustful looks, that were
much more trying to bear. How he longed to be able to burst
upon their astounded minds with the pent-up intelligence that
was silently racking and splitting his little bosom! But if he
did—the terrible firm of Quirk, Gammon and Snap—Oh! the
very thought of them glued his lips together. There was *one*,
however, of whom he might surely make a confidant—the excellent Huckaback, with whom he had had no opportunity of
communicating since Sunday night. That gentleman was as
close a prisoner at the establishment of DIAPER and SARSENET,
in Tottenham-court Road, as Titmouse at Messrs. Tag-rag's,
of which said establishment he was as great an ornament as
was Titmouse of that of Messrs. Tag-rag's. They were about
the same height, and equals in puppyism of manners, dress,
and appearance; but Titmouse was much the better-looking.

With equal conceit apparent in their faces, that of Huckaback, square, and flat, and sallow, had an expression of ineffable impudence, that made a lady shudder, and a gentleman feel a tingling sensation in his right toe. About his small black eyes there was a glimmer of low cunning; but he is not of sufficient importance to be painted any further. When Titmouse left the shop that night, a little after nine, he hurried to his lodgings, to make himself as imposing in his appearance before Messrs. Quirk, Gammon and Snap as his time and means would admit of. Behold, on a table lay a letter from Huckaback. It was written in a flourishing mercantile hand; and here is a copy of it:

" DEAR TIT,

" I hope you are well, which is what I can only middling say in respect of me. Such a row with my governors as I have had to-day! I thought that, as I had been in the House near upon Eighteen Months at £25 per annum, I might naturally ask for £30 a year (which is what my Predecessor had), when, would you believe it, Mr. Sharpeye (who is going to be taken in as a Partner), to whom I named the thing, ris up in rage against me, and I were had up into the counting-house, where both the governors was, and they gave it me in such a way that you never saw nor heard of; but it wasn't all on their own side, as you know me too well to think of. You would have thought I had been a going to rob the house. They said I was most oudacious, and all that, and ungrateful, and what would I have next? Mr. Diaper said times was come to such a pitch! since when he was first in the business, for salaries, says he, is risen to double, and not half the work done that was, and no gratitude—(cursed old curmudgeon!) He said if I left them just now, I might whistle for a character, except one that I should not like; but if he don't mind I'll give him a touch of law about that—which brings me to what happened to-day with *our* lawyers, Titty, the people at Saffron Hill, whom I thought I would call in on to-day, being near the neighborhood with some light goods, to see how affairs was getting on, and stir them up a bit "—

This almost took Titmouse's breath away—

—" feeling most *interested* on your account, as you know, dear Tit, I do. I said I wanted to speak to one of the gentlemen on business of wital importance; whereat I was quickly shown into a room where two gents was sitting. Having put down my parcel for a minute on the table I said I was a very intimate friend of yours, and had called in to see how things went on about the advertisement; whereat you never saw in your life how struck they looked, and stared at one another in speechless silence, till they said to me what concerned me about the business? or something of that nature, but in such a way that *ris a rage* in me directly, all for your sake (for I did not like the looks of things;) and says I, I said, we would let them know we were not to be gammoned; whereas up rose the youngest of the two, and ringing the bell, he says to a tight-laced young gentleman with a pen behind his ear, ' Show him to the door,' which I was at once; but, in doing so, let out a little of my mind to them. They're no better then they should be, you see if they are; but when we touch the property, we'll show them who is their masters, which consoles me. Good-bye, keep your sperrits up, and I will call and tell you more about it on Sunday. So farewell (I write this at Mr. Sharpeye's desk, who is coming down from dinner directly). —Your true friend,

" R. HUCKABACK.

" P.S.—Met a young Jew last night with a lot of prime cigars, and (knowing he *must* have stole them, they looked so good at the price), I bought one shilling's worth for me, and two shillings' worth for you, your salary being higher, and to say nothing of your chances."

All that part of the foregoing letter which related to its amiable writer's interview with Messrs. Quirk, Gammon and Snap, Titmouse read in a kind of spasm—he could not draw a breath, and felt a choking sensation coming over him. After awhile, "I may spare myself," thought he, "the trouble of rigging out—Huckaback has done my business for me with Messrs. Quirk, Gammon and Snap—mine will only be a walk in vain!" And this cursed call of Huckaback's, too, to have happened after what occurred last night between Titmouse and them!! and so urgently as he had been enjoined to keep the matter to himself! Of course, Huckaback would seem to have been sent by him; seeing he appeared to have assumed the hectoring tone which Titmouse had tried so vainly over-night, and now so bitterly repented of; and he had no doubt grossly insulted the arbiters of Titmouse's destiny (for he knew Huckaback's impudence)—he had even said that he (Titmouse) would not be GAMMONED by them! But time was pressing—the experiment must be made; and with a beating heart he scrambled into a change of clothes—bottling up his wrath against the unconscious Huckaback till he should see that worthy. In a miserable state of mind he set off soon after for

Saffron Hill at a quick pace which soon became a trot, and often sharpened into a downright run. He saw, heard and thought of nothing, as he hurried along Oxford Street and Holborn, but Quirk, Gammon Snap, and Huckaback, and the reception which the latter might have secured for him—if, indeed, he was to be received at all. The magical words *Ten Thousand a Year*, had not disappeared from the field of his troubled vision; but how faintly and dimly they shone!—like the Pleiades coldly glistening through intervening mists far off—oh! at what a stupendous, immeasurable, and hopeless distance! Imagine those stars gazed at by the anguished and despairing eyes of the bereaved lover, madly believing one of them to contain HER who has just departed from his arms, and from this world, and you may form a notion of the agonizing feelings—the absorbed contemplation of one dear, dazzling, but distant object, experienced on this occasion by Mr. Titmouse. No, no: I don't mean seriously to pretend that so grand a thought as this *could* be entertained by his little optics intellectual; you might as well suppose the tiny eye of a black beetle to be scanning the vague, fanciful, and mysterious figure and proportions of Orion, or a chimpanzee to be perusing and pondering over the immortal *Principia*. I repeat, that I have no desire of the sort, and am determined not again foolishly to attempt fine writing, which I now perceive to be entirely out of my line. In language more befitting me and my subject, I may be allowed to say that there is no getting the contents of a quart into a pint pot: that Titmouse's mind was a half pint—and it was brimful. All the while that I have been going on thus, however, Titmouse was hurrying down Holborn at a rattling rate. When at length he had reached Saffron Hill, he was in a bath of perspiration. His face was quite red; he breathed hard; his heart beat violently; he had got a stitch in his side; and he could not get his gloves on his hot and swollen hands. He stood for a moment with his hat off, wiping his reeking forehead, and endeavoring to recover himself a little, before entering the dreaded presence to which he had been hastening. He even fancied, for a moment, that his eyes gave out sparks of light! While thus pausing, St. Andrew's Church struck ten, half electrifying Titmouse, who bolted up the hill, and was soon standing opposite the door. How the sight of it smote him, as it reminded him of the way in which, on the preceding night, he had bounced out of it! But that could not now be helped; so *ring* went the bell; as softly, however, as he could; for he recollected that it was a very loud bell, and he did not wish to offend. He stood for

some time, and nobody answered. He waited for nearly two
minutes, and trembled, assailed by a thousand vague fears.
He might not, however, have rung loudly enough—so—again,
a little louder, did he venture to ring. Again he waited.
There seemed something threatening in the great brass plate
on the door, out of which "QUIRK, GAMMON AND SNAP" appeared to look at him ominously.   While he thought of it, by
the way, there was something very serious and stern in all
their faces—he wondered that he had not noticed it before.
What a drunken beast he had been to go on in their presence
as he had! thought he; then Huckaback's image flitted across
his disturbed fancy.   "Ah!" thought he, "that's the thing!
—that's it, depend upon it; this door will never be opened to
me again—he's done for me!"   He breathed faster, clinched
his fist, and involuntarily raised it in a menacing way, when
he heard himself addressed—"Oh! dear me, sir, I *hope* I
haven't kept you waiting," said the old woman whom he had
before seen, fumbling in her pocket for the door-key. She
had been evidently out shopping, having a plate in her left
hand, over which her apron was partially thrown. "Hope
you've not been ringing long, sir!"
   "Oh, dear! no, ma'am," replied Titmouse, with anxious
civility, and a truly miserable smile—"Afraid I may have
kept *them* waiting," he added, almost dreading to hear the answer.
   "Oh, no, sir, not at all—they've all been gone since a little
after nine; but there's a letter I was to give you!" She opened
the door; Titmouse nearly dropped with fright.   "I'll get it
for you, sir—let me see, where did I put it?—Oh, in the clerk's
room, I think." Titmouse followed her in.   "Dear me—
where can it be?" she continued, peering about and then snuffing the long wick of the candle which she had left burning for
the last quarter of an hour, during her absence. "I *hope* none
of the clerks has put it away in mistake! Well, it isn't *here*,
anyhow."
   "Perhaps, ma'am, it's in their *own* room," suggested Titmouse, in a faint tone.
   "Oh, p'r'aps it is!" she replied; "we'll go and see"—and
she led the way, followed closely by Titmouse, who caught his
breath as he passed the green-baize door. Yes, there was the
room—the scene of last night was transacted there, and came
crowding over his recollection—there was the green-shaded
candlestick—the table covered with paper—an arm-chair near
it, in which, probably, Mr. Quirk had been sitting only an
hour before to write the letter they were now in quest of, and

which might be to forbid him their presence forever! How dreary and deserted the room looked, thought he, as he peered about it in search of the dreaded letter!

"Oh, here it is!—well, I never!—who could have put it here, now? I'm sure I didn't. Let me see—it was, no doubt "—said the old woman, holding the letter in one hand and putting the other to her head.

"Never mind, ma'am," said Titmouse, stretching his hand toward her—"now we've got it, it don't much signify." She gave it to him. "Seem particularly anxious for me to get it —did they?" he inquired, with a strong effort to appear unconcerned—the dreaded letter quite quivering, the while, in his fingers.

"No, sir—Mr. Quirk only said I was to give it to you when you called. B'lieve they sent it to you, but the clerk said he couldn't find your place out; by the way (excuse me, sir), but yours *is* a funny name! How I heard 'em laughing at it, to be sure! What makes people give such queer names? Would you like to read it here, sir?—you're welcome. '

"No, thank you, madame—it's of not the *least* consequence," he replied, with a desperate air; and tossing it with attempted carelessness into his hat, which he put on his head, he very civilly wished her good-night, and departed—very nearly inclined to sickness, or faintness, or something of the sort, which the fresh air might perhaps dispel. He quickly espied a lamp at a corner, which promised to afford him an uninterrupted opportunity of inspecting his letter. He took it out of his hat. It was addressed—simply:

"Mr. Titmouse, *Cocking* Court, Oxford Street," (which accounted, perhaps, for the clerk's having been unable to find it); and having been opened with trembling eagerness, thus it read:—

"Messrs. Quirk, Gammon and Snap present their compliments to Mr. Titmouse, and are anxious to save him the trouble of his intended visit this evening.

"They exceedingly regret that obstacles (which it is to be hoped, however, may not prove *ultimately* insurmountable) exist in the way of their prosecuting their intended inquiries on behalf of Mr. Titmouse.

"Since their last night's interview with him, circumstances, which they could not have foreseen, and over which they have no control, have occurred, which render it unnecessary for Mr. T. to give himself any more anxiety in the affair—at least, not until he shall have heard from Messrs. Q. G. and S. If any

thing of importance *should* hereafter transpire, it is not improbable that Mr. T. may hear from them.

"They were favored, this afternoon, with a visit from Mr.
T.'s friend—a Mr. Hucklebottom.

"*Saffron Hill, Wednesday Evening, 12th July, 18—.*"

When poor Titmouse had finished reading over this vague,
frigid, and disheartening note a second time, a convulsive sob
or two pierced his bosom, indicative of its being indeed swollen
with sorrow; and at length overcome by his feelings, he cried
bitterly—not checked even by the occasional exclamations of
one or two passers-by. He could not at all control himself.
He felt as if he could have almost relieved himself by banging
his head against the wall! A tumultuous feeling of mingled
grief and despair prevented his thoughts, for a long while,
from settling on any one idea or object. At length, when the
violence of the storm had somewhat abated, on concluding a
third perusal of the death-warrant to all his hopes, which he
held in his hand, his eye lighted upon the strange word which
was intended to describe his friend Huckaback; and it instantly
changed both the kind of his feelings, and the direction in
which they had been rushing. Grief became rage; and the
stream foamed in quite a new direction — namely, toward
Huckaback. That fellow he considered to be the sole cause of
the direful disaster which had befallen him. He utterly lost
sight of one circumstance, which one should have thought
might have occurred to his thought at such a time—viz., his
own offensive and insolent behavior overnight to Messrs. Quirk,
Gammon and Snap. But so it was;—yes, upon the devoted
(but unconscious) head of Huckaback was to descend the
lightning rage of Tittlebat Titmouse. The fire that was
thus quickly kindled within, soon dried up the source of his
tears. He crammed the letter into his pocket, and started
off at once in the direction of Leicester Square, breathing rage
at every step—*viresque acquirens eundo.* His hands kept convulsively clinching together as he pelted along. Hotter and
hotter became his rage, as he neared the residence of Huckaback. When he had reached it, he sprung upstairs; knocked
at his *quondam* friend's door: and on the instant of its being
— doubtless somewhat surprisedly — opened by Huckaback,
who was undressing, Titmouse sprung toward him, let fly a
goodly number of violent blows upon his face and breast—and
down fell Huckaback upon the bed behind him, insensible,
and bleeding profusely from his nose.

"There! there!"—gasped Titmouse, breathless and exhausted, discharging a volley of oaths and opprobrious epithets at the victim of his fury. "Do it again! You will, won't you! *You'll* go—and meddle again in other people's—you—cu-cu-cursed officious "—But his rage was spent—the paroxysm was over; the silent and bleeding figure of Huckaback was before his eyes; and he gazed at him, terror-stricken. What had he done! He sunk down on the bed beside Huckaback—then started up, wringing his hands, and staring at him in an ecstasy of remorse and fright. It was rather singular that the noise of such an assault should have roused no one to inquire into it; but so it was. Frightened almost out of his bewildered senses, he closed and bolted the door; and addressed himself, as well as he was able, to the recovery of Huckaback. Propping him up, and splashing cold water on his face, Titmouse at length discovered symptoms of revival, which he anxiously endeavored to accelerate by putting to the lips of the slowly awakening victim of his violence some cold water in a tea-cup. He swallowed a little; and soon afterward, opening his eyes, stared on Titmouse with a dull eye and bewildered air.

"What's been the matter?" at length he faintly inquired.

"Oh, Hucky! so glad to hear you speak again. It's I—I—Titty! I did it! Strike me, Hucky, as soon as you're well enough! Do—kick me—anything you choose! I won't hinder you!" cried Titmouse, sinking on his knees, and clasping his hands together, as he perceived Huckaback rapidly reviving.

"Why, what *is* the matter?" repeated that gentleman, with a wondering air, raising his hand to his nose, from which the blood was still trickling. The fact is, that he had lost his senses, not so much from the violence of the injuries he had received, as from the suddenness with which they had been inflicted.

"I did it all—yes, I did!" continued Titmouse, gazing on him with a look of agony and remorse.

"Why, I can't be awake—I can't!" said Huckaback, rubbing his eyes, and then staring at his stained shirt-front and hands.

"Oh, yes, you are—you are!" groaned Titmouse; "and I'm going *mad* as fast as I can! Do what you like to me! Lick me if you please! Call in a constable! Send me to jail! Say I came to rob you—anything—I don't care what becomes of me!"

"Why, what *does* all this jabber mean, Titmouse?" inquired Huckaback, sternly, apparently meditating reprisals.

"Oh, yes, I see! Now you *are* going to give it me! I won't stir. So hit away, Hucky·"

"Why—are you mad?" inquired Huckaback, grasping him by the collar rather roughly.

"Yes, quite! Mad!—ruined!—gone to the devil all at once!"

"And what if you are? What did it matter to *me*? What brought you to me, here?" continued Huckaback, in a tone of increasing vehemence. "What have I done to offend you? How *dare* you come *here*? And at this time of night, too? Eh?"

"What, indeed! Oh, lud, oh, lud, oh, lud! Kick me, I say —strike me! You'll do me good, and bring me to my senses. *Me* to do all this to you! And we've been such precious good friends always. I'm a brute, Hucky—I've been mad, stark mad, Hucky—and that's all I can say."

Huckaback stared at him more and more, and began at length to suspect how matters stood—namely, that the Sunday's incident had turned Titmouse's head—he having also, no doubt, heard some desperate bad news during the day, smashing all his hopes. A mixture of emotions kept him silent. Astonishment — apprehension — doubt—pride—pique —resentment. He had been *struck*—his blood had been drawn—by the man there before him on his knees, formerly his friend—now, he supposed, a madman.

"Why, curse me, Titmouse, if I can make up my mind what to do to you!" he exclaimed. "I—I suppose you're going mad, or gone mad, and I must forgive you. But get away with you—out with you, or—or—I'll call in—"

"Forgive me—forgive me, dear Hucky! Don't send me away—I shall go and drown myself if you do."

"What the d—l do I care if you do? You'd much better have gone and done it before you came here. Nay, be off and do it now, instead of blubbering here in this way."

"Go on! Hit away—it's doing me good—the worse the better!" sobbed Titmouse.

"Come, come—none of this noise here. I'm tired of it."

"But, pray, don't send me away from you. I shall go straight to the devil if you do. I've no friend but you, Hucky. Yet I've been such a villain to you?—But it is quite put the devil into me, when all of a sudden I found it was *you*."

"Me!—why, what *are* you after?" interrupted Huckaback, with an air of angry wonder.

"Oh, dear, dear!" groaned Titmouse; "if I've been a brute to you, which is quite true, you've been the ruin of me clean! I'm clean done for, Huck. Cleaned out! You've done my business for me; knocked it all on the head. I sha'n't never hear any more of it—they've said as much in their letter—they say that you've called—"

Huckaback now began to have a glimmering notion of his having been, in some considerable degree, connected with the mischief of the day—an unconscious agent in it. He audibly drew in his breath, as it were, as he more and more distinctly recollected his visit to Messrs. Quirk, Gammon and Snap; and adverted more particularly to his *threats*, uttered, too, in Titmouse's name, and as if by his authority. Whew! here was a kettle of fish.

Now, strange and unaccountable as, at first thought, it may appear, the very circumstance which one would have thought calculated to assuage his resentment against Titmouse— namely, that he had really *injured* Titmouse most seriously, (if not indeed irreparably), and so *provoked* the drubbing which had just been administered to him—had quite the contrary effect. Paradoxical as it may seem, matter of clear mitigation was at once converted into matter of aggravation. —Were the feelings which Huckaback then experienced akin to that which often produces hatred of a person whom one has injured? May it be thus accounted for? That there is a secret satisfaction in the mere consciousness of being a sufferer—a martyr—and that, too, in the presence of a person whom one perceives to be aware that he has wantonly injured one; that one's bruised spirit is soothed by the sight of his remorse—by the consciousness that he is punishing himself infinitely more severely than *we* could punish him; and of the claim one has obtained to the *sympathy* of everybody who sees, or may hear of one's suffering (that rich and grateful balm to injured feeling). But, when, as in the case of Huckaback, feelings of this description (in a coarse and small way, to be sure, according to his kind) were suddenly encountered by a consciousness of his having *deserved* his sufferings; when the martyr felt himself quick sinking into the culprit and offender; when, I say, Huckaback felt an involuntary consciousness that the gross indignities which Titmouse had just inflicted on him had been justified by the provocation—nay, far less than his mischievous and impudent interference had deserved;—and when feelings of this sort, moreover, were sharpened by a certain tingling sense of physical pain from the blows which he had received—the result was, that the sleeping lion of Huckaback's courage was very near awakening.

"*I've half a mind, Titmouse*"—said Huckaback, knitting his brows, and appearing inclined to raise his arm. There was an ominous pause for a moment or two, during which

3

Titmouse's feelings also underwent a slight alteration. His allusion to Huckaback's ruinous insult to Messrs. Quirk, Gammon and Snap unconsciously converted his remorse into rage, which it rather, perhaps, resuscitated. He rose from his knees. "Ah!" said he, in quite an altered tone, "you *may* look fierce! you may!—you'd better strike me, Huckaback—do! Finish the mischief you've begun this day! Hit away—you're quite safe,"—and he secretly prepared himself for the mischief which—did not come.

"You *have* ruined me! you have, Huckaback!" continued Titmouse, with increasing vehemence; "and I shall be cutting my throat—nay," striking his fist on the table, "I will!"

"You don't say so!" exclaimed Huckaback, apprehensively. "No, Titmouse, don't—don't think of it; it will all come right yet, depend on't; you see if it don't!"

"Oh, no! it's all done for—it's all up with me!"

"But what's been done?—let us hear," said Huckaback, as he passed a wet towel to and fro over his ensanguined features. It was by this time clear that the storm which had for some time given out only a few faint fitful flashes or flickerings in the distance, had passed away. Titmouse, with many grievous sighs, took out the letter which had produced the paroxysms I have been describing, and read it aloud. "And only see how they've spelled your name, Huckaback—look!" he added, handing his friend the letter.

"How *particular* vulgar!" exclaimed Huckaback, with a contemptuous air, which, overspreading his features, half-closed as was his left eye, and swollen as were his cheek and nose, would have made him a queer object to one who had leisure to observe such matters. "And so this is all they say of *me*," he continued. "How do you come to know that I've been doing you a mischief? All I did was just to look in, as respectful as possible, to ask how you was, and they very civilly told me you was very well, and we parted—"

"Nay, now, that's a lie, Huckaback, and you know it!" interrupted Titmouse.

"It's true, so help me—!" vehemently asseverated Huckaback.

"Why, perhaps you'll deny that you wrote and told me all you said," interrupted Titmouse, indignantly, feeling in his pocket for Huckaback's letter, which that worthy had at the moment quite forgotten having sent, and certainly seemed rather nonplused on being reminded of.

"Oh—ay, if you mean *that*—hem!" he stammered.

"Come, you know you're a liar, Huck—but it's no good now; liar or no liar, it's all over."

"The pot and kettle, anyhow, Tit, as far as that goes—but let's spell over this letter; we haven't studied it yet; I'm a hand, rather, at getting at what's said in a letter!—Come "—and they drew their chairs together, Huckaback reading over the letter slowly, alone; Titmouse's eyes traveling incessantly from his friend's countenance to the letter, and so back again, to gather what might be the effect of its perusal.

"There's a glimpse of daylight yet, Titty!" said Huckaback, as he concluded reading it.

"Now! Is there really? Do tell me, Hucky—"

"Why, first and foremost, how uncommon polite they are, (except that they haven't manners enough to spell my name right!—")

"Really—and so they are!" exclaimed Titmouse, rather elatedly.

"And then, you see, there's another thing—if they'd meant to give the thing the go-by altogether, what could have been easier than to have said so?—but they haven't said anything of the sort, so they don't mean to give it all up."

"Lord, Huck! what would I give for such a head as yours! What you say is quite true," said Titmouse, still more cheerfully.

"To be sure, they do say there's an *obstacle*—an obstacle, you see—nay, it's obstacles, which is several, and that "—Titmouse's face fell.

"But they say again, that it's—it's—curse their big words —they say it's—to be got over in time."

"Well—that's something, isn't it?"

"To be sure it is; and a'n't anything better than nothing? But then, again, here's a stone in the other pocket; they say there's a *circumstance!* Don't you hate circumstances, Titty? —I do."

"So do I!—What does it mean? I've often heard—isn't it a *thing?* And that may be—anything."

"Oh, there's a great dif—hem! And they go on to say it's happened since you was there—"

"Curse me, then, if that don't mean *you*, Huckaback!" interrupted Titmouse, with returning anger.

"No, that can't be it; they said they'd no control over the circumstance;—now they *had* over me; for they ordered me to the door, and I went; a'n't that so, Titty?—Lord, how my eye does smart, to be sure!"

"And don't I smart all over, inside and out, if it comes to that?" inquired Titmouse, dolefully.

"There's nothing particular in the rest of the letter—only uncommon civil, and saying if anything turns up you shall hear."

"*I* could make that out myself—so there's nothing in that" —said Titmouse, quickly.

"Well—if it *is* all over—what a pity! Such things as we could have done, Titty, if we'd got the thing—eh?"

Titmouse groaned at this glimpse of the heaven he seemed shut out of forever.

"Can't you find anything—nothing at all comfortable-like, in the letter?" he inquired, with a deep sigh.

Huckaback again took up the letter and spelled it over. "Well," said he, striving to give himself an appearance of thinking, "there's something in it that, after all, I don't seem quite to get to the bottom of—they've seemingly taken a deal of pains with it."

[And undoubtedly it *was* a document that had been pretty well considered by its framers before being sent out; though, probably, they had hardly anticipated its being so soon afterward subjected to the scrutiny of the acute intellects which were now engaged upon it.]

"And then, again, you know they are lawyers; and do *they* ever write anything that hasn't got more in it than anybody can find out? These gents that wrote this, they're a trick too keen for the thieves, even—and how can *we*—hem!—but I wonder if that fat, old, bald-headed gent, with sharp eyes, was Mr. Quirk—"

"To be sure it was," interrupted Titmouse, with a half shudder.

"Was it? Well, then, I'd advise Old Nick to look sharp before he tackles that old gent, that's all!"

"Give me Mr. Gammon for my money—such an *uncommon* gentleman-like—he's quite taken to me—"

"Ah, that, I suppose, was him with the black velvet waist-coat and white hands! But *he* can look stern, too, Tit! You should have seen him ring, when—hem!—But what was I saying about the letter? Don't you see they say they'll be sure to write if anything turns up?"

"So they do, to be sure! Well—I'd forgot that!" interrupted Titmouse, brightening up.

"Then, isn't there their advertisement in the *Flash!* They hadn't their eye on anything when they put it there, I dare say!—They can't get out of that, anyhow!"

"I begin to feel all of a sweat, Hucky; I'm sure there's something in the wind yet!" said Titmouse, drawing nearer still to his comforter. "And more than that—would they have said half they did to me last night—"

"Eh! halloo, by the way! I've not heard of what went on last night! So you went to 'em? Well—tell us all that happened—and nothing but the truth, be *sure* you don't; come, Titty!" said Huckaback, snuffing the candle, and then turning eagerly to his companion.

"Well—they'd such a number of queer-looking papers before them, some with old German-text writing, and others with zigzag marks—and they were so uncommon polite—they all three got up as I went in, and made me bows, one after the other, and said, 'Yours most obediently, Mr. Titmouse,' and a great many more such things."

"Well—and then?"

"Why, Hucky, so help me—! and 'pon my soul, that old gent, Mr. Quirk, told me"—Titmouse's voice trembled at the recollection—"he says, 'Sir, you're the real owner of Ten Thousand a year.'"

"Lawks!" ejaculated Huckaback, opening wider and wider his eyes and ears as his friend went on.

"'And a title—a *lord* or something of that sort—and you've a great many country seats; and there's been £10,000 a year saving up for you ever since you was born—and heaps of interest.'"

"Lord, Tit! you take my breath away," gasped Huckaback, his eyes fixed intently on his friend's face.

"Yes; and they said I might marry the most beautifulest woman that ever my eyes saw, for the asking."

"You'll forget poor Bob Huckaback, Tit!" murmured his friend, despondingly.

"Not I—"

"Have you been to Tag-rag's to-day, after hearing all this?"

[The thermometer seemed to have been plunged out of hot water into cold—Titmouse was down to zero in a trice.]

"Oh!—that's it! 'Tis all gone again! What a fool I am! We've clean forgot this cursed letter—and that leads me to the end of what took place last night. That cursed shop was what we split on!"

"Split on the shop! eh? What's the meaning of that?" inquired Huckaback, with eager anxiety.

"Why, that's the thing," continued Titmouse, in a faltering tone, and with a depressed look—"That was what I wanted to know myself; for they said I'd better go back!/

So I said, 'Gents,' said I, 'I'll be —— if I go back to the shop any more;' and I snapped my fingers at them—so! (for you know what a chap I am when my blood's up). And they all turned gashly pale—they did, upon my life—you never saw anything like it! And one of them said then, in a humble way, 'Wouldn't I please to go back to the shop, just for a day or two, till things is got to rights a bit.' 'Not a day, nor a minute!' says I, in an immense rage. 'We think you'd better, really,' said they. 'Then,' says I, 'if that's your plan, curse me if I won't cut with you all, and I'll employ some one else!' and—would you believe me?—out I went, bang! into the street!!''

" You *did*, Tit!!''

" They shouldn't have given me so much brandy and water as they did; I didn't well know what I was about, what with the news and the spirits!''

" And you went into the street?'' inquired Huckaback, with a kind of horror.

" I did, indeed.''

" They'd given you the sperrits to see what kind of a chap you'd be if you got the property—only to try you, depend on it!''

" Lord! I—I dare say they did!'' examined Titmouse, elevating his head with sudden amazement, totally forgetting that that same brandy and water he had asked for—" and me never to think of it at the time!''

" Now are you quite sure you wasn't in a *dream* last night, all the while?''

" Oh, dear, I wish I had been—I do, indeed, Hucky!''

" Well—you went into the street—what then?'' inquired Huckaback, with a sigh of exhausted attention.

" Why, when I'd got there, I was fit to bite my tongue off, as one may suppose; but, just as I was a-turning to go in again, who should come up to me but Mr. Gammon, saying, he humbly hoped there was no offense.''

" Oh, glorious! So it was all set right again, then, eh?''

" Why—I—I can't quite exactly say that much, either—but—when I went back (being obligated by Mr. Gammon being so pressing), the other two was sitting as pale as death; and though Mr. Gammon and me went on our knees to the old gent, it wasn't any use for a long time; and all that he could be got to say was, that perhaps I might look in again to-night—(but they first made me swear a solemn oath on the Bible never to tell any one anything about the fortune)—and then—*you* went, Huckaback, and you did the business; they of course concluding I'd sent you!'"

"Oh, bother! that can't be. Don't you see how civilly they speak of me in their letter? They're afraid of me, you may depend on it. By the way, Tit, how much did you promise to come down, if you got the thing?"

"*Come down!*—I—really—by Jove, I didn't! No—I'm sure I didn't!"—answered Titmouse, as if new light had burst in upon him.

"Why, Tit, I never seed such a goose! That's it, depend upon it—it's the whole thing! That's what they're driving at in the note!—Why, Tit, where was your wits? D'ye think such gents as them—great lawyers, too—will work for nothing?—You write and tell them you will come down handsome —say a couple of hundreds, besides expenses—Gad! 'twill set you on your pins again, Titty!—Rot me! now I think of it, if I didn't dream last night that you was a Member of Parliament or something of that sort."

"A Member of Parliament! And so I shall, if all this turns up well."

"You see if my dream don't come true! You see, Titty, I'm *always* a-thinking of you, day and night. Never was two fellows that was such close friends as we was from the beginning."

[They had been acquainted with each other about a year.]

"Hucky, what a cruel scamp I was to behave to you in the way I did—curse me, if I couldn't cry to see your eye bunged up in that way!"

"Pho! dear Titty, I knew you loved me all the while—and meant no harm; you wasn't your self when you did it—and besides, I deserve ten times more. If you had killed me I should have liked you as much as ever!"

"Give us your hand, Hucky! Let's forgive one another!" cried Titmouse, excitedly; and their hands were quickly locked together.

"If we don't mismanage the thing, we shall be all right yet, Titty; but you won't do anything without speaking to me first —will you, Titty?"

"The thoughts of it all going right again is enough to set me wild, Hucky!—But what shall we do to set the thing going again?"

"*Quarter past one!*" quivered the voice of the paralytic watchman beneath, startling the friends out of their excited colloquy; his warning being at the same time silently seconded by the long-wicked candle, burning within half an inch of its

socket. They hastily agreed that Titmouse should immediately write to Messrs. Quirk, Gammon and Snap a proper
[*i. e.*, a most abject] letter, solemnly pledging himself to obey
their injunctions in everything for the future, and offering
them a handsome reward for their exertions, if successful.

"Well—good-night, Huck! good-night," said Titmouse,
rising. "I'm not the least sleepy—I sha'n't sleep a wink all
night long! I shall sit up to write my letter—you haven't got
a sheet of paper here, by the way?—I've used all mine."
[That was, he had, some months before, bought a sheet to
write a letter, and had so used it.]

Huckaback produced a sheet, somewhat crumpled, from a
drawer. "I'd give a hundred if I had them!" said he; "I
sha'n't care a straw for the hiding I've got to-night—though
I'm a *leetle* sore after it, too—and what the deuce am I to say
to-morrow to Messrs. Diaper—"

"Oh, you can't hardly be at a loss for a lie that'll suit *them*,
surely!—So good-night, Hucky—good-night!"

Huckaback wrung his friend's hand, and was in a moment
or two alone. "Haven't my fingers been itching all the while
to be at the fellow!" exclaimed he, as he shut the door.
"But, somehow, I've got too soft a sperrit, and can't bear to
hurt any one;—and then—if the chap gets his £10,000 a year
—why—hem! Titty a'n't such a bad fellow, in the main, after
all.

If Titmouse had been many degrees higher in the grade of
society, *he would still have met with his Huckaback :*—a trifle
more polished, perhaps; but hardly more quick-sighted or
effective than, in his way, had been the vulgar being he had
just quitted.

Titmouse hastened homeward. How it was he knew not;
but the feelings of elation with which he had quitted Huckaback did not last long; they rapidly sunk in the cold night-air,
lower and lower, the further he got from Leicester Square.
He tried to recollect *what it was* that had made him take so
very different a view of his affairs from that with which he had
entered Huckaback's room. He had still a vague impression
that they were not desperate; that Huckaback had told him
so, *and somehow proved it;* but how he knew not—he could not
recollect. As Huckaback had gone on from time to time,
Titmouse's little mind seemed to him to comprehend and appreciate what was said, and to gather encouragement from it;
but now—consume it!—he stopped—rubbed his forehead—
what the deuce WAS it? By the time that he had reached his
own door, he felt in as deplorable and despairing a humor as

ever. He sat down to write his letter at once; but, after many vain efforts to express his meaning—his feelings being not in the least degree relieved by the many oaths he uttered—he at length furiously dashed his pen, point-wise, upon the table, and thereby destroyed the only implement of the sort which he possessed. Then he tore, rather than pulled off his clothes; blew out his candle with a furious *puff!* and threw himself on his bed—but in so doing banged the back of his head against the back of the bed—and which suffered most, for some time after, probably Mr. Titmouse was best able to tell.

Hath, then—oh, Titmouse! fated to undergo much!—the blind jade Fortune, in her mad vagaries—she, the goddess whom thou hast so long foolishly worshiped—at length cast her sportful eye upon thee and singled thee out to become the envy of millions of admiring fools, by reason of the pranks she will presently make thee exhibit for her amusement? If this be indeed, as at present it promises, her intent, she truly, to me calmly watching her movements, appears resolved first to wreak her spite upon thee to the uttermost, and make thee pass through intense sufferings! Oh, me! Oh, me! Alas!

CHAPTER III.

THE means by which Messrs. Quirk, Gammon and Snap became possessed of the important information which put them into motion, as we have seen, to find out by advertisement one yet unknown to them, it will not be necessary, for some time—and which will prove to have originated in a very remarkable accident—for me to explain. Theirs was a keen house, truly, and dealing principally in the criminal line of business; and they would not, one may be sure, have lightly committed themselves to their present extent, namely, in inserting such an advertisement in the newspapers, and, above all, going so far in their disclosures to Titmouse. Their prudence in the latter step, however, was very questionable to themselves even; and they immediately afterward deplored together the precipitation with which Mr. Quirk had communicated to Titmouse the nature and extent of his possible good fortune. It was Mr. Quirk's own doing, however, and after as much expostulation as the cautious Gammon could venture to use. I say they had not *lightly* taken up the affair; they had not "acted unadvisedly." They were fortified, first, by the opinions of Mr. Mortmain, an able and experienced conveyancer, who thus wound up an abstrusely learned opinion on the voluminous "case" which had been submitted to him:—

"* * Under all these circumstances, and assuming as above, I am decidedly of opinion that the title to the estate in question is at this moment not in their present possessor (who represents the younger branch of the Dreddlington family), but in the descendants of Stephen Dreddlington, through the female line; which brings us to Gabriel Tittlebat Titmouse. This person, however, seems not to have been at all aware of the existence of his rights, or he could hardly have been concerned in the pecuniary arrangements mentioned at fol. 33 of the case. Probably something may be heard of his heir by making careful inquiry in the neighborhood where he was last heard of, and issuing advertisements for his heir-at-law; care, of course, being taken not to be so specific in the terms of such advertisement as to attract the notice of A. B. (the party now in possession.) If such person should, by the means above suggested, be discovered, I advise proceedings to be commenced forthwith, under the advice of some gentleman of experience at the common-law bar.

"MOULDY MORTMAIN.

"*Lincoln's Inn,*
   "*January* 19, 18—."

This was sufficiently gratifying to the "house," but to make assurance doubly sure, before embarking in so harassing and expensive an enterprise—one which lay a good deal, too, without the sphere of their practice, which, as already mentioned, was chiefly in criminal law—the same *case*, without Mr. Mortmain's opinion, was laid before a younger conveyancer, who, having much less business than Mr. Mortmain, would, it was thought, "look into the case fully," though receiving only one third of the fee which had been paid to Mr. Mortmain. And Mr. FUSSY FRANKPLEDGE—that was his name—*did* "look into the case fully," and in doing so turned over two thirds of his little library, and also gleaned—by note and verbally—the opinions upon the subject of some half dozen of his "learned friends," to say nothing of the magnificent air with which he indoctrinated his eager and confiding pupils upon the subject. At length his imp of a clerk bore the precious result of his master's labors to Saffron Hill, in the shape of an "opinion," three times as long as, and indescribably more difficult to understand than the opinion of Mr. Mortmain, and which, if it demonstrated anything beyond the prodigious *cram* which had been undergone by its writer for the purpose of producing it, demonstrated this—namely, that neither the party indicated by Mr. Mortmain, nor the one then actually in possession, had any more right to the estate than the aforesaid Mr. Frankpledge, but that the happy individual so entitled was some third person. Messrs. Quirk and Gammon, a good deal flustered hereat, hummed and hawed on perusing these contradictory opinions of counsel learned in the law, and the proper result followed—*i. e.*, a "CONSULTATION," which was to solder up all the differences between Mr. Mortmain and Mr. Frankpledge, or, at all events, strike out some light which might guide their clients on their adventurous way.

Now, Mr. Mortmain had been Mr. Quirk's conveyancer, whenever such functionary's services had been required, for about twenty years, and Quirk was ready to suffer death in defense of any opinion of Mr. Mortmain. Mr. Gammon swore by Frankpledge, who had been at school with him, and was a "rising man." Mortmain belonged to the old school—Frankpledge steered by the new lights. The former could point to some forty cases in the Law Reports, which had been ruled in conformity with his previously given opinion, and some twenty which had been overruled thereby; the latter gentleman, although he had been only five years in practice, had writtten an *opinion* which had led to a suit—which had ended in a difference of opinion between the Court of King's Bench and the Common Pleas, the credit of having done which was, however, some time afterward, a little bit tarnished by the decision of a Court of Error, without hearing the other side, *against* the opinion of Mr. Frankpledge. But—

Mr. Frankpledge quoted so many cases and went to the bottom of everything and gave so much for his money—and was so civil—

Well, the consultation came off at length at Mr. Mortmain's chambers, at eight o'clock in the evening. A few minutes before that hour Messrs. Quirk and Gammon were to be seen in the clerk's room, in civil conversation with that prim functionary, who explained to them that *he* did all Mr. Mortmain's drafting—pupils were *so* idle; that Mr. Mortmain did not score out much of what he, the aforesaid clerk, had drawn; that he noted up Mr. Mortmain's new cases for him in the reports, Mr. M. having so little time, and that the other day the Vice-Chancellor called on Mr. Mortmain—with several other matters of that sort, calculated to enhance the importance of Mr. Mortmain, who, as the clerk was asking Mr. Gammon, in a good-natured way, how long Mr. Frankpledge had been in practice, and where his chambers were—made his appearance, with a cheerful look and a bustling gait, having just walked

down from his house in Queen's Square, with a comfortable
bottle of old port on board. Shortly afterward Mr. Frankpledge arrived, followed by his little clerk, bending beneath
two bags of books, unconscious bearer of as much law as had
well-nigh split thousands of learned heads, and broken tens
of thousands of hearts in the making of, being destined to have
a similar but far greater effect in the applying of; and the consultation began.

As Frankpledge entered, he could not help casting a sheep's
eye toward a table that glistened with *such* an array of
" papers," (a tasteful arrangement of Mr. Mortmain's clerk
before every consultation), and down sat the two conveyancers
and the two attorneys. I devoutly wish I had time to describe
the scene at length, but greater events are pressing upon me.
The two conveyancers fenced with one another for some time
very guardedly and good-humoredly, pleasant was it to observe
the conscious condescension of Mortmain, the anxious energy
and volubility of Frankpledge. When Mr. Mortmain said
anything that seemed weighty or pointed, Quirk looked with
an elated air, a quick triumphant glance, at Gammon, who, in
his turn, whenever Mr. Frankpledge quoted an "old case"
from Bendloe, Godsbolt, or the Year Books (which, having
always piqued himself on his almost exclusive acquaintance
with the modern cases, he made a point of doing), gazed at
Quirk with a smile of placid superiority. Mr. Frankpledge
talked almost the whole time; Mr. Mortmain, immovable in
the view of the case which he had taken in his "opinion,"
listened with an attentive, good-natured air, ruminating pleasantly the while upon the quality of the port he had been
drinking, the first of the bin which he had tasted, and upon
the decision which the Chancellor might come to on a case
brought into court on his advice, and which had been argued
that afternoon. At last Frankpledge unwittingly fell foul of
a favorite crotchet of Mortmain's—and at it they went, hammer and tongs, for nearly twenty minutes (it had nothing
whatever to do with the case they were consulting upon). In
the end Mortmain of course adhered to his points, and Frankpledge intrenched himself in his books; each slightly yielded
to the views of the other on immaterial points, or what could
have appeared the use of the consultation? but did that which
both had resolved upon doing from the first, *i. e.*, sticking to
his original opinion. Both had talked an amazing deal of deep
law, which had at least one effect: viz., it fairly drowned both
Quirk and Gammon, who, as they went home, with not, it
must be owned, the clearest perceptions in the world of what

had been going on (though, before going to the consultation, each had really known something about the case) stood each stoutly by his conveyancer's opinion, each protesting that he had never been once misled—Quirk by Mortmain, or Gammon by Frankpledge—and each resolved to give his man more of the conveyancing business of the house than he had before. I grieve to add that they parted that night with a trifle less of cordiality than had been their wont. In the morning, however, this little irritation and competition had passed away, and they agreed, before giving up the case, to take the final opinion of Mr. Tresayle—the great Mr. Tresayle. He was, indeed, a wonderful conveyancer—a perfect miracle of real-property law learning. He had had such an enormous practice for forty-five years that for the last ten he had never put his nose out of chambers for pure want of time, and at last of inclination, and had been so conversant with Norman-French and law Latin, in the old English letter, that he had almost entirely forgotten how to write the modern English character. His opinions made their appearance in three different kinds of handwriting. First, one that none but he and his own clerk could make out; secondly, one that none but he himself could read; and thirdly, one that neither he nor his clerk nor any one on earth could decipher. The use of any one of these styles depended on—the difficulty of the case to be answered. If it were an easy one, the answer was very judiciously put into No. I.; if rather difficult, it of course went into No. II.; and if exceedingly difficult, and also important, it was very properly thrown into No. III., being a question that really ought not to have been asked, and did not deserve an answer. The fruit within these uncouth shells, however, was precious. Mr. Tresayle's law was supreme over everybody's else. It was currently reported that Lord Eldon even, who was himself slightly acquainted with such subjects, reverently deferred to the authority of Mr. Tresayle, and would lie winking and knitting his shaggy eyebrows half the night if he thought that Mr. Tresayle's opinion on a case and his own differed. This was the great authority to whom, as in the last resort, Messrs. Quirk, Gammon and Snap resolved to appeal. To his chambers they, within a day or two after their consultation at Mr. Mortmain's, dispatched their case, with a highly respectable fee, and a special compliment to his clerk, hoping to hear from that awful quarter within a month—which was the earliest average period within which Mr. Tresayle's opinions found their way to his patient but anxious clients. It came at length, with a note from Mr. Prim, his clerk, intimating that they would find him, *i. e.*, the aforesaid Mr. Prim, at chambers the next morning, prepared to explain the opinion to them, having just had it read over to him by Mr. Tresayle, for it proved to be in No. II. The opinion occupied about two pages, and the handwriting bore a strong resemblance to Chinese or Arabic, with a quaint intermixture of the uncial Greek character—it was impossible to contemplate it without a certain feeling of awe. In vain did old Quirk squint at it, from all corners, for nearly a couple of hours, having first called in the assistance of a friend of his, an old attorney of upward of fifty years' standing, nay—even Mr. Gammon, foiled at length, could not for the life of him refrain from a soft curse or two. Neither of them could make anything of it—as for Snap, they never showed it to him; it was not within his province—*i. e.*, the Insolvent Debtors' Court, the Old Bailey, the Clerkenwell Sessions, the Police Officers, the inferior business of the Common Law Courts, and the worrying of the clerks of the office—a department in which he was perfection itself.

To their great delight, Mr. Tresayle's opinion completely corroborated that of Mr. Mortmain, neither whose nor Mr. Frankpledge's had been laid before him. Nothing could be more terse, perspicuous, and conclusive than the great man's opinion. Mr. Quirk was in raptures, and immediately sent out for an engraving of Mr. Tresayle, which had lately come out, for which he paid 5s., and ordered it to be framed and hung up in his own room, where already grinned a quaint resemblance, in black profile, of Mr. Mortmain. In special good humor he assured Mr. Gammon, who was plainly somewhat crest-fallen about Mr. Frankpledge, that everybody must have a beginning, and even he himself (Mr. Quirk) had been once only a beginner.

Once fairly on the scent, Messrs. Quirk and Gammon soon began secretly but energetically to push their inquiries. They discovered that Gabriel Tittlebat Titmouse, having spent the chief portion of his blissful days as a cobbler at Whitehaven, had died in London, somewhere about the year 17—. At this point they stood for a long while, in spite of two advertisements, to which they had been driven with the greatest reluctance, for fear of attracting the attention of those most interested in thwarting their efforts. Even that part of the affair had been managed somewhat skillfully. It was a stroke of Mr. Gammon's to advertise not for "Heir-at-Law," but "*Next of Kin*," as the reader has seen. The former might have challenged a notice of unfriendly curiosity, which the latter was hardly calculated to attract. At length—at the "third time of asking"—up turned Tittlebat Titmouse, in the way which we have seen. His relationship with Mr. Gabriel Tittlebat Titmouse was indisputable; in fact, he was that "deceased person's" son and heir-at-law. The reader may guess the chagrin and disgust of Mr. Gammon at the appearance, manner and character of the person whom he fully believed, on first seeing him at Messrs. Tag-rags' to be the rightful owner of the fine estates held by one who, as against Titmouse, had no more real title to them than had Mr. Tag-rag, and for whom their house was to undertake the very grave responsibility of instituting such proceedings as would be requisite to place Mr. Titmouse in the position which they believed him entitled to occupy—having to encounter a hot and desperate opposition at every point from those who had nine tenths of the law—to wit, *possession*—on their side, on which they stood as upon a rock, and with immense means for carrying on the war defensive. That Messrs. Quirk, Gammon and Snap did not contemplate undertaking all this, without having calculated upon its proving well worthy their while, was only reasonable. They were going voluntarily to become the means of conferring immense benefits upon one who was a total stranger to them—who had not a penny to expend upon the prosecution of his own rights. Setting aside certain difficulties which collected themselves into two awkward words, MAIN-TENANCE and CHAMPERTY, and stared them in the face whenever they contemplated any obvious method of securing the just reward of their enterprise and toils—setting aside all this, I say, it might turn out, only after a ruinous expenditure had been incurred, that the high authorities which had sanctioned their proceedings, in point of law, had expressed their favorable opinions on a state of facts, which, however satisfactorily they looked on paper, could not be properly substantiated, if keenly sifted, and determinedly resisted. All this, too—all their time, labor, and money, to go for nothing—on behalf of a vulgar, selfish, ignorant, presumptuous, ungrateful puppy, like Titmouse. Well, indeed, therefore, might Mr. Gammon, as we have seen he did, give himself and partners a forty-eight hours' interval between his interview with Titmouse and formal introduction of him to the firm, in which to consider their position and mode of procedure. The taste of his quality which that first interview afforded them all—so far surpassing all that the bitter description of him given to them by Mr. Gammon had prepared them for—filled them with inexpressible disgust, and would have induced them to throw up the whole affair—so getting rid both of it and him together. But then, on the other hand, there were certain very great advantages, both of a professional and even directly pecuniary kind, which it would have been madness, indeed, for any office lightly to throw away. It was really, after all, an unequal struggle between feeling and interest. If they should succeed in unseating the present wrongful possessor of a very splendid property, and putting in his place the rightful owner, by means alone of their own professional ability, perseverance and heavy pecuniary outlay (a fearful consideration, truly; but Mr. Quirk had scraped together some thirty thousand pounds), what recompense could be too great for such resplendent services? To say nothing of the *éclat* which it would gain for their office, in the profession and in the world at large, and the substantial and permanent advantages, if, as they ought to be, they were intrusted with the general management of the property by the new and inexperienced and confiding owner—ay, but there was the rub! What a disheartening and disgusting specimen of such new owner had disclosed itself to their anxiously expecting, but soon recoiling, eyes—always, however, making due allowances for one or two cheering indications, on Mr. Titmouse's part, of a certain rapacious and litigious humor, which might pleasantly and profitably occupy their energies for some time to come. Their position and interests had long made them sharp observers, but when did ever before, low and disgusting qualities force themselves into revolting prominence as his had done in the very moment of an expected display of the better feelings of human nature—such as enthusiastic gratitude? They had in their time had to deal with some pleasant specimens of humanity, to be sure, but when with any more odious and impracticable than Titlebat Titmouse threatened to prove himself? What hold could they get upon such a character as his? Beneath all his coarseness and weakness there was a glimmer of low cunning which might suffice to keep their superior and practiced astuteness in full play. These were difficulties, cheerless enough in the contemplation, truly; but, nevertheless, the partners could not bear the idea of escaping from them by throwing up the affair altogether. Then came the question—How were they to manage Titmouse?—how acquire an early and firm hold of him, so as to convert him into a *capital client*? His fears and his interests were obviously the engines with which their experienced hands were to work, and several long and most anxious consultations had Messrs. Quirk, Gammon and Snap had on this important matter. The first great question with them was—To what extent, and when they should acquaint him with the nature of his expectations?

Gammon was for keeping him comparatively in the dark till success was within reach, during that interval, which might be a long one, by alternately stimulating his hopes and fears; by persuading him to an entire dependence on them; by persuading him of the extent of their exertions and sacrifices on his behalf—they *might* do something; mold him a little into shape fit for their purposes, and persuade him that his affairs must needs go to ruin but in their hands. Something like this was the scheme of the cautious, acute, and placid Gammon. Mr. Quirk, with whom had originated the whole discovery, thought thus: Tell the fellow at once the whole extent of what we can do for him: viz., turn a half-starving linen-draper's shopman into the owner of £10,000 a year, and of a great store of ready money. This will in a manner stun him into submission, and make him at once and for all what we want him to be. He will immediately fall prostrate with reverend gratitude—looking at us, moreover, as three gods, who at our will can shut him out of heaven. " *That's* the way," said Mr. Quirk, and Mr. Quirk had been forty years in practice—had made the business what it was—still held half of it in his own hands, two thirds of the remaining half being Gammon's and the residue Snap's; and Gammon, moreover, had a very distinct perception that the funds for carrying on the war would come out of the tolerably well-stored pockets of their senior partner. So, after a long discussion, he openly yielded his opinion to that of Mr. Quirk—cherishing, however, a very warm respect for it in his own bosom. As for Snap, that distinguished member of the firm was very little consulted in the matter, which had not yet been brought into that stage where his powerful energies could come into play. He had of course, however, heard a good deal of what was going on, and knew that ere long there would be the copying out and serving of the Lord knows how many copies of declarations in ejectment, motions against the casual ejector, and so forth—so far at least as he was " up to " all those quaint and anomalous proceedings. It had, therefore, been at length agreed that the communication to Titmouse, on his first interview, of the full extent of his splendid expectations, should depend upon the discretion of Mr. Quirk. The reader has seen the unexpected turn which matters took upon that important occasion, and if it proved Quirk's policy to be somewhat inferior in point of discretion and long-sightedness to that of Gammon, still it must be owned that the latter had cause to admire the rapid generalship with which the consequences of Quirk's false move had been retrieved by him—not ill seconded by Snap. What could have been more judicious than his reception of Titmouse on the occasion of his being led in again by the subtle Gammon?

The next and greatest matter was, how to obtain any hold upon such a person as Titmouse had shown himself, so as to secure to themselves, in the event of success, the remuneration to which they considered themselves entitled. Was it so perfectly clear that if he felt disposed to resist it they could compel him to pay the mere amount of their bill of costs?

Suppose he should turn round upon them, and have their BILL TAXED—Quirk grunted with fright at the bare thought. Then there was a slapping *quiddam honorarium* extra—undoubtedly for *that* they must, they feared, trust to the honor and gratitude of Titmouse; and a pretty taste of his quality they had already experienced. Such a disposition as *his*, to have to rely upon for the prompt settlement of a bill of thousands of pounds of costs, and, besides that, to have it to look to for the payment of at least some five or perhaps ten thousand pounds *douceur*—nay, and this was not all. Mr. Quirk had, as well as Mr. Gammon, cast many an anxious eye on the following passages from a certain work entitled *Blackstone's Commentaries:*

" MAINTENANCE is an officious intermeddling in a suit that no way belongs to one, by ' maintaining ' or assisting either party with money, or otherwise, to prosecute or defend it.* * It is an offense against public justice, as it keeps alive strife and contention, and perverts the remedial process of the law into an engine of oppression.* * The punishment by common-law is fine and imprisonment, and by statute 32 Hen. VIII. c. 9, a forfeiture of £10.

" CHAMPERTY—(*campi partitio*)—is a species of Maintenance, and punished in the same manner, being a bargain with a plaintiff or defendant ' *campum partiri,*' to divide the land, or other matter sued for between them, if they prevail at law, whereupon the champertor is to carry on the suit at his own expense.* * These pests of civil society, that are perpetually endeavoring to disturb the repose of their neighbors, and officiously interfering in other men's quarrels, even at the hazard of their own fortunes, were severely animadverted on by the Roman law, and they were punished by the forfeiture of a third part of their goods, and perpetual infamy."*

---

* *Blackstone's Commentaries*, vol. iv. pp. 134-5.

These were pleasant passages surely!—
Many were the conversations and consultations which the
partners had had with Messrs. Mortmain and Frankpledge
respectively, upon the interesting question, whether there were
any mode of at once securing themselves against the ingrati-
tude of Titmouse, and protecting themselves against the penalties of the law. It made old Mr. Quirk's bald head even flush
all over whenever he thought of their bill being taxed, or contemplated himself the inmate of a prison (above all, at his
advanced time of life) with mournful leisure to meditate upon
the misdeeds that had sent him thither, to which profitable
exercise the legislature would have specially stimulated him by
a certain *fine* above mentioned. As for Gammon, he knew
there *must* be a way of doing the thing somehow or another;
for his friend Frankpledge felt infinitely less difficulty in the
way than Mortmain, whom he considered a timid and old-
fashioned practitioner. The courts, said Mr. Frankpledge,
were now setting their faces strongly against the doctrine of
Maintenance, as being founded on a by-gone state of things:
cessante ratione cessat et ipsa lex, was his favorite maxim.
There was no wrong without a remedy, he said, and was there
not a *wrong* in the case of a poor man wrongfully deprived of
his own? And how could this be *remedied*, if the old law of
Maintenance stood like a bugbear in the way of humane and
spirited practitioners? Was no one to be able to take up the
cause of the oppressed, encouraged by the prospect of an ample
recompense? If it was said—let the claimant sue in *formâ
pauperis ;* but then he must swear that he is not worth five
pounds; and a man may not be able to take that oath, and yet
be unequal to the commencement of a suit requiring the outlay of thousands. Moreover, a pretty prospect it was for such
a suitor (*in formâ pauperis*) if he should happen to be non-
suited—to be " put to his election, whether to be whipped or
pay the costs."* Thus reasoned within himself that astute
person, Mr. Frankpledge; and at length satisfied himself that
he had framed an instrument which would " meet the case "
—that " would hold water." To the best of my recollection,
it was a BOND, conditioned to pay the sum of ten thousand
pounds to Messrs. Quirk, Gammon and Snap, within two
months of Titmouse's being put into possession of the rents
and profits of the estate in question. The *condition* of that
bond was, as its framer believed, drawn in a masterly manner,

* * *

* *Blackstone*, vol. iii, p. 400, where it is stated, however, that " that
practice is now disused."

and his draft was lying before Messrs. Quirk, Gammon and
Snap, on the Wednesday morning (*i. e.* the day after Titmouse's interview with them), and had succeeded at length in
exciting the approbation of Mr. Quirk himself; when—whew!
—down came a note from Mr. Frankpledge, to the effect that,
" since preparing the draft bond," he had had " reason *slightly
to modify* his original opinion," owing to his " having lighted
upon a LATE CASE," in which an instrument, precisely similar
to the one which he had prepared for his admiring clients, had
been held " totally ineffectual and void both at law and in
equity." I say, Mr. Frankpledge's note was to that effect, for
so ingeniously had he framed it—so effectually concealed his
retreat beneath a little cloud of contradictory authorities, like
as the ink-fish, they say, eludeth his pursuers—that his clients
cursed the law, not their draftsman: and, moreover, by prudently withholding the *name* of the " late case," he at all
events, for a while, had prevented their observing that it was
senior to some eight or ten cases which (indefatigable man!)
he had culled for them out of the legal garden, and arrayed on
the back of his draft. Slightly disconcerted were Messrs. Quirk
and Gammon, it may be believed, at this new view of the " result of the authorities." " Mortmain is always right!" said
Quirk, looking hard at Gammon; who observed simply that
one day Frankpledge would be as old as Mortmain then was—
by which time (thought he) I also know where *you* will be,
my old friend, if there's any truth in the Scriptures. In this
pleasant frame of mind were the partners, when the impudent
apparition of Huckaback presented itself, in the manner which
has been described. Huckaback's commentary upon the disgusting text of Titmouse overnight (as a lawyer would say, in
an analogy to a well-known term, " Coke upon Littleton ")
produced an effect upon their minds which may be guessed at.
It was while their minds were under these two soothing influences, *i. e.* of the insolence of Huckaback and the vacilla-
tion of Frankpledge, that Mr. Gammon had penned the note
to Titmouse (surely, under the circumstances, one of extraordinary temper and forbearance) which had occasioned Titmouse the agonies which I have been attempting faintly to
describe;—and that Quirk, summoning Snap into the room,
had requested him to give orders for denial to Titmouse if he
should again make his appearance at the office; which injunction Snap forthwith delivered in the clerk's room, in a tone
and manner that were a very model of the *imperative mood.*

A day or two afterward, Mr. Quirk (who was a man that
stuck like a limpet to a rock to any point which occurred to

him), in poring over that page in the fourth volume of Blackstone's Commentaries, where were to be found the passages
which have been already quoted (and which both Quirk and
Gammon had long had off by heart), as he sat one day at dinner, at home, whither he had taken the volume in question,
fancied he had at last hit upon a notable crotchet, which, the
more he thought of, the more he was struck with, determining
to pay a visit in the morning to Mr. Mortmain. The spark of
light that had twinkled till it kindled in the tinder of his mind,
was struck by his hard head out of the following sentence of
the text in question:—

" A man *may*, however, maintain the suit of his near kinsman, servant, or POOR NEIGHBOR, out of *charity and compassion*, with impunity; *otherwise*, the punishment is," etc.,
etc.*

Now, it seemed to Mr. Quirk, that the words which I have
placed in italics and small capitals, exactly met the case of
poor Tittlebat Titmouse. He stuck to that view of the case,
till he *almost* began to think that he really had a kind of a
sort of a charity and compassion for poor Tittlebat—kept out
of his rights—tyrannized over by a vulgar draper in Oxford
Street—where, too, no doubt, he was half-starved.—" It's a
great blessing that one's got the means—and the inclination,
to serve one's poor neighbors "—thought Quirk, as he slowly
swallowed another glass, of the *wine that maketh glad the
heart of man*—and also *softens* it;—for the more he drank,
the more and more pitiable became his mood—the more sensitive was he to compassionate suggestions; and by the time he
had finished the decanter, he was actually in tears. These
virtuous feelings brought their own reward, too—for, from
time to time, they conjured up, as it were, the faint rainbow
image of a bond conditioned for the payment of TEN THOU-
SAND POUNDS!

To change the metaphor a little—by the time that old Quirk
had reached his office in the morning, the heated iron had
cooled; if his heart had retained any of the maudlin softness
of the preceding evening, the following pathetic letter from
Titmouse might have made a very deep impression upon it,
and fixed him, in the benevolent and disinterested mind of the
old lawyer, as indeed his " poor neighbor." The following is
an exact copy of it. It had been written by Titmouse, all out
of his own head; and with his own hand had he left it, at the
late hour on the night before.

* *Blackstone's Commentaries*, vol. iv. p. 186.

" *To Messrs.* QUERK, GAMON *and* SNAPE.

" GENTS,

" Y^r Esteem'd Favor lies now before Me, which *must Say* have Given me Much Concern, seeing I Thought it was All Made up betwixt us That was of Such an *Unpleasant Nature* on Tuesday night (ultimo) w^h I most humbly Own (and Acknowledge) was all alone and *intirely* of My Own Fault, and Not in the Least Your's which behaved to me, Must say, In the most Respectful and superior manner that was possible to think Of, for I truly Say I never was In the Company of Such Imminent and superior Gents before in my life w^h will take my Oath sincerely Of, Gents. Please to consider the Brandy (w^h *do* think *was Uncommon Stiff*) such a flustrum As I Was In before, to, w^h was Evident to All of Us there then Assemblid and very natral like to be the Case Seeing I have nevir known what Peas of Mind was since I behaved in Such a *Oudacious* way w^h truly was the case I can't Deny to Such Gents as Yourselfs that were doing me such Good Fortune And Kindness to me as it would Be a Dreadful *sin and shame* (such as Trust I can never be Guilty of) to be (w^h am not) and never Can Be insensible Of, Gents do Consider all this Favorably because of my humble, Amends w^h I here Make with the greatest Trouble in my Mind that I have Had Ever Since, it was all of the Sperrits I tooke w^h made me Go On at such a Rate w^h was always (beg to Assure y^r most resp^e house) the Case Since my birth I took Sperrits never so little Since I had the Meazles when I was 3 Years Old as I Well Recollect and hope it will be Born in Mind what is Often Said, and I'm Sure I've read it Somewhere Else that People that Is Drunk Always speaks the *Direct Contrarywise* of their True and Real Thoughts. (w^h am certain never was any Thing Truer in my case) so a I get the Money or What not, do whatever you Like w^h are quite welcome to Do if you please, and no questions Asked, don't Mind saying by The Way It shall Be As Good as £200 note in The way of your Resp^e House if I Get the Estate of w^h am much in Want of. Mr. Gamon (w^h is the most Upright gent that ever I came across in All my Life) will tell you that I Was Quite Cut up when he came After me in that kind Way and told him Then how I loved y^r Respect^e House and would do all In My Power to Serve You, which see if I Don't, I was in Such a rage with that Fellow (He's only in a *Situation* in Tottenham C^t Road) Huckaback which is his true name it was an *oudacious* thing, and have given him such a Precious Good hiding last Night as you never saw when on his Bendid Knees He asked the pardon of your Respectable House, say^g

nothing Of Me w^h w^d not allow because I said I would Not
Forgive Him because he had not injured me: But you, w^h I
wonder at his *Impudence* in Calling on Professional Gents like
you, if I get The Estate shall never cease to Think well of you
and mean While how full of Trouble I am *Often Thinking
Of Death* which is the End of Every Thing And Then in that
Case who will the Property Go to Seeing I Leave never a
Brother or Sister Behind me. And Therefore Them That w^d
Get it I Feel Sure of w^d Not do So Well by you (if You will
Only believe Me) So Gents. This is All at present That I will
Make So Bold to trouble you With About my Unhappy Affairs
Only to say That am *used* most Intolerably Bad now In The
Shop quite Tyrannicall And Mr. Tag-Rag as Set Them All
Against Me and I shall Never Get Another Situat^n for want of
a Cha^r which he will give me say^s not^g at Present of the Sort
of Victules w^h give me Now to Eat Since Monday last, For
Which am Sure the Devil must have Come In to That Gentle-
man (Mr. Tag-Rag, he was only himself in a Situation in Hol-
born once, gett^g the Business by marry^g the widow w^h wonder
At for he is nothing Particular to Look At.) A am y^rs
  Humbly to Command Till Death (always
Humbly Begging pardon for the bad Conduct w^h was guilty of
when In Liquor Especially On an Empty Stomach, Having
Taken Nothing all that Day excepting what I could not Eat),
  " Your's most Resp^y
    " Tittlebat Titmouse.
" P.S. Will Bring that young Man with Tears In his Eyes
to Beg y^r pardon Over again If You Like w^h will Solemnly
Swear if Required That he did It all of His *own* Head And
that Have given It him For it in the Way That is Written
Above And humbly Trust You Will make Me So happy Once
more by Writing To Me (if it is only a Line) To say You Have
Thought No more of it. T. T. No. 9 Closet C^t. Oxford
Street. 14/7/18—"

This touching epistle, I was saying, might have brought
tears into Mr. Quirk's eyes, if he had been *used* to the melting
mood, which he was not; having never been seen to shed a
tear but once—when five sixths of his little bill of costs (£196,
15s. 4d.) were taxed off in an action on a Bill of Exchange for
£20. As it was, he tweedled the letter about in his hands for
about five minutes, in a musing mood, and then stepped with
it into Mr. Gammon's room. That gentleman took the letter
with an air of curiosity, and read it over; at every sentence (if
indeed a sentence there was in it) bursting into soft laughter.

" Ha, ha, ha!" he laughed on concluding it—"a comical gentleman, Mr. Titmouse, upon my honor!"

" Funny—is't it rather?" interposed Mr. Quirk, standing with his hands fumbling about in his breeches pocket.

" What a crawling despicable little rascal!—ha, ha, ha!

" Why—I don't quite say that, either," said Quirk, doubtingly—" I don't exactly look at it in *that* light!"

" My dear sir!" exclaimed Gammon, leaning back in his chair, and laughing rather heartily (at least for him).

" You can't leave off that laugh of yours," said Quirk, a little tartly; " but I must say I don't see anything in the letter to laugh at so particularly. It is written in a most respectful manner, and shows a proper feeling toward the house."

" Ay! see how he speaks of *me*!" interrupted Gammon, with such a smile!—

" And doesn't he speak so of me? and all of us?"

" He'll let the house tread on him till he can tread on the house, I dare say."

" But you must own, Mr. Gammon, it shows we've licked him into shape a bit—eh?"

" Oh, it's a little vile creeping reptile now, and so it will be to the end of the chapter—of our proceedings; and when we've *done* everything—really, Mr. Quirk! if one *were* apt to lose one's temper, it would be to see such a *thing* as that put into possession of such a fortune."

" That may be, Mr. Gammon; but I really—hem!—trust—I've a higher feeling!—To right—the injured—" He could get no further.

" Hem!" exclaimed Gammon.

The partners smiled at one another. A touch, or an attempted touch at *disinterestedness!*—and at Quirk's time of life!

" But he's now in a humor for *training*, at all events—isn't he?" exclaimed Quirk—" we've something now to go to work upon—gradually."

" Isn't that a leaf of *my* book, Mr. Quirk?—isn't that exactly what—"

" Well, well — what does it signify?" interrupted Quirk rather petulantly—" I've got a crochet that'll do for us, yet, about the matter of law, and make all right and tight—so I'm going to Mortmain."

" I've got a little idea of my own of that sort, Mr. Quirk," said Gammon—" I've got an extract from Co-Litt—. I can't imagine how either of them could have missed it; and, as Frankpledge dines with me to-day, we shall talk it all over.

But, by the way, Mr. Quirk, I should say, with all œeference, that we'll take no more notice of this fellow till we've got some screw tight enough—''

'' Why—all that may be very well; but you see, Gammon, the fellow seems the real heir, after all—and if *he* don't get it, *no one can ;* and if *he* don't—*we* don't! eh?''

'' There's a very great deal of force in that observation, Mr. Quirk,'' said Gammon, emphatically:— and, tolerably well pleased with one another, they parted. , If Quirk might be compared to an old file, Gammon was the *oil !*—so they got on, in the main, very well together. It hardly signifies what was the result of their interview with their two conveyancers. They met the next morning on ordinary business; and as each made no allusions whatever to the '' crotchet '' of the day before, it may be safely inferred that each had been satisfied by his conveyancer of having found out a mare's-nest:

'' I think, by the way,'' said Mr. Gammon to Mr. Quirk, before they parted on the previous evening, '' it may be as well, all things considered, to acknowledge the receipt of the fellow's note—eh?—*Can't* do any harm, you know, and civility costs nothing—hem!''

'' The very thing I was thinking of,'' replied Quirk, as he always did on hearing any suggestion from Mr. Gammon. So by that night's post was dispatched (postpaid) the following note to Mr. Titmouse:

'' Messrs. Quirk, Gammon, and Snap have the pleasure of acknowledging the receipt of Mr. Titmouse's polite letter of last night's date; and earnestly beg that he will not distress himself about the little incident that occurred at their office on Tuesday night, and which they assure him they have quite forgotten. They made all allowances, however their feelings suffered at the time. They beg Mr. T. will give them credit for not losing sight of his interests, to the best of their ability; obstructed as they are, however, by numerous serious difficulties. If they should be in any degree hereafter overcome, he may rest assured of their promptly communicating with him; and till then they trust Mr. T. will not inconvenience himself by calling on, or writing to them.

'' *Saffron Hill*, 15*th July*, 18—.

'' P.S.—Messrs. Q. G. and S. regret to hear that any unpleasantness has arisen (Gammon could hardly write for laughing) between Mr. Titmouse and his friend Mr. Hicklebagle, who, they assure him, manifested a very warm interest in behalf of Mr. T., and conducted himself with the greatest propriety on the occasion of his calling upon Messrs. Q. G. and S. They happened at that moment to be engaged in matters of the highest importance; which will, they trust, explain any appearance of abruptness they might have exhibited toward that gentleman. Perhaps Mr. Titmouse will be so obliging as to intimate as much to Mr. Hickerbag."

There was an obvious reason for this polite allusion to Huckaback. Gammon thought it very possible that that gentleman might be in Mr. Titmouse's confidence, and exercise a powerful influence over him hereafter; and which influence Messrs. Quirk, Gammon and Snap might find it well worth their while to secure beforehand.

The moment that Titmouse, with breathless haste, had read over this mollifying document, which being directed to his lodgings correctly; he obtained as soon as he had reached his lodgings after quitting Mr. Tag-rag, about ten o'clock, he hastened to his friend Huckaback. That gentleman (who seemed now virtually recognized by Messrs. Quirk, Gammon, and Snap as Titmouse's confidant) shook his head ominously, exclaiming—"Blarney, blarney!" and a bitter sneer settled on his disagreeable features, till he had read down to the postscript! the perusal of which effected a sudden change in his feelings. He declared, with a great oath, that Messrs. Quirk, Gammon, and Snap were "perfect gentlemen," and would "do the right thing, Titmouse might depend upon it;" an assurance which greatly cheered Titmouse, to whose keen discernment it never once occurred to refer Huckaback's altered tone to the right cause, viz., the lubricating quality of the postscript; and since Titmouse did not allude to it, no more did Mr. Huckaback, although his own double misnomer stuck a little in his throat. So effectual indeed had been that most skillful postscript upon the party whom it had been aimed at that he exerted himself unceasingly to revive Titmouse's confidence in Messrs. Quirk, Gammon and Snap; and so far succeeded, that Titmouse returned to his lodgings at a late hour, a somewhat happier, if not a *wiser* man than he had left them. By the time, however, that he got into bed, having once more spelled over the note in question, he felt as despondent as ever, and thought that Huckaback had not known what he had been talking about. He also adverted to an *apparently* careless allusion by Huckaback to the injuries which had been inflicted upon him by Titmouse on the Wednesday night; and which, by the way, Huckaback determined it should be no fault of his if Titmouse easily forgot! He hardly knew why—

but he disliked this particularly.—Whom had he, however, in the world, but Huckaback? In company with him alone, Titmouse felt that his pent-up feelings could discharge themselves. Huckaback had certainly a wonderful knack of keeping up Titmouse's spirits, whatever cause he fancied he might really have for depression. In short, he longed for the Sunday morning—ushering in a day of rest and sympathy. Titmouse would indeed then have to look upon an agitating and miserable week, what with the dismal upsetting of his hopes, in the manner I have described, and the tyrannical treatment he experienced at Tag-rag and Co.'s.

Mr. Tag-rag began, at length, in some degree, to relax his *active* exertions against Titmouse, simply because of the trouble it gave him to keep them up. He attributed the pallid cheek and depressed manner of Titmouse entirely to the discipline which had been inflicted upon him at the shop, and was gratified at perceiving that all his other young men seemed, especially in his presence, to have imbibed his hatred of Titmouse? What produced in Tag-rag his hatred of Titmouse? Simply what had taken place on the Monday. Mr. Tag-rag's dignity and power had been doggedly set at naught by one of his shopmen, who had since refused to make the least submission, or offer any kind of apology. Such conduct struck at the root of subordination in his establishment. Again, there is perhaps nothing in the world so calculated to enrage a petty and vulgar mind to the highest pitch of malignity as the calm persevering defiance of an inferior, whom it strives to *despise,* while it is only *hating,* which it at the same time feels to be the case. Tag-rag now and then looked toward Titmouse as he stood, behind the counter, as if he could have murdered him. Titmouse attempted once or twice, during the week, to obtain a situation elsewhere, but in vain. He could expect no character from Tag-rag; and when the 10th of August should have arrived, what was to become of him? These were the kind of thoughts often passing through his mind during the Sunday, which he and Huckaback spent together in unceasing conversation on the one absorbing event of the last week. Titmouse, poor little puppy, had dressed himself with just as much care as usual; but as he was giving the finishing touches at his toilet, pumping up grievous sighs every half minute, the sum of his reflections might be stated in the miserable significance of a quaint saying of Poor Richard's—"How hard is it to make an empty sack stand upright!"

Although the sun shone as vividly and beautifully as on the preceding Sunday, to Titmouse's saddened eye there seemed a

sort of gloom everywhere. Up and down the Park he and
Huckaback walked toward the close of the afternoon; but Titmouse had not so elastic a strut as before. He felt empty and
sinking. Everybody seemed to know what a sad pretender he
was; and they quitted the magic circle much earlier than had
been usual with Titmouse. What with the fatigue of a long
day's saunter, the vexation of having had but a hasty, inferior,
and unrefreshing meal, which did not deserve the name of dinner, and their unpleasant thoughts, both seemed depressed as
they walked along the streets. At length they arrived at the
open doors of a gloomy-looking building, into which two or
three sad and prim-looking people were entering. After walking a few paces past the door—"Do you know, Huck," said
Titmouse, stopping, "I've often thought that—that—there's
something in *Religion.*"

"To be sure there is, for those that like it—who doubts it?
It's all very well in its place, no doubt," replied Huckaback
with much surprise, which increased, as he felt himself slowly
being swayed around toward the building in question. "But
what of that?"

"Oh, nothing; but—hem! hem!" replied Titmouse, sinking his voice to a whisper—"a touch of—religion—would not
be so much amiss just now, I feel—uncommon inclined that
way, somehow."

"Religion's all very well, Titty, dear!—for them that has
much to be thankful for; but devil take me! what have either
you or me to be—"

"But, Huck—how do you know but we might *get* something to be thankful for, by praying?—I've often heard of
great things;—Come."

Huckaback stood for a moment irresolute, twirling about his
cane, and looking rather distastefully toward the dingy building. "To be sure," he said, faintly. Titmouse drew him
nearer; but he suddenly started back.—"No! oh, 'tis only a
meeting-house, Tit! Curse Dissenters, how I hate 'em! No
—I won't pray in a meeting-house, let me be bad as I may.
Give me a regular-like, respectable church, with a proper
steeple, and parson, and prayers, and all that."

Titmouse secretly acknowledged the force of these observations; and the intelligent and piously disposed couple, with
perhaps a just, but certainly a somewhat sudden regard for
orthodoxy, were not long before they had found their way into
a church where evening service was being performed. They
ascended the gallery stair; and seeing no reason to be ashamed
of being at church, down they both went, with loud clattering

steps and a bold air, into the very central seat in the front of the gallery, which happened to be vacant. Titmouse paid a most exemplary attention to what was going on, kneeling sitting and standing with exact propriety, in the proper places, joining audibly in the responses, and keeping his eye pretty steadily on the prayer-book, which he found lying there. He even rebuked Huckaback for whispering (during one of the most solemn parts of the service) that "there was a pretty gal in the next pew!"—He thought that the clergyman was an uncommon fine preacher, and said some things that he *must* have meant for him, Titmouse, in particular.

"Curse me, Hucky!" said he, heatedly, as soon as they had quitted the church, and were fairly in the street—"Curse me if—if—ever I felt so comfortable-like in my mind before, as I do now—I'll go next Sunday again."

"Lord, Tit, you don't really mean—it's deuced dull work!"

"Hang me if I don't though! and if anything should come of it—if I do but get the estate—(I wonder, now, where Mr. *Gammon* goes to church. I should like to know!—I'd go there regularly)—But if I *do* get the thing—you see if I don't—"

"Ah, I don't know; it's not much use praying for money, Tit; I've tried it myself, once or twice, but it didn't answer!"

"I'll take my oath you was staring at the gals all the while, Hucky!"

"Ah, Titty!" exclaimed Huckaback, and winked his eye, and put the tip of his forefinger to the tip of his nose, and laughed.

Titmouse continued in what he doubtless imagined to be a devout frame of mind, for several minutes after quitting the church. But close by the aforesaid church, the devil had a thriving little establishment, in the shape of a cigar-shop; in which a showily dressed young Jewess sat behind the counter, right underneath a glaring gas-light—with a thin strip of greasy black velvet across her forehead, and long ringlets that rested on her shoulders—bandying slang with two or three other such puppies as Titmouse and Huckaback. Our friends entered and purchased a cigar apiece, which they lighted on the spot; and after each of them had exchanged an impudent wink with the Jewess, out they went, puffing away—all the remains of their piety! When they had come to the end of their cigars they parted, each speeding homeward. Titmouse, on reaching his lodgings, sunk into profound depression. He felt an awful conviction that his visit to the cigar-shop had entirely spoiled the effects of his previous attendance at the church, and that, if so disposed, he might now sit and whistle for his ten thousand a year. Thoughts such as these drove him nearly distracted. If, indeed, he had foreseen having to go through such another week as the one just over, I think it not impossible that before the arrival of the ensuing Sunday Mr. Titmouse might have afforded a little employment to that ancient but gloomy functionary, a coroner and his jury. At that time, however, inquests of this sort were matter-of-fact and melancholy affairs enough; which I doubt not would have been rather a *dissuasive* from suicide, in the estimation of one who might be supposed ambitious of the *éclat* of a modern inquest; where, indeed, such strange antics are played by certain new performers as would suffice to revive the corpse (if it were a corpse that had ever had a spark of sense or spirit in it) and make it kick the coroner out of the room. But to one of so high an ambition as Tittlebat Titmouse, how delightful would it not have been, to anticipate becoming (what had been quite impracticable during life) the object of public attention after his death—by means of a flaming dissertation by the coroner on his own zeal, and spirit—the nature and extent of his rights, powers, and duties;—when high doctors are browbeaten, the laws set at defiance, and public decency plucked by the beard; and the torn and bleeding hearts of surviving relatives still further agonized by an exposure, all quivering under the recent stroke, to the gaping vulgar! Indeed, I sometimes think that the object of certain coroners, nowadays, is twofold; first public—to disgust people with suicide, by showing what horrid proceedings will take place over their carcasses; and secondly, private—to get the means of studying anatomy by *post-mortems*, which the said coroner never could procure in his own practice: which enables us to account for some things one has lately seen, viz., that if a man come to his death by means of a wagon crushing his legs, the coroner institutes an exact examination of the *lungs* and *heart*. I take it to be getting now into a rule—the propriety whereof, some people think, can not be doubted—namely, that bodies ought now to be opened only to prove that they ought not to have been opened; an inquest must be held, in order to demonstrate that it need not have been held, except that certain fees thereby find their way into the pocket of the aforesaid coroner, which would otherwise not have done so. In short, such a coroner as I have in my eye may be compared to a great ape squatting on a corpse, furiously chattering and spitting at all around it; and I am glad that it hath at last had wit enough first to *shut the door* before proceeding to its horrid tricks.

Touching, by the way the *moral* of suicide, it is a way which some have of *cutting* the Gordian knot of the difficulties of life; which having been done, possibly the very first thing that is made manifest to the spirit, after taking its mad leap in the dark, is—how very easily the said knot might have been UN-TIED; nay, that it was *on the very point* of being untied, if the impatient spirit had stayed only a moment longer:—a dismal discovery which may excite ineffable grief at the folly and horror of the crime of which such spirit has been guilty. But ah! it is too late! The triumphant fiend has secured his victim!

I said it was not *impossible* that Mr. Titmouse might, under the circumstances alluded to, have done the deed which has called forth the above very natural and profound reflections; but upon the whole, it is hardly *probable*, for he knew that by doing so he would (first) irreparably injure society, by depriving it of an enlightened and invaluable member; (secondly), inflict great indignity on his precious body, of which, during life, he had always taken the most affectionate care, by consigning it to burial in a cross-road, at night time, with a stake run through it,* and moreover peril the little soul that had just leaped out of it, by not having any burial-service said over his aforesaid remains; and (lastly) lose all chance of enjoying Ten Thousand a Year—at least upon earth. I own I was a little startled (as I dare say was the reader) at a passage of mournful significance in Mr. Titmouse's last letter to Messrs. Quirk, Gammon and Snap, viz.—"How full of trouble I am, *often thinking of death,* which is the end of everything;" but on carefully considering the context, I am disposed to think that the whole was only a device of Titmouse's, either to rouse the fears, or stimulate the feelings, or excite the hopes, of the three arbiters of his destiny to whom it was addressed. Mr. Gammon, he thought, might be thereby moved to pity; while Mr. Quirk would probably be operated upon by fears, lest the sad contingency pointed at might deprive the house of one who would richly repay their exertions; and by hopes of indefinite advantage, if they could by any means prevent its happening. I have often questioned Titmouse on the subject, but he would only wink his eye, and say that he "knew *what to be at*" as well as any one! That these gentlemen really *did* keenly scrutinize, and carefully weigh every expression in the letter, ridiculous as it was, and contemptible as, I fear, it showed its writer to be, is certain; but it did not occur to them

* This mode of treating the remains of a *felo de se,* was (on the 8th July, 1823) abolished by Act of Parliament.

to compare with it, at least, the spirit and intention of their own answer to it. Did the latter document contain less cunning and insincerity, because it was couched in somewhat superior phraseology? They could conceal their selfish and overreaching designs, while poor Titmouse exposed all his little mean-mindedness and hypocrisy, simply because he had not learned how to conceal it effectually. 'Twas indeed a battle for the very same object, but between unequal combatants. Each was trying to take the other in. If Messrs. Quirk, Gammon and Snap despised and loathed the man to whom they exhibited such anxious courtesy, Titmouse hated and feared those whom his interests compelled him for a while to conciliate. Was there, in fact, a pin to choose between them--except, perhaps, that Titmouse was, in a manner, excused by his necessities?—but in the meanwhile his circumstances were becoming utterly desperate. He continued to endure great suffering at Mr. Tag-rag's during the day—the constant butt of the ridicule and insult of his amiable companions, and the victim of his employer's vile and vulgar spirit of hatred and oppression. His spirit (such as it was), in short, was very nearly broken. Though he seized every opportunity that offered, to inquire for another situation, he was unsuccessful; for all whom he applied to spoke of the *strict character* they should require, "before taking a new hand into their establishment." His occupations at nights, after quitting the shop, were two only—either to call upon Huckaback (whose sympathy, however, he was exhausting rapidly) or solace his feelings by walking down to Saffron Hill, and lingering about the closed office of Messrs. Quirk, Gammon and Snap—there was a kind of gratification even in that! He once or twice felt flustered even in catching a glimpse of the old housekeeper returning from some little errand. How he would have rejoiced to get into her good graces, and accompany her into even the kitchen—when he would be on the premises at least, and conversing with one of the establishment of those who he believed could, with a stroke of their pens, turn this wilderness of a world into a paradise for him! But he dared not make any overtures in that quarter, for fear of their getting to the notice of the dreaded Messrs. Quirk, Gammon and Snap.

At length, no more than three or four shillings stood between him and utter destitution; and the only person in the world whom he could apply to for even the most trivial assistance, was Huckaback—whom, however, he knew to be scarcely any better off than himself; and whom, moreover, he felt to be treating him more and more coldly, as the week wore on without his hearing of any the least tidings from Saffron Hill. Huckaback evidently felt now scarcely any interest or pleasure in the visits of his melancholy friend, and was plainly disinclined to talk about his affairs. At length he quite turned up his nose, with disgust, whenever Titmouse took out the well-worn note of Messrs. Quirk, Gammon and Snap, which was almost dropping in pieces with being constantly carried about in his pocket, taken in and out, and folded and unfolded, for the purpose of conning over its contents, as if there might yet linger in it some hitherto undiscovered source of consolation. Poor Titmouse, therefore, looked at it on every such occasion with as eager and vivid an interest as ever; but it was glanced at by Huckaback with a half-averted eye, and a cold, drawling, yawning " Ya—a—as—I see—I—dare—say!" As his impressions of Titmouse's bright prospects were thus being rapidly effaced, his smarting recollection of the drubbing he had received became distincter and more frequent; his feelings of resentment more lively, and not the less so, because the expression of them had been stifled (while he had considered the star of Titmouse to be in the ascendant), till the time for setting them into motion and action had gone by. In fact, the presence of Titmouse, suggesting such thoughts and recollections, became intolerable to Huckaback; and Titmouse's perceptions (dull as they naturally were, but a little quickened by recent suffering) gave him more and more distinct notice of this circumstance, at the precise time when he meditated applying for the loan of a few shillings. These feelings made him as humble toward Huckaback, and as patient of his increasing rudeness and ill-humor, as he felt abject toward Messrs. Quirk, Gammon and Snap; for, unless he could succeed in wringing some trifling loan from Huckaback (if he really had it in his power to advance him *anything*), he could not conjecture what was to become of him. Various faint but unadroit hints and feelers of his had been thrown away; for Huckaback either did not, or could not, comprehend them. But at length a sudden and fearful pressure compelled him to speak out. Gripe, the collector, called one morning for the poor's rates due from Mrs. Squallop (Titmouse's landlady) and cleaned her out of almost every penny of ready money which she had by her. This threw the good woman upon her resources, to replenish her empty pocket—and down she came upon Titmouse—or rather, up she went to him; for his heart sunk within him one night on his return from the shop, having only just taken off his hat and lit his candle, as he heard the fat old termagant's well-known heavy step ascend-

4

ing the stairs, and approaching nearer and nearer to his door. Her loud imperative single knock vibrated through his heart, and he was ready to drop.

"Oh, Mrs. Squallop! How d'ye do, Mrs. Squallop?" commenced Titmouse, faintly, when he had opened the door; "Won't you take a chair?" offering to the panting dame almost the only chair he had.

"No—I a'n't come to stay, Mr. Titmouse, because d'ye see, in coorse you've got a pound, at least, ready for me, as you promised long ago—and never more welcome; there's old Gripe been here to-day, and his hodious rates—('drat the poor, say I! them as can't work should starve!—rates is a robbery!)—but howsomdever, he's cleaned *me* out to-day; so, in coorse, I come up to *you*. Got it?"

"I—I—I—'pon my life, Mrs. Squallop, I'm uncommon sorry—"

"Oh, bother your sorrow, Mr. Titmouse!—out with the needful, for I can't stop palavering here."

"I—I can't, so help me ——!" gasped Titmouse, with the calmness of desperation.

"You can't! And marry, sir, why not, may I make bold to ask?" inquired Mrs. Squallop after a moment's pause, striving to choke down her rage.

"P'r'aps you can get blood out of a stone, Mrs. Squallop; it's what I can't," replied Titmouse, striving to screw his courage up to the sticking place to encounter one who was plainly bent upon mischief. "I've got two shillings—there they are," throwing them on the table; "and cuss me if I've another rap in the world; there, ma'am!"

"You're a liar, then, that's flat!" exclaimed Mrs. Squallop, slapping her hand upon the table, with a violence that made the candle quiver on it, and almost fall down. "*You* have the *himperance*," said she, commencing the address she had been preparing in her own mind ever since Mr. Gripe had quitted her house, "to stand there and tell me you've got nothing in the world but them *two shillings!* Heugh! Out on you, you oudacious fellow!—you jack-a-dandy! *You* tell me you haven't got more than them two shillings, and yet turns out every Sunday morning of your life like a lord, with your pins, and your rings, and your chains, and your fine coat, and your gloves, and your spurs, and your dandy cane—ough! you whipper-snapper! You're a cheat — you're a swindler, jack-a-dandy! You're the contempt of the whole court, you are, you jack-a-dandy! You've got all my rent on your back, and have had every Sunday for three months, you cheat!—you low fellow! you ungrateful chap! You're a-robbing the widow and fatherless! Look at me, and my six fatherless children down there, you good-for-nothing, nasty, proud puppy!—eugh! it makes me sick to see you. *You* dress yourself out like my lord mayor! You've bought a gold chain with my rent, you rascally cheat! *You* dress yourself out!—Ha, ha!—you're a nasty, mean-looking, humpty, dumpty, carroty-headed—"

"You'd better not say *that* again, Mrs. Squallop," quoth Titmouse, with a fierce glance.

"Not say it again!—ha, ha! Hoighty-toighty, carroty-haired jack-a-dandy!—Why, you hop-o-my-thumb! d'ye think I won't say whatever I choose, and in my own house? You're a Titmouse by name and by nature; there a'n't a cockroach crawling down-stairs that a'n't more respectable-like and better behaved than you. You're a himpudent cheat, and dandy, and knave, and a liar, and red-haired rascal—and that in your teeth! Ough! Your name stinks in court. You're a-taking of everybody in as will trust you to a penny's amount. There's poor old Cox, the tailor, with a sick wife and children, whom you've cheated this many months, all of his not having spirit to summons you! But *I'll* set him upon you; you see if I don't—and I'll have my own, too, or I wouldn't give *that* for the laws!" shouted Mrs. Squallop, at the same time snapping her fingers in his face, and then pausing for breath after her eloquent invective.

"Now, what *is* the use," said Titmouse, gently, being completely cowed—"now, what good *can* it do to go on in this way, Mrs. Squallop?"

"Missus me no missus, Mr. Titmouse, but pay me my rent, you jack-a-dandy! You've got my rent on your back and on your little finger; and I'll have it off you before I've done with you, I warrant you. I'm your landlady, and I'll have you up; I'll have old Thumbscrew here the first thing in the morning, and distrain everything, and you, too, you jackdaw, if any one would buy you, which they won't! I'll have my rent at last; I've been too easy with you, you ungrateful chap; for, mark, even Gripe this morning says, Haven't you a gentleman lodger up above? get him to pay you your own, says he; and so I will. I'm sick of all this, and I'll have my rights. Here's my son, Jem, a far better-looking chap than you, though he *hasn't* got hair like a sandy mop all under his chin, and he's obligated for to work from one week's end to another, in a paper cap and fustian jacket; and you—you painted jackanapes! But now I have got you, and I'll turn

you inside out, though I know there's nothing in you! But
I'll try to get at your fine coats, and spurs, and trousers, your
chains and pins, and make something of them before I've done
with you, you jack-a-dandy!"—and the virago shook her fist
at him, looking as though she had not yet uttered even half
that was in her heart toward him.

[Alas, alas, unhappy Titmouse, much-enduring son of sorrow! I perceive that you now feel the sharpness of an angry
female tongue; and indeed to me, not in the least approving
of the many coarse and heart-splitting expressions which she
uses, it seems, nevertheless, that she is not very far off the
mark in much that she hath said; for in truth in your conduct there is not a little that to me, piteously inclined toward
you as I am, yet appeareth obnoxious to the edge of this woman's reproaches. But think not, O bewildered and not-with-
sufficient-distinctness-discerning-the-nature-of-things Titmouse! that she hath only a sharp and bitter tongue. In this
woman behold a mother, and it may be that she will soften before you, who have plainly, as I hear, neither father nor mother. Oh, me!]

Titmouse trembled violently; his lips quivered; and the long
pent-up tears forced their way at length over his eyelids and
fell fast down his cheeks.

"Ah, you may well cry! you may! But it's too late! it's
my turn to cry now! Don't you think that I feel for my own
flesh and blood, that is my six children? And isn't what's
mine theirs? And aren't you keeping the fatherless out of
their own? It's too bad of you, it is! and you know it is,"
continued Mrs. Squallop, vehemently.

"*They've* got a mother—a kind—good—mother—to take
—care of them," Titmouse sobbed; "but there's been no one
in the—the—world that cares a straw for *me*—this twenty—
years!" He fairly wept aloud.

"Well, then, more's the pity for *you*. If you had, they
wouldn't have let you make such a puppy of yourself—and at
your landlady's expense, too. You know you're a fool," said
Mrs. Squallop, dropping her voice a little; for she was a
MOTHER after all, and she knew that what poor Titmouse had
just stated was quite true. She tried hard to feed the fire of
her wrath, by forcing into her thoughts every aggravating topic
against Titmouse that she could think of; but it became every
moment harder and harder to do so, for she was consciously
softening rapidly toward the weeping and miserable little object, on whom she had been heaping such violent and bitter
abuse. He was a great fool, to be sure—he was very fond of

fine clothes—he knew no better—he had, however, paid his
rent well enough till lately—he was a very quiet, well-disposed
lodger, for all *she* had known—he had given her youngest child
a pear not long ago. Really, thought Mrs. Squallop, I may
have gone a *leetle* too far.

"Come—it a'n't no use crying in this way. It won't put
money into your pocket, nor my rent into mine. You know
you've wronged me, and I *must* be paid," she added, but in a
still lower tone. She tried to cough away a certain rising disagreeable sensation about her throat, that kept increasing; for
Titmouse, having turned his back to hide the extent of his
emotions, seemed half choked with suppressed sobs.

"So you won't speak a word—not a word—to the woman
you've injured so much?" inquired Mrs. Squallop, trying to
assume a harsh tone; but her eyes were a little obstructed with
tears.

"I—I—*can't* speak," sobbed Titmouse—"I—I feel ready
to drop—everybody hates me"—here he paused; and for
some moments neither spoke. "I've been kept on my legs
the whole day about the town by Mr. Tag-rag, and had no
dinner. I—I—wish I was *dead!* I do!—you may take all I
have—here it is," continued Titmouse, with his foot pushing
toward Mrs. Squallop the old hair trunk that contained all
his little finery. "I sha'n't want them much longer, for I'm
turned out of my situation."

This was too much for Mrs. Squallop, and she was obliged
to wipe her full eyes with the corner of her apron, without
saying a word. Her heart smote her for the misery she had
inflicted on one who seemed quiet broken down. Pity suddenly flew, fluttering his wings—soft dove!—into her heart,
and put to flight in an instant all her enraged feelings.
"Come, Mr. Titmouse," said she, in quite an altered tone,
"never mind *me;* I'm a plain-spoken woman enough, I dare
say—and often say more than I mean—for I—I know I a'n't
over particular when my blood's up—but—Lord!—I—I
wouldn't hurt a hair of your head, poor chap!—for all I've
said—no, not for double the rent you owe me. Come! don't
go on so, Mr. Titmouse—what's the use?—it's all quite—over
—I'm sorry—Lud! if I'd *really* thought"—she almost sobbed
—"you'd been so—so—why, I'd have waited till to-morrow
night before I'd said a word. But, Mr. Titmouse, since you
haven't had any dinner, won't you have a mouthful of something—a bit of bread and cheese?—I'll soon fetch you up a bit
and a drop of beer—we've just had it in for our suppers."

"No, thank you—I can't—I can't eat!" sobbed Titmouse.

"Oh, bother it, but you *shall!* I'll go down and fetch it up in half a minute, as sure as my name is Squallop!" And out of the room and down-stairs she bustled, glad of a moment to recover herself.

"Lord-a-mercy!" said she, on entering her room, to her eldest daughter, and a neighbor who had just come in to supper—and while she hastily cut a thick hunch of bread, and a good slice of cheese—"there I've been a-rating that poor little chap, up at the top room (my dandy lodger, you know), like anything—and I really don't think he's had a morsel of victuals in his belly this precious day; and I've made him cry, poor soul! as if his heart would break. Pour us out half a pint of that beer, Sally—a *good* half pint, mind!—I'm going to take it upstairs directly. I've gone a deal too far with him I do think; but it's all of that nasty old Gripe; I've been wrong all the day through it! How I hate the sight of old Gripe! What odious-looking people they do get to collect the rates and taxes, to be sure!—Poor chap," she continued, as she wiped out a plate with her apron, and put into it the bread and cheese, with a knife—"he offered me a chair when I went in, so uncommon civil-like, it took a good while before I could get myself into the humor to *give it* him as I wanted. And he's no father nor mother (half of which has happened to *you*, Sal, and the rest will happen one of these days, you know!) and he's not such a very bad lodger, after all, though he *does* get a little behindhand now and then, and though he turns out every Sunday like a lord, poor fool—as my poor husband used to say, ' with a shining back and empty belly.' "

"But that's no reason why honest people should be kept out of their own, to feed his pride," interposed her neighbor, a skinny old widow, who had never had chick nor child, and was always behindhand with her own rent; but whose effects were not worth distraining upon. "I'd get hold of some of his fine crincum-crancums and gimcracks, for security like, if I were you. I would, indeed."

"Why—no, poor soul—*I* don't hardly like: he's a vain creature, and puts everything he can on his back, to be sure; but he a'n't quite a *rogue*, neither."

"Ah, ha, Mrs. Squallop—you're such a simple soul!—Won't my fine gentleman make off with his finery after to-night?"

"Well, I shouldn't have thought it! To be sure, he may! Really, there *can't* be much harm in asking him (in a proper kind of way) to deposit one of his fine things with me, by way of security—that ring of his, you know—eh?—Well, I'll *try* it anyhow," said Mrs. Squallop, as she set off upstairs.

"I know what *I* should do, if so be he was a lodger of *mine*, that's all," said her visitor (as Mrs. Squallop quitted the room) vexed to find their supper so considerably and unexpectedly diminished, especially as to the pot of porter, which she strongly suspected would not be replenished.

"There," said Mrs. Squallop, setting down on the table what she had brought for Titmouse, "there's a bit of supper for you; and you're welcome to it, I'm sure, Mr. Titmouse."

"Thank you, thank you—I can't eat," said he, casting, however, upon the victuals a hungry eye, which belied what he said, while in his heart he longed to be left alone with them for about three minutes.

"Come, don't be ashamed—fall to work—it's good wholesome victuals," said she, lifting the table near to the edge of the bed, on the side of which he was sitting, and taking up the two shillings lying on the table—" and capital good beer, I warrant me; you'll sleep like a top after it."

"You're uncommon kind, Mrs. Squallop; but I sha'n't get a wink of sleep to-night for thinking—"

"Oh, bother your thinking! Let me begin to see you eat a bit. Well, I suppose you don't like to eat and drink before me, so I'll go." [Here arose a sudden conflict in the good woman's mind, whether or not she would act on the suggestion which had been put into her head down-stairs. She was on the point of yielding to the impulse of her own good-natured though coarse feelings; but at last—] "I—I—dare say, Mr. Titmouse, you mean what's right and straightforward," she stammered.

"Yes, Mrs. Squallop—you may keep those two shillings; they're the last farthing I have left in the whole world."

"No—hem! hem!—ahem! I was just suddenly a-thinking —now can't you guess, Mr. Titmouse?"

"What, Mrs. Squallop?" inquired Titmouse, meekly but anxiously.

"Why—suppose now—if it were only to raise ten shillings with old Balls, round the corner, on one of those fine things of yours—your ring, say." [Titmouse's heart sunk within him.] "Well, well—never mind—don't fear," said Mrs. Squallop, observing him suddenly turn pale again. "I—I only thought—but never mind! It don't signify—good-night! we can talk about that to-morrow—good-night—a good night's rest, Mr. Titmouse!" and the next moment he heard her heavy step descending the stairs. Several minutes had elapsed be-

fore he could recover from the agitation into which he had
been thrown by her last proposal; but within ten minutes of
her quitting the room, there stood before him, on the table,
an *empty* plate and jug.

CHAPTER IV.

"THE beast! the fat old toad!" thought he, the instant
that he had finished masticating what had been supplied to
him by real charity and good-nature—"the vulgar wretch!—
the nasty canting old hypocrite!—I saw what she was driving
at all the while! She had her eyes on my ring! She'd have
me pawn it at old Balls's—ha, ha!—Catch me! that's all!—
Seven shillings a week for this nasty hole!—I'll be bound I pay
nearly half the rent of the whole house—the old cormorant!—
out of what she gets from me! How I hate her! More than
half my salary goes into her greasy pocket! Cuss me if I
couldn't have kicked her down-stairs — porter, bread and
cheese, and all—while she was standing canting there — A
sniveling old beldame!—Take my ring!! Lord!—" Here he
began to undress. "Ha! I'm up to her; she'll be coming
here to-morrow, with that devil Thumbscrew, to distrain, I'll
be sworn. Well—I'll take care of *these* anyhow;" and kneeling down and unlocking his trunk, he took out of it his guard-
chain, breast-pin, studs, and ring, carefully folded them up in
paper, and depositing them in his trousers' pockets, resolved
henceforth their nightly resting-place should be—under his
pillow; while during the day they should accompany his person whithersoever he went. Next he bethought himself of the
two or three important papers to which Mr. Gammon had
referred: and, with tremulous eagerness, read them over once
or twice, but without being able to extract from them the
slightest clew to their real character and bearing. Then he
folded them up in a half-sheet of writing-paper, which he proceeded to stitch carefully beneath the lining of his waistcoat;
after which he blew out his slim candle, and with a heavy sigh
got into bed. For some moments after he had blown out the
candle did the image of it remain on his aching and excited
retina: and just so long did the thoughts of *ten thousand
a year* dwell on his fancy, fading, however, quickly away amid
the thickening gloom of doubts, and fears, and miseries, which
oppressed him. There he lies, stretched on his bed, a wretched figure, lying on his breast, his head buried beneath his
feverish arms. Anon, he turns round upon his back, stretches
his wearied limbs to their uttermost, folds his arms on his

breast, then buries them beneath the pillow, under his head.
Now he turns on his right side, then on his left—presently he
starts up, and with a muttered curse shakes his little pillow,
flinging it down angrily. He can not sleep—he can not rest
—he can not keep still. Bursting with irritability, he gets
out of bed, and steps to the window, which opening wide, a
slight gush of fresh air cools his hot face for a moment or two.
His wearied eye looks up and beholds the moon shining overhead in cold splendor, turning the clouds to gold as they flit
past her, and shedding a softened luster upon the tiled roofs
and irregular chimney-pots—the only objects visible to him.
No sound is heard, but occasionally the dismal cry of a disappointed cat, the querulous voice of the watchman, and the echo
of the rumbling hubbub of Oxford Street. O miserable Titmouse! of what avail is it for thee thus to fix thy sorrowful
lack-luster eye upon the cold Queen of Night!

    *   *   *   *   *   *   *

At that moment there happened to be also gazing at the
same glorious object, but at some two hundred miles' distance
from London, a somewhat different person, with very different
feelings, and in very different circumstances. It was one of
the angels of the earth—a pure-hearted and very beautiful
girl; who, after a day of peaceful, innocent, and charitable
employment, and having just quitted the piano, where her
exquisite strains had soothed and delighted the feelings of her
brother, harassed with political anxieties, had retired to her
chamber for the night. A few moments before she was presented to the reader she had extinguished her taper, and dismissed her maid without her having discharged more than
half her accustomed duties—telling her that she should finish
undressing by the light of the moon, which then poured her
soft radiance into every corner of the spacious but old-fashioned
chamber in which she sat. Then she drew her chair to the
window-recess, and pushing open the window, sat before it,
half undressed as she was, her hair disheveled, her head leaning on her hand, gazing on the scenery before her with tranquil admiration. Silence reigned absolutely. Not a sound
issued from the ancient groves which spread far and wide on
all sides of the fine old mansion in which she dwelt—solemn
solitudes, not yet less soothing than solemn. Was not the
solitude enhanced by a glimpse she caught of a restless fawn,
glancing in the distance across the avenue, as he silently
changed the tree under which he slept? Then the gentle
breeze would enter her window, laden with sweet scents of
which he had just been rifling the coy flowers beneath, in their

dewy repose, tended and petted during the day by her own delicate hand. Beautiful moon!—Cold and chaste in thy skyey palace, studded with briliiant and innumerable gems, and shedding down thy rich and tender radiance upon this lovely seclusion—was there upon the whole earth a more exquisite countenance then turned toward thee than hers? Wrap thy white robe, dearest Kate, closer round thy fair bosom, lest the amorous night breeze do thee hurt, for he groweth giddy with the sight of thy charms. Thy rich tresses, half uncurled, are growing damp—so it is time that thy blue eyes should seek repose. Hie thee, then, my love!—to yon antique couch, with its quaint carvings and satin draperies dimly visible in the dusky shade, inviting thee to sleep, and having first bent in cheerful reverence before thy Maker—to bed!—to bed!—sweet Kate, nothing disturbing thy serene thoughts, or agitating that beautiful bosom. Hush! hush!— Now she sleeps! It is well that thine eyes are closed in sleep; for BEHOLD—SEE! the brightness without is disappearing; sadness and gloom are settling on the face of nature; the tranquil night is changing her aspect; clouds are gathering, winds are moaning; the moon is gone:—but sleep on, sweet Kate—sleep on, dreaming not of dark days before thee—Oh, that thou couldst sleep on till the bightness returned!

 * * * * * * *

After having stood thus leaning against the window for nearly half an hour, Titmouse, heavily sighing, returned to bed—but there he tossed about in wretched restlessness till nearly four o'clock in the morning. If he now and then sunk into forgetfulness for a while, it was only to be harassed by the dreadful image of Mrs. Squallop, shouting at him, tearing his hair, cuffing him, flinging a pot of porter in his face, opening his boxes, tossing his clothes about, taking out his invaluable ornaments; by Tag-rag kicking him out of the shop, and Messrs. Quirk, Gammon and Snap dashing past him in a fine carriage, with six horses, and paying no attention to him as he ran shouting and breathless after them; Huckaback following, kicking and pinching him behind. These were the few little bits of different colored glass in a mental kaleidoscope, which, turned capriciously round, produce those innumerable fantastic combinations out of the simple and ordinary events of the day, which we call *dreams*—tricks of the wild sisters Fancy, when sober Reason has left her seat for a while. But this is fitter for the Royal Society than the bedroom of Tittlebat Titmouse, and I beg the reader's pardon.

About six o'clock Titmouse rose and dressed himself, and,

slipping noiselessly and swiftly down-stairs and out of the court, in order to avoid all possibility of encountering his land-lady or his tailor, soon found himself in Oxford Street. Not many people were stirring there. One or two men who passed him were smoking their morning's pipe, with a half-awakened air, as if they had only just got out of a snug bed, in which they always slept every moment that they lay upon it. Tit-mouse almost envied them. What a squalid figure he looked as he paced up and down, till at length he saw the porter of Messrs. Tag-rag and Co. opening the shop-door. He soon entered it, and commenced another joyous day in that delight-ful establishment. The amiable Mr. Tag-rag continued un-altered.

"You're at liberty to take yourself off, sir, this very day—this moment, sir, and a good riddance," said he, bitterly, dur-ing the course of the day, after demanding of Titmouse how he dared to give himself such sullen airs; "and then we shall see how charming easy it is for gents like you to get another sitiwation, sir! Your looks and manner is quite a recommen-dation, sir! If I was you, sir, I'd raise my terms. You're worth double what I give, sir!" Titmouse made no reply. "What do you mean, sir, by not answering me—eh, sir?" suddenly demanded Tag-rag, with a look of fury.

"I don't know what you'd have me say, sir. What am I to say, sir?" inquired Titmouse, with a sigh.

"What, indeed! I should like to catch you! Say, indeed! Only say a word—and out you go, neck and crop. Attend to that old lady coming in, sir. And mind, sir, I've got my eye on you!" Titmouse did as he was bid, and Tag-rag, a bland smile suddenly beaming in his attractive features, hurried down toward the door, to receive some lady-customers, whom he observed alighting from a carriage, and at that moment you would have sworn that he was one of the kindest-hearted, sweetest-tempered men in the world.

When at length *this* day had come to a close, Titmouse, in-stead of repairing to his lodgings, set off, with a heavy heart, to pay a visit to his excellent friend Huckaback, whom he knew to have received his quarter's salary the day before, and from whom he faintly hoped to succeed in extorting some trifling loan. "If you want to learn the value of money, *try to borrow some*," says Poor Richard—and Titmouse was now going to learn that useful but bitter lesson. Oh, how disheartening was Mr. Huckaback's reception of him. That gentleman, in answering the modest knock of Titmouse, suspecting who was his visitor, opened the door but a little way, and in that little

way, with his hand on the latch, he stood, with a plainly repulsive look.

"Oh! it's you, Titmouse, is it?" he commenced, coldly.

"Yes. I—I just want to speak a word to you—only a word
or two, Hucky, if you aren't busy?"

"Why, I was just going to go—but what d'ye want, Titmouse?" he inquired, in a freezing manner not stirring from
where he stood.

"*Let* me come inside a minute," implored Titmouse, feeling as if his heart were really dropping out of him, and, in a
most ungracious manner, Huckaback motioned him in.

"Well," continued Huckaback, with a chilling distrustful
look.

"Why, Huck, I know you're a good-natured chap—you
couldn't, just for a short time, lend me ten shill—"

"No, curse me if I can, and that's flat!" briskly interrupted
Huckaback, finding his worst suspicions confirmed.

"Why, Hucky, wasn't you only yesterday paid your salary?"

"Well!—suppose I was!—what then? You're a monstrous
cool hand, Titmouse! I never! So I'm to lend you, when I'm
starving myself? I've received such a lot, haven't I?"

"I thought we'd always been friends, Hucky," said Titmouse, faintly, "and so we shouldn't mind helping one another a bit. Don't you remember, I once lent you half a
crown?"

"Half a crown!—and that's nine months ago!"

"Do, Hucky, do. 'Pon my soul, I've not a sixpence in the
whole world."

"Ha, ha! A pretty chap to borrow! You can pay so well!
By George, Titmouse, you're a cool hand!"

"If you won't lend me, I must starve."

"Go to *my uncle's*." (Titmouse groaned aloud.) "Well
—and why not? What of that?" continued Huckaback,
sharply and bitterly. "I dare say it wouldn't be the first
time you've done such a trick no more than me. I've been
obligated to do it. Why shouldn't you? A'n't there that
ring?"

"Oh, Lord! oh, Lord! that's just what Mrs. Squallop said
last night."

"Whew! *She's* down on you, is she! And you have the
face to come to me! *You*—that's a-going to be sold up, come
to borrow! Lord, that's good, anyhow! A queer use that to
make of one's friends;—it's a taking them in, I say!"

"Oh, Huck, Huck, if you only knew what a poor devil—"

"Yes, that's what I was a-saying, but it a'n't ' poor devils '

one lends money to, so easily, I warrant me; though you *a'n'*
such a poor devil—you're only shamming! Where's your
guard-chain, your studs, your breast-pin, your ring, and all
that? Sell 'em? if not, anyhow, *pawn* 'em. Can't eat your
cake and have it; fine back must have empty belly with us
sort of chaps."

If you'll only be so uncommon kind as to lend me—this
once—ten shillings," continued Titmouse, in an imploring
tone, "I'll bind myself by a solemn oath, to pay you the very
first moment I get what's due to me from Tag-rag and Co."—
Here he was almost choked by the sudden recollection that
he had almost nothing to receive.

"You've some property in the moon, too, that's coming to
you, you know!" said Huckaback, with an insulting sneer.

"I know what you're driving at," said poor Titmouse, and
he continued, eagerly, "and if anything *should* ever come up
from Messrs. Quirk, Gam—"

"Yough! Faugh! Pish! Stuff!" burst out Huckaback,
in a tone of contempt and disgust; "*never* thought there was
anything in it, and now *know* it! It's all in my eye, and all
that!"

"Oh, Hucky, Hucky! You don't say so!" groaned Titmouse, bursting into tears; "you did not *always* say so?"

"It's enough that I say it *now*, then; will that do?" interrupted Huckaback, impetuously.

"Oh, Lord, Lord! what is to become of me?" cried Titmouse, with a face full of anguish.

[At this moment the following was the course of thought
passing through the mind of Mr. Huckaback:—it is not *certain*
that nothing will come of the fellow's affair with Messrs. Quirk,
Gammon and Snap. It was hardly likely that they would
have gone as far as Titmouse represented (lawyers as they
were) unless they had seen very substantial grounds for doing
so. Besides even though Titmouse might not get ten thousand a year, he might yet succeed in obtaining a very splendid
sum of money, and if he (Huckaback) could but get a little
slice out of it, Titmouse was now nearly desperate, and would
promise anything, and if he could but be wheedled into giving
anything in writing—Well, thought Huckaback, I'll try it,
however!]

"Ah, Titmouse, you're civil enough *now*, and would *promise*
anything," said Huckaback, appearing to hesitate, but when
you get your money you'd forget everything about it—"

"Forget my promise! Dear Hucky! only try me—do try
me but once, that's all! 'Pon my precious life, ten shillings

is worth more to me now than a hundred pounds may be by and by."

"Ay, so you say *now ;* but d'ye mean to tell me that, if I was now to advance you ten shillings out of my poor little salary," continued Huckaback, apparently carelessly, "you'd for instance, pay me a hundred pounds out of your thousands!"

"Oh, Lord! only you try me—do try me!" said Titmouse, eagerly.

"Oh, I dare say," interrupted Huckaback, smiling incredulously, and chinking some money in his trousers' pocket. Titmouse heard it, and (as the phrase is) his teeth watered, and he immediately swore such a tremendous oath as I dare not set down in writing that if Huckaback would that evening lend him ten shillings Titmouse would give him one hundred pounds out of the very first moneys he got from the estate.

"Ten shillings is a slapping slice out of my little salary—I shall have, by George, to go without a many things I'd intended getting; it's worth ten pounds to me just now."

"Why, dear Hucky! 'pon my soul, 'tis worth a hundred to *me !* Mrs. Squallop will sell me out, bag and baggage, if I don't give her something to-morrow!"—

"Well, if I really thought—would you mind giving me, now, a bit of black and white for it?"

"I'll do anything you like; only let me feel the ten shillings in my fingers!"

"Well, no sooner said than done, if you're a man of your word," said Huckaback, in a trice producing a bit of paper, and a pen and ink, "So only just for the fun of it; but—Lord! what stuff!—I'm only bargaining for a hundred pounds of moonshine. Ha, ha! I shall never see the color of your money, not I; so I may as well say two hundred when I'm about it, as one hundred—"

"Why, hem! Two hundred, Huck, *is* rather a large figure; one hundred's odds enough, I'm sure!" quoth Titmouse, meekly.

"P'r'aps, Tit, you forget the *licking* you gave me the other day," said Huckaback, with sudden sternness. "Suppose I was to go to an attorney, and get the law of you, what a sight of damages I should have—three hundred pounds at least!"

Titmouse appeared even yet hesitating.

"Well, then!" said Huckaback, flinging down his pen, "suppose I have them yet—"

"Come, come, Hucky, 'tis all past and gone, all that—"

"Is it? Well, I never! I shall never be again the same

man I was before that 'ere licking. I've a sort of a—a—of a—feeling inside as if my breast was—I shall carry it to my grave—curse me if I sha'n't!''

[It never once occurred to Titmouse, not having his friend Mr. Gammon at his elbow, that the plaintiff in the action of *Huckaback* v. *Titmouse* might have been slightly at a loss for a *witness* of the assault; but something quite as good in its way—a heaven-sent suggestion—*did* occur to him.]

"Ah," said Titmouse suddenly, "that's true; and uncommon sorry am I; but still, a hundred pounds is a hundred pounds and a large sum for the use of ten shillings, and a licking; but never you think it's all moonshine about my business with Messrs. Quirk, Gammon and Snap! You should only have heard what *I've* heard to-day from those gents; hem! but I won't split *again* either.''

"Eh? What? Heard from those gents at Saffron Hill?'' interrupted Huckaback, briskly; "come, Titty, out with it—out with it; no secrets between friends, Titty!''

"No, I'll be hanged if I do—I won't spoil it all again, and now since I've let out as much, which I didn't mean to do, I'll tell you something else—ten shillings is no use to me, I must have a pound.''

"Titty, Titty!'' exclaimed Huckaback, with unaffected concern.

"And won't give more than fifty for it when I get my property either''—[Huckaback whistled aloud, and with a significant air buttoned up the pocket which contained the money; intimating that now the negotiation was all at an end, for that Titmouse's new terms were quite out of the question:] "for I know where I can get twenty pounds easily, only I like to come to a *friend* first.''

"You aren't behaving much like a friend to one as has always been a fast friend of yours, Titty! *A pound!*—I haven't got it to part with, that's flat, so, if that's your figure, why, you must even go to your other friend, and leave poor Hucky?''

"Well, I don't mind saying only ten shillings,'' quoth Titmouse, fearing that he had been going on *rather* too fast.

"Ah, that's something reasonable-like, Titty! and to meet you like a friend, I'll take fifty pounds instead of a hundred; but you won't object now to—you know—a deposit; that ring of yours—well, well! it don't signify, since it goes against you; so now, here goes, a bit of paper for ten shililngs, ha, ha!'' and taking a pen, after a pause, in which he called to mind as

much of the phraseology of money securities as he could, he
drew up the following stringent document:

" *Know all Men* That you are Bound to *Mr. R. Huckaback*
Promising The Bearer (on *Demand*) To pay Fifty Pounds in
cash out of the Estate, *if you get it.*   (Value received.)
" (Witness,) 22d July, 18—.
          " R. HUCKABACK."

" There, Titty—if you're an honest man, and would do as
you would be done by," said Huckaback, after signing his
own name as above, handing the pen to Titmouse, " sign
that; just to show your honor, like—for, in course, I sha'n't
ever come on you for the money—get as much as you may."
   A blessed thought occurred to poor Titmouse in his extremity, viz., that there was *no stamp* on the above instrument,
(and he had never seen a promissory note or bill of exchange
without one); and he signed it instantly, with many fervent
expressions of gratitude.   Huckaback received the valuable
security with apparently a careless air, and after cramming it
into his pocket, as if it had been in reality only a bit of waste
paper, counted out ten shillings into the eager hand of Titmouse, who, having thus most unexpectedly succeeded in his
mission, soon afterward departed—each of this pair of worthies
fancying that he had succeeded in cheating the other.   Huckaback, having very cordially shaken Titmouse by the hand,
heartily damned him upon shutting the door on him, and then
anxiously perused and reperused his " security," wondering
whether it was possible for Titmouse at any time thereafter to
evade it, and considering by what means he could acquaint
himself with the progress of Titmouse's affairs.   The latter
gentleman, as he hurried homeward, dwelt for a long while
upon only one thought—how fortunate was the omission of his
friend to have a stamp upon his security.   When and where,
thought he, was it that he had heard that nothing would do
without a stamp?   However, he had got the ten shillings safe,
and Huckaback might wait for his fifty pounds till—but in the
meanwhile he, Titmouse, seemed to stand a fair chance of going to the dogs; the ten shillings, which he had just obtained
with so much difficulty, were to find their way immediately
into the pockets of his landlady, whom it might pacify for a
day or two, and what quarter was he now to look to for the
smallest assistance?   What was to become of him?   Titmouse
was a miserable fool; but thoughts such as these, in such

circumstances as his, would force themselves into the mind of even a fool! How could he avoid—oh, horrid thought!—soon parting with, or at least pawning, his ring and his other precious trinkets? He burst into a perspiration at the mere thought of seeing them hanging ticketed for sale in the window of old Balls! As he slowly ascended the stairs which led to his apartment, he felt as if he were following some unseen conductor to a dungeon.

He was not aware that all this while, although he heard nothing from them, he occupied almost exclusively the thoughts of those distinguished practitioners in the law, Messrs. Quirk, Gammon and Snap. They, in common with Huckaback, had an intense desire to share in his anticipated good fortune, and determined to do so according to their opportunities. The excellent Huckaback (a model of a usurer on a small scale) had promptly and adroitly seized hold of the very first opportunity that presented itself, for securing a little return hereafter for the ten shillings, with which he had so generously parted when he could so ill afford it; while Messrs. Quirk, Gammon and Snap were racking their brains, and, from time to time, those of Messrs. Mortmain and Frankpledge, to discover some instrument strong and large enough to cut a fat slice for themselves out of the fortune they were endeavoring, for that purpose, to put within the reach of Mr. Titmouse.

A rule of three mode of stating the matter would be thus: as the inconvenience of Huckaback's parting with his ten shillings and his waiver of damages for a very cruel assault. were to his contingent gain, hereafter, of £50; so were Messrs. Quirk, Gammon and Snap's risk, exertions, outlay and benefit conferred on Titmouse, to their contingent gain of ten thousand pounds. The principal point of difference between them was—as to the mode of *securing* their future recompense: in which it may have been observed by the attentive reader, with respect to the precipitancy of Huckaback and hesitating caution of Messrs. Quirk, Gammon and Snap, that—" *thus fools*" (*e. g.* Huckaback) " *rushed in where angels*" (*i. e.* Messrs. Quirk, Gammon and Snap) "*feared to tread.*" Let me not, however, for a moment, insinuate that both these parties were actuated by only one motive, *i. e.* to make a prey of this little monkey *millionaire* that was to be. 'Tis true that Huckaback appears to have driven rather a hard bargain with his distressed friend (and almost every one that, being similarly situated, has occasion for such services as Titmouse sought from Huckaback, will find himself called upon to pay

pretty nearly the same price for them), but it was attended
with one good effect; for the specific interest in Titmouse's
future prosperity, acquired by Huckaback, quickened his energies and sharpened his wits in the service of his friend. But
for this, indeed, it is probable that Mr. Huckaback's door
would have become as hopelessly closed against Titmouse as
was that of Messrs. Quirk, Gammon and Snap. Some two or
three nights after the little transaction between the two
friends which I have been describing, Huckaback called upon
Titmouse, and after greeting him rather cordially, told him
that he had come to put him up to a trick upon the Saffron
Hill people, that would tickle them into a little activity in his
affairs. The trick was—the sending a letter to those gentlemen calculated to—but why attempt to characterize it? I have
the original document lying before me, which was sent by Titmouse the very next morning to Messrs. Quirk, Gammon and
Snap; and here follows a *verbatim* copy of it:—

" *No. 9 Closet Court,*
" *Oxford Street.*

" *To Messrs.* QUIRK & CO.

" Gents,—Am sorry *to* Trouble You, But Being *Drove quite
desperate* at my Troubles (which have bro^t me to my Last
Penny a Week ago) and Mrs. Squallop my Landlady w^d dis-
train on Me only that There Is nothing to distrain on, Am
Determined to Go Abroad in a Week's Time, and shall Never
come Any More back again with Great Grief w^h Is What I now
Write To tell You Of (Hoping you will please Take No notice
of it) So Need give Yourselves No Further Concern with my
Concerns Seeing The Estate is Not To Be Had and Am Sorry
you Sh^d Have Had so Much trouble with My Affairs w^h c^d not
Help. Sh^d have Much liked The Thing, only it was Not Worth
Stopping For, or Would, but Since It Was not God's Will be
Done *which it will.* Have raised a Trifle On my Future Pros-
pects (w^h am Certain There is Nothing In) from a *True
Friend* " [need it be guessed at whose instance these words
found their way into the letter?] " w^h was certainly uncom-
mon inconvenient to That Person But H^d do Anything to Do
me good As he says Am going to raise A Little More from a
Gent That does *Things of that Nature* w^h will help me with
Expense in Going Abroad (which place I Never mean to Return from). Have fixed for the 10th To Go on w^h Day Shall
Take leave Of Mr. Tag-rag (who on my Return Shall be glad
to See Buried or in the Workhouse). Have wrote This letter

Only to Save Y^r Respectable Selves trouble w^h Trust You w^d not have Taken.

              " And Remain,
                      " Gents,
                  " Y^r humble Unworthy servant,
                              " T. TITMOUSE.

" *P. S.*—Hope you will Particularly Remember me to Mr. Gammon. What is to become of me, know nothing, being so troubled. Am Humbly Determined not to employ any Gents in This matter except y^r most Respectable House. and sh^d be most Truly Sorry to Go Abroad wh^h *am really Often thinking of in earnest.* (Unless something Speedily Turns Up, favorable), T. T.—Sh^d like (by the way) to know if you sh^d be so Disposed what y^r resp^e house w^d take for my Chances Down (*Out and out*) In a Round Sum (*Ready Money*). And hope if they Write It will be by next Post or Shall be Gone Abroad."

Old Mr. Quirk, as soon as he had finished the perusal of this skillful document, started, a little disturbed, from his seat and bustled into Mr. Gammon's room with Mr. Titmouse's open letter in his hand. " Gammon," said he, " just cast your eye over this, will you? Really, we must look after Titmouse or he'll be gone!" Mr. Gammon took the letter rather eagerly, read deliberately through it, and then looked up at his fidgety partner, who stood anxiously eying him, and smiled.

" Well, Gammon, I really think—eh? Don't you—"

" Upon my word, Mr. Quirk, this nearly equals his former letter, and it also seems to have produced on you the desired effect."

" Well, Gammon, and what of that? Because my heart don't happen to be *quite* a piece of flint, you're always—"

" You might have been a far wealthier man than you are but for that soft heart of yours, Mr. Quirk," said Gammon, with a bland smile. (!)

" I know I might, Gammon—I know it. I thank my God I'm not so keen after business that I can't feel for this poor soul—really, his state's quite deplorable!"

" Then, my dear sir, put your hand into your pocket at once, as I was suggesting last night, and allow him a weekly sum."

" A—hem! hem! Gammon "—said Quirk, sitting down, thrusting his hands into his waistcoat pockets, and looking very earnestly at Gammon.

" Well, then," replied that gentleman, shrugging his shoul-

ders, in answer to the mute appeal—" write and say you *won't*
—'tis soon done, and so the matter ends."

" Why, Gammon, you see, if he goes abroad," said Quirk,
after a long pause—" we lose him forever."

" Pho!—go abroad! He's too much for you, Mr. Quirk—
he is indeed, ha, ha!"

" You're fond of a laugh at my expense, Gammon; it's
quite pleasant—you can't think how I like that same laugh of
yours!"

" I beg your pardon, Mr. Quirk—but you really misunderstand me; I was laughing only at the absurd inconsistency of
the fellow: he's a most transparent little fool, and takes *us* for
such. Go abroad! Ridiculous pretense!—In his precious
postscript he undoes all—he says he is only often *thinking* of
going—pshaw!—That the wretch is in great distress is very
probable; but it must go hard with him before he either com-
mits suicide or goes abroad, I warrant him: I've no fears on
that score—but there *is* a point in the letter that may be worth
considering—I mean the fellow's hint about borrowing money
on his prospects."

" Yes, to be sure—the very thing that struck *me*." [Gam-
mon faintly smiled.]   " I never thought much about the *other*
part of the letter—all stuff about going abroad—pho!—But to
be sure, if he's trying to raise money, he may get into keen
hands.—Do you really think he *has*?"

" Oh, no—of course it's only a little lie of his—or he must
have found out some greater fool than himself, which I had
not supposed possible. But however that may be, I really
think, Mr. Quirk, it's high time that we should take some decided step."

" Well—yes, it may be," said Quirk, slowly—" and I must
say that Mortmain encouraged me a good deal the day before
yesterday."

" Well, and you know what Mr. Frankpledge—"

" Oh, as to Frankpledge—hem!"

" What of Mr. Frankpledge, Mr. Quirk?" inquired Gammon, rather tartly.

" There! There!—Always the way.—But what does it signify? Come, come, Gammon, we know each other too well to
quarrel!—I don't mean anything disrespectful to Mr. Frankpledge, but when Mortmain has been one's conveyancer these
twenty years, and never once—hem!—but, however, he tells
me that we are now standing on sure ground, or that he don't
know what sure ground is, and sees no objection to our even
taking preliminary steps in the matter, which indeed I begin

to think it high time to do!—And as for securing ourselves in respect of any advances to Titmouse—he suggests our taking a bond, conditioned—say for the payment of £500 or £1000 on demand, under cover of which one might advance him, you know, just such sums as, and when we pleased; one could stop when one thought fit: one could begin with three or four pounds a week, and increase as his prospects improved—eh?"

"You know *I've* no objection to such an arrangement; but consider, Mr. Quirk, we must have patience; it will take a long while to get our verdict, you know, and perhaps as long to *secure* it afterward; and this horrid little wretch all the while on our hands; what the deuce to do with him, I really don't know!"

"Humph, humph!" grunted Quirk, looking very earnestly and uneasily at Gammon.

"And what I chiefly fear is this—suppose he should get dissatisfied with the amount of our advances, and, knowing the state and prospects of the cause, should *then* turn restive?"

"Ay, confound it, Gammon, all that should be looked to, shouldn't it?" interrupted Quirk, with an exceedingly chagrined air.

"To be sure," continued Gammon, thoughtfully. "By that time he may have got substantial friends about him, whom he could persuade to become security to us for further and past advances."

"Nay, now that you name the thing, Gammon; it was what I was thinking of only the other day:" he dropped his voice— "Isn't there one or two of our own clients, hem!—"

"Why, certainly, there's old Fang; I don't think it impossible he might be induced to do a little usury—it's all he lives for, Mr. Quirk; and the security is good in reality, though perhaps not exactly marketable."

"Nay; but, on second thoughts, why not do it myself, if anything *can* be made of it?"

"That, however, will be for future consideration. In the meantime, we'd better send for Titmouse, and manage him a little more—discreetly, eh? We did not exactly hit it off last time, did we, Mr. Quirk?" said Gammon, smiling rather sarcastically. "We must keep him at Tag-rag's if the thing *can* be done for the present, at all events."

"To be sure; he couldn't then come buzzing about us, like a gad-fly; he'd drive us mad in a week, I'm sure."

"Oh, I'd rather give up everything than submit to it. It can't be difficult for us, I should think, to bind him to our own terms—to put a bridle in the ass's mouth? Let us say that we insist on his signing an undertaking to act implicitly according to our directions in everything."

"Ay, to be sure; on pain of our instantly turning him to the right about. I fancy it will do now!"

"And now, Mr. Quirk," said Gammon, with as much of peremptoriness in his tone as he could venture upon to Mr. Quirk, "you really must do me the favor to leave the management of this little wretch to me. You see, he seems to have taken—Heaven save the mark!—a fancy to me, poor fellow —and—and—it must be owned, we miscarried sadly the other night, on a certain grand occasion—eh?"

Quirk shook his head dissentingly.

"Well, then," continued Gammon, "one thing I am determined on: one or the other of us shall undertake Titmouse, solely and singly. Pray, for Heaven's sake, tackle him yourself—a disagreeable duty! You know, my dear sir, how invariably I leave everything of real importance and difficulty to your very superior tact and experience."

"Come, come, Gammon, that's a drop of sweet oil—"

Quirk might well say so, for he felt its softening, smoothing effects already.

"Upon my word and honor, Mr. Quirk, I'm in earnest. Pshaw!—and you must know it. I know you too well, my dear sir, to attempt to—"

"Certainly, I must say, those must get up *very* early that can find Caleb Quirk napping"—Gammon felt at that moment that for several years *he* must have been a very early riser. And so the matter was arranged in the manner which Gammon had wished and determined upon, *i. e.* that Mr. Titmouse should be left entirely to his management; and, after some little discussion as to the time and manner of the meditated advances, the partners parted. On entering his own room, Quirk, closing his door, stood leaning against the side of the window, with his hands in his pockets, and his eyes instinctively resting on his banker's book, which lay on the table. He was in a very brown study: the subject on which his thoughts were busied being the prudence or imprudence of leaving Titmouse thus in the hands of Gammon. It might be all very well for Quirk to *assert* his self-confidence when in Gammon's presence, but he did not really feel it. He never left Gammon after any little difference of opinion, however friendly, without a secret suspicion that somehow or another Gammon had been too much for him, and always gained his purposes, without giving Quirk any handle of dissatisfaction. In fact, Quirk was thoroughly afraid of Gammon, and Gammon knew it. In the present instance an undefinable but increasing suspicion and dissatisfaction forced him presently back again into Gammon's room.

"I say, Gammon, you understand, eh?—*Fair play*, you know," he commenced, with a shy embarrassed air, ill concealed under a forced smile.

"Pray, Mr. Quirk, what may be your meaning?" inquired Gammon with unusual tartness, with an astonished air, and blushing violently, which was not surprising; for ever since Quirk had quitted him, Gammon's thoughts had been occupied with only one question, viz., how he should go to work with Titmouse to satisfy him that he (Gammon) was the only member of the firm that had a real disinterested regard for him, and so acquire a valuable control over him. Thus occupied, the observation of Quirk had completely taken Gammon aback; and he lost his presence of mind, of course his temper quickly following. "Will you favor me, Mr. Quirk, with an explanation of your extraordinarily absurd and offensive observation?" said he, reddening more and more as he looked at Mr. Quirk.

"You're a queer hand, Gammon," replied Quirk, with almost an equally surprised and embarrassed air, for he could not resist a sort of conviction that Gammon had fathomed what had been passing in his mind.

"What did you mean, Mr. Quirk, by your singular observation just now?" said Gammon, calmly, having recovered his presence of mind.

"Mean? Why, that—we're *both* queer hands, Gammon, ha, ha, ha!" answered Quirk, with an anxious laugh.

"I shall leave Titmouse entirely—*entirely*, Mr. Quirk, in your hands; I will have nothing whatever to do with him. I am quite sick of him and his affairs already; I can not bring myself to undertake such an affair, and that was what I was thinking of—when—"

"Eh? indeed! Well, to be sure! Only think!" said Quirk, dropping his voice, looking to see that the two doors were shut, and resuming the chair which he had lately quitted. "What do you think has been occurring to *me* in my own room, just now? Whether it would suit us better to throw this monkey overboard, put ourselves confidentially in communication with the party in possession, and tell him that—hem!—for a—eh? You understand?—a con-si-de-ra-tion—a *suitable* con-si-de-ra-tion."

"Mr. Quirk! Heavens!" Gammon was really amazed.

"Well? You needn't open your eyes so very wide, Mr. Gammon—why shouldn't it be done? You know we shouldn't

be satisfied with a trifle, of course.   But suppose he'd agree to
buy our silence with four or five thousand pounds, really, it's
well worth considering!   Upon my soul, Gammon, it *is* a
hard thing on him; no fault of his, and it is very hard for him
to turn out, and for such a—eugh!—such a wretch as Titmouse; you'd feel it yourself, Gammon, if you were in his
place, and I'm sure you'd think that four or five thous—"
   " But is not Titmouse our POOR NEIGHBOR?" said Gammon, with a sly smile.
   " Why, that's only one way of looking at it, Gammon! Perhaps the man we are going to eject does a vast deal of good
with the property; certainly he bears a very high name in the
county—and fancy Titmouse with ten thousand a year!—"
   " Mr. Quirk, Mr. Quirk, it's not to be though of for a moment—not for a moment," interrupted Gammon, seriously,
and even somewhat peremptorily—" nothing should persuade
me to be any party to such—"
   At this moment Snap burst into the room with a heated appearance, and a chagrined air—
   " *Pitch* v. *Grub*—"
   [This was a little pet action of poor Snap's: it was for slander uttered by the defendant (an hostler) against the plaintiff (a
waterman on a coach-stand), charging the plaintiff with having *the mange*, on account of which a woman refused to marry
him.]
   " Pitch v. Grub just been tried at Guildhall.   Witness bang
up to the mark—words and special damage proved; slapping
speech from Sergeant Shout.   Verdict for plaintiff—but only
one farthing; and Lord Widdrington said, as the jury had
given one farthing for damages, *he* would give him another for
costs,* and that would make a halfpenny; on which the defendant's attorney tendered me a halfpenny on the spot.
Laughter in court—move for new trial first day of next term,
and tip his lordship a rattler in the next Sunday's *Flash !*"
   " Mr. Quirk, once for all, if these kind of actions are to go
on I'll leave the firm, come what will. " [It flickered across his

---

* I suppose myself to be alluding here to a very oppressive statute,
passed to clip the wings of such gentlemen as Mr. Snap, by which it is
enacted, that, in actions for slander, if the jury find a verdict under
forty shillings. *e. g.* as in the case of the text, for one farthing, the
plaintiff shall be entitled to recover from the defendant only as much
costs as damages *i. e.* another farthing; a provision which has made
many a poor pettifogger sneak out of court with a flee in his ear. Since
this was written, a still more stringent statute hath been made, which,
'tis to be hoped, will put down the nuisance.

mind that Titmouse would be a capital client to start with on his own account.] "I protest our names will quite stink in the profession."

"Good, Mr. Gammon, good!" interposed Snap, warmly; "your little action for the usury penalties the other day came off so uncommon well!"

"Let me tell you, Mr. Snap," interrupted Gammon, reddening—

"Pho! Come! Can't be helped—fortune of the war"—interrupted the head of the firm—"*Is Pitch solvent!*—of course we've security for costs out of pocket."

Now, the fact was, that poor Snap had picked up Pitch at one of the police offices, and, in his zeal for business, had undertaken his case on pure speculation, relying on the apparent strength of the plaintiff's case—Pitch being only a waterman attached to a coach-stand. When, therefore, the very ominous question of Mr. Quirk met Snap's ear, he suddenly happened (at least, he thought so) to hear himself called for from the clerk's room, and bolted out of Mr. Gammon's room rather unceremoniously.

"Snap will be the ruin of the firm, Mr. Quirk," said Gammon, with an air of disgust. "But I really must get on with the brief I'm drawing: so, Mr. Quirk, we can talk about Titmouse to-morrow!"

The brief he was drawing up was for a defendant who was going to nonsuit the plaintiff (a man with a large family, who had kindly lent the defendant a considerable sum of money) solely because of the *want of a stamp*.

Quirk differed in opinion with Gammon, and, as he resumed his seat at his desk, he could not help writing the words, "*Quirk and Snap*," and thinking how well such a firm would sound and work—for Snap was verily a chip of the old block!

There will probably never be wanting those who will join in abusing and ridiculing attorneys and solicitors. Why? In almost every action at law, or suit in equity, or proceeding which may, or may not, lead to one, each client conceives a natural dislike for his opponent's attorney or solicitor. *If the plaintiff succeeds*, he hates the defendant's attorney for putting him (the said plaintiff) to so much expense, and causing him so much vexation and danger; and, when he comes to settle with his own attorney, there is not a little heart-burning in looking at his bill of costs, however reasonable. *If the plaintiff fails*, of course it is through the ignorance and unskillfulness of his attorney or solicitor; and he hates almost equally his own and his opponent's attorney. Precisely so is it with a successful or unsuccessful *defendant*. In fact, an attorney or solicitor is almost always obliged to be acting *adversely to some one* of whom he at once makes an enemy; for an attorney's weapons must necessarily be pointed almost invariably at our pockets! He is, necessarily, also called into action in cases when all the worst passions of our nature—our hatred and revenge, and our self-interest—are set in motion. Consider the mischief that might be constantly done on a grand scale in society, if the vast majority of attorneys and solicitors were not honorable and able men! Conceive them, for a moment, disposed everywhere to stir up litigation, by availing themselves of their perfect acquaintance with almost all men's circumstance — artfully inflaming irritable and vindictive clients, kindling, instead of stifling, family dissensions, and fomenting public strife—why, were they to do only a hundredth part of what it is thus in their power to do, our courts of justice would soon be doubled, together with the number of our judges, counsel, and attorneys; new jails must be built to hold the ruined litigants—and the insolvent court enlarged and in constant session throughout the year.

But not all of this body of honorable and valuable men are entitled to this tribute of praise. There are a few QUIRKS, several GAMMONS, and many SNAPS in the profession of the law—men whose characters and doings often make fools visit the sins of individuals upon the whole species; nay, there are far worse, as I have heard—but I must return to my narrative.

On Friday night, the 18th July, 18—, the state of Mr. Titmouse's affairs was this: he owed his landlady £1, 9s. his washer-woman 6s.; his tailor £1, 8s.,—in all three guineas; besides 10s. to Huckaback (for Tittlebat's notion was that on repayment at any time of 10s., Huckaback would be bound to deliver up to him the document or voucher which he had given him), and a weekly accruing rent of 7s. to his landlady, besides some very small sums for washing, tea, bread, and butter, etc. To meet these serious liabilities, he had—*not one farthing*.

On returning to his lodgings that night, he found a line from Thumbscrew, his landlady's broker, informing him that, unless by ten o'clock on the next morning his arrears of rent were paid, she should distrain, and she would also give him notice to quit at the end of the week; that nothing could induce her to give him further time. He sat down in dismay on reading this threatening document; and, in sitting down, his eyes fell on a bit of paper lying on the floor, which must have been thrust under the door. From the marks on it, it was evident that he must have trod upon it in entering. It proved to be a summons from the Court of Requests, for £1, 8s. due to Job Cox, his tailor. He deposited it mechanically on the table; and for a minute he dared hardly breathe.

This seemed something really like a *crisis.*

After a silent agony of half an hour's duration, he rose trembling from his chair, blew out his candle, and in a few minutes' time might have been seen standing with a pale and troubled face before the window of old Balls, the pawnbroker, peering through the suspended articles—watches, sugar-tongs, rings, brooches, spoons, pins, bracelets, knives and forks, seals, chains, etc.—to see whether any one else than old Balls were within. Having at length watched out a very pale and wretched-looking woman, Titmouse entered to take her place: and after interchanging a few faltering words with the white-haired and hard-hearted old pawnbroker, produced his guard-chair, his breast-pin, and his ring, and obtained three pounds two shillings and sixpence on the security of them. With this sum he slunk out of the shop, and calling on Cox, his tailor, paid his trembling old creditor the full amount of his claim (£1, 8s.) together with 4s., the expense of the summons—simply asking a receipt, without uttering another word, for he felt almost choked. In the same way he dealt with Mrs. Squallop, his landlady—not uttering one word in reply to her profuse and voluble apologies, but pressing his lips between his teeth till the blood came from them, while his heart seemed bursting within him. Then he walked upstairs, with a desperate air—with eighteen-pence in his pocket—*all his ornaments gone* —his washer-woman yet unpaid—his rent going on—several other little matters unsettled; and the 10th of August approaching, when he expected to be dismissed penniless from Mr. Tag-rag's, and thrown on his own resources for subsistence. When he had regained his room, and having shut the door, had reseated himself at his table, he felt for a moment as if he could have yelled. Starvation and Despair, two fiends, seemed sitting beside him in shadowy ghastliness, chilling and palsying him—petrifying his heart within him. WHAT WAS HE TO DO? Why had he been born? Why was he so much more persecuted and miserable than any one else? Visions of his ring, his breast-pin, his studs, stuck in a bit of card with their price written above, and hanging exposed to his view in old Balls's window, almost frenzied him. Thoughts such as these at length began to suggest others of a dreadful nature. * * * The means at that instant within his reach. * * * A

sharp knock at the door startled him out of the stupor into
which he was sinking. He listened for a moment, as if he
were not certain that the sound was a real one. There seemed
a ton-weight upon his heart, which a mighty sigh could lift for
an instant, but not remove; and he was in the act of heaving
a second such sigh, as he languidly opened the door—expecting to encounter Mr. Thumbscrew, or some of his myrmidons,
who might not know of his recent settlement with his landlady.

"Is this Mr.—Tit—Titmouse's!" inquired a genteel-looking young man.

"Yes," replied Titmouse, sadly.

"Are you Mr. Titmouse?"

"Yes," he replied, more faintly than before.

"Oh—I have brought you, sir, a letter from Mr. Gammon,
of the firm of Quirk, Gammon and Snap, solicitors, Saffron
Hill," said the stranger, unconscious that his words shot a flash
of light into a little abyss of sorrow before him. "He begged
me to give this letter into your hands and said he hoped you'd
send him an answer by the first morning's post."

"Yes—oh—I see—certainly—to be sure—with pleasure—
how is Mr. Gammon?—uncommon kind of him—very humble
respects to him—take care to answer it," stammered Titmouse
in a breath, hardly knowing whether he was standing on his
head or his heels, and not quite certain where he was.

"Good-evening, sir," replied the stranger, evidently a little
surprised at Titmouse's manner, and withdrew. Titmouse
shut his door. With prodigious trepidation of hand and flutter of spirits, he opened the letter—an inclosure meeting his
eyes in the shape of a bank-note.

"Oh, Lord!" he murmured, turning white as the sheet of
paper he held. Then the letter dropped from his hand, and
he stood as if stupefied for some moments; but presently rapture darted through him; a five-pound bank-note was in his
hand, and it had been inclosed in the following letter:—

"35 *Thavies' Inn, 29th July,* 18—.

"MY DEAR MR. TITMOUSE,

"Your last note, addressed to our firm, has given me the
greatest pain, and I hasten, on my return from the country,
to forward you the inclosed trifle, which I sincerely hope will
be of temporary service to you. May I beg the favor of your
company on Sunday evening next, at seven o'clock, to take a
glass of wine with me? I shall be quite alone and disengaged;
and may have it in my power to make you some important
communications, concerning matters in which, I assure you, I

feel a very deep interest on your account. Begging the favor of an early answer to-morrow morning, I trust you will believe me, ever, my dear sir, your most faithful humble servant,

"OILY GAMMON.

"TITTLEBAT TITMOUSE, ESQ."

The first balmy drop of the long-expected golden shower had at length fallen upon the panting Titmouse. How polite—nay, how affectionate and respectful—was the note of Mr. Gammon! and, for the first time in his life, he saw himself addressed

"TITTLEBAT TITMOUSE, ESQUIRE."

If his room had been large enough to admit of it, Titmouse would have skipped round it again and again in his frantic ecstasy. Having at length read over and over again the blessed letter of Mr. Gammon, he hastily folded it up, crumpled up the bank-note in his hand, clapped his hat on his head, blew out his candle, rushed down-stairs as if a mad dog were at his heels, and in three or four minutes' time was standing breathless before old Balls, whom he almost electrified by asking, with an eager and joyous air, for a return of the articles which he had only an hour before pawned with him; at the same time laying down the duplicates and the bank-note. The latter, old Balls scrutinized with most anxious exactness, and even suspicion—but it seemed perfectly unexceptionable; so he gave him back his precious ornaments, and the change out of his note, *minus* a trifling sum for interest. Titmouse then started off at top speed to Huckaback; but it suddenly occurring to him as possible that that gentleman, on hearing of his good fortune, might look for an immediate repayment of the ten shillings he had recently lent to Titmouse, he stopped short —paused—and returned home. There he had hardly been seated a moment, when down he pelted again, to buy a sheet of paper and a wafer or two, to write his letter to Mr. Gammon; which having obtained, he returned at the same speed, almost overturning his fat landlady, who looked after him as if he were a mad cat scampering up and down-stairs, and fearing that he had gone suddenly crazy. The note he wrote to Mr. Gammon was so exceedingly extravagant, that, candid as I have (I trust) hitherto shown myself in the delineation of Mr. Titmouse's character, I can not bring myself to give the said letter to the reader—making all allowance for the extraordinary excitement of its writer.

Sleep that night and morning found and left Mr. Titmouse

the assured exulting master of TEN THOUSAND A YEAR.
Of this fact, the oftener he read Mr. Gammon's letter, the
stronger became his convictions. 'Twas undoubtedly rather a
large inference from small premises; but it secured him unspeakable happiness, *for a time*, at a possible cost of future
disappointment and misery, which he did not pause to consider. The fact is, that logic (according to Dr. Watts, *the
right use of reason*) is not a practical art. No one regards it
in actual life; observe, therefore, folks on all hands constantly acting like Tittlebat Titmouse in the case before us. His
conclusion was—that he had become the certain master of ten
thousand a year; his *premises* were what the reader has seen.
I do not, however, mean to say, that if the reader be a youth
hot from the University, he may not be able to prove, by a
very refined and ingenious argument, that Titmouse was, in
what he did above, a fine natural logician; for I recollect that
some great logician hath demonstrated, by a famous argument,
that there is NOTHING in the world; and no one that I have
heard of hath ever been able to prove the contrary.

By six o'clock the next morning, Titmouse had, with his
own hand, dropped his answer into the letter-box upon the
door of Mr. Gammon's chambers in Thavies' Inn; in which
answer he had, with numerous expressions of profound respect
and gratitude, accepted Mr. Gammon's polite invitation. A
very happy man felt Titmouse, as he returned to Oxford
Street; entering Messrs. Tag-rag's premises with alacrity, just
as they were being opened, and volunteering his assistnce in
numerous things beyond his usual province, with singular
briskness and energy; as if conscious that by doing so he was
greatly gratifying Messrs. Quirk, Gammon and Snap, whose
wishes upon the subject he knew. He displayed such unwonted cheerfulness and patient good-nature throughout the
day, that one of his companions, a serious youth, in a white
neckerchief, black clothes, and with a sanctified countenance
—the only professing pious person in the establishment—took
an occasion to ask him, in a mysterious whisper, "whether he
had not got *converted;*" and whether he would, at six o'clock
in the morning, accompany the speaker to a room in the
neighborhood, where he (the youth aforesaid) was going to
conduct an exhortation and prayer meeting! Titmouse refused—but not without a few qualms; for luck certainly
seemed to be smiling on him, and he felt that he ought to be
grateful for it; but then, he at length reflected, the proper
place for that sort of thing would be a regular church—to
which he resolved to go. This change of manners Tag-rag,

however, looked upon as assumed only to affront *him;* seeing
nothing but impertinence and defiance in all that Titmouse
did—as if the nearer Titmouse got to the end of his bondage
—*i. e.* the 10th of August—the lighter-hearted he grew. He
resolved religiously to keep his counsel; to avoid even—at all
events for the present—communicating with Huckaback.

On the ensuing Sunday he rose at an earlier hour than usual,
and took nearly twice as long a time as usual to dress—by reason of his often falling into many delightful reveries. By
eleven o'clock he might have been seen entering the gallery of
St. Andrew's Church, Holborn; where he considered that
doubtless Mr. Gammon, who lived in the neighborhood, might
attend. He asked three or four pew-openers, both below and
above, if they knew which was Mr. Gammon's pew—Mr.
Gammon of Thavies' Inn; not dreaming of presumptuously
going to the pew, but of sitting in some place that commanded
a view of it. Mr. Gammon, I need hardly say, was quite unknown there—no one had ever heard of such a person: nevertheless Titmouse, albeit a little galled at being, in spite of his
elegant appearance, slipped into a back pew, remained—but
his thoughts wandered grievously the whole time. The service over, he sauntered in the direction of Hyde Park, to
saunter in which he seemed now to have a sort of *claim.* How
soon might he become, instead of a mere spectator as heretofore, a partaker in its glories! The dawn of the day of fortune
was on his long-benighted soul; and he could hardly subdue
his excited feelings. Punctual to his appointment, as the
clock struck seven he made his appearance at Mr. Gammon's,
with a pair of span-new white kid gloves on, and was speedily
ushered, a little flurried, by a comfortable-looking elderly
female servant, into Mr. Gammon's room. Mr. Titmouse was
dressed just as when he was first presented to the reader sally-
ing forth into Oxford Street. Mr. Gammon, who was sitting
reading the *Sunday Flash* at a table on which stood a couple
of decanters, several wine-glasses, and two or three dishes of
fruit, rose and received his distinguished visitor with the most
delightful affability.

"I am most happy, Mr. Titmouse, to see you in this friendly way," said he, shaking him by the hand.

"Oh, don't name it, sir," quoth Titmouse, rather indistinctly, and hastily running his hand through his hair.

"I've nothing, you see, to offer you but a little fruit, and a
glass of fair port or sherry."

"Particular fond of *them,* sir," replied Titmouse, endeavoring to clear his throat; for in spite of a strong effort to appear

at his ease, he was unsuccessful; so that when Gammon's keen eye glanced at the bedizened figure of his guest, a bitter smile passed over his face, without having been observed. "*This*," thought he as his eye passed from the ring glittering on the little finger of the right hand, to the studs and breast-pin in the shirt front, and thence to the guard-chain glaring entirely outside a damson-colored satin waistcoat, and the spotless white glove which yet glistened on the left hand—"This is the writer of the dismal epistle of the other day, announcing his desperation and destitution!"

"Your health, Mr. Titmouse!—help yourself!" said Mr. Gammon, in a cheerful and cordial tone; Titmouse pouring out a glass only three quarters full, raised it to his lips with a slightly tremulous hand, and returned Mr. Gammon's salutation. When had Titmouse tasted a glass of wine before?—a reflection, occurring not only to himself, but also to Gammon, to whom it was a circumstance that might be serviceable. "You see, Mr. Titmouse, mine's only a small bachelor's establishment, and I can not put my old servant out of the way by having my friends to dinner"—[quite forgetting that the day before he had entertained at least six friends, including Mr. Frankpledge—but the idea of going through a dinner *with* Mr. *Titmouse!*]

And now, O inexperienced Titmouse, unacquainted with the potent qualities of wine, I warn you to be cautious how you drink many glasses, for you can not calculate the effect which they will have upon you; and, indeed, methinks that with this man you have a game to play which will not admit of much wine being drunk. Be you, therefore, on your guard; for wine is like a strong serpent, who will creep unperceivedly into your empty head, and coil himself up therein, until at length he moves about—and all things are as naught to you!

"Oh, sir, 'pon my honor, I beg you won't name it—all one to me, sir!—Beautiful wine this, sir."

"Pretty fair, I think—certainly rather old;—but what fruit will you take—currant or cherries?"

"Why—a—I've so lately dined," replied Titmouse, alluding to an exceedingly slight repast at a coffee-shop about two o'clock. He could have preferred the cherries, but did not feel quite at his ease how to dispose of the stones nicely—gracefully—so he took a very few red currants upon his plate, and eat them slowly, and with a modest air.

"Well, Mr. Titmouse," commenced Gammon with an air of concern, "I was really much distressed by your last letter."

"Uncommon glad to hear it, sir—know you would, sir—you're so kind-hearted;—all quite true, sir!"

"I had no idea that you were reduced to such straits," said Gammon, in a sympathizing tone, but setting his eye involuntarily on the ring of Titmouse.

"Quite dreadful, sir—'pon my soul, dreadful; and such usage at Mr. Tag-rag's!"

"But you mustn't think of going abroad—away from all your friends, Mr. Titmouse."

"*Abroad*, sir!" interrupted Titmouse with anxious but subdued eagerness; "never thought of such a thing."

"Oh! I—I thought—"

"There isn't a word of truth in it, sir; and if you've heard so it must have been from that oudacious fellow that called on you—he's *such* a liar—if you knew him as well as I do, sir!" said Titmouse with a confident air, quite losing sight of his letter to Messrs. Quirk, Gammon and Snap—"No, sir—shall stay and stick to friends that stick to me."

"Take another glass of wine, Mr. Titmouse," interrupted Gammon, cordially, and Titmouse obeyed him; but while he was pouring it out, a sudden recollection of his letter flashing across his mind, satisfied him that he stood detected in a flat lie before Mr. Gammon; and he blushed scarlet.

"Do you like the sherry?" inquired Gammon, perfectly aware of what was passing through the mind of his guest, and wishing to divert his thoughts. Titmouse answered in the affirmative; and proceeded to pour forth such a number of apologies for his own behavior at Saffron Hill, and that of Huckaback on the subsequent occasion, as Gammon found it difficult to stop, over and over again assuring him that all had been forgiven and forgotten. Then Titmouse came to the remittance of the five pounds—

"Don't mention it, my dear sir," interrupted Gammon very blandly; "it gave me, I assure you, far greater satisfaction to send it, than you to receive it. I hope it has a little relieved you?"

"I think so, sir! I was, 'pon my life, on my last legs."

"When things come to the worst, they often mend, Mr. Titmouse! I told Mr. Quirk (who to do him justice came at last into my views) that, however premature, and perhaps imprudent it might be in us to go so far, I could not help relieving your present necessities, even out of my own resources."

[Oh, Gammon, Gammon!]

"How uncommon kind of you, sir!" exclaimed Titmouse.

"Not in the least, my dear sir—(pray fill another glass,

Mr. Titmouse!) You see, Mr. Quirk is quite a man of business —and our profession too often affords instances of persons whose hearts contract as their purses expand, Mr. Titmouse— ha! ha! Indeed, those who make their money as hard as Mr. Quirk, are apt to be slow at parting with it, and *very* suspicious."

"Well, I hope no offense, sir; but really I thought as much, directly I saw that old gent."

"Ah—but *now* he is embarked, heart and soul, in the affair."

"No! *Is* he really, sir?" inquired Titmouse, eagerly.

"That is," replied Gammon, quickly, "so long as I am at his elbow, urging him on—for he wants some one who—hem! In fact, my dear sir, ever since I had the good fortune to make the discovery, which happily brought us acquainted with each other, Mr. Titmouse" [it was old Quirk who had made the discovery, and Gammon had for a long time thrown cold water on it], "I have been doing all I could with him, and I trust I may say have at last got the thing into shape."

"I'll take my oath, sir," said Titmouse, excitedly, "I never was so much struck with any one in all my born days as I was with you, sir, when you first came to my emp—to Mr. Tag-rag's sir—Lord, sir, how uncommon sharp you seemed!" Gammon smiled with a deprecating air, and sipped his wine in silence; but there was a great sweetness in the expression of his countenance. Poor Titmouse's doubts, hopes, and fears were rapidly subsiding into *a reverence* for Gammon! * * *

"I certainly quite agree with Mr. Quirk," said Gammon presently, "that the difficulties in our way are of the most serious description. To speak, for an instant only, of the risk we ourselves incur personally—would you believe it, my dear Mr. Titmouse?—in such a disgraceful state are our laws, that we can't gratify our feelings by taking up your cause, without rendering ourselves liable to imprisonment for Heaven knows how long, and a fine that would be ruin itself, if we should be found out!"

Titmouse continued silent, his wine-glass in his hand arrested in its way to his mouth, which, together with his eyes, were opened to their widest extent, as he stared with a kind of terror upon Mr. Gammon.—"*Are* we, then, unreasonable, my dear sir, in entreating you to be cautious—nay, in insisting on your compliance with our wishes, in all that we shall deem prudent and necessary, when not only your own best interests, but our characters, liberties, and fortunes are staked on the issue of this great enterprise? I am sure," con-

tinued Gammon, with great emotion, "you will feel for us,
Mr. Titmouse. I see you do!" Gammon put his hand over
his eyes, in order, apparently, to conceal his emotion, but
really to observe what effect he had produced upon Titmouse.
The conjoint influence of Gammon's wine and eloquence not
a little agitated Titmouse, in whose eyes stood tears.

"I'll do anything—anything, sir," he almost sobbed.

"Oh! all we wish is to be allowed to serve you effectually;
and to enable us to do that—"

"Tell me to get into a soot-bag, and lie hid in a coal-hole,
and see if I won't do it!"

"What! a coal-hole? Would you, then, even stop at Tag-
rag and Co.'s?"

"Ye-e-e-e-s, sir—hem! hem! That is till the *tenth* of next
month, when my time's up."

"Ay!—ay!—oh, I understand! Another glass, Mr. Titmouse," said Gammon, pouring himself out some more wine;
and observing, while Titmouse followed his example, that
there was an unsteadiness in his motions of a very different description from that which he had exhibited at the commencement of the evening—at the same time wondering what the
deuce they should do with him after the *tenth* of August.

"You see, I have the utmost confidence in you, and had so
from the first happy moment when we met; but Mr. Quirk is
rather sus— In short, to prevent misunderstanding (as he
says) Mr. Quirk is anxious that you should give a *written*
promise." (Titmouse looked eagerly about for writing materials.) "No, not now, but in a day or two's time. I confess, my dear Mr. Titmouse, if *I* might have decided on the
matter, I should have been satisfied with your verbal promise;
but, I must say, Mr. Quirk's gray hairs seem to have made
him quite—eh! you understand? Don't you think so, Mr.
Titmouse?"

"To be sure! 'pon my honor, Mr. Gammon!" replied Titmouse; not very distinctly understanding, however, what he
was so energetically assenting to.

"I dare say you wonder why we wish you to stop a few
months longer at your present hiding-place—at Tag-rag's?"

"*Can't*, possibly!—after the tenth of next month, sir," replied Titmouse, eagerly.

"But as soon as we begin to fire off our guns against the
enemy—Lord, my dear sir, if they could only find out, you
know, where to get at you—you would never live to enjoy your
ten thousand a year! They'd either poison or kidnap you—
get you out of the way, unless you keep out of *their* way: and

if you will but consent to keep snug at Tag-rag's for a while, who'd suspect where you was? We could easily arrange with your friend Tag-rag that you should—"

"My stars! I'd give something to hear you tell Tag-rag—why, I wonder what he'll do!"

"Make you very comfortable, and let you have your own way in everything—that you may rely upon?"

"Go to the play, for instance, whenever I want, and do all that sort of thing?"

"Nay, try! anything!—And as for money, I've persuaded Mr. Quirk to consent to our advancing you a certain sum per week, from the present time, while the case is going on "—(Titmouse's heart began to beat fast)—" in order to place you above absolute inconvenience; and when you consider the awful sums we shall have to disburse—cash out of pocket—(the tongues of counsel, you know, are set on gold springs, and only gold keys open their lips!)—for court-fees, and other indispensable matters, I should candidly say that four thousand pounds of hard cash out of pocket, advanced by our firm in your case, would be the very lowest." (Titmouse stared at him with an expression of stupid wonder.) "Yes—four thousand pounds, Mr. Titmouse, at the very least—the *very* least." Again he paused, keenly scrutinizing Titmouse's features by the light of the candles, which just then were brought in. "You seem surprised, Mr. Titmouse."

"Why—why—where's all the money to come from, sir?" exclaimed Titmouse, aghast.

"Ah! that is indeed a fearful question," replied Gammon, with a very serious air; "but at my request, our firm has agreed to make the necessary advances; and also (for *I* could not bear the sight of your distress, Mr. Titmouse!) to supply your necessities liberally in the meantime, as I was saying."

"Won't you take another glass of wine, Mr. Gammon?" suddenly inquired Titmouse, with a confident air.

"With all my heart, Mr. Titmouse! I'm delighted that you approve of it. I paid enough for it, I can warrant you."

"Cuss me if ever I tasted such wine! Uncommon! Come —no heel-taps, Mr. Gammon—here goes—let's drink—success to the affair!"

"With all my heart, my dear sir—with all my heart. Success to the thing—amen!" and Gammon drained his glass; so did Titmouse. "Ah! Mr. Titmouse, you'll soon have wine enough to float a frigate—and indeed what not—with ten thousand a year?"

"And all the back-rents, you know—ha, ha!"

"Yes—to be sure!—the back-rents! The sweetest estate that is to be found in all Yorkshire! Gracious, Mr. Titmouse!" continued Gammon, with an excited air—"What may you not do? Go where you like—do what you like—get into Parliament—marry some lovely woman!"

"Lord, Mr. Gammon!—you a'n't dreaming? Nor I? But now, in course, *you* must be paid handsome for your trouble! —Only say how much—Name your sum! What you please! You only give me all you've said."

"For my part I wish to rely entirely on your mere word of honor. Between gentlemen, you know—my dear sir—"

"You only try me, sir."

"But you see, Mr. Quirk's getting old, and naturally is anxious to provide for those whom he will leave behind him— and so Mr. Snap agreed with him—two to one against me, Mr. Titmouse—of course they carried the day—two to one."

"Only say the figure, sir!" cried Titmouse, eagerly.

"A single year's income, only—ten thousand pounds will hardly—"

"Ten thousand pounds! By jingo, that *is* a slice out of the cake! Oh, Lord!" quoth Titmouse, looking aghast.

"A mere crumb, my dear sir!—a trifle! Why, *we* are going to give *you* that sum at least every year—and indeed it was suggested to our firm, that unless you gave us at least a sum of twenty-five thousand pounds—in fact, we are recommended to look out for some other heir."

"Oh, dear! oh, Mr. Gammon," cried Titmouse, hastily— "it's not to be thought of, sir!"

"So I said; and as for throwing it up—to be sure we shall have ourselves to borrow large sums to carry on the war—and unless we have your bond for at least ten thousand pounds, we can not raise a farthing."

"Well—curse me, if you sha'n't do what you like!—Give me your hand, and do what you like, Mr. Gammon!"

"Thank you, Mr. Titmouse! How I like a glass of wine with a friend in this quiet way!—you'll always find me rejoiced to show—"

"Your hand! By George—Didn't I take a liking to you from the first? But to speak my mind a bit—as for Mr. Quirk —excuse me—but he's a cur—cur—mudg—mudg—mudg— eon—hem!"

"Hope you've not been so imprudent, my dear Titmouse," threw in Mr. Gammon, rather anxiously, "as to borrow money—eh?"

"Devil knows, and devil cares! No stamp, I know—bang

up to the mark,"—here he winked an eye, and put his finger
to his nose—"wide awake—Huck—uck—uck—uck! how his
name sti—sticks.   Your hand, Mr. Gammon—here—this, this
way—what are you bobbing your head about for?   Ah, ha!—
The floor—'pon my life—how funny—it's like being at sea—
up, down—oh, dear!"—he clapped his hand to his head.
[Pythagoras has finely observed, that a man is not to be considered dead drunk till he lies on the floor, and stretches out
his arms and legs to prevent his going lower.]

See-saw, see-saw, up and down, up and down, went everything about him.   Now he felt sinking through the floor, then
gently rising to the ceiling.   Mr. Gammon seemed getting into
a mist and waving about the candles in it.   Mr. Titmouse's
head swam; his chair seemed to be resting on the waves of the
sea.

"I'm afraid the room's rather close, Mr. Titmouse," hastily
observed Gammon, perceiving from Titmouse's sudden paleness and silence but too evident symptoms that his powerful
intellect was for a while paralyzed.   Gammon started to the
window and opened it.   Paler, however, and paler became
Titmouse.   Gammon's game was up much sooner than he had
calculated on.

"Mrs. Brown! Mrs. Brown! order a cab instantly, and tell
Tomkins"—that was the inner porter—"to get his son ready
to go home with this gentleman—he's not very well."   He
was obeyed.   It was, in truth, all up with Titmouse—at least
for a while.

As soon as Gammon had thus got rid of his distinguished
guest, he ordered the table to be cleared of the glasses, and
tea to be ready within half an hour.   He then walked out to
enjoy the cool evening; on returning, sat pleasantly sipping
his tea, now and then dipping into the edifying columns of the
Sunday Flash, but oftener ruminating upon his recent conversation with Titmouse, and speculating upon certain possible results to himself personally; and a little after eleven
o'clock, that good man, at peace with all the world—calm and
serene, retired to repose.   He had that night rather a singular
dream; it was of a snake encircling a monkey, as if in gentle
and playful embrace.   Suddenly tightening its folds, a crackling sound was heard; the writhing coils were then slowly un-
wound—and, with a shudder, he beheld the monster licking
over the motionless figure, till it was covered with a viscid
slime.   Then the serpent began to devour its prey; and, when
gorged and helpless, behold, it was immediately fallen upon
by two other snakes.   To his disturbed fancy, there was a dim

resemblance between their heads and those of Quirk and Snap—they all three became intertwisted together—and writhed and struggled till they fell over the edge of a dark and frightful precipice—he woke—thank God; it was only a dream.

CHAPTER V.

WHEN, after his return from Mr. Gammon's chambers, at Thavies' Inn, Titmouse woke at an early hour in the morning, he was laboring under the ordinary effects of unaccustomed inebriety. His mouth and lips were perfectly parched; there was a horrid weight pressing on his aching eyes, and upon his throbbing head. His pillow seemed undulating beneath him, and everything swimming around him; but when, to crown the whole, he was roused from a momentary nap by the insupportable—the loathed importunities of Mrs. Squallop, that he would just sit up and partake of three thick rounds of hot buttered toast, and a great basin of smoking tea, which would do him *so* much good, and settle his stomach—at all events, if he'd only have a thimbleful of good gin in it—poor Titmouse was fairly overcome. He lay in bed all that day, during which he underwent very severe sufferings; and it was not till toward night that he began to have anything like a distinct recollection of the evening he had spent with Mr. Gammon; who, by the way, had sent one of the clerks, during the afternoon, to inquire after him. He did not get out of bed on the Tuesday till past twelve o'clock, when, in a very rickety condition, he made his appearance at the shop of Messrs. Tag-rag and Co; on approaching which he felt a sudden faintness, arising from mingled apprehension and disgust.

"What are you doing here, sir?—You're no longer in my employment, sir," exclaimed Tag-rag, attempting to speak calmly, as he hurried down the shop white with rage, to meet Titmouse, and planted himself right in the way of his languid and pallid shopman.

"Sir!" faintly exclaimed Titmouse, with his hat in his hand.

"Very much obliged, sir—very! by the offer of your valuable services," said Tag-rag. "But—*that's* the way out again, sir—that!—there!—good-morning, sir—good-morning, sir!—that's the way out"—and he egged on Titmouse, till he had got him fairly into the street—with infinite difficulty restraining himself from giving him a parting kick. Titmouse stood for a moment before the door, trembling and aghast, looking in a bewildered manner at the shop; but Tag-rag again making his appearance, Titmouse slowly walked away and returned to his lodging. Oh, that Mr. Gammon had witnessed the scene—thought he—and so have been satisfied that it had been Tag-rag who had put an end to his service, not he himself who had quitted it!

The next day, about the same hour, Mr. Gammon made his appearance at the establishment from which Titmouse had been expelled so summarily, and inquired for Mr. Tag-rag, who presently presented himself—and recognizing Mr. Gammon, who naturally reminded him of Titmouse, changed color a little.

"What did you please to want, sir?" inquired Mr. Tag-rag, with a would-be resolute air, twirling round his watch-key with some energy.

"Only a few minutes' conversation, sir, if you please," said Mr. Gammon, with such a significant manner as a little disturbed Mr. Tag-rag; who, with an ill-supported sneer, bowed very low, and led the way to his own little room. Having closed the door, he with an exceedingly civil air, begged Mr. Gammon to be seated; and then occupied the chair opposite to him, and awaited the issue with ill-disguised anxiety.

"I am very sorry, Mr. Tag-rag," commenced Gammon, with his usual elegant and feeling manner, "that any misunderstanding should have arisen between you and Mr. Titmouse."

"You're a lawyer, sir, I suppose?" Mr. Gammon bowed. "Then you must know, sir, that there are always two sides to a quarrel."

"Yes—you are right, Mr. Tag-rag; and, having already heard Mr. Titmouse's version, may I be favored with *your* account of your reasons for dismissing him? For he tells us that yesterday you dismissed him suddenly from your employment, without giving any warn—"

"So I did, sir; and what of that?" inquired Tag-rag, tossing his head with an air of defiance. "Things are come to a pretty pass indeed, when a man can't dismiss a drunken, idle, impudent, impertinent—abusive vagabond—"

"Do you seriously charge him with being such a character, and can you *prove* your charges, Mr. Tag-rag?" inquired Gammon, gravely.

"Prove 'em! yes, sir, a hundred times over; so will all my young men!"

"And in a court of justice, Mr. Tag-rag?"

"Oh! he is going to *law*, is he? That's why you're come here—ah, ha!—when you can make a silk purse out of a sow's ear, you may get your bill out of Mr. Tittlebat Titmouse!—ha, ha, ha!'' laughed Tag-rag, hoping thereby to conceal how much he was really startled.

"Well—that's *our* lookout, Mr. Tag-rag: to Mr. Titmouse, his character is as valuable as Mr. Tag-rag's is to him. In short, he has placed himself in our hands, and we are resolved to go on with the case, if it cost us a hundred pounds—we are indeed, Mr. Tag-rag.''

"Why—he's not a penny in the world to go to law with!'' exclaimed Tag-rag, with an air of mingled wonder, scorn, and alarm.

"But you forget, Mr. Tag-rag, that if Mr. Titmouse's account should turn out to be correct, it will be *your* pocket that must pay all the expenses, amounting probably to twenty times the sum which the law may award to Mr. Titmouse.''

"*Law*, sir!—It's not justice!—I hate law.—Give me common sense and common honesty!''

"Both of them would condemn your conduct, Mr. Tag-rag; for I have heard a full account of what Mr. Titmouse has suffered at your hands—of the cause of your sudden warning to him, and your still more sudden dismissal of yesterday. Oh, Mr. Tag-rag! upon my honor, it won't do—not for a moment—and should you go on, rely upon what I tell you, that it will cost you dear.''

"And suppose, sir,'' said Tag-rag, in a would-be contemptuous tone—"I should have witnesses to prove all I've said—which of us will look funny then, sir?''

"Which, indeed! However, since that is your humor, I can only assure you that Mr. Titmouse defies you to prove any misconduct on his part. We have taken up his cause, and, as you may perhaps find, we shall not easily let it drop.''

"I mean no offense, sir,'' said Tag-rag, in a mitigated tone; "but I must say, that ever since *you* first came here, Titmouse has been quite another person. He seems not to know who I am, nor to care either—and he's perfectly unbearable.''

"My dear sir, what has he *said* or *done*?—that, you know, is what you must be prepared to prove.''

"Well, sir! and which of us is likely to be best off for witnesses?—Think of that, sir—I've eighteen young men—''

"We shall chance that, sir,'' replied Gammon, shrugging his shoulders; "but again, I ask, what did you dismiss him for? and I request a plain, straightforward answer.''

"What did I dismiss him for? Haven't I eyes and ears? First and foremost he's the most odious-mannered fellow I ever came near—and—he hadn't a shirt to his back when I first took him—the ungrateful wretch!—Sir, it's not against the law, I suppose, to *hate* a man;—and if it isn't, how I hate Titmouse!"

"Mr. Tag-rag"—said Gammon, lowering his voice, and looking very earnestly at his companion—"can I say a word to you in confidence—the strictest confidence!"

"What's it about, sir?" inquired Tag-rag, with an apprehensive air.

"I dare say you may have felt, perhaps, rather surprised at the interest which I—in fact our office, the office of Quirk, Gammon and Snap, in Saffron Hill—appear to have taken in Mr. Titmouse."

"Why, sir, it's *your* lookout to see how you're to be paid for what you're doing—and I dare say lawyers generally keep a pretty sharp lookout in that direction."

Gammon smiled, and continued—"It may, perhaps, a little surprise you, Mr. Tag-rag, to hear that your present (ought I to say, your *late?*) shopman, Mr. Tittlebat Titmouse, is at this moment probably the very luckiest man in this kingdom."

"Why—you don't mean to say he's drawn a prize in the lottery?"—exclaimed Tag-rag, pricking up his ears.

"Pho! my dear sir, *that* is a mere trifle compared with the good fortune that has befallen him. I solemnly assure you that I believe he will turn out to be the undoubted owner of an estate worth at least ten thousand a year, besides a vast accumulation of ready money!"

"Ten thousand a year! — My Titmouse! — Tittlebat Titmouse!—Ten thousand a year!" faltered Tag-rag, after a pause, having gone as pale as death.

"I have as little doubt of the fact, as I have that you yesterday turned him out-of-doors, Mr. Tag-rag!"

"But—who could have dreamed it? How was—*really*, Mr. Gammon!—how *was* I to know it?"

"That's the fact, however," said Gammon, shrugging his shoulders. Tag-rag wriggled about in his chair, put his hands in and out of his pockets, scratched his head, and continued staring open-mouthed at the bearer of such astounding intelligence. "Perhaps, however, all this is meant as a joke, sir," —said he—"And if so—it's—it's—a very—"

"It's one of his solicitors, who were fortunate enough to make the discovery, that tells you. I repeat what I have already told you, Mr. Tag-rag, that an estate of ten thousand a year is the very least—"

"Why, that's two hundred thousand pounds, sir!"—exclaimed Tag-rag, with an awe-struck air.

"At the very least—"

"Lord, Mr. Gammon!—Excuse me, sir, but how *did* you find it out?"

"Mere accident—a mere accidental discovery, sir, in the course of other professional inquiries!"

"And does Mr. Titmouse know it?"

"Ever since the day after that on which I called on him here!" replied Gammon, pointedly.

"You don't say so!"—exclaimed Tag-rag, and then continued silent for nearly half a minute, evidently amazed beyond all power of expression.

"Well"—at length he observed—"I *will* say this—he's the most amiable young gentleman—the *very amiablest* young gentleman I—ever—came near. I always thought there was something uncommon superior-like in his looks."

"Yes—I think he *is* of rather an amiable turn," observed Gammon, with an expressive smile—"and so intelligent—"

"Intelligent! Mr. Gammon! you should only have known him as I have known him!—Well, to be sure I—Lord! His only fault was, that he was above his business; but when one comes to think of it, how could it be otherwise? From the time I first clapped eyes on him—I—I—knew he was—a superior article—quite superior—you know what I mean, sir?—He couldn't help it, of course!—to be sure—he never was much liked by the other young men; but that was jealousy!—all jealousy; I saw that all the while." Here he looked at the door, and added in a very low tone, "Many sleepless nights has their bad treatment of Mr. Titmouse cost me!—Even I, now and then, used to look and speak sharply to him—just to keep him, as it were, down to the mark of the others—he was so uncommon handsome and genteel in his manner, sir. Hang me, if I didn't tell Mrs. Tag-rag the very first day he came to me, that he was a gentleman born—or ought to have been one."

Now, do you suppose, acute reader, that Mr. Tag-rag was insincere in all this? By no means. He spoke the real dictates of his heart, unaware of the sudden change which had taken place in his feelings. It certainly has an ugly look of improbability—but it was *the nature of the beast ;* his eye suddenly caught a glimpse of the golden calf, and he instinctively fell down and worshiped it. "Well—at all events," said Mr. Gammon, scarcely able to keep a serious expression on his face—"though he's not lived much like a gentleman hitherto, yet he will live for the future like a *very great gentleman*—and spend his money like one, too."

"I—I—dare say—he will!—I wonder how he *will* get through a quarter of it!—what do *you* think he'll do, sir?"

"Heaven only knows—he may very shortly do just what he likes! Go into the House of Commons, or—"

"Lord, sir!—I feel as if I shouldn't be quite right again for the rest of the day!—I own to you, sir, that all yesterday and to-day I've been on the point of going to Mr. Titmouse's lodgings to apologize for—for—Good gracious me! one can't take it all in at once—Ten thousand a year!—Many a lord hasn't got more—some not as much, I'll be bound!—Dear me, what will he do!—Well, one thing I'm *sure* of—he'll never have a truer friend than plain Thomas Tag-rag, though I've not always been a-flattering him—I respected him too much!—The many little things I've borne with in Titmouse, that in any one else I'd have—But why didn't he tell me, sir? We should have understood one another in a moment."—Here he paused abruptly; for his breath seemed suddenly taken away, as he reviewed the series of indignities which he had latterly inflicted on Titmouse—the kind of life which that amiable young gentleman had led in his establishment.

Never had the keen Gammon enjoyed anything more exquisitely than the scene which I have been describing. To a man of his practical sagacity in the affairs of life and knowledge of human nature, nothing could appear more ludicrously contemptible than the conduct of poor Tag-rag. How differently are the minds of men constituted! How Gammon despised Tag-rag!

"*Now*, may I take it for granted, Mr. Tag-rag, that we understand each other?" replied Gammon.

"Yes, sir," replied Tag-rag, meekly. "But do you think Mr. Titmouse will ever forgive or forget the little misunderstanding we've lately had? If I could but explain to him how I have been acting a part toward him—all for his good!"

"You may have opportunities for doing so, if you are really so disposed, Mr. Tag-rag; for I have something seriously to propose to you. Circumstances render it desirable that for some little time this important affair should be kept as quiet as possible; and it is Mr. Titmouse's wish and ours—as his confidential professional advisers—that for some few months he should continue in your establishment, and apparently in your service as before."

"In my service!—my service!" interrupted Tag-rag, opening his eyes to their utmost. "I sha'n't know how to behave in my own premises! Have a man with ten thousand a year behind my counter, sir? I might as well have the Lord Mayor! Sir, it can't—it can't be. Now, if Mr. Titmouse chose to become a *partner* in the house—ay, there might be something in that—he needn't have any trouble—be only a sleeping partner." Tag-rag warmed with the thought. "Really, sir, that wouldn't be so much amiss—would it?" Gammon assured him that it was out of the question; and gave him some of the reasons for the proposal which he (Mr. Gammon) had been making. While Gammon fancied that Tag-rag was paying profound attention to what he was saying, Tag-rag's thoughts had shot far ahead. He had an only child—a daughter, about twenty years old—Miss Tabitha Tag-rag; and the delightful possibility of her by and by becoming Mrs. Titmouse, put her amiable parent into a perspiration. Into the proposal just made by Mr. Gammon he fell with great eagerness, which he attempted to conceal — for what innumerable opportunities would it not afford him for bringing about the desire of his heart—for throwing the lovely young couple into each other's way—endearing them to each other! Oh, delightful! It really looked almost as if fate had determined that the thing should come to pass! If Mr. Titmouse did not dine with him, Mrs. and Miss Tag-rag at Satin Lodge, Clapham, on the very next Sunday, it should, Tag-rag resolved, be owing to no fault of *his*. Mr. Gammon having arranged everything exactly as he had desired, and having again enjoined Mr. Tag-rag to absolute secrecy, took his departure. Mr. Tag-rag, in his excitement, thrust out his hand and grasped that of Gammon, which was extended toward him somewhat coldly and reluctantly. Tag-rag attended him with extreme obsequiousness to the door; and on his departure walked back rapidly to his own room, and sat down for nearly half an hour in deep thought. Abruptly rising, at length he clapped his hat on his head, and saying that he should soon be back, hurried out to call upon his future son-in-law, full of affectionate anxiety concerning his health—and vowing within himself, that henceforth it should be the study of his life to make his daughter and Titmouse happy! There could be no doubt of the reality of the event just communicated to him by Mr. Gammon; for he was one of a well-known firm of solicitors; he had had an interview on "important business" with Titmouse a fortnight ago, and that could have been nothing but the prodigious event just communicated to himself. Such things had happened to others —why not to Tittlebat Titmouse? In short, Tag-rag had no doubt on the matter.

He found Titmouse not at home; so he left a most particularly civil message, half a dozen times repeated, with Mrs.
Squallop (to whom also he was especially civil) to the effect
that he, Mr. Tag-rag, should be only too happy to see Mr.
Titmouse at No. 375 Oxford Street, whenever it might suit
his convenience; that he had something very particular to say
to him about the unpleasant and unaccountable occurrence of
yesterday; that he was most deeply concerned to hear of Mr.
Titmouse's indisposition, and anxious to learn from himself
that he had recovered, etc., etc., etc.;—all which, together
with one or two other little matters, which Mrs. Squallop could
not help putting together, satisfied that shrewd lady that
" something was in the wind about Mr. Titmouse;" and made
her reflect rather anxiously on one or two violent scenes she
had had with him, and which *she* was now ready entirely to
forget and forgive.   Having thus done all that at present was
in his power to forward the thing, the anxious and excited
Tag-rag returned to his shop; on entering which, one Lutestring, his principle young man, eagerly apprised him of a
claim which he had, as he imagined, only the moment before
established to the thanks of Mr. Tag-rag, by having " bundled
off, neck and crop, that hodious Titmouse," who, about five
minutes before, had, it seemed, had the " impudence " to
present himself at the shop-door, and walk in as if nothing
had happened!! [Titmouse had so presented himself, in consequence of a call from Mr. Gammon, immediately after his interview with Tag-rag.]

" You—ordered—Mr. Titmouse—off!!" exclaimed Tag-rag,
starting back aghast, and stopping his voluble and officious assistant.

" Of course, sir—after what happened yester—"

" Who authorized you, Mr. Lutestring?" inquired Tag-rag,
striving to choke down the rage that was rising within him.

" Why, sir, I *really* supposed that—"

" You supposed! You're a meddling, impertinent, disgusting—"   Suddenly his face was overspread with smiles as three
or four elegantly dressed customers entered, whom he received
with profuse obeisances.   But when their backs were turned,
he directed a lightning look toward Lutestring, and retreated
once more to his room, to meditate on the agitating events of
the last hour.   The extraordinary alteration in Mr. Tag-rag's
behavior was attributed by his shopmen to his having been
frightened out of his wits by the threats of Titmouse's lawyer
—for such it was clear the stranger was; and more than one

of them stored it up in their minds as a useful precedent
against some future occasion.

Twice afterward during the day did Tag-rag call at Titmouse's lodgings—but in vain; and on returning the third
time felt not a little disquieted. He determined, however, to
call the first thing on the ensuing morning; if he should then
fail of seeing Mr. Titmouse, he was resolved to go to Messrs.
Quirk, Gammon and Snap—and besides, address a very affectionate letter to Mr. Titmouse. How totally changed had become all his feelings toward that gentleman within the last few
hours! The more Tag-rag reflected on Titmouse's conduct,
the more he saw in it to approve of. How steady and regular
had he been in his habits! how civil and obliging! how patient
of rebuke! how pleasing in his manners to the customers!
Surely, surely, thought Tag-rag, Titmouse can't have been
four long years in my employ without getting a—sort of a—
feeling—of attachment to me—he'd have left long ago if he
hadn't! It was true there had now and then been tiffs between them; but who could agree always? Even Mrs. Tag-
rag and he, when they were courting, often fell out with one
another. Tag-rag was now ready to forget and forgive all—he
had never meant any harm to Titmouse. He believed that
poor Tittlebat was an orphan, poor soul! alone in the wide
world—*now* he would become the prey of designing strangers.
Tag-rag did not like the appearance of Gammon. No doubt
that person would try and ingratiate himself as much as possible with Titmouse! Then Titmouse was remarkably good-
looking. " I wonder what Tabby will think of him when she
sees him!" How anxious Tittlebat must be to see her—*his*
daughter! How could Tag-rag make Tittlebat's stay at his
premises (for he could not bring himself to believe that on the
morrow he could not set all right, and disavow the impudent
conduct of Lutestring) agreeable and delightful? He would
discharge the first of his young men that did not show Titmouse proper respect. What low lodgings poor Tittlebat lived
in! Why could he not take up his quarters at Satin Lodge?
They always had a nice spare bedroom. Ah! *that* would be a
stroke! How Tabby could endear herself to him! What a
number of things Mrs. Tag-rag could do to make him comfortable!

About seven o'clock Tag-rag quitted his premises in Oxford
Street for his country house; and, occupied with these and
similar delightful and anxious thoughts and speculations, hurried along Oxford Street on his way to the Clapham Stage,
without thinking of his umbrella, though it rained fast. When

he had taken his place on the coach-box, beside old Crack (as
he had done almost every night for years), he was so unusually
silent that Crack naturally thought that his best passenger
was going to become bankrupt, or compound with his creditors,
or something of that sort.   Mr. Tag-rag could hardly keep
his temper at the slow pace old Crack was driving at—just
when Tag-rag could have wished to gallop the whole way.
Never had he descended with so much briskness, as when the
coach at length drew up before the little green gate, which
opened on the nice little gravel walk, which led up to the little
green wooden porch, which sheltered the slim door which admitted you into Satin Lodge. As Tag-rag stood for a moment
wiping his wet shoes upon the mat, he could not help observing, for the first time, by the inward light of ten thousand a
year, how uncommon narrow the passage was; and thinking
that Satin Lodge would never do when he should be the
father-in-law of a man worth ten thousand a year; he could
easily let that house and take a larger one.   As he hung his
hat upon the peg, the mischievous insolence of Lutestring occurred to him; and he deposited such a prodigious, but half-
suppressed execration upon that gentleman's name, as must
have sunk a far more buoyant sinner many fathoms deeper
than usual into a certain hot and deep place that shall be
nameless.

Mrs. and Miss Tag-rag were sitting in the front parlor, intending to take tea as soon as Mr. Tag-rag should have arrived.
It was not a large room, but furnished prettily, according to
the taste of the owners.   There was only one window, and it
had a flaunting white summer curtain.   The walls were orna-
mented with three pictures, in slight gilt frames, being portraits of Mr., Mrs., and Miss Tag-rag; and I do not wish to
say more of these pictures, than that in each of them the *dress*
was done with singular exactness and fidelity—the faces seeming to have been painted in, in order to set off and complete
the picture of the dress.   The skinny little Miss Tag-rag sat
at the worn-out jingling piano-forte, playing—oh, horrid and
doleful sound!—*The Battle of Prague.*   Mrs. Tag-rag, a fat
showily dressed woman of about fifty, her cap having a prodigious number of artificial flowers in it, sat reading a profitable volume, entitled *Groans from the Bottomless Pit to
Awaken Sleeping Sinners,* by the REV. DISMAL HORROR—a
very rousing young dissenting preacher lately come into that
neighborhood, and who had almost frightened into fits half the
women and children, and one or two old men, of his congregation; given out, among several similarly cheering intimations,

that they must all necessarily be damned unless they immediately set about making themselves as miserable as possible in this world. Only the Sunday before, he had pointed out, with awful force and distinctness, how cards and novels were the devil's traps to catch souls; and balls and theaters short and easy cuts to—

He had proved to his trembling female hearers, in effect, that there was only one way to heaven—through his chapel; that the only safe mode of spending their time on earth was reading such blessed works as that which he had just published, and going to prayer-meetings almost daily. But when a Sunday or two before, he preached a funeral sermon, to '' improve the death ''—such being his impressive phrase—of a Miss Snooks (who had kept a circulating library in the neighborhood), and who having been to the theater on the Thursday night, was taken ill of a bowel attack on the Friday, and was a '' lifeless corpse when the next Sabbath dawned ''—you might have heard a beetle sneeze within any of the walls all over the crowded chapel. Two thirds of the women present, struck with the awful judgment upon the deceased Miss Snooks, made solemn vows never again to enter the accursed walls of a theater; many determined no longer to subscribe to the circulating library, ruining their precious souls with light and amusing reading; and almost all resolved forthwith to become active members of a sort of religious tract society, which Mr. Horror had just established in the neighborhood, for the purpose of giving the sick and starving poor *spiritual* food, in the shape of tracts (chiefly written by himself), which might '' wean their affections away from this vain world,'' and '' fix them on better things,'' rejoicing, in the meanwhile, in the bitter pangs of destitution. All this sort of thing Mr. Horror possibly imagined to be advancing the cause of real religion! In short, he had created a sort of spiritual fever about the place, which was then just at its height in worthy Mrs. Tag-rag.

'' Well, Dolly, how are you to-night?'' inquired Tag-rag, with unusual briskness, on entering the room.

'' Tolerable, thank you, Tag,'' replied Mrs. Tag-rag, mournfully, with a sigh, closing the cheerful volume she had been perusing—it having been recommended the preceding Sunday from the pulpit by its pious and gifted author, Mr. Horror, to be read and prayed over every day by every member of his congregation.

'' And how are *you*, Tabby?'' said Tag-rag, addressing his daughter. '' Come and kiss me, you little slut—come!''

"No, I sha'n't, pa! Do let me go on with my practicing"
—and twang! went those infernal keys.

"D'ye hear, Tab? Come and kiss me, you little minx—"

"Really, pa, how provoking—just as I am in the middle of
the *Cries of the wounded!* I sha'n't—that's flat."

The doting parent could not, however, be denied; so he
stepped to the piano, put his arm around his dutiful daughter's neck, kissed her fondly, and then stood for a moment behind her, admiring her brilliant execution of *The Trumpet of
Victory.* Having changed his coat, and put on an old pair of
shoes, Tag-rag was comfortable for the evening.

"Tabby plays wonderful well, Dolly, don't she?" said Tag-
rag, as the tea things were being brought in, by way of beginning a conversation, while he drew his chair nearer to his wife.

"Ah! I'd a deal rather see her reading something serious—
for life is short, Tag, and eternity's long."

"Botheration!—Stuff!—Tut!"

"You may find it out one day, my dear, when it's too
late—"

"I'll tell you what, Dolly," said Tag-rag, angrily, "you're
coming a great deal too much of that sort of thing—my house
is getting like a Methodist meeting-house. I can't bear it—I
can't! What the deuce is come to you all in these parts, lately?" Mr. Tag-rag had been induced, some three years before, to quit the Church of England and take up with Mr.
Dismal Horror; but his zeal by no means kept pace with that
of his wife.

"Ah, Tag-rag," replied his wife, with a sigh, "I can only
pray for you—I can do no more—"

"Oh!" exclaimed Tag-rag, with an air of desperate disgust,
thrusting his hands into his pockets, and stretching his legs to
their utmost extent under the table. "I'll tell you what,
Mrs. T.," he added, after awhile, "too much of one thing is
good for nothing; you may choke a dog with pudding:—I
sha'n't renew my sitting at Mr. Horror's."

"Oh, dear, dear pa, do! That's a love of a pa!" interposed Miss Tag-rag, twirling round on her music-stool. "All
Clapham's running after him—he's quite the rage! There's
the Dugginses, the Pips, the Jones, the Maggots—and, really,
Mr. Horror does preach such dreadful things, it's quite delightful to look round and see all the people with their eyes and
mouths wide open—and ours is such a good pew for seeing—
and Mr. Horror is such a bee-yeautiful preacher—isn't he,
ma?"

"Yes, love, he is—but I wish I could see you profit by him, and preparing for death—"

"Why, ma, how *can* you go on in that ridiculous way? You know I'm not twenty yet!"

"Well, well! poor Tabby!" here Mrs. Tag-rag's voice faltered—"a day will come, when—"

"Play me the *Devil among the Tailors* or *Copenhagen Waltz*, something of that sort, Tabby," said her father, furiously, "or I shall be sick!—I can't bear it! Curse Mr. Hor—"

"Well!—Oh, my!—I never!—Mr. Tag-rag!" exclaimed his astounded wife.

"Play away, Tab, or I'll go and sit in the kitchen! They're cheerful *there!* The next time I come across Mr. Horror, if I don't give him a bit of my mind—" here he paused, and slapped his hand with much energy upon the table. Mrs. Tag-rag wiped her eyes, sighed, and resumed her book. Miss Tag-rag began to make tea, her papa gradually forgetting his rage, as he fixed his dull gray eyes fondly on the pert skinny countenance of his daughter.

"By the way, Tag," exclaimed Mrs. Tag-rag suddenly, but in the same mournful tone, addressing her husband, "you haven't of course forgot the flowers for my new bonnet?"

"Never once thought of it," replied Tag-rag, doggedly.

"You haven't! Good gracious! what am I to go to chapel in next Sunday!" she exclaimed, with sudden alarm, closing her book, "and our seat in the very front of the gallery—bless me! I shall have a hundred eyes on me!"

"Now that you're coming down a bit, and dropped out of the clouds, Dolly," said her husband, much relieved, "I'll tell you a bit of news that will, I fancy, rather—"

"Come! what is it, Tag?" eagerly inquired his wife.

"What should you say of a chance of a certain somebody" (here he looked unutterable things at his daughter) "that shall be nameless, becoming mistress of ten thousand a year.

"Why"—Mrs. Tag-rag changed color—"has any one fallen in love with Tab?"

"What should you say, Mrs. T., of our Tab marrying a man with ten thousand a year? There's for you! Isn't *that* better than all your—"

"Oh, Tag, don't say that; but"—here she hastily turned down the leaf of *Groans from the Bottomless Pit,* and tossed that inestimable work upon the sofa—"do tell me, lovey! what *are* you talking about?"

"What indeed, Dolly!—I'm going to have him here to dinner next Sunday."

Miss Tag-rag having been listening with breathless eagernes
to this little colloquy between her prudent and amiable parents, unconscious of what she was about, poured all the tea
into the sugar-basin instead of her papa's tea-cup.

"Have *who*, dear Tag?" inquired Mrs. Tag-rag, impatiently.

"Who? why whom but my Tittlebat Titmouse! You've
seen him, and heard me speak of him often, you know—"

"What!—*that* odious, nasty—"

"Hush, hush!" involuntarily exclaimed Tag-rag, with an
apprehensive air—"That's all past and gone—I was always a
little too hard on him. Well, at all events, he's turned up all
of a sudden master of ten thousand a year. He has, indeed—
may this piece of toast choke me if he hasn't!"

Mrs. Tag-rag and her daughter sat in speechless wonder.

"Where did he see Tab, Taggy?" inquired at length Mrs.
Tag-rag.

"Oh—I—I—why—you see—I don't exactly think *that*
signifies so much—He *will* see her, you know, next Sunday."

"So then he's positively coming?" inquired Mrs. Tag-rag
with a fluttered air.

"Y—e—s—I've no doubt."—(I'll discharge Lutestring to-
morrow, thought Tag-rag with a sharp inward spasm.)

"But aren't we counting our chickens, Taggy, before they're
hatched? If Titmouse is all of a sudden become such a
catch, he'll be snapped up in a minute, you know, of course—"

"Why, you see, Dolly—we're first in the market, I'm sure
of that—his attorney tells me he's to be kept quite snug and
quiet under my care for months, and see no one—"

"My gracious!" exclaimed Mrs. Tag-rag, holding up both
her hands—"if *that* don't look like a special interposition of
Providence, now—"

"So *I* thought, Tabby, while Mr. Gammon was telling
me!" replied her husband.

"Ah, Tag, there are many of 'em, if we were only to be
on the lookout for them!"

"I see it all! It's designed by Providence to get them soon
together! When once Mr. Titmouse gets sight of Tabby, and
gets into her company—eh! Tab, lovey! *you'll* do the rest,
hem!"

"La, pa! how you go on!" simpered Miss Tag-rag.

"You must do your part, Tab," said her father—"we'll
do ours. He'll bite, you may depend on it, if you manage
well!"

"What sort of a looking young man is he, dear pa?" inquired Miss Tag-rag blushing, and her heart fluttering very fast.

" Oh, you *must* have seen him, sweetest—"

" How could I ever notice any one of the lots of young men at the shop, pa?—I don't at all know him."

" Well—he's the handsomest, most genteel-looking young fellow I ever came across; he's long been an ornament to my establishment, for his good looks and civil and obliging manners—quite a treasure! You should have seen how he *took* with ladies of rank always!—"

" Dear me," interrupted Mrs. Tag-rag, anxiously addressing her daughter, " I hope, Tabby, that Miss Nix will send home your lilac-colored frock by next Sunday!"

" If she *don't*, ma, I'll take care she never makes anything more for *me*, that's poz!" replied Miss Tag-rag, earnestly.

" We'll call there to-morrow, love, and hurry her on," said her mother; and from that moment until eleven o'clock, when the amiable and interesting trio retired to rest, nothing was talked of but the charming Titmouse, and the good fortune he so richly deserved, and how long the courtship was likely to last.   Mrs. Tag-rag, who for the last month or so, had always remained on her knees before getting into bed for at least ten minutes, on this eventful evening compressed her prayers, I regret to say, into one minute and a half's time (as for Tag-rag, a hardened heathen, for all he had taken to hearing Mr. Horror, he always tumbled prayerless into bed the moment he was undressed); while, for once in a way, Miss Tag-rag, having taken only half an hour to put her hair into papers, popped into bed directly she had blown the candle out, without saying *any* prayers—or even thinking of finishing the novel which lay under her pillow, and which she had got on the sly from the circulating library of the late Miss Snooks.   For several hours she lay in a delicious reverie, imagining herself become Mrs. Tittlebat Titmouse, riding about Clapham in a handsome carriage, going to the play every night; and what would the three Miss Knippses say when they heard of it—they'd burst.   And such a handsome man, too!

She sunk, at length, into unconsciousness, amid a soft confusion of glistening white satin—favors—bride-maids—Mrs. Tittlebat Tit—Tit—Tit—Tit—Tit—mouse.

Titmouse, about half past nine o'clock, on the ensuing morning, was sitting in his little room in a somewhat troubled humor, musing on many things, and little imagining the intense interest he had excited in the feelings of the amiable occupants of Satin Lodge, when a knock at his door started him

out of his reverie. Guess his amazement to see, on opening
it, Mr. Tag-rag!

"Your most obedient, sir," commenced that gentleman, in
a subdued and obsequious manner, plucking off his hat the instant he saw Titmouse. "I hope you're better, sir!—Been
very uneasy, sir, about you."

"Please to walk in, sir," replied Titmouse, not a little flustered—"I'm better, sir, thank you."

"Happy to hear it, sir!—But am also come to offer humble
apologies for the rudeness of that upstart that was so rude to
you yesterday, at my premises—know whom I mean, eh?—
Lutestring—I shall get rid of him, I do think—"

"Thank you, sir—But—but—when I was in your employ—"

"*Was* in my employ!" interrupted Tag-rag with a sigh,
gazing earnestly at him—"It's no use trying to hide it any
longer! I've all along seen you was in a world too good for—in
fact, quite above your situation in my poor shop! I *may* have
been wrong, Mr. Titmouse," he continued, diffidently, as he
placed himself on what seemed the only chair in the room
(Titmouse sitting on a common wooden stool)—"but I did it
for the best—eh?—don't you understand me, Mr. Titmouse?"
Titmouse continued looking on the floor incredulously, sheepishly, and somewhat sullenly.

"Very much obliged, sir—but must say you've rather a
funny way of showing it, sir. Look at the sort of life you've
led me for this—"

"Ah! knew you'd say so! But I can lay my hand on my
heart, Mr. Titmouse, and declare to God—I can, indeed, Mr.
Titmouse—" Titmouse preserved a very embarrassing silence.
—"*See* I'm out of your good books—But—won't you forget
and forgive, Mr. Titmouse? I *meant* well. Nay, I humbly
beg forgiveness for everything you've not liked in me. Can I
say more? Come, Mr. Titmouse, you've a noble nature, and
I ask forgiveness!" cried Tag-rag softly and earnestly: you
would have thought that his life depended on his success in
what he was doing!

"You—you ought to do it before the whole shop, if you're
in earnest," replied Titmouse, a little relenting—"for they've
all seen your goings-on."

"Them!—the brutes!—the vulgar fellows, eugh!—you and
I, Mr. Titmouse, are a *leetle* above them! D'ye think we
ought to mind what *servants* say?—Only you say the word,
and I make a clean sweep of 'em all; you shall have the premises to yourself, Mr. Titmouse, within an hour after any of
those chaps shows you the least glimmer of disrespect."

"Ah! I don't know—you've used me most uncommon bad, 'pon my soul!—far worse than they have—you've nearly broke my heart, sir! You have!"

"Well, my womankind at home are right, after all! They told me all along I was going the wrong way to work, when I said how I tried to keep your pride down, and prevent you from having your head turned by knowing your good looks! Over and over again, my little girl has said, with tears in her dear eyes, 'you'll break his spirit, dear papa—if he *is* handsome, wasn't it God that made him so?'" The little frostwork which Titmouse had thrown around his heart began to melt like snow under sunbeams. "Ah, Mr. Titmouse, Mr. Titmouse! the women are always right, and *we're* always wrong," continued Tag-rag, earnestly, perceiving his advantage. "Upon my soul, I could kick myself for my stupidity, and cruelty too!"

"Ah, I should think so! No one knows what I have suffered! And now that I'm—I suppose you've heard it all, sir? —what's in the wind—and all that?"

"Yes, sir—Mr. Gammon (that most respectable gentleman) and I have had a long talk yesterday about you, in which he did certainly tell me everything—nothing like confidence, Mr. Titmouse, when gentleman meets gentleman, you know! Oh, Lord! the news is really delightful! delightful!"

"*Isn't* it, sir?" eagerly interrupted Titmouse, his eyes glistening with sudden rapture.

"Ah! ten thous—I *must* shake hands with you, my dear Mr. Titmouse;" and for the first time in their lives their hands touched, Tag-rag squeezing that of Titmouse with energetic cordiality; while he added, with a little emotion in his tone— "Thomas Tag-rag may be a plain-spoken and wrong-headed man, Mr. Titmouse—but he's a warm heart, I assure you!"

"And did Mr. Gammon tell you *all*, sir?" eagerly interrupted Titmouse.

"Everything—everything; quite confidential, I assure you, for he saw the interest I felt in you!"

"And did he say about my—hem!—eh? my stopping a few weeks longer with you?" inquired Titmouse, chagrin overspreading his features.

"I think he did, indeed, Mr. Titmouse! He's quite bent on it, sir! And so would any true friend of yours be—because you see "—here he dropped his voice, and looked very mysteriously at Titmouse—"in short, I quite agree with Mr. Gammon!"

"Do you indeed, sir!" exclaimed Titmouse, with rather an uneasy look.

"I do, i' faith! Why, they'd give thousands and thousands to get you out of the way—and what's money to them! But they must look very sharp that get at you in the premises of Thomas Tag-rag, I warrant 'em—Talking of that, ah, ha!—it *will* be a funny thing to see YOU, Mr. Titmouse—Squire Titmouse—ah, ha, ha!"

"You won't hardly expect me to go out with *goods*, I suppose, sir?"

"Ha, ha, ha!—Ha, ha, ha!—Might as well ask me if I'd clean that beast Lutestring's shoes! No, no, my dear Mr. Titmouse, you and I have done with each other as master and servant; it's only as friends that we know each other now!—You may say and do whatever you like, and come and go when and where you like!—It's true it will make my other hands rather jealous, and get me into trouble; but what do I care? Suppose they *do* all give me warning for your sake? Let 'em go, say I!" He snapped his fingers with an air of defiance. "*Your* looks and manners would keep a shopful of customers—one Titmouse is worth a hundred of them."

"'Pon my soul, you speak most uncommon gentleman-like, sir, certainly!" said Titmouse, with a little excitement—"and if you'd only *always*—but that's all past and gone; and I've no objections to say at once, that all the articles I may want in your line I'll have at your establishment, pay cash down, and ask for no discount. And I'll send all my friends, for, in course, sir, you know I shall have lots of them!"

"Don't forget your oldest, your truest, your humblest friend, Mr. Titmouse," said Tag-rag, with a cringing air.

"That I won't!" replied Titmouse, heatedly.

[It flashed across his mind that a true and old friend would be only too happy to do him some such trifling service as to lend him a ten-pound note.]

"Hem!—Now, *are* you such a friend, Mr. Tag-rag?" cried he, sheepishly.

"Am I?—can you doubt me? Try me! See what I could not do for you! Friend, indeed!" and he looked quite fondly at Titmouse.

"Well, I believe you, sir! And the fact is, a—a—a—you see, Mr. Tag-rag, though all this heap of money's *coming* to me, I'm precious low just *now*—"

"Ye—e—e—s, Mr. Titmouse," quoth Tag-rag, anxiously; his dull gray eye fixed on that of Titmouse steadfastly.

" Well—if you've a mind to prove your words, Mr. Tag-rag, and don't mind advancing me a ten-pound note—"

" Hem!" involuntarily uttered Tag-rag, so suddenly and violently that it made Titmouse almost start off his seat. Then Tag-rag's face flushed over, he twirled about his watch-key rapidly, and wriggled about in his chair with visible agitation.

" Oh, you aren't going to do it! If so, you'd better say it at once," quoth Titmouse, rather cavalierly.

" Why—*was* ever anything so unfortunate?" stammered Tag-rag. " That cursed lot of French goods I bought only yesterday, to be paid for this very morning—and it will drain me of every penny!"

" Ah—yes!—True! Well, it don't much signify," said Titmouse, carelessly, running his hand through his bushy hair. " In fact, I needn't have bothered an old friend at all, now I think of it—Mr. Gammon says he's my banker to any amount. I beg pardon, I'm sure—"

Tag-rag was in a horrid dilemma. He felt so flustered by the suddenness and seriousness of the thing that he could not see his way plain in any direction.

" Let me see," at length he stammered; and pulling a ready-reckoner out of his pocket, he affected to be consulting it, as if to ascertain merely the state of his banker's account, but really desiring a few moments' time to collect his thoughts. 'Twas in vain, however; nothing occurred to him; he saw no way of escape; his old friend the devil deserted him for a moment—supplying him with no ready lie to meet the exigency. He must, he feared, cash up! " Well," said he—" it certainly *is* rather unfortunate, just at this precise moment; but I'll step to the shop, and see how my ready-money matters stand. It sha'n't be a trifle, Mr. Titmouse, that shall stand between us. But—if I *should* be hard run—perhaps—eh? Would a five-pound note do?"

" Why—a—a—certainly, if it wouldn't suit you to advance the ten—"

" I dare say," interrupted Tag-rag, a trifle relieved, " I shall be able to accommodate you. Perhaps you'll step on to the shop presently, and then we can talk over matters!—By the way, did you ever see anything so odd? forgot the main thing; come and take your mutton with me at Clapham, next Sunday—my womankind will be quite delighted. Nay, 'tis *their* invitation—ha, ha!"

" You're uncommon polite," replied Titmouse, coloring

with pleasure. Here seemed the first pale primrose of the coming spring—an invitation to Satin Lodge.

"The politeness—the favor—will be yours, Mr. Titmouse! I'm quite proud of your coming! We shall be quite alone; have you all to ourselves; only me, my wife, and daughter— an only child, Mr. Titmouse—*such* a child! She's really often said to me, ' I wonder '—but I won't make you vain, eh! May I call it a fixture?"

"'Pon my life, Mr. Tag-rag, you're monstrous uncommon polite. It's true, I was going to dine with Mr. Gammon—"

"Oh! pho! (I mean no disrespect, mind!) he's only a bachelor—*I've* got ladies in the case, and all that—eh, Mr. Titmouse? and a *young* one!"

"Well, thank you, sir. Since your so pressing—"

"That's it! An engagement, poz!—Satin Lodge—for Sunday next," said Tag-rag, rising and looking at his watch. "Time for me to be off. See you soon at the shop? Soon arrange that little matter of business, eh? You understand? Good-bye! good-bye!" and shaking Titmouse cordially by the hand, Tag-rag took his departure. As he hurried on to his shop he felt in a most painful perplexity about this loan of five pounds. It was truly like squeezing five drops of blood out of his heart. But what was to be done? Could he offend Titmouse? Where was he to stop, if he once began? Dare he ask for security? Suppose the whole affair should after all turn into smoke?

Now, consider the folly of Tag-rag. Here was he in all this terrible pucker about advancing *five pounds* on the strength of prospects and chances which he had deemed safe for adventuring *his daughter* upon—her, the only object on earth (except money) that he regarded with anything like sincere affection. How was this? The splendor of the future possible good fortune of his daughter might, perhaps, have dazzled and confused his perceptions. Then, again, *that* was a *remote* contingent venture, but this sudden appeal to his pocket—the demand of an immediate outlay and venture—was an instant pressure, and he felt it severely. Immediate profit was everything to Tag-rag—'twas his very life's blood! He was, in truth, a *tradesman to his heart's core*. If he could have seen the immediate *quid pro quo*, or could, at all events, have got, if only by way of earnest, as it were, a bit of poor Titmouse's heart, and locked it up in his desk, he would not have cared so much; it would have been a little in his line; here was a FIVE-POUND NOTE going out forthwith, and nothing immediate,

visible, palpable, replacing it. Oh! Titmouse had unconsciously pulled Tag-rag's very heart-strings!

Observe, discriminating reader, that there is all the difference in the world between a TRADESMAN and a MERCHANT;
and, moreover, that it is not every *tradesman* that is a Tag-
rag.

All these considerations combined to keep Tag-rag in a perfect fever of doubt and anxiety, which several hearty curses
(I regret to say) failed in effectually relieving. By the time,
however, that Titmouse had made his appearance at Mr. Tag-
rag's shop, with a sufficiently sheepish air, and was beginning
to run the gantlet of grinning contempt from the choice
youths on each side of the shop, Tag-rag had determined on
the course he should pursue in the very embarrassing matter
above referred to. To the amazement of all present he bolted
out of a little counting-house or side-room, hastened to meet
Titmouse with outstretched hand and cordial speech, drew him
into his little room, and shut the door. There Tag-rag informed his flurried young friend that he had made arrangements (with a little inconvenience, which, however, between
friends, signified nothing) for lending Titmouse five pounds.

"And as life's uncertain, my dear Mr. Titmouse," said
Tag-rag, as Titmouse, with ill-disguised ecstasy, put the five-
pound note into his pocket—"even between the dearest
friends—eh? Understand? It's not *you* I fear, nor you me,
because we've confidence in each other. But if anything
should happen those we leave behind us"—Here he took out
of his desk an " I. O. U. £5," ready drawn up and dated—" a
mere slip—a word or two—is satisfaction to both of us."

"Oh, yes, sir! yes, sir!—anything!" said Titmouse; and
hastily taking the pen proffered him, signed his name; on
which Tag-rag felt a little relieved. Lutestring was then
summoned into the room, and thus (not a little to his disgust
and astonishment) addressed by his imperious employer.
"Mr. Lutestring, you will have the goodness to see that Mr.
Titmouse is treated by every person in my establishment with
the utmost possible respect. Whoever treats this gentleman
with the slightest disrespect isn't any longer a servant of mine.
D'ye hear me, Mr. Lutestring?" added Tag-rag, sternly, observing a very significant glance of intense hatred which Lutestring directed toward Titmouse. " D'ye hear me, sir?"

"Oh, yes, sir! yes, sir! your orders shall be attended to,"
he replied, in as insolent a tone as he could venture upon, and
leaving the room with a half-audible whistle of contempt,
while a grin overspread his features, he had within five min-

utes filled the mind of every shopman in the establishment with feelings of mingled wonder, hatred, and fear toward Titmouse. What, thought they, could have happened? What was Mr. Tag-rag about? This was all of a piece with his rage at Lutestring the day before. "D—n Titmouse!" said or thought every one of them!

Titmouse, for the remainder of the day, felt, as may be imagined, but little at his ease, for—to say nothing of his insuperable repugnance to the discharge of any of his former duties; his uneasiness under the oppressing civilities of Mr. Tag-rag, and the evident disgust toward him entertained by his companions; many most important considerations arising out of recent and coming events—his altering circumstances—were momentarily forcing themselves upon his attention. The first of these was his *hair*; for Heaven seemed to have suddenly given him the long-coveted means of changing its detested hue, and the next was *an eyeglass*, without which, he had long felt his appearance and appointments to be painfully incomplete. Early in the afternoon, therefore, on the readily admitted plea of important business, he obtained the permission of the obsequious Mr. Tag-rag to depart for the day, and instantly directed his steps to the well-known shop of a fashionable perfumer and perruquier in Bond Street—well known to those, at least, who were in the habit of glancing at the enticing advertisements in the newspapers. Having watched through the window till the coast was clear (for he felt a natural delicacy in asking for a hair dye before people who could in an instant perceive his urgent occasion for it), he entered the shop, where a well-dressed gentleman was sitting behind the counter reading. He was handsome, and his elaborately curled hair was of a heavenly black (so at least Titmouse considered it) that was better than a thousand printed advertisements of the celebrated fluid which formed the chief commodity there vended. Titmouse, with a little hesitation, asked this gentleman what was the price of their article "for turning *light* hair black"—and was answered— "only seven and sixpence for the smaller sized bottle." One was in a twinkling placed upon the counter, where it lay like a miniature mummy, swathed, as it was, in manifold advertisements. "You'll find the fullest directions within, and testimonials from the highest nobility to the wonderful efficacy of the 'CYANOCHAITANTHROPOPOION.' "*

* This fearful-looking word, I wish to inform my lady readers, is an original and monstrous amalgamation of three or four Greek words—

" *Sure* it will do, sir?" inquired Titmouse, anxiously.

" Is *my* hair dark enough to your taste, sir?" said the gentleman, with a calm and bland manner—" because I owe it entirely to this valuable specific."

" Do you, indeed, sir?" inquired Titmouse, adding, with a sigh, " but, between ourselves, look at mine!"—and, lifting off his hat for a moment, he exhibited a great crop of bushy, carroty hair.

" Whew! rather ugly that, sir!"—exclaimed the gentleman, looking very serious—" What a curse to be born with such hair, isn't it?"

" 'Pon my life I think so, sir!" answered Titmouse, mournfully; " and do you really say, sir, that this what's-it's-name turned yours of that beautiful black?"

" Think? 'Pon my honor, sir—certain; no mistake, I assure you! I was fretting myself into my grave about the color of my hair! Why, sir, there was a nobleman in here (I don't like to mention names) the other day, with a head that seemed as if it had been dipped into water, and then powdered with brick dust; but—I assure you, the Cyanochaitanthropopoion was too much for it—it turned black in a very short time. You should have seen his lordship's ecstasy—[the speaker saw that Titmouse would swallow anything; so he went on with a confident air]—and in a month's time he had married a beautiful woman whom he had loved from a child, but who had vowed she could never bring herself to marry a man with such a head of hair."

" How long does it take to do all this, sir?" interrupted Titmouse, eagerly, with a beating heart.

" Sometimes two—sometimes three days. In four days' time, I'll answer for it, your most intimate friend would not know you. My wife did not know me for a long while, and wouldn't let me salute her—ha, ha." Here another customer entered, and Titmouse laying down the five-pound note he had squeezed out of Tag-rag, put the wonder-working vial into his pocket, and on receiving his change, departed, bursting with eagerness to try the effects of the Cyanochaitanthropopoion. Within half an hour's time he might have been seen driving a hard bargain with a pawnbroker for a massive-look-

Κυανοχαιτανθρωποποιων—denoting a fluid " *that can render the human hair black.*" Whenever a barber or perfumer determines on trying to puff off some villainous imposition of this sort, strange to say, he goes to some starving scholar, and gives him half a crown to coin a word like the above, that shall be equally unintelligible and unpronounceable, and therefore attractive and popular.

ing eyeglass, which, as it hung suspended in the window, he had for months cast a longing eye upon, and he eventually purchased it (his eyesight, I need hardly say, was perfect) for only fifteen shillings. After taking a hearty dinner in a little dusky eating-house in Rupert Street, frequented by fashionable-looking foreigners, with splendid heads of curling hair and mustaches, he hastened home, eager to commence the grand experiment. Fortunately, he was undisturbed that evening. Having lighted his candle, and locked his door, with tremulous fingers he opened the papers enveloping the little vial, and glancing over their contents, got so inflamed with the number-less instances of its efficacy, detailed in brief but glowing terms —as—the " Duke of * * * * * *—the Countess of * * * * * *— the Earl of, etc. etc. etc. etc.—the lovely Miss ——, the cele-brated Sir Little Bull's-eye (who was so gratified that he al-lowed his name to be used)—all of whom, from having hair of the reddest possible description, were now possessed of raven-hued locks "—that he threw down the paper, and hurriedly got the cork out of the bottle. Having turned up his coat cuffs he commenced the application of the Cyanochaitanthro-popoion, rubbing it into his hair, eyebrows, and whiskers, with all the energy he was capable of, for upward of half an hour. Then he read over again every syllable on the papers in which the vial had been wrapped; and about eleven o'clock, having given sundry curious glances at the glass, got into bed full of exciting hopes and delightful anxieties concerning the success of the great experiment he was trying. He could not sleep for several hours. He dreamed a rapturous dream—that he bowed to a gentleman with coal-black hair, whom he fancied he had seen before—and suddenly discovered that he was only looking at *himself* in a glass!!—This woke him. Up he jumped— sprung to his little glass breathlessly—but, ah! merciful Heavens! he almost dropped down dead! His hair was per-fectly *green*—there could be no mistake about it. He stood there staring in the glass in speechless horror, his eyes and mouth distended to their utmost for several minutes. Then he threw himself on the bed, and felt fainting. Up he present-ly jumped again in a kind of ecstasy—rubbed his hair desper-ately and wildly about—again looked into the glass—there it was, rougher than before, but eyebrows, whiskers and head— all were, if anything, of a more vivid and brilliant green. Despair came over him. What had all his past troubles been to this?—what was to become of him? He got into bed again and burst into a perspiration. Two or three times he got into and out of bed, to look at himself again—on each occasion deriving only more terrible confirmation than before of the disaster that had befallen him. After lying still for some minutes he got out of bed, and kneeling down, tried to say his prayers, but it was in vain—and he rose half choked. It was plain that he must have his head shaved, and wear a wig—that was making an old man of him at once. Getting more and more disturbed in his mind, he dressed himself, half determined on starting off to Bond Street, and breaking every pane of glass in the shop-window of the cruel impostor who had sold him the liquid that had so frightfully disfigured him. As he stood thus irresolute, he heard the step of Mrs. Squallop approaching his door, and recollected that he had ordered her to bring up his tea-kettle about that time. Having no time to take his clothes off he thought the best thing he could do would be to pop into bed again, draw his night-cap down to his ears and eyebrows, pretend to be asleep, and, turning his back toward the door, have a chance of escaping the observation of his landlady. No sooner thought of than done. Into bed he jumped, and drew the clothes over him—not aware, however, that in his hurry he had left his legs, with boots and trousers exposed to view—an unusual spectacle to his landlady, who had, in fact, scarcely ever known him to be in bed at so late an hour before. He lay as still as a mouse. Mrs. Squallop, after glancing with surprise at his legs, happening to direct her eyes toward the window, beheld a small vial, only half of whose dark contents were remaining—oh, gracious!—of course it must be POISON, and Mr. Titmouse must be dead!—In a sudden fright she dropped the kettle, plucked the clothes off the trembling Titmouse, and cried out—" Oh, Mr. Titmouse! Mr. Titmouse! what *have* you been—"

" Well, ma'am, what the devil do you mean? How dare—" commenced Titmouse, suddenly sitting up, and looking furiously at Mrs. Squallop. An inconceivably strange and horrid figure he looked. He had all his day clothes on; a white cotton night-cap was drawn down to his very eyes, like a man going to be hanged; his face was very pale, and his whiskers were of a bright green color.

" Lord a-mighty!" exclaimed Mrs. Squallop, faintly, the moment that this strange apparition presented itself, and, sinking on the chair, she pointed with a dismayed air to the ominous-looking object standing on the window shelf. Titmouse, from that, supposed she had found out the true state of the case.

" Well—*isn't* it an infernal shame, Mrs. Squallop?" said he, getting off the bed, and, plucking off his night-cap, exhibited the full extent of his misfortune. "What d'ye think of *that!*" he exclaimed, staring wildly at her. Mrs. Squallop gave a faint shriek, turned her head aside, and motioned him away.

"I shall go mad—I SHALL!" cried Titmouse, tearing his green hair.

"Oh, Lord!—oh, Lord!" groaned Mrs. Squallop, evidently expecting him to leap upon her. Presently, however, she a little recovered her presence of mind, and Titmouse, stuttering with fury, explained to her what had taken place. As he went on, Mrs. Squallop became less and less able to control herself, and at length burst into a fit of convulsive laughter, and sat holding her hands to her fat shaking sides, as if she would have tumbled off her chair. Titmouse was almost on the point of striking her. At length, however, the fit went off, and, wiping her eyes, she expressed the greatest commiseration for him, and proposed to go down and fetch up some soft soap and flannel, and try what " a good hearty wash would do." Scarce sooner said than done—but, alas, in vain. Scrub, scrub—lather, lather, did they both; but, the instant the soap-suds were washed off there was the head as green as ever.

"Oh, murder! murder! what *am* I to do, Mrs. Squallop?" groaned Titmouse, having taken another look at himself in the glass.

"Why—really I'd be off to a police-office, and have 'em all taken up, if as how I was *you!*" quoth Mrs. Squallop.

"No—See if I don't take that bottle, and make the fellow that sold it me swallow what's left—and I'll smash in his shop front besides!"

"Oh, you won't—you mustn't—not on no account! Stop at home a bit, and be quiet, it may go off with all this washing, in the course of the day. Soft soap is an uncommon strong thing for getting colors out—but—a—a—excuse me, Mr. Titmouse—why wasn't you satisfied with the hair God Almighty had given you? D'ye think He didn't know a deal better than you what was best for you? I'm blest if I don't think this is a judgment on you."

"What's the use of your standing preaching to me in this way, Mrs. Squallop?" said Titmouse, first with amazement, and then with fury in his manner—"A'n't I half mad without it? Judgment or no judgment—where's the harm of my wanting black hair any more than black trousers? That a'n't *your own* hair, Mrs. Squallop—you're as gray as a badger underneath—'pon my soul. I've often remarked it."

"I'll tell you what, Mr. Himperance!" furiously exclaimed

Mrs. Squallop, "you're a liar! And you deserve what you've got! It *is* a judgment, and I hope it will stick by you—so take *that* for sauce, you vulgar fellow!" (snapping her fingers at him.) "Get rid of your green hair if you can! It's only carrot *tops* instead of carrot *roots*—and some likes one, some the other—ha! ha! ha!"

"I'll tell you what, Mrs. Squ—" he commenced, but she had gone, having slammed to the door behind her, with all her force; and Titmouse was left alone in a half-frantic state, in which he continued for nearly two hours. Once again he read over the atrocious puffs which had overnight inflated him to such a degree, and he now saw that they were all lies. This is a sample of them:—

"This divine fluid (as it was enthusiastically styled to the inventor, by the lovely Duchess of Doodle) possesses the inestimable and astonishing quality of changing hair, of whatever color, to a dazzling jet black; at the same time imparting to it a rich glossy appearance, which wonderfully contributes to the imposing *tout ensemble* presented by those who use it. That well-known ornament of the circle of fashion, the young and lovely Mrs. Fitzfrippery, owned to the proprietor that to this surprising fluid it was that she was indebted for those unrivaled raven ringlets which attracted the eyes of envying and admiring crowds," and so forth. A little further on—"This exquisite effect is not *in all cases* produced instantaneously; much will of course depend (as the celebrated M. Dupuytren, of the Hotel Dieu, at Paris, informed the inventor) on the physical idiosyncrasy of the party using it, with reference to the constituent particles of the coloring matter constituting the fluid in the capillary vessels. Often a single application suffices to change the most hopeless-looking head of red hair to as deep a black; but not unfrequently the hair *passes through intermediate shades and tints*—all, however, ultimately settling into a deep and permanent black."

This passage not a little revived the drooping spirits of Titmouse. Accidentally, however, an asterisk at the last word in the above sentence directed his eye to a note at the bottom of the page, printed in such minute type as baffled any but the strongest sight and most determined eye to read, and which said note was the following:—

"Though cases *do*, undoubtedly, occasionally occur, in which the native inherent indestructible qualities of the hair defy all attempts at change or even modification, and resist even *this* potent remedy: of which, however, in all his experience " (the wonderful specific has been invented for about *six*

6

months) "the inventor has known but very few instances." But to this exceedingly select class of unfortunate incurables, poor Titmouse, alas! entertained a dismal suspicion that *he* belonged!

"Look, sir! Look! Only look here what your cussed stuff has done to my hair!" said Titmouse, on presenting himself soon after to the gentleman who had sold him the infernal liquid; and, taking off his hat, exposed his green hair. The gentleman, however, did not appear at all surprised or discomposed.

"Ah—yes! I see—I see. You're in the intermediate stage. It differs in different people—"

"Differs, sir! I'm going mad. I look like a green monkey —Cuss me if I don't!"

"In *me*, now, the color was a strong *yellow*. But, have you read the explanations that are given in the wrapper?"

"Read 'em?" echoed Titmouse, furiously—" I should think so! Much good they do *me!* Sir, you're a humbug!—an impostor! I'm a sight to be seen for the rest of my life! Look at me, sir! Eyebrows, whiskers, and all!"

"*Rather* a singular appearance, just at present, I must own," said the gentleman, his face turning suddenly red all over with the violent effort he was making to prevent an explosion of laughter. He soon, however, recovered himself, and added, coolly—" If you'll only persevere—"

"Persevere be d——d!" interrupted Titmouse, violently clapping his hat on his head, "I'll teach you to *persevere* in taking in the public! I'll have a warrant out against you in no time!"

"Oh, my dear sir, I'm accustomed to all this!" said the gentleman, coolly.

"The—devil—you—are!" gasped Titmouse, quite aghast.

"Oh, often—often, while the liquid is performing the first stage of the change; but, in a day or two afterward, the parties generally come back smiling into my shop, with heads as black as crows!"

"No! But really—do they, sir?" interrupted Titmouse, drawing a long breath.

"Hundreds, I may say thousands, my dear sir!" And one lady gave me a picture of herself, in her black hair, to make up for her abuse of me when it was a puce color—Fact, honor!"

"But do you recollect any one's hair turning *green*, and then getting black?" inquired Titmouse, with trembling anxiety.

"Recollect any? Fifty at least. For instance, there was Lord Albert Addlehead—but why should I name names? I know hundreds! But everything is honor and confidential *here!*"

"And did Lord What's-his-name's hair go green, and then black; and was it at first as light as mine?"

"His hair was redder, and in consequence it became greener, and now is blacker than ever yours will be."

"Well, if I and my landlady have this morning used an ounce we've used a quarter of a pound of soft soap in—"

"Soft soap!—soft soap!" cried out the gentleman, with an air of sudden alarm—"That explains all" (he forget how well it had already been explained by him). "By Heavens, sir!—soft soap! You may have ruined your hair forever!" Titmouse opened his eyes and mouth with a start of terror, it not occurring to his reflecting mind that the intolerable green had preceded and caused, not followed, the use of the soft soap. "Go home, my dear sir! God bless you—go home, as you value your hair; take this small bottle of DAMASCUS CREAM, and rub it in before it's too late, and then use the remainder of the—"

"Then you don't think it's already too late?" inquired Titmouse, faintly, and having been assured to the contrary— having asked the price of the Damascus cream, which was "*only* three and sixpence" (stamp included)—he paid it with a rueful air, and took his departure. He sneaked along the streets with the air of a pickpocket, fearful that every one he met was an officer who had his eye on him. He was not, in fact, very far off the mark; for many a person smiled, and stared, and turned round to look at him as he went along.

CHAPTER VI.

TITMOUSE slunk upstairs to his room in a sad state of depression, and spent the next hour in rubbing into his hair the Damascus cream. He rubbed till he could hardly hold his arms up any longer from sheer fatigue. Having risen at length to mark, from the glass, the progress he had made, he found that the only result of his persevering exertions had been to give a greasy shining appearance to the hair, that remained as green as ever. With a half-uttered groan he sunk down upon a chair, and fell into a sort of abstraction, which was interrupted by a sharp knock at his door. Titmouse started up, trembled, and stood for a moment or two irresolute, glancing fearfully at the glass, and then, opening the door, let in Mr. Gammon, who started back a pace or two, as if he had been shot, on catching sight of the strange figure of Tit-

mouse. It was useless for Gammon to try to check his laughter; so, leaning against the door-post, he yielded to the impulse, and laughed without intermission for at least two minutes. Titmouse felt desperately angry, but feared to show it,
and the timid, rueful, lackadaisical air with which he regarded
the dreaded Mr. Gammon, only prolonged and aggravated the
agonies of that gentleman. When at length he had a little
recovered himself, holding his left hand to his side, with an
exhausted air, he entered the little apartment, and asked Titmouse what in the name of heaven he had been doing to
himself: " *Without this* " (in the absurd slang of the lawyers)
that he suspected most vehemently all the while quite well
what Titmouse had been about; but he wished to hear Titmouse's own account of the matter!—Titmouse, not daring to
hesitate, complied—Gammon listening in an agony of suppressed laughter. He looked as little at Titmouse as he could, and
was growing a trifle more sedate, when Titmouse, in a truly
lamentable tone, inquired, "What's the good, Mr. Gammon,
of ten thousand a year with such a horrid head of hair as
this?" On hearing which Gammon jumped off his chair,
started to the window, and laughed for one or two minutes
without ceasing. This was too much for Titmouse, who
presently cried aloud in a lamentable manner; and Gammon,
suddenly ceasing his laughter, turned round and apologized in
the most earnest manner; after which he uttered an abundance
of sympathy for the sufferings which " he deplored being unable to alleviate." He even restrained himself when Titmouse
again and again asked if he could not "have the law of the
man who had so imposed on him." Gammon diverted the
thoughts of his suffering client, by taking from his pocket
some very imposing packages of paper, tied round with red
tape. From time to time, however, he almost split his nose
with efforts to restrain his laughter, on catching a fresh
glimpse of poor Titmouse's emerald hair. Mr. Gammon was
a man of business, however; and in the midst of all this distracting excitement, contrived to get Titmouse's signature to
sundry papers of no little consequence; among others, first,
to a bond conditioned for the payment of £500; secondly,
another for £10,000; and lastly, an agreement (of which he
gave Titmouse an alleged copy) by which Titmouse, in consideration of Messrs. Quirk, Gammon and Snap using their
best exertions to put him in possession of the estate, etc., etc.,
bound himself to conform to their wishes in everything, on
pain of their instantly throwing up the whole affair, looking
out for another heir-at-law (!) and issuing execution forthwith

against Titmouse for all expenses incurred under his retainer. I said that Gammon gave his confiding client an *alleged* copy of this agreement;—it was not a real copy, for certain stipulations appeared in each that were not intended to appear *in* the other, for reasons which were perfectly satisfactory to Messrs. Quirk, Gammon and Snap. When Gammon had got to this point he thought it the fitting opportunity for producing a second five-pound note. He did so, and put Titmouse thereby into an ecstasy, which pushed out of his head for a while all recollection of what had happened to his hair. He had at that moment nearly eleven pounds in hard cash! Gammon easily obtained from him an account of his little money transactions with Huckaback—of which, however, all he could tell was—that for ten shillings down, he had given a written engagement to pay fifty pounds on getting the estate. Of this Gammon made a careful memorandum, explaining the atrocious villainy of Huckaback—and, in short, that if he (Titmouse) did not look very sharply about him, he would be robbed right and left; so that it was of the utmost consequence to him early to learn how to distinguish between false and true friends. Gammon went on to assure him that the instrument he had given to Huckaback was probably, in point of law, not worth a farthing, on the ground of its being both fraudulent and usurious; and intimated something, which Titmouse did not very distinctly comprehend, about the efficacy of a bill in equity for a *discovery*, which, at a very insignificant expense, (not exceeding £100) would enable the plaintiff in equity to put the defendant in equity (*i. e.* Huckaback) in the way of declaring, on his solemn oath, that he had advanced the full sum of £50; and having obtained this important and satisfactory result, Titmouse would have the opportunity of disproving the statement of Huckaback—*if he could ;* which of course he could not. By this process, however, a little profitable employment would have been afforded to a certain distinguished firm in Saffron Hill—and that was *something*—to Gammon.

"But, by the way, talking of money," said Titmouse suddenly, "you can't think how surprising handsome Mr. Tagrag has behaved to me!"

"Indeed, my dear sir!" exclaimed Gammon, with real curiosity, "what has he done?"

"Advanced me five pounds—all of his own head!"

"Are you serious, Mr. Titmouse?" inquired Gammon.

Titmouse produced the change which he had obtained for Tag-rag's five-pound note, minus only the prices of the

Cyanochaitanthropopoion, the Damascus cream, and the eye-glass. Gammon merely stroked his chin in a thoughtful manner. So occupied, indeed, was he with his reflections, that though his eye was fixed on the ludicrous figure of Titmouse, which so shortly before had occasioned him such paroxysms of laughter, he did not feel the least inclination even to a smile. Tag-rag advance Titmouse five pounds! Throwing as much smiling indifference into his manner as was possible, he asked Titmouse the particulars of so strange a transaction. Titmouse answered (how truly the reader can judge) that Mr. Tag-rag had, in the very handsomest way, volunteered the loan of five pounds, and moreover offered him any further sum he might require!

"What a charming change, Mr. Titmouse!" exclaimed Gammon, with a watchful eye and anxious smile.

"Most delightful, 'pon my soul!"

"Rather sudden, too!—eh?—Mr. Titmouse?"

"Why—no—no; I should say, 'pon my life, certainly not. The fact is, we've long misunderstood each other. He's had an uncommon good opinion of me all the while—people *have* tried to set him against me; but it's no use, he's found them out—he told me so! And he's not only said, but *done* the handsome thing. He's turned up, by Jove, a trump all of a sudden—though it looked an ugly card."

"Ha, ha, ha!—very!—how curious!" exclaimed Mr. Gammon, mechanically revolving several important matters in his mind.

"I'm going, too, to dine at Satin Lodge, Mr. Tag-rag's country house, next Sunday."

"Indeed! It will be quite a change for you, Mr. Titmouse!"

"Yes, it will, by Jove; and—a—a—what's more—there's—hem!—you understand?"

"Go on, I beg, my dear Mr. Titmouse—"

"There's a lady in the case—not that she's *said* anything; but a nod's as good as a wink to a blind horse—eh! Mr. Gammon?"

"I should think so—Miss Tag-rag will have money, of course?"

"You've hit it. Lots. But I've not made up my mind."

[I'd better undeceive this poor devil at once, as to this sordid wretch Tag-rag (thought Gammon) otherwise the cunning old rogue may get a very mischievous hold upon him! And a *lady in the case!* The old scamp has a daughter! Whew! this will never do! The sooner I enlighten my young friend the better—though at a little risk.]

"It's very important to be able to tell who are real and who false friends, as I was saying just now, my dear Tit-mouse," said Gammon, seriously.

"I think so. Now look, for instance, there's that fellow Huckaback. I should say *he*—"

"Pho! pho! my dear sir, a mere beetle—he's not worth thinking of, one way or the other. But, can't you guess another sham friend, who has changed so suddenly."

"Do you mean Mr. Tag-rag—eh?"

"I mention no names, but it's rather odd that when I am speaking of hollow-hearted friends, *you* should at once name Mr. Tag-rag."

"The proof of the pudding—handsome is that handsome does; and I've got £5 of his money, at any rate."

"Of course, he took no security for such a trifle, between such close friends as you and him?"

"Oh—why—now you mention it—But 'twas only a line—one line."

"I knew it, my dear sir," interrupted Gammon, calmly, with a significant smile—"Tag-rag and Huckaback, they're on a par—ah, ha, ha! My dear Titmouse, you are too honest and confiding!"

"What keen eyes you lawyers have, to be sure! Well—I never "—he was evidently somewhat staggered. "I—I—must say," he presently added, looking gratefully at Gammon, "I think I *do* now know of a true friend, that sent me two five-pound notes, and never asked for any security."

"My dear sir, you really pain me by alluding to such a matter!"

[Oh, Gammon, is not this too bad! What are the papers which you know are now in your pocket, signed only this very evening by Titmouse?]

"You are not a match for Tag-rag, Titmouse; because he was *made* for a tradesman—you are not. Do you think he would have parted with his £5 but for value received? Oh, Tag-rag! Tag-rag!"

"I—I really begin to think, Mr. Gammon—'pon my soul, I do think you're right."

"Think!—Why—for a man of your acuteness—how could he imagine you could forget the long course of insult and tyranny which you have endured under him; that he should change all of a sudden—just now, when—"

"Ay, by Jove! just when I'm coming into my property,' interrupted Titmouse, quickly.

"To be sure—to be sure! Just now, I say, to make this sudden change! Bah! bah!"

"I hate Tag-rag, always did. Now, he's trying to take me in, just as he does everybody; but I've found him out. I won't lay out a penny with him!"

"Would you, do you think, ever have seen the inside of Satin Lodge, if you hadn't—"

"Why, I don't know; I really think—hem!"

"*Would* you, my dear sir?—But now a scheme occurs to me—a very amusing idea, indeed! Ah, ha, ha!—Shall I tell you a way of proving to his own face how insincere and interested he is toward you? Go to dinner, by all means, eat his good things, hear all that the whole set of them have to say, and just before you go (it will require you to have your wits about you) pretend, with a long face, that our affair is all a bottle of smoke; say that Messrs. Quirk, Gammon and Snap have told you the day before that they had made a horrid mistake, and you were the wrong man—"

"'Pon my life, I—I really," stammered Titmouse, "daren't —I couldn't—I couldn't keep it up—he'd half kill me. Besides, there will be Miss Tag-rag—it would be the death of her, I know."

"Miss Tag-rag! Gracious Heavens! What on earth can you have to do with *her?* *You*—why, if you really succeed in getting this fine property, she might make a very suitable wife for one of your grooms—ha, ha!—But for *you*—absurd!"

"Ah! I don't know—she may be a devilish fine girl, and the old fellow will have a tolerable penny to leave her—and a bird in the hand—eh? Besides, I know what she's all along thought—hem!—but that doesn't signify."

"Pho! pho! Ridiculous! Ha, ha, ha! Fancy Miss Tag-rag Mrs. Titmouse! Your eldest son—ah, ha, ha! Tag-rag Titmouse, Esq. Delightful! Your honored father a draper in Oxford Street!" All this might be very clever, but it did not seem to *tell* upon Titmouse, whose little heart had been reached by a cunning hint of Tag-rag's concerning his daughter's flattering estimate of Titmouse's personal appearance. The reason why Gammon attacked so seriously a matter which appeared so chimerical and preposterous, was this—that, according to his present plan, Titmouse was to remain for some considerable while at Tag-rag's, and, with his utter weakness of character, might be worked upon by Tag-rag and his daughter, and get inveigled into an engagement which might be productive, hereafter, of no little embarrassment. He succeeded, however, at length, in obtaining Titmouse's promise to adopt his suggestion, and thereby discover the true nature of the feelings entertained toward him at Satin Lodge. He shook Titmouse energetically by the hand, and left him perfectly certain, that if there was one person in the world worthy of his esteem, and even reverence, that person was OILY GAMMON, ESQ.

As he bent his steps toward Saffron Hill he reflected rather anxiously on several matters that had occurred to him during the interview which I have just described. On reaching the office he was presently closeted with Mr. Quirk, to whom, first and foremost, he exhibited and delivered the documents to which he had obtained Titmouse's signature, and which, the reader will allow me to assure him, were of a somewhat different texture from a certain legal instrument or security which I laid before him some little time ago.

"Now, Gammon," said the old gentleman, as soon as he had locked up in his safe the above-mentioned documents—"now, Gammon, I think we may be up and at 'em; load our guns, and blaze away," and he rubbed his hands.

"Perhaps so, Mr. Quirk," replied Gammon; "but we must, for no earthly consideration, be premature in our operations! Let me, by the way, tell you one or two little matters that have just occurred to Titmouse!"—Then he told Mr. Quirk of the effects which had followed the use of the potent Cyanochaitanthropopoion, at which old Quirk almost laughed himself into fits. When, however, Gammon, with a serious air, mentioned the name of Miss Tag-rag, and his grave suspicions concerning her, Quirk bounced up out of his chair, almost startling Gammon out of *his*. If he had just been told that his banker had broke he could scarce have shown more emotion.

The fact was, that he, too, had a DAUGHTER—an only child —whom he had destined to become Mrs. Titmouse.

"A designing old villain!" he exclaimed at length, and Gammon agreed with him; but, strange to say, with all his acuteness, never adverted to the real cause of Quirk's sudden and vehement exclamation. When Gammon told him of the manner in which he had opened Titmouse's eyes to the knavery of Tag-rag, and the expedient he had suggested for its demonstrations, Quirk could have worshiped Gammon, and could not help rising and shaking him very energetically by the hand, much to his astonishment. After a long consultation, two things were agreed upon by the partners; to look out fresh lodgings for Titmouse, and remove him presently altogether from the company and influence of Tag-rag. Some time after

they had parted, Quirk came with an eager air into Mr. Gammon's room, with a most important suggestion: viz., whether
it would not be impossible for them to get Tag-rag to *become*
a surety to them, by and by, on behalf of Titmouse? Gammon was delighted! He heartily commended Mr. Quirk's
sagacity, and promised to turn it about in his thoughts very
carefully. Not having been let entirely into Quirk's policy
(of which the reader has, however, just had a glimpse) Mr.
Gammon did not see the difficulties which kept Quirk awake
almost all that night: viz., how to protect Titmouse from the
machinations of Tag-rag and his daughter, and yet keep Tag-
rag sufficiently interested in, and intimate with, Titmouse, to
entertain, by and by, the idea of becoming surety for him to
them, the said Messrs. Quirk, Gammon and Snap; and—
withal—how to manage Titmouse all the whole, so as to forward their objects, and also that of turning his attention toward Miss Quirk; all this formed really rather a difficult problem!—Quirk looked down on Tag-rag with honest indignation,
as a mean and mercenary fellow, with unprincipled schemes,
thank Heaven, he already saw through, and from which he
resolved to rescue his innocent and confiding client, who was
made for better things—*to wit, Miss Quirk.*

When Titmouse rose the next morning (Saturday) behold
—he found his hair had become of a variously shaded purple
or violet color! Astonishment and apprehension by turns possessed him, as he stared into the glass, at this unlooked-for
change of color, and hastily dressing himself, after swallowing
a very slight breakfast, off he went once more to the scientific
establishment in Bond Street, to which he had been indebted
for his recent delightful experiences. The distinguished inventor and proprietor of the Cyanochaitanthropopoion was behind the counter as usual—calm and confident as ever.

"Ah! I see—as I said! as I said!" quoth he, with a sort of
glee in his manner. "Isn't it?—coming round quicker than
usual—Really, I'm selling more of the article than I can possibly make."

"Well,"—at length said Titmouse, as soon as he had recovered from the surprise occasioned by the sudden volubility
with which he had been assailed on entering—"then *is* it really going on tolerable well?" taking off his hat, and looking
anxiously into a glass that hung close by.

"*Tolerable* well, my dear sir! Delightful! Perfect!
Couldn't be better! If you'd studied the thing, you'd know,
sir, that purple is the middle color between green and black.
Indeed, black's only purple and green mixed, which explains

the whole thing!'' Titmouse listened with infinite satisfaction to this philosophical statement.

'' Remember, sir—my hair is to come like yours—eh? you recollect, sir? Honor—that was the bargain, you know!''

'' I have very little doubt of it, sir—nay, I am certain of it, knowing it by experience.''

[The scamp had been hired expressly for the purpose oi lying thus in support of the Cyanochaitanthropopoion; his own hair being a natural black.]

'' I'm going to a grand dinner to-morrow, sir,'' said Titmouse, ''with some devilish great people, at the west end of the town—eh? you understand? will it do by that time? Would give a trifle to get my hair a shade darker by that time—for—bem!—most lovely girl—eh? you understand the thing?—devilish anxious, and all that sort of thing, you know!''

'' Yes—I do,'' replied the gentleman of the shop, in a confidential tone; and opening one of the glass doors behind him, took out a bottle considerably larger than the first, and handed it to Titmouse. '' This,'' said he, '' will complete the thing; it combines chemically with the purple particles, and the result is generally arrived at in about two days' time —''

'' But it will do *something* in a night's time—eh?—surely?''

'' I should think so! But here it is—it is called the TETA-RAGMENON ABRACADABRA.''

'' What a name!'' exclaimed Titmouse with a kind of awe. '' 'Pon honor, it almost takes one's breath away—''

'' It will do more, sir; it will take your red hair away! By the way, only the day before yesterday, a lady of high rank, (between ourselves, Lady Caroline Carrot) whose red hair always seemed as if it would have set her bonnet in a blaze—ha, ha!—came here, after two days use of the Cyanochaitanthropopoion, and one day's use of this Tetaragmenon Abracadabra—and asked me if I knew her. Upon my soul I did not, till she solemnly assured me she was really Lady Caroline!''

'' *How* much is it?'' eagerly inquired Titmouse, thrusting his hand into his pocket, with no little excitement.

'' Only nine-and-sixpence.''

'' Oh, my stars, what a price! Nine-and-six—''

'' Ah, but would you have believed it, sir? This extraordinary fluid cost a great German chemist his whole life to bring to perfection; and it contains expensive materials from all the four corners of the world!''

'' That may be—but really—I've laid out a large figure with you, sir, this day or two! Couldn't you say eight sh—''

"We never abate, sir; it's not *our* style of doing business," replied the gentleman, in a manner that quite overawed poor Titmouse, who at once bought this, the third abomination; not a little depressed, however, at the heavy prices he had paid for the three bottles, and the uncertainty he felt as to the ultimate issue. That night he was so well satisfied with the progress which the hair on his head was making (for, by candle-light, it really looked much darker than could have been expected) that he resolved—at all events for the present—to leave well alone; or at the utmost, to try the effects of the Tetaragmenon Abracadabra only upon his eyebrows and whiskers. Into them he rubbed the new specific; which, on the bottle being opened, surprised him in two respects: first, it was perfectly colorless; secondly, it had a most infernal smell. However, it was no use hesitating; he had bought and paid for it; and the papers it was folded in gave an account of its success that was really irresistible and unquestionable. Away, therefore, he rubbed; and when he had finished, got into bed, in humble hope as to the result, which would be disclosed by the morning's light. But, alas! would you have believed it? When he looked at himself in the glass, about six o'clock (at which hour he awoke) I protest it is a fact, that his eyebrows and whiskers were as white as snow; which, combining with the purple color of the hair on his head, rendered him one of the most astounding objects (in human shape) the eye of man had ever beheld. There was the wisdom of age seated in his eyebrows and whiskers, unspeakable youthful folly in his features, and a purple crown of WONDER on his head.

Really, it seemed as if the devil were wreaking his spite on Mr. Titmouse; nay, perhaps it was the devil himself who had served him with the bottles in Bond Street. Or was it a mere ordinary servant of the devil—some greedy, impudent, unprincipled speculator, who, desirous of acting on the approved maxim—*Fiat experimentum in corpore vili*—had pitched on Titmouse (seeing the sort of person he was) as a godsend, quite reckless what effect he produced on his hair, so as the stuff was paid for, and its effects noted? It might possibly have been sport to the gentleman of the shop, but it was near proving death to poor Titmouse, who really might have resolved on throwing himself out of the window, only that he saw it was not big enough for a baby to get through. He turned aghast at the monstrous object which his little glass presented to him; and sunk down upon the bed with a feeling as if he were now fit for death. As before. Mrs. Squallop made her appearance with his kettle for breakfast. He was sitting at the table dressed, and with his arms folded, with a reckless air, not at all caring to conceal the new and still more frightful change which he had undergone since she saw him last. Mrs. Squallop stared at him for a second or two in silence; then, stepping back out of the room, suddenly drew to the door and stood outside, laughing vehemently.

" I'll kick you down-stairs!" shouted Titmouse, rushing to the door, pale with fury, and pulling it open.

" Mr.—Mr.—Titmouse, you'll be the death of me—you will —you will!" gasped Mrs. Squallop, almost black in the face, and the water running out of the kettle, which she was unconsciously holding in a slant. After a while, however, they got reconciled. Mrs. Squallop had fancied he had been but rubbing chalk on his eyebrows and whiskers; and seemed dismayed, indeed, on hearing the true state of the case. He implored her to send out for a small bottle of ink; but as it was Sunday morning none could be got; and she teased him to try a little blacking! He did—but, of course, it was useless. He sat for an hour or two in an ecstasy of grief and rage. What would he now have given never to have meddled with the hair which Heaven had thought fit to send him into the world with? Alas, with what mournful force Mrs. Squallop's words again and again recurred to him! To say that he eat breakfast would be scarcely correct. He drank a single cup of cocoa, and eat about three inches' length and thickness of a roll, and then put away his breakfast things on the window shelf. If he had been in the humor to go to church, how could he? He would have been turned out as an object involuntarily inciting everybody to laughter!

Yet, poor soul, in this extremity of misery, he was not utterly neglected; for he had that morning quite a little levee. First came Mr. Snap, who, having quite as keen and clear an eye for his own interest as his senior partners, had early seen how capable was acquaintance with Titmouse of being turned to his (Snap's) great advantage. He had come, therefore, dressed very stylishly, to do a little bit of toadying on the sly (on his own exclusive account) and had brought with him, for the edification of Titmouse, a copy of that day's *Sunday Flash*, which contained a long account of a bloody fight between Birmingham Bigbones and London Littlego, for £500 a side (sixty rounds had been fought, both men killed, and their seconds had bolted to Boulogne). Poor Snap, however, though he had come with the best intentions, and the most anxious wish to evince profound respect for the future master

of ten thousand a year was quite taken by storm by the very
first glimpse he got of Titmouse, and could not for a long while
recover himself. He had come to ask Titmouse to dine with
him at a tavern in the Strand, where there was to be capital
singing in the evening; and also to accompany him, on the
ensuing morning, to the Old Bailey, to hear "a most interesting trial" for bigamy, in which Snap was concerned for the
prisoner—a miscreant, who had been married to five living
women. Snap conceived (and very justly) that it would give
Titmouse a striking idea of his (Snap's) importance, to see
him so much, and apparently so familiarly concerned with
well-known counsel. In his own terse and quaint way, he was
explaining to Titmouse the various remedies he had against
the Bond Street impostor, both by indictment and action on
the case; nay (getting a little, however, beyond his depth)
he assured the eager Titmouse, that a bill of discovery would
lie in equity, to ascertain what the Tetaragmenon Abracadabra
was composed of, with a view to his preferring an indictment
against the owner, when his learned display was interrupted
by a double knock, and—oh, mercy on us!—enter Mr. Gammon.

Whether he or Snap felt more disconcerted, I can not
say; but Snap *looked* the most confused and sneaking. Each
told the other a lie, in as easy, good-natured a way as he could
assume, concerning the object of his visit to Titmouse. Thus
they were going on, when—another knock—and, "Is this Mr.
Titmouse's?" inquired a voice, which brought a little color
into the face of both Gammon and Snap; for it was absolutely
old Quirk, who bustled breathless into the room, on his first
visit, and seemed completely confounded by the sight of both
his partners. What with this, and the amazing appearance
presented by Titmouse, Mr. Quirk was so overwhelmed that
he scarce spoke a syllable. Each of the three partners felt
(in his own way) exquisite embarrassment. Huckaback, some
time afterward, made his appearance, but *him* Titmouse unceremoniously dismissed in a twinkling in spite of a vehement
remonstrance. But presently, behold another arrival—Mr.
Tag-rag, who had come to announce that his carriage (*i. e.* a
queer, rickety, little one-horse chaise, with a tallow-faced boy
in it, in faded livery) was waiting to convey Mr. Titmouse to
Satin Lodge, and take him a long drive in the country! Each
of these four worthies could have spit in the other's face;
first, for *detecting*, and, secondly, for *rivaling* him in his
schemes upon Titmouse. A few minutes after the arrival of
Tag-rag, Gammon, half-choked with disgust, and despising

himself even more than his fellow-visitors, slunk off, followed almost immediately by Quirk, who was dying to consult him on this new aspect of affairs which had presented itself. Snap (who, ever since the arrival of Messrs. Quirk and Gammon, had felt like an ape on hot irons) very shortly followed in the footsteps of his partners, having made no engagement whatever with Titmouse; and thus the enterprising and determined Tag-rag was left master of the field. He had in fact come to *do business*, and business he determined to do. As for Gammon, during the short time he had stayed, how he had endeared himself to Titmouse, by explaining (not aware that Titmouse had confessed all to Snap) the singular change in the color of his hair to have been occasioned simply by the intense mental anxiety through which he had lately passed! The anecdotes he told of sufferers, whose hair a single night's agony had changed to all the colors of the rainbow! Though Tag-rag outstayed all his fellow-visitors, in the manner which has been described, he could not prevail upon Titmouse to accompany him in his '' carriage,'' for Titmouse pleaded a pressing engagement (*i. e.* a desperate attempt he purposed making to obtain some *ink*) but pledged himself to make his appearance at Satin Lodge at the appointed hour (half past three for four o'clock). Away, therefore, drove Tag-rag, delighted that Satin Lodge would so soon contain so resplendent a visitor—indignant at the cringing, sycophantic attentions of Messrs. Quirk, Gammon and Snap, against whom he resolved to put Titmouse on his guard, and infinitely astonished at the extraordinary change that had taken place in the color of Titmouse's hair. Partly influenced by the explanation which Gammon had given of the phenomenon, Tag-rag resigned himself to feelings of simple wonder. Titmouse was doubtless passing through stages of physical transmogrification, corresponding with the marvelous change that was taking place in his circumstances;—and for all he (Tag-rag) knew, other and more extraordinary changes were going on; Titmouse might be growing at the rate of half an inch a day, and soon stand before him a man more than six feet high! Considerations such as these invested Titmouse with intense and overpowering interest in the estimation of Tag-rag; *how* could he make enough of him at Satin Lodge that day? If ever that hardened sinner felt inclined to utter an inward prayer, it was as he drove home—that Heaven would array his daughter in angel hues to the eyes of Titmouse!

My friend Tittlebat made his appearance at the gate of Satin Lodge at about a quarter to four o'clock. Good gracious, how he had dressed himself out! He considerably exceeded his appearance when first presented to the reader.

Miss Tag-rag had been before her glass ever since the instant of her return from chapel, up to within ten minutes' time of Titmouse's arrival. An hour and a half at least had she bestowed on her hair, disposing it in little corkscrew and somewhat scanty curls, that quite glistened in bear's grease, hanging on each side of a pair of lean and sallow cheeks. The color which ought to have distributed itself over her cheeks, in roseate delicacy, had thought fit to collect itself into the tip of her sharp little nose. Her small gray eyes beamed with the gentle and attractive expression that was perceptible in her father's, and her projecting under lip reminded everybody of that delicate feature in her mother. She was very short, and her figure rather skinny and angular. She wore her lilac-colored frock; her waist being pinched in to a degree that made you think of a fit of colic when you looked at her. A long red sash, tied in a most elaborate bow, gave a very brilliant air to her dress generally. She had a thin gold chain round her neck, and wore long white gloves; her left hand holding her pocket-handkerchief, which she had suffused with bergamot that scented the whole room. Mrs. Tag-rag had made herself very splendid, in a red-silk gown and staring head-dress; in fact, she seemed *on fire*. As for Mr. Tag-rag, whenever he was dressed in his Sunday clothes, he looked the model of a dissenting minister: in his black coat, waistcoat, and trousers, and primly tied white neckerchief, with no shirt-collar visible.

For a quarter of an hour had this interesting trio been standing at their parlor window, in anxious expectation of Titmouse's arrival; their only amusement being the numberless dusty stage-coaches driving every five minutes close past their gate (which was about ten yards from their house), at once enlivening and ruralizing the scene. Oh, that poor laburnum—laden with dust, drooping with drought, and evidently in the very last stage of a decline—that was planted beside the little gate! Tag-rag spoke of cutting it down; but Mrs. and Miss Tag-rag begged its life a little longer—and then *that* subject dropped. How was it that, though both the ladies had sat under a thundering discourse from Mr. Dismal Horror that morning—they had never once since thought or spoke of him or his sermon—never even opened his " *Groans?*" The reason was plain. They thought of Titmouse, who was bringing " airs from heaven;" while Horror brought only " blasts from hell "—and *those* they had every day in the week (his sermons on the Sunday, his " *Groans* " on the week day).

At length Miss Tag-rag's little heart fluttered violently, for her papa told her that Titmouse was coming up the road—and so he was. Not dreaming that he could be seen, he stood beside the gate for a moment, under the melancholy laburnum; and, taking a dirty-looking silk handkerchief out of his hat, slapped it vigorously about his boots (from which circumstance it may be inferred that he had walked) and replaced it in his hat. Then he unbuttoned his surtout, adjusted it nicely, and disposed his chain and eyeglass just so as to let the tip only of the latter be seen peeping out of his waistcoat; twitched up his collars, plucked down his wristbands, drew the tip of a white pocket-handkerchief out of the pocket in the breast of his surtout, pulled a white glove half-way on his left hand; and, having thus given the finishing touches to his toilet, opened the gate, and—Tittlebat Titmouse, Esquire, the great guest of the day, for the first time in his life (swinging a little ebony cane about with careless grace) entered the domain of Mr. Tag-rag.

The little performance I have been describing, though every bit of it passing under the eyes of Tag-rag, his wife, and his daughter, had not excited a smile; their anxious feelings were too deep to be reached or stirred by light emotions. Miss Tag-rag turned very pale and trembled.

"La, pa!" said she, faintly, "how could you say he'd got white eyebrows and whiskers? Why—they're a beautiful *black !*"

Tag-rag was speechless; the fact was so—for Titmouse had fortunately succeeded in obtaining a little bottle of ink, which he had applied with great effect. As Titmouse approached the house (Tag-rag hurrying out to open the door for him) he saw the two ladies standing at the windows. Off went his hat, and out dropped the silk handkerchief, not a little disconcerting him for the moment. Tag-rag, however, soon occupied his attention at the door with anxious civilities, shaking him by the hand, hanging up his hat and stick, and then introducing him to the sitting-room. The ladies received him with the most profound courtesies, which Titmouse returned with a quick embarrassed bow, and an indistinct—"I hope you're well, mem?"

If they had had presence of mind enough to observe it, the purple color of Titmouse's hair must have surprised them not a little; all they could see, however, was—the angelic owner of ten thousand a year.

The only person tolerably at his ease, and he *only* tolerably, was Mr. Tag-rag; and he asked his guest—

"Wash your hands, Titmouse, before dinner?" Titmouse said he had washed them before he had come out. [The day was hot, and he had walked five miles at a slapping pace.] In a few minutes, however, he felt a little more assured; for it was impossible for him not to perceive the awful deference with which he was treated.

"Seen the *Sunday Flash*, mem?" said he, modestly, addressing Mrs. Tag-rag.

"I—I—that is—not *to-day*," she replied, coloring.

"Vastly amusing, isn't it?" interposed Tag-rag, to prevent mischief—for he knew his wife would as soon have taken a cockatrice into her hand.

"Ye—e—s," replied Titmouse, who had not even glanced at the copy which Snap had brought him. "An uncommon good fight between Birmingham Big—"

Tag-rag saw his wife getting redder and redder. "No news stirring about Ministers, is there?" said he, with a desperate attempt at a diversion.

"Not that I have heard," replied Titmouse. Soon he got a little further, and said how cheerful the stages going past must make the house. Tag-rag agreed with him. Then there was a little pause.

"Been to church, mem, this morning, mem?" timidly inquired Titmouse of Miss Tag-rag.

"Yes, sir," she replied, faintly coloring, casting her eyes to the ground, and suddenly putting her hand into that of her mother—with such an innocent, engaging simplicity—like a timid fawn lying as close as possible to its dam!*

"We always go to *chapel*, sir," said Mrs. Tag-rag, confidently, in spite of a very fierce look from her husband; "the gospel isn't preached in the Church of England. We sit under Mr. Horror—a heavenly preacher! You've heard of Mr. Horror?"

"Yes, mem! Oh, yes! Capital preacher!" replied Titmouse, who of course (being a true churchman) had never in his life heard of Mr. Horror, or any other dissenter.

"When *will* dinner be ready, Mrs. T. ?" inquired Tag-rag, abruptly, and with a very perceptible dash of sternness in his tone; but dinner was announced the very next moment. He took his wife's arm, and in doing so, gave it a sudden vehement

---

* " Vitas hinnuleo me similis, Chloe,
    Quærenti pavidam montis avils
  Matrem.
        et corde et genibus tremit."
                              HOR. i. 23.

pressure, which, coupled with a furious glance, explained to her the extent to which she had incurred his anger. She thought, however, of Mr. Horror, and was silent.

Titmouse's proffered arm the timid Miss Tag-rag scarcely touched with the tip of her finger, as she walked beside him to dinner. Titmouse soon got tolerably composed and cheerful at dinner (which consisted of a little piece of nice roast beef, with plenty of horse-radish, Yorkshire pudding, a boiled fowl, a plum-pudding made by Mrs. Tag-rag, and custards which had been superintended by Miss Tag-rag) and, to oblige his hospitable host and hostess, eat till he was fit to burst. Miss Tag-rag, though really very hungry, eat only a very small slice of beef and a quarter of custard, and drank a third of a glass of sherry after dinner. She never once spoke, except in hurried answers to her papa and mamma; and, sitting exactly opposite Titmouse (with only a plate of greens and a boiled fowl between them) was continually coloring whenever their eyes happened to encounter one another, on which occasion hers would suddenly drop, as if overpowered by the brilliance of his. Titmouse began to love her very fast. After the ladies had withdrawn, you should have heard the way that Tag-rag went on with Titmouse—I can liken the two to nothing but an old fat spider and a little fly.

> " Will you come into my parlor?
> Said the spider to the fly;"

and it might have been well for Titmouse to have answered, in the language of the aforesaid fly:—

> " No, thank you, sir, I really feel
> No curiosity."

Titmouse, however, swallowed with equal facility Mr. Tag-rag's hard port and his soft blarney; but *all* fools have large swallows. When at length Tag-rag alluded to the painfully evident embarrassment of his " poor Tabby," and said he had " now found out what had been so long the matter with her " [ay, even this went down] and hemmed, and winked his eye, and drained his glass, Titmouse began to get flustered, blushed, and hoped Mr. Tag-rag would soon " join the ladies." They did so (Tag-rag stopping behind to lock up the wine and the remains of the fruit). Miss Tag-rag presided over the tea-things. There were muffins, and crumpets, and reeking hot buttered toast; Mrs. Tag-rag would hear of no denial, so poor Titmouse, after the most desperate resistance, was obliged to swallow a round of toast, half a muffin, and an entire crumpet,

and four cups of hot tea; after which he felt a very painful degree of turgidity, and a miserable conviction that he should be
able to eat and drink nothing more for the remainder of the
week.

After the tea things had been removed, Tag-rag, directing
Titmouse's attention to the piano, which was open (with some
music on it ready to be played from), asked him whether he
liked music. Titmouse, with great eagerness, hoped Miss T.
would give them some music; and she, after holding out a long
and vigorous siege, at length asked her papa what it should be.

"*The Battle of Prague*," said her papa.

"*Before Jehovah's awful throne*," hastily interposed her
mamma.

"The Battle," sternly repeated her papa.

"It's Sunday night, Mr. T.," meekly rejoined his wife.

"Which will *you* have, Mr. Titmouse?" inquired Tag-rag,
with *The Battle of Prague* written in every feature of his face.
Titmouse almost burst into a state of perspiration.

"A little of both, sir, if you please."

"Well," replied Tag-rag, slightly relaxing, "that will do.
Split the difference—eh? Come, Tab, down with you. Titmouse, will you turn over the music for her?"

Titmouse rose, and having sheepishly taken his station beside Miss Tag-rag, the performance commenced with *Before
Jehovah's awful throne!* But, mercy upon us! at what a rate
she rattled over that "pious air." If its respectable com-
poser had been present, he must have gone into a fit; but there
was no help for it—the heart of the lovely performer was in
The Battle of Prague, to which she presently did most ample
justice. So much were her feelings engaged in that sublime
composition, that the bursting of one of the strings—twang!
in the middle of the "*cannonading*," did not at all disturb
her; and, as soon as she had finished the exquisite "finale,"
Titmouse was in such a tumult of excitement, from different
causes, that he could have shed tears. Though he had never
once turned over at the right place, Miss Tag-rag thanked him
for his services with a smile of infinite sweetness. Titmouse
vowed that he had never heard such splendid music—begged
for more; and away went Miss Tag-rag, hurried away by her
excitement. Rondo after rondo, march after march, for at
least half an hour; at the end of which old Tag-rag suddenly
kissed her with passionate fondness. Though Mrs. Tag-rag
was horrified at the impiety of all this, she kept a very anxious
eye on the young couple, and interchanged with her husband,
every now and then, very significant looks. Shortly after nine,

spirits, wine, and hot and cold water, were brought in. At the sight of them Titmouse looked alarmed—for he knew that he must take something more, though he would have freely given five shillings to be excused—for he felt as if he could not hold one drop more. But it was in vain. Willy-nilly, a glass of gin and water stood soon before him; he protested he could not touch it unless Miss Tag-rag would " take something "— whereupon, with a blush, she " thought she *would* " take a wine-glassful of sherry and water. This was provided her. Then Tag-rag mixed a tumbler of port wine negus for Mrs. Tag-rag, and a great glass of mahogany-colored brandy and water for himself; and then he looked round, and felt perfectly happy. As Titmouse advanced with his gin and water, his spirits got higher and higher, and his tongue more fluent. He once or twice dropped the " Mr.," when addressing Tag-rag; several times smiled, and once even winked at the embarrassed Miss Tag-rag. Mr. Tag-rag saw it and could not control himself—for he had got to the end of his first glass of brandy and water, and mixed himself a second quite *as* strong as the former.

" Tab! ah, Tab! what *has* been the matter with you all these months?"—and he winked his eye at her and then at Titmouse.

" Papa!" exclaimed Miss Tag-rag, blushing up to her very temples.

" Ah, Titmouse—Titmouse—give me your hand," said Tag-rag; " you'll forget us all when you're a great man—but we shall always remember you."

" You're very good—very!" said Titmouse, cordially returning the pressure of Tag-rag's hand.—At that instant it suddenly occurred to him to adopt the suggestion of Mr. Gammon. Tag-rag was going on very fast, indeed, about the disinterested nature of his feelings toward Titmouse; toward whom, he said, he had always felt just as he did at that moment—'twas in vain to deny it.

" I am sure your conduct shows it, sir," commenced Titmouse, feeling a shudder like that with which a timid bather approaches the margin of the cold stream. " I could have taken my oath, sir, you would have refused to let me come into your house, when you heard of it—"

" Ah, ha!—that's *rather* an odd idea, too. If I felt a true friendship for you as plain Titmouse, it's so likely I should have *cut* you just when—ahem! My dear sir! it was *I* that thought *you* wouldn't have come into *my* house! A likely thing!"

Titmouse was puzzled. His perceptions, never very quick or clear, were now undoubtedly somewhat obfuscated with what he had been drinking. In short, he did not understand that Tag-rag had not understood *him;* and felt rather baffled.

"What surprising ups and downs there are in life, Mr. Titmouse!" said Mrs. Tag-rag, respectfully—"they're all sent from above, to try us! No one knows how they'd behave, if as how (in a manner) they were turned upside down."

"I—I hope, mem, I haven't done anything to show that *I*—"

"Oh! my dear Titmouse," anxiously interrupted Tag-rag, inwardly cursing his wife, who, finding she always went wrong in her husband's eyes whenever she spoke a word, determined for the future to stick to her negus—"the fact is, there's a Mr. Horror here that's for sending decent people to ——. He's filled my wife with all sorts of—nay, if she isn't bursting with cant—so never mind her. *You* done anything wrong! You're a pattern of modesty and propriety—your hand, my dear Titmouse!"

"Well—I'm a happy man again," resumed Titmouse, resolved now to go on with his adventure. "And when did they tell you of it, sir?"

"Oh, a few days ago—a week ago," replied Tag-rag, trying to recollect.

"Why — why — sir — a'n't you mistaken?" inquired Titmouse, with a depressed, but at the same time a surprised air. "It only happened this morning, after you left—"

"Eh? eh? ah, ha! What *do* you mean, Mr. Titmouse?" interrupted Mr. Tag-rag, with a faint attempt at a smile. Mrs. Tag-rag and Miss Tag-rag also turned exceedingly startled faces toward Titmouse, who felt as if a house were going to fall down on him.

"Why, sir," he began to cry (an attempt which was greatly aided by the maudlin condition to which drink had reduced him) "till to-day, I thought I was heir to ten thousand a year, and it seems I'm not; it's all a mistake of those cursed people at Saffron Hill!"

Tag-rag's face changed visibly, and showed the desperate shock he had just sustained. His inward agony was forcing out on his slanting forehead great drops of perspiration.

"What a capital joke, Mr. Titmouse, ah, ha!" he gasped, hastily passing his handkerchief over his forehead. Titmouse, though greatly alarmed, stood to his gun pretty steadily.

"I—I wish it was a joke! It's been no joke to *me*, sir.

There's another Tittlebat Titmouse, it seems, in Shoreditch, that's the right—"

"Who told you this, sir? Pho, I don't—I can't believe it," said Tag-rag, in a voice tremulous between suppressed rage and fear.

"True though, 'pon my life! It *is*, so help me—"

"How dare you swear before ladies, sir? You're insulting them, sir!" cried Tag-rag, trembling with rage. "And in my presence, sir? You're not a gentleman!" He suddenly dropped his voice, and, in a trembling and most earnest manner, asked Titmouse whether he was really joking or serious.

"Never more serious in my life, sir; and enough to make me so, sir!" replied Titmouse in a lamentable manner.

"You mean to tell me it's all a mistake, then, and you're no more than you always were?" inquired Tag-rag, with a desperate attempt to speak calmly.

"Oh, yes, sir! Yes!" cried Titmouse, mournfully; "and if you'll only be so kind as to let me serve you as I used. You know it was no fault of *mine*, sir. They *would* tell me it was so!"

'Tis impossible to conceive a more disgusting expression than the repulsive features that Tag-rag wore at that moment, while he gazed in ominous and agitated silence at Titmouse. His lips quivered, and he seemed incapable of speaking.

"Oh, ma, I do feel *so* ill!" faintly exclaimed Miss Tag-rag, turning deadly pale. Titmouse was on the verge of dropping on his knees and confessing the trick, greatly agitated at the effect produced on Miss Tag-rag, when Tag-rag's heavy hand was suddenly placed on his shoulder, and he whispered in a fierce under-tone, "You're an impostor, sir!" which arrested Titmouse, and made something like a MAN of him. He was a fearful fool, but he did not want for mere *pluck;* and now it was roused. Mrs. Tag-rag exclaimed, "Oh, you shocking scamp!" as she passed Titmouse, and led her daughter out of the room.

"Then an impostor, sir, a'n't fit company for *you*, of course, sir!" said Titmouse, rising, and trembling with mingled apprehension and anger.

"Pay me my five-pound note!" almost shouted Tag-rag, furiously tightening his grasp by which he held Titmouse's collar.

"Well, sir, and I will, if you'll only take your hand off? Halloo, sir—What the de—Leave go, sir! Hands off! Are you going to murder me? I'll pay you, and done with you, sir," stammered Titmouse;—when a faint scream was heard, plainly from Miss Tag-rag, overhead, and in hysterics. Then the seething caldron boiled over. "You *infernal* scoundrel!" said Tag-rag, almost choked with fury; and suddenly seizing Titmouse by the collar, scarce giving him time, in passing, to get hold of his hat and stick, he urged him along through the passage, down the gravel walk, threw open the gate, thrust him furiously through it, and sent after him such a blast of execration, as was enough to drive him a hundred yards down the road. Titmouse did not fully recover his breath or his senses for a long while afterward. When he did, the first thing he felt was an inclination to fall down on his knees on the open road, and worship the sagacious and admirable GAMMON, who had so exactly predicted what had come to pass!

And now, Mr. Titmouse, for some little time I have done with you. Away!—give room to your betters. But don't think that I have yet "rifled *all* your sweetness," or am *yet* about to "fling you like a noisome weed away."

CHAPTER VII.

WHILE the lofty door of a house in Grosvenor Street might be imagined yet quivering under the shock of a previously announced dinner-arrival, one of the servants who were standing behind a carriage which approached from the direction of Piccadilly slipped off, and in a twinkling, with a thun-thun-thunder - under-under, — thunder-runder-runder, thun - thun-thun! and a shrill thrilling *whir-r-r* of the bell, announced the arrival of the Duke of ——, the last guest. It was a large and plain carriage, but perfectly well known; and before the door of the house at which it had drawn up had been opened, displaying some four or five servants standing in the hall, in simple but elegant liveries, half a dozen passengers had stopped to see get out of the carriage an elderly, middle-sized man, with a somewhat spare figure, dressed in plain black clothes, with iron-gray hair, and a countenance which, once seen, was not to be forgotten. That was a great man; one, the like of whom many previous centuries had not seen; whose name shot terror into the hearts of all the enemies of old England all over the world, and fond pride and admiration into the hearts of his fellow-countrymen.

"A quarter to eleven!" he said, in a quiet tone, to the servant who was holding open the carriage-door—while the bystanders took off their hats; a courtesy which he acknowledged, as he slowly stepped across the pavement, by touching his hat in a mechanical sort of way with his forefinger. The house-door then closed upon him; the handful of cn-lookers passed away; off rolled the empty carriage, and all without was quiet as before. The house was that of Mr. Aubrey, one of the members for the borough of YATTON, in Yorkshire—a man of rapidly rising importance in Parliament. Surely his was a pleasant position—that of an independent country gentleman, a member of one of the most ancient noble families in England, with a clear unincumbered rent-roll of ten thousand a year; and already, in only his thirty-fourth year, spokesman of his class, and promising to become one of the ablest debaters in the House! Parliament having been assembled, in consequence of a particular emergency, at a much earlier period than usual, the House of Commons, in which Mr. Aubrey had the evening before delivered a well-timed and powerful speech, had adjourned for the Christmas recess, the House of Lords being about to follow its example that evening; an important division, however, being first expected to take place at a late hour. Mr. Aubrey was warmly complimented on his success by several of the select and brilliant circle then assembled; and who were all in high spirits—on account of a considerable triumph just obtained by their party, and to which Mr. Aubrey was assured, by even the Duke of ——, his exertions had certainly not a little contributed. While his Grace was energetically intimating to Mr. Aubrey his opinion to this effect, there were two lovely women listening to him with intense eagerness —they were the wife and sister of Mr. Aubrey. The former was an elegant and interesting woman—with raven hair, and a complexion of dazzling fairness—of nearly eight-and-twenty; the latter was a really beautiful girl, somewhere between twenty and twenty-one. Both were dressed with the utmost simplicity and elegance. Mrs. Aubrey, most dotingly fond of her husband, and a blooming young mother of two as charming children as were to be met with in a day's walk all over both the parks, was, in character and manners, all pliancy and gentleness; while about Miss Aubrey there was a dash of spirit that gave an infinite zest to her beauty. Her blue eyes beamed with the richest expression of feeling—in short, Catherine Aubrey was, both in face and figure, a downright English beauty; and she knew—truth must be told—that such she appeared to the Great Duke whose cold aquiline eye she often *felt* to be settled upon her with satisfaction. The fact was, that he had penetrated at a first glance beneath the mere surface of an arch, sweet and winning manner, and detected a certain strength of character in Miss Aubrey which gave him more than usual interest in her, and spread over his iron-cast features a pleasant expression, relaxing their sternness.   It might indeed be said, that, before her, in his person,

> " Grim-visaged war hath smooth'd his wrinkled front."

'Twas a subject for a painter, that delicate and blooming girl, her auburn hair hanging in careless grace on each side of her white forehead, while her eyes

> " That might have soothed a tiger's rage,
>   Or thaw'd the cold heart of a conqueror,"

were fixed with absorbed interest on the stern and rigid countenance which she reflected had been, as it were, a thousand times darkened with the smoke of the grisly battle-field.   But I must not forget that there are others in the room; and amongst them, standing at a little distance, is Lord De la Zouch, one of Mr. Aubrey's neighbors in Yorkshire.   Apparently he is listening to a brother peer talking to him very earnestly about the expected division; but Lord De la Zouch's eye is fixed on you, lovely Kate—and how little can you imagine what is passing through his mind?   It has just occurred to him that his sudden arrangement for young Delamere—his own son and heir, come up the day before from Oxford—to call for him about half past ten, and take his place in Mrs. Aubrey's drawing-room, while he, Lord De la Zouch, goes down to the House—may be attended with certain consequences.   He is speculating on the effect of your beauty bursting suddenly on his son—who has not seen you for nearly two years; all this gives him anxiety—for, dear Kate, he knows that your forehead would wear the ancient coronet of the De la Zouches with grace and dignity.   But Delamere is as yet too young and if he gets the image of Catherine Aubrey into his head, it will, fears his father, instantly cast into the shade and displace all the stern visages of those old poets, orators, historians, philosophers, and statesmen, who ought, in Lord De la Zouch and his son's tutor's judgment, to occupy exclusively the head of the aforesaid Delamere for some five years to come. That youngster—happy fellow!—frank, high-spirited, and enthusiastic—and handsome to boot—was heir to an ancient title and great estates; all that his father had considered in looking out for an alliance was—youth, health, beauty, blood—here they all were;—and *fortune* too—bah! what did it signify to his son—but at any rate, 'twas not to be thought of for some years.

   " Suppose," said he aloud, though in a musing manner " one were to say—twenty-four—"

" *Twenty-four !*" echoed his companion with amazement; " my dear De la Zouch, what the deuce do you mean? *Eighty-four* at the very lowest."

" Eh! what? oh—yes, of course—I should say ninety—I mean—hem!—*they* will muster about twenty-four only."

" Ah—I beg your pardon!—*there* you're right, I dare say." Here the announcement of dinner put an end to the colloquy of the two statesmen. Lord De la Zouch led down Miss Aubrey with an air of the most delicate and cordial courtesy; and felt almost disposed, in the heat of the moment, to tell her that he had arranged all in his own mind—that if *she* willed it, she had *his* hearty consent to become the future Lady De la Zouch. He was himself the eleventh who had come to the title in direct descent from father to son; 'twas a point he was not a little nervous and anxious about—he detested collateral succession—and he made himself infinitely agreeable to Miss Aubrey as he sat beside her at dinner! The Duke of —— sat on the right-hand side of Mrs. Aubrey, seemingly in high spirits, and she appeared proud enough of her supporter. It was a delightful dinner-party, elegant without ostentation, and select without pretense of exclusiveness. All were cheerful and animated, not merely on account of the over-night's parliamentary victory, which I have already alluded to, but also in contemplation of the coming Christmas; how, and where, and with whom each was to spend that " righte merrie season," being the chief topic of conversation. As there was nothing peculiar in the dinner, and as I have no turn for describing such matters in detail—the clatter of plate, the jingling of silver, the sparkling of wines, and so forth—I shall request the reader to imagine himself led by me quietly out of the dining-room into the library—thus escaping from all the bustle and hubbub attendant upon such an entertainment as is going on in the front of the house. We shall be alone in the library—here it is; we enter it, and shut the door. 'Tis a spacious room, all the sides covered with books, of which Mr. Aubrey is a great collector —and the clear red fire (which we must presently replenish, or it will go out) is shedding a subdued ruddy light on all the objects in the room, very favorable for our purpose. The ample table is covered with books and papers; and there is an antique-looking arm-chair drawn opposite to the fire, in which Mr. Aubrey has been indulging in a long reverie till the moment of quitting it to go and dress for dinner. This chair I shall sit in myself; you may draw out from the recess for yourself, one of two little sloping easy-chairs, which have been placed there by Mrs. and Miss Aubrey for their own sole use, considering that they are excellent judges of the period at which Mr. Aubrey has been long enough alone, and at which they should come in and gossip with him. We may as well draw the dusky green curtains across the window, through which the moon shines at present rather too brightly.—So now, after coaxing up the fire, I will proceed to tell you a little bit of pleasant family history.

The Aubreys are a Yorkshire family—the younger branch of the ancient and noble family of the Dreddlingtons. Their residence, YATTON, is in the north-eastern part of the country, not above fifteen or twenty miles from the sea. The hall is one of those old structures, the sight of which throws you back at least a couple of centuries in our English history. It stands in a park, crowded with trees, many of them of great age and size, and under which some two hundred head of deer perform their capricious and graceful gambols. In approaching from London, you strike off the great north road into a broad by-way; after going down which for about a mile, you come to a struggling little village called Yatton, at the further extremity of which stands a little aged gray church, with a tall thin spire; an immense yew-tree, with a kind of friendly gloom, over-shadowing, in the little church-yard, nearly half the graves. Rather in the rear of the church is the vicarage-house, snug and sheltered by a line of fir-trees. After walking on about eighty yards, you come to the high park-gates, and see a lodge just within, on the left-hand side, sheltered by an elm-tree. You then wind your way for about two thirds of a mile along a gravel walk, amongst the thickening trees, till you come to a ponderous old crumbling-looking red-brick gate-way of the time of Henry VII., with one or two deeply set stone windows in the turrets, and moldering stone-capped battle-ments peeping through high-climbing ivy. There is an old escutcheon immediately over the point of the arch; and as you pass underneath, if you look up you can see the groove of the old portcullis still remaining. Having passed under this castellated remnant, you enter a kind of court, formed by a high wall completely covered with ivy, running along in a line from the right-hand turret of the gate-way till it joins the house. Along its course are a number of yew-trees. In the center of the open space is a quaintly disposed grass-plat, dotted about with stunted box, and in the center of that stands a weather-beaten stone sun-dial. The house itself is a large irregular pile of dull-red brick-work, with great stacks of chim-neys in the rear; the body of the building has evidently been erected at different times. Some part is evidently in the style of Queen Elizabeth's reign, another in that of Queen Anne; and it is plain that on the site of the present structure has formerly stood a castle. There are, indeed, traces of the old moat still visible round the rear of the house. One of the ancient towers, with small deep stone windows, still remains, giving its venerable support to the right-hand extremity of the building, as you stand with your face to the door. The long frontage of the house consists of two huge masses of dusky-red brick-work (you can hardly call them *wings*) connected together by a lower building in the center, which contains the hall. There are three or four rows of long thin deep windows, with heavy-looking wooden sashes. The high-pitched roof is of slate, and has deep projecting eaves, forming, in fact, a bold wooden cornice running along the whole length of the building, which is some two or three stories high. At the left extremity stand a clump of ancient cedars of Lebanon, feathering in evergreen beauty down to the ground. The hall is large and lofty; the floor is of polished oak, almost the whole of which is covered with thick matting; it is wainscoted all round with black oak; some seven or eight full-length pictures, evidently of considerable antiquity, being let into the panels. Quaint figures these are to be sure; and if they resemble the ancestors of the Aubrey family, those ancestors must have been singular and startling persons! The faces are quite white and staring—all as if in wonder; and they have such long thin legs! ending in sharp-pointed shoes. On each side of the ample fire-place stands a figure in full armor; and there are also ranged along the wall old helmets, cuirasses, swords, lances, battle-axes and cross-bows; the very idea of wearing, wielding, and handling which makes your arms ache while you exclaim, "they *must* have been giants in those days!" On one side of this hall, a door opens into the dining-room, beyond which is the library; on the other side a door leads you into a noble room, where stands a very fine organ. Out of both the dining-room and drawing-room you pass up a staircase contained in an old square tower; two sides of each of them, opening on the old quadrangle, lead into a gallery running all round it, and into which all the bedrooms open. —But I need not go into further detail. Altogether it is truly a fine old mansion. Its only constant occupant is Mrs. Aubrey, the mother of Mr. Aubrey, in whose library we are now seated. She is a widow, having survived her husband, who twice was one of the county members, about fifteen years. Mr. Aubrey is her first-born child, Miss Aubrey her last; four intervening children she has followed to the grave—the grief and suffering consequent upon which have sadly shaken her constitution, and made her, both in actual health and in appearance, at least ten years older than she really is—for she has, in point of fact, not long since entered her sixtieth year. What a blessed life she leads at Yatton! Her serene and cheerful temper makes every one happy about her; and her charity is unbounded, but dispensed with a most just discrimination. One way or another, almost a fourth of the village are direct pensioners upon her bounty. You have only to mention the name of Madam Aubrey, the lady of Yatton, to witness involuntary homage paid to her virtues. Her word is law; and well indeed it may be. While Mr. Aubrey, her husband, was to the last somewhat stern in his temper and reserved in his habits, bearing withal a spotless and lofty character, *she* was always what she still is, meek, gentle, accessible, charitable, and pious. On his death she withdrew from the world, and has ever since resided at Yatton—never having quitted it for a single day. There are in the vicinity one or two stately families, with ancient name, sounding title and great possessions; but for ten miles round Yatton, old Madam Aubrey, the squire's mother, is the name that is enshrined in people's kindliest and most grateful feelings, and receives their readiest homage. 'Tis perhaps a very small matter to mention, but there is at the hall a great white old mare, Peggy, that for these twenty years, in all weathers, hath been the bearer of Madam's bounty. A thousand times hath she carried Jacob Jones (now a pensioned servant, whose hair is as white as Peggy's) all over the estate, and also oft beyond it, with comfortable matters for the sick and poor. Most commonly there are a couple of stone bottles filled with cowslip, currant, ginger, or elderberry wine, slung before old Jones over the well-worn saddle—to the carrying of which Peggy has got so accustomed that she does not go comfortably without them. She has so fallen into the habits of old Jones, who is an inveterate gossip (Madam having helped to make him such by the numerous inquiries she makes of him every morning as to every one in the village and on the estate, and which inquiries he must have the means of answering) that slow as he jogs along, if ever she meets or is overtaken by any one, she stops of her own accord, as if to hear what they and her rider have to say to one another. She is a great favorite with all, and gets a mouthful of hay or grass at every place she stops at, either from the children or the old people. When old Peggy comes to die, she will be missed by all the folk around Yatton. Madam Aubrey, growing, I am sorry to say, very feeble, can not go about as much as she used, and betakes herself oftener and oftener to the old family coach; and when she is going to drive about the neighborhood, you may almost always see it stop at the vicarage for old Dr. Tatham, who generally accompanies her. On these occasions she always has a bag containing Testaments and Prayer-books, which are principally distributed as rewards to those whom the parson can recommend as deserving of them. For these five-and-twenty years she has never missed giving a copy of each to every child in the village on the estate, on its being confirmed; and the old lady looks around very keenly every Sunday, from her pew, to see that these Bibles and Prayer-books are reverently used. I could go on for an hour and longer, telling you these and other such matters of this exemplary lady; but we shall by and by have some opportunities of seeing and knowing more of her personally. Her features are delicate, and have been very handsome; and in manner she is very calm, and quiet, and dignified. She looks all that you could expect from what I have told you. The briskness of youth, the sedate firmness of middle age, have years since given place, as you will see with some pain, to the feebleness produced by ill health and mental suffering—for she mourned after her children with all a fond and bereaved mother's love. Oh! how she dotes upon her surviving son and daughter! And are they not worthy of such a mother?

Mr. Aubrey is in his thirty-fourth year; and inherits the mental qualities of both his parents—the demeanor and person of his father. He has a reserve that is not cynical, but only diffident; yet it gives him, at least at first sight, and till you have become familiar with his features, which are of a cast at once refined and aristocratic, yet full of goodness, an air of hauteur, which is very—very far from his real nature. He has in truth the soft heart and benignant temper of his mother, joined with the masculine firmness of character which belonged to his father; which, however, is in danger of being seriously impaired by *inaction*. Sensitive he is, perhaps to a fault. There is a tone of melancholy or pensiveness in his composition, which has probably increased upon him from his severe studies, ever since his youth. He is a man of superior intellect, and is a capital scholar. At Oxford he plucked the prize of Double First from a host of strong competitors, and has since justified the expectations which were entertained of him. He has made several really valuable contributions to historic literature—indeed, I think he is even now engaged upon some researches calculated to throw much light upon the obscure origin of several of our political institutions. He has entered upon *politics* with uncommon—perhaps with an excessive—ardor. I think he is likely to make an eminent figure in Parliament; for he is a man of very clear head, very patient, of business-like habits, ready in debate, and, moreover, has a very impressive delivery as a public speaker. He is generous and charitable as his admirable mother, and careless, even to a fault, of his pecuniary interests. He is a man of perfect simplicity and purity of character. Above all, his virtues are the virtues which have been sublimed by Christianity—as it were, the cold embers of morality warmed into religion. He stands happily equidistant from infidelity and fanaticism. He has looked for light from above, and has heard a voice saying, "*This* is the way, walk thou in it." His piety is the real source of that happy consistent dignity, and content, and firmness, which have earned him the respect of all who know him, and will bear him through whatever may befall him. He who standeth upon this rock can not be moved, perhaps not even touched, by the surges of worldly reverses—of difficulty and distress. In a manner Mr. Aubrey is calm and gentleman-like; in person he is rather above the middle height, and of slight make. From the way in which his clothes hang about him, a certain sharpness at his shoulders catching the eye of an observer—you would feel an anxiety about his health, which would be increased by hearing of the mortality in his family; and your thoughts are perhaps pointed in the same direction, by a glance at his long, thin, delicate, white hands. His countenance has a serene manliness about it when in repose, and great acuteness and vivacity when animated. His hair, not very full, is black as jet, and his forehead ample and marked.

Mr. Aubrey has been married about six years; 'twas a case of love at first sight. Chance threw him in the way of Agnes St. Clair, within a few weeks after she had been bereaved of her only parent, Colonel St. Clair, a man of old but impoverished family, who fell in the Peninsular War. Had he lived only a month or two longer, he would have succeeded to a considerable estate; as it was, he left his only child comparatively penniless; but Heaven had endowed her with personal beauty, with a lovely disposition, and superior understanding. It was not till after a long and anxious wooing, backed by the cordial entreaties of Mrs. Aubrey, that Miss St. Clair consented to become the wife of a man, who, to this hour, loves her with all the passionate ardor with which she had first inspired him. And richly she deserves his love, for she does, indeed, dote upon him: she studies, or rather, perhaps, anticipates his every wish; in short, had the whole sex been searched for one calculated to make happy the morbidly fastidious Aubrey, the choice must surely have fallen on Miss St. Clair; a woman whose temper, whose tastes, and whose manners were at once in delicate and harmonizing unison and contrast with his own. She has hitherto brought him but two children—and those very beautiful children, too—a boy between four and five years old, and a girl about two years old. If I were to hint my own impressions I should say there was a probability—but be that as it may, 'tis an affair we have nothing to do with at present.

Of Catherine Aubrey you had a momentary moonlight glimpse, at a former period of this history;* and you have seen her this evening under other, and perhaps not less interesting circumstances. Now, where have you beheld a more exquisite specimen of budding womanhood?—but I feel that I shall get extravagant if I begin to dwell upon her charms. You have seen her—judge for yourself; but you do not *know* her as I do; and I shall tell you that her personal beauty is but a faint emblem of the beauties of her mind and character. She is Aubrey's youngest—now his only sister; and he cherishes her with the tenderest and fondest regard. Neither he, nor his mother—with both of whom she spends her time alternately—can bear to part with her for ever so short an interval. She is the gay, romping playmate of the little Aubreys; the demure secretary and treasurer of her mother. I say *demure*, for there is a sly humor and archness in Kate's composition, which flickers about even her gravest moods. She is calculated equally for the seclusion of Yatton and the splendid atmosphere of Almack's; but for the latter she seems at present to have little inclination. Kate is a girl of decided character, of strong sense, of high principle; all of which are irradiated, not overborne, by her sparkling vivacity of temperament. She has real talent; and her mind has been trained, and her tastes directed, with affectionate skill and vigilance by her gifted brother. She has many accomplishments; but the only one I shall choose here to name is—music. *She* was one to sing and play before a man of the most fastidious taste and genius! I defy any man to hear the rich tones of Miss Aubrey's voice without feeling his heart moved. Music is with her a matter not of *art* but of *feeling*—of passionate feeling; but hark!—hush!—surely—yes, that is Miss Aubrey's voice—yes, that is her clear and brilliant touch; the ladies have ascended to the drawing-room, and we must presently follow them. How time

* See *ante*, p. 105.

has passed! I had a great deal more to tell you about the family, but we must take some other opportunity.

Yes, it *is* Miss Aubrey, playing on the new and superb piano given by her brother last week to Mrs. Aubrey. Do you see with what a careless grace and ease she is giving a very sweet but difficult composition of Haydn? The lady who is standing by her to turn over her music, is the celebrated Countess of Lydsdale. She is still young and beautiful; but beside Miss Aubrey she presents a somewhat painful contrast! 'Tis all the difference between an artificial and a natural flower. Poor Lady Lydsdale! you are not happy with all your fashion and splendor; the glitter of your diamonds can not compensate for the loss of the sparkling spirits of a younger day; they pale their ineffectual fires beside the fresh and joyous spirit of Catherine Aubrey! You sigh—

"Now, I'll sing you quite a new thing," said Miss Aubrey, starting up, and turning over her portfolio till she came to a sheet of paper, on which were some verses in her own hand-writing: "The words were written by my brother, and I have found an old air that exactly suits them!" Here her fingers, wandering lightly and softly over the keys, gave forth a beautiful symphony in the minor; after which, with a rich and soft voice, she sung the following:—

PEACE.

I.

Where, O where
Hath gentle PEACE found rest?
Builds she in bower of lady fair?—
But LOVE—he hath possession there;
Not long is *she* the guest.

II.

Sits she crown'd
Beneath a pictured dome?
But there AMBITION keeps his ground,
And Fear and Envy skulk around;
This can not be her home!

III.

Will she hide
In scholar's pensive cell?
But *he* already hath his bride:
Him MELANCHOLY sits beside—
With her she may not dwell!

IV.

Now and then,
Peace, wandering, lays her head
On regal couch, in captive's den—
But nowhere finds she rest with men,
Or only with the dead!

To these words, trembling on the beautiful lips of Miss Aubrey, was listening an unperceived auditor, with eyes devouring her every feature, and ears absorbing every tone of her thrilling voice. It was young Delamere, who had only a moment or two before Miss Aubrey had commenced singing the above lines, alighted from his father's carriage, which was then waiting at the door to carry off Lord De la Zouch to the House of Lords. Arrested by the rich voice of the singer, he stopped short before he had entered the drawing-room in which she sat, and, stepping to a corner where he was hid from view, though he could distinctly see Miss Aubrey, there he remained as if rooted to the spot. He, too, had a soul for music; and the exquisite manner in which Miss Aubrey gave the last verse, called up before his excited fancy the vivid image of a dove fluttering with agitated uncertainty over the sea of human life, even like the dove over the waters enveloping the earth in olden time. The mournful minor into which she threw the last line, excited a heart susceptible of the liveliest emotions to a degree which it required some effort to control, and almost a fear to relieve. When Miss Aubrey had quitted the piano, Mrs. Aubrey followed, and gave a very delicate sonata from Haydn. Then sat down Lady Lydsdale, and dashed off, in an exceedingly brilliant style, a *scena* from the new opera, which quickly reduced the excited feelings of Delamere to a pitch admitting of his presenting himself. While this lowering process was going on, Delamere took down a little volume from a tasteful little cabinet of books immediately behind him, and which proved to be a volume of the *Faery Queen*. He found many pencil-marks, evidently made by a light female hand; and turning to the fly-leaf, beheld, in a small elegant handwriting, the name of "*Catherine Aubrey.*" His heart fluttered; he turned toward the piano, and beheld the graceful figure of Miss Aubrey standing beside Lady Lydsdale, in an attitude of delighted earnestness—for her ladyship was undoubtedly a very brilliant performer—totally unconscious of the admiring eye that was fixed upon her. After gazing at her for some moments, he gently pressed the autograph to his lips; and solemnly vowed within himself, in the most deliberate manner possible, that if he could not marry

Catherine Aubrey, he would never marry anybody; he would, moreover, quit England forever; and deposit a broken heart in a foreign grave—and so forth. Thus calmly resolved—or rather to such a resolution did his thoughts tend—that sedate person, the Honorable Geoffry Lovel Delamere. He was a high-spirited, frank-hearted fellow; and, like a good-natured fool, whom bitter knowledge of the world has not cooled down into contempt for a very considerable portion of it, trusted and loved almost every one whom he saw. At that moment there was only one person in the whole world that he hated, viz., the miserable individual—if any such there were—who might have happened to forestall him in the affections of Miss Aubrey. The bare idea made his breath come and go quickly, and his cheek flush. Why, he felt that he had a sort of *right* to Miss Aubrey's heart; for had they not been born, and had they not lived almost all their lives, within a few miles of each other? Had they not often played together?—were not their family estates almost contiguous?—Delamere advanced into the room, assuming as unconcerned an air as he could; but he felt not a little tried when Miss Aubrey, on seeing him, gayly and frankly extended her hand to him, supposing him to have only the moment before entered the house. Poor Delamere's hand slightly quivered as he felt it clasping the soft lilied fingers of her whom he had thus resolved to make his wife; what would he not have given to have carried them to his lips! Now, if I were to say that in the course of that evening, Miss Aubrey did not form a kind—of a sort—of a faint—notion of the possible state of matters with young Delamere, I should not be treating the reader with that eminent degree of candor for which I think he, or she, is at present disposed to give me credit. But Kate was deeply skilled in human nature, and settled the matter by one very just reflection, viz., that Delamere was, in contemplation of law, a mere *infant*—i. e. he wanted yet several weeks of twenty-one! and, therefore, that it was not likely that, etc., etc., etc. And, besides—pooh!—pooh!—'tis a mere *boy*, at College—how ridiculous!—So she gave herself no trouble about the affair; exhibited no symptoms of caution or coyness, but conducted herself just as if he had not been present.

He was a handsome young fellow, too!—

During the evening, Mr. Delamere took an opportunity of asking Miss Aubrey who wrote the verses, which he pointed to, as they lay on the piano. The handwriting, she said, was hers, but the verses were composed by her brother. He asked for the copy, with a slight trepidation. She readily gave it

to him—he receiving it with (as he supposed) a mighty unconcerned air. He read it over that night, before getting into
bed, at least six times; and it was the very first thing he looked
at on getting out of bed in the morning. Now, Miss Aubrey
certainly wrote an elegant hand—but as for *character*, of
course it had none. He could scarce have distinguished it
from the handwriting of any of his cousins or friends—How
should he? All women are taught the same hard, angular,
uniform hand—but good, bad, or indifferent, this was *Kate
Aubrey's* handwriting—and her pretty hand had rested on the
paper while writing—that was enough. He resolved to turn
the verses into every kind of Greek and Latin meter he knew
of—

In short, that here was a "course of true love" *opened*,
seems pretty evident; but whether it will "run smooth" is
another matter.

Their guests having at length departed, Mr. Aubrey, his
wife and sister, soon afterward rose to retire. He went, very
sleepy, straight to his dressing-room; they to the nursery—(a
constant and laudable custom with them)—to see how the
children were going on, as far as they could learn, from their
drowsy attendants. Little Aubrey would have reminded you
of one of the exquisite sketches of children's heads by Reynolds
or Lawrence, as he lay breathing imperceptibly, with his rich
flowing hair spread upon the pillow, in which his face was
partly hid, and his arms stretched out. Mrs. Aubrey put her
finger into one of his hands, which was half open, and which
closed as it were instinctively upon it with a gentle pressure.
"Look, Kate," softly whispered Mrs. Aubrey. Miss Aubrey
leaned forward and kissed his little cheek with an ardor that
almost awoke him. After a glance at a tiny head partly visible above the clothes, in an adjoining bed, and looking like a
rosebud almost entirely hid amongst the leaves, they withdrew.

"The little loves!—how one's heart thrills with looking at
them!" said Miss Aubrey, as they descended.

"Kate!" whispered Mrs. Aubrey, with an arch smile, as
they stood at their respective chamber doors, which adjoined,
"Mr. Delamere is improved—is not he?—Ah, Kate!—I understand!"

"Agnes, how can you?"—hastily answered Miss Aubrey,
with cheeks suddenly crimsoned. "I never heard such nonsense."

"Night, night, Kate! think over it!" said Mrs. Aubrey,
and kissing her beautiful sister-in-law, the next moment the

blooming wife had entered her bedroom. Miss Aubrey slipped into her dressing-room, where Harriet, her maid, was sitting asleep before the fire. Her lovely mistress did not for a few minutes awake her; but placing her candlestick on the toilet-table, stood in a musing attitude.

"It's so perfectly *ridiculous*," at length she said aloud, and up started her maid. Within a quarter of an hour Miss Aubrey was in bed, but by no means asleep.

The next morning, about eleven o'clock, Mr. Aubrey was seated in the library, in momentary expectation of his letters; and a few moments before the postman's *rat-tat* was heard, Mrs. and Miss Aubrey made their appearance, as was their wont, in expectation of anything that might have been upon the cover, in addition to the address—

"CHARLES AUBREY, ESQ., M. P., etc. etc. etc. the words, letters, or figures, "Mrs. Aubrey," or "Miss Aubrey," in the corner. In addition to this, 'twas not an unpleasant thing to skim over the contents of *his* letters! as one by one he opened them; and laid them aside; for both these fair creatures were daughters of Eve, and inherited a *little* of her curiosity. Mr. Aubrey was always somewhat nervous and fidgety on such occasions, and wished them gone; but they only laughed at him, so he was fain to put up with them. On this morning there were more than Mr. Aubrey's usual number of letters; and in casting her eye over them, Mrs. Aubrey suddenly took up one that challenged attention; is bore a black seal, had a deep black bordering, and had the frank of Lord Alkmond, at whose house in Shropshire they had for months been engaged to spend the ensuing Christmas, and were intending to set off on their visit the very next day. The ominous missive was soon torn open; it was from Lord Alkmond himself, who in a few hurried lines announced the sudden death of his brother; so that there was an end of their visit to the Priory.

"Well!" exclaimed Mr. Aubrey, calmly, rising after a pause, and standing with his back to the fire, in a musing posture.

"Has he left any family, Charles?" inquired Mrs. Aubrey with a sigh, her eyes still fixed on the letter.

"I—I really don't know—poor fellow! We lose a vote for Shellington—we shall, to a certainty," he added, with an air of chagrin visibly stealing over his features.

"How politics harden the heart, Charles! Just at this moment to be—" quoth Mrs. Aubrey.

"It *is* too bad, Agnes, I own—but you see," said Mr. Aubrey, affectionately; but added suddenly, "stay, I don't know either, for there's the Grassingham interest come into the field since the last—"

"Charles, I do really almost think," exclaimed Mrs. Aubrey with sudden emotion, stepping to his side, and throwing her arms round him affectionately, "that if *I* were to die, I should be forgotten in a fortnight, if the House were sitting—"

"How *can* you say such things, my love?" inquired Aubrey, kissing her forehead.

"When Agnes was born, you know," she murmured inarticulately. Her husband folded her tenderly in his arms in silence. On the occasion she alluded to, he had nearly lost her; and they both had reason to expect that another similar season of peril was not *very* distant.

"Now, Charles, you *can't* escape," said Miss Aubrey, presently assuming a cheerful tone; "now for dear old Yatton!—"

"Yes, Yatton! Positively you must!" added Mrs. Aubrey, smiling through her tears.

"What! Go to Yatton?" said Mr. Aubrey, shaking his head and smiling. "Nonsense! Why we must set off to-morrow: they've had no warning!"

"What warning does mamma require, Charles?" inquired his sister eagerly. "Isn't the dear old place always in apple-pie order?"

"How you love the 'dear old place,' Kate!" exclaimed Aubrey, in such an affectionate tone as brought his sister in an instant to his side, to urge on her suit; and there stood the lord of Yatton embraced by these two beautiful women, his own heart (*inter nos*) seconding every word they uttered.

"How my mother would stare!" said he at length irresolutely, looking from one to the other, and smiling at their eagerness.

"What a bustle everything will be in!" exclaimed Kate. "I fancy I'm there already! The great blazing fires—the holly and mistletoe. We must all go, Charles—children and all!"

"Why, really, I hardly know—"

"Oh! I've settled it all," quoth Kate, seeing that she had gained her point, and resolved to press her advantage, "and what's more, we've no time to lose; this is Tuesday—Christmas-day is Saturday—we must of course stop a night on the way; but hadn't we better have Griffiths in, to arrange all?" Aubrey rang the bell.

"Request Mr. Griffiths to come to me," said he to the servant who answered the summons.

Within a very few minutes that respectable functionary had

made his appearance and received his instructions. The march
to Shropshire was countermanded—and hey! for Yatton!—for
which they were to start the next day about noon. Mr. Griffiths's
first step was to pack off Sam, Mr. Aubrey's groom, by the
Tally-ho, the first coach to York, starting at two o'clock that
very day, with letters announcing the immediate arrival of the
family. These orders were received by Sam (who had been
born and bred at Yatton) while he was bestowing, with vehement sibilation, his customary civilities on a favorite mare of
his master's. Down dropped his curry-comb; he jumped into
the air; snapped his fingers; then he threw his arms round
Jenny, and tickled her under the chin. "Dang it," said he,
as he threw her another feed of oats, "I wish thee were going
wi' me—dang'd if I don't!" Then he hastily made himself
"a *bit* tidy;" presented himself very respectfully before Mr.
Griffiths, to receive the wherewithal to pay his fare; and having obtained it, off he scampered to the Bull and Mouth, as if
it had been a neck-and-neck race between him and all London,
which should get down to Yorkshire first. A little after one
o'clock, his packet of letters was delivered to him; and within
another hour Sam was to be seen (quite comfortable, with a
draught of spiced ale given him by the cook, to make his hasty
dinner "sit well") on the top of the Tally-ho, rattling rapidly
along the great north road.

"Come, Kate," said Mrs. Aubrey, entering Miss Aubrey's
room, where she was giving directions to her maid, "I've ordered
the carriage to be at the door as soon as it can be got ready;
we must go off to Coutts's—see!" She held in her hand two
slips of paper, one of which she gave Miss Aubrey. 'Twas a
check for one hundred pounds—her brother's usual Christmas-
box—"and then we've a quantity of little matters to buy this
afternoon. Come, Kate, quick! quick!"

Now, poor Kate had nearly spent all her money, which circumstance, connected with another that I shall shortly mention, had given her not a little concern. At her earnest request, her brother had, about a year before, built her a nice
little school, capable of containing some eighteen or twenty
girls, on a slip of land between the vicarage and the park wall
of Yatton, and old Mrs. Aubrey and her daughter found a
resident school-mistress, and, in fact, supported the little
establishment, which, at the time I am speaking of, contained
some seventeen or eighteen of the villagers' younger children.
Miss Aubrey took a prodigious interest in this little school,
scarce a day passing without her visiting it when she was at
Yatton; and what Kate wanted, was the luxury of giving a

Christmas present to both mistress and scholars. That, however, she would have had some difficulty in effecting but for this her brother's timely present, which had quite set her heart at ease. On their return, the carriage was crowded with the things they had been purchasing—articles of clothing for the feebler old villagers; work-boxes, samplers, books, testaments, prayer-books, etc., etc., etc., for the school; the sight of which I can assure the reader, made Kate far happier than if they had been the costliest articles of dress and jewelry.

The next day was a very pleasant one for traveling—"frosty, but kindly." About one o'clock there might have been seen standing before the door the roomy yellow family carriage, with four post-horses, all in traveling trim. In the rumble sat Mr. Aubrey's valet and Mrs. Aubrey's maid—Miss Aubrey's, and one of the nursery-maids, going down by the coach which had carried Sam—the Tally-ho. The coach-box was piled up with that sort of luggage which, by its lightness and bulk, denotes lady traveling: inside were Mrs. and Miss Aubrey, muffled in furs, shawls, and pelisses; a nursery-maid with little Master and Miss Audrey, equally well protected from the cold; and the vacant seat awaited Mr. Aubrey, who at length made his appearance, having been engaged till the latest moment in giving and repeating specific instructions concerning the forwarding of his letters and papers. As soon as he had taken his place, and all had been snugly disposed within, the steps were doubled up, the door was closed, the windows were drawn up—crack! crack! went the whips of the two postilions, and away rolled the carriage over the dry hard pavement.

" Now that's what I call's doing it *uncommon* comfortable," said a pot-boy to one of the footmen at an adjoining house, where he was delivering the porter for the servants' dinner; " how *werry* nice and snug them two looks in the rumble behind!"

" *We* goes to-morrow," carelessly replied the gentleman he was addressing.

" It's a fine thing to be gentlefolk," said the boy, taking up his pot-board.

" Ya as," drawled the footman, twitching up his shirt collar.

On drawing up to the posting-house, which was within about forty miles from Yatton, the Aubreys found a carriage and four just ready to start, after changing horses; and whose should this prove to be but Lord De la Zouch's, containing himself, his lady, and his son. Mr. Delamere. His lordship

and son both alighted on accidentally discovering who had
overtaken them; and coming up to Mr. Aubrey's carriage
windows, exchanged surprised and cordial greetings with its
occupants—whom Lord De la Zouch imagined to have been by
this time on their way to Shropshire.   Mr. Delamere manifested a surprising eagerness about the welfare of little Agnes
Aubrey, who happened to be lying fast asleep in Miss Aubrey's
lap; but the evening was fast advancing, and both the traveling parties had yet before them a considerable portion of their
journey.   After a hasty promise on the part of each to dine
with the other before returning to town for the season—a
promise which *Mr. Delamere* at all events resolved should not
be lost sight of—they parted.   'Twas eight o'clock before Mr.
Aubrey's eye, which had been for some time on the lookout,
caught sight of Yatton woods; and when it did, his heart
yearned toward them.   The moon shone brightly and cheerily, and it was pleasant to listen to the quickening clattering
tramp of the horses upon the dry, hard highway, as the travelers rapidly neared a spot endeared to them by every early
and tender association.   When they had got within half a mile
of the village, they overtook the vicar, who had mounted his
nag, and been out on the road to meet the expected comers,
for an hour before.   Aubrey roused Mrs. Aubrey from her
nap, to point out Dr. Tatham, who by that time was cantering along beside the open window.   'Twas refreshing to see
the cheerful old man—who looked as ruddy and hearty as ever.
  "God bless you all!   All well?" he exclaimed, riding close
to the window.
  "Yes; but how is my mother?" inquired Aubrey.
  "High spirits—high spirits!   Was with her this afternoon!
Have not seen her better for years!   So surprised!   Ah! here's
an old friend—Hector!"
  "Bow-wow-wow-wow!   Bow—Bow-wow!"
  "Papa! papa!" exclaimed the voice of little Charles, struggling to get on his father's lap to look out of the window,
"that is Hector!   I know it is!   He is come to see *me!*   I
want to look at him!"
  Mr. Aubrey lifted him up as he desired, and a huge black-
and-white Newfoundland dog almost leaped up to the window
at sight of him clapping his little hands, as if in eager recog-
nition, and then scampered and bounded about in all directions, barking most boisterously, to the infinite delight of little
Aubrey.   This messenger had been sent on by Sam, the
groom, who had been on the lookout for the travelers for
some time; and the moment he caught sight of the carriage,

pelted down the village, through the park, at top speed, up to the Hall, there to communicate the good news of their safe arrival. The travelers thought that the village had never looked so pretty and picturesque before. The sound of the carriage dashing through it, called all the cottagers to their doors, where they stood bowing and courtesying. It soon reached the park-gates, which were thrown wide open in readiness for its entrance. As they passed the church, they heard its bells ringing a merry peal to welcome their arrival; its faint chimes went to their very hearts.

" My darling Agnes, here we are again in the old place," said Mr. Aubrey in a joyous tone, affectionately kissing Mrs. Aubrey and his sister, as, after having wound their way up the park at almost a gallop, they heard themselves rattling over the stone pavement immediately under the old turreted gateway. On approaching it, they saw lights glancing about in the hall windows; and before they had drawn up, the great door was thrown open, and several servants (one or two of them gray-headed) made their appearance, eager to release the travelers from their long confinement. A great wood fire was crackling and blazing in the ample fire-place in the hall opposite the door, casting a right pleasant and cheerful light over the various antique objects ranged around the walls; but the object on which Mr. Aubrey's eye instantly settled was the venerable figure of his mother, standing beside the fire-place with one or two female attendants. The moment that the carriage door was opened, he stepped quickly out (nearly tumbling, by the way, over Hector, who appeared to think that the carriage-door had been opened only to enable him to jump into it, which he prepared to do).

" God bless you, madam!" said he, tenderly, as he received his mother's fervent but silent greeting, and imagined that the arms folded round him were somewhat feebler than when he had last felt them embracing him. With similar affection was the good old lady received by her daughter and daughter-in-law.

" Where is my pony, grandmamma?" quoth little Aubrey, running up to her (he had been kept quiet for the last eighty miles or so, by the mention of the aforesaid pony, which had been sent to the Hall as a present to him some weeks before). " Where is it? I want to see my little pony directly! Mamma says you have got a little pony for me with a long tail; I *must* see it before I go to bed; I must indeed—is it in the stable?"

" You shall see it in the morning, my darling—the very

fi st thing," said Mrs. Aubrey, fervently kissing her beautiful
little grandson, while tears of joy and pride ran down her
cheek. She then pressed her lips on the delicate but flushed
cheek of little Agnes, who was fast asleep: and as soon as they
had been conducted toward their nursery, Mrs. Aubrey, followed by her children, led the way to the dining-room—the
dear delightful old dining-room, in which all of them had
passed so many happy hours of their lives. It was large and
lofty; and two antique branch silver candlesticks, standing on
sconces upon each side of a strange old straggling carved mantel-piece of inlaid oak, aided by the blaze given out by two immense logs of wood burning beneath, thoroughly illuminated
it. The walls were oak-paneled, containing many pictures,
several of them of great value; and the floor also was of polished oak, over the center of which, however, was spread a
thick richly colored Turkey carpet. Opposite the door
was a large mullioned bay-window, then, however, concealed
behind an ample flowing crimson curtain. On the further
side of the fire-place stood a high-backed and roomy arm-chair,
almost covered with Kate's embroidery, and in which Mrs.
Aubrey had evidently, as usual, been sitting till the moment
of their arrival—for on a small ebony table beside it lay her
spectacles and an open volume. Nearly fronting the fire-
place was a recess, in which stood an exquisitely carved black
ebony cabinet, inlaid with white and red ivory. This Miss
Aubrey claimed as her own, and had appropriated it to her
own purposes ever since she was seven years old. "You dear
old thing!" said she, throwing open the folding-doors—
"Everything just as I left it! Really, dear mamma, I could
skip about the room for joy! I wish Charles would never
leave Yatton again!"

"It's rather lonely, my love, when *none* of you are with
me," said Mrs. Aubrey. "I feel getting older—"

"Dearest mamma," interrupted Miss Aubrey, quickly. "*I*
won't leave you again! I'm quite tired of town—I am indeed!"

Though fires were lighted in their several dressing-rooms, of
which they were more than once reminded by their respective
attendants, they all remained seated before the fire in carriage
costume (except that Kate had thrown aside her bonnet, her
half-unfurled tresses hanging in negligent profusion over her
thickly furred pelisse) eagerly conversing about the little incidents of their journey, and the events which had transpired at
Yatton since they had quitted it. At length, however, they
retired to perform the refreshing duties of the dressing-room,

before sitting down to supper. Of that comfortable meal, within twenty minutes' time or so, they partook with hearty relish. What mortal, however delicate, could resist the fare set before them—the plump capon, the delicious grilled ham, the poached eggs, the floury potatoes, home-baked bread, white and brown—custards, mince-pies, home-brewed ale, as soft as milk, as clear as amber—mulled claret—and so forth? The travelers had evidently never relished anything more, to the infinite delight of old Mrs. Aubrey; who observing, soon afterward, irrepressible symptoms of fatigue and drowsiness, ordered them all off to bed—Kate sleeping in the same chamber in which she sat when the reader was permitted to catch a moonlight glimpse of her, as already more than once referred to.

They did not make their appearance the next morning till after nine o'clock, Mrs. Aubrey having read prayers before the assembled servants, as usual, nearly an hour before—a duty her son always performed when at the Hall—but on this occasion he had overslept himself. He found his mother in the breakfast-room, where she was soon joined by her daughter and daughter-in-law, all of them being in high health and spirits. Just as they were finishing breakfast, little Aubrey burst into the room in a perfect ecstasy—for old Jones had taken him round to the stables, and shown him the little pony which had been bought for him only a few months before. He had heard it neigh—had seen its long tail—had patted its neck —had seen it eat—and now his vehement prayer was, that his papa, and mamma, and Kate would immediately go and see it, and take his little sister also.

Breakfast over, they separated. Old Mrs. Aubrey went to her own room to be attended by her housekeeper; the other two ladies retired to their rooms—Kate principally engaged in arranging her presents for her little scholars: and Mr. Aubrey repaired to his library—as delightful an old snuggery as the most studious recluse could desire—when he was presently attended by his bailiff. He found everything was going on as he could have wished. With one or two exceptions, his rents were paid most punctually; the farms and lands kept in capital condition. To be sure, an incorrigible old poacher had been giving his people a little trouble, as usual, and was committed for trial at the Spring Assizes; a few trivial trespasses had been committed in search of fire-wood, and other small matters; which, after having been detailed with great minuteness by his zealous and vigilant bailiff, were dispatched by Mr. Aubrey with a " pooh, pooh!"—then there was Gregory, who held the smallest farm on the estate, at its southern extremity—he was three quarters' rent in arrear—but he had a sick wife and seven children—so he was at once forgiven all that was due on the ensuing quarter day.—"In fact," said Mr. Aubrey, "don't ask him for any more rent. I'm sure the poor fellow will pay when he's able."

Some rents were to be raised; others lowered; and some half dozen of the poorer cottages were to be forthwith put into good repair, at Mr. Aubrey's expense. The two oxen had been sent, on the preceding afternoon, from the home farm to the butcher's, to be distributed on Christmas-eve among the poorer villagers, according to orders brought down from town by Sam, the day before. Thus was Mr. Aubrey engaged for an hour or two, till luncheon-time, when good Dr. Tatham made his welcome appearance, having been engaged most of the morning in touching up an old Christmas sermon.

He had been vicar of Yatton for nearly thirty years, having been presented to it by the late Mr. Aubrey, with whom he had been intimate at college. He was a delightful specimen of a country parson. Cheerful, unaffected, and good-natured, there was a dash of quaintness or roughness about his manners that reminded you of the crust in very fine old port. He had been a widower, and childless, for fifteen years. His parish had been ever since his family, whom he still watched over with an affectionate vigilance. He was respected and beloved by all. Almost every man, woman, and child that had died in Yatton, during nearly thirty years, had departed with the sound of his kind and solemn voice in their ears. He claimed a sort of personal acquaintance with almost all the grave-stones in his little church-yard; and when he looked at them, his conscience bore him witness, that he had done his duty by the dust that slept underneath. He was at the bedside of a sick person almost as soon as the doctor—no matter what sort of weather, or at what hour of the day or night. Methinks I see him now, bustling about the village, with healthy ruddy cheek, a clear, cheerful eye, hair white as snow; with a small stout figure, clothed in a suit of somewhat rusty black (knee-breeches and gaiters all round the year), and with a small shovel-hat. No one lives in the vicarage with him but an elderly woman, his housekeeper, and her husband, whose chief business is to look after the doctor's old mare and the little garden; in which I have often seen him and his master, with his coat off, digging for hours together. He rises at five in the winter, and four in the summer, being occupied till breakfast with his studies; for he was an excellent scholar, and has not forgotten, in the zealous discharge of his sacred duties, the pursuits of literature and philosophy, in which he gained no inconsiderable distinction in his youth. He derives a moderate income from his living; but it was even more than sufficient for his necessities. Ever since Mr. Aubrey's devotion to politics has carried him away from Yatton for a considerable portion of each year, Dr. Tatham had been the right-hand counselor of old Mrs. Aubrey, in all her pious and charitable plans and purposes. Every New-year's-day, there came from the Hall to the vicarage six dozen of fine old port wine—a present from Mrs. Aubrey; but the little doctor (though he never tells her so) scarce drinks six bottles of them in a year. Two dozen of them go, within a few days' time, to a poor brother parson in an adjoining parish, who, with his wife and three children—all in feeble health—can hardly keep body and soul together, and who, but for this generous brother would not probably taste a glass of wine throughout the year, except on certain occasions when the very humblest may moisten their poor lips with wine—I mean the SACRAMENT—the sublime and solemn festival given by One who doth not forget the poor and destitute, however in their misery they may sometimes think to the contrary!—the remainder of his little present Dr. Tatham distributes in small quantities among such of his parishioners as may require it, and may not happen to have come under the intimate notice of Mrs. Aubrey. Dr. Tatham has known Mr. Aubrey ever since he was about five years old. 'Twas the doctor that first taught him Greek and Latin; and, up to his going to college, gave him the frequent advantage of his learned experience.—But surely I have gone into a very long digression, and must return.

While Miss Aubrey, accompanied by her sister-in-law, and followed by a servant carrying a great bag, filled with articles brought from London the day before, went to the school which I have before mentioned, in order to distribute her prizes and presents, Mr. Aubrey and Dr. Tatham set off on a walk through the village.

"I must really do something for that old steeple of yours, Doctor," said Aubrey, as arm in arm they approached the church. "It looks crumbling away in many parts."

"If you'd only send a couple of masons to repair the *porch*, and make it weather-tight, it would satisfy me for some years to come," said the Doctor.

"Well—we'll look at it," replied Aubrey; and, turning aside, they entered the little church-yard.

"How I love this old yew-tree!" he exclaimed as they

passed under it; "it casts a kind of tender gloom around that always makes me pensive, not to say melancholy!" A sigh escaped him, as his eye glanced at the family vault, which was almost in the center of the shade, where lay his father, three brothers, and a sister, and where, in the course of nature, a few short years would see the precious remains of his mother deposited. But the Doctor who had hastened forward alone for a moment, finding the church door open, called out to Mr. Aubrey, who soon stood within the porch. It certainly required a little repairing, which Mr. Aubrey said should be looked to immediately. "See—we're all preparing for to-morrow," said Dr. Tatham, leading the way into the little church, where the grizzle-headed clerk was busy decorating the pulpit, reading-desk, and altar-piece, with the cheerful emblems of the season.

"I never see these," said the Doctor, taking up one of the sprigs of mistletoe lying on a form beside them, "but I think of your own Christmas verses, Mr. Aubrey, when you were younger and fresher than you now are—don't you recollect them?"

"Oh—pooh!"

"But I remember them," rejoined the Doctor; and he began:

> "'Hail! silvery, modest mistletoe,
> Wreath'd round winter's brow of snow,
> Clinging so chastely, tenderly:
> Hail holly, darkly, richly green,
> Whose crimson berries blush between
> The prickly foliage, modestly.
> Ye winter-flowers, bloom sweet and fair,
> Though Nature's garden else be bare—
> Ye vernal glistening emblems, meet
> To twine a Christmas coronet!'"

"That will do, Doctor," interrupted Aubrey, smiling— "what a memory you have for trifles!"

"Peggy! Peggy!—you're sadly overdoing it," said the Doctor, calling out to the sexton's wife, who was busy at work in the Squire's pew—a large square pew in the nave, near the pulpit. "Why, do you want to hide the Squire's family from the congregation? You're quite putting a holly hedge all round!"

"Please you, sir," quoth Peggy, "I've got so much I don't know where to put it—so, in course, I put it here!"

"Then," said the Doctor, with a smile, looking round the church, "let John get up and stick some of it into those old hatchments; and," looking up at the clerk, busy at work in the pulpit, " don't you put quite so much up there in my candlesticks!"

With this the parson and the squire took their departure. As they passed slowly up the village, which already wore a sort of holiday aspect, they met on all hands with a cordial and respectful greeting. The quiet little public-house turned out some four or five stout steady fellows—all tenants of Mr. Aubrey's—with their pipes in their hands, and who took off their hats, and bowed very low. Mr. Aubrey went up and entered into conversation with them for some minutes—their families and farms, he found, were well and thriving. There was quite a little crowd of women about the shop of Nick Steele, the butcher, who, with an extra hand to help him, was giving out the second ox which had been sent from the Hall, to the persons whose names had been given in to him from Mrs. Aubrey. Further on some were cleaning their little windows, others sweeping their floors, and sprinkling sand over them; most were sticking holly and mistletoe in their windows and over their mantel-pieces. Everywhere, in short, was to be seen that air of quiet preparation for the solemnly cheerful morrow, which fills a thoughtful observer with feelings of pensive but exquisite satisfaction.

Mr. Aubrey returned home toward dusk, cheered and enlivened by his walk. His sudden plunge into the simplicity and comparative solitude of country life—and that country Yatton—had quite refreshed his feelings, and given a tone to his spirits. Of course Dr. Tatham was to dine at the Hall on the morrow; if he did not, indeed, it would have been for the first time during the last five-and-twenty years.

Christmas-eve passed pleasantly and quietly enough at the Hall. After dinner the merry little ones were introduced, and their prattle and romps occupied an hour right joyously. As soon as, smothered with kisses, they had been dismissed to bed, old Mrs. Aubrey composed herself in her great chair to her usual after-dinner's nap, while her son, his wife, and sister, sitting fronting the fire—a decanter or two, and a few wine-glasses and dessert, remaining on the table behind them—sat conversing in a subdued tone, now listening to the wind roaring in the chimney—a sound which not a little enhanced their sense of comfort—then criticising the disposition of the evergreens with which the room was plenteously decorated, and laying out their movements during the ensuing fortnight. Mrs. Aubrey and Kate were, with affectionate earnestness, contrasting to Aubrey the peaceful pleasures of a country life with the restless excitement and endless anxieties of a London political life, to which they saw him more and more addicting himself; he all the while playfully parrying their attacks, but secretly acknowledging the truth and force of what they said, when hark—a novel sound from without, which roused the old lady from her nap. What do you think, dear reader, it was? The voices of little girls singing what seemed to be a Christmas hymn; yes, they caught the words—

> " Hark! the herald angels sing,
> Glory to the new-born king;
> Peace on earth, and mercy mild—"

" Why, surely—it must be your little school-girls," said old Mrs. Aubrey, looking at her daughter, and listening.

" I do believe it is!" quoth Kate, her eyes suddenly filling with tears, as she sat eagerly inclining her ear toward the window.

" They must be standing on the grass-plot just before the window," said Mr. Aubrey: the tiny voices were thrilling his very heart within him. His sensitive nature might be compared to a delicate Æolian harp, which gave forth, with the slightest breath of accident or circumstance,

> " The still, sad music of humanity."

In a few moments he was almost in tears—the sounds were so unlike the fierce and turbulent cries of political warfare to which his ears had been latterly accustomed! The more the poor children sung, the more was he affected. Kate's tears fell fast, for she had been in an excited mood before this little incident occurred. " Do you hear, mamma," said she, " the voice of the poor little thing that was last taken into the school? The little darling!" Kate tried to smile away her emotion; but 'twas in vain. Mr. Aubrey gently drew aside the curtain and pulled up the central blind—and there, headed by their matron, stood the little singers exposed to view, some eighteen in number, ranged in a row on the grass, their small white shawls glistening in the moonlight. The oldest seemed not more than ten or twelve years old, while the younger ones could not be more than five or six. They seemed all singing from their very hearts. Aubrey stood looking at them with very deep interest.

As soon as they had finished their hymn they were conducted into the housekeeper's room, according to orders sent for that purpose from Mrs. Aubrey, and each of them received a little present of money, besides a full glass of Mrs. Jackson's choicest raisin wine, and a currant bun: Kate slipping half a guinea

into the hand of their mistress, to whose wish to afford gratification to the inmates of the Hall was entirely owing the little incident which had so pleased and surprised them.

" A happy Christmas to you, dear papa and mamma!" said little Aubrey, about eight o'clock the next morning, pushing aside the curtain, and trying to clamber up on the high bed where Mr. and Mrs. Aubrey were still asleep—soon, however, they were awoke by the welcome sound!—the morning promised a beautiful day. The air, though cold, was clear; and the branches of the trees visible from their windows were all covered with hoar-frost, which seemed to line them as if with silver fringe. The little bells of Yatton church were ringing a merry peal, but how different in tone and strength from the clangor of the London church-bells!—Christmas was indeed at last arrived—and cheerful were the greetings of those who soon after met at the bountiful breakfast-table. Old Mrs. Aubrey was going to church with them—in fact, not even a domestic was to be left at home that could possibly be spared. By the time that the carriage, with the fat and lazy-looking gray horses, was at the Hall door, the sun had burst out in beauty from an almost cloudless sky. The three ladies rode alone; Aubrey preferring to walk, accompanied by his little son, as the ground was dry and hard, and the distance very short. A troop of some twelve or fourteen servants, male and female, presently followed; and then came Mr. Aubrey, leading along the heir of Yatton—a boy of whom he might well be proud, as the future possessor of his name, his fortune, and his honors. When he had reached the church, the carriage was returning home. Almost the whole congregation stood collected before the church door, to see the Squire's family enter, and reverend were the courtesies and bows with which old Mrs. Aubrey and her lovely companions were received. Very soon after they had taken their places, Mr. Aubrey and his son made their appearance; objects they were of the deepest interest, as they passed along to their pew. A few minutes afterward little Dr. Tatham entered the church in his surplice (which he almost always put on at home) with a face, serious to be sure, but yet overspread with an expression even more bland and benignant than usual. He knew there was not a soul among the little crowd around him that did not really love him, and that did not know how heartily he returned their love. All eyes were of course on the Squire's pew, Mrs. Aubrey was looking well—her daughter and daughter-in-law were thought by all to be by far the most beautiful women in the world—what must people think of them in London? Mr. Aubrey looked, they thought, pleased and happy, but rather paler, and even a little thinner; and as for the little Squire, with his bright eyes, his rosy cheeks, his arch smile, his curling auburn hair—and so like his father and mother—he was the pride of Yatton!

Dr. Tatham read prayers, as he always did, with great distinctness and deliberation, so that everybody in the church, young and old, could catch every syllable; and he preached, considerately enough, a very short sermon—pithy, homely, and affectionate. He reminded them that he was then preaching his thirty-first Christmas-day sermon from that pulpit! The service and sacrament over, none of the congregation moved from their places till the occupants of the Squire's pew had quitted it, but as soon as they had got outside of the door the good people poured out after them, and almost lined the way from the church door to the gate at which the carriage stood, receiving and answering a hundred kind inquiries concerning themselves, their families, and their circumstances.

Mr. Aubrey stayed behind, desirous of taking another little ramble with Dr. Tatham through the village, for the day was indeed bright and beautiful, and the occasion inspiriting. There was not a villager within four or five miles of the Hall who did not sit down that day to a comfortable little relishing dinner, at least one third of them being indebted for it directly to the bounty of the Aubreys. As soon as Dr. Tatham had taken off his gown he accompanied Mr. Aubrey in cheerful mood, in the briskest spirits. 'Twas delightful to see the smoke come curl·ing out of every chimney, scarce any one visible, suggesting to you that they were all housed, and preparing for or partaking of their roast beef and plum-pudding. Now and then the bustling wife would show her heated red face at the door, and hastily courtesy as they passed, then returning to dish up her little dinner.

"Ah, ha; Mr. Aubrey!—isn't such a day as this worth a whole year in town?" exclaimed Dr. Tatham.

"Both have their peculiar influences, Doctor; the pleasure of the contrast would be lost if—Contrast! Believe me, in the language of Virgil— Ah! how goes on old blind Bess, Doctor?" interrupted Aubrey, as they approached the smallest cottage in the village—in fact the very last.

"She's just the same as she has been these last twenty years. Shall we look in on the old creature?"

"With all my heart. I hope, poor soul! that *she* has not been overlooked on this festive occasion."

"Trust Mrs. Aubrey for that! I'll answer for it, we shall find old Bess as happy, in her way, as she can be."

This was a stone-blind old woman, who had been bedridden for the last twenty years. She had certainly passed her hundredth year—some said two or three years before—and had lived in her present little cottage for nearly half a century, having grown out of the recollection of almost all the inhabitants of the village. She had long been a pensioner of Mrs. Aubrey's, by whom alone, indeed, she was supported. Her great age, her singular appearance, and a certain rambling way of talking that she had, earned her the reputation in the village of being able to say strange things; and one or two of the old gossips knew of things coming to pass according to what—poor old soul—she had predicted!

Dr. Tatham gently pushed open the door. The cottage consisted, in fact, of but one room, and that a very small one, and lighted by one only little window. The floor was clean, and evidently just fresh sanded. On a wooden stool, opposite a fire-place, on which a small saucepan pot was placed, sat a girl about twelve years old (a daughter of the woman who lived nearest), crumbling some bread into a basin, with some broth in it. On a narrow bed against the wall, opposite the window, was to be seen the somewhat remarkable figure of the solitary old tenant of the cottage. She was sitting up, resting against the pillow, which was placed on end against the wall. She was evidently a very tall woman, and her long, brown, wrinkled, shriveled face, with prominent cheek-bones and bushy white eyebrows, betokened the possession, in earlier days, of a most masculine expression of features. Her hair, white as snow, was gathered back from her forehead, under a spreading plain white cap; and her sightless eyes, wide open, stared forward with a startling and somewhat sinister expression. She was wrapped round in a clean white bed-gown, and her long thin arms lay straight before her on the outside of the bed-clothes. Her lips were moving, as if she were talking to herself.

" She's a strange-looking object, indeed!" exclaimed Mr. Aubrey, as he and Dr. Tatham stood watching her for a few moments in silence.

" Dame! Dame!" said the Doctor, loudly, approaching her bedside, " how are you to-day? It's Christmas-day—I wish you a merry Christmas."

" Ay, ay—merry, merry! More the merrier! I've seen a hundred and nine of them!"

" You seem very happy, dame."

" They won't give me my broth—my broth," said she, peevishly.

"It's coming, granny," called out the shrill voice of the girl sitting before the fire, quickening her emotions.

"Here's the Squire come to see you, dame, and he wishes you a happy Christmas," said Dr. Tatham.

"What! the Squire? Alive yet? Ah, well-a-day! well-a-day," said she, in a feeble, mournful tone, slowly rubbing together her long, skinny, wrinkled hands, on the backs of which the veins stood out like knotted whip-cord. She repeated the last words several times, in a truly doleful tone, gently shaking her head.

"Granny's been very sad, sir, to-day, and cried two or three times," said the little girl, stirring about the hot broth.

"Poor Squire! doth he not look sad?" inquired the old woman.

"Why should I, dame? What have I to fear?" said Mr. Aubrey.

"Merry in the Hall! all, merry! merry! But no one has heard it but old blind Bess. Where's the Squire?" she added, suddenly turning her face full toward where they were standing—and it seemed whitened with emotion. Her staring eyes were settled on Mr. Aubrey's face, as if she were reading his very soul.

"Here I am, dame," said he, with a great deal of curiosity, to say the least of it.

"Give me your hand, Squire," said she, stretching out her left arm, and working about her talon-like fingers, as if in eagerness to grasp Mr. Aubrey's hand, which he gave her.

"Never fear! never, never! Happy in the Hall! I see all! How long—"

"Why, dame, this is truly a very pleasant greeting of yours," interposed Dr. Tatham, with a smile.

"Short and bitter! long and sweet! Put your trust in God, Squire."

"I hope I do, granny," replied Mr. Aubrey, seriously.

"I see! I hear!—my broth!—where is it?"

"Here it is, granny," said the girl.

"Good-day, dame," said Mr. Aubrey, gently disengaging his hand from hers, and before they had left the cottage she began to swallow very greedily the broth with which the little girl fed her.

"This is the sort of way in which this old superannuated creature has frightened one or two of—"

"Is it, indeed?" inquired Mr. Aubrey, with a sort of mechanical smile. Dr. Tatham saw that he was in a somewhat serious humor.

"She's alarmed *you*, I protest!—I protest she has!" exclaimed the Doctor, with a smile, as they walked along. Now, he knew the disposition and character of Aubrey intimately; and was well aware of a certain tendency he had to superstition.

"My dear Doctor, I assure you that you are mistaken—I am indeed not *alarmed*—but at the same time I will tell you something not a little singular. Would you believe that a month or two ago, when in the town, I dreamed that I heard some one uttering something very much like the words which this old woman has just been uttering?"

"Ah! ha, ha!" laughed the Doctor; and, after a second or two's pause, Aubrey, as if ashamed of what he had said, echoed the laugh, and their conversation passed on to political topics, which kept them engaged for the remainder of their walk, Mr. Aubrey quitting his companion at the door of the vicarage, to be rejoined by him at five o'clock, the dinner hour at the Hall. As Mr. Aubrey walked along the park, the shades of evening casting a deepening gloom around him, his thoughts involuntarily recurred to the cottage of old blind Bess, and he felt vague apprehensions flitting with darkening shade across his mind. Though he was hardly weak enough to attach any definite meaning or importance to the gibberish he had heard, it still had left an unpleasant *impression*, and he was vexed at feeling a wish that the incident—trifling as he was willing to believe it—should not be mentioned by Dr. Tatham at the Hall; and still more, on recollecting that he had *purposely abstained* from requesting the good Doctor not to do so. All this implied that the matter had occupied his thoughts to a greater extent than he secretly relished. On reaching, however, the Hall door, this brief pressure on his feelings quickly ceased; for on entering he saw Mrs. Aubrey, his sister, and his two children, at high romps together in the hall, and he heartily joined in them.

CHAPTER VIII.

By five o'clock the little party were seated at the cheerful dinner-table, covered with the glittering old family plate, and that kind of fare, at once substantial and luxurious, which befitted the occasion. Old Mrs. Aubrey, in her simple white turban and black velvet dress, presided with a kind of dignified cheerfulness which was delightful to see. Kate had contrived to make herself look more lovely even than usual, wearing a dress of dark-blue satin, tastefully trimmed with blonde, and

which exquisitely comported with her beautiful complexion.
Oh, that Delamere had been sitting opposite to, or beside her!
The more matured proportions of her blooming sister-in-law
appeared to infinite advantage in a rich green velvet dress,
while a superb diamond glistened with subdued luster on her
beautiful bosom. She wore no ornaments in her dark hair,
which was, as indeed might be said of Kate, " when unadorned,
adorned the most." The gray-headed old butler, as brisk as
his choicest champagne, with which he perpetually bustled
round the table, and the two steady-looking old family servants, going about their business with quiet celerity—the delicious air of antique elegance around them—this was a Christmas dinner after one's own heart! Oh, the merry and dear old
Yatton! And as if there were not loveliness enough already
in the room, behold the door suddenly pushed open as soon as
the dessert is on the table, and run up to his gay and laughing mother, her little son, his ample snowy collar resting
gracefully on his crimson velvet dress. 'Tis her hope and
pride—her first-born—the little squire; but where is his sister?
—where is Agnes? 'Tis even as Charles says—she fell asleep
in the very act of being dressed, and they were obliged to put
her to bed; so Charles is alone in his glory. You may well
fold your delicate white arm around him, mamma!—

His little gold cup is nearly filled to join in the first toast:
are you all ready? The worthy Doctor has poured Mrs.
Aubrey's glass and Kate's glass full up to the brim:—*Our
next Christmas.*

Yes, your next Christmas! The vigilant eye of Dr. Tatham
alone perceived a faint change of color in Mr. Aubrey's cheek
as the words were uttered; and his eye wandered for an instant, as if tracing across the room the image of old blind
Bess; but 'twas gone in a moment; Aubrey was soon in much
higher spirits than usual. Well he might be. How could
man be placed in happier circumstances than he was? As
soon as the ladies had withdrawn, together with little Aubrey,
the Doctor and Mr. Aubrey drew their chairs before the fire,
and enjoyed a long hour's pleasant chat on matters domestic
and political. As to the latter, the parson and the squire were
stout Tories; and a speech which Aubrey had lately delivered
in the House, on the Catholic claims, had raised him to a pitch
of eminence in the parson's estimation, where he had very few
men in the country to keep him company. The Doctor here
got on very fast indeed, and was just assuring the Squire that
he saw dark days in store for Old England from the machinations of the Papists; and that, for his part, he should rejoice

to "seal his testimony with his blood," and would go to the
stake not only without flinching, but rejoicing—(all which I
verily believe *he* verily believed he would have done)—and
coveting the crown of martyrdom—when Aubrey caught the
sounds of his sister playing on the organ, a noble ·instrument,
which a year or two before, at her urgent request, he had purchased and placed in the drawing-room, whither he and the
Doctor at once repaired.   'Twas a spacious and lofty room,
well calculated for the splendid instrument which occupied the
large recess fronting the door.   Miss Aubrey was playing
Handel, and with an exquisite perception of his matchless
power and beauty.   Hark! did you ever hear the grand yet
simple recitative she is now commencing?

" *In the days of Herod the king, behold, there came wise
men from the East to Jerusalem,*
" *Saying— Where is he that is born King of the Jews ? for
we have seen his star in the East, and are come to worship
him.*"

The Doctor officiated as chaplain that evening.   The room
was almost filled with servants, many of whose looks very
plainly showed the merry doings that had been going on in the
servants' hall; some of them could scarce keep their eyes open;
one or two sat winking at each other, and so forth.   Under
the circumstances, therefore, the Doctor, with much judgment, read very short prayers, and immediately afterward
took his departure for his snug little vicarage.

The next morning, which proved as fine as the preceding,
Mr. Aubrey was detained in-doors with his letters, and one or
two other little matters of business in his library, till luncheon
time.   " What say you, Kate, to a ride round the estate?"
said he, on taking his seat.   Miss Aubrey was delighted, and
forthwith the horses were ordered to be got ready as soon as
possible.

" You must not mind a little rough riding, Kate," said
Aubrey; " for we've got to go over some ugly places.   I'm
going to meet Waters at the end of the avenue, about that old
sycamore—we must have it down at last."

" Oh, no, Charles, no; I thought we had settled that last
year," replied Kate, earnestly.

" Pho! if it had not been for you, Kate, it would have been
down two years ago at least.   Its hour is come at last; 'tis indeed, so no pouting!   It is injuring the other trees; and, beside, it spoils the prospect from the back of the house."

" 'Tis only Waters that puts all these things into your head,

Charles, and I shall let him know *my* opinion on the subject
when I see him! Mamma, haven't *you* a word to say for the
old—''

But Mr. Aubrey, not deeming it discreet to await the new
force which was being brought against him, started off to go
round and see a newly purchased horse, just brought to the
stables.

Kate, who really became everything, looked charming in
her blue riding-habit, sitting on her horse with infinite ease
and grace—a capital horsewoman. The exercise soon brought
a rich bloom upon her cheek; and as she cantered along the
road by the side of her brother, no one that met them but
must have been struck with her beauty. Just as they had
dropped into an easy walk—

"Charles," said she, observing two horsemen approaching
them, "who can these be? Heavens! did you ever see such
figures? And how they ride!''

"Why, certainly," replied her brother, smiling, "they look
a brace of undoubted Cockneys! what can they be doing in
these parts?''

"Dear me, what puppies!" exclaimed Miss Aubrey, lowering her voice as they neared the persons she spoke of.

"They *are* certainly a most extraordinary couple! Who
can they be?" said Mr. Aubrey, a smile forcing itself into his
features. One of the two was dressed in a light blue surtout,
with the tip of a white pocket-handkerchief seen peeping out
of a pocket in the front of it. His hat, with scarce any brim
to it, was stuck aslant on the top of a bushy head of queer-
colored hair. His shirt collars were turned down completely
over his stock, displaying a great quantity of dirt-colored hair
under his chin; while a pair of mustaches, of the same color,
were sprouting upon his upper lips. A quizzing-glass was
stuck in his right eye, and in his hand he carried a whip with
a shining silver head. The other was almost equally distinguished by the elegance of his appearance. He had a glossy
hat, a purple-colored velvet waistcoat, two pins connected by
little chains in his stock, a bottle-green surtout, sky-blue
trousers. In short, who should these be but our old friends
Messrs. Titmouse and Snap? Whoever they might be, it was
plain that they were perfect novices on horseback, and their
horses had every appearance of having been much fretted and
worried by their riders. To the surprise of Mr. Aubrey and
his sister, these two personages attempted to rein in, as they
neared, with the evident intention of speaking to them.

"Pray—a—sir, will you, sir, tell us," commenced Titmouse, with a desperate attempt to appear at his ease, as he tried to make his horse stand still for a moment—"isn't there a place called—called "—here his horse, whose sides were constantly being galled by the spurs of its unconscious rider, began to back a little, then to go on one side, and, in Titmouse's fright, his glass dropped from his eye, and he seized hold of the pommel. Nevertheless, to show the lady how completely he was at his ease all the while, he leveled a great many oaths and curses at the unfortunate eyes and soul of his wayward brute; who, however, not in the least moved by them, but infinitely disliking the spurs of its rider and the twisting round of its mouth by the reins, seemed more and more inclined for mischief, and backed close up to the edge of the ditch.

"I'm afraid, sir," said Mr. Aubrey, kindly, "you are not much accustomed to riding. Will you permit *me*—"

"Oh, yes—ye—ye—s, sir, I am uncommon—whee-o-uy! whuoy!"—(then a fresh volley of oaths.) "Oh, dear, 'pon my soul—ho!—what—what *is* he going to do! Snap! Snap!" —'Twas, however, quite in vain to call on that gentleman for assistance; for he had grown as pale as death, on finding that his own brute seemed strongly disposed to follow the infernal example of the other, and was particularly inclined to rear up on its hind legs. The very first motion of the sort brought Snap's heart (not large enough, perhaps, to choke him) into his mouth. Titmouse's beast suddenly inclined the contrary way, and throwing its hind feet into the air, sent its terrified rider flying, head over heels, into the very middle of the hedge, from which he dropped into the wet ditch. Both Mr. Aubrey and his groom dismounted, and secured the horse, who, having got rid of its ridiculous rider, stood quietly enough. Titmouse proved to be more frightened than hurt. His hat was crushed flat on his head, and half the left side of his face covered with mud—as, indeed, were his clothes all the way down. The groom (almost splitting with laughter) helped him on again; and as Mr. and Miss Aubrey were setting off—"I think, sir," said the former, politely, "you were inquiring for some place?"

"Yes, sir," quoth Snap. "Isn't there a place called Ya— Yat—Yat—(be quiet, you brute)—Yatton about here?"

"Yes, sir—straight on," replied Mr. Aubrey. Miss Aubrey hastily threw her veil over her face, to conceal her laughter, spurred her horse, and she and her brother were soon out of sight of the strangers.

"I say, Snap," quoth Titmouse, when he had in a measure

cleansed himself, and they had both got a little composed, " see that lovely gal?"

" Fine girl—devilish fine!" replied Snap.

" I'm blessed if 1 don't think—'pon my life, I believe we've met before!"

" Didn't seem to know you though!—"

" Ah! I don't know—how uncommon infernal unfortunate to happen just at the moment when—" Titmouse became silent; for all of a sudden he recollected when and where, and under what circumstances he had seen Miss Aubrey before, and which his vanity would not allow of his telling Snap. The fact was, that she had once accompanied her sister-in-law to Messrs. Tag-rag and Company's, to purchase some small matter of mercery. Titmouse had helped her, and his absurdity of manner had provoked a smile, which Titmouse a little misconstrued; for when, a Sunday or two afterward, he met her in the Park, the little fool had the presumption to nod to her—she having not the slightest notion who he was— and of course not having, on the present occasion, the least recollection of him. The reader will remember that this little incident made a deep impression on the mind of Mr. Titmouse.

The coincidence was really not a little singular—but to return to Mr. Aubrey and his sister. After riding a mile or two further up the road, they leaped over a very low mound or fence, which formed the extreme boundary of that part of the estate, and having passed through a couple of fields, they entered the lower extremity of that fine avenue of elms, at the higher end of which stood Kate's favorite tree, and also Waters and his under-bailiff—who looked to her like a couple of executioners, only awaiting the fiat of her brother. The sun shone brightly upon the doomed sycamore—" the ax was laid at its root." As they rode up the avenue Kate begged very hard for mercy; but for once her brother seemed obdurate— the tree, he said, *must* come down—'twas all nonsense to think of having it standing any longer!—

" Remember, Charles," said she, passionately, as they drew up, " how we've all of us romped and sported under it! Poor papa also—"

" See, Kate, how rotten it is," said her brother; and riding close to it, with his whip he snapped off two or three of its feeble silvery-gray branches—" it's high time for it to come down."

" It fills the grass all around with little branches, sir, when ever there's the least breath of wind," said Waters.

"It won't hardly hold a crow's weight on the topmost branches, sir," said Dickons, the under-bailiff.

"Had it any leaves last summer?" inquired Mr. Aubrey.

"I don't think, sir," said Waters, "it had a hundred all over it!"

"Really, Kate, 'tis such a melancholy, unsightly object, when seen from any part of the Hall "—turning round on his horse to look at the rear of the Hall, which was at about eighty yards' distance. "It looks such an old withered thing among the fresh green trees around it—'tis quite a painful contrast." Kate had gently urged on her horse while her brother was speaking, till she was close beside him.

"Charles," said she, in a low whisper, "does not it remind you a little of poor old mamma, with her gray hairs, among her children and grandchildren? *She* is not out of place among *us*—is she?" Her eyes filled with tears. So did her brother's.

"Dearest Kate," said he, with emotion, affectionately grasping her little hand, "you have triumphed! The old tree shall never be cut down in my time! Waters, let the tree stand, and if anything *is* to be done to it—let the greatest *care* be taken of it." Miss Aubrey turned her head aside to conceal her emotion. Had they been alone she would have flung her arms round her brother's neck.

"If I were to speak my mind," said Waters, seeing the turn things were taking, "I should say, with our young lady, the old tree's quite a kind of ornament in this here situation, and (as one might say) it sets off the rest." [It was he who had been worrying Mr. Aubrey for these last three years to have it cut down.]

"Well," replied Mr. Aubrey, "however that may be, let me hear no more of cutting it down.—Ah! what does old Jolter want here?" said he, observing an old tenant of that name, almost bent double with age, hobbling toward them. He was wrapped up in a coarse thick blue coat; his hair was long and white; his eyes dim and glassy with age.

"I don't know, sir—I'll go and see," said Waters. "What's the matter, Jolter?" he inquired, stepping forward to meet him.

"Nothing much, sir," replied the old man, taking off his hat, and bowing very low toward Mr. and Miss Aubrey.

"Put your hat on, my old friend," said Mr. Aubrey, kindly.

"I only come to bring you this bit of paper, sir, if you please," said the old man, addressing Waters. "You said, a while ago, as how I was always to bring you papers that were

left with me, and this "—taking one out of his pocket—" was
left with me only about an hour ago. It's seemingly a lawyer's
paper, and was left by an uncommon gay young chap. He
ask me my name, and then he looked at the paper, and read it
all over to me, but I couldn't make anything of it."

"What is it?" inquired Mr. Aubrey, as Waters cast his eye
over a sheet of paper, partly printed and partly written.

"Why, it seems the old story, sir—that slip of waste land,
sir. Mr. Tomkins is at it again, sir."

"Well, if he chooses to spend money in that way, I can't
help it," said Mr. Aubrey, with a smile. "Let me look at
the paper." He did so. "Yes, it seems the same kind of
thing as before. Well," handing it back, "send it to Mr.
Parkinson, and tell him to look to it, and, at all events, take
care that poor old Jolter comes to no trouble by the business.
How's the old wife, Jacob?"

"She's dreadful bad with rheumatis, sir, but the stuff that
Madam sends her does her a woundy deal of good, sir, in her
inside."

"Well, we must try if we can't send you some more; and,
harkee, if the goodwife doesn't bet better soon, send us up
word to the Hall, and we'll have the doctor call on her.
Now, Kate, let us away homeward." And they were soon
out of sight.

I do not intend to deal so unceremoniously or summarily as
Mr. Aubrey did with the document which had been brought to
his notice by Jolter, then handed over to Waters, and by him,
according to orders, transmitted then next day to Mr. Parkinson, Mr. Aubrey's attorney. It was what is called a "DE-
CLARATION IN EJECTMENT;" touching which, in order to throw
a ray or two of light upon a document which will make no
small figure in this history, I shall try to give the reader a little information on the point; and hope that a little attention
to what now follows will be repaid in due time.

If _Jones_ claims a _debt_ or _goods_, or _gamades_ from _Smith_, one
would think that, if he went to law, the action would be entitled "Jones _versus_ Smith;" and so it is. But behold, if it
be LAND which is claimed by Jones from Smith, the style and
name of the cause stand thus:—"DOE, on the demise of Jones,
versus ROE." Instead, therefore, of Jones and Smith fighting
out the matter in their own proper names, they set up a couple
of puppets (called "John Doe" and "Richard Roe") who
fall upon one another in a very quaint fashion, after the manner of Punch and Judy. John Doe pretends to be the real
plaintiff, and Richard Roe the real defendant. John Doe says

that the land which Richard Roe has is his (the said John
Doe's) because *Jones* (the real plaintiff) gave him a lease of it;
and *Jones* is then called " the lessor of the plaintiff. " John
Doe further says that one Richard Roe (who calls himself by
the very significant and expressive name of a " *Casual Ejector*,"
came and turned him out, and so John Doe brings his action
against Richard Roe. 'Tis a fact that whenever land is sought
to be recovered in England, this anomalous and farcical proceeding must be adopted. It is the duty of the *real* plaintiff
(Jones) to serve on the *real* defendant (Smith) a copy of the
queer document which I shall proceed to lay before the reader;
and also to append to it an affectionate note, intimating the
serious consequences which will ensue upon inattention or con-
tumacy. The " Declaration," then, which had been served
upon old Jolter, was in the words, letters, and figures following—that is to say:—

" IN THE KING'S BENCH.
" Michaelmas Term, —th Geo.—

" YORKSHIRE, to-wit:—Richard Roe was attached to answer
John Doe of a plea wherefore the said Richard Roe, with force
and arms, etc., entered into two messuages, two dwelling-
houses, two cottages, two stables, two outhouses, two yards,
two gardens, two orchards, twenty acres of land covered with
water, twenty acres of arable land, twenty acres of pasture
land, and twenty acres of other land, with the appurtenances,
situated in the parish of *Yatton*, in the county of Yorkshire,
which TITTLEBAT TITMOUSE, Esquire, had demised to the said
John Doe for a term which is not yet expired, and ejected him
from his said farm, and other wrongs to the said John Doe
there did, to the great damage of the said John Doe, and
against the peace of our Lord the King, etc.; and Thereupon
the said John Doe, by OILY GAMMON, his attorney, com-
plains,—

" That whereas the said TITTLEBAT TITMOUSE, on the —th
day of August, in the year of our Lord 18—, at the parish
aforesaid, in the county aforesaid, had demised the same tenements, with the appurtenances, to the said John Doe, to have
and to hold the same to the said John Doe and his assigns
thenceforth, for and during, and unto the full end and term
of twenty years thence next ensuing, and fully to be completed
and ended: By virtue of which said demise, the said John Doe
entered into the said tenements, with the appurtenances, and
became and was thereof possessed for the said term, so to him
thereof granted as aforesaid. And the said John Doe being so

thereof possessed, the said Richard Roe afterward, to-wit, on the day and year aforesaid, at the parish aforesaid, in the county aforesaid, with force and arms, etc., entered into the said tenements, with the appurtenances, which the said TITTLEBAT TITMOUSE had demised to the said John Doe in manner and for the term aforesaid, which is not yet expired, and ejected the said John Doe from his said farm; and other wrongs to the said John Doe then and there did, to the great damage of the said John Doe, and against the peace of our said Lord the now King. Wherefore the said John Doe saith that he is injured, and hath sustained damage to the value of £50, and therefore he brings his suit, etc.

"SQUEAL, for the Plaintiff.

GROWL, for the Defendant.

{ Pledges of } John Den.
{ Prosecution. } Richard Fenn.

"MR. JACOB JOLTER,

"I am informed that you are in possession of, or claim title to, the premises in this Declaration of Ejectment mentioned, or to some part thereof: And I, being sued in this action as a *casual ejector* only, and having no claim or title to the same, do advise you to appear, next Hilary Term, in His Majesty's Court of Common Pleas at Westminster, by some attorney of that Court; and then and there, by a rule to be made by the same Court, to cause yourself to be made defendant in my stead; otherwise, I shall suffer judgment to be entered against me by default, and you will be turned out of possession.

"Your loving friend,

"RICHARD ROE.

"Dated this 8th day of December, 18—."

———

You may regard the above document in the light of a deadly and destructive missile, thrown by an unperceived enemy into a peaceful citadel, attracting no particular notice from the innocent, unsuspecting inhabitants—among whom, nevertheless, it presently explodes, and all is terror, death and ruin.

Mr. Parkinson, Mr. Aubrey's solicitor, who resided at Grilston, the post-town nearest to Yatton, from which it was distant about six or seven miles, was sitting on the evening of Tuesday, the 28th of December, 18—, in his office, nearly finishing a letter to his London agents, Messrs. Runnington and Company—one of the most eminent firms in the profession—and which he was desirous of dispatching by that night's mail. Among other papers which have come into my hands in con-

nection with this history, I have happened to light on the
letter Mr. Parkinson was writing; and as it is not long, and
affords a specimen of the way in which business is carried on
between town and country attorneys and solicitors, here fol-
loweth a copy of it:—

" Grilston, 28th Dec., 18—

" DEAR SIRS,

" *Re Middleton.*

" Have you got the marriage-settlements between these parties ready? If so, please send them as soon as possible; for
both the lady's and gentleman's friends are (as usual in such
cases) very pressing for them.

" *Puddinghead* v. *Quickwit.*

" Plaintiff bought a horse of defendant in November last,
' warranted sound,' and paid for it on the spot £64.   A week
afterward his attention was accidentally drawn to the animal's
head; and, to his infinite surprise, he discovered that the left
eye was a *glass eye*, so closely resembling the other in color,
that the difference could not be discovered except on a very
close examination.   I have seen it myself, and it is indeed
wonderfully well done.   My countrymen are certainly pretty
sharp hands in such matters—but this beats anything I ever
heard of.   Surely this is a breach of the warranty?   Or is it to
be considered a *patent* defect, which would not be within the
warranty?—Please take pleader's opinion, and particularly as
to whether the horse could be brought into court to be viewed
by the court and jury, which would have a great effect.   If
your pleader thinks the action will lie, let him draw declaration, *venue*—Lancashire (for my client would have no chance
with a Yorkshire jury).   If you think the *venue* is transitory,
and that defendant would not be successful in a motion,
change it.   *Qu.*—Is the man who sold the horse to defendant
a competent witness for the plaintiff, to prove that, when he
sold it to defendant, it had but one eye, and that on this account the horse was sold for less?

" *Mule* v. *Stott.*

" I can not get these parties to come to an amicable settlement.   You may remember, from the two former actions,
that it is for damages on account of two geese of defendant
having been found trespassing on a few yards of Chatmoss belonging to the plaintiff.   Defendant now contends that he is
entitled to common, *pour cause de vicinage.   Qu.*—Can this
be shown under Not Guilty, or must it be pleaded specially?—

8

About two years ago, by the way, a pig belonging to plaintiff got into defendant's flower-garden, and did at least £3 worth of damage—Can this be in any way set off against the present action? There is now no hope of avoiding a third trial, as the parties are now more exasperated against each other than ever, and the expense (as at least fifteen witnesses will be called on each side) will amount to upward of £250. You had better retain Mr. Cacklegander.

" Re Lords Oldacre and De la Zouch.

"Are the deeds herein engrossed? As it is a matter of magnitude, and the foundation of extensive and permanent family arrangements, pray let the greatest care be taken to secure accuracy. Please take special care of the stamps—"

Thus far had the worthy writer proceeded with his letter, when Waters made his appearance, delivering to him the declaration in ejectment which had been served upon old Jolter, and also the instructions concerning it which had been given by Mr. Aubrey. After Mr. Parkinson had asked particularly concerning Mr. Aubrey's health, and what had brought him so suddenly to Yatton, he cast his eye hastily over the " Declaration "—and at once came to the same conclusion concerning it which had been arrived at by Waters and Mr. Aubrey, viz., that it was another little arrow out of the quiver of the litigious Mr. Tomkins. As soon as Waters had left, Mr. Parkinson thus proceeded to conclude his letter:—

" Doe dem. Titmouse v. Roe.

"I inclose you Declaration herein, served yesterday. No doubt it is the disputed slip of waste land adjoining the cottage of old Jacob Jolter, a tenant of Mr. Aubrey of Yatton, that is sought to be recovered. I am quite sick of this petty annoyance, as also is Mr. Aubrey, who is now down here. Please call on Messrs. Quirk, Gammon and Snap, of Saffron Hill, and settle the matter finally, on the best terms you can; it being Mr. Aubrey's wish that old Jolter (who is very feeble and timid) should suffer no inconvenience. I observe a new lessor of the plaintiff, with a very singular name. I suppose it is the name of some prior holder of the little property at present held by Mr. Tomkins.

"Hoping soon to hear from you (particularly about the marriage-settlement), I am,

"Dear Sirs,

"(With all the compliments of the season)

"Yours truly,

"JAMES PARKINSON.

"P.S.—The oysters and codfish came to hand in excellent order, for which please accept my best thanks.

"I shall remit you in a day or two £100 on account."

This letter, lying among some twenty or thirty similar ones on Mr. Runnington's table, on the morning of its arrival in town, was opened in its turn; and then, in like manner, with most of the others, handed over to the managing clerk, in order that he might inquire into and report upon the state of the various matters of business referred to. As to the last item in Mr. Parkinson's letters, there seemed no particular reason for hurrying; so two or three days had elapsed before Mr. Runnington, having some other little business to transact with Messrs. Quirk, Gammon and Snap, bethought himself of looking at his Diary, to see if there was something else that he had to do with them. Putting, therefore, the Declaration in *Doe d. Titmouse* v. *Roe* into his pocket, it was not long before he was at the office in Saffron Hill—and in the very room in it which had been the scene of several memorable interviews between Mr. Tittlebat Titmouse and Messrs. Quirk, Gammon and Snap. I shall not detail what transpired on that occasion between Mr. Runnington and Messrs. Quirk and Gammon, with whom he was closeted for nearly an hour. On quitting the office his cheek was flushed, and his manner somewhat excited. After walking a little way in a moody manner, and with a slow step, he suddenly jumped into a hackney-coach, and within a quarter of an hour's time had secured an inside place in the Tally-ho coach, which started for York at two o'clock that afternoon—much doubting within himself, the while, whether he ought not to have set off at once in a post-chaise and four. He then made one or two calls in the Temple; and, hurrying home to the office, made hasty arrangements for his sudden journey into Yorkshire. He was a calm and experienced man—in fact, a first-rate man of business, and you may be assured that this rapid and decisive movement of his had been the result of some very startling disclosures made to him by Messrs. Quirk and Gammon.

Now, let us glide back to the delightful solitude which we reluctantly quitted so short a time ago.

Mr. Aubrey was a studious and ambitious man; and in acceding so readily to the wishes of his wife and sister, to spend the Christmas recess at Yatton, had been not a little influenced by one consideration, which he had not thought it worth while to mention—namely, that it would afford him an opportunity of addressing himself with effect to a very important and com-

plicated question, which was to be brought before the House
shortly after its reassembling, and of which he then knew
scarcely anything at all.   For this purpose he had had a quantity of Parliamentary papers, etc., etc., etc., packed up and
sent down by coach; and he quite gloated over the prospect of
their being duly deposited upon his table, in the tranquil leisure
of his library at Yatton.   But quietly as he supposed all this
to have been managed, Mrs. Aubrey and Kate had a most accurate knowledge of his movements; and resolved within themselves (being therein comforted and assisted by old Mrs.
Aubrey) that, as at their instances Mr. Aubrey had come
down to Yatton, so they would take care that he should have
not merely nominal, but real holidays, unless he thought fit to
rise at an early hour in the morning (which Mrs. Aubrey,
junior, took upon herself to say *she* would take care should
never be the case), it was decreed that he should not be allowed
to waste more than two hours a day in his library.   'Twas
therefore in vain for him to sit at breakfast with an eye aslant
and thought-laden brow, as if meditating a long day's seclusion; somehow or another, he never got above an hour to himself.   He was often momentarily petulant on these occasions,
and soon saw through the designs of his enemies: but he so
heartily and tenderly loved them—so thoroughly appreciated
the affection which dictated their little maneuvers—that he
soon surrendered at discretion, and, in fact, placed himself
almost entirely at their mercy; resolving to make up for lost
time on his return to town, and earnestly hoping that the interests of the nation would not suffer in the meanwhile!   In
short, the ladies of Yatton had agreed on their line of operations: that almost every night of their stay in the country
should be devoted either to entertaining or visiting their neighbors; and, as a preparatory movement, that the days (weather
permitting) should be occupied with exercise in the open air
making " morning " calls on neighbors at several miles' distance from the Hall, and from each other; and from which
they generally returned only in time enough to dress for dinner.   As soon, indeed, as the *York True Blue* (the leading
county paper) had announced the arrival at Yatton of " Charles
Aubrey, Esq., M. P., and his family, for the Christmas recess," the efforts of Mrs. and Miss Aubrey were most powerfully seconded by a constant succession of visitors—by

" Troops of friends,"

as the lodge-keeper could have testified; for he and his buxom
wife were continually opening and shutting the great gates.

On the Monday after Christmas-day (*i. e.* the day but one following) came cantering up to the Hall Lord De la Zouch and Mr. Delamere, of course staying to luncheon, and bearing a most pressing invitation from Lady De la Zouch, zealously backed by themselves, for the Aubreys to join a large party at Fotheringham Castle on New-year's-eve. This was accepted —a day and a night were thus gone at a swoop. The same thing happened with the Oldfields, their nearest neighbors; with Sir Percival Pickering at Luddington Court, where was a superb new picture-gallery to be critically inspected by Mr. Aubrey; the Earl of Oldacre, a college friend of Mr. Aubrey's —the venerable Lady Stratton, the earliest friend and school-fellow of old Mrs. Aubrey, and so forth. Then Kate had several visits to pay on her own account; and, being fond of horseback, she did not like riding about the country with only a groom in attendance on her; so her brother *must* accompany her on these occasions. The first week of their stay in the country was devoted to visiting their neighbors and friends in the way I have stated; the next was to be spent in receiving them at Yatton, during which time the old Hall was to ring with merry hospitality.

Then there was a little world of other matters to occupy Mr. Aubrey's attention, and which naturally crowded upon him, living so little at Yatton as he had latterly. He often had a kind of levee of his humbler neighbors, tenants, and constituents; and on these occasions his real goodness of nat-ure, his simplicity, his patience, his forbearance, his sweetness of temper, his benevolence, shone conspicuous. With all these more endearing qualities, there was yet a placid dignity about him that chilled undue familiarity and repelled presumption. He had here no motive or occasion for ostentation, or, as it is called, popularity-hunting. In a sense it might be said of him, that he was "monarch of all he surveyed." It is true, he was member for the borough—an honor, however, for which he was indebted to the national influence of his commanding position—one which left him his own master, not converting him into a paltry delegate, hand-cuffed by pledges on public questions, and laden with injunctions concerning petty local interests only—liable, moreover, to be called to an account at any moment by ignorant and insolent demagogues — but a member of Parliament training to become a statesman, pos-sessed of a free will, and therefore capable of independent and enlightened deliberations; placed by his fortune above the reach of temptation—but I shall not go any further, for the portraiture of a member of Parliament of those days suggests

such a humiliating and bitter contrast, that I shall not ruffle
either my own or my reader's temper by touching it any further.   On the occasions I have been alluding to, Mr. Aubrey
was not only condescending and generous, but practically acute
and discriminating: qualities of his, these latter, so well
known, however, as to leave him at length scarce any opportunities of exercising them. His quiet but decisive interference
put an end to a number of local unpleasantnesses and annoyances, and caused his increasing absence from Yatton to be
very deeply regretted.   Was a lad or a wench taking to idle
and dissolute courses?   A kind, or, as the occasion required, a
stern expostulation of his—for he was a justice of the peace
moreover—brought them to their senses.   He had a very
happy knack of reasoning and laughing quarrelsome neighbors into reconciliation and good humor.   He had a very keen
eye after the practical details of agriculture; he was equally
quick at detecting an inconvenience, and appreciating—sometimes even suggesting—a remedy; and had, on several occasions, brought such knowledge to bear very effectively upon
discussions in Parliament.   His constituents, few in number
undoubtedly, and humble, were quite satisfied with and proud
of their member; and his unexpected appearance diffused
among them real and general satisfaction.   As a landlord, he
was beloved by his numerous tenantry; and well he might—
for never was there so easy and liberal a landlord; he might at
any time have increased his rental by £1500 or £2000 a year, as
his steward frequently intimated to him—but in vain.   "Ten
thousand a year," said Mr. Aubrey, "is far more than my
necessities require—it affords me and my family every luxury
that I can conceive of, and its magnitude reminds me constantly that hereafter I shall be called upon to give a very
strict and solemn account of *my* stewardship."   I would I had
time to complete, as it ought to be completed, this portraiture
of a true Christian gentleman!

As he rode up to the Hare and Hounds Inn, at Grilston,
one morning, to transact some little business, and also to look
in on the Farmers' Club, which was then holding one of its
fortnightly meetings (all touching their hats and bowing to
him on each side of the long street as he slowly passed up it)
he perceived one of his horse's feet limp a little.   On dis-
mounting, therefore, he stopped to see what was the matter,
while the groom took up the foot to examine it.

"Dey-vilish fine horse!" exclaimed the voice of one standing close beside him, and in a tone of most disagreeable confidence.   The exclamation was addressed to Mr. Aubrey; who,

on turning to the speaker, beheld a young man—'twas Titmouse—dressed in a style of the most extravagant absurdity. One hand was stuck into the hinder pocket of a stylish topcoat (the everlasting tip of a white pocket-handkerchief glistening at the mouth of his breast-pocket) and the other held a cigar in his mouth from which, as he addressed Mr. Aubrey with an air of signal assurance, he slowly expelled the smoke that he had inhaled. Mr. Aubrey turned toward him with a cold and surprised air, without replying, at the same time wondering where he had seen the ridiculous object before.

"The horses in these parts aren't to be compared with them at London—eh, sir?" quoth Titmouse, approaching closer to Mr. Aubrey and his groom, to see what the latter was doing—who, on hearing Titmouse's last sally, gave him a very significant look.

"I'm afraid the people here won't relish your remarks, sir!" replied Mr. Aubrey, hardly able to forbear a smile, at the same time with an astonished air scanning the figure of his companion from head to foot.

"Who cares?" inquired Titmouse, with a very energetic oath. At this moment up came a farmer, who, observing Mr. Aubrey, made him a very low bow. Mr. Aubrey's attention being at the moment occupied with Titmouse, he did not observe the salutation; not so with Titmouse, who, conceiving it to have been directed to himself, acknowledged it by taking off his hat with great grace! Mr. Aubrey followed into the house, having ordered his groom to bring back the horse in an hour's time.

"Pray," said he mildly to the landlady, "who is the person smoking the cigar outside?"

"Why, sir," she replied, "he's a Mr. *Brown;* and has another with him here—who's going up to London by this afternoon's coach—this one stays behind a day or two longer. They're queer people, sir. Such dandies! Do nothing but smoke, and drink brandy and water, sir; only that t'other writes a good deal."

"Well, I wish you would remind him," said Mr. Aubrey, smiling "that, if he thinks fit to speak to *me* again, or in my presence, I am a magistrate, and have the power of fining him ive shillings for every oath he utters."

"What! sir, has he been speaking to *you?* Well, I never— ie's the most forward little upstart I ever seed!" said she, lropping her voice; "and the sooner he takes himself off from here the better; for he's always winking at the maids and talk ing impudence to them. I'se box his ears, I warrant him, one of these times!" Mr. Aubrey smiled and went upstairs.

"There don't seem much wrong," quoth Titmouse to the groom, with a condescending air, as soon as Mr. Aubrey had entered the house.

"Much you know about it, I don't guess!" quoth Sam, with a contemptuous smile.

"Who's your master, fellow?" inquired Titmouse, knocking off the ashes from the tip of his cigar.

"A gentleman. What's *yours?*"

"Curse your impudence, you vagabond—" The words were hardly out of his mouth before Sam, with a slight tap of his hand, had knocked Titmouse's glossy hat off his head, and Titmouse's purple-hued hair stood exposed to view, provoking the jeers and laughter of one or two by-standers. Titmouse appeared about to strike the groom; who, hastily giving the bridles of his horses into the hands of an hostler, threw himself into boxing attitude; and, being a clean, tight-built stout young fellow, looked a very formidable object, as he came squaring nearer and nearer to the dismayed Titmouse; and on behalf of the outraged honor of all the horses of Yorkshire, was just going to let fly his *one-two*, when a sharp tapping at the bow-window overhead startled him for a moment, interrupting his war-like demonstrations: and, on casting up his eyes, he beheld the threatening figure of his master, who was shaking his whip at him. He dropped his guard, touched his hat very humbly, and resumed his horses' bridles; muttering, however, to Titmouse, "If thou'rt a man come down into t' yard, and I'll mak thee think a horse kicked thee, a liar as thou art!"

"Who's that gentleman gone upstairs?" inquired Titmouse of the landlady, after he had sneaked into the inn.

"Squire Aubrey of Yatton," she replied, tartly. Titmouse's face, previously pale, flushed all over. "Ay, ay," she continued sharply—"thou *must* be chattering to the grand folks, and thou'st nearly put thy foot into 't at last, I can tell thee; for that's a magistrate, and thou'st been a-swearing afore him."

Titmouse smiled rather faintly; and entering the parlor, affected to be engaged with a county newspaper; and he remained very quiet for upward of an hour, not venturing out of the room till he had seen off Mr. Aubrey and his formidable Sam.

It was the hunting season; but Mr. Aubrey, though he had as fine horses as were to be found in the county, and which were always at the service of his friends, partly from want of inclination and partly from the delicacy of his constitution, never shared in the sports of the field. Now and then, however, he rode to cover, to see the hounds throw off, and exchange greetings with a great number of his friends and neighbors on such occasions collected together. This he did the morning after that on which he had visited Grilston, accompanied, at their earnest entreaty, by Mrs. Aubrey and Kate. I am not painting angels, but describing frail human nature; and truth forces me to say, that Kate knew pretty well that on such occasions she appeared to no little advantage. I protest I love her not the less for it—but is there a beautiful woman under the sun who is not aware of her charms, and of the effect they produce upon our sex? Pooh! I never will believe to the contrary. In Kate's composition this ingredient was but an imperceptible alloy in virgin gold. Now, how was it that she came to think of this hunting appointment? I do not exactly know; but I recollect that when Lord De la Zouch last called at Yatton, he happened to mention it at lunch, and to say that he and one Geoffry Lovel Delamere—but however that may be, behold on a bright Thursday morning, Aubrey and his two lovely companions made their welcome appearance at the field, all superbly mounted, and most cordially greeted by all present. Miss Aubrey attracted universal admiration; but there was one handsome youngster, his well-formed figure showing to great advantage in his new pink and leathers that made a point of challenging her special notice, and in doing so, attracting that of all his envious fell'-sportsmen; and that was Delamere. He seemed infinitely more taken up with the little party from Yatton than with the serious business of the day. His horse, however, had an eye to business; and with erected ears, catching the first welcome signal sooner than its gallant rider, sprung off like light, and would have left its abstracted rider behind had he not been a first-rate seat. In fact, Kate herself was not quite sufficiently on her guard; and her eager filly suddenly put in requisition all her rider's little strength and skill to rein her in—which having done, Kate's eye looked rather anxiously after her late companion, who, however, had already cleared the first hedge, and was fast making up to the scattering scarlet crowd. Oh, the bright, exhilarating scene!

"Heigh-ho!" said Kate, with a slight sigh, as soon as Delamere had disappeared—"I was very nearly off."

"So was somebody else, Kate!" said Mrs. Aubrey, with a sly smile.

"This is a very cool contrivance of yours, Kate—bringing us here this morning," said her brother, rather gravely.

"What *do* you mean, Charles?" she inquired, slightly reddening. He good-naturedly hit her shoulder with his whip,
laughed, urged his horse into a canter, and they were all soon
on their way to General Grim's, an old friend of the late Mr.
Aubrey's.

The party assembled on New-year's-eve at Fotheringham
Castle, the magnificent residence of Lord De la Zouch, was
numerous and brilliant. The Aubreys arrived about five
o'clock; and on their emerging from their chambers into the
drawing-room, about half past six—Mr. Aubrey leading in his
lovely wife and his very beautiful sister—they attracted general attention. He himself looked handsome, for the brisk
country air had brought out a glow upon his too frequently
sallow countenance—sallow with the unwholesome atmosphere,
the late hours, the wasting excitement of the House of Commons; and his smile was cheerful, his eye bright and penetrating.   There is nothing that makes such quick triumphant way
in English society as the promise of speedy political distinction.
It will supply to its happy possessor the want of family and
fortune—it rapidly melts away all distinctions; the obscure
but eloquent commoner finds himself suddenly standing in
the rarefied atmosphere of privilege and exclusiveness—the
familiar equal, often the conscious superior, of the haughtiest
peer of the realm.   A single successful speech in the House of
Commons opens before its utterer the shining doors of fashion
and greatness, as if by magic.   It is as it were POWER stepping into its palace, welcomed by gay crowds of eager obsequious expectants.   Who would not press forward to grasp in
anxious welcome the hand that, in a few short years, may dis-
pense the glittering baubles sighed after by the great, and the
more substantial patronage of office, which may point public
opinion in any direction?   But, to go no further, what if to
all this be added a previous position in society, such as that
occupied by Mr. Aubrey! There were several very fine women,
married and single, in that splendid drawing-room; but there
were two girls, in very different styles of beauty, who were soon
allowed by all present to carry off the palm between them—I
mean Miss Aubrey and Lady Caroline Caversham, the only
daughter of the Marchioness of Redborough, both of whom
were on a visit at the castle of some duration.   Lady Caroline
and Miss Aubrey were of about the same age, and dressed
almost exactly alike, viz., in white satin; only Lady Caroline
wore a brilliant diamond necklace, whereas Kate had chosen
to wear not a single ornament.

Lady Caroline was a trifle the taller, and had a very stately carriage. Her hair was black as jet—her features were refined and delicate; but they wore a very cold, haughty expression. After a glance at her half-closed eyes, and the swan-like curve of her snowy neck, you unconsciously withdrew from her, as from an inaccessible beauty. The more you looked at her, the more she satisfied your critical scrutiny; but your *feelings* went not out toward her—they were, in a manner, chilled and repulsed. Look, now, at our own Kate Aubrey—nay, never fear to place her beside yon supercilious divinity—look at her, and your *heart* acknowledges her loveliness; your soul thrills at sight of her bewitching blue eyes—eyes now sparkling with excitement, then languishing with softness, in accordance with the varying emotions of a sensitive nature—a most susceptible heart. How her sunny curls harmonize with the delicacy and richness of her complexion! Her figure, observe, is, of the two, a trifle fuller than her rival's—stay, don't let your admiring eyes settle so intently upon her budding form, or you will confuse Kate—turn away, or she will shrink from you like the sensitive plant! Lady Caroline seems the exquisite but frigid production of a skillful statuary, who had caught a divinity in the very act of disdainfully setting her foot for the first time upon this poor earth of ours; but Kate is a living and breathing beauty—as it were, fresh from the hand of God himself!

Kate was very affectionately greeted by Lady De la Zouch, a lofty and dignified woman of about fifty; so also by Lord De la Zouch; but when young Delamere welcomed her with a palpable embarrassment of manner, a more brilliant color stole into her cheek, and a keen observer might have noticed a little, rapid, undulating motion in her bosom, which told of some inward emotion. And a keen observer Kate at that moment had in her beautiful rival; from whose cheek, as that of Kate deepened in its roseate bloom, faded away the color entirely, leaving it the hue of the lily. Her drooping eyelids could scarcely conceal the glances of alarm and anger which she darted at her plainly successful rival in the affections of the future Lord De la Zouch. Kate was quickly aware of this state of matters; and it required no little self-control to appear *un*aware of it. Delamere took her down to dinner, and seated himself beside her, and paid her such pointed attentions as at length really distressed her; and she was quite relieved when the time came for the ladies to withdraw. That she had not a secret yearning toward Delamere, the frequent companion of her early days, I can not assert, because I know it would be contrary to the fact. Circumstances had kept him on the

Continent for more than a year between the period of his quitting Eton and going to Oxford, where another twelvemonth
had slipped away without his visiting Yorkshire: thus two
years had elapsed—and behold Kate had become a woman and
he a man! They had mutual predispositions toward each
other, and 'twas mere accident which of them first manifested
symptoms of fondness for the other—the same result must
have followed, namely (to use a great word), reciprocation.
Lord and Lady De la Zouch idolized their son, and were old
and very firm friends of the Aubrey family; and, if Delamere
really formed an attachment to one of Miss Aubrey's beauty,
accomplishments, talent, amiability, and ancient family—why
should he not be gratified? Kate, whether she would or not,
was set down to the piano, Lady Caroline accompanying her
on the harp—on which she usually performed with mingled
skill and grace; but on the present occasion, both the fair performers found fault with their instruments—then with themselves—and presently gave up the attempt in despair. But
when, at a later period of the evening, Kate's spirits had been
a little exhilarated with dancing, and she sat down, at Lord
De la Zouch's request, and gave that exquisite song from *The
Tempest*—" Where the bee sucks,"—all the witchery of her
voice and manner had returned; and as for Delamere, he
would have given the world to marry her that minute, and so
forever extinguish the hopes of—as he imagined—two or three
nascent competitors for the beautiful prize then present.

That Kate was good as beautiful, the following little incident, which happened to her on the ensuing evening, will show.
There was a girl in the village at Yatton, about sixteen or
seventeen years old, called Phœbe Williams; a very pretty
girl, and who had spent about two years at the Hall as a
laundry-maid, but had been obliged, some few months before
the time I am speaking of, to return to her parents in the village, ill of a decline. She had been a sweet-tempered girl in
her situation, and all her fellow-servants felt great interest in
her, as also did Miss Aubrey. Mrs. Aubrey sent her daily,
jellies, sago, and other such matters, suitable for the poor
girl's condition; and about a quarter of an hour after her return from Fotheringham, Miss Aubrey, finding one of the female servants about to set off with some of the above-mentioned articles, and hearing that poor Phœbe was getting
rapidly worse, instead of retiring to her room to undress,
slipped on an additional shawl, and resolved to accompany the
servant to the village. She said not a word to either her mother, her sister-in-law, or her brother; but simply left word with

her maid where she was going, and that she should quickly return. It was snowing smartly when Kate set off; but she cared not, hurried on by the impulse of kindness, which led her to pay perhaps a last visit to the humble sufferer. She walked alongside of the elderly female servant, asking her a number of questions about Phœbe, and her sorrowing father and mother. It was nearly dark as they quitted the park gates, and snowing, if anything, faster than when they had left the Hall. Kate, wrapping her shawl still closer round her slender figure, and her face pretty well protected by her veil, hurried on, and they soon reached Williams's cottage. Its humble tenants were, as may be imagined, not a little surprised at her appearance at such an hour, and in such inclement weather, and so apparently unattended. Poor Phœbe, worn to a shadow, was sitting opposite the fire, in a little wooden arm-chair, and propped up by a pillow. She trembled, and her lips moved on seeing Miss Aubrey, who sitting down on a stool beside her, after laying aside her snow-whitened shawl and bonnet, spoke to her in the most gentle and soothing strain imaginable. What a contrast in their two figures! 'Twould have been no violent stretch of imagination to say, that Catherine Aubrey at that moment looked like a ministering angel sent to comfort the wretched sufferer in her extremity. Phœbe's father and mother stood on each side of the little fire-place, gazing with tearful eyes upon their only child, soon about to depart from them forever. The poor girl was indeed a touching object. She had been very pretty, but now her face was white and wofully emaciated—the dread impress of consumption was upon it. Her wasted fingers were clasped together on her lap, holding between them a little handkerchief, with which, evidently with great effort, she occasionally wiped the dampness from her face.

"You're very good, ma'am," she whispered, "to come to see me, and so late. They say it's a sad, cold night."

"I heard, Phœbe, that you were not so well, and I thought I would just step along with Margaret, who has brought you some more jelly. Did you like the last?"

"Y-e-s, ma'am," she replied, hesitatingly; "but it's *very* hard for me to swallow anything now, my throat feels so sore." Here her mother shook her head and looked aside; for the doctor had only that morning explained to her the nature of the distressing symptom which her daughter was alluding to—as evidencing the very last stage of her fatal disorder.

"I'm very sorry to hear you say so, Phœbe," replied Miss

Aubrey. "Do you think there's anything else that Mrs.
Jackson could make for you?"

"No, ma'am, thank you; I feel it's no use trying to swallow anything more."

"While there's life," said Kate, in a subdued, hesitating
tone, "there's hope—they say." Phœbe shook her head
mournfully. "Don't stop long, dear lady—it's getting very
late for you to be out alone. Father will go—"

"Never mind me, Phœbe—I can take care of myself. I
hope you mind what good Dr. Tatham says to you? You know
this sickness is from God, Phœbe. He knows what is best for
His creatures."

"Thank God, ma'am, I think I feel resigned. I know it is
God's will; but I am very sorry for poor father and mother—
they'll be so lone-like when they don't see Phœbe about."
Her father gazed intently at her, and the tears ran trickling
down his cheeks; her mother put her apron before her face,
and shook her head in silent anguish. Miss Aubrey did not
speak for a few moments.

"I see you have been reading the prayer-book mamma
gave you when you were at the Hall," said she at length,
observing the little volume lying open on Phœbe's lap.

"Yes, ma'am—I was *trying;* but somehow, lately, I can't
read, for there's a kind of mist comes over my eyes, and I
can't see."

"That's weakness, Phœbe," said Miss Aubrey, quickly but
tremulously.

"May I make bold, ma'am," commenced Phœbe, languidly, after a hesitating pause, "to ask *you* to read the little
psalm I was trying to read a while ago? I should so like to
hear *you.*"

"I'll try, Phœbe," said Miss Aubrey, taking the book,
which was open at the sixth psalm. 'Twas a severe trial, for
her feelings were not a little excited already. But how could
she refuse the dying girl? So she began, a little indistinctly,
in a very low tone, and with frequent pauses; for the tears
every now and then quite obscured her sight. She managed,
however, to get as far as the sixth verse, which was thus:

"*I am weary of my groaning; every night wash I my bed,
and water my couch with tears; my beauty is gone for very
trouble.*"

Here Kate's voice suddenly stopped. She buried her face
for a moment or two in her handkerchief, and said hastily: "I
can't read any more, Phœbe!" Every one in the little room
was in tears, except poor Phœbe, who seemed past that.

"It's time for me to go now, Phœbe. We'll send some one early in the morning to know how you are," said Miss Aubrey, rising and putting on her bonnet and shawl. She contrived to beckon Phœbe's mother to the back of the room, and silently slipped a couple of guineas into her hands; for she knew the mournful occasion there would soon be for such assistance! She then left, peremptorily declining the attendance of Phœbe's father—saying that it *must* be dark when she could not find the way to the Hall, which was almost in a straight line from the cottage, and a little more than a quarter of a mile off. It was very much darker, and it still snowed, though not so thickly as when she had come. She and Margaret walked side by side, at a quick pace, talking together about poor Phœbe. Just as she was approaching the extremity of the village, nearest the park—

"Ah, my lovely gals!" exclaimed a voice, in a low but most offensive tone—"alone? How uncommon—" Miss Aubrey for a moment seemed thunder-struck at so sudden and unprecedented an occurrence; then she hurried on with a beating heart, whispering to Margaret to keep close to her, and not to be alarmed. The speaker, however, kept pace with them.

"Lovely gals!—wish I'd an umbrella, my angels!—Take my arm? Ah! Pretty gals!"

"Who *are* you, sir?" at length exclaimed Kate, spiritedly, suddenly stopping, and turning to the rude speaker.

[Who else should it be but Tittlebat Titmouse!] "Who am I? Ah, ha! Lovely gals! one that loves the pretty gals."

"Do you know, fellow, who I am?" inquired Miss Aubrey, indignantly, flinging aside her veil, and disclosing her beautiful face, white as death, but indistinctly visible in the darkness, to her insolent assailant.

"No, 'pon my soul, no; but—lovely gal! lovely gal!—'pon my life, spirited gal!—do you no harm! Take my arm?—"

"Wretch! ruffian! How dare you insult a lady in this manner? Do you know who I am? My name, sir, is Aubrey—I am Miss Aubrey of the Hall! Do not think—"

Titmouse felt as if he were on the point of dropping down dead at that moment with amazement and terror; and when Miss Aubrey's servant screamed out at the top of her voice, "Help!—help, there!" Titmouse, without uttering a syllable more, took to his heels, just as the door of a cottage, at only a few yards' distance, opened, and out rushed a strapping farmer, shouting—"Hey! what be t'matter?" You may guess his astonishment on discovering Miss Aubrey, and his

fury at learning the cause of her alarm.   Out-of-doors he
pelted, without his hat, uttering a volley of fearful imprecations, and calling on the unseen miscreant to come forward;
for whom it was lucky that he had time to escape from a pair
of fists that in a minute or two would have beaten his little
carcass into a jelly! Miss Aubrey was so overcome by the
shock she had suffered, that but for a glass of water she might
have fainted. As soon as she had a little recovered from her
agitation, she set off home, accompanied by Margaret, and
followed very closely by the farmer, with a tremendous knotted
stick under his arm—(he wanted to have taken his double-
barreled gun)—and thus she soon reached the Hall, not a little
tired and agitated. This little incident, however, she kept to
herself, and enjoined her two attendants to do the same; for
she knew the distress it would have occasioned those whom she
loved. As it was, she was somewhat sharply rebuked by her
mother and brother who had just sent two men out in quest
of her, and whom it was singular that she should have missed.
This is not the place to give an account of the eccentric movements of our friend Titmouse; still there can be no harm in
my just mentioning that the sight of Miss Aubrey on horseback had half maddened the little fool; her image had never
been effaced from his memory since the occasion on which, as
already explained, he had first seen her; and as soon as he had
ascertained, through Snap's inquiries, who she was, he became
more frenzied in the matter than before, because he thought
he now saw a probability of obtaining her. "If like children," says Edmund Burke, "we will cry for the moon, why
like children we must—*cry on.*" Whether this was not something like the position of Mr. Tittlebat Titmouse, in his passion for CATHERINE AUBREY, the reader can judge. He had
unbosomed himself in the matter to his confidential adviser
Mr. Snap; who, having accomplished his errand, had the day
before returned to town, very much against his will, leaving
Titmouse behind him, to bring about, by his own delicate and
skillful management, a union between himself, as the future
lord of Yatton, and the beautiful sister of its present occupant.

CHAPTER IX.

MR. AUBREY and Kate were sitting together playing at
chess, about eight o'clock in the evening; Dr. Tatham and
Mrs. Aubrey, junior, looking on with much interest; old Mrs.
Aubrey being busily engaged writing. Mr. Aubrey was sadly

an overmatch for poor Kate—he being in fact a first-rate player; and her soft white hand had been hovering over the half dozen chessmen she had left, uncertain which of them to move, for nearly two minutes, her chin resting on the other hand, and her face wearing a very puzzled expression. "Come, Kate," said every now and then her brother, with that calm victorious smile which at such a moment would have tried any but so sweet a temper as his sister's. "If *I* were you, Miss Aubrey," was perpetually exclaiming Dr. Tatham, knowing as much about the game the while as the little Marlborough spaniel lying asleep at Miss Aubrey's feet. "Oh, dear!" said Kate, at length, with a sigh, "I really don't see how to escape—"

"Who can that be?" exclaimed Mrs. Aubrey, looking up and listening to the sound of carriage wheels.

"Never mind," said her husband, who was interested in the game—"come, come, Kate." A few minutes afterward a servant made his appearance, and coming up to Mr. Aubrey, told him that Mr. Parkinson and another gentleman had called, and were waiting in the library to speak to him on business.

"What can they want at this hour?" exclaimed Mr. Aubrey, absently, intently watching an expected move of his sister's, which would have decided the game. At length she made her long-meditated descent, in quite an unexpected quarter.

"Checkmate!" she exclaimed, with infinite glee.

"Ah!" cried he, rising, with a slightly surprised and chagrined air, "I'm ruined! Now, try your hand on the Doctor, while I go and speak to these people. I wonder what can possibly have brought them here. Oh, I see—I see; 'tis probably about Miss Evelyn's marriage-settlement—I'm to be one of her trustees." With this he left the room, and presently entered the library, where were two gentlemen, one of whom, a stranger, was in the act of pulling off his great-coat. It was Mr. Runnington; a tall, thin, elderly man, with short gray hair—his countenance bespeaking the calm, acute, clear-headed man of business. The other was Mr. Parkinson; a plain, substantial-looking, hard-headed country attorney.

"Mr. Runnington, my London agent, sir," said he to Mr. Aubrey, as the latter entered. Mr. Aubrey bowed.

"Pray, gentlemen, be seated," he replied with his usual urbanity of manner, taking a chair beside them.

"Why, Mr. Parkinson, you look very serious—both of you. What is the matter?" he inquired, surprisedly.

"Mr. Runnington, sir, has arrived, most unexpectedly to me," replied Mr. Parkinson, "only an hour or two ago, from London, on business of the last importance to you."

"*To me!*—well, what is it? Pray, say at once what it is—I am all attention," said Mr. Aubrey, anxiously.

"Do you happen," commenced Mr. Parkinson, very nervously, "to remember sending Waters to me on Monday or Tuesday last, with a paper which had been served by some one on old Jolter?"

"Certainly," replied Mr. Aubrey, after a moment's consideration.

"Mr. Runnington's errand is connected with that document," said Mr. Parkinson, and paused.

"Indeed!" exclaimed Mr. Aubrey, apparently a little relieved. "I assure you, gentlemen, you very greatly overestimate the importance I attach to anything that such a troublesome person as Mr. Tomkins can do, if I am right in supposing that it is he who—Well, then, what *is* the matter?" he inquired, quickly, observing Mr. Parkinson shake his head, and interchange a grave look with Mr. Runnington; "you can not think, Mr. Parkinson, how you will oblige me by being explicit."

"This paper," said Mr. Runnington, holding up that which Mr. Aubrey at once recollected as the one on which he had cast his eye on its being handed to him by Waters, "is a Declaration in Ejectment, with which Mr. Tomkins has nothing whatever to do. It is served virtually on *you*, and you are the real defendant."

"So I apprehend I was in the former trumpery action."

"Do you recollect, Mr. Aubrey," said Mr. Parkinson, with a trepidation which he could not conceal, "several years ago, some serious conversation which you and I had together on the state of your title—when I was preparing your marriage-settlements?"

Mr. Aubrey started, and his face was suddenly blanched.

"The matters we then discussed have suddenly acquired fearful importance. This paper occasions us, on your account, the profoundest anxiety." Mr. Aubrey continued silent, gazing on Mr. Parkinson with intensity. "Supposing, from a hasty glance at it, and from the message accompanying it, that it was merely another action of Tomkins about the slip of waste land attached to Jolter's cottage, I sent it up to London to my agents, Messrs. Runnington, requesting them to call on the plaintiff's attorney, and settle the action. He did so; and

—perhaps, you will explain the rest," said Mr. Parkinson to Mr. Runnington.

"Certainly," said that gentleman with a serious air, but much more calmly and firmly than Mr. Parkinson; "I called accordingly, early yesterday morning, on Messrs. Quirk, Gammon and Snap—they are a very well—but not enviably-known firm in the profession; and in a very few minutes my misconception of the nature of the business I had called to settle was set right. In short—" he paused, as if distressed at the intelligence he was about to communicate.

"Oh, pray, pray go on, sir," said Mr. Aubrey in a low tone.

"I am no stranger, sir, to your firmness of character; but I shall have to tax it, I fear, to its uttermost. To come at once to the point—they told me that I might undoubtedly *settle* the matter, if you would consent to give up immediate possession of *the whole Yatton estate*, and account for the mesne profits to their client, the right heir—as they contend—a Mr. Tittlebat Titmouse." Mr. Aubrey leaned back in his chair, overcome, for an instant, by this astounding intelligence; and all three of them preserved silence for more than a minute. Mr. Runnington was a man of a very feeling heart. In the course of his great practice he had had to encounter many distressing scenes; but probably none of them had equaled that in which, at the earnest entreaty of Mr. Parkinson, who distrusted his own self-possession, he now bore a leading part. The two attorneys interchanged frequent looks of deep sympathy for their unfortunate client, who seemed as if stunned by the intelligence they had brought him.

"I felt it my duty to lose not an instant in coming down to Yatton," resumed Mr. Runnington, observing Mr. Aubrey's eye again directed inquiringly toward him; "for Messrs. Quirk, Gammon and Snap are very dangerous people to deal with, and must be encountered promptly, and with the greatest possible caution. The moment that I had left them, I hastened to the Temple, to retain for you Mr. Subtle, the leader of the Northern Circuit; but they had been beforehand with me, and retained him nearly three months ago, together with another eminent king's counsel on the circuit. Under these circumstances, I lost no time in giving a special retainer to the Attorney-General, in which I trust I have done right, and in retaining as junior a gentleman whom I consider to be incomparably the ablest and most experienced lawyer on the circuit."

"Did they say anything concerning the nature of their

client's title?" inquired Mr. Aubrey, after some expressions of amazement and dismay.

"Very little—I might say, nothing. If they had been *never* so precise, of course I should have distrusted every word they said. They certainly mentioned that they had had the first conveyancing opinions in the kingdom, which concurred in favor of their client; that they had been for months prepared at all points, and accident only had delayed their commencing proceedings till now."

"Did you make any inquiries as to who the claimant was?" inquired Mr. Aubrey.

"Yes; but all I could learn was, that they had discovered him by mere accident; and that he was at present in very obscure and distressed circumstances. I tried to discover by what means they proposed to commence and carry on so expensive a contest; but they smiled significantly, and were silent." Another long pause ensued, during which Mr. Aubrey was evidently silently struggling with very agitating emotions.

"What is the meaning of their affecting to seek the recovery of only one insignificant portion of the property?" he inquired.

"It is their own choice—it may be from consideration of mere convenience. The title, however, by which they may succeed in recovering what they at present go for, will avail to recover every acre of the estate, and the present action will consequently decide everything!"

"And suppose the worst—that they are successful," said Mr. Aubrey, after they had conversed a good deal, and very anxiously, on the subject of a presumed infirmity in Mr. Aubrey's title, which had been pointed out to him in general terms, by Mr. Parkinson, on the occasion already adverted to —"what is to be said about the rental which I have been receiving all this time—ten thousand a year?" inquired Mr. Aubrey, looking as if he dreaded to hear his question answered.

"Oh! that's quite an after-consideration—let us fight the battle."

"I beg, Mr. Runnington, that you will withhold nothing from me," said Mr. Aubrey. "To what extent shall I be liable?"

Mr. Runnington paused.

"I am afraid that *all* the mesne profits, as they are called, which you have received"—commenced Mr. Parkinson—

"No, no," interrupted Mr. Runnington; "I have been

turning that matter over in my mind, and I think that the statute of limitations will bar all but the last six years—"

"Why, *that* will be sixty thousand pounds!" interrupted Mr. Aubrey, with a look of sudden despair. "Gracious Heavens, that is perfectly frightful!—frightful! If I lose Yatton, I shall not have a place to put my head in—not one farthing to support myself with! And yet to have to make up *sixty thousand pounds!*" The perspiration stood upon his forehead, and his eye was laden with alarm and agony. He slowly rose from his chair and bolted the door, that they might not, at such an agitating moment, be surprised or disturbed by any of the servants or his family.

"I suppose," said he, in a faint and tremulous tone, "that if this claim succeed, my mother will also share my fate—"

They shook their head in silence.

"Permit me to suggest," said Mr. Runnington, in a tone of the most respectful sympathy, "that sufficient for the day is the evil thereof."

"But the NIGHT follows!" said Mr. Aubrey, with a visible tremor; and his voice made the hearts of his companions thrill within them. "I have a frightful misgiving as to the issue of these proceedings! I ought not to have neglected the matter pointed out to me by Mr. Parkinson on my marriage. I feel as if I had been culpably lying ever since. But I really did not attach to it the importance it deserved; I never, indeed, distinctly appreciated the nature of what was then pointed out to me!"

"A thousand pities that a *fine* was not *levied*, is it not?" said Mr. Runnington.

"Ay indeed, it is!" replied Mr. Parkinson, with a sigh, and they spoke together for some time, and very earnestly, concerning the nature and efficacy of such a measure, which they explained to Mr. Aubrey.

"It comes to this," said he, "that in all probability, I and my family are at this moment "—he shuddered—" trespassers at Yatton!"

"That, Mr. Aubrey," said Mr. Parkinson earnestly, "remains to be proved! We really are getting on far too fast. One would think that the jury had already returned a verdict against us—that judgment had been signed—and that the sheriff was coming in the morning to execute the writ of possession in favor of our opponent." This was well meant by the speaker; but surely it was like talking of the machinery of the ghastly guillotine to the wretch in shivering expectation of

suffering by it on the morrow. An involuntary shudder ran
through Mr. Aubrey.

"Sixty thousand pounds!" he exclaimed, rising and walking to and fro. "Why, I am ruined beyond all redemption!
How can I ever satisfy it?" Again he paced the room several times, in silent agony. Presently he resumed his seat.
"I have, for these several days past, had a strange sense of
impending calamity," and yet, more calmly—"I have been
equally unable to account for, or get rid of it. It may be an
intimation from Heaven; I bow to its will!"

"We must remember," said Mr. Runnington "that '*possession is nine tenths of the law;*' which means, that your mere
possession will entitle you to retain it against all the world,
till a stronger title than yours to the right of possession be
made out. You stand on a mountain; and it is for your adversary to displace you, not by showing merely that you have
no real title, but that *he has*. If he could prove all your title-
deeds to be merely waste paper—that in fact you have no more
title than I have—he would not, by stopping there, advance his
own case an inch; he must *first* establish in himself a clear and
independent title; so that you are entirely on the defensive;
and rely upon it, that though never so many screws may be
loose, so acute and profound a lawyer as the Attorney-General
will impose every difficulty on—"

"Nay, but God forbid that any unconscientious advantage
should be taken on my behalf!" said Mr. Aubrey. Mr. Runnington and Mr. Parkinson both opened their eyes pretty wide
at this sally; the latter could not understand but that everything was fair in war; the former saw and appreciated the
nobility of soul which had dictated the exclamation.

"I suppose the affair will soon become public," said Mr.
Aubrey, with an air of profound depression, after much
further conversation.

"Your position in the country, your eminence in public
life, the singularity of the case, and the magnitude of the stake
—all are circumstances undoubtedly calculated soon to urge
the affair before the notice of the public," said Mr. Runnington.

"What disastrous intelligence to break to my family!" exclaimed Mr. Aubrey, tremulously. "With what fearful suddenness it has burst upon us! But something, I suppose," he
presently added with forced calmness, "must be done immediately?"

"Undoubtedly," replied Mr. Runnington. "Mr. Parkinson and I will immediately proceed to examine your title-deeds,

the greater portion of which are, I understand, here in the Hall, and the rest at Mr. Parkinson's; and prepare, without delay, a case for the opinion of the Attorney-General, and also of the most eminent conveyancers of the kingdom. Who, by the way," said Mr. Runnington, addressing Mr. Parkinson— "who was the conveyancer that had the abstracts before him, on preparing Mr. Aubrey's marriage-settlement?"

"Oh, you are alluding to the ' *Opinion* ' I mentioned to you this evening?" inquired Mr. Parkinson. "I have it at my house, and will show it you in the morning. The doubt he expressed on one or two points gave me, I recollect, no little uneasiness—as *you* may remember, Mr. Aubrey."

"I certainly do," he replied, with a profound sigh; "but though what you said reminded me of something or another that I had heard when a mere boy, I thought no more of it. I think you also told me that the gentleman who wrote the opinion was a nervous fidgety man, always raising difficulties in his clients' titles—and one way or another, the thing never gave me any concern—scarcely ever even occurred to my thoughts, till to-day! What infatuation has been mine! But you will take a little refreshment, gentlemen, after your journey?" said Mr. Aubrey suddenly, glad of the opportunity it would afford him of reviving his own exhausted spirits by a cup of wine, before returning to the drawing-room. He swallowed several glasses of wine without any immediately perceptible effect; and the bearers of the direful intelligence just communicated to the reader, after a promise by Mr. Aubrey to drive over to Grilston early in the morning, and bring with him such of his title-deeds as were then at the Hall, took their departure, leaving him outwardly calmer, but with a fearful oppression at his heart. He made a powerful effort to control his feelings, so as to conceal, for a while at least, the dreadful occurrence of the evening. His face, however, on re-entering the drawing-room, which his mother, attended by Kate, had quitted for her bedroom, somewhat alarmed Mrs. Aubrey; whom, however, he at once quieted, by saying that he certainly *had* been annoyed—" excessively annoyed "—at a communication just made to him; " and which might, in fact, prevent his sitting again for Yatton."

"Oh, that's the cause of your long stay? There, Doctor, am I not right?" said Mrs. Aubrey, appealing to Dr. Tatham. "Did I not tell you that this was something connected with politics? Charles, I do *hate* politics—give *me* a quiet home!" A pang shot through Mr. Aubrey's heart; but he felt that he had. for the present. succeeded in his object.

Mr. Aubrey's distracted mind was indeed, as it were,
buffeted about that night on a dark sea of trouble; while
the beloved being beside him lay sleeping peacefully; all unconscious of the rising storm.   Many times, during the dismal
night, would he have risen from his bed to seek a momentary
relief by walking to and fro, but that he feared disturbing her,
and disclosing the extent and depths of his distress.   It was
nearly five o'clock in the morning before he at length sunk
into sleep; and of one thing I can assure the reader, that however that excellent man might have shrunk—and shrunk he
did—from the sufferings that seemed in store for him, and
those who were far dearer to him than life itself, he did not
give way to one repining or rebellious thought.   On the contrary, his real frame of mind, on that trying occasion, may be
discovered in one short prayer, which he more than once was
on the point of expressing aloud in words—" Oh, my God! in
my prosperity I have ever acknowledged Thee; forsake me not
in my adversity."

At an early hour in the morning his carriage drew up at Mr.
Parkinson's door; and he brought with him, as he had
promised, a great number of title-deeds and family documents.
On these, as well as on many others which were in Mr. Parkinson's custody, that gentleman and Mr. Runnington were anxiously engaged during almost every minute of that day and
the ensuing one; at the close of which, they had between them
drawn up the rough draft of a case, with which Mr. Runnington set off for town by the mail; undertaking to lay it immediately before the Attorney-General, and also before one or two
of the greatest conveyancers of the day, commended to their
best and earliest attention.   He pledged himself to transmit
their opinions, by the very first mail, to Mr. Parkinson; and
both those gentlemen immediately set about active preparations for defending the ejectment.   The " eminent conveyancer " fixed upon by Messrs. Runnington and Parkinson was
Mr. Tresayle, whose clerk, however, on looking into the
papers, presently carried them back to Messrs. Runnington,
with the startling information that Mr. Tresayle had, a few
months ago, "advised on the other side."   The next person
whom Mr. Runnington thought of was—singularly enough—
Mr. Mortmain, who, on account of his eminence, was occasionally employed, in heavy matters, by the firm.   His clerk,
also, on the ensuing morning returned the papers, assigning a
similar reason to that which had been given by Mr. Tresayle's
clerk!   All this formed a sad corroboration, truly, of Messrs.
Quirk and Gammon's assurance to Mr. Runnington, that they

had " had the first conveyancing opinions in the kingdom;"
and evidenced the formidable scale on which their operations
were being conducted. There were, however, other " eminent
conveyancers " besides the two above mentioned; and in the
hands of Mr. Mansfield, who, with a less extended reputation,
but an equal practice, was a far abler man, and a much higher
style of conveyancer than Mr. Mortmain, Mr. Runnington
left his client's interests with the utmost confidence. Not
satisfied with this, he laid the case also before Mr. Crystal, the
junior whom he had already retained in the cause—a man
whose lucid understanding was not ill indicated by his name.
Though his manner in court was not particularly forcible or
attractive, he was an invaluable acquisition in an important
case. To law he had for some twenty years applied himself
with unwearying energy; and he consequently became a ready,
accurate, and thorough lawyer, equal to all the practical
exigencies of his profession. He brought his knowledge to
bear on every point presented to him with beautiful precision.
He was equally quick and cautious—artful to a degree—But I
shall have other opportunities of describing him; since on him,
as on every working junior, will devolve the real conduct of
the defendant's case in the memorable action of *Doe on the
demise of Titmouse* v. *Roe.*

As Mr. Aubrey was driving home from the visit to Mr. Parkinson which I have just above mentioned, he stopped his carriage on entering the village, because he saw Dr. Tatham coming out of Williams's cottage, where he had been paying a
visit to poor dying Phœbe.

The little Doctor was plunthering on, ankle-deep in snow,
toward the vicarage, when Mr. Aubrey (who had sent home
his carriage with word that he should presently follow) came
up with him, and greeting him with unusual fervor, said that
he would accompany him to the vicarage.

" You are in very great trouble, my dear friend," said the
Doctor, seriously—" I saw it plainly last night; but of course
I said nothing. Come in with me! Let us talk freely with
one another; for, *as iron sharpeneth iron, so doth the countenance of a man his friend.* Is it not so?"

" It is indeed, my dear Doctor," replied Mr. Aubrey, suddenly softened by the affectionate simplicity of the Doctor's
manner. How much the good Doctor was shocked by the
communication which Mr. Aubrey presently made to him, the
reader may easily imagine. He even shed tears, on beholding
the forced calmness with which Mr. Aubrey depicted the
gloomy prospect that was before him. 'Twas not in vain

however, that the pious and venerable pastor led the subdued
and willing mind of his beloved companion to those sources of
consolation and support which a true Christian can not approach in vain.   Upon his bruised and bleeding feelings were
poured the balm of true religious consolation; and Mr. Aubrey
quitted his reverend companion with a far firmer tone of mind
than that with which he had entered the vicarage.   But when
he passed through the park-gates, the sudden reflection that
he was probably no longer the proprietor of the dear old
familiar objects that met his eye at every step almost overpowered him.

On entering the Hall, he was informed that one of the
tenants, Peter Johnson, had been sitting in the servants' hall
for nearly two hours waiting to see him.   Mr. Aubrey repaired
at once to the library, and desired the man to be shown in.
This Johnson had been for some twenty-five years a tenant of
a considerable farm on the estate, had scarcely ever been a few
weeks behindhand with his rent, and had always been considered one of the most exemplary persons in the whole neighborhood.   He had now, poor fellow, got into trouble, indeed;
for he had, a year or two before, been persuaded to become
security for his brother-in-law, a tax-collector; and had, alas!
the day before, been called upon to pay the three hundred
pounds in which he stood bound—his worthless brother-in-law
having absconded with nearly £1000 of the public money.
Poor Johnson, who had a large family to support, was in deep
tribulation, bowed down with grief and shame; and after a
sleepless night, had at length ventured down to Yatton, and
with a desperate boldness asked the benevolent squire to advance him £200 toward the money, to save himself from being
cast into prison.   Mr. Aubrey heard his sad story to the end
without one single interruption; though to a more practiced
observer than the troubled old farmer, the workings of his
countenance, from time to time, must have told his inward
agitation.   "I lend this poor soul £200!" thought he, "who
am penniless myself?   Shall I not be really acting as *his* dis-
honest relative has been acting, and making free with money
that belongs to another?"

"I assure you, my worthy friend," said he at length, with
a little agitation of manner, "that I have just now a very
serious call upon me—or you know how gladly I would have
complied with your request."

"Oh, sir, have mercy on me!   I've an ailing wife and seven
children to support," said poor Johnson, wringing his hands.

"Can't I do anything with the Government—"

"No, sir; I'm told they're so mighty angry with my rascally brother, they'll listen to nobody. It's a hard matter for me to keep things straight at home without this, sir, I've so many mouths to fill; and if they take me off to prison, Lord! what's to become of us all?"

Mr. Aubrey's lips quivered. Johnson fell on his knees, and the tears ran down his cheeks. "I've never asked a living man for money before, sir; and if you'll only lend it me, God Almighty will bless you and yours; you'll save us all from ruin; I'll work day and night to pay it back again!"

"Rise—rise, Johnson," said Mr. Aubrey, with emotion. "You shall have the money, my friend, if you will call to-morrow," he added, with a deep sigh, after a moment's hesitation.

He was as good as his word.

Had Mr. Aubrey been naturally of a cheerful and vivacious turn the contrast now afforded by his gloomy manner must have alarmed his family. As it was, however, it was not so strong and marked as to be attended with that effect, especially as he exerted himself to the utmost to conceal his distress. That *something* had gone wrong, he freely acknowledged, and as he spoke of it always in connection with political topics, he succeeded in parrying their questions, and checking suspicion. But, whenever they were all collected together, could he not justly compare them to a happy group, unconscious that they stood on a mine which was about to be fired?

About a week afterward, namely, on the 12th of January, arrived little Charles's birthday, when he became five years old, and Kate had for some days been moving heaven and earth to get up a children's party in honor of the occasion. After considerable riding and driving about, she succeeded in persuading the parents of some eight or ten children—two little daughters, for instance, of the Earl of Oldacre (beautiful creatures they were, to be sure)—little Master and the two Miss Bertons, the children of one of the county members—Sir Harry Oldfield, an orphan of about five years of age, the infant possessor of a magnificent estate—and two or three little girls besides—to send them all to Yatton for a day and a night, with their governesses and attendants.

'Twas a charming little affair. It went off brilliantly, as the phrase is, and repaid all Kate's exertions. She, her mother, and brother and sister, all dined at the same table, at a very early hour, with the merry little guests, who (with a laughable crowd of attendants behind them, to be sure) behaved remarkably well on the occasion. Sir Harry (a little

thing about Charles's age—the black ribbon round his waist,
and also the half-mourning dress worn by his maid, who stood
behind him, showed how recent was the event which made him
an orphan) proposed little Aubrey's health, in (I must own) a
somewhat stiff speech, demurely dictated to him by Kate
(who sat between him and her beautiful little nephew). She
then performed the same office for Charles, who stood on a
chair while delivering his eloquent acknowledgment of the
toast.

[Oh! that anguished brow of thine, Aubrey (thank God it
is unobserved!) but it tells *me* that the iron is entering thy
soul!]

And the moment that he had done—Kate folding her arms
around him and kissing him—down they all jumped, and a
merry throng scampered off to the drawing-room (followed
by Kate), where blind-man's buff, husbands and wives, and
divers other little games kept them in constant enjoyment.
After tea they were to have dancing—Kate mistress of the
ceremonies—and it was quite laughable to see how perpetually
she was foiled in her efforts to form the little sets. The girls
were orderly enough—but their wild little partners were quite
uncontrollable. The instant they were placed, and Kate had
gone to the instrument and struck off a note or two—heigh!—
there was a scrambling little crowd, jumping and laughing,
and chattering and singing! Over and over again she formed
them into sets, with the like results. But at length a young
lady, one of their governesses, took Miss Aubrey's place at the
piano, leaving the latter to superintend the performances in
person. She at length succeeded in getting up something like
a country-dance, led off by Charles and little Lady Anne
Cherville, the eldest daughter of the Earl of Oldacre, a beautiful child of about five years old, and who, judging from appearances, bade fair, in due time, to become another Lady
Caroline Caversham. You would have laughed outright to
watch the coquettish airs which this little creature gave herself
with Charles, whom yet she evidently could not bear to see
dancing with another.

"Now I shall dance with somebody else!" he exclaimed,
suddenly letting go Lady Anne, and snatching hold of a sweet
little thing, Miss Berton, that was standing modestly beside
him. The discarded beauty walked with a stately air and a
swelling heart, toward Mrs. Aubrey, who sat beside her husband on the sofa; and on reaching her, she stood for a few
moments silently watching her late partner busily and gayly
engaged with her successor—and then burst into tears.

"Charles!" called out Mrs. Aubrey; who had watched the whole affair, and could hardly keep her countenance—"come here directly, Charles."

"Yes, mamma!" he exclaimed—quite unaware of the serious aspect which things were assuming—and without quitting the dance, where he was (as his jealous mistress too plainly saw, for, despite her grief, her eye seemed to follow all his motions) skipping about with infinite glee with a *third* partner —a laughing sister of his last partner.

"Come here, Charles," said Mr. Aubrey, and in an instant his little son, all flushed and breathless, was at his side.

"Well, dear papa!" said he, keeping his eye fixed on the little throng he had just quitted, and where his deserted partner was skipping about alone.

"What have you been doing to Lady Anne, Charles?" said his father.

"Nothing, dear papa!" he replied, still wistfully eying the dancers.

"You know you left me, and went to dance with Miss Berton; you did, Charles!" said the offended beauty.

"That is not behaving like a little gentleman, Charles," said his father. The tears came into the child's eyes.

"I'm *very* sorry, dear papa, I *will* dance with her"—

"No, not now," said Lady Anne, haughtily.

"Oh, pooh! pooh!—kiss and be friends," said Mrs. Aubrey, laughing, "and go and dance as prettily as you were doing before." Little Aubrey put his arms round Lady Anne, kissed her, and away they both started to the dance again. While the latter part of this scene was going on, Mr. Aubrey's eye caught the figure of a servant who simply made his appearance and then retired (for such had been Mr. Aubrey's orders, in the event of any messenger coming from Grilston). Hastily whispering that he should return soon, he left the room. In the hall stood a clerk from Mr. Parkinson; and on seeing Mr. Aubrey, he took out a packet and retired—Mr. Aubrey, with evident trepidation, repairing to his library. With a nervous hand he broke the seal, and found the following letter from Mr. Parkison, with three other inclosures:—

"*Grilston, 12th Jan.,* 18—

"My Dear Sir,

"I have only just received, and at once forward to you, copies of the three opinions given by the Attorney-General, Mr. Mansfield, and Mr. Crystal. I lament to find that they are all of a discouraging character. They are quite independent of each other, having been laid before their respective writers at the same moment; yet you will observe that all three of them have hit upon precisely the same point, viz., that the descendants of Geoffry Dreddlington had no right to succeed to the inheritance till there was a failure of the heirs of Stephen Dreddington. If, therefore, our opponents have contrived to ferret out any one who satisfies that designation (I can not conjecture how they can ever have got upon the scent), I really fear we must prepare for a very serious struggle. I have been quietly pushing my inquiries in all directions, with a view to obtaining a clew to the case intended to be set up against us, and which you will find very shrewdly guessed at by the Attorney-General. *Nor am I the only party,* I find, in the field, who has been making pointed inquiries in your neighborhood; but of this more when we meet to-morrow.

"I remain,

"Yours very respectfully,

"J. PARKINSON.

"CHARLES AUBREY, ESQ., M. P."

Having read this letter, Mr. Aubrey sunk back in his chair and remained motionless for more than a quarter of an hour. At length he roused himself and read over the opinions; the effect of which—as far as he could comprehend their technicalities—he found had been but too correctly given by Mr. Parkinson. Some suggestions and inquiries put by the acute and experienced Mr. Crystal, suddenly revived recollections of one or two incidents even of his boyish days, long forgotten, but which, as he reflected upon them, began to reappear to his mind's eye with sickening distinctness. Wave after wave of apprehension and agony passed over him, chilling and benumbing his heart within him; so that, when his little son came some time afterward running up to him, with a message from his mamma, that she hoped he could come back to see them all play at snapdragon before they went to bed, he answered him mechanically, hardly seeming sensible even of his presence. At length, with a groan that came from the depths of his heart, he rose and walked to and fro, sensible of the necessity of exerting himself, and preparing himself, in some degree, for encountering his mother, his wife, and his sister. Taking up his candle, he hastened to his dressing-room, where he hoped, by the aid of refreshing ablutions, to succeed in effacing at least the stronger of those traces of suffering which his glass displayed to him as it reflected the image of his agitated countenance. A sudden recollection of the critical and delicate situation of his idolized wife glanced through his heart like a keen arrow. He sunk upon the sofa, and, clasping his hands, looked indeed forlorn. Presently the door was pushed hastily but gently open, and, first looking in to see that it was really he of whom she was in search, in rushed Mrs. Aubrey, pale and agitated, having been alarmed by his long-continued absence from the drawing-room, and the look of the servant from whom she had learned that his master had been for some time gone upstairs.

"Charles! my love! my sweet love!" she exclaimed, rushing up to him, sitting down beside him, and casting her arms round his neck. Overcome by the suddenness of her appearance and movements, for a moment he spoke not.

"For mercy's sake—as you love me!—tell me, dearest Charles, what has happened!"

"Nothing—love—nothing," he replied; but his look belied his speech.

"Oh! am not I your wife, dearest? Charles, I shall really go distracted if you do not tell me what has happened. I know that something—something dreadful—" He put his arm round her waist, and drew her tenderly toward him. He felt her heart beating violently. He kissed her cold forehead, but spoke not.

"Come, dearest! let me share your sorrows," said she in a thrilling voice. "Can not you trust your Agnes? Has not Heaven *sent* me to share your anxieties and griefs?"

"I love you, Agnes! ay, more than ever man loved woman!" he faltered, as he felt her arms folding him in closer and closer embrace; and she gazed at him with wild agitation, expecting presently to hear of some fearful catastrophe.

"I can not bear this much longer, dearest—I feel I can not," said she, rather faintly. "*What* has happened? What, that you dare not tell *me?* I can bear anything, while I have you and my children! You have been unhappy, my own Charles, for many days past. I have felt that you were!—I will not part with you till I know all!"

"You soon *must* know all, my sweet love; and I take Heaven to witness, that it is principally on your account, and that of my children, that I—in fact, I did not wish any of you to have known it till—"

"You are never going—to fight a duel?" she gasped, turning as white as death.

"Oh! no, no, Agnes! I solemnly assure you! If I could have brought myself to engage in such an unhallowed affair, would *this* scene ever first have occurred? No, no, my own

love! Must I then tell you of the misfortune that has overtaken us?" His words somewhat restored her, but she continued to gaze at him in mute and breathless apprehension.
Let me then conceal nothing, Agnes—they are bringing an
action against me, which, if successful, may cause us all to
quit Yatton—and it may be forever."

"Oh, Charles!" she murmured, her eyes riveted upon his,
while she unconsciously moved still nearer to him and trembled. Her head dropped upon his shoulder.

"Why is this?" she whispered after a pause.

"Let us, dearest, talk of it another time. I have now told
you what you asked me." He poured her out a glass of
water. Having drunk a little she appeared revived.

"Is all lost? Do, my own Charles—let me know really the
worst!"

"We are young, Agnes, and have the world before us.
Health and honor are better than riches. You and our little
loves—*the children which God has given us*—are *my* riches,"
said he, gazing with unspeakable tenderness at her. "Even
should it be the will of Heaven that this affair should go
against us—so long as they can not separate us from each
other, they can not really hurt us." She suddenly kissed him
with frantic energy, and an hysteric smile gleamed over her
pallid excited features.

"Calm yourself, Agnes!—calm yourself, for my sake!—as
you love me!" His voice quivered. "Oh, how very weak
and foolish I have been to yield to—"

"No, no, no!" she gasped, evidently laboring with hysteric
oppression. "Hush!" said she, suddenly starting, and wildly
leaning forward toward the door which opened into the gallery
leading into the various bedrooms. He listened—the mother's
ear had been quick and true. He presently heard the sound
of many children's voices approaching; they were the little
party, accompanied by Kate, on their way to bed, and little
Charles's voice was loudest, and his laugh the merriest of them
all. A wild smile gleamed on Mrs. Aubrey's face; her hand
grasped her husband's with convulsive pressure; and she suddenly sunk, rigid and senseless, upon the sofa. He seemed for
a moment stunned at the sight of her motionless figure. Soon,
however, recovering his presence of mind, he rang the bell,
and one or two female attendants quickly appeared; and by
their joint assistance Mrs. Aubrey was carried to her bed in
the adjoining room, where, by the use of the ordinary remedies, she was presently restored to consciousness. Her first
languid look was toward Mr. Aubrey, whose hand she slowly

raised to her lips. She tried to throw a smile over her wan features—but 'twas in vain; and, after a few heavy and half-choking sobs, her overcharged feelings found relief in a flood of tears. Full of the liveliest apprehensions as to the effect of this violent emotion upon her, in her critical condition, he remained with her for some time, pouring into her ear every soothing and tender expression he could think of. He at length succeeded in bringing her into a somewhat more tranquil state than he could have expected. He strictly enjoined the attendants, who had not quitted their lady's chamber, and whose alarmed and inquisitive looks he had noticed for some time with anxiety, to preserve silence concerning what they had so unexpectedly witnessed, adding that something unfortunate had happened, of which they would hear but too soon.

"Are you going to tell Kate?" whispered Mrs. Aubrey, sorrowfully. "Surely, love, *you* have suffered enough through *my* weakness. Wait till to-morrow. Let her—poor girl!--have a *few* more happy hours!"

"No, Agnes—it was my own weakness which caused me to be surprised into this premature disclosure to you. And now I *must* meet her again to-night, and I can not control either my features or my feelings. Yes, poor Kate, she must know all to-night. I shall not be long absent, Agnes." And directing her maid to remain with her till he returned, he withdrew, and with slow step and heavy heart descended to the library; preparing himself for another heart-breaking scene—plunging another innocent and joyous creature into misery, which he believed to be inevitable. Having looked into the drawing-room as he passed it—and seen no one there—his mother having, as usual, retired at a very early hour—he rang his library bell, and desired Miss Aubrey's maid to request her mistress to come down to him there, as soon as she was at leisure. He was glad that the only light in the room was that given out by the fire, which was not very bright, and so would in some degree shield his features from, at all events, immediate scrutiny. His heart ached as, shortly afterward, he heard Kate's light step crossing the hall. When she entered, her eyes sparkled with vivacity, and a smile was on her beauteous cheek. Her dress was slightly disordered, and her hair half uncurled—the result of her sport with the little ones whom she had been seeing to bed.

"What merry little things, to be sure!" she commenced, laughingly—"I could not get them to lie still a moment—popping their little heads in and out of the clothes. A fine night I shall have with Sir Harry! for he is to be *my* tiny

9

little bedfellow, and I dare say I shall not sleep a wink all night. Why, Charles, how very—*very* grave you look to-night!" she added, quickly, observing his eye fixed moodily upon her.

" 'Tis you who are so very gay," he replied, endeavoring to smile. "I want to speak to you, dear Kate," he commenced, affectionately, "on a serious matter. I have received some letters to-night—" Kate colored suddenly and violently, and her heart beat; but, sweet soul! she was mistaken—very, very far off the mark her troubled brother was aiming at. "And relying on your strength of mind, I have resolved to put you at once in possession of what I myself know. Can you bear bad news well, Kate?"

She turned very pale, and drawing her chair nearer to her brother, said: "Do not keep me in suspense, Charles—I can bear anything but suspense—that *is* dreadful! What has happened? Oh, dear," she added, with sudden alarm, "where are mamma and Agnes?" she started to her feet.

"I assure you they are both well, Kate. My mother is now doubtless asleep, and as well as she ever was; Agnes is in her bedroom—certainly much distressed at the news which I am going—"

"Oh, why, Charles, did you tell *anything* distressing to *her?*" exclaimed Miss Aubrey, with an alarmed air.

"We came together by surprise, Kate! Perhaps, too, it would have been worse to have kept her in suspense; but she is recovering!—I shall soon return to her.—And now, my dear Kate—I know your strong sense and spirit—a very great calamity hangs over us. Let you and me," he grasped her hands affectionately, "stand it steadily, and support those who can not!"

"Let me at once know all, Charles. See if I do not hear it as becomes your sister," she said, with forced calmness.

"If it should become necessary for all of us to retire into obscurity—into humble obscurity, dear Kate—how do you think you could bear it?"

"If it will be an honorable obscurity—nay, 'tis quite impossible to be *dis*honorable obscurity," said Miss Aubrey, with a momentary flash of energy.

"Never, never, Kate! The Aubreys may lose everything on earth but the jewel HONOR, and love for one another!"

"Let me know all, Charles; I see that something or other shocking has happened," said Miss Aubrey, in a low tone, with a look of the deepest apprehension.

"I will tell you the worst, Kate—a strange claim is set up

—by one I never heard of—to the whole of the property we now enjoy!"

Miss Aubrey started, and the slight color that remained faded entirely from her cheek.

" But is it a *true* claim, Charles?" she inquired, faintly.

" That remains to be proved. But I will disguise nothing from you—I have woful apprehensions—"

" Do you mean to say that Yatton *is not ours!*" inquired Miss Aubrey, catching her breath.

" So, alas! my dearest Kate, it is said!"

Miss Aubrey looked bewildered, and pressed her hand to her forehead.

" How shocking! —shocking!—shocking!" she gasped.— " What is to become of mamma?"

" God Almighty will not desert her in her old age. He will desert none of us, if we only trust in him," said her brother.

Miss Aubrey remained gazing at him intently, and continued perfectly motionless.

" Must we then all leave Yatton?" said she, faintly, after a while.

" If this claim succeeds—but we shall leave it *together*, Kate."

She threw her arms round his neck, and wept bitterly.

" Hush, hush, Kate!" said he, perceiving the increasing violence of her emotions, " restrain your feelings for the sake of my mother—and Agnes."

His words had the desired effect; the poor girl made a desperate effort. Unclasping her arms from her brother's neck, she sat down in a chair, breathing hard, and, after a few minutes' pause, she said, faintly: " I am better now. Do tell me more, Charles! Let me have something to *think* about— only don't say anything about—about mamma and Agnes!" In spite of herself a visible shudder ran through her frame.

" It seems, Kate," said he, with all the calmness he could assume—" at least they are trying to prove—that our branch of the family has succeeded to the property prematurely—that there is living an heir of the elder branch—that his case has been taken up by powerful friends; and—let me tell you the worst at once—even the lawyers consulted by Mr. Parkinson on my behalf take a most alarming view of the possibilities of the case that may be brought against us—"

" But is mamma provided for?" whispered Miss Aubrey, almost inarticulately. " When I look at her again I shall almost break my heart!"

" No, no, Kate, you won't! Heaven will give you strength,"

said her brother in a tremulous voice.   "Remember, my only
sister—my dearest Kate! you must support *me* in my trouble,
as I will support you—we will support one another—"

"We will—we will!" interrupted Miss Aubrey—instantly
checking, however, her rising excitement.

"You bear it bravely, my noble girl!" said Mr. Aubrey,
fondly, after a brief interval of silence.

She turned from him her head, and moved her hand—in
deprecation of expressions that might utterly unnerve her.
Then she convulsively clasped her hands over her forehead;
and, after a minute or two, turned toward him with tears in
her eyes, but tranquilized features.   The struggle had been
dreadful, though brief—her noble spirit recovered itself.

'Twas like some fair bark, in mortal conflict with the
black and boiling waters and howling hurricane; long quivering on the brink of destruction, but at last outliving the
storm, righting itself, and suddenly gliding into safe and
tranquil waters!

The distressed brother and sister sat conversing for a long
time, frequently in tears, but with infinitely greater calmness
and firmness than could have been expected.   They agreed
that Dr. Tatham should very early in the morning be sent for,
and implored to take upon himself the bitter duty of breaking
the matter as gradually and safely as possible to their mother;
its effects upon whom her children anticipated with the most
vivid apprehension.   They both considered that an event of
such publicity and importance could not possibly remain long
unknown to her, and that it was, on the whole, better that the
trial should be got over as soon as possible.   They then retired
—Kate to a sleepless pillow, and her brother to spend a greater
portion of the night in attempts to soothe and console his suffering wife; each of them having first knelt in humble reverence, and poured forth the breathings of a stricken and bleeding heart, before Him who hath declared that He HEARETH
and ANSWERETH prayer.

Ah! who can tell what a day or an hour may bring forth.

"It won't kindle—not a bit on't—it's green and full o' sap.
Go out and get us a log that's dry and old, George—and let's
try to have a bit of a blaze in t' ould chimney, this bitter
night," said Isaac Tonson, the gamekeeper at Yatton, to the
good-natured landlord of the Aubrey Arms, the little—and
only—inn of the village.   The suggestion was instantly attended to.

"How Peter's a-feathering of his geese to-night, to be

sure!'' exclaimed the landlord on his return, shaking the snow off his coat, and laying on the fire a great, dry, old log of wood, which seemed very acceptable to the hungry flames; for they licked it cordially the moment it was placed amongst them, and there was very soon given out a cheerful blaze. 'Twas a snug room, the brick floor covered with fresh sand; and on a few stools and benches, with a table in the middle, on which stood a large can and ale-glasses, with a plate of tobacco, sat some half dozen men enjoying their pipe and glass. In the chimney-corner sat Thomas Dickons, the faithful under-bailiff of Mr. Aubrey, a big, broad-shouldered, middle-aged man, with a hard-featured face and a phlegmatic air. In the opposite corner sat the little grizzle-headed clerk and sexton, old Hallelujah—(as he was called, but his real name was Jonas Higgs). Beside him sat Pumpkin, the gardener at the Hall, a very frequent guest at the Aubrey Arms o' nights—always attended by Hector, the large Newfoundland dog already spoken of, and who was now lying stretched on the floor at Pumpkin's feet, his nose resting on his forefeet, and his eyes, with great gravity, watching the motions of a skittish kitten under the table. Opposite to him sat Tonson, the gamekeeper, —a thin, wiry, beetle-browed fellow, with eyes like a ferret; and there were also one or two farmers, that lived in the village.

"Let's ha' another can o' ale, afore ye sit down," said Tonson, "we can do with another half a gallon, I'm thinking!'' This order also was quickly attended to; and then the landlord, having seen to the door, and fastened the shutters close, took his place on a vacant stool, and resumed his pipe.

"So she do take a very long grave, Jonas?'' inquired Dickons, of the sexton, after some little pause.

"Ay, Mr. Dickons, a' think she do, t' ould girl! I always thought she would. 'Tis a reg'lar *man's* size, I warrant you; and when parson saw it, a' said, he thought 'twere too big; but I ax'd his pardon, and said I hadn't been sexton for thirty years without knowing my business—ha, ha!''

"I suppose, Jonas, you mun ha' seen her walking about i' t' village in your time— *Were* she such a big-looking woman?'' inquired Pumpkin, as he shook the ashes out of his pipe, and replenished it.

"Forty years ago I used to see her—she were then an old woman, wi' white hair, and leaned on a stick—I never thought she'd a lasted so long,'' replied Higgs, emptying his glass.

"She've had a pretty long spell on't,'' quoth Dickons, after slowly emptying his mouth of smoke.

"A hundred and two," replied the sexton; "so saith her coffin-plate—a' seed it to-day."

"What were her name?" inquire Tonson—"I never knew her by any name but blind Bess."

"Her name be *Elizabeth Crabtree,* on the coffin," replied Higgs; "and she's to be buried to-morrow."

"She were a strange old woman," said Hazel, one of the farmers, as he took down one of the oat-cakes that were hanging overhead, and breaking off a piece, held it with the tongs before the fire to toast, and then put it into his ale.

"Ay, she were," quoth Pumpkin; "I wonder what she thinks o' such things *now*—may be she's paying dear for her tricks!"

"Tut, Pumpkin," said Tonson, "let t' ould creature rest in her grave peaceably!"

"Ay, Master Tonson," quoth the clerk, in his reading-desk twang—"*there be no knowledge, nor wisdom, nor device!*"

"'Tis very odd," observed Pumpkin, "but this dog that's lying at my feet never could a' bear going past her cottage late o' nights; and the night she died—Lord! you should have heard the howl Hector gave—and a' didn't then know she were gone."

"No! but were't really so?" inquired Dickons—several of the others taking their pipes out of their mouths, and looking earnestly at Pumpkin.

"I didn't half like it, I assure you," quoth Pumpkin.

"Ha, ha, ha!—ha, ha!" laughed the gamekeeper—

"Ay, marry you may laugh—but I'll stake half a gallon o' ale you daren't go by yourself to the cottage where she's lying —*now*, mind—i' the dark."

"I'll do it," quoth Higgs, eagerly, preparing to lay down his pipe.

"No, no—*thou'rt* quite used to dead folk," replied Pumpkin — and, after a little faint drollery, they dropped into silence.

"Bess dropped off sudden like at last, didn't she?" inquired the landlord.

"She went out, as they say, like the snuff of a candle," replied Jobbins, one of the farmers; "no one were with her but my Missus at the time. The night afore she took to the rattles all of a sudden. My Sall (that's done for her this long time, by madam's orders) says old Bess were a good deal shaken by a chap from London, that came down about a week before Christmas."

" Ay, ay," quoth one, " I've heard o' that—what was it?—what passed atwixt them?"

" Why, a' don't well know—but he seemed to know summat about t' ould girl's connections, and he had a book, and wrote down something; and he axed her, so Sall do tell me, such a many things about old people, and things that are long gone by!"

" What were the use on't?" inquired Dickons; " for Bess hath been silly this ten years, to my sartain knowledge."

" Why, a' couldn't tell. He seemed very 'quisitive, too, about t' old creature's Bible and prayer-book (she kept 'em in that ould bag of hers)—and Sall said she talked a good deal to the chap in her mumbling way, and seemed to know some folk he asked her about. And Sall saith she hath been, in a manner, dismal ever since, and often a-crying and talking to herself."

" I've heard," said the landlord, " that squire and parson were wi' her on Christmas-day—and that she talked a deal o' strange things, and that the squire did seem, as it were, *struck* a little, you know—struck, like!"

" Why, so my Sall do say; but it may be all her own head," replied Jobbins.

Here a pause took place.

" Madam," said the sexton, " hath given orders for a decent burying to-morrow."

" Well, a' never thought any wrong of ould Bess, for my part," said one—and another—and another; and they smoked their pipes for some minutes in silence.

" Talking o' strangers from London," said the sexton presently; " who do know anything o' them two chaps that were at church last Sunday? Two such peacock chaps I never seed afore in *my* time—and grinning all service time!"

" Ay, *I'll* tell you something of 'em," said Hazel—a big broad-shouldered farmer, who plucked his pipe out of his mouth with sudden energy—" They're a brace o' good ones, to be sure, ha, ha! Some week or ten days ago, as I were a-coming across the field leading into the lane behind the church, I seed these same two chaps, and on coming nearer (they not seeing me for the hedge) Lord bless me! would ye believe it? —if they wasn't a-teasing my daughter Jenny, that were coming along wi' some physic from the doctor for my old woman! One of em seemed a-going to put his arm round her neck, and t'other came close to her on t'other side, a-talking to her and pushing her about." Here a young farmer, who had but seldom spoken, took his pipe out of his mouth and exclaiming, "Lord bless me!" sat listening with his mouth wide open.

"Well, a' came into the road behind 'em, without their seeing me; and "—(here he stretched out a thick, rigid, muscular arm, and clinched his teeth)—"a' got hold of each by the collar, and one of 'em I shook about, and gave him a kick i' the breech that sent him spinning a yard or two on the road, he clapping his hand behind him, and crying, to be sure— 'You'll smart for this—a good hundred pound damages!' or summat o' that sort. T'other dropped on his knees, and begged for mercy; so a' just spit in his face, and flung him under t' hedge, telling him if he stirred till I were out o' sight, I'd crack his skull for him; and so I would!" Here the wrathful speaker pushed his pipe again between his lips, and began puffing away with great energy; while he who had appeared to take so great an interest in the story, and who was the very man who had flown to the rescue of Miss Aubrey, when she seemed on the point of being similarly treated, told that circumstance exactly as it occurred, amid the silent but excited wonder of those present—all of whom, at its close, uttered vehement execrations, and intimated the summary and savage punishment which the cowardly rascal would have experienced at the hands of each and every one of them, had they come across him.

"I reckon," said the landlord, as soon as the swell had a little subsided, "they must be the two chaps that put up here, some time ago, for an hour or so. You should ha' seen 'em get on and off the saddle—that's all! Why, a' laughed outright! The chap with the hair under his chin got on upon the wrong side, and t'other seemed as if he thought his beast would a' *bit* him!"

"Ha, ha, ha!" laughed all.

"I thought they'd a' both got a fall before they'd gone a dozen yards!"

"They've taken a strange fancy to my church-yard," said the sexton, setting down his glass, and then preparing to fill his pipe again; "they've been looking about among 'em— among t' ould grave-stones, up behind t' ould yew-tree, yonder; and one of them writ something, now and then, in a book; so they're book-writers, in coorse!"

"That's scholars, I reckon," quoth Dickons; "but rot the larning of such chaps as them!"

"I wonder if they'll put a picture o' the Hall in their book," quoth the sexton. "They axed a many questions about the people up there, especially about the squire's father, and some ould folk, whose names I knew when they spoke of 'em—but I hadn't heard o' them for this forty year. And one of 'em (he were the shortest, and such a chap, to be sure!—just like the monkey that were dressed i' the man's clothes last Grilston fair) talked uncommon fine about young *Miss*—"

"If *I'd* a heard him tak' her name into his dirty mouth, his teeth should a' gone after it!" said Tonson.

"Lord! he didn't say any harm—only silly like—and t'other seemed now and then not to like his going on so. The little one said Miss were a lovely gal, or something like that, and hoped they'd become by and by better friends—ah, ha!"

"What! wi' that chap?" said Pumpkin—and he looked as if he were meditating putting the little sexton up the chimney, for the mere naming of such a thing.

"I reckon they're fro' London, and brought toon tricks wi' 'em—for I never heard o' such goings-on as theirs down *here* afore," said Tonson.

"One of 'em—him that axed me all the questions, and write i' t' book, seemed a sharp enough chap in his way; but I can't say much for the little one," said Higgs. "Lud, I couldn't hardly look in his face for laughing, he seemed such a fool!—He had a riding-whip wi' a silver head, and stood smacking his legs (you should ha' seen how tight his clothes was on his legs—I warrant you, Tim Timkins never seed such a thing, I'll be sworn) all the while, as if a' liked to hear the sound of it."

"If I'd a' been beside him," said Hazel, "I'd a saved him that trouble—only I'd a' laid it into *another* part of him!"

"Ha, ha, ha!" they laughed—and presently passed on to other matters.

"Hath the squire been doing much lately in Parliament?" inquired the sexton of Dickons.

"Why, yes—he's trying hard to get that new road made from Harkley Bridge to Hilton."

"Ah, that would save a good four mile, if a' could manage it!"

"I hear the Papists are trying to get the upper hand again, which the Lud forbid!" said the sexton, after another pause.

"The squire hath lately made a speech in that matter, that hath finished them," said Dickons.

"What would they be after?" inquired the landlord of Dickons, of whom, in common with all present, he thought great things.

"They *say* they wants nothing but what's their own, and liberty, and that like—"

"If thou wert a shepherd, Master Higgs," replied Dickons, "and wert to be asked by ten or dozen wolves to let them in among thy flock of sheep, they saying how quiet and kind they would be to 'em—would'st let 'em in, or keep 'em out—eh?"

"Ay, ay—that be it—'tis as true as gospel!" said the clerk.

"So you a'n't to have that old sycamore down, after all, Master Dickons?" inquired Tonson.

"No; miss hath carried the day against the squire and Mr. Waters; and there stands the old tree, and it hath to be looked better after than it were afore."

"Why hath miss taken such a fancy to it? 'Tis an old crazy thing."

"If thou hadst been there when she did beg, as I may say, its life," replied Dickons, with a little energy—"and hadst seen her, and heard her voice, that be as smooth as cream, thou would'st never have forgotten it, I can tell thee!"

"There isn't a more beautiful lady i' th' country, I reckon, than the squire's sister?" inquired the sexton.

"No, nor in all England: if there be, I'll lay down a hundred pounds."

"And where's to be found a young lady that do go about i' t' village like she?—She were wi' Phœbe Williams t'other night, all through the snow, and i' t' dark."

"If I'd only laid hands on that chap!" interrupted the young farmer, her rescuer.

"I wonder she do not choose some one to be married to, up in London," said the landlord.

"She'll be having some delicate high quality chap, I reckon, one o' these fine days," said Hazel.

"She will be a dainty dish, truly, for whomever God gives her to," quoth Dickons.

"Ay, she will," said more than one, in an earnest tone.

"Now, to my mind," said Tonson, "saving your presence, Master Dickons, I know not but young madam be more to my taste; she be in a manner somewhat fuller—plumper-like, and her skin be *so* white, and her hair as black as a raven's."

"There's not another two such women to be found in the whole world," said Dickons, authoritatively. Here Hector suddenly rose up, and went to the door, where he stood snuffing in an inquisitive manner.

"Now, what do that dog hear, I wonder?" quoth Pumpkin, curiously, stooping forward.

"Blind Bess," replied Tonson, winking his eye, and laughing. Presently there was a sharp rapping at the door; which the landlord opened, and let in one of the servants from the

Hall, his clothes white with snow, his face nearly as white, with manifest agitation.

" Why, man, what's the matter?" inquired Dickons, startled by the man's appearance. " Art frightened at anything?"

" Oh, Lord! oh, Lord!" he commenced.

" What is it, man? Art drunk?—or mad?—or frightened? Take a drop o' drink," said Tonson. But the man refused it.

" Oh, my friends, sad work at the Hall!"

" What's the matter?" cried all at once, rising and standing round the new-comer.

" If thou be'st drunk, John," said Dickons, sternly, " there's a way of sobering thee—mind that."

" Oh, Master Dickons, I don't know what's come to me, for grief and fright! The squire, they do say, and all of us, are to be turned out o' Yatton!"

" *What!*" exclaimed all in a breath.

" There's some one else lays claim to it. We must all go! Oh, Lud! oh, Lud!" No one spoke for near a minute; and consternation was written on every face.

" Sit thee down here, John," said Dickons at length, " and let us hear what thou hast to say—or thou wilt have us all be going up in a body to the Hall."

Having forced on him part of a glass of ale, he began: " There hath been plainly mischief brewing, *somewhere*, this many days, as I could tell by the troubled face o' the squire; but he kept it to himself. Lawyer Parkinson and another have been latterly coming in chaises from London; and last night the squire got a letter that seems to have finished all. Such trouble there were last night with the squire, and young madam and miss! And to-day the parson came, and were a long while alone with old Madam Aubrey, who hath since had a stroke, or a fit, or something of that like (the doctors have been there all day from Grilston), and likewise young madam hath taken to her bed, and is ill."

" And what of the squire and miss?" inquired some one, after all had maintained a long silence.

" Oh, 'twould break your heart to see them," said the man, bursting into tears: " they are both as pale as death: he so dreadful sorrowful, but quiet like, and she now and then wringing her hands, and both them going from the bedroom of old madam to young madam's. Nay, an' there had been half a dozen deaths i' th' house, it could not be worse. Neither the squire nor miss hath touched food the whole day!"

There was, in truth, not a dry eye in the room, nor one

whose voice did not seem somewhat obstructed with his emotions.

"Who told thee about the squire's losing the estate?" inquired Dickons.

"We heard of it but an hour or so agone. Mr. Parkinson (it seems by the squire's orders) told Mr. Waters, and he told it to us; saying as how it was useless to keep such a thing secret, and that we might all know the occasion of so much trouble.

"Who's to ha' it then, instead of the squire?" at length inquired Tonson, in a voice half choked with rage and grief.

"Lord only knows at present. But whoever 'tis, there isn't one of us sarvants but will go with the squire and his—if it be even to prison, *that* I can tell ye."

"I'm Squire *Aubrey's* gamekeeper," quoth Tonson, his eye kindling as his countenance darkened, "and no one's else! It shall go hard if any one else hath a game—"

"But if there's law in the land, sure the justice must be wi' t' squire—he and his family have had it so long," said one of the farmers.

"I'll tell you what, masters," said Pumpkin, mysteriously: "I shall be somewhat better pleased when Jonas here hath got that old creature Bess safe under ground."

"Blind Bess?" exclaimed Tonson, with a very serious, not to say disturbed, countenance. "I wonder—sure! sure! that ould witch can have had no hand in all this—"

"Poor old soul, not she! There be no such things as witches nowadays," exclaimed Jonas. "Not she, I warrant me! She hath been ever befriended by the squire's family. *She* do it!"

"The sooner we get her under ground, for all that, the better, say I!" quoth Tonson, striking his hand on the table.

"The parson hath a choice sermon on ' The Flying away of Riches,' " said Higgs in a quaint, sad manner; " 'tis to be hoped he'll preach from it next Sunday!—"

Soon after this, the little party dispersed, each oppressed with greater grief and amazement than he had ever known before. Bad news fly swiftly—and that which had just come from the Hall, within a very few hours of its having been told at the Aubrey Arms, had spread grief and consternation among high and low for many miles round Yatton.

CHAPTER X.

WOULD you have believed it? Notwithstanding all that had happened between Titmouse and Tag-rag, they positively got reconciled to one another—a triumphant result of the astute policy of Mr. Gammon. As soon as he had heard Titmouse's infuriated account of his ignominious expulsion from Satin Lodge, he burst into a fit of hearty but gentle laughter which at length subsided into an inward chuckle that lasted the rest of the day; and which was occasioned, first, by gratification at the impression which his own sagacity had evidently produced upon the powerful mind of Titmouse; secondly, by an exquisite appreciation of the mingled meanness and stupidity of Tag-rag. I do not mean it to be understood, that Titmouse had given Mr. Gammon such a terse and clear account of the matter as I imagine myself to have given to my reader; but still he told quite enough to put Mr. Gammon in full possession of the true state of the case. Good: but then—instantly reflected Gammon—what are we now to do with Titmouse?—where was that troublesome little ape to be caged, till it suited the purposes of his proprietors (as Messrs. Quirk, Gammon and Snap might surely be called, for they had caught him, however they might fail to tame him) to let him loose upon society, to amuse and astonish it by his antics?—That was the question occupying the thoughts of Mr. Gammon while his calm, clear, gray eye was fixed upon Titmouse, apparently very attentive to what he was saying. That gentleman had first told the story of his wrongs to Snap, who instantly, rubbing his hands, suggested an indictment at the Clerkenwell Sessions—an idea which infinitely delighted Titmouse, but was somewhat sternly " pooh-pooh-pooed!" by Mr. Gammon as soon as he heard of it—Snap thereat shrugging his shoulders with a disconcerted air, but a bitter sneer upon his sharp, hard face. Like many men of little but active minds, early drilled to particular callings, Snap was equal to the mechanical conduct of business—the mere working of the machinery—but, as the phrase is, could never see an inch beyond his nose. Every petty conjuncture of circumstances that admitted of litigation, at once suggested its *expediency*, without reference to other considerations, or connection with, or subordination to, any general purpose or plan of action. A creature of small impulses, he had no idea of foregoing a momentary advantage to secure an ulterior object—which, in fact, he could not keep for a moment before his thoughts, so as to have any influence on his movements. What a different man now, was Gammon!

To speak after the manner of physiologists, several of my characters—Titmouse, Tag-rag (with his amiable wife and daughter), Huckaback, Snap, and old Quirk himself—may be looked on as reptiles of a low order in the scale of being, whose simple structures almost one dash of the knife would suffice to lay thoroughly open. Gammon, however, I look upon as of a much higher order; possessing a far more complicated structure, adapted to the discharge of superior functions; and who, consequently, requireth a more careful dissection. But let it not be supposed that I have yet done with *any* of my characters.

Gammon saw that Tag-rag, under proper management, might be made very useful. He was a moneyed man; a selfish man; and, after his sort, an ambitious man. He had an only child, a daughter, and if Titmouse and he could only be by any means once more brought together, and a firm friendship cemented between them, Gammon saw several very profitable uses to which such an intimacy might be turned, in the happening of any of several contingencies which he contemplated as possible. In the event, for instance, of larger outlays of money being required than suited the convenience of the firm—could not Tag-rag be easily brought to accommodate his future son-in-law of £10,000 a year? Suppose, for instance, that after all their case should break down, and all their pains, exertions, and expenditure be utterly thrown away? Now, if Tag-rag could be quietly brought some fine day, to the point of either making some actual advance, or entering into security for Titmouse—ah! that *would* do, said both Quirk and Gammon. But then Titmouse was a very unsafe instrument—an incalculable fool, and might commit himself too far!

"You forget, Gammon," said old Mr. Quirk. "I don't fear this girl of Tag-rag's—because only let Titmouse see—hem," he suddenly paused, and looked a little confused.

"To be sure—I see," replied Gammon, quietly, and the thing passed off. "If either Miss Quirk or Miss Tag-rag becomes Mrs. Titmouse," thought he, "I am not the man I take myself for."

A few days after Titmouse's expulsion from Satin Lodge, without his having ever gone near Tag-rag's premises in Oxford Street, or, in short, seen or heard anything about him, or any one connected with him, he removed to small but very respectable lodgings in the neighborhood of Hatton Garden, provided for him by Mr. Quirk. Mrs. Squallop was quite affected while she took leave of Titmouse, who gave her son sixpence to take his two boxes down-stairs to the hackney-coach drawn up opposite to the entrance of Closet Court.

" I've always felt like a mother toward you, sir, in my humble way," said Mrs. Squallop, in a very respectful manner, and courtesying profoundly.

" A—I've not got any small silver by me, my good woman:" Titmouse with a fine air, as he drew on his white kid glove.

" Lord, Mr. Titmouse!" sad the woman, almost bursting into tears, " I wasn't asking for money, neither for me nor mine—only one can't help, as it were, feeling at parting with an old lodger, you know, sir—"

" Ah—ya—as—and all that! Well, my good woman, good-day, good-day."

" Good-bye, sir—God bless you; now you're going to be a rich man!—Excuse me, sir."—And she seized his hand and shook it.

" You're a—devilish—impudent—woman—'pon my soul!" exclaimed Titmouse, his features filled with amazement at the presumption of which she had been guilty; and he strode down the stairs with an air of offended dignity.

" Well—I never!—*That* for you, you little brute," said Mrs. Squallop, snapping her fingers as soon as she had heard his last step on the stairs—" Kind or cruel, it's all one to you, you're a nasty jackanapes, only fit to stand in a tailor's window to show his clothes—and I'll be sworn you'll come to no good in the end. Let you be *rich* as you may, you'll always be the fool you always were!"

Had the good woman been familiar with the Night Thoughts of Young, she might have expressed herself somewhat tersely in a line of his—

" Pigmies are pigmies still, though perch'd on Alps,"

And, by the way, who can read the next line—

" And pyramids are pyramids in vales,"

without thinking for a moment, with a kind of proud sympathy, of certain *other* characters in this history? Well! but let us pass on.

The day after that on which Mr. Gammon had had a long interview with Titmouse, at the new lodgings of the latter,—when, after a very skillful effort, he had succeeded in reconciling Titmouse to a renewal of his acquaintance with Tagrag, upon that gentleman's making a complete and abject apology for his late monstrous conduct, Mr. Gammon wended

his way toward Oxford Street, and soon introduced himself
once more to Mr. Tag-rag, who was standing leaning against
one of the counters in his shop in a musing position, with a
pen behind his ear, and his hands in his breeches pockets.
Ten days had elapsed since he had expelled the little impostor
Titmouse from Satin Lodge, and during that interval he had
neither seen nor heard anything whatever of him.   On now
catching the first glimpse of Mr. Gammon, he started from
his musing posture, not a little disconcerted, and agitation
overspread his coarse deeply pitted face with a tallowy hue.
What was in the wind! Mr. Gammon coming to him, so long
after what had occurred?   Mr. Gammon who, having found
out his error, had discarded Titmouse!   Tag-rag had a mortal
dread of Gammon, who seemed to him to glide like a dangerous snake into the shop, so quietly and *so deadly!*   There
was something so calm and imperturbable in his demeanor, so
blandly crafty, so ominously gentle and soft in the tone of his
voice, so penetrating in his eye, and he could throw such an
infernal smile over his features!   Tag-rag might be likened to
the ox, suddenly shuddering as he perceives the glistening
folds of the rattlesnake noiselessly moving toward, or around
him, in the long grass.   One glimpse of his blasting beauty of
hue, and—Horror! all is over.

If the splendid bubble of Titmouse's fortune *had* burst in
the manner which he had represented, why Gammon here now?
thought Tag-rag.   It was with, in truth, a very poor show of
contempt and defiance that, in answer to the bland salutation
of Gammon, he led the way down the shop into the little room
which had been the scene of such an extraordinary communication concerning Titmouse on a former occasion.

Gammon commenced, in a mild tone, with a very startling
representation of the criminal liability which Tag-rag had incurred by his wanton outrage upon Mr. Titmouse, his own
guest, in violation of all the laws of hospitality.   Tag-rag
furiously alleged the imposition which had been practiced on
him by Titmouse; but seemed quite collapsed when Gammon
assured him that the circumstance would not afford him the
slightest justification.   Having satisfied Tag-rag that he was
entirely at the mercy of Titmouse, who might subject him to
both fine and imprisonment, Mr. Gammon proceeded to open
his eyes to their widest stare of amazement by assuring him
that Titmouse had been hoaxing him, and that he was really
in the dazzling position in which he had been first represented
by Gammon to Tag-rag; that every week brought him nearer
to the full and uncontrolled enjoyment of an estate in York-

shire, worth £10,000 a year at the very lowest; that it was becoming an object of increasing anxiety to them (Messrs. Quirk,
Gammon and Snap) to keep him out of the hands of money-
lenders, who, as usual in such cases, had already scented out
their victim, and so forth.—Tag-rag turned very white, and
felt sick at heart in the midst of all his wonder. Oh, and his
daughter had lost the golden prize! and through *his* misconduct! He could have sunk into the cellar!—Mr. Gammon
declared that he could not account for the singular conduct of
Mr. Titmouse on the melancholy occasion in question, except
by referring it to the excellent wines which he had too freely
partaken of at Satin Lodge, added (said Gammon, with an
exquisite expression of features that perfectly fascinated Tag-
rag) to a "certain tender influence" which had fairly laid
prostrate the faculties of the young and enthusiastic Titmouse;
that there could be no doubt of his real motive in the conduct
alluded to, namely, a desire to test the sincerity and disinterestedness of a "certain person's" attachment before he let all
his fond and passionate feelings go out toward her—[At this
point the perspiration burst from every pore in the body of
Tag-rag]—and that no one could deplore the unexpected issue
of his little experiment so much as now did Titmouse.

Tag-rag really, for a moment, scarcely knew where he was,
who was with him, nor whether he stood on his head or his
heels, so delightful and entirely unexpected was the issue of
Mr. Gammon's visit. As soon as his faculties had somewhat
recovered themselves from their temporary confusion, almost
breathless, he assured Gammon that no event in the whole
course of his life had occasioned him such poignant regret as
his treatment of Titmouse on the occasion in question; that he
had undoubtedly followed unwittingly (he was ashamed to
own) the example of Titmouse, and drunk far more than his
usual quantity of wine; besides which he had undoubtedly
noticed, as had Mrs. T., the state of things between Mr. Titmouse and his daughter—talking of whom, by the way, he
could assure Mr. Gammon that they had both been ill ever
since that unfortunate evening, and had never ceased to condemn his—Tag-rag's monstrous conduct on that occasion. As
for his daughter, she was growing thinner and thinner every
day, and he thought he must send her to the country for a
short time; in fact—poor girl!—she was plainly pining away!

To all this Mr. Gammon listened with a calm, delightful,
sympathizing look, that quite transported Tag-rag, and satisfied him that Mr. Gammon implicitly believed every word that
was being said to him. But when he proceeded to assure Tag-

rag that this visit of his had been undertaken at the earnest
instance of Mr. Titmouse himself (who, by the way, had removed to lodgings which would do for the present, so as they
were only near to their office, for the purpose of frequent communication on matters of business between him and their firm),
who had urged him, Mr. Gammon, to tender the olive branch,
in the devout hope that it might be accepted.   Tag-rag's excitement knew scarce any bounds; and he could almost have
started into the shop, and given orders to his shopmen to sell
every article, for the rest of the day, one and a half per cent.
under what they had been selling before!   Mr. Gammon wrote
down Titmouse's direction, and assured Mr. Tag-rag that a
call from him would be gratefully received by Mr. Titmouse.
"There's no accounting for these things, Mr. Tag-rag—is
there?" said Mr. Gammon, with an arch smile, as he prepared
to depart—Tag-rag squeezing his hands with painful energy as
Gammon bade him adieu, saying he should not be himself for
the rest of the day, and bowing the aforesaid Mr. Gammon
down the shop with as profound an obsequiousness as if he had
been the Lord High Chancellor, or even the Lord Mayor.   As
soon as Gammon had got fairly into the street, and to a safe
distance, he burst into little gentle paroxysms of laughter,
every now and then, that lasted him till he had regained his
office in Saffron Hill.

   The motive so bold and skillfully suggested by Gammon to
Tag-rag, as that impelling Titmouse to seek a reconciliation
with him, was greedily credited by Tag-rag.   'Tis certainly
very easy for a man to believe what he wishes to be true.   Was
it *very* improbable that Tag-rag, loving only one object on
earth (next to money, which indeed he really did love with
the best and holiest energies of his nature), namely, his daughter; and believing her to be possessed of qualities calculated to
excite every one's love—should believe that she had inspired
Titmouse with the passion of which he had just been hearing—
a passion that was consuming him, that could not be quenched
by even the gross outrage which—but faugh! *that* Tag-rag
shuddered to think of.   He clapped his hat on his head, and
started off to Titmouse's lodgings, and fortunately caught that
gentleman just as he was going out to dine at a neighboring
tavern.   If Tag-rag had been a keen observer, he could hardly
have failed to discover aversion toward himself written in every
feature and gesture of Titmouse; and also how difficult it was
to be concealed.   But his eagerness overbore everything, and
took Titmouse quite by storm.   Before Tag-rag had done with
him, he had obliterated every trace of resentment in his little

friend's bosom. Thoroughly as Gammon thought he had prepared him for the encounter, and armed him at all points—
'twas of no avail. Tag-rag poured such a monstrous quantity
of flummery down the gaping mouth and insatiate throat of
the little animal, as at length produced its desired effect. Few
can resist flattery, however coarsely administered; but as for
Titmouse, he felt the soft fluid deliciously insinuating itself
into every crevice of his little nature, for which it seemed, indeed, to have a peculiar affinity; 'twas a balm, 'twas an opiate
soothing his wounded pride, lubricating all his inner man;
nay, flooding it, so as at length to extinguish entirely the very
small glimmering spark of discernment which nature had
lighted in him. "To be fore*warned* is to be fore*armed*," says
the proverb; but it was not verified in the present instance.
Titmouse would have dined at Satin Lodge on the very next
Sunday, in accordance with the pressing invitations of Tag-
rag, but that he happened to recollect having engaged himself
to dine that evening with Mr. Quirk, at his residence in
Camberwell—ALIBI HOUSE. As I have already intimated in
a previous part of this history, that most respectable old
gentleman, Mr. Quirk, with the shrewdness natural to him,
and which had been quickened by his great experience, had
soon seen through the ill-contrived and worse-concealed designs upon Titmouse of Mr. Tag-rag; and justly considered
that the surest method of rendering them abortive would be to
familiarize Titmouse with a superior style of things, such as
was to be found at Alibi House—and a more lovely and attractive object for his best affections in Miss Quirk—Dora
Quirk, the luster of whose charms and accomplishments there
could be no doubt, he thought, would instantly efface the
image of that poor, feeble, vulgar creature, Miss Tag-rag; for
such old Quirk knew her to be, though he had, in fact, never
for a moment set eyes upon her. Mr. Tag-rag looked rather
blank at hearing of the grand party there was to be at Alibi
House, and that Titmouse was to be introduced to the only
daughter of Mr. Quirk, and could not, for the life of him,
abstain from dropping something, vague and indistinct to be
sure, about "entrapping unsuspecting innocence," and "interested attentions," and other similar expressions—all of
which, however, were lost upon Titmouse. Tapping with an
auctioneer's hammer on a block of granite, would make about
as much impression upon it as hint, innuendo, or suggestion,
upon a blockhead. So it was with Titmouse. He promised
to dine at Satin Lodge on the Sunday after, with which poor
Mr. Tag-rag was obliged to depart content; having been un-

able to get Titmouse up to Clapham on either of the intervening evenings, on which, he told Mr. Tag-rag, he was particularly engaged with an intimate friend—in fact, one of the
solicitors; and Tag-rag left him, after shaking him by the
hand with the utmost cordiality and energy.   He instantly
conceived a lively hatred of old Mr. Quirk and his daughter,
who seemed taking so unfair an advantage.   However, what
could be done?   Many times during his interview, did he
anxiously turn about in his mind the expediency of proffering
to lend or give Titmouse a five-pound note, of which he had
one or two in his pocket-book; but no—'twas too much for
human nature—he *could* not bring himself to it; and quitted
Titmouse as rich a man as he had entered his lodgings.

The gentleman to whom Titmouse alluded was in fact Mr.
Snap, who had early evinced a great partiality for him, and
lost no opportunity of contributing to his enjoyment.   He was
a sharp-sighted person, and quickly detected many qualities in
Titmouse kindred to his own.   He sincerely commiserated
Titmouse's situation, than which what could be more lonely
and desolate?   Was he to sit night after night, in the length-
ening nights of autumn and winter, with not a soul to speak
to, not a book to read (that was at least interesting or worth
reading); nothing, in short, to occupy his attention?   " No,"
said Snap to himself; " I will do as I would be done by; I will
come and draw him out of his dull hole; I will show him life—
I will give him an early insight into the habits and practices of
the great world, in which he is so soon to cut a leading figure!
I will early familiarize him with the gayest and most exciting
modes of London life!"   The very first taste of this cup of
pleasure was exquisitely relished by Titmouse, and he felt a
proportionate gratitude to him whose kind hand had first
raised it to his lips.   Scenes of which he had heretofore only
heard and read—after which he had often sighed and yearned,
were now opening daily before him, limited as were his means;
and he felt perfectly happy.   When Snap had finished the
day's labors of the office, from which he was generally released
about eight or nine o'clock in the evening, he would repair to
his lodgings, and decorate himself for the evening's display;
after which, either he would go to Titmouse, or Titmouse
come to him, as might have been previously agreed upon between them; and then—

" The *town* was all before them, where to choose."

Sometimes they would, arm in arm, each with his cigar in
his mouth, saunter for hours together along the leading streets

and thoroughfares, making acute observations and deep reflections upon the ever-moving and motley scenes around them.
Most frequently, however, they would repair, at half price, to
the theaters; for Snap had the means of securing almost a
constant supply of "orders" from the underlings of the
theaters, also in respect to the *Sunday Flash*, with which
Messrs. Quirk and Gammon were connected, and other newspapers. Ah, 'twas a glorious sight to see these two gentlemen
saunter into a vacant box, conscious that the eyes of two
thirds of the house were fixed upon them in admiration, and
conducting themselves accordingly—as swells of the first
water. One such night counterbalanced, in Titmouse's estimation, a whole year of previous obscurity and wretchedness!
The theater over, they would repair to some cloudy tavern,
full of noise and smoke, and the glare of gas-light—redolent
of the fragrant fumes of tobacco, spirits, and porter, intermingled with the tempting odors of smoking kidneys, mutton-
chops, beefsteaks, oysters, stewed cheese, toasted cheese,
Welsh rabbits; where those who are chained to the desk and
the counter during the day revel in the license of the hour,
and eat, and drink, and smoke to the highest point either of
excitement or stupefaction, and enter into all the slang of the
day—of the turf, the ring, the cockpit, the theaters, and shake
their sides at comic songs. To enter one of these places when
the theater was over, was a luxury indeed to Titmouse; figged
out in his very uttermost best, with satin stock and double
breast-pins; his glossy hat cocked on one side of his head, his
tight blue surtout, with the snowy handkerchief elegantly
drooping out of the breast-pocket; straw-colored kid gloves,
tight trousers, and shining boots; his ebony silver-headed cane
held carelessly under his arm; to walk into the middle of the
room with a sort of haughty ease and indifference, or nonchalance, and after deliberately scanning, through his eye-
glass, every box, with its occupants, at length drop into a
vacant nook, and with a languid air summon the bustling
waiter to receive his commands. The circumstances of his
almost always accompanying Snap on these occasions, who was
held in great awe by the waiters, to whom his professional
celebrity was well known (for there was scarce an interesting,
a dreadful, or a nasty scene at any of the police-offices in
which Snap's name did not figure in the newspapers as " on
behalf of the prisoner)" got Titmouse almost an equal share
of consideration, and aided the effect produced by his own
commanding appearance. As for Snap, whenever he was
asked who his companion was, he would whisper in a very

significant tone and manner,—"Devilish high chap!" From
these places they would repair, not unfrequently, to certain
other scenes of nightly London life, which, I thank God! the
virtuous reader can form no notion of, though they are,
strange to say, winked at, if not patronized by the police and
magistracy, till the metropolis is choked with them. Thus
would Snap and Titmouse pleasantly pass away their time till
one, two, three, and often four o'clock in the morning; at
which hours they would, with many yawns, skulk homeward
through the deserted and silent streets, their clothes redolent
of tobacco smoke, their stomachs overcharged, their heads
often muddled, swimming, and throbbing with their multifarious potations—having thus spent a "*jolly night*," and
"*seen life.*" 'Twas thus that Snap greatly endeared himself
to Titmouse, and secretly (for he enjoined upon Titmouse, as
the condition of their continuance, strict secrecy on the subject
of these nocturnal adventures) stole a march upon his older
competitors for the good opinion of Titmouse—Messrs. Quirk,
Tag-rag, and even the astute and experienced Gammon himself.   Such doings as these required, however, as may easily
be believed, some slight augmentations of the allowance made
to Titmouse by Messrs. Quirk and Gammon; and 'twas fortunate that Snap was in a condition, having a few hundreds at
his command, to supply the necessities of Titmouse, receiving
with a careless air, on the occasion of such advances, small
slips of paper by way of acknowledgments; some on stamped
paper, others on unstamped paper—promissory notes and
I. O. U's.   Inasmuch, however, as Snap was not always possessed of a stamp on the occasion of a sudden advance, and
having asked the opinion of his pleader (a sharp fellow who
had been articled at the same time as himself to Messrs. Quirk
and Gammon) as to whether an instrument in this form—
"I. O. U. so much—*with interest,*" would be available
without a stamp, and being informed that it was a very
doubtful point, Snap ingeniously met the difficulty by quietly
adding to the principal what might become due in respect of
interest: *e. g.* if £5 were lent, the acknowledgment would
stand for £15—these little slips of paper being generally signed
by Titmouse in moments of extreme exhilaration, when he
never thought of scrutinizing anything that his friend Snap
would lay before him.   For the honor of Snap I must say that
I hardly think he deliberately purposed to perpetrate the fraud
which such a transaction appears to amount to; all he wanted
was—so he satisfied himself at least—to have it in his power to
recover the full amount of principal *really* advanced, with

interest, on one or other of those various securities, and hold the surplus as trustee for Titmouse. If, for instance, any unfortunate difference should hereafter arise between himself and Titmouse, and he should refuse to recognize his pecuniary obligations to Snap, the latter gentleman would be provided with short and easy proofs of his demands against him. 'Twas thus, I say, that Snap rendered himself indispensable to Titmouse, whom he bound to him by every tie of gratitude; so that, in short, they became sworn friends.

I will always say for Gammon, that he strenuously endeavored, from whatever motive, to urge upon Titmouse the necessity of his acquiring, at all events, a smattering of the elements of useful education. Beyond an acquaintance with the petty operations of arithmetic requisite for counter-transactions, I will venture to say that poor Titmouse had no serviceable knowledge of any kind. Mr. Gammon repeatedly pressed him to put himself under competent teachers of the ordinary branches of education; but Titmouse as often evaded him, and at length flatly refused to do anything of the kind. He promised, however, to read such books as Mr. Gammon might recommend, who thereupon sent him several; but a book before Titmouse was much the same as a plate of sawdust before a hungry man. Mr. Gammon, himself a man of considerable acquirements, soon saw the true state of the case, and gave up his attempts in despair and disgust. Not that he ever suffered Titmouse to perceive the faintest indications of such feelings toward him; on the contrary, Gammon ever manifested the same bland and benignant demeanor, consulting his wishes in everything, and striving to instill into him feelings of love, tempered by respect, as toward the most powerful—the only real, disinterested friend he had; and to a very great extent he succeeded.

Titmouse spent several hours in preparing for an effective first appearance at the dinner-table at Alibi House. Since dining at Satin Lodge he had considerably increased his wardrobe both in quantity and style. He now sported a pair of tight black trousers, with pumps and gossamer silk stockings. He wore a crimson velvet waistcoat, with a bright blue satin under-waistcoat, a shirt-frill standing out somewhat fiercely at right angles with his breast, and a brown dress-coat cut in the extreme of the fashion, the long tails coming to a point just about the backs of the knees. His hair (its purple hue still pretty distinctly perceptible) was disposed with great elegance. He had discarded mustaches; but had a very promising imperial. The hair underneath his chin came out curling on

each side of it, above his stock, like two little tufts or horns.
Over his waistcoat he wore his mosaic-gold watch-guard, and
a broad black watered ribbon, to which was attached his eye-
glass—in fact, if he had dressed himself in order to sit to a
miniature painter for his likeness, he could not have taken
greater pains, or secured a more successful result. The only
points about his appearance with which he was at all dissatisfied, were his hair—which was not yet the thing which he
hoped in due time to see it—his thick red stumpy hands, and
his round shoulders. The last matter gave him considerable
concern, for he felt that it seriously interfered with a graceful
carriage; and that the defect in his figure had been, after all,
not in the least remedied by the prodigious padding of his
coat. His protuberant eyes, of very light hue, had an expression that entirely harmonized with that of his open mouth;
and both together—quite independently of his dress, carriage,
and demeanor—(there is nothing like being candid)—gave you
the image of a—complete fool. Having at length carefully
adjusted his hat on his head, and drawn on his white kid
gloves, he enveloped himself in a stylish cloak, with long black
silk tassels, which had been lent to him by Snap; and about
four o'clock, forth sallied Mr. Titmouse, carefully picking his
way, in quest of the first coach that could convey him to Alibi
House, or as near to it as might be. He soon found one, and,
conscious that his appearance was far too splendid for an outside place, got inside. All the way along his heart was in a
little flutter of vanity, excitement, and expectation. He was
going to be introduced to Miss Quirk—and probably, also, to
several people of great consequence—as the heir apparent to
£10,000 a year. Two very respectable female passengers, his
companions all the way, he never once deigned to interchange
a syllable with. Four or five times did he put his head out of
the window, calling out, in a loud peremptory tone—" Mind,
coachman—Alibi House—Mr. Quirk's—Alibi House—Do you
hear, demme?" After which he would sink back into the seat
with a magnificent air, as if he had not been used to give himself so much trouble. The coach at length stopped. " Halibi
'Ouse, sir," said the coachman, in a most respectful tone—
" this is Mr. Quirk's, sir." Titmouse stepped out, dropped
eighteen pence into the man's hand, and opening the gate,
found himself in a straight and narrow gravel walk, of about
twenty yards in length, with little obstinate-looking stunted
shrubs on each side. 'Twas generally known among Mr.
Quirk's friends by the name of the *Rope-walk*. Titmouse
might have entered before as fine-looking a house, but only to

deliver a bundle of drapery or hosiery; never before had he entered such a one as a guest. It was, in fact, a fair-sized house, at least treble that of Satin Lodge, and had a far more stylish appearance. When Titmouse pulled the bell the door was quickly plucked open by a big footman, with showy shoulder-knot and a pair of splendid red plush breeches, who soon disposed of Titmouse's cloak and hat, and led the way to the drawing-room, before our friend, with a sudden palpitation of the heart, had had a moment's time even to run his hands through his hair. "Your name, sir?" inquired the man, sud-denly pausing—with his hand upon the handle of the door.

"Mr. Titmouse."

"I—*beg* your pardon, sir; *what* name?"

Titmouse, clearing his throat, repeated his name—open went the door, and—"Mr. Ticklemouse," said the servant very loudly and distinctly—ushering in Titmouse; on whom the door was the next instant closed. He felt amazingly flustered —and he would have been still more so if he could have been made aware of the titter which pervaded the fourteen or twenty people assembled in the room, occasioned by the droll mis-nomer of the servant, and the exquisitely ridiculous appear-ance of poor Titmouse. Mr. Quirk, dressed in black, with knee-breeches and silk stockings, immediately bustled up to him, shook him cordially by the hand, and led him up to the assembled guests. "My daughter—Miss Quirk; Mrs. Alder-man Addlehead; Mrs. Deputy Diddledaddle; Mrs. Alias, my sister;—Mr. Alderman Addlehead; Mr. Deputy Diddledaddle; Mr. Bluster; Mr. Slang; Mr. Hug; Mr. Flaw; Mr. Viper; Mr. Ghastly; Mr. Gammon you know." Miss Quirk was about four- or five-and-twenty—a fat young lady, with flaxen hair curled formally all over her head and down to her shoul-ders, so that she very much resembled one of those great wax dolls seen in bazaars and shop windows, especially if looked at through a strong magnifying glass. Her complexion was beautifully fair; her eyes small; her face quite round and fat. From the die-away manner in which she moved her head, and the languid tone of her voice, it was obvious that she was a very sentimental young lady. She was dressed in white, and wore a massive gold chain—her fat arms being half covered with long kid gloves. She was sitting on the sofa, from which she did not rise when Titmouse was introduced to her—and the moment after hid her face behind the album which had been lying on her knee, and which she had been showing to the ladies on each side of her; for, in fact, neither she nor any one else could, without the greatest difficulty, refrain from laughing at the monkeyfied appearance of Titmouse. The Alderman was a stout, stupid, little man—a fussy old prig— with small angry-looking black eyes, and a short red nose; as for his head, it seemed as though he had just smeared some sticky fluid over it, and then dipped it into a flour tub, so thickly laden was it with powder. Mr. Deputy Diddledaddle was tall and thin, and serious and slow of speech, with the solemn composure of an undertaker. Mr. Bluster was a great Old Bailey barrister, about fifty years old, the leader constantly employed by Messrs. Quirk, Gammon and Snap; and was making at least a thousand a year. He had an amazingly truculent-looking countenance, coarse to a degree, and his voice matched it; but on occasions like the present—*i. e.* in elegant society—he would fain drop the successful terrors of his manner, and appear the mild, dignified gentleman. He therefore spoke in a very soft, cringing way, with an anxious smile; but his bold insolent eye and coarse mouth—what could disguise or mitigate their expression? Here he was, playing the great man; making himself, however, most particularly agreeable to Messrs. Quirk and Gammon. Slang was of the same school; fat, vulgar, confident, and empty; telling obscene jokes and stories, in a deep bass voice. He sung a good song, too—particularly of that class which required the absence of ladies—and of *gentlemen*. Hug (Mr. Toady Hug) was also a barrister; a glib little Jewish-looking fellow, creeping into considerable criminal practice. He was a sneaking backbiter, and had a blood-hound scent after an attorney. See him, for instance, at this moment, in close and eager conversation with Mr. Flaw, who, rely upon it, will give him a brief before the week is over. Viper was the editor of the *Sunday Flash;* a cold, venomous, little fellow. He was of opinion that everything was wrong—moral, physical, intellectual, and social; that there was really no such thing, or at least ought not to be, as religion; and as to political rights, that everybody ought to be uppermost at once. He had failed in business twice and disreputably, then had become a Unitarian parson, but, having seduced a young female member of his congregation, he was expelled from his pulpit. An action being brought against him by the mother of his victim, and heavy damages obtained, he attempted to take the benefit of the Insolvent Debtors' Act—but, on account of Miss ——, was remanded for eighteen months. That period he employed in writing a shockingly blasphemous work, for which he was prosecuted, and sentenced to a heavy fine and imprisonment; on being released from which, saturated with gall and bitterness against all mankind, he took to political writing of a very violent character, and was at length picked up, half starved, by his present patron, Mr. Quirk, and made editor of the *Sunday Flash.* Is not all this history written in his sallow, sinister-eyed, bitter-expressioned countenance? Woe to him who gets into a discussion with Viper! There were one or two others present, particularly a Mr. Ghastly, a third-rate tragic actor, with a tremendous mouth, only one eye, and a very hungry look. He never spoke, because no one spoke to him, for his clothes seemed rather rusty-black. The only man of gentle-man-like appearance in the room was Mr. Gammon; and he took an early opportunity of engaging poor Titmouse in con-versation, and setting him comparatively at his ease—a thing which was attempted by old Quirk, but in such a fidgety-fussy way as served only to fluster Titmouse the more. Mr. Quirk gave a dinner-party of this sort regularly every Sunday; and they formed the happiest moments of his life—occasions on which he banished from his thoughts the responsible anxieties of his profession, and, surrounded by a select circle of choice spirits, such as were thus collected together, partook joyously of the

" Feast of reason, and the flow of soul."

" This is a very beautiful picture, Titmouse, isn't it?" said Gammon, leading him to the further corner of the drawing-room, where hung a small picture with a sort of curtain of black gauze before it, which Gammon lifting up, Titmouse beheld a picture of a man suspended from the gallows, his hands tied with cords before him, his head forced aside, and covered down to the chin with a white night-cap. 'Twas done with sickening fidelity, and Titmouse gazed at it with a shud-der. " Charming thing, isn't it?" said Gammon, with a very expressive smile.

" Y—e—e—s," replied Titmouse, his eyes glued to the horrid object.

" Very striking, a'n't it?" quoth Quirk, bustling up to them; " 'twas painted for me by a first-rate artist, whose brother I very nearly saved from the gallows. Like such things?" he inquired, with a matter-of-fact air, drawing down the black gauze.

" Yes, sir, uncommon—most uncommon."

" Well, I'll show you something *very* interesting! Heard of Gilderoy, that was hanged last year for forgery? Gad, my daughter's got a brooch with a lock of his hair in it, which he gave me himself—a client of mine: within an ace of get-

ting him off—flaw in the indictment—found it out myself—
did, by gad! Come along, and I'll get Dora to show it to
you!" and putting Titmouse's arm in his he led him up to the
interesting young lady.

"Dora, just show my friend Titmouse that brooch of yours,
with Gilderoy's hair."

"Oh, my dear papa, 'tis such a melancholy thing!" said
she, at the same time detaching it from her dress, and handing
it to her papa, who, holding it in his hands, gave Titmouse,
and one or two others who stood beside, a very interesting account of the last hours of the deceased Gilderoy.

"He was *very* handsome, papa, wasn't he?" inquired Miss
Quirk with a sigh, and a very pensive air.

"Wasn't bad-looking; but good looks and the condemned
cell don't long agree together."

"Ah, papa!" exclaimed Miss Quirk in a mournful tone,
and, leaning back on the sofa, raised her handkerchief to her
eyes.

"You are too sensitive, my love!" whispered her aunt, Mrs.
Alias, squeezing the hand of her niece, who, struggling against
her feelings, presently revived.

"We were looking just now," said Mr. Hug, addressing
Mr. Quirk, "at a very interesting addition to Miss Quirk's
album—that letter of Grizzlegut."

"Ah, very striking! Value it beyond everything! Shall
never forget Grizzlegut! Very nearly got off! 'Twas an 'etc.'
that nearly saved his life, through being omitted in the indictment. 'Fore gad, we thought we'd got 'em!"

They were alluding to an autograph letter which had been
addressed to Mr. Quirk by Grizzlegut (who had been executed
for high treason a few weeks before) the night before he
suffered. He was a blood-stained scoundrel of the deepest dye,
and ought to have been hanged and quartered half a dozen
times.

"Will you read it aloud, Mr. Hug?" inquired Miss Quirk;
and the barrister, in a somewhat pompous tone, read the following memorable document:—

                                   "*Condemned Cell, Newgate,*
                              "*Friday night, half past 11 o'clock,*
                                            "*1st May, 18—*

"SIR,

"At this awful moment, when this world is closing rapidly
upon me and my fellow-sufferers, and the sound of the wretches
putting up the Grim Gallows are audible to my listening ears,

and on the morrow the most horrible death that malicious tyrants can inflict awaits me, my soul being calm and full of fortitude, and beating responsive to the call of GLORIOUS LIBERTY, I feel prouder than the King upon his throne. I feel that I have done much to secure the liberties of my *injured country.*

> " ' For liberty, glorious Liberty,
> Who'd fear to die?'

"Many thanks to you, sir, for your truly indefatigable efforts on my behalf, and the constant exercise of a skill that nearly secured us a Glorious Acquittal. What a Flame we would have raised in England! That should have blasted the enemies of True Freedom. I go to Hereafter (if, indeed, there be a hereafter), as we shall soon know, not with my soul crammed with Priestcraft, but a Bold Briton, having laid down my life for my country, knowing that Future Ages will do me Justice.

"Adieu, Tyrants, adieu! Do your worst!! My soul defies you!!!

> " I am, Sir,
> " Your humble, obliged, and
> " Undismayed servant,
> " ARTHUR GRIZZLEGUT.

" To CALEB QUIRK, ESQ.

> " Tyrants grim
> Will on the morrow cut me limb from limb,
> While Liberty looks on with terrible eye,
> And says, *I will avenge him by and by.*
> " ARTHUR GRIZZLEGUT."

The reading of the above produced a great sensation. " That man's name will be enrolled among the Sidneys and the Hampdens of his country!" said Viper, with a grim and excited air. " That letter deserves to be carved on a golden tablet! The last four lines are sublime! He was a martyr to principles that are silently and rapidly making their way in this country."—How much further he would have gone on in this strain, seeing no one present had resolution enough to differ with or interrupt him, even if they had been so disposed, I know not; but fortunately dinner was announced—a sound which startled old Quirk out of a posture of intense attention to Viper, and evident admiration of his sentiments. He gave his arm with an air of prodigious politeness to the gaunt Mrs. Alderman Addlehead, whose distinguished lord led down Mrs. Quirk—and the rest followed in no particular order — Tit-

mouse arm in arm with Gammon, who took care to place him,
next to himself (Gammon). It was really a dashing sort of
dinner. Quirk had, indeed, long been celebrated for his Sunday dinners. Titmouse had never seen anything like it; and
was quite bewildered—particularly at the number of different
shaped and colored glasses, etc., etc., etc., placed opposite to
him. He kept a constant eye on the movements of Gammon,
and did whatever he did, as if the two had been moved by the
same set of springs, and was thus saved innumerable embarrassments and annoyances. What chiefly struck his attention
was a prodigious number of dishes, great and small, as if half
a dozen dinners had been crowded into one; the rapidity with
which they were changed, and plates removed, in constant
succession; the incessant invitations to take wine that were
flying about during the whole of dinner. For a considerable
while Titmouse was too much flurried to enjoy himself; but a
few glasses of champagne succeeded in elevating his spirits to
the proper pitch—and would soon have driven them far beyond it. Almost everybody, except the great folk at the top
of the table, asked him to take wine; and he constantly filled
his glass. In fact Gammon, recollecting a scene at his own
chamber, soon perceived that, unless he interfered, Titmouse
would be drunk long before dinner was over. He had not imagined the earth to contain so exquisite a drink as champagne;
and he could have fallen down and worshiped it, as it came
fizzing and flashing out of the bottle. Gammon earnestly assured him that he would be ill if he drank so much—that
many eyes were upon him—and that it was not the custom to
do more than merely sip from his wine-glass when challenging
or challenged. But Titmouse had taken a considerably
greater quantity on board, before Gammon thus interfered,
than that gentleman was aware of, and began to get very
voluble. Guess the progress he had made, when he called out
with a confident air—"Mr. Alderman! Your health!"—
whether more to that great man's astonishment or disgust I
can not undertake to say; but after a steady stare for a moment or two at Titmouse, "Oh! I shall be very happy, indeed, *Mr. Gammon*," he called out, looking at the latter gentleman, and drinking with *him*. That signified nothing,
however, to Titmouse, who, indeed, did not see anything at
all pointed or unusual, and gulped down his wine as eagerly
as before.

"Cool puppy, that, Miss Quirk, must say," snuffled the
offended Alderman to Miss Quirk.

"He's young, dear Mr. Aldermar," said she, sweetly and

mildly—"and when you consider the immense fortune he is coming into—ten thousand a year, my papa says—"

"That don't make him less a puppy—nor a brute," inter· rupted the ruffled Alderman, still more indignant; for his own forty thousand pounds, the source of all his social eminence, sunk into insignificance at the sound of the splendid income just about to drop into the lap of Titmouse. Mr. Bluster, who headed the table on Miss Quirk's left-hand side, and who felt that he *ought* to be, but knew that in the presence of the Alderman he *was* not, the great man of the day, observing the irritation under which his rival was suffering, immediately raised his threatening double glasses to his eyes, and in a tone of ostentatious condescension, looking down the table to Titmouse, called out, "Mr. Titmash—may I have the honor of drinking wine with you?"

"Ya—as, brother Bumptious," replied Titmouse, who could never bear his name mispronounced, and he raised *his* glass to his eye; "was just going to ask *you !*" All this was done in such a loud and impudent tone and manner, as made Gammon still more uneasy for his young companion. But his sally had been received by the company as a very smart retort, and produced a roar of laughter, every one being glad to see Mr. Bluster snubbed, who bore it in silent dignity, though his face showed his chagrin and astonishment; and he very heartily agreed, for once in his life, with the worshipful person opposite to him in his estimate of our friend Titmouse. "Mr. Titmouse! Mr. Titmouse! my daughter wonders you won't take wine with her," said Mr. Quirk in a low tone—"will you join us? we're going to take a glass of champagne."

"Oh! 'pon my life—delighted,"—quoth Titmouse.

"Dora, my dear! Mr. Titmouse will take wine with you!—Jack" (to the servant), "fill Miss Quirk's and Mr. Titmouse's glasses to the brim."

"Oh, no! dearest papa."

"Pho! pho!—nonsense—the first time of asking, you know, ah, ha!"

"Well! If it *must* be," and with what a graceful inclination—with what a sly searching glance and fascinating smile did she exchange courtesies with Titmouse! He felt disposed to take wine with her a second time immediately; but Gammon restrained him. Mr. Toady Hug, having become acquainted with the brilliant prospects of Titmouse, earnestly desired to exert his little talents to do the agreeable and ingratiate himself with Mr. Titmouse; but there was a counteracting force in another direction, the attorney, Mr. Flaw, who had

the greatest practice at the Clerkenwell Sessions, sat beside
him, and received his most respectful and incessant attentions;
Hug, speaking over to him in a low confidential whisper, constantly casting a furtive glance toward Bluster and Slang, to
see whether they were observing him. In " strict confidence,"
he assured Mr. Flaw how his case, the other day, might have
been won, if such and such a course had been adopted, " which
would have been the line *he* " (Hug) " would have taken;"
and which he explained with anxious energy. " I must say,
Flip regularly threw the case away—no doubt of it! By the
way, what became of that burglary case of yours, on Friday?"

" Found guilty, poor fellows!"

" You don't say so?"

" Fact, by Jove, though!"

" How *could* Gobble have lost that verdict? I assure you
I would have bet ten to one on your getting a verdict; for I
read over your brief as it lay beside me, and upon my honor,
Mr. Flaw, it was admirably got up. Everything depends on
the brief—"

" Glad you thought so, sir," replied Flaw, wondering how
it was that he had never before thought of giving a brief to
Mr. Hug.

" It's a great mistake of counsel not to pay the utmost attention to their briefs. For my part," continued Mr. Hug in
a still lower tone, " I make a point of reading every syllable
in my brief, however long it is."

" It's the only way, depend on it, sir. We attorneys, you
know, see and know so much of the case, conversing confidentially with the prisoners—"

" Ay, and beyond that. Your practical suggestions, my
dear sir, are often— Now, for instance, in the brief I was
alluding to there was, I recollect—one most—uncommonly
acute suggestion."

" Which was it, sir?" inquired the attorney, briskly, his
countenance showing the progress of Hug's lubricating process.

" Oh—why—a—a—hem!" stammered Hug, somewhat nonplused—" No; it would hardly be fair to Gobble, and I'm
sorry indeed—"

" Well, well—it can't be helped *now*—but I must say that
once or twice latterly I've thought, myself, that Mr. Gobble
has rather— By the way, Mr. Hug, shall you be in town this
week till the end of the sessions?"

" Ye—e—s!" hastily whispered Hug, after glancing guiltily
toward his brethren, who, though they did not seem to do so,
were really watching him closely.

"I'm happy to hear it! You've heard of Aaron Doodle, who was committed for that burglary at ——? Well, I defend him, and shall be happy to give you the brief. Do you lead Mr. Dolt?" Hug nodded. "Then he will be your junior. Where are your chambers, Mr. Hug?"

"No. 4, Cant Court, Gray's Inn. When, my dear sir, does the case come on?"

"Thursday—perhaps Wednesday."

"Then *do* come and breakfast with me, and we can talk it over, you know, so nicely together."

"Sir, you're *very* polite. I will do myself the pleasure—" replied Mr. Flaw—and took wine with Mr. Hug.

This little stroke of business over, the disengaged couple were at liberty to do the general conversation of the table. Mr. Bluster and Mr. Slang kept the company in almost a constant roar, with descriptions of scenes in court, in which *they* had, of course, been the principal actors; and according to their own accounts they must be wonderful fellows. Such brothers of judges!—Such bafflers and browbeaters of witnesses!—Such bamboozlers of juries!

You should have seen the sneering countenance of Hug all the while. He never once smiled or laughed at the brilliant sallies of his brethren, and did his best to prevent his new patron, Mr. Flaw, from doing so—constantly putting his hand before his mouth, and whispering into Mr. Flaw's ear at the very point of the joke or story—and the smile would disappear from the countenance of Mr. Flaw.

The Alderman laughed till the tears ran out of his little eyes, which he constantly wiped with his napkin. Amidst the general laughter and excitement, Miss Quirk, leaning her chin on her hand, her elbow resting on the table, several times directed soft, languishing looks toward Titmouse, unobserved by any one but himself; and they were not entirely unsuccessful, although Titmouse was wonderfully taken with the stories of the two counselors, and believed them to be two of the greatest men he had ever seen or heard of, and at the head of their profession.

"'Pon my soul—I hope, sir, you'll have those two gents in *my* case?" said he earnestly to Gammon.

"Unfortunately, your case will not come on in their courts," said Gammon, with a very expressive smile.

"Why, can't it come on where I choose?—or when you like?" inquired Titmouse surprisedly.

Mr. Quirk had been soured during the whole of dinner, for he had anxiously desired to have Titmouse sit beside him at

10

the bottom of the table; but in the little hubbub attendant upon coming down to dinner and taking places, Titmouse slipped out of sight for a minute; and when all were placed, Quirk's enraged eye perceived him sitting in the middle of the table beside Gammon. Gammon *always* got hold of Titmouse. Old Quirk could have flung a decanter at his head.— In his own house!—at his own table! Always anticipating and circumventing him.

"Mr. Quirk, I don't think we've taken a glass of wine together yet, have we?" said Gammon with a bland and cordial manner, at the same time pouring himself out a glass of wine. He perfectly well knew what was annoying his respected partner, whose look of quaint embarrassment, when so suddenly assailed, infinitely amused him. "Catch me asking you here again, Master Gammon," thought Quirk, "the next time that Titmouse dines here!" The reason why Mr. Snap had not been asked was, that Quirk had some slight cause to suspect his having conceived the notion of paying his addresses to Miss Quirk—a thing at any time not particularly palatable to Mr. Quirk; but in the present conjuncture of circumstances quite out of the question, and intolerable even in the idea. Snap was not slow in guessing the reason of his exclusion, which had greatly mortified, and also not a little alarmed him. As far as he could venture, he had, during the week, endeavored to "set" Titmouse "against" Miss Quirk, by such faint disparaging remarks and insinuations as he dared venture upon with so difficult a subject as Titmouse, whom he at the same time inflamed by representations of the splendid matches he might very soon command among the highest women of the land. By these means Snap had, to a certain extent, succeeded; but the few melting glances which had fallen upon Titmouse's sensitive bosom from the eyes of Miss Quirk, were beginning to operate a slight change in his feelings. The old Alderman, on the intimation that the "ladies were going to withdraw," laid violent hands on Miss Quirk (he was a "privileged" old fool), and insisted on her singing his favorite song,—"*My Friend and Pitcher*." His request was so warmly seconded by the rest of the company, Titmouse as loud and eager as any, that she was fain to comply. She sung with some sweetness and much self-possession. She carried Titmouse's feelings along with her from the beginning, as Gammon, who was watching him, perceived.

"Most uncommon lovely gal, isn't she?" whispered Titmouse, with great vivacity.

"Very!" replied Gammon, dryly, with a slight smile.

" Shall I call out *encore?* A'n't that the word? 'Pon my soul, most lovely gal! she must sing it again."

" No, no—she wishes to go—'tis not usual; she will sing it for you, I dare say, this evening, if you ask her."

" Well—most charming gal!—Lovely!"—

" Have patience, my dear Titmouse," said Gammon, in a low whisper; " in a few months' time you'll soon be thrown into much higher life than this—among *really* beautiful, and rich, and accomplished women "—[and, *thought* Gammon, you'll resemble a monkey that has found his way into a rich tulip-bed!]

" Fancy Miss Tag-rag standing beside her," whispered Titmouse, scornfully.

" Ha, ha!" gently laughed Gammon—" both of them, in their way, are very worthy persons; but "—Here the ladies withdrew. 'Twas no part of Gammon's plans that Titmouse should become the son-in-law of either Quirk or Tag-rag. Mr. Gammon had formed already vastly different plans for him!

As soon as Quirk had taken the head of the table, and the gentlemen drawn together, the bottles were pushed round very briskly, accompanied by no less than three different sorts of snuff-boxes, all belonging to Mr. Quirk—all of them presents from clients. One was a huge affair of Botany Bay wood, with a very flaming inscription on the inside of the lid; from which it appeared that its amiable donors, who were trying the effect of a change of climate on their moral health at the expense of a grateful country, owed their valuable lives to the professional skill and exertions of " Caleb Quirk, Esq." In short, the other two were trophies of a similar description, of which their possessor was justly not a little proud; and as he saw Titmouse admiring them, it occurred to him as very possible that, within a few months' time, he should be in possession of a magnificent *gold* snuff-box, in acknowledgment of the services he should have rendered to his distinguished guest and client. Titmouse was in the highest possible spirits. This, his first glimpse into high life, equaled all his expectations. Round and round went the bottles—crack went joke after joke. Slang sung song upon song, of, however, so very coarse and broad a character as infinitely disgusted Gammon, and apparently shocked the Alderman—though I greatly distrust that old sinner's sincerity in the matter. Then Ghastly's performances commenced. Poor fellow! he exerted himself to the utmost to earn the good dinner he had just devoured; but when he was in the very middle of one of his most impassioned

scenes—undoubtedly " tearing a passion to rags,"—Mr. Quirk
interrupted, impatiently—" Come, come, Ghastly, we've had
enough of that sort—it don't suit at all!—Lord bless us!—
don't *roar* so, man!"

Poor Ghastly instantly resumed his seat, with a chagrined
and melancholy air.

" Give us something funny," snuffled the Alderman.

" Let's have the chorus of Pigs and Ducks," said Quirk;
" you do that *remarkable* well. I could fancy the animals
were running, and squealing, and quacking all about the
room." The actor did as he was desired, commencing with a
sigh, and was much applauded. At length Gammon happened
to get into a discussion with Mr. Bluster on some point connected with the Habeas Corpus Act, in which our friend Gammon, who never got heated in discussion, and was very accurate in whatever he knew, had glaringly the best of it. His
calm, smiling self-possession almost drove poor Bluster frantic.
The less he knew, of course, the louder he talked, the more
vehement and positive he became; at length offering a *bet* that
he was right; at which Gammon bowed, smiled and closed the
discussion. While engaged in it he had of course been unable
to keep his eyes upon Titmouse, who drank, consequently, like
a little fish, never letting the bottle pass him. Every one
about him filled his glass every time—why should not he?

Hug sat next to Viper; feared him, and avoided discussion
with him; for, though they agreed in their politics, which
were of the loosest and lowest radical description, they had a
personal antipathy each to the other. In spite of their wishes,
they at length got entangled in a very virulent controversy,
and said so many insulting things to each other that the rest
of the company, who had for some time been amused, got at
length—not disgusted—but alarmed, for the possible results.
Mr. Quirk, therefore, interfered.

" Bravo! bravo! bravo!" he exclaimed, as Viper concluded
a most envenomed passage; " that will do, Viper—whip it into
the next *Flash*—'twill be a capital leader! It will produce a
sensation! And in the meantime, gentlemen, let me request
you to fill your glasses—bumpers—for I have a toast to propose, in which you'll all feel interested when you'll hear who's
the subject of it. It is a gentleman who is likely soon to be
elevated to a station which Nature has formed him—hem!
hem!—to adorn—"

" Mr. Quirk's proposing your health, Titmouse!" whispered
Gammon to his companion, who, having been very restless for
some time, had at length become quite silent—his head rest-

ing on his hand, his elbow on the table—his eyes languidly
half open, and his face exceedingly pale.   Gammon saw that
he was in truth in a very ticklish condition.

"I—wish—you'd—let me—go out—I'm devilish ill"—said
Titmouse, faintly.   Gammon made a signal to Quirk, who instantly ceased his speech; and, coming down to Titmouse, he
and Gammon hastily led him out of the room, and into the
nearest bed-chamber, where he began to be very ill, and so
continued for several hours.   Old Quirk, who was a long-
headed man, was delighted by this occurrence; for he saw that
if he insisted on Titmouse's being put to bed, and passing the
night—and perhaps the next day—at Alibi House, it would
enable Miss Quirk to bring her attractions to bear upon him
effectively, by exhibiting those delicate and endearing attentions which are so soothing, and indeed necessary to an invalid.
Titmouse continued severely indisposed during the whole of
the night; and, early in the morning, it was thought advisable
to send for a medical man, who pronounced Titmouse to be in
danger of a bilious fever, and to require rest, and care, and
medical attendance for some days to come.   This was rather
"too much of a good thing" for old Quirk—but there was no
remedy.   Foreseeing that Titmouse would be thrown constantly, for some little time to come, into Miss Quirk's company,
her prudent parent enjoined upon Mrs. Alias, his sister, the
necessity of impressing on his daughter's mind the great uncertainty that, after all, existed as to Titmouse's prospects;
and the consequent necessity there was for her to regulate her
conduct with a view to either failure or success—to keep her
affections, as it were, in abeyance.   But the fact was, that Miss
Quirk had so often heard the subject of Titmouse's brilliant
expectations talked of by her father, and knew so well his
habitual prudence and caution, that she looked upon Titmouse's speedy possession of ten thousand a year as a matter
almost of certainty.   She was a girl of some natural shrewdness, but of an early inclination to maudlin sentimentality.
Had she been blessed with the vigilant and affectionate care of
a mother as she grew up (her mother having died when Miss
Quirk was but a child), and been thrown among a different set
of people from those who constantly visited at Alibi House—
and of whom a very *favorable* specimen has been laid before
the reader—Miss Quirk might really have become a very sensible and agreeable girl.   As it was, her manners had contracted a certain coarseness, which at length overspread her
whole character, and the selfish and mercenary motives by
which she could not fail to perceive all her father's conduct

regulated, infected herself. She resolved, therefore, to be governed by the considerations so urgently pressed upon her by both her father and her aunt.

It was several days before Titmouse was allowed, by his medical men, to quit his bedroom; and it is impossible for any woman not to be touched by the sight of a sudden change effected in a man by severe indisposition and suffering—even be that man so poor a creature as Titmouse. He was very pale and considerably reduced by the severe nature of his complaint, and of the powerful medicines which had been administered to him. When he made his first appearance before Miss Quirk, one afternoon, with somewhat feeble gait, and a languid air that mitigated, if it did not obliterate, the foolish and conceited expression of his features, she really regarded him with considerable interest; and, though she might hardly have owned it even to herself, his expected good fortune invested him with a kind of subdued radiance. *Ten thousand a year!*—Miss Quirk's heart fluttered! By the time that he was well enough to take his departure, she had, at his request, read over to him nearly half of that truly interesting work—the Newgate Calendar; she had sung to him, and played to him, whatever he asked her; and, in short, she felt that if she could but be certain that he would gain his great lawsuit, and step into ten thousand a year, she could *love* him. She insisted, on the day of his quitting Alibi House, that he should write in her album; and he very readily complied. It was nearly ten minutes before he could get a pen to suit him. At length he succeeded, and left the following interesting memento of himself in the very centre of a fresh page:—

> " Tittlebat Titmouse is My name,
>   England is My Nation,
> London is My dwelling-Place,
>   And Christ is My Salvation,
>   " TITTLEBAT TITMOUSE,
>   " halibi lodge."

Miss Quirk turned pale with astonishment and vexation on seeing this elegant and interesting addition to her album. Titmouse, on the contrary, looked at it with no little pride, for having had a capital pen, and his heart being in his task, he had produced what he conceived to be a very superior specimen of penmanship: in fact, the signature was by far the best he had ever written. When he had gone Miss Quirk was twenty times on the point of tearing out the leaf which had been so dismally disfigured, but on her father coming home in

the evening, he laughed heartily—"and as to tearing it out,"
said he, "let us first see which way the verdict is."

Titmouse became, after this, a pretty frequent visitor at
Alibi House; growing more and more attached to Miss Quirk,
who, however, conducted herself toward him with much judgment.   His inscription on her album had done a vast deal toward cooling down the ardor with which she had been disposed
to regard even the future owner of ten thousand a year.   Poor
Snap seemed to have lost all chance, being treated with greater
coldness by Miss Quirk on every succeeding visit to Alibi
House.   At this he was sorely discomfited, for she would have
whatever money her father might die possessed of, besides a
commanding interest in the partnership business.   'Twas a
difficult thing for him to preserve his temper in his close
intimacy with Titmouse, who had so grievously interfered with
his prospects.

The indisposition I have been mentioning prevented Titmouse from paying his promised visit to Satin Lodge.   On
returning to his lodgings from Alibi House he found that
Tag-rag had either called or sent every day to inquire after
him with the most affectionate anxiety; and one or two notes
lying on his table apprised him of the lively distress which the
ladies of Satin Lodge were enduring on his account, and implored him to lose not a moment in communicating the state
of his health, and personally assuring them of his safety.
Though the image of Miss Quirk was continually before his
eyes, Titmouse, nevertheless, had cunning enough not to drop
the slightest hint to the Tag-rags of the true state of his feelings.   Whenever any inquiry, with ill-disguised anxiety, was
made by Mrs. Tag-rag concerning Alibi House and its inmates,
Titmouse would, to be sure, mention Miss Quirk, but in such
a careless and slighting way as gave great consolation and encouragement to Tag-rag, his wife and daughter.   When at
Mr. Quirk's he spoke somewhat unreservedly of the amiable
inmates of Satin Lodge.   These two mansions were almost the
only private residences visited by Titmouse, who spent his time
much in the way which I have already described.   How he got
through his days I can hardly tell.   At his lodgings he got up
very late, and went to bed very late.   He never read anything
excepting occasionally a song-book lent him by Snap, or a
novel, or some such book as "Boxiana," from the circulating
library.   Dawdling over his dress and his breakfast, then
whistling and humming, took up so much of every day as he
passed at his lodgings.   The rest was spent in idling about the
town, looking in at shop windows, and now and then going to

some petty exhibition. When evening came he was generally joined by Snap, when they would spend the night in the manner I have already described. As often as he dared he called at Messrs. Quirk, Gammon and Snap's office at Saffron Hill, and worried them not a little by inquiries concerning the state of his affairs, and the cause of the delay in commencing proceedings. As for Huckaback, by the way, Titmouse cut him entirely, saying that he was a devilish low fellow, and it was no use knowing him. He made many desperate efforts, both personally and by letter, to renew his acquaintance with Titmouse, but in vain. I may as well mention, by the way, that as soon as Snap got scent of the little money transaction between his friend and Huckaback, he called upon the latter, and tendering him twelve shillings, demanded up the document which he had extorted from Titmouse. Huckaback held out obstinately for some time—but Snap was too much for him, and talked in such a formidable strain about an indictment for conspiracy (!) and fraud, that Huckaback at length consented, on receiving twelve shillings, to deliver up the document to Snap, on condition of Snap's destroying it on the spot. This was done, and so ended all intercourse—at least on this side of the grave—between Titmouse and Huckaback.

The sum allowed by Messrs. Quirk and Gammon to Titmouse was amply sufficient to have kept him in comfort; but it never would have enabled him to lead the kind of life which I have described—and he would certainly have got very awkwardly involved had it not been for the kindness of Snap in advancing him, from time to time, such sums as his exigencies required. In fact, matters went on as quietly and smoothly as possible for several months—till about the middle of November, when an event occurred that seemed to threaten the total demolition of all his hopes and expectations.

He had not seen or heard from Messrs. Quirk or Gammon for nearly a fortnight; Snap he had not seen for nearly a week. At length he ventured to make his appearance at Saffron Hill, and was received with a startling coldness—a stern abruptness of manner, that frightened him out of his wits. All the three partners were alike—as for Snap, the contrast between his present and his former manner was perfectly shocking; he seemed quite another person. The fact was, that the full statement of Titmouse's claims had been laid before Mr. Subtle, the leading counsel retained in his behalf, for his opinion, before actually commencing proceedings; and the partners were indeed thunder-struck on receiving that opinion: for Mr. Subtle pointed out a radical deficiency of proof in a matter which, as soon as their attention was thus pointedly called to it, Messrs. Quirk and Gammon were amazed at their having overlooked, and still more at its having escaped the notice of Mr. Tresayle, Mr. Mortmain and Mr. Frankpledge. Mr. Quirk hurried with the opinions to the first two gentlemen, and after a long interview with each, they owned their fears that Mr. Subtle was right, and that the defect seemed incurable; but they showed their agitated clients that *they* had been guilty of neither oversight nor ignorance, inasmuch as the matter in question was one of *evidence* only—one which a *nisi prius* lawyer, with a full detail of "proofs" before him, could hardly fail to light upon—but which, it would be found, had been assumed and taken for granted in the cases laid before conveyancers. They promised to turn it over in their minds, and to let Messrs. Quirk and Gammon know if anything occurred to vary their impression. Mr. Tresayle and Mr. Mortmain, however, preserved an ominous silence. As for Frankpledge, he had a knack, somehow or another, of always coming to the conclusion wished and hoped for by his clients, and, after prodigious pains, wrote a very long opinion, to show that there was nothing in the objection. Neither Mr. Quirk nor Mr. Gammon could understand the process by which Mr. Frankpledge arrived at such a result, but, in despair, they laid his opinion before Mr. Subtle, in the shape of a second case for his opinion. It was, in a few days' time, returned to them, with only a line or two—thus:—

"With every respect for the gentleman who wrote this opinion, I can not perceive what it has to do with the question. I see no reason whatever to depart from the view I have already taken of this case.—J. S."

Here was something like a dead lock, indeed!

"We're done, Gammon!" said Quirk, with a dismayed air. Gammon seemed lost, and made no answer.

"Does anything—eh? anything occur to you? Gammon, I *will* say this for you—you're a long-headed fellow!" Still Gammon spoke not.

"Gammon! Gammon! I really believe—you begin to see something."

"*It's to be done*, Mr. Quirk!" said Gammon, at length, with a grave and apprehensive look, and a cheek paler than before.

"Eh? how? Oh, I see!—Know what you mean, Gammon,' replied Quirk, with a hurried whisper, glancing at both doors to see that they were safe.

"We must resume our intercourse with Titmouse, and let

matters go on as before," said Gammon, with a very anxious, but at the same time a determined air.

"I—I wonder if what has occurred to *you* is what has occurred to me?" inquired Quirk, in an eager whisper.

"Pooh! pooh! Mr. Quirk."

"Gammon, dear Gammon, no mystery! You know I have a deep stake in this matter!"

"So have I, Mr. Quirk," replied Gammon, with a sigh. "However"—Here the partners put their heads close together, and whispered to each other in a low, earnest tone for some minutes. Quirk rose from his seat, and took two or three turns about the room in silence, Gammon watching him calmly.

To his inexpressible relief and joy, within a few hours of the happening of the above colloquy, Titmouse found himself placed on precisely his former footing with Messrs. Quirk, Gammon and Snap.

In order to bring on the cause for trial at the next spring assizes, it was necessary that the declaration in ejectment should be served on the tenant in possession before Hilary Term; and, in a matter of such magnitude, it was deemed expedient for Snap to go down and personally effect the service in question. In consequence, also, of some very important suggestions as to the evidence given by the junior in the cause, it was arranged that Snap should go down about a week before the time fixed upon for effecting the service, and make minute inquiries as to one or two facts which it was understood could be established in evidence. As soon as Titmouse heard of this movement, that Snap was going direct to Yatton, the scene of his, Titmouse's, future greatness, he made the most pertinacious and vehement entreaties to Messrs. Quirk and Gammon to be allowed to accompany him, even going down on his knees. There was no resisting this, but they exacted a solemn pledge from him that he would place himself entirely at the disposal of Snap; go under some feigned name, and, in short, neither say nor do anything tending to disclose their real character or errand.

Snap and Titmouse established themselves at the Hare and Hounds Inn at Grilston; and the former immediately began, cautiously and quietly, to collect such evidence as he could discover. One of the first persons to whom he went was old blind Bess. His many pressing questions at length stirred up in the old woman's mind recollections of long-forgotten names, persons, places, scenes, and associations, thereby producing an agitation not easily to be got rid of, and which had by no means subsided when Dr. Tatham and Mr. Aubrey paid her the Christmas-day visit, which has been already described.

CHAPTER XI.

THE reader has had already pretty distinct indications of the manner in which Titmouse and Snap conducted themselves during their stay in Yorkshire, and which, I fear, have not tended to raise either of these gentlemen in the reader's estimation. Titmouse manifested a very natural anxiety to see the present occupants of Yatton; and it was with infinite difficulty that Snap could prevent him from sneaking about in the immediate neighborhood of the Hall, with the hope of seeing them. His first encounter with Mr. and Miss Aubrey was entirely accidental, as the reader may remember; and when he found that the lady on horseback near Yatton, and the lady whom he had striven to attract the notice of in Hyde Park were one and the same beautiful woman, and that that beautiful woman was neither more nor less than the sister of the present owner of Yatton, the marvelous discovery created a mighty pother in his little feelings. The blaze of Kate Aubrey's beauty in an instant consumed the images both of Tabitha Tag-rag and Dora Quirk. It even for a while outshone the splendors of ten thousand a year: such is the inexpressible and incalculable power of woman's beauty over everything in the shape of man—over even so despicable a sample of him as Tittlebat Titmouse.

While putting in practice some of those abominable tricks to which, under Snap's tutelage, Titmouse had become accustomed in walking the streets of London, and from which even the rough handling they had got from farmer Hazel could not turn him, Titmouse at length, as has been seen, most unwittingly fell foul of that fair creature, Catherine Aubrey herself, who seemed truly like an angelic messenger returning from her errand of sympathy and mercy, and suddenly beset by a little imp of darkness. When Titmouse discovered who was the object of his audacious and revolting advances, his soul was petrified within him; and it was fortunate that the shriek of Miss Aubrey's attendant at length startled him into a recollection of a pair of heels, to which he was that evening indebted for an escape from a most murderous cudgeling, which might have been attended with one effect not contemplated by him who inflicted it; viz., the retention of the Aubreys in the possession of Yatton. Titmouse ran for nearly half a mile on the high-road toward Grilston, without stopping. He dared not venture back to Yatton, with the sound of the lusty farmer's voice in his ears, to get back from the Aubrey Arms the horse which had brought him that afternoon from Grilston, to which place he walked on, through the snow and darkness; reaching his inn in a perfect panic, from which, at length, a tumbler of stiff brandy and water, with two or three cigars, somewhat relieved him. Forgetful of the solemn pledge which he had given to Messrs. Quirk, Gammon and Snap, not to disclose his name or errand, and it never once occurring to him that, if he would but keep his own counsel, Miss Aubrey could never identify *him* with the ruffian who had assailed her, he spent the interval between eight and twelve o'clock, at which latter hour the coach by which he had resolved to return to London would pass through Grilston, in indicting the following letter to Miss Aubrey:—

" Grilston, January 6th, 18—.

" HONOURED MISS,

" Hoping No Offence Will Be Taken where None is meant, (*which am Sure of*,) This I send To say Who I Am which, Is the Right And True Owner of Yatton which You Enjoy Amongst You All At This present (Till The Law Give it to *Me*) Which It quickly Will And which It Ought to Have done When I were First born And Before Yr Respect. Family ever Came into it, And All which Yr. hond. Brother Have so unlawfully Got possession Of must Come Back to Them Whose Due It is wh. Is myself as will be Sone provd. And wh. am most truly Sorry Of *on your own Acct.* (Meaning (hond. Miss,) you Alone) as Sure as Yatton is Intirely Mine So My Heart Is *yours* and No Longer my Own Ever since I Saw You first as Can Easily prove but wh. doubtless You Have forgot Seeing You Never New, seeing (as Mr. Gammon, My Sollicitor And a Very Great Lawyer, say) *Cases Alter Circumstances*, what Can I say More Than that I Love you *Most Amazing* Such As Never Thought Myself Capable of Doing Before and wh. cannot help Ever Since I First saw Yor. most *Lovely* and *Divine* and *striking* Face wh. have Stuck In my Mind Ever Since Day and Night Sleeping and Waking I will Take my Oath Never Of Having Lov'd Any one Else, though (must Say) have Had a Wonderful Many *Offers* From Females of *The Highest Rank* Since my Truly Wonderful Good fortune got talked About every Where but have *Refused Them All* for *yr sake*, And Would All the World But you. When I Saw You on Horseback It was All my Sudden confusion In Seeing you (The Other Gent. was One of my Resp^e. Solicitors) w^h

Threw Me off in that Ridiculous Way w^h was a Great Mortifi-
cation And made My brute Of A horse *go on so* For I Remem-
bered You and was Wonderful struck *with Your Improv'd
Appearance* (As that Same Gent. can Testify) And you was
(Hon^d. Miss) Quite Wrong *To Night* when You Spoke so
Uncommon Angry To Me, Seeing If I Had Only Known What
Female it Was (meaning *yourself which I respect So*) out so
Late Alone I should Have spoke quite Different So hope You
Will Think Nothing More Of that Truly *Unpleasant Event*
Now (Hon^d. Madam) What I have To say Is if You Will
Please To Condescend To Yield To My Desire We Can Live
Most uncommon Comfortable at Yatton Together w^h. Place
shall Have Great Pleasure in *Marrying You From* and I may
(*perhaps*) Do Something Handsome for y^r. respectable Brother
And Family, w^h. can Often Come to see us And Live in the
Neighborhood, if You Refuse me, Will not say What shall
Happen to *Those* which (am Told) *Owe me a Precious Long
Figure* wh. May (*perhaps*) Make a Handsome Abatement in,
if You And I *Hit it*.

" Hoping You Will Forget What Have So Much Griev^d. me
And Write p^r. return of Post,
        " Am, hon^d. Miss
    " Y^r most Loving of Devoted Servant,
        " (Till Death)
            "TITTLEBAT TITMOUSE.
" (*Private*) "

This equally characteristic and disgusting production its accomplished writer sealed twice, and then left, together with
sixpence, in the hands of the landlady of the Hare and Hounds,
to be delivered at Yatton Hall the first thing in the morning.
The good woman, however—having no particular wish to
oblige such a strange puppy, whom she was only too glad to
get rid of, and having a good deal to attend to—laid the letter
aside on the chimney-piece, and entirely lost sight of it for
nearly a fortnight. Shortly after the lamentable tidings concerning the impending misfortunes of the Aubrey family had
been communicated to the inhabitants of Grilston she forwarded the letter (little dreaming of the character in which
its writer was likely ere long, to reappear at Grilston), together
with one or two others, a day or two after Miss Aubrey had
had the interview with her brother which I have described to
the reader; but it lay unnoticed by any one—above all by the
sweet sufferer whose name was indicated on it—among a great

number of miscellaneous letters and papers which had been suffered to accumulate on the library table.

Mr. Aubrey entered the library one morning alone, for the purpose of attending to many matters which had been long neglected. He was evidently thinner: his face was pale, and his manner dejected: still there was about him an air of calmness and resolution. Through the richly pictured old stained-glass window, the molten sunbeams were streaming in a kind of tender radiance upon the dear old familiar objects around him. All was silent. Having drawn his chair to the table, on which were lying a confused heap of letters and papers, he felt a momentary repugnance to enter upon the task which he had assigned to himself, of opening and attending to them; and walked slowly for some time up and down the room, with folded arms, uttering occasionally profound sighs. At length he sat down, and commenced the disheartening task of opening the many letters before him. One of the first he opened was from Peter Johnson—the old tenant to whom he had lent the sum of two hundred pounds; and it was full of expressions of gratitude and respect. Then came a letter, a fortnight old, bearing the frank of Lord ——, the Secretary of State for Foreign Affairs. He opened it and read:—

                      " *Whitehall*, 16*th January*, 18—.

"MY DEAR AUBREY,

" You will remember that Lord ——'s motion stands for the 28th. We will venture to calculate upon receiving your powerful support in the debate. We expect to be much pressed with the Duke of ——'s affair, which you handled shortly before the recess with such signal ability and success. When you return to town you must expect a renewal of certain offers, which I most sincerely trust, for the benefit of the public service, will not be *again* declined.

              " Ever yours faithfully,
                        " C——

" (Private and confidential.)
"CHARLES AUBREY, ESQ., M. P."

Mr. Aubrey laid down the letter calmly as soon as he had read it; and, leaning back in his chair, seemed lost in thought for several minutes. Presently he reapplied himself to his task, and opened and glanced over a great many letters; the contents of several of which occasioned him deep emotion. Some were from persons in distress whom he had assisted, and who implored a continuance of his aid; others were from ardent political friends—some sanguine, others desponding—concerning the prospects of the session. Two or three hinted that it was everywhere reported that he had been offered one of the under-secretaryships, and had declined; but that it was, at the king's desire, to be pressed upon him. Many letters were on private, and still more on country business, and with one of them he was engaged, when a servant entered with one of that morning's county papers. Tired with his task, Mr Aubrey rose from his chair as the servant gave him the paper, and, standing before the fire, unfolded the *Yorkshire Stingo*, and glanced listlessly over its miscellaneous contents. At length his eye lighted upon the following paragraph:—

".The rumors so deeply affecting a member for a certain borough in this county, and to which we alluded in our last paper but one, turn out to be well founded. A claimant has started up to the very large estates at present held by the gentleman in question; and we are very much misinformed if the ensuing spring assizes will not effect a considerable change in the representation of the borough alluded to, by relieving it from the Tory thralldom under which it has been so long oppressed. We have no wish to be hard upon a falling man; and, therefore, shall make no comment upon the state of mind in which that person may be presumed to be, who must be conscious of having been so long enjoying the just rights of others. Some extraordinary disclosures may be looked for when the trial comes on. We have heard from a quarter on which we are disposed to place reliance that the claimant is a gentleman of decided Whig principles, and who will prove a valuable accession to the Liberal cause."

Mr. Aubrey was certainly somewhat shocked by brutality such as this; but, on Miss Aubrey's entering the room, he quietly folded up the paper and laid it aside, fearful lest his sister's feelings should be pierced by so coarse and cruel a paragraph, which, in fact, had been concocted in London in the office of Quirk, Gammon and Snap, who were, as before stated, interested in the *Sunday Flash*, which was in some sort connected, through the relationship of the editors, with the *Yorkshire Stingo*. The idea had been suggested by Gammon, of attempting to enlist the *political* feeling of a portion of the county in favor of their client.

" Here are several letters for *you*, Kate," said her brother, picking several of them out. The very first she took up, it having attracted her attention by the double seal and the vulgar style of the handwriting, was that from Titmouse, which has just been laid before the reader. With much sur-

prise she opened the letter, her brother being similarly engaged with his own; and her face getting gradually paler and
paler as she went on, at length she flung it on the floor, with
a passionate air, and burst into tears. Her brother, with
astonishment, exclaimed,—"Dear Kate, what is it?" and he
rose and stooped to pick up the letter.

"Don't—don't, Charles!" she cried, putting her foot upon
it, and flinging her arms round his neck. "It is an audacious letter—a vulgar, a cruel letter, dear Charles!" Her
emotion increased as her thoughts recurred to the heartless
paragraph concerning her brother with which the letter concluded. "I could have overlooked everything but *that*,"
said she, unwittingly. With gentle force he succeeded in getting hold of the painfully ridiculous and contemptible effusion.
He attempted faintly to smile several times as he went on.

"Don't—don't, dearest Charles! I can't bear it. Don't
smile—it's very far from your heart; you do it only to assure
me."

Here Mr. Aubrey read the paragraph concerning himself.
His face turned a little paler than before, and his lips quivered
with suppressed emotion. "He is evidently a *very* foolish fellow!" he exclaimed, walking toward the window, with his
back to his sister, whom he did not wish to see how much he
was affected by so petty an incident.

"What does he allude to, Kate, when he talks of your
having spoken angrily to him, and that he did not know you?"
he inquired, after a few moments' pause, returning to her.

"Oh, dear!—I am so *grieved* that you should have noticed
it—but since you ask me"—and she told him the occurrence
alluded to in the letter. Mr. Aubrey drew himself up unconsciously as Kate went on, and she perceived him becoming still
paler than before, and *felt* the kindling anger of his eye.

"Forget it—forget it, dearest Charles!—So despicable a
being is really not worth a thought," said Kate, with increasing anxiety; for she had never in her life before witnessed
her brother the subject of such powerful emotions as then
made rigid his slender frame. At length, drawing a long
breath—

"It is fortunate, Kate," said he, calmly, "that *he* is not a
gentleman, and that I *endeavor to be*—a Christian." She
flung her arms round him, exclaiming,

"There spoke my own noble brother!"

"I shall preserve this letter as a curiosity, Kate," said he
presently; and with a pointed significance of manner that
arrested his sister's attention, he added—"It is rather singu-

lar, but some time before you came in I opened a letter in which your name is mentioned—I can not say in a *similar* manner, and yet—in short, it is from Lord De la Zouch, inclosing one—"

Miss Aubrey suddenly blushed scarlet, and trembled violently.

"Don't be agitated, my dear Kate, the inclosure is from Lady De la Zouch; and if it be in the same strain of kindness that pervades Lord De la Zouch's letter to *me*—"

"I would rather that *you* opened and read it, Charles"—she faltered, sinking into a chair.

"Come, come, dear Kate—play the woman!" said her brother, with an affectionate air.—"To say that there is nothing in these letters that I believe will interest you—very deeply gratify and interest your feelings—would be—"

"I know—I—I—suspect—I—" faltered Miss Aubrey with much agitation—"I shall return."

"Then you shall take these letters with you, and read, or not read them, as you like," said her brother, putting the letters into her hand with a fond and sorrowful smile, that soon, however, flitted away—and, leading her to the door, he was once more alone; and, after a brief interval of reverie, he wrote answers to such of the many letters before him as he considered earliest to require them.

Notwithstanding the judgment and tenderness with which Dr. Tatham discharged the very serious duty which, at the entreaty of his afflicted friends he had undertaken, of breaking to Mrs. Aubrey the calamity with which she and her family were menaced, the effects of the disclosure had been most disastrous. They had paralyzed her; and Mr. Aubrey, who had long been awaiting its issue, in sickening suspense, in an adjoining room, was hastily summoned in to behold a mournful and heart-rending spectacle. His venerable mother—she who had given him life at the mortal peril of her own; she whom he cherished with unutterable tenderness and reverence; she who doted upon him as upon the light of her eyes; from whose dear lips he had never heard a word of unkindness or severity; whose heart had never known an impulse but of gentle, noble, unbounded generosity toward all around her—this idolized being now lay suddenly prostrated and blighted before him—

Poor Aubrey yielded to this long and violent agony, in the presence of her who could apparently no longer hear, or see, or be sensible of what was passing in the chamber.

"My son," said Dr. Tatham, after the first burst of his friend's grief was over, and he knelt down beside his mother

with her hand grasped in his, "despise not the chastening of
the Lord; neither be weary of His correction:
"For whom the Lord loveth. He correcteth, even as a father
the son in whom he delighteth.
"The Lord will not cast off forever.
"But though He cause grief, yet will He have compassion,
according to the multitude of His mercies.
"For He doth not afflict willingly, nor grieve the children of
men."

It was with great difficulty that Dr. Tatham could render
himself audible while murmuring these soothing and solemn
passages of Scripture in the ear of his distracted friend, beside
whom he knelt.

Mrs. Aubrey had suffered a paralytic seizure, and lay motionless and insensible; her features slightly disfigured, but
partially concealed beneath her long silvery gray hair, which
had, in the suddeness of the fit, strayed from beneath her cap.

"But what am I about?" at length exclaimed Mr. Aubrey,
with a languid and alarmed air—"has medical assistance—"

"Dr. Goddart and Mr. Whateley are both sent for by
several servants, and will doubtless be very quickly here," replied Dr. Tatham; and while he yet spoke, Mr. Whateley—
who, when hastened on by the servant who had been sent for
him, was entering the park on a visit to young Mrs. Aubrey,
who was also seriously ill and in peculiarly critical circumstances—entered the room and immediately resorted to the
necessary measures.   Soon afterward, also, Dr. Goddart
arrived; but, alas, how little could they do for the venerable
sufferer!

During the next and for many ensuing days the lodge was
assailed by very many anxious and sympathizing inquirers, who
were answered by Waters, whom Mr. Aubrey—oppressed by
the number of friends who hurried up to the Hall, and insisted upon seeing him to ascertain the extent to which the
dreadful rumors were correct—had stationed there during the
day to afford the requisite information.   The Hall was pervaded by a gloom that could be felt.   Every servant had a
woe-begone look, and moved about as if a funeral were stirring.   Little Charles and Agnes, almost imprisoned in their
nursery, seemed quite puzzled and confused at the strange unusual seriousness, and quietness, and melancholy faces everywhere about them.   Kate romped not with them as had been
her wont; but would constantly burst into tears as she held
them on her knee or in her arms, trying to evade the continual
questioning of Charles.   " I think it will be time for *me* to cry

too, by and by!" said he to her one day, with an air half in
jest and half in earnest that made poor Kate's tears flow
afresh. Sleepless nights and days of sorrow soon told upon
her appearance. Her glorious buoyancy of spirits, that ere-
while, as it were, had filled the whole Hall with gladness—
where were they now? Ah, me! the rich bloom had disappeared from her beautiful cheek; but her high spirit, though
oppressed, was not broken, and she stood firmly and calmly
amid the scowling skies and lowering tempests. You fancied
you saw her auburn tresses stirred upon her pale but calm brow
by the breath of the approaching storm; and that she also felt
it, but trembled not, gazing on it with a bright and steadfast
eye. Her *heart* might be indeed bruised and shaken; but
her *spirit* was, ay, unconquerable. My glorious Kate, how
my heart goes forth toward you!

And thou, her brother, who art of kindred spirit; who art
supported by philosophy, and exalted by religion, so that thy
constancy can not be shaken or overthrown by the black and
ominous swell of trouble which is increasing and closing around
thee, I know that thou wilt outlive the storm—and yet it rocks
thee!

A month or two may see thee and thine expelled from old
Yatton, and not merely having lost everything, but with a
liability to thy successor that will hang round thy neck like a
millstone. What, indeed, is to become of you all? Whither
will you go? And your suffering mother, should she survive
so long, is her precious form to be borne away from Yatton?

Around thee stand those who, if thou fallest, will perish—
and that thou knowest; around thee calm, sorrowful, but erect
figure, are a melancholy group—thy afflicted mother—the wife
of thy bosom—thy two little children—thy brave and beautiful
sister—Yet think not, Misfortune! that over this man thou
art about to achieve thy accustomed triumphs. Here, behold
thou hast a MAN to contend with; nay, more, a CHRISTIAN
MAN, who hath calmly girded up his loins against the coming
fight!

'Twas Sabbath evening, some five weeks or so after the happening of the mournful events above commemorated, Kate,
having spent, as usual, several hours keeping watch beside the
silent and motionless figure of her mother, had quitted the
chamber for a brief interval, thinking to relieve her oppressed
spirits by walking, for a little while, up and down the long
gallery. Having slowly paced backward and forward once or
twice, she rested against the little oriel window at the furthest
extremity of the gallery and gazed, with saddened eye, upon

the setting sun, till at length, in calm grandeur, it disappeared beneath the horizon. 'Twas to Kate a solemn and mournful sign; especially followed as it was by the deepening shadows and gloom of evening. She sighed; and with her hands crossed on her bosom, gazed, with a tearful eye, into the darkening sky, where glittered the brilliant evening star. Thus she remained, a thousand pensive and tender thoughts passing through her mind, till the increasing chills of evening warned her to retire. "I will go," said she to herself, as she walked slowly along, "and try to play the evening hymn—I may not have *many* more opportunities!" With this view she gently opened the drawing-room door, and, glancing around, found that she should be alone. The fire gave the only light. She opened the organ with a sigh, and then sat down before it some minutes without touching the keys. At length she struck them very gently, as if fearful of disturbing those who, she soon recollected, were too distant to hear her. Ah! how many associations were stirred up as she played over the simple and solemn air! At length, in a low and rather tremulous voice, she began—

> " Soon will the evening star, with silver ray,
>   Shed its mild radiance o'er the sacred day;
>   Resume we, then, ere night and silence reign,
>   The rites which holiness and Heaven ordain—"

She sung the last line somewhat indistinctly; and, overcome by a flood of tender recollections, ceased playing; then, leaning her head upon her hand, she shed tears. At length she resumed—

> " Here humbly let us hope our Maker's smile
>   Will crown with sweet success our earthly toil—
>   And here on each returning Sabbath join—"

Here poor Kate's voice quivered—and, after one or two ineffectual attempts to sing the next line, she sobbed, and ceased playing. She remained for several minutes, her face buried in her handkerchief, shedding tears. At length, "I'll play the last verse," thought she, "and then sit down before the fire, and read over the evening service (feeling for her little prayer-book), before I return to poor mamma!" With a firmer hand and voice, she proceeded—

> " Father of Heaven! in whom our hopes confide,
>   Whose power defends us, and whose precepts guide—
>   In life our guardian, and in death our friend,
>   Glory supreme be thine, till time shall end!"

She played and sung these lines with a kind of solemn energy; and she felt as if a ray of heavenly light had trembled for a moment upon her upturned eye. She had not been, as she had supposed, alone; in the furthest corner of the room had been all the while sitting her brother—too exquisitely touched by the simplicity and goodness of his sweet sister to apprise her of his presence. Several times his feelings had nearly overpowered him; and as she concluded he arose from his chair, and approaching her, after her first surprise was over,—"Heaven bless you, dear Kate!" said he, taking her hands in his own. Neither of them spoke for a few moments.

"I could not have sung a line, or played, if I had known that you were here," said she.

"I thought so, Kate."

"I don't think I shall ever have the heart to play again!" —They were both silent.

"Be assured, Kate, that submission to the will of God," said Mr. Aubrey, as (he with his arm round his sister) they walked slowly to and fro, "is the great lesson to be learned from the troubles of life; and for that purpose they are sent. Let us bear up a while; the waters will not go over our heads!"

"I hope not," replied his sister, faintly, and in tears.

"How did you leave Agnes, Charles?"

"She was asleep; she is still very feeble—" Here the door was suddenly opened, and Miss Aubrey's maid entered hastily, exclaiming,

"Are you here, ma'am?—or sir?"

"Here we are," they replied, hurrying toward her; "what is the matter?"

"Oh, madam is *talking!* She began speaking all of a sudden. She did, indeed, sir. She's talking, and—" continued the girl, almost breathless.

"My mother talking!" exclaimed Aubrey, with an amazed air.

"Oh yes, sir! she is—she is indeed!"

Miss Aubrey sunk into her brother's arms, overcome for a moment with the sudden and surprising intelligence.

"Rouse yourself, Kate!" he exclaimed with animation; "did I not tell you that Heaven would not forget us? But I must hasten upstairs, to hear the joyful sounds with my own ears—and do you follow as soon as you can." Leaving her in the care of her maid, he hastened out of the room upstairs and was soon at the door of his mother's chamber. He stood for a moment in the door-way, and his straining ears caught the gentle tones of his mother's voice, speaking in a low but

cheerful tone. His knees trembled beneath him with joyfu
excitement. Fearful of trusting himself in her presence till he
had become calmer, he noiselessly sunk on the nearest chair,
with beating heart and straining ear—ay, every tone of that
dear voice thrilled through his heart. But I shall not torture
my own or my reader's heart by dwelling upon the scene that
ensued. Alas! the venerable sufferer's tongue was indeed
loosed—but reason had fled! He listened—he distinguished
her words. She supposed that all her children—dead and
alive—were romping about her; she spoke of him and his sister as she had spoken to them twenty years ago.

As soon as he had made this sad discovery, overwhelmed
with grief he staggered out of the room; and motioning his
sister, who was entering, into an adjoining apartment, communicated to her, with great agitation, the woful condition of
their mother.

CHAPTER XII.

THE chief corner-stone suddenly found wanting in the glittering fabric of Mr. Titmouse's fortune, so that to the eyes of
its startled architects, Messrs. Quirk, Gammon and Snap, it
seemed momentarily threatening to tumble about their ears,
was a certain piece of evidence which, being a matter-of-fact
man, I should like to explain to the reader before we get on
any further. In order, however, to do this effectually, I must
go back to an earlier period in the history than has been yet
called to his attention. If it shall have been unfortunate
enough to attract the hasty eye of the superficial and impatient
novel-reader, I make no doubt that by such a one certain portions of what has gone before, and which could not fail of attracting the attention of long-headed people, as being not
thrown in for nothing (and therefore to be borne in mind with
a view to subsequent explanation), have been entirely overlooked or forgotten. Now, I can fancy that the sort of reader
whom I have in my eye, as one whose curiosity it is worth some
pains to excite and sustain, has more than once asked himself
the following question, viz.—

How did Messrs. Quirk, Gammon and Snap first come to be
acquainted with the precarious tenure by which Mr. Aubrey
held the Yatton property? Why, it chanced in this wise:

Mr. Parkinson of Grilston, who has been already introduced
to the reader, succeeded to his late father in one of the most
respectable practices, as a country attorney and solicitor, in
Yorkshire. He was a highly honorable, painstaking man, and

deservedly enjoyed the entire confidence of all his numerous and influential clients. Some twelve years before the period at which this history commences, Mr. Parkinson, who was a very kind-hearted man, had taken into his service an orphan boy of the name of Steggars, at first merely as a sort of errand-boy and to look after the office. He soon, however, displayed so much sharpness, and acquitted himself so creditably in any-thing that he happened to be concerned in, a little above the run of his ordinary duties, that in the course of a year or two he became a sort of clerk, and sat and wrote at the desk it had formerly been his sole province to dust. Higher and higher did he rise, in process of time, in his master's estimation; and at length became quite a *factotum*—as such, acquainted with the whole course of business that passed through the office. Many interesting matters connected with the circumstances and connections of the neighboring nobility and gentry were thus constantly brought under his notice, and now and then set him thinking whether the knowledge thus acquired could not, in some way, and at some time or another, be turned to his own advantage; for I am sorry to say that he was utterly unworthy of the kindness and confidence of Mr. Parkinson, who little thought that in Steggars he had to deal with—a rogue in grain. Such being his character, and such his oppor-tunities, this worthy made a practice of minuting down, from time to time, anything of interest or importance in the affairs which thus came under his notice—even laboriously copying long documents, when he thought them of importance enough for his purpose, and had the opportunity of doing so without attracting the attention of Mr. Parkinson. He thus silently acquired a mass of information which might have enabled him to occasion great annoyance, and even inflict serious injury; and the precise object he had in view was either to force him-self, hereafter, into partnership with his employer (provided he could get regularly introduced into the profession), or even compel his master's clients to receive him into their confidence, adversely to Mr. Parkinson, making it worth his while to keep the secrets of which he had become possessed. So careful ought to be, and indeed generally are, attorneys and solicitors, as to the characters of those whom they thus receive into their employ. On the occasion of Mr. Aubrey's intended marriage with Miss St. Clair, with a view to the very liberal settlements which he contemplated, a full abstract of his title was laid by Mr. Parkinson before his conveyancer, in order to advise and prepare the necessary instruments. Owing to inquiries sug-gested by the conveyancer, additional statements were laid before him, and produced an opinion of a somewhat unsatisfactory description, from which I shall lay before the reader the following paragraph:—

"There seems no reason for supposing that any descendant of Stephen Dreddlington is now in existence; still, *as it is by no means physically impossible that such a person may be in esse*, it would unquestionably be most important to the security of Mr. Aubrey's title to establish clearly the validity of the conveyance by way of mortgage, executed by Harry Dreddlington, and which was afterward assigned to Geoffry Dreddlington on his paying off the money borrowed by his deceased uncle; since the descent of Mr. Aubrey from Geoffry Dreddlington would, in that event, clothe him with an indefeasible title at law, by virtue of that deed, and any equitable rights which were originally outstanding, would be barred by lapse of time. But the difficulty occurring to my mind on this part of the case is, that unless Harry Dreddlington, who executed that deed of mortgage, survived his father (a point on which I am surprised that I am furnished with no information), the deed itself would have been mere waste parchment, as in reality the conveyance of a person who *never had any interest* in the Yatton property—and, of course, neither Geoffry Dreddlington, nor his descendant, Mr. Aubrey, could derive any right whatever under such an instrument. In that case, such a contingency as I have above hinted at—I mean the existence of any legitimate descendant of Stephen Dreddlington—*might have a most serious effect upon the rights of Mr. Aubrey.*"

Now, every line of this opinion, and also even of the Abstract of Title upon which it was written, did this quick-sighted young scoundrel copy out and deposit, as a great prize, in his desk, among other similar notes and memoranda, little wotting his master the while of what he was doing. Some year or two afterward, the relationship subsisting between Mr. Parkinson and his clerk Steggars was suddenly determined by a somewhat untoward event; viz., by the latter's decamping with the sum of £700 sterling, being the amount of money due on a mortgage which he had been sent to receive from a client of Mr. Parkinson's. Steggars fled with it—but first having bethought himself of the documents to which I have been alluding and which he carried with him to London. Hot pursuit was made after the unfortunate delinquent, who was taken into custody two or three days after his arrival in town, while he was walking about the streets, with the whole of the sum which he had embezzled, *minus* a few pounds, upon his person, in bank-notes. He quickly found his way into Newgate.

His natural sagacity assured him that his case was rather an ugly one; but hope did not desert him.

" Well, my kiddy," said Grasp, the grim-visaged, gray-headed turnkey, as soon as he had ushered Steggars into his snug little quarters; " here you are, you see—isn't you?"

" I think I am," replied Steggars, with a sigh.

" Well—and if you want to have a chance of not going across the water till you're a many years older, you'll get yourself *defended*, and the sooner the better, d'ye see. There's *Quirk, Gammon and Snap*—my eyes! how they *do* thin this here place of ours, to be sure! The only thing's to get 'em soon; 'cause, ye see, they're so run after. Shall I send them to you?"

Steggars answered eagerly in the affirmative. In order to account for this spontaneous good nature on the part of Grasp, I must explain that old Mr. Quirk had for years secured a large criminal practice by having in his interest most of the officers attached to the police-offices and Newgate, to whom he gave, in fact, systematic gratuities, in order to get their recommendations to the persecuted individuals who came into their power. Very shortly after Grasp's messenger had reached Saffron Hill, with the intelligence that " there was *something now in the trap*," old Quirk bustled down to Newgate, and was introduced to Steggars, with whom he was closeted for some time. He took a lively interest in his new companion, whose narrative of his flight and capture he listened to in a very kind and sympathizing way, and promised to do for him whatever his little skill and experience *could* do. He hinted, however, that, as Mr. Steggars must be aware, a *little* ready money would be required, in order to fee counsel—whereat Steggars looked very dismal indeed, and, knowing the state of his exchequer, imagined himself already on shipboard, on his way to Botany Bay. Old Mr. Quirk asked him if he had no friends who would raise a trifle for a " chum in trouble,"—and on answering in the negative, he observed the enthusiasm of the respectable old gentleman visibly and rapidly cooling down.

" But I'll tell you what, sir," said poor Steggars suddenly, " if I haven't money, I may have *money's worth* at my command; I've a little box, that's at my lodging, which those that got me know nothing of—and in which there is a trifle or two about the families and fortunes of some of the first folk in Yatton, that would be precious well worth looking after, to those that know how to follow up such matters."

Old Quirk hereat pricked up his ears, and asked his young friend how he got possessed of such secrets.

"Oh, fy! fy!" said he, gently, as soon as Steggars had told him the practices of which I have already put the reader in possession.

"Ah—you may say fy! fy! if you like," quoth Steggars, earnestly; "but the thing is, not how they were come by, but what can be done with them, now they're got. For example, there's a certain member of parliament in Yorkshire that, high as he may hold his head, has no more right to the estates that yield him a good ten thousand a year than I have, but keeps some folk out of their own that could pay some other folk a round sum to be put in the way of getting their own;" and that was only *one* of the good things he knew of. Here old Quirk rubbed his chin, hemmed, fidgeted about in his seat, took off his glasses, wiped them, replaced them; and presently went through that ceremony again. He then said that he had the honor of being concerned for a great number of gentlemen in Mr. Steggars's "present embarrassed circumstances," but who had always been able to command at least a five-pound note, at starting, to run a heat for liberty.

"Come, come, old gentleman," quoth Steggars, earnestly. "I don't want to go over the water before my time, if I can help it, I assure you; and I see you know the value of what I've got! Such a gentleman as you can turn every bit of paper I have in my box into a fifty-pound note."

"All this is moonshine, my young friend," said old Quirk, in an irresolute tone and manner.

"Ah! is it, though! To be able to tell the owner of a fat ten thousand a year that you can spring a mine under his feet at any moment—eh?—and no one ever know how you came by your knowledge. And if they wouldn't do what was handsome, couldn't you *get the right heir*—and wouldn't *that*—Lord! it would make the fortunes of half a dozen of the first houses in the profession!" Old Quirk got a little excited.

"But mind, sir—you see "—said Steggars, "if I get off, I'm not to be cut out of the thing altogether—eh? I shall look to be taken into your employ, and dealt handsomely by—"

"Oh, Lord!" exclaimed Quirk, involuntarily—adding, quickly, "Yes, yes! to be sure! only fair; but let us first get you out of your present difficulty, you know!" Steggars, having first exacted from him a written promise to use his utmost exertions on his (Steggars's) behalf, and secure him the services of two of the most eminent Old Bailey counsel—viz., Mr.

Bluster and Mr. Slang—gave Mr. Quirk the number of the house where his precious box was, and a written order to the landlord to deliver it up to the bearer; after which Mr. Quirk shook him cordially by the hand, and having quitted the prison, made his way straight to the house in question, and succeeded in obtaining what he asked for.   He faithfully performed his agreement with Steggars; for he retained both Bluster and Slang for him, and got up their briefs with care; but, alas! although these eminent men exerted all their great powers, they succeeded not in either bothering the judge, bamboozling the jury, or browbeating the witnesses (the principal one of whom was Mr. Parkinson); Steggars was found guilty, and sentenced to be transported for life.   Enraged at this issue, he sent a message the next day to Mr. Quirk requesting a visit from him.   When he arrived, Steggars, in a very violent tone, demanded that his papers should be returned to him.   'Twas in vain that Mr. Quirk explained to him again and again his interesting position with reference to his goods, chattels, and effects—*i. e.* that, as a convicted felon, he had no further concern with them, and might dismiss all anxiety on that score from his mind.   Steggars hereat got more furious than before, and intimated plainly the course he should feel it his duty to pursue—that, if the papers in question were not given up to him as he desired, he should at once write off to his late employer, Mr. Parkinson, and acknowledge how much further he (Steggars) had wronged him and his clients than he supposed of. Old Quirk very feelingly represented to him that he was at liberty to do anything that he thought calculated to relieve his excited feelings; and then Mr. Quirk took a final farewell of his client, wishing him health and happiness.

"I say, Grasp!" said he, in a whisper, to that grim functionary, as soon as he had secured poor Steggars in his cell, "that bird is a little ruffled just now—isn't he, think you?"

"Lud, sir, the nat'ralist thing in the world, considering—"

"Well—if he should want a letter taken to any one, whatever he may say to the contrary, you'll send it on to Saffron Hill—eh?   Understand?—He may be injuring himself, you know;" and old Quirk, with one hand clasped the huge arm of Grasp in a familiar way, and with the forefinger of the other touched his own nose, and then winked his eye.

"All right!" quoth Grasp, and they parted.   Within a very few hours' time Mr. Quirk received, by the hand of a trusty messenger, from Grasp, a letter written by Steggars to Mr. Parkinson—a long and eloquent letter to the purport and effect which Steggars had intimated.   Mr. Quirk read it with much satisfaction, for it disclosed a truly penitent feeling, and a desire to undo as much mischief as the writer had done. He (Mr. Quirk) was not in the least exasperated by certain very plain terms in which his own name was mentioned; but, making all due allowances, quietly put the letter in the fire as soon as he had read it. In due time Mr. Steggars, whose health had suffered from close confinement, caught frequent whiffs of the fresh sea-breeze, having set out, under most favorable auspices, for Botany Bay, to which distant but happy place he had been thus fortunate in securing, so early, an *appointment for life.*

Such, then, were the miserable means by which Mr. Quirk became acquainted with the exact state of Mr. Aubrey's title; on first becoming apprised of which, Mr. Gammon either felt, or affected, great repugnance to taking any part in the affair. He appeared to suffer himself, at length, however, to be over-persuaded by Quirk into acquiescence; and, that point gained —having ends in view of which Mr. Quirk had not the least conception, and which, in fact, had but suddenly occurred to Mr. Gammon himself—worked his materials with a caution, skill, energy, and perseverance, which soon led to important results. Guided by the suggestions of acute and experienced counsel, after much pains and considerable expense, they succeeded in discovering that precious specimen of humanity, Tittlebat Titmouse, who hath already figured so prominently in this history. When they came to set down on paper the result of all their researches and inquiries, in order to submit it in the shape of a case for the opinion of Mr. Mortmain and Mr. Frankpledge, in the manner which has been already described, it looked perfect on paper, as many a faulty pedigree and abstract of title had looked before, and will yet look. It was quite possible for even Mr. Tresayle himself to overlook the defect which had been pointed out by Mr. Subtle. That which is stated to a conveyancer as *a fact*—any particular event, for instance, as of a death, a birth, or a marriage, at a particular time, which the very nature of the case renders highly probable—he may easily assume to be so. But when the same statement comes under the acute and experienced eye of a *nisi prius* lawyer, who knows that he will have to *prove* his case, step by step, the aspect of things is soon changed. "De non *apparentibus,* et de non *existentibus,*" saith Lord Coke, "eadem est ratio." The first practitioner at the common law before whom the case came, in its roughest and earliest form, in order that he might "lick it into shape," and "advise generally," preparatory to its "being laid before

counsel," was Mr. Traverse, a young pleader, whom Messrs.
Quirk and Gammon were disposed to take by the hand. He
wrote a very showy, but superficial and delusive opinion; and
put the intended *protégé* of his clients, as it were by a kind of
hop, step, and jump, into possession of the Yatton estates.
Quirk was quite delighted on reading it; but Gammon shook
his head with a somewhat sarcastic smile, and said he would
at once prepare a case for the opinion of Mr. Lynx, whom he
had pitched upon as the junior counsel in any proceedings
which might be instituted in a court of law. Lynx (of whom
I shall speak hereafter) was an experienced, hard-headed,
vigilant, and accurate lawyer; the very man for such a case,
requiring, as it did, most patient and minute examination.
With an eye fitted

> " To inspect a mite, not comprehend the heaven,"

he *crawled,* as it were, over a case; and thus, like as one can
imagine that a beetle creeping over the floor of St. Paul's
would detect minute flaws and fissures that would be invisible
to the eye of Sir Christopher Wren himself, spied out defects
that much nobler optics would have overlooked. To come to
plain matter-of-fact, however, I have beside me the original
opinion written by Mr. Lynx, and shall treat the reader to a
taste of it—giving him sufficient to enable him to appreciate
the ticklish position of affairs with Mr. Titmouse. To make
it not altogether unintelligible, let us suppose the state of the
pedigree to be something like this (as far as concerns our
present purpose):—

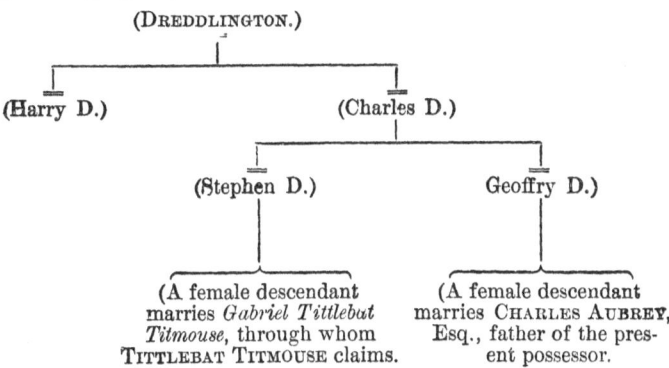

(DREDDLINGTON.)

(Harry D.)   (Charles D.)

(Stephen D.)   Geoffry D.)

(A female descendant   (A female descendant
marries *Gabriel Tittlebat*   marries CHARLES AUBREY,
Titmouse, through whom   Esq., father of the pres-
TITTLEBAT TITMOUSE claims.   ent possessor.

Be pleased now, unlearned reader, to bear in mind that
" *Dreddlington,*" at the top of the above table, is the common

ancestor; having two sons, the elder " *Harry D.*," the younger
" *Charles D*;" which latter has, in like manner, two sons,
" *Stephen D*," the elder son, and " *Geoffry D*," the younger
son; that Mr. Aubrey, at present in possession, claims under
" *Geoffry D.*" Now it will be incumbent on Titmouse, in
the first instance, to establish in himself a clear independent
title to the estates; it being sufficient for Mr. Aubrey (possession being nine tenths of the law) to falsify Titmouse's
proofs, or show them defective—" because," saith a very
learned sergeant who hath writ a text-book upon the Action of
Ejectment, " the plaintiff in an act of ejectment must recover
upon the strength of his own title, not the weakness of his
adversary's."

Now things standing thus, behold the astute Lynx advising
(*inter alia*) in manner following; that is to say—

" It appears clear that the lessor of the plaintiff (*i. e.* Tittlebat Titmouse) will be able to prove that Dreddlington (the
common ancestor) was seized of the estate at Yatton in the
year 1740; that he had two sons, Harry and Charles, the
former of whom, after a life of dissipation, appears to have
died without issue; and that from the latter (Charles) are
descended Stephen, the ancestor of the lessor of the plaintiff,
and Geoffry, the ancestor of the defendant. Assuming,
therefore, that the descent of the lessor of the plaintiff from
Stephen can be made out, as there appears every reason to
expect [on this point Lynx had written four brief pages], a
clear *prima facie* case will be established on the part of the
lessor of the plaintiff. As, however, it is suspected that Harry
D. executed a conveyance in fee of the property, in order to
secure the loan contracted by him from Aaron Moses, it will
be extremely important to ascertain, and, if possible, procure
satisfactory evidence that his decease occurred before the
period at which, by his father's death, that conveyance could
have become operative upon the property: since it is obvious
that, should he have survived his father, *that instrument,
being outstanding*, may form a complete answer to the case of
the lessor of the plaintiff. The danger will be obviously increased, should the debt to Aaron Moses prove to have been
paid off, as is stated to be rumored, by Geoffry D., the
younger son of Charles D.: for, should that turn out to be
the case, he would probably have taken a conveyance to himself, or to trustees for his benefit, from Aaron Moses—which
being in the power of the defendant, Mr. Aubrey, would enable
him to make out a title to the property, paramount to that
now attempted to be set up on behalf of Mr. Titmouse. Every

possible exertion, therefore, should be made to ascertain the precise period of the death of Harry D. The registries of the various parishes in which the family may have at any time resided should be carefully searched; and an examination made in the churches and church-yards, of all tombstones, escutcheons, etc., belonging or supposed to belong to the Dreddlington family, and by which any light can be thrown upon this most important point. It appears clear that Dreddlington (the common ancestor) died on the 7th August, 1742: —the question, therefore, simply is, *whether the death of his ildest son (Harry) took place prior or subsequent to that period.* It is to be feared that the defendant may be in possession of some better evidence on this point than is possessed by the lessor of the plaintiff. The natural presumption certainly seems to be, that the son, being the younger and stronger man, was the survivor."

The above mentioned opinion of Mr. Lynx, together with that of Mr. Subtle entirely corroborating it (and which was alluded to in a late chapter of this history), a pedigree, were lying on the table, one day, at the office at Saffron Hill. before the anxious and perplexed parties, Messrs. Quirk and Gammon.

Gammon was looking attentively, and with a very chagrined air, at the pedigree; and Quirk was looking at Gammon.

" Now, Gammon," said the former, " just let me see again where the exact hitch is—eh? You'll think me perhaps infernally stupid, but—curse me if I can see it!"

" See it, my dear sir? Here, *here!*" replied Gammon, with sudden impatience, putting his finger two or three times to the words " *Harry D.*"

" Lord bless us! Don't be so sharp with one, Gammon! I know as well as you that that's *about* where the crack is; but what is the precise thing we're in want of, eh?"

" Proof, my dear sir, of the death of Harry Dreddlington some time—no matter when—previous to the 7th August, 1742; and in default thereof, Mr. Quirk, we are all flat on our backs, and had better never have stirred in the business."

" You know, Gammon, you're better *up* in these matters than I—(only because I've not been able to turn my attention to 'em since I first began business)—so just tell me, in a word, what good's to be got by showing that fellow to have died in his father's life-time?"

" You don't show your usual acuteness, Mr. Quirk," replied Gammon, blandly. " It is to make waste paper of that confounded conveyance which he executed, and which Mr. Aubrey has, and with which he may, at a stroke, cut the ground from under our feet."

"The very thought makes one feel quite funny—don't it, Gammon," quoth Quirk, with a flustered air.

"It may well do so, Mr. Quirk. Now we *are* fairly embarked in a cause where success will be attended with so many splendid results, Mr. Quirk—though I'm sure you'll always bear me up in saying how very unwilling I was to take advantage of the villainy of that miscreant Steg—hem—"

"Gammon, Gammon, you're always harking back to that—I'm tired of hearing on't!"

"Well, now we're in it, I don't see why we should allow ourselves to be baffled by trifles. The plain question is, undoubtedly, whether we are to stand still or go on." Mr. Quirk gazed at Mr. Gammon with an anxious and puzzled look.

"How d'ye make out—in a legal way, you know, Gammon —*when* a man died—I mean, of a *natural* death?" inquired Quirk, who was familiar enough with the means of proving the exact hour of certain *violent* deaths at Debtor's Door.

"Oh, there are various methods of doing so, my dear sir," replied Gammon, carelessly. "Entries in family-bibles and prayer-books, registers, tombstones—ay, by the way, AN OLD TOMBSTONE," continued Gammon, musingly, "that would settle the business!"

"An old tombstone!" echoed Quirk, briskly. "Lord, Gammon, so it would! That's an *idea!*—I call that a decided idea, Gammon. 'Twould be the very thing!"

"The very thing!" repeated Gammon, pointedly. They remained silent for some moments.

"Snap could not have looked about him sharply enough, when he was down at Yatton!" at length observed Quirk, in a low tone, flushing all over as he uttered the last words, and felt Gammon's cold gray eye settled on him like that of a snake.

"He could not, indeed, my dear sir," replied Gammon, while Quirk continued gazing earnestly at him, now and then wriggling about in his chair, rubbing his chin, and drumming with his fingers on the table.—"And now that you've suggested the thing, it's not to be wondered at—you know, it would have been an old tombstone—a sort of fragment of a tombstone, perhaps—so deeply sunk in the ground, propably, as easily to have escaped observation, eh? Does not it strike *you* so, Mr. Quirk?" All this was said by Gammon in a musing manner and in a very low tone of voice; and he was delighted to find his words sinking into the eager mind of his companion.

"Ah, Gammon!" exclaimed Quirk, with a sound of partly a sigh, and partly a whistle, (the former being the exponent of the *true* state of his feelings, *i. e.* anxiety—the latter of what he wished to *appear* the state of his feelings, *i. e.* indifference).

"Yes, Mr. Quirk?"

"You're a deep devil, Gammon—I *will* say that for you!" replied Quirk, glancing toward each door, and, as it were, unconsciously drawing his chair a little closer to that of Gammon.

"Nay, my dear sir!" said Gammon, with a deferential and deprecating smile, "you give me credit for an acuteness I feel I do not deserve. If, indeed, I had not had *your* sagacity to rely upon, ever since I have had the honor of being connected with you—ah, Mr. Quirk, you know you lead—I follow—"

"Gammon, Gammon! Come—your name's *Oily*—"

"In moments like these, Mr. Quirk, I say nothing that I do not feel," interrupted Gammon, gravely, putting to his nose the least modicum of snuff which he could take with the tip of his finger out of the huge box of Mr. Quirk, who just then was thrusting immense pinches every half minute up his nostrils.

"It will cost a great deal of money to find that same tombstone, Gammon!" said Quirk, in almost a whisper, and paused, looking intently at Gammon.

"I think this is a different kind of snuff from that which you usually take, Mr. Quirk, isn't it?" inquired Gammon, as he inserted the tips of his fingers into the box.

"The same—the same," replied Quirk, mechanically.

"You are a man better equal to serious emergencies than any man I ever came near," said Gammon; "I perceive that you have hit the nail on the head, as indeed you always do."

"Tut! Stuff, Gammon; you're every bit as good a hand as I am." Gammon smiled, shook his head, and shrugged his shoulders.

"'Tis that practical sagacity of yours," said Gammon— "you know it as well as I can tell you—that has raised you to your present professional eminence." He paused, and looked very sincerely at his senior partner.

"Well, I must own I think I *do* know a trick or two," quoth Quirk, with a sort of *grunt* of gratification.

"Ay, and further, there are *some* clever men that never can keep their own counsel, but are like a hen that has just laid an egg, and then goes foolishly cackling about everywhere, and then her egg is taken away; but *you*—"

11

"Ha, ha!" laughed Quirk; "that's *devilish* good, Gammon!—Capital! Gad, I think I see the hen! Ha, ha!"

"Ha, ha!" echoed Gammon, gently. "But to be serious, Mr. Quirk; what I was going to say was, that I thoroughly appreciate your admirable caution in not confiding to any one —no, not even to me—the exact means by which you intend to extricate us from our present dilemma." Here Quirk got very fidgety, and twirled his watch-key violently.

"Hem! But—hem! Ay—a—a," he grunted, looking with an uneasy air at his calm astute companion; "I didn't mean so much as all *that*, either, Gammon; for two heads, in my opinion, are better than one. You *must* own that, Gammon!" said he, not at all relishng the heavy burden of responsibility which he felt that Gammon was about to devolve upon his (Quirk's) shoulders exclusively.

"'Tis undoubtedly rather a serious business on which we are now entering," said Gammon; "and I have always admired a saying which you years ago told me of that great man Machiavel—"

[Oh, Gammon! Gammon! You well know that poor old Mr. Quirk never heard of the name of that same Machiavel till this moment!]

"That when great affairs are stirring a master-move should be confined to the master-mind that projects it. I understand! I see! I will not, therefore, inquire into the precise means by which I am satisfied you will make it appear, in due time (while I am engaged getting up the subordinate, but very harassing details of the general case), that *Henry Dreddlington died before the 7th of August*, 1742." Here, taking out his watch—"Bless me, Mr. Quirk, how time passes!—Two o'clock! I ought to have been at Messrs. Gregson's a quarter of an hour ago."

"Stop—a moment or two can't signify! It—it," said Quirk, hesitatingly, "it was *you*, wasn't it, that thought of the tombstone?"

"I!—my dear Mr. Quirk"—interrupted Gammon, with a look of astonishment and deference.

"Come, come—honor among thieves, you know, Gammon!" said Quirk, trying to laugh.

"No—it shall never be said that I attempted to take the credit of"—commenced Gammon; when a clerk entering put an end to the colloquy between the partners, each of whom, presently, was sitting alone in his own room—for Gammon found that he was too late to think of keeping his engagement with Messrs. Gregson; if indeed he had ever made any—which,

in fact, he had *not.* Mr. Quirk sat in a musing posture for
nearly half an hour after he and Gammon had separated.
" Gammon *is* a deep one! I'll be shot if ever there was his
equal," said Quirk to himself, at length; and starting off his
chair, with his hands crossed behind him, he walked softly to
and fro. " I know what he's driving at—though he thought
I didn't! He'd let me scratch my hands in getting the black-
berries, and then he'd come smiling in to eat 'em! But—
share and share alike—share profit, share danger, Master
Gammon;—you may find that Caleb Quirk is a match for Oily
Gammon—I'll have you in for it, one way or another!" Here
occurred a long pause in his thoughts. " Really I doubt the
thing's growing unmanageable—the prize can't be worth the
risk!—*Risk*, indeed—'fore gad—it's neither more nor less
than—" Here a certain picture hanging, covered with black
crape, in the drawing-room at Alibi House, seemed to have
glided down from its station, and to stand before his eyes with
the crape drawn aside—a ghastly object—eugh! He shuddered, and involuntarily closed his eyes. " How devilish odd
that I should just *now* have happened to think of it!" he
inwardly exclaimed, sinking into his chair, in a sort of cold
sweat.

" D—n the picture!" at length he exclaimed, almost aloud,
getting more and more flustered—" I'll burn it! It sha'n't
disgrace my drawing-room any longer!" Here Quirk almost
fancied that some busy little fiend sat squatting before the
grisly picture, writing the words " CALEB QUIRK " at the
bottom of it; and a sort of sickness came over him for a moment. Presently he started up, and took down one of several
well-worn dingy-looking books that stood on the shelves—a
volume of Burns's Justice. Resuming his seat, he put on his
glasses, and with a little trepidation turned to the head
" Forgery," and glanced over it, divided as it was into two
great heads—" Forgery *at Common Law*, and Forgery *by
Statute*," with many able observations of the learned compiler,
and important " *cases* " cited. At length his eye lighted upon
a paragraph that seemed suddenly to draw his heart up into
his throat, producing a sensation that made him involuntarily
clap his hand upon his neck.

" Oh, Gammon!" he muttered, drawing off his glases, sinking back in his chair, and looking toward the door that opened
into Gammon's room, in which direction he extended his right
arm, and shook his fist. " You *precious* villain!—I've an
uncommon inclination," at length thought he, " to go down
slap to Yorkshire—say nothing to anybody—make peace with

the enemy, and knock up the whole thing!—For a couple of thousand pounds—a trifle to the Aubreys, I'm sure. Were *I* in his place I shouldn't grudge it; and why should he?—By Jove," he got a little heated—" that *would* be, as Gammon has it, a master-move! and confined, egad! to the master-mind that thought of it!—Why should he ever know of the way in which the thing blew up? Really 'twould be worth half the money to do Gammon so hollow for once—by George, it would! —Gammon, that would slip Caleb Quirk's neck so slyly into the halter, indeed!"

" I'll tell you what, Mr. Quirk," said Gammon, suddenly re-entering the room after about an hour's absence, during which he too had, like his senior partner, been revolving many things in his mind—" it has occurred to me that I had better immediately go down to Yatton, *alone.* "

Hereat Mr. Quirk opened both his eyes and his mouth to their very widest; got very red in the face, and stared at his placid partner with a mingled expression of fear and wonder. " Hang me, Gammon!" at length he exclaimed, desperately slapping his fist upon the table—" if I don't think you're the very devil himself!"—and he sunk back in his chair, verily believing, in the momentary confusion of his thoughts, that what had been passing through his mind was known to Gammon; or that what had been passing through his (Quirk's) mind had also been occurring to Gammon, who had resolved upon being beforehand in putting his purposes into execution. Gammon was at first completely confounded by Quirk's reception of him, and stood for a few moments, with his hands elevated, in silence. Then he approached the table, and his eye caught the well-thumbed volume of Burns's Justice, open at the head, " FORGERY!"—and the quick-sighted Gammon saw how matters stood at a glance—the process by which the result he had just witnessed had been arrived at.

" Well, Mr. Quirk, what new vagary now?" he inquired, with an air of smiling curiosity.

" Vagary be ——!" growled old Quirk, sullenly, without moving in his chair.

Gammon stood for a moment or two eying him with a keen scrutiny. " What!" at length he inquired, good-humoredly, " do you then really grudge me any share in the little enterprise?"

" Eh?" quickly interrupted Quirk, pricking up his ears. " Do you intend to play *Mackivel!* eh? What must you go down alone to Yatton for, Gammon?" continued Quirk, anxiously.

"Why, simply as a sort of pioneer—to reconnoiter the church-yard—eh? I thought it might have been of service; but if—"

"Gammon, Gammon, your hand! I understand," replied Quirk, evidently vastly relieved—most cordially shaking the cold hand of Gammon.

"But understand, Mr. Quirk," said he, in a very peremptory manner, "no one upon earth is to know of my visit to Yatton except yourself."

He received a solemn pledge to that effect, and presently the partners separated, a little better satisfied with each other. Though not a word passed between them for several days afterward on the topic chiefly discussed during the interview above described, the reader may easily imagine that neither of them dropped it from his thoughts. Mr. Quirk paid one or two visits to the neighborhood of Houndsditch (a perfect hot-bed of clients), where resided two or three gentlemen of the Jewish persuasion, who had been placed, from time to time, under considerable obligations by the firm of Quirk, Gammon and Snap, in respect of professional services rendered both to themselves and to their friends. One of them, in particular, had a painful consciousness that it was in old Mr. Quirk's power at any time, by a whisper, to place his—the aforesaid Israelite's—neck in an unsightly noose that every now and then might be seen dangling from a beam opposite Debtor's Door, Newgate, about eight o'clock in the morning; him, therefore, every consideration of interest and gratitude combined to render subservient to the reasonable wishes of Mr. Quirk. He was a most ingenious little fellow, and had a great taste for the imitative arts—so strong a taste, in fact, that it had once or twice placed him in some jeopardy with the Goths and Vandals of the law, who characterized the noble art in which he excelled by a very ugly and formidable word, and annexed the most barbarous penalties to its practice. What passed between him and old Quirk on the occasion of their interviews, I know not; but one afternoon, the latter, on returning to his office, without saying anything to anybody, having bolted the door, took out of his pocket several little pieces of paper, containing pretty little picturesque devices of a fragmentary character, with antique letters and figures on them—crumbling pieces of stone, some looking more and some less sunk in the ground, and overgrown with grass: possibly they were designs for ornaments to be added to that tasteful structure—Alibi House—possibly intended to grace Miss Quirk's album. However this might be, after he had looked

at them and carefully compared them one with another for
some time, he folded them up in a sheet of paper, sealed it up
—with certainly not the steadiest hand in the world—and then
deposited it in an iron safe.

CHAPTER XIII.

YATTON, the recovery of which was the object of these secret
and formidable movements and preparations, not to say machinations, was all this while the scene of deep affliction.   The
lamentable condition of his mother plunged Mr. Aubrey, his
wife, and sister, into profounder grief than had been occasioned
by the calamity which menaced them all in common.   Had he
been alone he would have encountered the sudden storm of
adversity with unshrinking, nay, cheerful firmness; but could
it be so, when he had ever before him those whose ruin was
involved in his own?—Poor Mrs. Aubrey, his wife, having been
two or three weeks confined to her bed, during which time
certain fond hopes of the husband had been blighted, was
almost overpowered, when languid and feeble, supported by
Mr. Aubrey and Kate, she first entered the bedroom of the
venerable sufferer.   What a difference, indeed, was there between the appearance of all of them at that moment, and on
the Christmas-day, when, a happy group, they were cheerfully
enjoying the festivities of the season!   Kate was now pale, and
somewhat thinner; her beautiful features exhibited a care-worn
expression; yet there was a serene luster in her blue eye and
a composed resolution in her air, which bespoke the superiority
her soul.   What it had cost her to bear with any semblance
of self-possession, or fortitude, the sad spectacle now presented
by her mother!   What a tender and vigilant nurse was she, to
one who could no longer be sensible of, or appreciate, her
attentions!   How that sweet girl humored all her mother's
little eccentricities and occasional excitement, and accommodated herself to every-varying phases of her mental malady.
She had so schooled her sensibilities and feelings as to be able
to maintain perfect cheerfulness and composure in her mother's
presence, on occasions which forced her brother and his shaken
wife to turn aside with an eye of agony—overcome by some
touching speech or wayward action of the unconscious sufferer,
who constantly imagined herself—poor soul!—to be living over
again her early married life, and that in her little grandchildren she beheld Mr. Aubrey and Kate as in their child-
hood!   She would gently chide Mr. Aubrey, her husband, for
his prolonged absence, asking many times a day whether he

had returned from London. Every morning old Jacob Jones was shown into her chamber, at the hour at which he had been accustomed in happier days to attend upon her. The faithful old man's eyes would be blinded with tears, and his voice choked, as he was asked how Peggy got over her yesterday's journey, and listened to questions, messages, and directions, which had been familiar to him twenty years before, about villagers and tenants who had long laid moldering in their humble graves—their way thither cheered and smoothed by her Christian charity and benevolence! 'Twas a touching sight to see her two beautiful grandchildren, in whose company she delighted, brought, with a timorous and half-reluctant air, into her presence. How strange must have seemed to them the gayety of the motionless figure always lying in the bed: a gayety which, though gentle as gentle could be, yet sufficed not to assure the little things, or set them at their ease. Though her mild features ever smiled upon them, and her voice was cheerful, still 'twas from a prostrate figure that never moved, and was always surrounded by calm, quiet figures, with sorrowful constraint in their countenances and gestures! Charles would stand watching her, with apprehensive eye— the finger of one hand raised to his lip, while his other retained the hand that had brought him in, as if fearful of its quitting hold of him; the few words he could be brought to speak were in a subdued tone and hurried utterance:—and when, having been lifted up to kiss his grandmamma, he and his sister were taken out of the chamber, their little breasts would heave a sigh which showed how relieved they were from their recent constraint.

How wofully changed was everything in the once cheerful old Hall! Mr. Aubrey sitting in the library, intently engaged upon books and papers—Mrs. Aubrey and Kate now and then, arm in arm, walking slowly up and down the galleries, or one of the rooms, or the hall, not with their former sprightly gayety, but pensive, and often in tears, and then returning to the chamber of their suffering parent. All this was sad work, indeed, and seemed, as it were, to herald in coming desolation!

But little variation occurred, for several weeks, in the condition of Mrs. Aubrey, except that she grew visibly feebler. One morning, however, about six weeks after her seizure, from certain symptoms the medical men intimated their opinion that some important change was on the eve of taking place, for which they prepared the family. She had been very restless during the night. After frequent intervals of uneasy sleep, she would awake with evident surprise and bewilder-

ment. Sometimes a peculiar smile would flit over her emaciated features; at others they would be overcast with gloom,
and she would seem struggling to suppress tears. Her voice,
too, when she spoke, was feeble and tremulous, and she would
sigh, and shake her head mournfully. Old Jacob Jones, not
being introduced at the accustomed hour, she asked for him.
When he made his appearance she gazed at him for a moment
or two with a puzzled eye, exclaiming, "Jacob! Jacob! is it
you?" in a very low tone, and then she closed her eyes, apparently falling asleep. Thus passed the day; her daughter
and daughter-in-law sitting on either side of the bed, where
they had so long kept their anxious and affectionate vigils—
Mr. Aubrey sitting at the foot of the bed—and Dr. Goddart
and Mr. Whateley in frequent attendance. Toward the evening Dr. Tatham also, as had been his daily custom through
her illness, appeared, and in a low tone read over the service
for the visitation of the sick. Shortly afterward Mr. Aubrey
was obliged to quit the chamber, in order to attend to some
very pressing matters of business; and he had been engaged
for nearly an hour, intending almost every moment to return
to his mother's chamber, when Dr. Tatham entered as Mr.
Aubrey was subscribing his name to a letter, and, with a little
earnestness, said, "Come, my friend, let us return to your
mother; methinks she is on the eve of some decisive change:
the issue is with God." Within a very few moments they
were both at the bedside of Mrs. Aubrey. A large chamber-
lamp, standing on the table at a little distance from the bed,
diffused a soft light over the room, rendering visible at a
glance the silent and sad group collected round the bed, all
with their eyes directed toward the venerable figure who lay
upon it. Mr. Aubrey sat beside his wife close to his mother,
and taking her thin, emaciated hand into his own, gently
raised it to his lips. She seemed dozing; but his action appeared to rouse her for a moment. Presently she fixed her eye
upon him—its expression, the while, slowly but perceptibly
changing and exciting strange feelings within him. He
trembled and removed not his eye from hers. He turned
very pale—for the whole expression of his mother's countenance, which was turned full toward him, was changing.
Through the clouded windows of the falling fabric, behold:
its long-imprisoned tenant, THE SOUL, had arisen from its
torpor, and was looking at him. Reason was reappearing.
It was, indeed, his mother, and *in her right mind*, that was
gazing at him. He scarcely breathed. At length surprise
and apprehension yielded before a gush of tenderness and

love. With what an unutterable look was his mother at that moment regarding him! His lip quivered—his eye overflowed —and, as he felt her fingers very gently compressing his own, his tears fell down. Gently leaning forward, he kissed her cheek and sunk on one knee beside the bed.

"Is it you, my son?" said she, in a very low tone, but in *her own* voice, and it stirred up instantly a thousand fond recollections, almost overpowering him. He kissed her hand with fervent energy, but spoke not. She continued gazing at him with mingled solemnity and fondness. Her eye seemed brightening as it remained fixed upon him. Again she spoke, in a very low but clear voice—every thrilling word being heard by every one around her—"*Or ever the silver cord be loosed, or the golden bowl be broken, or the pitcher be broken at the fountain, or the wheel broken at the cistern,—Then shall the dust return to the earth as it was; and the spirit shall return unto God who gave it.*" It would be in vain to attempt to describe the manner in which these words were spoken, and which fell upon those who heard them as though they were listening to one from the dead.

"My mother!—my mother!" at length faltered Aubrey.

"God bless thee, my son!" said she, solemnly. "And Catherine, my daughter— God bless thee"— she presently added, gently turning round her head toward the quarter whence a stifled sob issued from Miss Aubrey, who rose, trembling, and leaning over, kissed her mother. "Agnes, are you here—and your little ones?—God bless—" Her voice got fainter, and her eyes closed. Mr. Whateley gave her a few drops of ether, and she presently revived.

"God has been very good to you, madame," said Dr. Tatham, observing her eye fixed upon him, " to restore you thus to your children."

"I have been long absent—long!—I wake, my children, but to bid you farewell, forever, upon earth."

"Say not so, my mother—my precious mother!" exclaimed her son, in vain endeavoring to suppress his emotions.

"I do, my son! Weep not for me; I am old, and am summoned away from among you—" She ceased, as if from exhaustion; and no one spoke for some minutes.

"It may be that God hath roused me, as it were, from the dead, to comfort my sorrowful children with words of hope," said Mrs. Aubrey, with much more power and distinctness than before. "Hope ye, then, in God; for ye shall yet praise Him who is the health of your countenance, and your God!"

"We will remember, my mother, your words!" faltered her
son.

"Yes, my son—if days of darkness be at hand "—She
ceased.   Again Mr. Whateley placed to her white lips a glass
with some reviving fluid—looking ominously at Mr. Aubrey,
as he found that she continued insensible. Miss Aubrey sobbed
audibly; indeed, all present were powerfully affected.   Again
Mrs. Aubrey revived, and swallowed a few drops of wine and
water.   A heavenly serenity diffused itself over her emaciated
features.

"We shall meet again, my loves!—I can no longer see you
with the eyes of "—Mr. Whateley observing a sudden change,
came nearer to her.

"Peace! peace!" she murmured, almost inarticulately.   A
dead silence ensued, interrupted only by smothered sobs.   Her
children sunk on their knees, and buried their faces in their
hands, trembling.

Mr. Whateley made a silent signal to Dr. Tatham, that life
had ceased—that the beloved spirit had passed away.   "The
Lord gave, and the Lord hath taken away; blessed be the
name of the Lord!" said Dr. Tatham, with tremulous
solemnity.   Mrs. Aubrey and Miss Aubrey, no longer able to
restrain their feelings, wept bitterly, and, overpowered with
grief, were supported out of the room by Dr. Tatham and Mr.
Aubrey.   As soon as it was known that the venerable mother
of Mr. Aubrey was no more, universal reverence was testified
for her memory, and sympathy for the afflicted survivors by
even those high and low in the remoter parts of the neighborhood who had no personal acquaintance with the family.
Two or three days afterward the undertaker, who had received
orders from Mr. Aubrey to provide a simple and inexpensive
funeral, submitted to him a list of more than thirty names of
the nobility and gentry of the country, who had sent to him
to know whether it would be agreeable to the family for them
to be allowed to attend Mrs. Aubrey's remains to the grave.
After much consideration, Mr. Aubrey accepted of this spontaneous tribute of respect to the memory of his mother
'Twas a memorable and melancholy day on which the inter-
ment took place—one never to be forgotten at Yatton.   What
can be more chilling than the gloomy bustle of a great funeral, especially in the country, and when the deceased is one
whose memory is enshrined in the holiest feelings of all who
know her?   What person was there, for miles around, who
could not speak of the courtesies, the charities, the goodness
of Madam Aubrey!

*When the ear heard her, then it blessed her; and when the
eye saw her, it gave witness to her:*
  *Because she delivered the poor that cried, and the fatherless,
and him that had none to help him.*
  *The blessing of him that was ready to perish came upon her,
and she caused the widow's heart to sing for joy.*
  She was eyes to the blind, and feet was she to the lame.
  She was a mother to the poor.—

Pale as death, the chief mourner, wrapped in his black
cloak, is stepping into the mourning-coach. No one speaks to
him; his face is buried in his handkerchief; his heart seems
breaking. He thinks of her whose dear dust is before him;—
then of the beloved beings whom he has left alone in their
agony till his return—his wife and sister. The procession
moving slowly on—long, silent rows of the tenantry and villagers, old and young, male and female—not a dry eye among
them, nor a syllable spoken—stand on each side of the way;
no sound heard but of horses' feet and wheels crushing along
the wet gravel—for the day is most gloomy and inclement.
As they quit the gates, carriage after carriage follows in the
rear; and the sorrowful crowd increases around them. Many
have in their hands the bibles and prayer-books which had been
given them by her who now lies in yonder hearse; and a few
can recollect the day when the great lord of Yatton led her
along from the church to the Hall, his young and blooming
bride—in pride and joy—and they are now going to lay her
beside him again. They enter the little church-yard, and are
met by good Dr. Tatham in his surplice, bareheaded, and with
book in hand; with full eye and quivering lip he slowly pre-
cedes the body into the church. His voice frequently trem-
bles, and sometimes he pauses while reading the service. Now
they are standing bareheaded at the vault's mouth—the last
sad rites are being performed; and probably, as is thinking the
chief mourner, over the last of his race who will rest in that
tomb!
  Long after the solemn ceremony was over, the little church-
yard remained filled with mournful groups of villagers and
tenants, who pressed forward to the dark mouth of the vault,
to take their last look at the coffin which contained he remains
of her whose memory would live long in all their hearts.
"Ah, dear old madam," quoth Jonas Higgs to himself, as he
finished his dreary day's labors by temporarily closing up the
mouth of the vault, "they might have turned thee, by and
by, out of yonder Hall, but they shall not touch thee *here!*"

Thus died, and was buried, Madam Aubrey; *and she is not yet forgotten.*

How desolate seemed the Hall the next morning to the bereaved inmates, as, dressed in deep mourning, they met at the cheerless breakfast-table! Aubrey kissed his wife and sister—who could hardly answer his brief inquiries. The gloom occasioned throughout the Hall, for the last ten days, by the blinds being constantly drawn down, now that they were drawn up, had given way to a staring light and distinctness, that almost startled and offended the eyes of those whose hearts were dark with sorrow as ever. Every object reminded them of the absence of *one*—whose chair stood empty in its accustomed place. There, also, was her Bible on the little round table near the window. The mourners seemed relieved by the entrance, by and by, of the children; but they were also in mourning! Let us, however, withdraw from this scene of suffering, where every object, every recollection, every association, causes the wounded heart to bleed afresh.

Great troubles seem coming upon them; and now that *they have buried their dead out of their sight,* and when time shall begin to pour his balm into their present smarting wounds, I doubt not that they will look those troubles in the face calmly and with fortitude, not forgetful of the last words of her for whom they now mourn so bitterly, and whom, beloved and venerable being! God hath mercifully taken away from evil days that are to come.

After much and anxious consideration, they resolved to go, on the ensuing Sunday morning, to church, where neither Mrs. Aubrey nor Kate had been since the illness of her mother. The little church was crowded; almost every one present, besides wearing a saddened countenance, exhibited some outward mark of respect in their dress—some badge of mourning—such as their little means admitted of. The pulpit and reading-desk were hung in black, as also was Mr. Aubrey's pew—an object of deep interest to the congregation, who expected to see at least *some* member of the family at the Hall. They were not disappointed. A little before Dr. Tatham took his place in the reading-desk, the well-known sound of the family carriage-wheels was heard, as it drew up before the gate; and presently Mr. Aubrey appeared at the church door, with his wife and sister on either arm; all of them, of course, in the deepest mourning—Mrs. and Miss Aubrey's countenances concealed beneath their long crape veils. For some time after taking their seats they seemed oppressed with emotion, evidently weeping. Mr. Aubrey, however, exhibited great composure, though his countenance bore the traces of the suffering he had undergone. Mrs. Aubrey seldom rose from her seat; but Kate stood up, from time to time, with the rest of the congregation; her white handkerchief, however, might be seen frequently raised to her eyes, beneath her black veil. As the service went on she seemed to have struggled with some success against her feelings. To relieve herself for a moment from its oppressive closeness she gently drew aside her veil; and thus, for a few minutes, exhibited a countenance inexpressibly beautiful. She could not, however, long bear to face ﾟ congregation, every one of whom she felt to be looking on her and those beside her with affectionate sympathy, and rather quickly drew her veil again over her face, without again removing it. There was one person present on whom the brief glimpse of her beauty had produced a prodigious impression. As he gazed at her, the color gradually deserted his cheek; and his eye remained fixed upon her, even after she had drawn down her veil. He experienced emotions such as he had never known before. *So that was Miss Aubrey!*

Mr. Gammon—for he it was, and he had gone thither, under the expectation of seeing, for the first time, some of the Aubrey family—generally passed for a cold-blooded person; and in fact few men living had more control over their feelings, or more systematically checked any manifestations of them; but there was something in the person and circumstances of Miss Aubrey—for by a hurried inquiry of the person next to him he learned that it was she—which excited new feelings in him. Her slightest motion his eye watched with intense eagerness; and faint half-formed schemes, purposes, and hopes passed in rapid confusion through his mind, as he foresaw that circumstances would hereafter arise by means of which—

"Good heavens! how very—*very* beautiful she is!" said he to himself, as, the service over, her graceful figure, following her brother and his wife with slow sad step, approached the pew in which he was standing, on her way to the door. He felt a sort of cold shudder as her black dress rustled past, actually touching him. What was he doing and meditating against that lovely being? And for whom—disgusting reptile! —for Titmouse? He almost blushed with a conflict of emotions, as he followed almost immediately after Miss Aubrey, never losing sight of her till her brother, having handed her into the carriage, got in after her, and they drove off toward the Hall.

The reader will not be at a loss to account for the presence

of Gammon on this occasion, nor to connect it with a great
trial at the approaching York Assizes. As he walked back to
Grilston to his solitary dinner, he was lost in thought; and on
arriving at the inn, repaired at once to his room, where he
found a copy of the *Sunday Flash*, which had, according to
orders, been sent to him from town, under his assumed name,
"Gibson." He eat but little, and that mechanically; and
seemed to feel, for once, little or no interest in his newspaper.
He had never paid the least attention to the eulogia upon Miss
Aubrey of the little idiot Titmouse, nor of Snap, of whom he
entertained but a very little higher opinion than of Titmouse.
One thing was clear, that from that moment Miss Aubrey
formed a new element in Mr. Gammon's calculations; and for
aught I know, may occasion very different results from those
originally contemplated by that calm and crafty person.

As it proved a moonlight night, he resolved at once to set
about the important business which had brought him into
Yorkshire; and for that purpose set off about eight o'clock on
his walk to Yatton. About ten o'clock he might have been
seen gliding into the church-yard, like a dangerous snake.
The moon continued to shine—and at intervals with brightness sufficient for his purpose, which was simply to reconnoiter,
as closely as possible, the little church-yard—to ascertain what
it might contain, and *what were its capabilities.* At length
he approached the old yew-tree, against whose huge trunk he
leaned with folded arms, apparently in a reverie. Hearing
a noise as of some one opening the gate by which he had entered, he glided further into the gloom behind him; and turning his head in the direction whence the sound came, he beheld
some one entering the church-yard. His heart beat quickly,
and he suspected that he had been watched; yet there was
surely no harm in being seen, at ten o'clock at night, looking
about him in a country church-yard. It was a gentleman who
entered, dressed in deep mourning; and Gammon quickly
recognized in him Mr. Aubrey—the brother of her whose beautiful image still shone before his mind's eye. What could he
be wanting there?—at that time of night? Gammon was not
kept long in doubt; for the stranger slowly bent his steps toward a large high tomb, in fact the central object, next to the
yew-tree, in the church-yard—and stood gazing at it in silence
for some time.

"That is, no doubt, where Mrs. Aubrey was buried the
other day," thought he, watching the movements of the
stranger, who presently raised his handkerchief to his eyes,
and for some moments seemed indulging in great grief. Gam-

mon distinctly heard either a sob or a sigh. "He must have been very fond of her," thought Gammon. "Well, if we succeed, the excellent old lady will have escaped a great deal of trouble—that's all." "If *we succeed!*" That reminded him of what he had for a few moments lost sight of, namely, his own object of coming thither; and he felt a sudden chill of remorse, which increased upon him till he almost trembled, as his eye continued fixed on Mr. Aubrey, and he thought also of Miss Aubrey—and the misery—the utter ruin into which he was seeking to plunge them both — the unhallowed means which they—which he—contemplated resorting to for that purpose.

Gammon's condition was becoming every moment more serious; for VIRTUE, in the shape of Miss Aubrey, began to shine every moment in more radiant loveliness before him—and he almost felt an inclination to sacrifice every person connected with the enterprise in which he was engaged, if it would give him a chance of winning the favor of Miss Aubrey. Presently, however, Mr. Aubrey, evidently heaving a deep sigh, bent his steps slowly back again, and quitted the church-yard. Gammon watched his figure out of sight, and then, for the first time since Mr. Aubrey's appearance, breathed freely. Relieved from the pressure of his presence, Gammon began to take calmer and juster views of his position; and he reflected that if he pushed on the present affair to a successful issue, he should be much more likely, than by prematurely ending it, to gain his objects. He therefore resumed his survey of the scene around him; and which presented appearances highly satisfactory, judging from the expression which now and then animated his countenance. At length he wandered round to the other end of the church, where a crumbling wall, half covered with ivy, indicated that there had formerly stood some building apparently of earlier date than the church. Such was the fact. Gammon soon found himself standing in a sort of inclosure, which had once been the site of an old chapel. And here he had not been long making his observations before he achieved a discovery of so extraordinary a nature; one so unlikely, under the circumstances, to have happened; one so calculated to baffle ordinary calculations concerning the course of events, that the reader may well disbelieve what I am going to tell him, and treat it as absurdly improbable. In short, not to keep him in suspense, Gammon positively discovered evidence of the death of Harry Dreddlington in his father's life-time, by means of just such a looking tombstone as he had long imaged to himself, and as he had

resolved that old Quirk should have got prepared before th
cause came into court. He almost stumbled over it. 'Twas
an old slanting stone, scarce two feet above the ground, partly
covered with moss, and partly hid by rubbish and old damp
grass. The moon shone brightly enough to enable Gammon,
kneeling down, to decipher, beyond all doubt, what was requisite to establish that part of the case which had been wanting. For a moment or two he was disposed to doubt whether
he was not dreaming. When, at length, he took out pencil
and paper, his hands trembled so much that he felt some difficulty in making an exact copy of the inestimable inscription.
Having done this, he drew a long breath as he replaced the
pencil and paper in his pocket-book, and almost he heard a
whispering sound in the air — "Verdict for the plaintiff."
Quitting the church-yard, he walked back to Grilston at a
much quicker rate than that at which he had come, his discovery having wonderfully elated him, and pushed all other
thoughts entirely out of his mind. But, thought he, doubtless the other side are aware of the existence of this tombstone
—they can hardly be supposed ignorant of it; they must have
looked up their evidence as well as we—and their attention has
been challenged to the existence or non-existence of proof of
the time of the death of Harry Dreddlington:—well—if they
are aware of it, they know that it cuts the ground from under
them and turns their conveyance, on which, doubtless, they
are relying, into waste paper; if they are *not*, and are under
the impression that that deed is valid and effectual, our proof
will fall on them like a thunder-bolt. "Gad,"—he held his
breath, and stopped in the middle of the road—"how immensely important is this little piece of evidence! Why, if they
knew of it—why in Heaven's name is it there still? What
easier than to have got rid of it?—why, they may still: what
can that stupid fellow Parkinson have been about? Yet, is it
because it has become unimportant, on account of their being
in possession of other evidence? What *can* they have to set
against so plain a case as ours is, with this evidence? Gad,
I'll not lose one day's time; but I'll have half a dozen competent witnesses to inspect, and speak to that same tombstone
in court." Such were some of the thoughts which passed
through his mind as he hastened homeward; and on his
arrival, late as it was—only the yawning hostler being up to let
him in—he sat down to write a letter off to Mr. Quirk, and
made it into a parcel to go by the mail in the morning,
acquainting him with the truly providential discovery he had
just made, and urging him to set about getting up the briefs

for the trial without delay; he himself purposing to stop at
Grilston a day or two longer, to complete one or two other
arrangements of an important nature. As soon as Mr. Quirk
had read this letter, he devoutly thanked God for His goodness; and hurrying to his strong-box, unlocked it, took out a
small sealed packet, and committed it to the flames.

Mr. Aubery, as soon as he had recovered from the first
shock occasioned by the communication by Mr. Parkinson of
the proceedings against him, set about acquainting himself,
as minutely as he could, with the true state of the case. He
had requested Mr. Parkinson to obtain from one of the counsel
in London, Mr. Crystal, a full account of the case, in an elementary form, for his own guidance; and on obtaining a remarkably clear and luminous statement, and also consulting
the various authorities cited in it—such, at least, as could be
supplied to him by Mr. Parkinson—the vigorous practical understanding of Mr. Aubrey, aided by his patient application,
soon mastered the whole case, and enabled him to appreciate
the peril in which he was placed. Since he could derive no
title through the conveyance of Harry Dreddlington (which
had been got in by Geoffry Dreddlington), owing to the death
of the former in his father's life-time, as he (Mr. Aubrey) understood from his advisers could be easily proved by the present
claimant of the property; the right of accession of Geoffry
Dreddlington's descendants depended entirely upon the fact
whether or not Stephen Dreddlington had really died without
issue; and as to that, certain anxious and extensive inquiries
instituted by Messrs. Runnington and Mr. Parkinson, in pur-
suance of the suggestions of their able and experienced counsel, had led them to entertain serious doubts concerning the
right of Geoffry's descendants to have entered into possession.
By what means his opponents had obtained their clew to the
state of his title, neither he nor any of his advisers could frame
a plausible conjecture. It was certainly possible that Stephen
Dreddlington, who was known to have been a man, like his
uncle Harry, of wild and eccentric habits, and to have been
supposed to leave no issue, might have married privately some
woman of inferior station, and left issue by her, who, living in
obscurity and at a distance from the seat of the family property, could have no opportunity of inquiring into or ascertaining their position with reference to the estates, till some acute
and enterprising attorneys like Messrs. Quirk, Gammon and
Snap, happening to get hold of them, and family papers in
their possession, had taken up their case. When, with impressions such as these, Mr. Aubrey perused and reperused the

opinions of the conveyancer given on the occasion of his (Mr. Aubrey's) marriage, he was confounded at the supineness and indifference which he had even twice exhibited, and felt disposed now greatly to overvalue the importance of every adverse circumstance. The boldness again and systematic energy with which the case of the claimant was prosecuted, and the eminent legal opinions which were alleged, and with every appearance of truth, to concur in his favor, afforded additional grounds for rational apprehension. He looked the danger, however, full in the face, and as far as lay in his power prepared for the evil day which might so soon come upon him. Certain extensive and somewhat costly alterations which he had been on the point of commencing at Yatton, he abandoned. But for the earnest interference of friends, he would at once have given up his establishment in Grosvenor Street, and applied for the Chiltern Hundreds, in order to retire from political life. Considering the possibility of his soon being declared the wrongful holder of the property, he contracted his expenditure as far as he could, without challenging unnecessary public attention; and paid into his banker's hands all his Christmas rents, sacredly resolving to abstain from drawing out one farthing of what might soon be proved to belong to another. At every point occurred the dreadful question—If I am declared never to have been the rightful owner of the property, how am I to discharge my frightful liabilities to him who is? Mr. Aubrey had nothing except the Yatton property. He had but an insignificant sum in the funds; Mrs. Aubrey's settlement was out of lands at Yatton, as also was the little income bequeathed to Kate by her father. Could anything, now, be conceived more dreadful under these circumstances than the mere danger—the slightest probability—of their being deprived of Yatton?—and with a debt of at the very least SIXTY THOUSAND POUNDS, due to him who had been wrongfully kept out of his property? That was the millstone which seemed to drag them all to the bottom. Against *that*, what could the kindness of the most generous friends, what could his own most desperate exertions, avail? All this had poor Aubrey constantly before his eyes, together with—his wife, his sister, his children. What was to become of *them?* It was long before the real nature and extent of his danger became known amongst his friends and neighbors. When, however, they were made aware of it, an extraordinary interest and sympathy were excited throughout almost the whole county. Whenever his attorney, Mr. Parkinson, appeared in public, he was besieged by most anxious inquiries concerning his distin-

guished client, whose manly modesty and fortitude, under the
pressure of his sudden and almost unprecedented difficulty and
peril, endeared him more than ever to all who had an opportunity of appreciating his position. With what intense and
absorbing interest were the ensuing assizes looked for! At
length they arrived.

The ancient city of York exhibited, on the commission day
of the Spring Assizes for the year 18—, the usual scene of animation and excitement. The High Sheriff, attended by an
imposing retinue, went out to meet the Judges, and escorted
them, amidst the shrill clanguor of trumpets, to the castle,
where the commission was opened with the usual formalities.
The Judges were Lord Widdrington, the Lord Chief Justice
of the King's Bench, and Mr. Justice Grayley, a puisne judge
of the same court—both admirable lawyers. The former was
possessed of the more powerful intellect. He was what may
be called a great scientific lawyer, referring everything to *principle* as extracted from precedent. Mr. Justice Grayley was
almost unrivaled in his knowledge of the *details* of the law,
his governing maxim being *ita lex scripta.* Here his knowledge was equally minute and accurate, and most readily applied to every case brought before him. Never sat there upon
the bench a more painstaking judge—one more anxious to do
right equally in great things as in small. Both were men of
rigid integrity; 'tis a glorious thing to be able to add—when,
for centuries, have other than men of rigid integrity sat upon
the English Bench? Lord Widdrington, however, in temper
was stern, arbitrary, and overbearing, and his manners were
disfigured not a little by coarseness; while his companion was
a man of exemplary amiability, affability, and forbearance.
Lord Widdrington presided at the Civil Court (where, of
course, would come on the important cause in which we are
interested), and Mr. Justice Grayley in the Criminal Court.

Soon after the sitting of the court, on the ensuing morning
—"Will your lordship allow me," rose and inquired the
sleek, smiling, and portly Mr. Subtle, dead silence prevailing
as soon as he had mentioned the name of the cause about
which he was inquiring, "to call your attention to a cause of
Doe on the demise of Titmouse v. *Jolter*—a special jury cause,
in which there are a great many witnesses to be examined on
both sides—and to ask that a day may be fixed for it to come
on?"

"Whom do you appear for, Mr. Subtle?" inquired his lordship.

"For the plaintiff, my lord."

" And who appears for the defendant?"

" The Attorney-General leads for the defendant, my lord,"
replied Mr. Sterling, who, with Mr. Crystal, was also retained
for the defendant.

" Well, perhaps you can agree between yourselves upon a
day, and in the meantime similar arrangements may be made
for any other special jury causes that may require it." After
due consultation, Monday week was agreed upon by the parties
and fixed by his lordship for the trial of the cause. During
the Sunday preceding it, York was crowded with persons of
the highest distinction from all parts of the county, who felt
interested in the result of the great cause of the assizes.
About midday a dusty traveling carriage-and-four dashed into
the streets from the London road, and drove up to the principal inn; it contained the Attorney-General (who just finished
reading his brief as he entered York) and his clerk. The
Attorney-General was a man of striking and highly intellectual
countenance; but he looked on alighting somewhat fatigued
with his long journey. He was a man of extraordinary natural talents, and also a first-rate lawyer—one whose right to
take the wool-sack, whenever it should become vacant, was
recognized by all the profession. His professional celebrity
and his coming down special on the present occasion added to
the circumstance of his being well known to be a personal
friend of his client, Mr. Aubrey—whence it might be inferred
that his great powers would be exerted to their utmost—was
well calculated to enhance the interest, if that were possible,
of the occasion which had brought him down at so great an
expense, and to sustain so heavy a responsibility as the conduct of a cause of such magnitude.

He came to lead against a formidable opponent. Mr.
SUBTLE was the leader of the Northern Circuit, a man of
matchless tact and practical sagacity, and most consummately skillful in the conduct of a cause. The only thing he ever
looked at was the verdict, to the gaining of which he directed
all his energies, and sacrificed every other consideration. As
for display, he despised it. A *speech*, as such, was his aversion. He entered into a friendly, but exquisitely crafty *conversation* with the jury; for he was so quick at perceiving the
effect of his address on the mind of each of the twelve, and
dexterous in accommodating himself to what he detected to
be the passing mood of each, that they felt as if they were all
the while reasoning with and being convinced by him. His
placid, handsome, smiling countenance, his gentlemanly bearing and insinuating address, full of good-natured cheerful con-

fidence in his cause, were irresistible. He flattered, he soothed, he fascinated the jury, producing an impression upon their minds which they often felt indignant at his opponent attempting to efface. In fact, as a *nisi prius* leader he was unrivaled, as well in stating as in arguing a case, as well in examining as cross-examining a witness. It required no little practical skill to form an adequate estimate of Mr. Subtle's skill in the management of a cause; for he did everything with such a smiling, careless, unconcerned air, in the great pinch and strain of a case, equally as in the pettiest details, that you would be apt to suspect that none but the easiest and most straightforward cases fell to his lot.

Titmouse, Titmouse, methinks the fates favored you in assigning to you Mr. Subtle!

Next came Mr. QUICKSILVER, a man of great but wild energy, who received what may be called a *muffling* retainer. What a contrast was he to Mr. Subtle! The first and the last thing he thought of in a cause was—himself. His delight was to make the jury feel as if a whirlwind were raging about them and he the spirit who had raised it. His object was either to dazzle or overpower them. He wrapped himself round in the gleaming garment of display, the gaudy patchwork of multifarious superficial acquirements. This was the strange, noisy object, flinging about wildly, in all directions, the firebrands and arrows of sarcasm and invective, which occupied their eye and ear till he had ceased; neither he nor they were thinking all the while of his dismayed and injured client, till reminded of him by the adverse charge of the judge, accompanied by a slight sneer and shrug of the shoulders from Mr. Subtle. Why, then, was such a man retained in the cause? 'Twas a fancy of Quirk's, a vast political admirer of Quicksilver's, who had made one or two most splendid speeches for him in libel cases brought against the *Sunday Flash*. Gammon most earnestly expostulated, but Quirk was inexorable; and himself carried his retainer to Mr. Quicksilver. Gammon, however, was somewhat consoled by the reflection that this wild elephant would be, in a manner, held in check by Mr. Subtle and Mr. Lynx, who, he hoped, would prevent any serious mischief from happening. Lynx possessed the qualities which his name would suggest to you. I have partly described him already. He was a man of minute accuracy, and "got up" every case in which he was engaged as if his life had depended on the result. Nothing escaped him. He kept his mind constantly even with the current of the cause. He was a man to *steer* a leader, if ever that leader should get, for an instant, on the wrong tack, or be uncertain as to his course. His suggestion and interference—rare, indeed, with such a man as Mr. Subtle, incessant with Mr. Quicksilver—were always worth attending to, and consequently received with deference.

For Mr. Aubrey also was retained a formidable bar. Mr. Attorney-General was a man much superior, in point of intellect and legal knowledge, to Mr. Subtle. His mind was distinguished by its tranquil power. He had a rare and invaluable faculty of arraying before his mind's eye all the facts and bearings of the most intricate case, and contemplating them, as it were, not successively, but simultaneously. His perception was quick as light; and, at the same time—rare, most rare accompaniment!—his judgment sound, his memory signally retentive. Inferior, possibly, to Mr. Subtle in rapid and delicate appreciation of momentary advantages, he was sagacious where Mr. Subtle was only ingenious. Mr. Attorney-General had as much weight with the judge as Mr. Subtle with the jury. With the former, there was a candor and straightforwardness—a dignified simplicity—which insensibly won the confidence of the judge; who, on the other hand, felt himself obliged to be ever on his guard against the slippery sophistries of Mr. Subtle, whom he thus got to regard with constant suspicion.

Mr. STERLING, the second counsel for the defendant, was a king's counsel, and a rival of Mr. Subtle upon the circuit. He was a man of great power; and, on important occasions, no man at the bar could acquit himself with more distinction. As a speaker, he was eloquent and impressive, perhaps deficient in vivacity; but he was a man of clear and powerful intellect; prompt in seizing the bearings of a case; a capital lawyer; and possessing, even on the most trying occasions, imperturbable self-possession.

Mr. CRYSTAL, with some faults of manner and bearing, was an honorable high-minded man; clear-sighted and strong-headed; an accurate and ready lawyer; vigilant and acute.

See, then, the combatants in this memorable encounter: for *Titmouse*—MR. SUBTLE, MR. QUICKSILVER, MR. LYNX; for *Mr. Aubrey*—MR. ATTORNEY-GENERAL, MR. STERLING, MR. CRYSTAL.

The consultation of each party was long and anxious.   •

About eight o'clock on the Sunday evening, at Mr. Subtle's lodgings, Messrs. Quirk, Gammon and Snap, accompanied by Mr. Mortmain, whom they had brought down to watch the case, made their appearance shortly after Mr. Quicksilver and Mr. Lynx.

"Our case seems complete, *now*," said Mr. Subtle, casting a penetrating and most significant glance at Messrs. Quirk and Gammon, and then at his juniors, to whom, before the arrival of their clients and Mr. Mortmain, he had been mentioning the essential link which a month before he had pointed out as missing, and the marvelous good fortune by which they had been able to supply it at the eleventh hour.

"That tombstone's a godsend, Subtle, isn't it?" said Quicksilver, with a grim smile. Lynx neither smiled nor spoke. He was a very matter-of-fact person. So as the case came out clear and nice in court, he cared about nothing more. But whatever might be the insinuation or suspicion implied in the observation of Mr. Subtle, the reader must, by this time, be well aware how little it was warranted by the facts.

"I shall open it very quietly," said Mr. Subtle, putting into his pocket his penknife, with which he had been paring his nails, while Mr. Quicksilver had been talking very fast. "What do you think, Mr. Lynx? Had I better allude boldly to the conveyance executed by Harry Dreddlington, and which becomes useless as soon as we prove his death in his father's life-time?"

"Ah! there's that blessed tombstone again," interposed Quicksilver.

"Or," resumed Mr. Subtle, "content myself with barely making out our pedigree, and let it come from the other side?"

"I think, perhaps, that the latter would be the quieter and safer course," replied Lynx.

"By the way, gentlemen," said Mr. Subtle, suddenly addressing Messrs. Quirk, Gammon and Snap, "how do *we* come to know anything about the mortgage executed by Harry Dreddlington?"

"Oh! *that*, you know," replied Quirk, quickly, "we first got scent of in Mr. ——." Here he paused suddenly, and turned quite red.

"It was suggested," said Gammon, calmly, "by one of the gentlemen whose opinions we have taken in the case—I forget by whom—that, from some recital, it was probable that there existed such an instrument; and that put us on making inquiry."

"Nothing more likely," added Mortmain, "than that it, or an abstract, or minute of it, should get into Stephen Dreddlington's hands."

"Ah! well! well!—I must say there's rather an air of mys-

tery about the case. But—about that tombstone—what sort
of witnesses will speak—"

"Will that evidence be requisite," inquired Lynx, "in the
plaintiff's case? All *we* shall have to do will be to prove the
fact that Harry died without issue, of which there's satisfactory evidence; and as to the *time* of his death, that will become material only if *they* put in the conveyance of Harry."

"True—true; ah! I'll turn that over in my mind. Rely
upon it, I'll give Mr. Attorney-General as little to lay hold of
as possible. Thank you, Mr. Lynx, for the hint. Now, gentlemen, one other question—What *kind of looking* people are
the witnesses who prove the latter steps of the pedigree of Mr.
Titmouse? Respectable? eh?—You know a good deal will depend on the credit they may obtain with the jury."

"They're very decent, creditable persons, you will find, sir,"
said Gammon.

"Good, good. Who struck the special jury?"

"We did, sir."

"Well, I must say that was a *very* prudent step for *you* to
take! considering the rank in life and circumstances of the respective parties! However, to be sure, if *you* didn't, they
would—so—well; good-night, gentlemen, good-night." So
the consultation broke up; and Messrs. Quirk, Gammon and
Snap returned home to their inn in a very serious and anxious
mood.

"You're a marvelous prudent person, Mr. Quirk," said
Gammon, in a somewhat fierce whisper, as they walked along;
"I suppose you would have gone on to explain the little matter of Steggars, and so have had our briefs thrown at our
heads—"

"Well, well, that *was* a slip." Here they reached their
inn. Titmouse was staying there; and in Messrs. Quirk,
Gammon and Snap's absence, he had got very drunk, and
quarreling under the archway with Boots; so they ordered him
to bed, they themselves sitting up till a very late hour in the
morning.

The consultation at the Attorney-General's had taken place
about three o'clock in the afternoon, within an hour after his
arrival; and had been attended by Messrs. Sterling, Crystal,
and Mansfield—by Mr. Runnington, and Mr. Parkinson, and
by Mr. Aubrey, whom the Attorney-General received with the
most earnest expressions of sympathy and friendship, listening
to every question and every observation of his with the utmost
deference.

"It would be both idle and unkind to disguise from you,

Aubrey," said he, " that our position is somewhat precarious. It depends entirely on the chance we may have of breaking down the plaintiff's case; for we have but a slender case of our own. I suppose they can bring proof of the death of Harry Dreddlington in his father's life-time?"

" Oh, yes, sir!" answered Mr. Parkinson, " there is an old tombstone behind Yatton Church which establishes that fact beyond all doubt; and a week or two ago no fewer than five or six persons have been carefully inspecting it; doubtless they will be called as witnesses to-morrow. "

" I feared as much. Then are ours no more than watching briefs. Depend upon it, they would not have carried on the affair with so high a hand if they had not pretty firm ground under foot! Messrs. Quirk, Gammon and Snap are tolerably well known in town—not *over*scrupulous, eh, Mr. Runnington?"

" Indeed, Mr. Attorney, you are right. I don't doubt they are prepared to go all lengths. "

" Well, we'll sift their evidence pretty closely, at any rate. So you really have reason to fear, as you intimated when you entered the room, that they have valid evidence of Stephen Dreddlington having left issue?"

" Mr. Snap told me," said Mr. Parkinson, " this morning, that they would prove issue of Stephen Dreddlington, and issue of that issue, as clean as a whistle—that was his phrase. "

" We mustn't take all for gospel that *he* would say. "

" They've got two houses filled with witnesses, I understand," said Mr Runnington.

" Do they seem Yorkshire people or strangers?"

" Why, most of them that I have seen," replied Parkinson, " seem strangers. "

" Ah, they will prove, I suppose, the later steps of the pedigree, when Stephen Dreddlington married at a distance from his native county. "

They then entered into a very full and minute examination of the case; after which—" Well," said the Attorney-General, evidently fatigued with his long journey, and rising from his chair, " we must trust to what will turn up in the chapter of accidents to-morrow. I shall be expected to dine with the Bar to-day," he added; " but immediately after dinner—say at seven o'clock, I shall be here, and at your service, if anything should be required." Then the consultation broke up. Mr. Aubrey had, at their earnest entreaty, brought Mrs. Aubrey and Kate from Yatton, on Saturday; for they declared themselves unable to bear the dreadful suspense in which they should

be left at Yatton. Yielding, therefore, to these their very
reasonable wishes, he had engaged private lodgings at the outskirts of the town. On quitting the consultation, which, without at the same time affecting overstrictness, he had regretted
being fixed for Sunday—but the necessity of the case appeared
to warrant it—he repaired to the magnificent MINSTER, where
the evening prayers were being read, and where were Mrs.
Aubrey and Kate. They were chanting the prayers as he entered, and was placed in a stall nearly opposite to where those
whom he loved so fondly were standing. The psalms allotted
for the evening were those in which the royal sufferer, David,
was pouring forth the deepest sorrows of his heart; and their
appropriateness to his own state of mind, added to the effect
produced by the melting melody in which they were conveyed
to his ears, excited in him, and, he perceived, also in those opposite, the deepest emotion. The glorious pile was beginning
to grow dusky with the stealing shadows of evening; and the
solemn and sublime strains of the organ, during the playing
of the anthem, filled the minds of all present who had any
pretensions to sensibility with mingled feelings of tenderness
and awe. Those in whom we are so deeply interested felt
their minds at once subdued and elevated; and as they quitted
the darkening fabric, through which the pealing tones of the
organ were yet reverberating, they could not help inquiring:
Should they ever enter it again—and in what altered circumstances might it be?

To return, however—though it is, indeed, like descending
from the holy mountain into the bustle and hubbub of the city
at its foot—Mr. Parkinson, being most unexpectedly and unfortunately summoned to Grilston that afternoon, in order to
send up some deeds of one of his distinguished clients to London, for the purpose of immediately effecting a mortgage, set
off in a post-chaise, at top speed, in a very unenviable frame
of mind; and by seven o'clock was seated in his office at Grilston, busily turning over a great number of deeds and papers,
in a large tin case, with the words " Right Honorable the Earl
of Yelverton " painted on the outside. Having turned over
almost everything inside, and found all that he wanted, he was
going to toss back again all the deeds which were not requisite
for his immediate purpose, when he happened to see one lying
at the very bottom, which he had not before observed. It
was not a large, but an old deed—and he took it up and hastily
examined it.

We have seen a piece of unexpected good fortune on the
part of Gammon and his client; and the reader will not be dis-

appointed at finding something of a similar kind befalling Mr. Aubrey, even at the eleventh hour. Mr. Parkinson's journey, which he had execrated a hundred times over, as he came down, produced a discovery which made him tremble all over with agitation and excitement, and begin to look upon it as almost owing to an interference of Providence. The deed he looked at bore an indorsement of the name of " *Dreddling-ton.*" After a hasty glance over its contents, he tried to recollect by what accident a document belonging to Mr. Aubrey could have found its way into the box containing Lord Yelverton's deeds; and it at length occurred to him that, about a twelvemonth before, Mr. Aubrey had proposed advancing several thousand pounds to Lord Yelverton, on mortgage of a portion of his lordship's property—but which negotiation had afterward been broken off; that Mr. Aubrey's title-deeds happened to be at the same time open and loose in his office —and he recollected having considerable trouble in separating the respective documents which had got mixed together. This one, after all, had been by some accident overlooked, till it turned up in this most timely and extraordinary manner! Having hastily effected the object which had brought him back to Grilston, he ordered a post-chaise and four, and within a quarter of an hour was thundering back, at top speed, on his way to York, which, the horses reeking and foaming, he reached a little after ten o'clock. He jumped out, with the precious deed in his pocket, the instant that his chaise-door was opened, and ran off, without saying more than—" I'm gone to the Attorney-General's." This was heard by many passers-by and persons standing round; and it spread far and wide that something of the utmost importance had transpired with reference to the great ejectment cause of Mr. Aubrey. Soon afterward, messengers and clerks belonging to Mr. Runnington and Mr. Parkinson were to be seen running to and fro, summoning Mr. Sterling, Mr. Crystal, Mr. Mansfield, and also Mr. Aubrey, to a second consultation at the Attorney-General's. About eleven o'clock they were all assembled. The deed which had occasioned all this excitement was one calculated indeed to produce that effect; and it filled the minds of all present with astonishment and delight. In a word, it was a deed of confirmation by old Dreddlington, the father of Harry Dreddlington, of the conveyance by the latter to Geoffry Dreddlington, who, in the manner already mentioned to the reader, had got an assignment of that conveyance to himself. After the Attorney-General had satisfied himself as to the account to be given of the deed—the custody from whence it came, namely, the attorney for the defendant, Mr. Parkinson undertaking to swear, without any hesitation, that whatever deeds of Mr. Aubrey's he possessed, he had taken from the muniment-room at Yatton—the second consultation broke up. Mr. Aubrey, on hearing the nature and effect of the instrument explained by the Attorney-General and Mr. Mansfield, and all his counsel, in short, concurring in opinion as to the triumphant effect which this instrument would produce on the morrow, may be pardoned for regarding it, in the excitement of the moment, as almost a direct interference of Providence. A few minutes before nine o'clock on the ensuing morning, the occasional shrill blasts of the trumpets announced that the judges were on their way to the castle, the approaches to which were crowded with carriages and pedestrians of a highly respectable appearance. As the castle clock finished striking nine, Lord Widdrington took his seat, and the swearing of the special jury commenced. The court was crowded almost to suffocation; all the chief places being filled with persons of distinction in the county. The benches on each side of the judge were occupied by ladies, who—especially the Countess of Oldacre and Lady De la Zouch—evinced a painful degree of anxiety and excitement in their countenances and demeanor. The bar also mustered in great force; the crown court being quite deserted, although a great murder case was going on there. The civil court was on the present occasion the point of attraction, not only on account of the interesting nature of the case to be tried, but of the keen contest that was expected between the Attorney-General and Mr. Subtle. The former, as he entered—his commanding features gazed at by many an anxious eye with hope, and a feeling that on his skill and learning depended that day the destination of the Yatton property—bowed to the judge, and then nodded and shook hands with several of the counsel nearest to him; then he sat down, and opening his bag, took out his huge brief, and began turning over its leaves with a calm and attentive air, occasionally turning round and conversing with his juniors. Every one present observed that the defendant's counsel and attorneys wore the confident looks of winning men; while their opponents, quick-sighted enough, also observed the circumstance, and looked, on that account alone, a shade more anxious than when they had entered the court. Mr. Subtle requested Gammon, whose ability he had soon detected, to sit immediately beneath him; next to Gammon sat Quirk, then Snap, and beside him Mr. Titmouse, with a staring sky-blue flowered silk handkerchief round his neck, a gaudy waistcoat, a tight surtout, and white kid gloves. He looked exceedingly pale, and dared hardly interchange a word with even Snap, who was just as irritable and excited as his senior partners. It was quickly known all over the court who Titmouse was. Mr. Aubrey scarcely showed himself in court all day, though he stood at the door near the bench, and could hear all that passed; Lord De la Zouch and one or two personal friends standing with him engaged, from time to time, in anxious conversation.

The jury having been sworn, Mr. Lynx rose, and in a few hurried sentences, to the lay audience utterly unintelligible, intimated the nature of the pleadings in the cause. The Attorney-General then rose, and requested that all the witnesses might leave the court. As soon as the little disturbance occasioned by this move had ceased, Mr. Subtle rose, and in a low but distinct tone said, "May it please your Lordship—Gentlemen of the Jury—In this cause I have the honor to appear before you as counsel for the plaintiff; and it now becomes my duty to state as briefly as I can the nature of his case. It is impossible, gentlemen, not to notice the unusual interest excited by the cause; and which may be accounted for by the very large estates in this county which are sought this day to be transferred to a comparative stranger, from the family who have long enjoyed them, and of whom I am anxious to say everything respectful; for you will very soon find that the name on the record is that of only the nominal defendant; and although all that is *professed* to be this day sought for is a very trifling portion of the property, your verdict will undoubtedly decide the question as to the true ownership and enjoyment of the large estates now held by the gentleman who is the substantial defendant—I mean Mr. Aubrey, the member of parliament for the borough of Yatton." Aware of the watchful and formidable opponent who would in due time answer him, and also of being himself entitled to the general reply—to the last word—Mr. Subtle proceeded to state the nature of the plaintiff's case with the utmost brevity and clearness. Scarcely any sound was heard but that of the pens of the short-hand writers, and of the counsel taking their notes. Mr. Subtle, having handed up two or three copies of the pedigree which he held in his hand to the judge and jury, pointed out with distinctness and precision every link in the chain of evidence which he intended to lay before the jury; and having done this—having presented as few salient points of attack to his opponent as he possibly could—he sat down, professing his entire ignorance of what case could be set up in

answer to that which he had opened. He had not been on
his legs quite half an hour; and when he ceased—how he had
disappointed every one present, except the judge and the bar!
Instead of a speech befitting so great an occasion—impressive
and eloquent—here had been a brief dry statement of a few
uninteresting facts—dates, births, deaths, marriages, registers,
entries, inscriptions, deeds, wills—without a single touch of
feeling or ray of eloquence. The momentary feeling of disappointment in the audience, however—almost all of whom, it
may easily be believed, were in the interest of the Aubreys—
quickly yielded to one of satisfaction and relief, as they thought
they might regard so meager a speech as heralding in as
meager a case. As soon as he sat down, Mr. Quicksilver rose
and called the first witness. "We're safe!" said the Attorney-General to Mr. Sterling and Mr. Crystal, with his hand
before his mouth, and with the very faintest whisper that could
be audible to those whom he addressed; and the witness having been sworn, they all resumed their seats and their writing.
The first and the subsequent witness established one or two
preliminary and formal points—the Attorney-General scarcely
rising to put a question to them. The third witness was examined by Mr. Subtle with apparent unconcern, but really
with exquisite anxiety. From the earnestness and attention
with which the words of the witness were watched and taken
down by both the judge and the counsel, who knew much better than the audience where the strain of the case commenced,
it must have appeared to the latter that either Mr. Subtle un-
derestimated, or his opponents overestimated, the value of the
evidence now in process of being extracted by Mr. Subtle, in
short, easy, pointed questions, and with a smiling unconcerned
countenance.

"Not so fast, sir," gruffly interposed Lord Widdrington,
addressing the witness.

"Take time, Mr. Jones," said Mr. Subtle, blandly, fearful
of ruffling or discomposing an important witness. The Attorney-General rose to cross-examine; pressed him quietly but
closely; varied the shape of his questions; now he soothed,
then he startled by his sternness; but sat down, evidently having produced no impression. Thus it was with one or two
succeeding witnesses; the Attorney-General on each occasion
resuming his seat after his abortive efforts, with perfect composure. At length, however, by a very admirable and well-
sustained fire of cross-questioning, he competely demolished a
material witness; and the hopes of all interested in behalf of
his clients rose high. Mr. Subtle, who had been all the while

paring his nails, and from time to time smiling with a careless air (though you might as safely have touched a tigress suckling her cubs as attempted at that moment to disturb him, so absorbed was he with intense anxiety), believing that he could establish the same facts by another and, as he believed, a better witness, did not re-examine; but calling that other, with an air of nonchalance, succeeded in extracting from him all that the other had failed in, and in baffling all the attempts of the Attorney-General to affect his credit or disturb his equanimity. At length, another witness being in the box—

"My Lord, I object to that question," said Mr. Attorney-General, as Mr. Subtle, amidst many indifferent and apparently irrelevant questions, quietly slipped in one of the greatest possible importance, had it been answered as he desired. 'Twas quite delightful to see the Attorney-General and his experienced and watchful juniors all rise at one and the same instant; showing how vain were the tricks and ingenuity of their sly opponent. Mr. Attorney-General stated his objection briefly and pointedly; Mr. Subtle answered him, followed by Quicksilver and Lynx; and then Mr. Attorney-General replied, with great force and clearness. This keen encounter of their wits over—

"I shall allow the question to be put," said Lord Widdrington, after a pause—"but I have great doubts as to its propriety. I will therefore take a note of Mr. Attorney-General's objection."

Four or five similar conflicts arose during the course of the plaintiff's case;—now concerning the competency of a witness—then as to the admissibility of a document, or the propriety of a particular question. On each of these occasions there were displayed on both sides consummate logical skill and acuteness, especially by the two leaders. Distinctions the most delicate and subtle were suggested with suddenness, and as promptly encountered; the most artful maneuvers to secure dangerous admissions resorted to, and baffled; the more recondite principles of evidence brought to bear with admirable readiness on both sides. To deal with them required indeed the practiced, penetrating, and powerful intellect of Lord Widdrington. Some points he disposed of promptly, to the satisfaction of both parties; on others he hesitated, and at length reserved them. Though none but the more experienced and able members of the bar could in the least degree enter into and appreciate the nature of these conflicts, they were watched with untiring attention and eagerness by all present, both ladies and gentlemen—by the lowly and the distinguished.

And though the intensity of the feelings of all was manifest by
a mere glimpse round the court, yet any momentary display
of eccentricity on the part of a witness, or petulance or re-
partee on the part of counsel, would occasion a momentary
merriment that in point of fact served only as a sort of *relief*
to the strained feelings of the audience, and instantly disappeared. The tombstone part of the case was got through
easily; scarce any attempt being made on the part of Mr. Aubrey's counsel to resist or interfere with it. But the great—
the hottest part of the fight—occurred at that point of the case
where Titmouse's descent from Stephen Dreddlington was
sought to be established. This gentleman, who had been a
very wild person, whose movements were very difficult to be
traced or accounted for, had entered the navy, and ultimately
died at sea, as had always been imagined, single and childless.
It was proved, however, that so far from such being the case,
he had married a person at Portsmouth, of inferior station;
and that by her he had a daughter, only two years before his
death, which happened at sea, as has been stated. Both mother and daughter, after undergoing great privation, and no
notice being taken of the mother by any of her late husband's
family, removed to the house of an humble and distant relative
n Cumberland, where the mother afterward died, leaving her
daughter, only fifteen years old. When she grew up, she lived
in some menial capacity in Cumberland, and ultimately married one Gabriel Tittlebat Titmouse; who, after living for some
years a cordwainer at Whitehaven, found his way to Grilston,
in Yorkshire, in the neighborhood of which town he had lived
for some years, in very humble circumstances. There he had
married; and about two years afterward his wife died, leaving
a son—our friend Tittlebat Titmouse. Both of them afterward came to London; where, in four or five years' time, the
father died, leaving the little Titmouse to flutter and hop
about in the wide world as best he could. During the whole
of this part of the case Mr. Gammon had evinced his deep
anxiety, and at a particular point—perhaps the crisis—his agitation was excessive; yet it was almost entirely concealed by
his remarkable self-control. The little documentary evidence
of which Gammon, at his first interview with Titmouse, found
him possessed, proved at the trial, as Gammon had foreseen,
of great importance. The evidence in support of this part of
the case, and which it took till two o'clock on the ensuing
afternoon to get through, was subjected to a most determined
and skillful opposition by the Attorney-General, but in vain
The case had been got up with the utmost care, under the ex-

cellent management of Lynx; and Mr. Subtle's consummate
tact and ability brought it, at length, fully and distinctly out
before the jury.

" That, my Lord," said he, as he sat down after re-examin-
ing his last witness, " is the case on the part of the plaintiff."
On this the judge and jury withdrew, for a short time, to
obtain refreshment. During their absence, the Attorney-
General, Mr. Sterling, Mr. Crystal, and Mr. Mansfield might
have been seen, with their heads all laid close together, engaged in anxious consultation—a group gazed at by the eager
eyes of many a spectator whose beating heart wished their
cause God-speed. The Attorney-General then withdrew for a
few moments, also to seek refreshment; and returning at the
same time with the judge, after a moment's pause rose, bowed
to the judge, then to the jury, and opened the defendant's
case. His manner was calm and impressive; his person was
dignified, and his clear, distinct voice fell on the listening ear
like the sound of silver. After a graceful allusion to the distinguished character of his friend and client, Mr. Aubrey (to
whose eminent position in the House of Commons he bore his
personal testimony), and to the magnitude of the interest now
at stake, he proceeded—" On every account, therefore, I feel
sensible, gentlemen, to an unusual and most painful extent,
of the very great responsibility now resting upon my learned
friends and myself, lest any miscarriage of mine should prejudice in any degree the important interests committed to us,
or impair the strength of the case which I am about to submit
to you on the part of Mr. Aubrey: a case which, I assure you,
unless some extraordinary mischance should befall us, will I
believe annihilate that which with so much pains, so much
tact, and so much ability, has just been laid before you by my
learned friend, Mr. Subtle, and establish the defendant in the
safe possession of that large property which is the subject of
the present most extraordinary and unexpected litigation.
But, gentlemen, before proceeding so far as that, it is fitting
that I should call your attention to the nature of the case set
up on the part of the plaintiff, and the sort of evidence by
which it has been attempted to be supported; and I am very
sanguine of being successful in showing you that the plaintiff's
witnesses are not entitled to the credit to which they lay claim;
and, consequently, that there is no case made out for the defendant to answer." He then entered into a rigorous analysis
of the plaintiff's evidence, contrasting each conflicting portion
with the other with singular force and cogency; and comment-
ing with powerful severity upon the demeanor and character

12

of many of the witnesses. On proceeding, at length, to open the case of the defendant—"And here, gentlemen," said he, "I am reminded of the observation with which my learned friend concluded—that he was entirely ignorant of the case which we meant to set up in answer to that which he had opened on the part of the plaintff. Gentlemen, it would have been curious, indeed, had it been otherwise—had my friend's penetrating eye been able to inspect the contents of our strong-box—and so become acquainted with the evidence on which my client rests his title to the property now in dispute. He has, however, succeeded in entitling himself to information on that point; and he shall have it—and to his heart's content." Here Mr. Subtle cast a glance of smiling incredulity toward the jury, and defiance toward the Attorney-General, "I will now concede to my learned friend every inch of the case which he has been endeavoring to make out; that he has completely established his pedigree. Mind, gentlemen, I concede this only for the purpose of the case which I am about to lay before you." He then mentioned the conveyance by Harry Dred-dlington of all his interest—

"You forget that he died in his father's life-time, Mr. Attorney-General," interposed Mr. Subtle, with a placid smile, and the air of a man who is suddenly relieved from a vast pressure of anxiety.

"Not a bit of it, gentlemen, not a bit of it—'tis a part of my case. My learned friend is quite right; Harry Dreddlington *did* die in his father's life-time;—but—" Here Mr. Subtle gazed at the Attorney-General with unaffected curiosity; and, when the latter came to mention "the *Deed of Confirmation* by the father of Harry Dreddlington," an acute observer might have observed a slight change of color in Mr. Subtle. Mr. Quicksilver went on writing—for he was entirely out of his depth, and therefore occupied himself with thinking over an article he was writing for some political review. Mr. Lynx looked at the Attorney-General as if he expected every instant to receive a musket-ball in his breast.

"What, '*confirm*' a *nullity*, Mr. Attorney-General?" interrupted Mr. Subtle, laying down his pen with a smile of derision; but a moment or two afterward, "Mr. Mortmain," said he, in a hasty whisper, "what do you think of this? Tell me —in four words—" Mortmain, his eye glued to the face of the Attorney-General the while, muttered hastily something about—*operating as a new grant—as a new conveyance.*

"Pshaw! I mean what's the *answer* to it?" muttered Mr. Subtle, impatiently; but his countenance preserved its expression of smiling nonchalance. "You will oblige me, Mr. Mortmain," he by and by whispered, in a quiet but peremptory tone, "by giving your utmost attention to the question as to the effect of this deed—so that I may shape my objection to it properly when it is tendered in evidence. If it really have the legal effect attributed to it, and which I suspect is the case, we may as well shut up our briefs. I *thought* there must be some such cursed point or other in the background."

Gammon saw the real state of Mr. Subtle's mind, and his cheek turned pale, but he preserved a smile on his countenance, as he sat with his arms folded. Quirk eyed him with undisguised agitation, scarce daring to look up at Mr. Subtle. Titmouse, seeing a little dismay in his camp, turned very white and cold, and sat still, scarce daring to breathe; while Snap looked like a terrier going to have its teeth pulled out.

At length the Attorney-General, after stating that, in addition to the case which he had intimated, as resting mainly on the deed of confirmation, he should proceed to prove the pedigree of Mr. Aubrey, sat down, having spoken about two hours and a half, expressing his conviction that when the defendant's evidence should have been closed, the jury, under his lordship's direction, would return a verdict for the defendant; and that, too, without leaving the jury-box, where, by their long and patient attention, they had so honorably acquitted themselves of the important duty imposed upon them by the constitution.

"James Parkinson!" exclaimed Mr. Sterling, quietly but distinctly as the Attorney-General sat down. "You are the attorney for the defendant?" inquired Mr. Sterling, as soon as the witness had been sworn. "Do you produce a conveyance between Harry Dreddlington and Moses Aaron?" etc. (specifying it). It was proved and put in, without much opposition. So also was—the assignment from Moses Aaron to Geoffry Dreddlington.

"Do you also produce a deed between Harry Dreddlington the elder and Geoffry Dreddlington?" and he mentioned the date and names of all the parties. Mr. Parkinson handed in the important document.

"Stay, stay; where did you get that deed, Mr. Parkinson?" inquired Mr. Subtle, sharply, extending his hand for the deed.

"From my office at Grilston, where I keep many of Mr. Aubrey's title-deeds."

"When did you bring it hither?"

"About ten o'clock last night, for the purpose of this trial."

"How long has it been at your office?"

"Ever since I fetched it, a year or two ago, with other deeds, from the muniment-room of Yatton Hall."

"How long have you been solicitor to Mr. Aubrey?"

"For this ten years, and my father was solicitor to his father for twenty-five years."

"Will you swear that this deed was in your office before the proceedings in this action were brought to your notice?"

"I have not the slightest doubt in the world."

"That does not satisfy me, sir. Will you *swear* that it was?"

"I *will*, sir," replied Mr. Parkinson, firmly. "It never attracted any more notice from me than any other of Mr. Aubrey's deeds, till my attention was drawn to it in consequence of these proceedings."

"Has any one access to Mr. Aubrey's deeds at your office but yourself?"

"None that I know of; I keep all the deeds of my clients that are at my office in their respective boxes, and allow no one access to them, except under my immediate notice, and in my presence."

Then Mr. Subtle sat down.

"My Lord, we now propose to put in this deed," said the Attorney-General, unfolding it.

"Allow me to look at it, Mr. Attorney," said Mr. Subtle. It was handed to him, and he, his juniors, and Mr. Mortmain, rising up, were engaged most anxiously in scrutinizing it for some minutes. Mortmain having looked at the stamp, sat down, and opening his bag, hastily drew out an old well-worn volume, which contained all the stamp acts that had ever been passed from the time of William the Third, when, I believe, the first of those blessings was conferred upon this country. First he looked at the deed—then at his book—then at the deed again; and at length might be seen with earnest gestures, putting Mr. Subtle in possession of his opinion on the subject. "My Lord," said Mr. Subtle, after a pause, "I object to this instrument being received as evidence, on account of the insufficiency of the stamp." This produced quite a sensation in court. Mr. Subtle then proceeded to mention the character of the stamp affixed to the deed, and read the act which was in force at the time that the deed bore date; and after a few additional observations, sat down, and was followed by Mr. Quicksilver and Mr. Lynx. Then arose the Attorney-General, having in the meantime carefully looked at the Act of Parliament, and submitted to his Lordship that the stamp was sufficient; being followed by his juniors. Mr. Subtle replied at some length.

"I certainly entertain some difficulty on the point," said his Lordship, "and will mention the matter to my brother Grayley." Taking with him the deed and Mr. Mortmain's Stamp Acts, his lordship left the court, and was absent a quarter of an hour—half an hour—three quarters of an hour; and at length returned.

"I have consulted," said he, as soon as he had taken his seat, amidst the profoundest silence, "my brother Grayley, and we have very fully considered the point. My brother happens, fortunately, to have by him a manuscript note of a case in which he was counsel, about eighteen years ago, and in which the exact point arose which exists in the present case." He then read out of a thick manuscript book, which he had brought with him from Mr. Justice Grayley, the particulars of the case alluded to, and which was certainly almost precisely similar to those then before the court. In the case referred to the stamp had been held sufficient; and so, his Lordship and his brother Grayley were of opinion, was the stamp in the deed then before him. The cloud which had settled upon the countenances of the Attorney-General and his party here flitted over to and settled upon those of his opponents. "Your Lordship will perhaps take a note of the objection," said Mr. Subtle, somewhat chagrined. Lord Widdrington nodded, and immediately made the requisite entry in his notes.

"*Now*, then, we propose to put in and read this deed," said the Attorney-General, with a smile of suppressed triumph, holding out his hand toward Mr. Lynx, who was spelling over it very eagerly—"I presume my learned friend will require only the operative parts to be read"—here Lynx, with some excitement, called his leader's attention to something which had occurred to him in the deed: up got Quicksilver and Mortmain, and presently—

"Not quite so fast, Mr. Attorney, if you please," said Mr. Subtle, with a little elation of manner—"I have another and I apprehend a clearly fatal objection to the admissibility of this deed, till my learned friend shall have accounted for an ERASURE"—

"Erasure!" echoed the Attorney-General, with much surprise—"Allow me to see the deed;" and he took it with an incredulous smile, which, however, disappeared as he looked more and more closely at the instrument: Mr. Sterling, Mr. Crystal, and Mr. Mansfield also looking extremely serious.

"I've hit them *now*," said Mr. Subtle to those behind him,

as he leaned back, and looked with no little triumph at his opponents—" By Jove! was there ever anything so lucky in this world before?" From what apparently inadequate and trifling causes often flow great results! The plain fact of the case was merely this: The attorney's clerk, in copying out the deed, which was one of considerable length, had written four or five words by mistake, and fearing to exasperate his master, by rendering necessary a new deed and stamp, and occasioning trouble and delay, neatly scratched out the erroneous words, and over the erasure wrote the correct ones. As he was the party who was intrusted with seeing to and witnessing the execution of the instrument, he of course took no notice of the alteration, and—see the result. The ownership of an estate of ten thousand a year about to turn upon the effect of this erasure!

"Hand me up the deed," said the Judge; and inspected it minutely for a minute or two.

"Has any one a magnifying-glass in court?" inquired the Attorney-General, with a look of increasing anxiety. No one happened to have one.

"Is it necessary, Mr. Attorney?" said Lord Widdrington, handing down the instrument to him with an ominous look.

"Well—you object, of course, Mr. Subtle—as I understand you—that this deed is void, on account of an erasure in a material part of it?" inquired Lord Widdrington.

"That is my objection, my Lord," said Mr. Subtle, sitting down.

"Now, Mr. Attorney," continued the Judge, turning to the Attorney-General, prepared to take a note of any observations he might offer. The spectators, the whole court—were aware that the great crisis of the case had arrived, and there was a sickening silence. The Attorney-General, with perfect calmness and self-possession, immediately addressed the court in answer to the objection. That there *was* an erasure, which, owing to the hurry with which the instrument had been looked at, had been overlooked, was indisputable; of course the Attorney-General's argument was, that it was an erasure in a part not material; but it was easy to see that he spoke with the air of a man who argues *contra spem*. What he said, however, was pertinent and forcible; the same might be said of Mr. Sterling and Mr. Crystal, but they were all plainly *graveled*. Mr. Subtle replied with cruel cogency; Mr. Quicksilver seized the opportunity—not choosing to see that the Judge was with them to make a most dangerous but showy speech; Mr. Subtle sitting beside him in the utmost distress, looking as if he could have withered him with a word. In consequence of some very

unguarded admissions of Quicksilver, down came upon him
Lord Widdrington; and Mr. Subtle—the only time during the
whole cause in which he lost his self-command—uttered a half-
stifled curse at the folly of Quicksilver, that could be heard by
half the bar, perhaps even by the Judge, who greatly relished
the exposure he was making of Quicksilver's indiscretion. At
length he sat down, with a somewhat foolish air, Mr. Subtle
turning his back full upon him before the whole court; but
when Lynx rose, and in a business-like way, with only a word
or two, put the point again fully before Lord Widdrington,
the scowl gradually disappeared from the brow of Mr. Subtle.

"Well," said Lord Widdrington, when Mr. Lynx had
done, "I own I feel no doubt at all upon the matter; but as
it is certainly of the greatest possible importance, I will just
see how it strikes my brother Grayley." With this he took
the deed in his hand, and quitted the court. He touched Mr.
Aubrey, in passing to his private room, holding the deed before him. After an absence of about ten minutes, Lord Widdrington returned.

"Silence! silence there!" bawled the crier; and the bustle
had soon subsided into profound silence.

"I entertain no doubt, nor does my brother Grayley," said
Lord Widdrington, "that I ought not to receive this deed in
evidence, without accounting for an erasure occurring in a
clearly essential part of it. Unless, therefore, you are prepared, Mr. Attorney, with any evidence as to this point, I shall
not receive the deed."

There was a faint buzz all over the court—a buzz of excitement, anxiety, and disappointment. The Attorney-General
consulted for a moment or two with his friends.

"Undoubtedly, my Lord, we are not prepared with any evidence to explain an appearance which has taken us entirely
by surprise. After this length of time, my Lord, of course—"

"Certainly—it is a great misfortune for the parties—a great
misfortune. Of course you tender the deed in evidence?" he
continued, taking a note.

"We do, my Lord, certainly."

You should have seen the faces of Messrs. Quirk, Gammon
and Snap as they looked at Mr. Parkinson, with an agitated
air, returning the rejected deed to the bag from which it had
been lately taken with so confident and triumphant an air!—
The remainder of the case, which had been opened by the
Attorney-General on behalf of Mr. Aubrey, was then proceeded
with: but in spite of all their assumed calmness, the disappointment and distress of his counsel were perceptible to all.

They were now dejected—they felt that the cause was lost, unless some extraordinary good fortune should yet befall them. They were not long in establishing the descent of Mr. Aubrey from Geoffry Dreddlington. It was necessary to do so; for grievously as they had been disappointed in failing to establish the title paramount, founded upon the deed of confirmation of Mr. Aubrey, it was yet an important question for the jury whether they believed the evidence adduced by the plaintiff to show title in himself.

"That, my Lord, is the defendant's case," said the Attorney-General, as his last witness left the box; and Mr. Subtle then rose to reply. He felt how unpopular was his cause; that almost every countenance around him bore a hostile expression. Privately, he loathed his case when he saw the sort of person for whom he was struggling. All his sympathies—for he was a very proud, haughty man—were on behalf of Mr. Aubrey, whom by name and reputation he well knew, with whom he had often sat in the House of Commons. Now, conspicuous before him, sat his little monkey-client, Titmouse —a ridiculous object; and calculated if there were any scope for the influence of prejudice, to ruin his own cause by the exhibition of himself before the jury. That was the vulgar idiot who was to turn the admirable Aubreys out of Yatton, and send them beggared into the world!—But Mr. Subtle was a high-minded English advocate; and if he had seen Miss Aubrey in all her loveliness, and knew her all depended upon his exertions, he could hardly have exerted himself more successfully than he did on the present occasion. And such, at length, was the effect which that exquisitely skillful advocate produced, in his address to the jury, that he began to bring about a change in the feelings of most around him: even the eye of scornful beauty began to direct fewer glances of indignation and disgust upon Titmouse, as Mr. Subtle's irresistible rhetoric drew upon their sympathies in his behalf. "My learned friend, the Attorney-General, gentlemen, dropped one or two expressions of a somewhat disparaging tendency, in alluding to my client, Mr. Titmouse; and shadowed forth a disadvantageous contrast between the obscure and ignorant plaintiff, and the gifted defendant. Good God, gentlemen! and is my humble client's misfortune to become his fault? If he be obscure and ignorant, unacquainted with the usages of society, deprived of the blessings of a superior education—if he have contracted vulgarity, *whose fault is it?*—Who has occasioned it? Who plunged him and his parents before him into an unjust poverty and obscurity, from which Providence is about this day to rescue him, and put him in possession of his own? Gentlemen, if topics like these must be introduced into this case, I ask you *who is accountable* for the present condition of my unfortunate client? Is he, or are those who have been, perhaps unconsciously, but still unjustly, so long reveling in the wealth that is his? Gentlemen, in the name of everything that is manly and generous, I challenge your sympathy, your commiseration, for my client." Here Titmouse, who had been staring up open-mouthed for some time at his eloquent advocate, and could be kept quiet no longer by the most vehement efforts of Messrs. Quirk, Gammon and Snap, rose up in an excited manner, exclaiming, "Bravo! bravo, sir! 'Pon my life, capital! It's quite true—bravo! bravo!" His astounded advocate paused at this unprecedented interruption. "Take the puppy out of court, sir, or I will not utter one word more," said he in a fierce whisper to Mr. Gammon.

"Who is that? Leave the court, sir! Your conduct is most indecent, sir! I have a great mind to commit you, sir!" said Lord Widdrington, directing an awful look down to the offender, who had turned of a ghastly whiteness.

"Have mercy upon me, my Lord! I'll never do it again," he groaned, clasping his hands, and verily believing that Lord Widdrington was going to take the estate away from him.

Snap at length succeeded in getting him out of court, and after the excitement occasioned by this irregular interruption had subsided, Mr. Subtle resumed:

"Gentlemen," said he, in a low tone, "I perceive that you are moved by this little incident; and it is characteristic of your superior feelings. Inferior persons, destitute of sensibility or refinement, might have smiled at eccentricities which occasion you only feelings of greater commiseration. I protest, gentlemen—" his voice trembled for a moment, but he soon resumed his self-possession; and after a long and admirable address, sat down confident of the verdict.

"If we lose the verdict, sir," said he, bending down and whispering into the ear of Gammon, "we may thank that execrable little puppy for it." Gammon changed color, but made no reply.

Lord Widdrington then commenced summing up the case to the jury, with his usual care and perspicacity. Nothing could be more beautiful than the ease with which he extricated the facts of the case from the meshes in which they had been alternately involved by Mr. Subtle and the Attorney-General. As soon as he had explained to them the general principles of law applicable to the case, he placed before them the facts proved by the plaintiff, and the answer of the defendant: every one in court trembled for the result if the jury took the same view which they felt compelled themselves to take. He suggested that they should retire to consider the case, taking with them the pedigrees which had been handed in to them; and added that, if they should require his assistance, he should remain in his private room for an hour or two. Both judge and jury then retired, it being about eight o'clock. Candles were lighted in the court, which continued crowded to suffocation. Few doubted which way the verdict would go. Fatigued as must have been most of the spectators with a two days' confinement and excitement—ladies as well as gentlemen—scarce a person thought of quitting till the verdict had been pronounced. After an hour and a half's absence, a cry was heard—" Clear the way for the jury;" and one or two officers, with their wands, obeyed the directions. As the jury were re-entering their box, struggling with a little difficulty through the crowd, Lord Widdrington resumed his seat upon the bench.

" Gentlemen of the jury, have the goodness," said the associate, " to answer to your names.—*Sir Godolphin Fitzherbert*—" and while their names were thus called over all the counsel took their pens, and, turning over their briefs with an air of anxiety, prepared to indorse on them the verdict. As soon as all the jurymen had answered a profound silence ensued.

" Gentlemen of the jury," inquired the associate, " are you agreed upon the verdict? Do you find your verdict for the plaintiff, or for the defendant?"

" FOR THE PLAINTIFF," replied the foreman; on which the officer, amidst a kind of blank dismayed silence, making at the same time some hieroglyphics upon the record, muttered— " *Verdict for the plaintiff.—Damages one shilling. Costs, forty shillings;* while another functionary bawled out, amidst the increasing buzz in the court, " Have the goodness to wait, gentlemen of the jury. You will be paid immediately." Whereupon, to the disgust and indignation of the unlearned spectators, and the astonishment of some of the gentlemen of the jury themselves—many of them the very first men of the county—Snap jumped up on the form, pulled out his purse with an air of exultation, and proceeded to remunerate Sir Godolphin Fitzherbert and his companions with the sum of two guineas each. Proclamation was then made, and the court adjourned till the next morning.

END OF PART I.

TEN THOUSAND A YEAR.

CHAPTER XIV.

"THE Attorney-General did his work very fairly, I thought —eh, Lynx?" said Mr. Subtle, as, arm in arm with Mr. Lynx, he quitted the castle gates, each of them on his way to their respective lodgings, to prepare for their next day's work.

"Yes—he's a keen hand, to be sure; he's given us *all* work enough, and I must say it's been a capital set-to between you! I'm *very* glad you got the verdict!"

"It wouldn't have done to be beaten on one's own dunghill, as it were—eh? By the way, Lynx, that was a good hit of yours about the erasure—I ought, really, if it had occurred to me at the time, to have given you the credit of it—'twas entirely yours, Lynx, I must say."

"Oh, no!" replied Lynx, modestly. "It was a mere accident my lighting on it; the merit was, the use you made of it!"

"To think of ten thousand a year turning on that same trumpery erasure!"—

"But are you sure of our verdict on that ground, Mr. Subtle? Do you think Widdrington was right in rejecting that deed?"

"'Right? to be sure he was! But I own I got rather uneasy at the way the Attorney-General put it—that the estate had once been vested, and could not be subsequently devested by an alteration or blemish in the instrument evidencing the passing of the estate—eh? That was a good point, Lynx."

"Ay, but as Lord Widdrington put it—that could be only where the defect was proved to exist after a complete and valid deed had been once established."

"True—true; that's the answer, Lynx; here, you see, the deed is disgraced in the first instance; no proof, in fact, that it ever *was* a deed—therefore mere waste paper."

"To be sure, *possession* has gone along with the deed—"

"Possession gone along with it?—What then!—That is to say, the man who has altered it, to benefit himself and his heirs, keeps it snugly in his own chest—and then that is of itself to be sufficient to—"

"Yes—and again, you know, isn't it the general rule that the party producing an instrument must account for the appearance of erasure or alteration to encounter the presumption of fraud?—it seems good sense enough!"

"It's really been a very interesting cause," said Mr. Subtle.

"Very. Some capital points—that of Mortmain's on the stamp act—"

"Pish, Lynx! there's nothing in it! I meant the cause itself had been an interesting one—uncommonly."

Mr. Subtle suddenly paused, and stood still. "God bless my soul, Lynx—I've made a blunder!"

"Eh!"

"Yes—by Jove, a blunder! Never did such a thing since I've had a cause before."

"A blunder? Impossible!—what is it?" inquired Lynx, briskly, pricking up his ears.

"It will be at least thirty or forty pounds out of our client's pocket. I forgot to ask Widdrington for the certificate for the costs of the special jury. I protest I never did such a thing before—I am quite annoyed; I hate to *overlook* anything."

"Oh! is that all?" inquired Lynx, much relieved—"then it's all right! While you were speaking to Mr. Gammon, immediately after the verdict had been given, I turned toward Quicksilver to get him to ask for the certificate—but he had seen a man with the new 'Times' containing the division on the Catholic claims, and had set off after him—so I took the liberty, as you seemed very earnestly talking to Mr. Gammon, to name it to the judge—and it's all right."

"Capital!—Then there isn't a point missed? And in a good two-days' fight that's something."

"D'ye think we shall keep the verdict, and get its fruits, Mr. Subtle?"

"We shall keep the verdict, I've no doubt; there's nothing in Widdrington's notes that we need be afraid of—but of course they'll put us to bring another ejectment, perhaps several."

"Yes—certainly—there *must* be a good deal of fighting before such a property as Yatton changes hands," replied Lynx, with a complacent air; for he saw a few pleasant pickings in store for him. "By the way," he continued, "our client's a sweet specimen of humanity, isn't he?"

"Faugh! odious little reptile! And did you ever in all your

life witness such a scene as when he interrupted me in the way he did?"

"Ha, ha! Never! But, upon my honor, what an exquisite turn you gave the thing—it was worth more than called it forth—it was admirable."

"Pooh—Lynx!" said Mr. Subtle, with a gratified air; "knack—mere knack—nothing more. My voice trembled—eh?—at least so I intended."

"Upon my soul, Mr. Subtle, I almost thought you were for the moment overcome, and going to shed tears."

"Ah, ah, ah!—Delightful! I was convulsed with inward laughter! *Shed tears!* Did the Bar take it, Lynx?" inquired Mr. Subtle; for though he hated display he loved *appreciation*, and by competent persons. "By the way, Lynx, the way in which you've got up the whole case does you vast credit—that opinion of yours on the evidence was—upon my word—the most masterly"—here he suddenly ceased and squeezed his companion's arm, motioning him thereby to silence. They had come up with two gentlemen, walking slowly, and conversing in a low tone, but with much earnestness of manner. They were, in fact, Mr. Aubrey and Lord De la Zouch. Mr. Subtle and Mr. Lynx crossed to the other side of the narrow street, and quickened their pace, so as soon to be out of sight and hearing of the persons they seemed desirous of avoiding. Mr. Subtle was, indeed, unable to bear the sight of the man whom his strenuous and splendid exertions during the last two days had tended to strip of his all—to thrust from the bright domain of wealth, prosperity, distinction, into—as it were—outer darkness—the outer darkness of poverty—of destitution.

"It's a bore for Mr. Aubrey, isn't it?" quoth the matter-of-fact Lynx.

"It's quite frightful!" replied Mr. Subtle, in a tone of voice and with a manner which showed how deeply he felt what he uttered. "And it's not only what he will lose, but what he will be liable to—the mesne profits—sixty thousand pounds."

"Oh!—you think, then, that we can't go beyond the *statute of limitations*—eh?—is that so clear?" Mr. Subtle looked sharply at Lynx, with an expression it would be difficult to describe. "Well"—continued the impenetrable Lynx—"at all events I'll look into it." He felt about as much *sentiment* in the matter as a pig eating acorns would feel interest in the antiquity of the oak from which they fell, and under whose venerable shade he was munching and stuffing himself.

"By the way, Lynx—aren't you with me in Higson and Mellington?"

"Yes—and it stands first for to-morrow morning."

"What's it about? I've not opened my papers, and—why, we've a consultation fixed for ten to-night."

"It's *libel* against a newspaper editor—the POMFRET COCKA-TRICE; and our client's a clergyman."

"What about?"

"Tithes—grasping, cruelty, and so forth."

"Justification?"

"No—not guilty only."

"Who leads for the defendant?"

"Mr. Quicksilver."

"Oh!—very well. We must have the consultation to-morrow morning, at the castle—ten minutes before the sitting of the court. I'm rather tired to-night." With this the great leader shook hands with his modest, learned, laborious junior—and entered his lodgings.

As soon as Titmouse had been ejected from the court, in the summary way with which the reader will remember, merely on account of his having, with slight indecorum, yielded to the mighty impulse of his agitated feelings, he began to cry bitterly, wringing his hands, and asking every one about him if they thought he could get in again, because it was his case that was going on. His eyes were red and swollen with weeping, and his little breast throbbed violently as he walked to and fro from one door of the court to the other. "Oh, gents will you get me in again?" said he, in passionate tones, approaching two gentlemen, who, with a very anxious and oppressed air, were standing together at the outside of one of the doors—in fact, Lord De la Zouch and Mr. Aubrey; and they quickly recognized in Titmouse the gentleman whose claims were being at that instant mooted within the court. "*Will* you get me in? You seem such *respectable* gents—'Pon my soul I'm going mad! It's my case that's going on! I'm Mr. Titmouse—"

"We have no power, sir, to get you in," replied Lord De la Zouch, haughtily; so coldly and sternly as to cause Titmouse involuntarily to shrink from him.

"The court is crowded to the very door, sir—and we really have no more right to be present in court, or get others into court, than you have," said Mr. Aubrey, with mildness and dignity.

"Thank you, sir! Thank you!" quoth Titmouse, moving with an apprehensive air away from Lord De la Zouch, toward

Mr. Aubrey "Know quite well who you are, sir; sorry to do all this; but law's law, and right's right, all the world over."

"I *desire* you to leave us, sir," said Lord De la Zouch, with irrepressible sternness; "you are very intrusive. How can we catch a syllable of what is going on while you are chattering in this way?" Titmouse saw that Mr. Aubrey looked toward him with a very different expression from that exhibited by his forbidding companion, and would perhaps have stood his ground, but for a glimpse he caught of a huge, powdered, broad-shouldered footman, in a splendid livery, one of Lord De la Zouch's servants, who, with a great thick cane in his hand, was standing at a little distance behind, in attendance on the carriage, which was standing in the castle yard. This man's face looked so ready for mischief that Titmouse slowly walked off. There were a good many standers-by, who seemed all to look with dislike and distrust at Titmouse. He made many ineffectual attempts to persuade the door-keeper, who had assisted in his extrusion, to readmit him; but the incorruptible janitor was proof against a sixpence—even against a shilling; and at length Titmouse gave himself up to despair, and thought himself the most miserable man in the whole world—as very probably, indeed, he was: for consider what a horrid interval of suspense he had to endure from the closing of Mr. Subtle's speech till the delivery of the verdict. But at length, through this portentous and apparently impenetrable cloud burst the rich sunlight of success.

"Mr. Titmouse!—Mr. Titmouse!—Mr. Tit—"

"Here! Here I am! Here!"—exclaimed the little fellow, jumping off the window-seat on which he had been sitting for the last hour in the dark, half stupefied with grief and exhaustion. The voice that called him was a blessed voice—a familiar voice—the voice of Mr. Gammon; who, as soon as the jury began to come back, on some pretense or other had quitted his seat between Quirk and Snap in order if the verdict should be for the plaintiff, to be the very first to communicate it to him. In a moment or two Mr. Gammon had grasped both Mr. Titmouse's hands. "My dear, dear Mr. Titmouse, I congratulate you. You are victorious! God grant you long life to enjoy your fortune! God bless you, Titmouse!" He wrung Titmouse's hands—and his voice trembled with the intensity of his emotions. Mr. Titmouse had gone very white, and for a while spoke not, but stood staring at Mr. Gammon, as if he was hardly aware of the importance of his communication.

"No—but—is it so? Honor bright?" at length he stam-mered.

"It is indeed! My long labors are at length crowned with success!—Hurrah, hurrah, Mr. Titmouse!"

"I've really *won?* It a'n't a joke or a dream?" inquired Titmouse, with quickly increasing excitement, and a joyous expression bursting over his features, which became suddenly flushed.

"A joke?—the best you'll ever have. A dream?—that will last your life. Thank God, Mr. Titmouse, the battle's ours; we've defeated all their villainy!"

"Tol de rol! Tol de rol! Tol de lol, lol, lol, rido!—Ah!" he added, in a loud truculent tone, as Lord De la Zouch and Mr. Aubrey slowly passed him—"done for, you know—'pon my life!—turned the tables!—*that* for you!" said he, snapping his fingers; but I need hardly say that he did so with perfect impunity so far as those two gentlemen were concerned, who were so absorbed with the grievous event which had just happened as scarcely to be aware of their being addressed at all.

"Aubrey, it's against you—all is lost; the verdict is for the plaintiff!" said Lord De la Zouch, in a hurried, agitated whisper, as he grasped the hand of Mr. Aubrey, whom he had quitted for an instant to hear the verdict pronounced. Mr. Aubrey for some moments spoke not.

"God's will be done!" at length said he in a low tone, or rather in a faint murmur. More than a dozen gentlemen, who came crowding out, grasped his hand with great energy and vehemence.

"God bless you, Aubrey! God bless you!"—said several voices, their speakers wringing his hand with great vehemence as they spoke.

"Let us go," said Lord De la Zouch, putting Mr. Aubrey's arm in his own, and leading him away from a scene of distressing excitement too powerful for his exhausted feelings.

"I am nothing of a fatalist," said Mr. Aubrey, after a pause of some minutes, during which they had quitted the castle gates, and his feelings had recovered from the shock which they had just before suffered:—"I am nothing of a fatalist, but I ought not to feel the least surprise at this issue, for I have long had a settled conviction that such *would* be the issue. For some time before I had the least intimation of the commencement of these proceedings, I was oppressed by a sense of impending calamity—"

"Well, that may be so; but it does not follow that the mischief is finally *done.*"

"I am certain of it!—But, dear Lord De la Zouch, how

much I owe to your kindness and sympathy!" said Mr. Aubrey, with a slight tremor in his voice.

"We are at this moment, Aubrey, firmer friends than we
ever were before. So help me Heaven! I would not lose your
friendship for the world; I feel it a greater honor than I am
worthy of—I do, indeed," said Lord De la Zouch, with great
emotion.

"There's a great gulf between us though, Lord De la Zouch,
as far as worldly circumstances are concerned—you a peer of
the realm, I a beggar."

"Forgive me, Aubrey, but it is idle to talk in that way; I
am hurt beyond measure at your supposing it possible that
under any circumstances—"

"Believe me, I feel the full value of your friendship—more
valuable at this moment than ever."

"That a serious calamity has fallen upon you is certain;—
which of us, indeed, is safe from such a calamity? But who
would bear it with the calm fortitude which *you* have already
evinced, my dear Aubrey?"

"You speak very kindly, Lord De la Zouch; I trust I shall
play the man, now that the time for playing a man's part has
come," said Mr. Aubrey, with an air of mingled melancholy
and resolution. "I feel an inexpressible consolation in the
reflection that I can not charge myself with anything unconscientious; and, as for the future, I put my trust in God. I
feel as if I could submit to the will of Heaven with cheerfulness—"

"Don't speak so despondingly, Aubrey—"

"Despondingly?" echoed Mr. Aubrey, with momentary
animation—"despondingly? My dear friend, I feel as if I
were indeed entering a scene black as midnight—but what is
it to the *valley of the shadow of death*, dear Lord De la Zouch,
which is before all of us, and at but a little distance! I assure
you I feel no vain-glorious confidence; yet I seem to be leaning
on the arm of an unseen but all-powerful supporter!"

"You are a hero, my dear Aubrey!" exclaimed Lord De la
Zouch, with sudden fervor.

"And that support will embrace those dearer to me than
life—dearer—far—far—" He ceased: his feelings quite overcame him, and they walked on for some time in silence. Soon
afterward they parted—for Lord De la Zouch perceived that
his unfortunate companion wished to be alone. He wrung
Mr. Aubrey's hands in silence; and having turned in the
direction of his hotel, Mr. Aubrey made for his lodgings. The
streets were occupied by passengers, some returning from the

castle after the great trial of the day; others standing here and
there, in little knots, conversing as he passed them; and he
felt conscious that the subject of their thoughts and conversation was himself and his fallen fortunes.   Several deep-
drawn sighs escaped him, as he walked on, the herald of such
dismal tidings, to those whom he loved: and he felt, but for
that which supported him from within, as it were, a fallen
angel so far as concerned this world's honors and greatness.
The splendors of human pomp and prosperity seemed rapidly
vanishing in the distance.   In the temporary depression of his
spirits he experienced feelings somewhat akin to those of the
heart-sickened exile, whose fond eyes are riveted upon the
mosques and minarets of his native city, bathed in the soft
sunlight of evening, where are the cherished objects of all his
tenderest thoughts and feelings; while his vessel is rapidly
bearing him from it, amid the rising wind, the increasing and
ominous swell of the waters, the thickening gloom of night—
whither?   The minster clock struck ten as he passed one of
the corners of the vast majestic structure, gray-glistening in
the faint moonlight.   The melodious chimes echoed in his ear,
and smote his subdued soul with a sense of peculiar solemnity
and awe; they forced upon him a reflection upon the transient
littleness of earthly things.   Then he thought of those dear
beings who were awaiting his return, and a gush of grief and
tenderness overflowed his heart, as he quickened his steps, with
an inward and fervent prayer that Heaven would support them
under the misfortune which had befallen them.   As he neared
the retired row of houses where his lodgings were situated he
imagined that he saw some one near the door of his lodgings,
as if on the lookout for his approach, and who, as he drew
nearer, at length entered his lodgings.   This was a person
whom Mr. Aubrey did not at all suspect—it was his worthy
friend Dr. Tatham, who, unable to quit Yatton in time to
hear the trial, had early that morning mounted his horse, and,
after a long and hard ride, reached York soon after Mr. Aubrey
had set off for the castle.   Though many of the country people then in York were aware that Mrs. and Miss Aubrey were
also there, a delicate consideration for their exquisitely distressing situation restrained them from intruding upon their
privacy, which had been evidently sought for by the species
of lodgings which Mr. Aubrey had engaged.   On the second
day the excellent Dr. Tatham had been their welcome and
instructive guest, scarce ever leaving them; Mr. Aubrey's
groom bringing word, from time to time, from his master how
the trial went on.   Late in the evening, urged by Kate, the

doctor had gone off to the castle, to wait till he could bring intelligence of the final result of the trial. He had not been observed by Mr. Aubrey amid the number of people who were about, and had at length fulfilled his mission, and been before-hand with Mr. Aubrey in communicating the unfortunate issue of the struggle. The instant that Mr. Aubrey had set his foot within the door he was locked in the impassioned embrace of his wife and sister. None of them spoke for some moments.

"Dearest Charles!—we've heard it all—we know it all!" at length they exclaimed in a breath. "Thank God, it is over at last—and we know the worst!—Are you well, dearest Charles?" inquired Mrs. Aubrey, with fond anxiety.

"Thank God, my Agnes, I am well!" said Mr. Aubrey, much excited—"and thank God that the dreadful suspense is at an end; and for the fortitude, my sweet loves, with which you bear the result. And how are *you*, my excellent friend?" continued he, addressing Dr. Tatham, and grasping his hands; "My venerable and pious friend—how it refreshes my heart to see you! as one of the chosen ministers of that God whose creatures we are, and whose dispensations we receive with reverend submission!"

"God Almighty bless you all, my dear friends!" replied Dr. Tatham, powerfully affected. "Believe that all this is from HIM! He has wise ends in view, though we see not nor com-prehend them! *Faint not when ye are rebuked of Him! If ye faint in the day of adversity, your strength is small!* But I rejoice to see your resignation!"—Aubrey, his wife and sis-ter, were for a while overcome with their emotions.

"I assure you all," said Aubrey, "I feel as if a very mountain had been lifted off my heart! How blessed am I in such a wife and sister!" A heavenly smile irradiated his pale features—and he clasped his wife and then his sister in his arms. They wept as they tenderly returned his embrace.

"Heaven," said he, "that gave us all, has taken all: why should we murmur? He will enable us, if we pray for His assistance, to bear with equanimity our present adversity, as well as our past prosperity! Come, Agnes! Kate! play the woman!"

Dr. Tatham sat silent by; but the tears ran down his cheeks. At length Mr. Aubrey gave them a general account of what had occurred at the trial—and which, I need hardly say, was listened to in breathless silence.

"Who is that letter from, love, lying on the table?" in-quired Mr. Aubrey, during a pause in the conversation.

"It's only from Johnson, dearest! to say the children are

quite well," replied Mrs. Aubrey. The ruined parents, as if by a common impulse, looked unutterable things at each other. Then the mother turned deadly pale, and her husband tenderly kissed her cold cheek; while Kate could scarcely restrain her feelings. The excitement of each was beginning to give way before sheer bodily and mental exhaustion; and Dr. Tatham, observing it, rose to take his departure. It was arranged that the carriage should be at the door by eight o'clock in the morning, to convey them back to Yatton—and that Dr. Tatham should breakfast with and then accompany them on horseback. He then took his departure for the night, with a very full heart; and those whom he had left soon afterward retired for the night; and having first invoked the mercy and pity of Heaven, sunk into slumber and brief forgetfulness of the perilous position in which they had been placed by the events of the day.

Somewhat different was the mode in which the night was spent by the victorious party. Gammon, as has been seen, was the first to congratulate Titmouse on his splendid success. The next was old Quirk—who, with a sort of conviction that he should find Gammon beforehand with him—bustled out of court, leaving Snap to pay the jury, settle the court fees, collect the papers, and so forth. Both Quirk and Snap (as soon as he was at liberty) exhibited a courtesy toward Titmouse which had a strong dash of reverence in it, such as was due to the possessor of ten thousand a year; but Gammon exhibited the tranquil matter-of-fact confidence of a man who had determined to be, and indeed knew that he *was* the entire master of Titmouse.

"I—wish you'd call a coach, or something of that sort, gents.—I'm devilish tired—I am, 'pon my soul!" said Mr. Titmouse, yawning, as he stood on the steps between Quirk and Gammon, waiting for Snap's arrival. He was, in fact, almost mad—bursting with excitement, and could not stand still for a moment. Now he whistled loudly and boldly; then he hummed a bar or two of some low comic song; and ever and anon drew on and off his damp gloves with an air of petulant impetuosity. Now he ran his hand through his hair with careless grace; and then with arms folded on his breast for a moment, looked eagerly, but with a would-be languid air, at two or three elegant equipages, which one by one, with their depressed and disappointed inmates, rolled off. At length Lord Widdrington, amid a sharp impetuous cry of "Make way for the judge there—make way for his lordship!" appeared in his robes, with a wearied air; and passing close by

Titmouse, was honored by him with a very fine bow indeed—
not being, however, in the least aware of the fact—as he passed
on to his carriage. The steps were drawn up, the door was
closed, and amid a sharp blast of trumpets, the carriage drove
slowly off, preceded and followed by the usual attendants. All
this pomp and ceremony made a very deep impression upon
the mind of Titmouse. " Ah," thought he, with a sudden
sigh of mingled excitement and exhaustion—" who knows but
I may be a judge some day? It's a devilish pleasant thing,
I'm sure! What a fuss he must make wherever he goes!
'Pon my life, quite delightful!" As there was no coach to be
had, Mr. Titmouse was forced to walk home, arm in arm with
Mr. Quirk and Mr. Gammon, and followed, at a little distance
by a knot of persons acquainted with his name and person,
and feeling toward him a strange mixture of emotions—dislike,
wonder, contempt, admiration. Goodness gracious! that
strange little gentleman was now worth, it was said, ten
thousand a year, and was squire of Yatton! Old Quirk shook
Titmouse's hand with irrepressible enthusiasm at least a dozen
times on their way to the inn; while Gammon now and ther
squeezed his arm, and spoke, in an earnest tone, of the difficulties yet to be overcome. On reaching the inn the landlady,
who was standing at the door, and had evidently been on the
lookout for her suddenly distinguished guest, received him
with several most profound courtesies, and most eager and
respectful inquiries about his health, as he had had no luncheon
—and asking what he would be pleased to have for his supper.
She added, moreover, that fearing his former bedroom might
not have been to his mind, she had changed it, and he would
that night sleep in the very best she had.

" We must make a night on't, eh?" quoth Mr. Quirk, with
an excited air. His partners assented to it, as did Mr. Titmouse; and cold beef, sausages, fowl, ham, beef-steaks, and
mutton-chops were ordered to be in readiness in half an hour's
time. Soon afterward Mr. Titmouse followed the chambermaid to his new bedroom.

" 'This is the room we always give to quality folk—when we
get them," said she, as she sat his candle on the drawers, and
looked with a little triumph around the room.

" Ah—yes!—'pon my soul—quite right—always do your
best for quality!—Lovely gal—eh?" Here he chucked her
under the chin, and seemed disposed to imprint a kiss upon
her cheek: but, with a " Lord, sir—that's not the way quality
folks behave!" she modestly withdrew. Titmouse, left alone

first threw himself on the bed; then started off, and walked
about; then sat down; then danced about; then took off his
coat; then threw himself on the bed again; hummed, whistled,
jumped up again—in a sort of wild ecstasy or delirium. In
short, it is plain that he was not master of himself. In fact,
his little mind was as agitated by the day's events as a small
green puddle by the road side for a while would be on a stone
being suddenly flung into it by a child. While Messrs. Quirk
and Snap were, after their sort, as excited as even Mr. Titmouse was, Gammon, retiring to his bedroom, and ordering
thither pens, ink, and paper, sat down and wrote the following letter:—

                           " York, 5th April, 18—.

    " MY DEAR SIR,—The very first leisure moment I have I
devote to informing you, as one of the most intimate friends
of our highly respected client, Mr. Titmouse, of this brilliant
event which has just occurred. After a most severe and protracted struggle of two days (the Attorney-General having
come down special on the other side) the jury, many of them
the chief gentlemen of the county, have within the last hour
returned a verdict in favor of our common friend, Mr. Titmouse—thereby declaring him entitled to the whole of the
estates at Yatton (ten thousand a year rent-roll, at least), and,
by consequence, to an immense accumulation of by-gone rents,
which must be made up to him by his predecessor, who, with
all his powerful party, and in spite of the unscrupulous means
resorted to to defeat the ends of justice, is dismayed beyond
expression at the result of this grand struggle—unprecedented
in the annals of modern litigation. The result has given
lively satisfaction in these parts—it is plain that our friend
Mr. Titmouse will very soon become a great lion in society.

    " To you, my dear sir, as an early and valued friend of our
interesting client, I sit down to communicate the earliest intelligence of this most important event, and I trust that you will,
with our respectful compliments, communicate this happy
event to your amiable family—who, I am persuaded, must
ever feel a very warm interest in our client's welfare. He is
now, naturally enough, much excited with his extraordinary
good fortune, to which we are only too proud and happy to
have contributed by our humble, but strenuous and long-
continued exertions. He begs me to express his most cordial
feelings toward you, and to say that, on his return to town,
Satin Lodge will be one of the very first places at which he will
call. In the meantime, I beg you will believe me, my dear

sir, with the best compliments of myself and partners, your most sincerely,   "OILY GAMMON.

"THOMAS TAG-RAG, ESQ., etc. etc. etc."

"That, I think, will about do"—quoth Gammon to himself, with a thoughtful air, as, having made an exact copy of the above letter, he sealed it up and directed it. He then came down-stairs to supper, having first sent the letter off to the post-office. What a merry meal was that same supper! Mr. Titmouse, Mr. Quirk and Mr. Snap eat almost to bursting: Gammon was more abstinent—but overpowered by the importunities of his companions, took a far greater quantity than usual of the bouncing bottled porter, the hard port and fiery sherry, which his companions drank as if they had been but water. Then came in the spirits—with hot water and cold; and to these all present did ample justice; in fact, it was very hard for any one to resist the other's entreaties. Mr. Gammon in due time felt himself *going*—but seemed as if, on such an occasion, he had no help for it. Every one of the partners, at different stages of the evening, made a speech to Titmouse, and proposed his health; who, of course, replied to each, and drank the health of each. Presently old Quirk sung a comic song, in a very dismal key; and then he and Snap joined in one called "*Handcuff* v. *Halter;*" at which Gammon laughed heartily and listened with that degree of pleased attention, which showed that he had resolved, for once at least, to bandon himself to the enjoyment of the passing hour. Then Titmouse began to speak of what he should do as soon as he had "touched the shiners"—his companions entering into all his little schemes with a sort of affectionate enthusiasm. At length old Mr. Quirk, after by turns laughing, crying, singing, and talking, leaned back in his chair, with his half-emptied tumbler of brandy and water in his hand, and fell fast asleep. Gammon also, in spite of all he could do, began—the deuce take it!—to feel and exhibit the effects of a hasty and hearty meal and his very unusual potations, especially after such long abstinence and intense anxiety as he had experienced during the previous two days. He had intended to have seen them all under the table; but he began gradually to feel a want of control over himself, his thoughts, and feelings, which a little disquieted him, as he now and then caught glimpses of the extent to which it was proceeding. "*In vino veritas*," properly translated, means—that when a man is fairly under the influence of liquor, you see a strong manifestation of his real character. The vain man is vainer; the voluble, more volu-

ble; the morose, more morose; the passionate, more passionate; the detractor, more detracting; the sycophant, more
sycophantic, and so forth.   Now Mr. Gammon was a cold,
cautious, long-headed schemer; and as the fumes of liquor
mounted up into his head they only increased the action and
intensity of those qualities for which, when sober, he was so
pre-eminently distinguished, only that there was a half-con-
scious want of coherency and subordination.   The impulse
and the habit were present; but there seemed a strange disturbing force: in short—what is the use of disguising matters?
—Mr. Gammon was getting very drunk, and he felt very sorry
for it—but it was too late.   In due time the dismal effort *not
to appear* drunk ceased—a great relief! Silent and more silent
he became; more and more observant of the motions of Snap
and Titmouse; more and more complicated and profound in
his schemes and purposes; and at length he felt as if, by some
incomprehensible means, he were taking *himself* in—inveigling
himself: at which point, after a vain attempt to understand his
exact position with reference to himself, he slowly, but *rather*
unsteadily rose from his chair; looked with an unsettled eye
at Titmouse for nearly a minute; a queer smile now and then
flitted across his features; and he presently rang the bell.
Boots having obeyed the summons, Gammon with a very
turbid brain followed him to the door, with a most desperate
effort to walk thither steadily—but in vain.   Having reached
his room, he sat down with a sort of suspicion that he had said
or done something to commit himself.   Vain was the attempt
to wind up his watch; and at length he gave it up with a faint
curse.   With only one stocking off, conceiving himself to be
undressed, after four or five times trying to blow out his candle
in vain, he succeeded and got into bed, his head, however, occupying the place in the bed assigned to his feet.   He lay
asleep for about half an hour—and then experienced certain
insupportable sensations.   He was indeed very miserable, and
lost all thoughts of what would become of Titmouse—of Quirk
and Snap—in his own indisposition.

    " I say, Snap," quoth Titmouse, with a grin, and putting
his finger to his nose as soon as Gammon had quitted the room
in the manner above described—" Mr. Quirk a'n't much company for us now, eh?   Shall we go out and have some fun?"

    " Walk will do us good—yes.   Go where you like, Tit-
mouse," replied Snap, who, though young, was a thoroughly
seasoned vessel, and could hold a great deal of drink without
seeming or *really being* much the worse for it.   As for Titmouse, happily for him! (seeing that he was so soon to have

the command of unlimited means, unless indeed the envious fates should in the meantime interpose to dash the brimful cup from his eager lips), he was becoming more and more accustomed to the effects of drink; which had, up to the moment I am speaking of, no other effect than to elevate his spirits up to the pitch of indefinite daring and enterprise. " 'Pon my life, Snap, couldn't we stand another tumbler—eh? Warm us for the night air?"

"What shall it be?" quoth Snap, ringing the bell— "whisky?"

" Devil knows, and devil cares!" replied Titmouse, recklessly; and presently there stood before the friends two steaming tumblers of what they had ordered. Immediately after disposing of them, the two gentlemen, quite *up to the mark*, as they expressed it—each with a cigar in his mouth—sallied forth in quest of adventures. Titmouse felt that he had now become a gentleman; and his taste and feelings prompted him to pursue, as early as possible, a gentlemanly line of conduct —particularly in his amusements. It was now past twelve; and the narrow old-fashioned streets of York, silent and deserted, formed a strong contrast to the streets of London at the same hour, and seemed scarcely to admit of much sport. But sport our friends were determined to have; and the night air aiding the effect of their miscellaneous potations, they soon became somewhat excited and violent. Yet it seemed difficult to get up a *row*—for no one was visible in any direction. Snap, however, by way of making a beginning, suddenly shouted " fire!" at the top of his voice, and Titmouse joined him; when having heard half a dozen windows hastily thrown up by the dismayed inhabitants whom the alarming sounds had aroused from sleep, they scampered off at their top speed. In another part of the town they yelled, and whistled, and crowed like cocks, and mewed like cats—the last two being accomplishments in which Titmouse was very eminent—and again took to their heels. Then they contrived to twist a few knockers off doors, pull bells, and break a few windows; and while exercising their skill in this last branch of the night's amusement, Titmouse, in the very act of aiming a stone which took effect in the middle of a bedroom window, was surprised by an old watchman waddling round the corner. He was a feeble, asthmatic old man; so Snap knocked him down at once, and Titmouse blew out the candle in his lantern, which he then jumped upon and smashed to pieces, and knocked its prostrate owner's hat over his eyes. Snap, on some strange unaccountable impulse, wrested the rattle out of the poor

creature's hand, and sprung it loudly. This brought several
other old watchmen from different quarters; and aged numbers prevailing against youthful spirit—the two gentlemen,
after a considerable scuffle, were overpowered and conveyed to
the cage. Snap having muttered something about demanding
to look at the *warrant,* and then about a malicious arrest and
false imprisonment, sunk on a form, and then down upon the
floor, and fell fast asleep. Titmouse for a while showed a very
resolute front, and swore a great many oaths that he would
fight the Boots at the inn for five shillings, if he dared show
himself; but all of a sudden his spirit collapsed, as it were,
and he sunk on the floor and was grievously indisposed for
some hours. About nine o'clock the contents of the cage—
viz., Snap, Titmouse, two farmers' boys who had been caught
stealing cakes, an old beggar, and a young pickpocket—were
conveyed before the Lord Mayor, to answer for their several
misdeeds. Snap was wofully crest-fallen. He had sent for
the landlord of the inn where they had put up to come, on
their behalf, to the Mansion House; but he told Quirk of the
message he had received. Mr. Quirk, finding that Gammon
could not leave his room through severe indisposition—the
very first time that Mr. Quirk had ever seen or heard of his
being so overtaken—set off, in a very mortified and angry
mood, in quest of his hopeful client and junior partner. They
were in a truly dismal pickle. Titmouse, pale as death, his
clothes disordered, and one of his shirt-collars torn off; Snap
sat beside him with a sheepish air, looking as if he could hardly keep his eyes open. At him Mr. Quirk looked with keen
indignation, but spoke not to him nor for him; for Titmouse,
however, he expressed great commiseration, and entreated his
lordship to overlook the little misconduct of which he (Titmouse) in a moment of extreme excitement, had been guilty,
on condition of making amends for the injury, both to person
and property, of which he had been guilty. By this time his
lordship had become aware of the names and circumstances of
the two delinquents; and, after lecturing them very severely,
he fined them five shillings apiece for being drunk, and permitted them to be discharged, on their promising never to
offend in the like way again, and paying three pounds by way
of compensation to the watchman and one or two persons
whose knockers they were proved to have wrenched off, and
windows to have broken. His lordship had delayed the case of
Messrs. Snap and Titmouse to the last; chiefly because, as
soon as he had found out who Mr. Titmouse was, it occurred
to him that he would make a sort of little start at the great

ball to be given by the Lady Mayoress that evening. As soon, therefore, as the charge had been disposed of, his lordship desired Mr. Titmouse to follow him, for a moment, to his private room. There, having shut the door, he gently chided Mr. Titmouse for the indiscretion of which he had been guilty, and of which it was not to have been expected that a gentleman of his consequence in the county would be guilty. His lordship begged him to consider the station which he was now called to occupy; and, in alluding to the signal event of the preceding day, warmly congratulated him upon it; and, by the way, his lordship trusted that Mr. Titmouse would, in the evening, favor the Lady Mayoress and himself with his company at the ball, where they would be very proud of the opportunity of introducing him to some of the gentry of the county, amongst whom his future lot in life was likely to be cast. Mr. Titmouse listened to all this as if he were in a dream. His brain (the little of it that he had) was yet in a most unsettled state; as also was his stomach. When he heard the words "Lady Mayoress," "ball," "Mansion House," "gentry of the county," and so forth, a dim vision of splendor flashed before his eyes; and, with a desperate effort, he assured the Lord Mayor that he should be very uncommon proud to accept the invitation, if he were well enough—but just then he was uncommon ill.

His lordship pressed him to take a glass of water, to revive him and settle his stomach; but Mr. Titmouse declined it, and soon afterward quitted the room; and, leaning on the arm of Mr. Quirk, set off homeward—Snap walking beside him in silence, with a very quaint disconcerted air—not being taken the least notice of by Mr. Quirk. As they passed along, they encountered several of the barristers on their way to court, and others, who recognized Titmouse; and with a smile, evidently formed a pretty accurate guess as to the manner in which the triumph of the preceding day had been celebrated. Mr. Quirk, finding that Mr. Gammon was far too much indisposed to think of quitting York, at all events till a late hour in the evening, and, indeed, that Titmouse was similarly situated—with a very bad grace consented to them stopping behind; and himself, with Snap—the former inside, the latter outside—having settled with most of the witnesses, leaving the remainder, with their own expenses at the inn, to be settled by Mr. Gammon—set off for town by the two o'clock coach. It was, indeed, high time for them to return; for the oppressed inmates of Newgate were getting wild on account of the protracted absence of their kind and confidential advisers. When they left, both Gammon and Titmouse were in bed. The former, however, began to revive shortly after the coach which conveyed away his respected co-partners and the guard's horn had ceased to be heard; and about an hour afterward he descended from his room, a great deal better for the duties of the toilet and a bottle of soda-water with a little brandy in it.

A cup of strong tea and a slice or two of dry toast set him entirely to rights, and then Gammon—the calm, serene, astute Gammon—was "himself again." Had he said anything indiscreet, or in any way committed himself overnight? —thought he, as he sat alone, with folded arms, trying to recollect what had taken place. He hoped not—but had no means of ascertaining. Then he entered upon a long and anxious consideration of the position of affairs since the great event of the preceding evening. The only definite object which he had had in view, personally, in entering into the affair, was the obtaining that ascendency over Titmouse, in the event of his becoming possessed of the magnificent fortune they were in quest of for him, which might enable him, in one way or another, to elevate his own position in society, and secure for himself permanent and solid advantages. In the progress of the affair, however, new views presented themselves to his mind.

Toward the close of the afternoon, Titmouse recovered sufficiently to make his appearance down-stairs. Soon afterward, Gammon proposed a walk, as the day was fine, and the brisk fresh country air would be efficacious in restoring Titmouse to his wonted health and spirits. His suggestion was adopted; and soon afterward might have been seen, Gammon, supporting on his arm his languid and interesting client, Mr. Titmouse, making their way to the river, along whose quiet and pleasing banks they walked for nearly a couple of hours in close conversation, during which, Gammon, by repeated and various efforts, succeeded in producing an impression on Titmouse's mind that the good fortune which seemed now within his reach had been secured for him by the enterprise, skill and caution of one, Mr. Gammon, only; who would, moreover, continue to devote himself to Mr. Titmouse's interest, and protect him from the designs of those who would endeavor to take advantage of him. Mr. Gammon also dropped one or two vague hints that his—Titmouse's—continuance in the enjoyment of the Yatton property would always depend upon the will and power of him, the aforesaid Gammon, in whose hands were most unsuspected, but potent weapons.

And, indeed, it is not at all impossible that such may prove to be really the case.

What a difference is there between man and man, in temper, and disposition, and intellect! Compare together the two individuals now walking slowly, arm in arm, beside the sweet Ouse; and supposing one to have designs upon the other—disposed to insnare and overreach him—what chance has the shorter gentleman? Compare even their countenances—what a difference!

Gammon heard with uneasiness of Titmouse's intention to go to the Lady Mayoress's ball that evening; and, for many reasons, resolved that he should not. In vain, however, did Gammon try to persuade him that he was asked only to be turned into ridicule, for that almost everybody there would be in the interest of the Aubreys, and bitterly opposed to him, Mr. Titmouse; in spite of these and all other representations, Titmouse expressed his determination to go to the ball; on which, Gammon, with a good-natured smile, exclaimed, "Well, well!"—and withdrew his opposition. Shortly after their return from their walk, they sat down to dinner, and Gammon, with a cheerful air, ordered a bottle of champagne, of which he drank about a glass and a half, and Titmouse the remainder. That put him into a humor to take more wine, without much pressing; and he swallowed, in rapid succession, a glass of ale and seven or eight glasses of port and sherry. By this time he had forgotten all about the ball, and clamored for brandy and water. Gammon, however, saw that his end was answered. Poor Titmouse was becoming rapidly more and more helpless; and within half an hour's time was assisted to his bedroom in a very bad state. Thus Gammon had the satisfaction of seeing his benevolent design accomplished, although it pained him to think of the temporary inconvenience occasioned to the unconscious sufferer, who had, however, escaped the devices of those who wished publicly to expose his inexperience; and as for the means which Gammon had resorted to in order to effect his purpose—why, he may be supposed to have had a remoter object in view, viz., early to disgust him with intemperance.

Alas! how disappointed were the Mayor and Mayoress that their queer little lion did not make his appearance in the gay and brilliant scene! How many had they told that he was coming! The three daughters were almost bursting with vexation and astonishment. They had been disposed to entertain a warmer feeling than that of mere curiosity toward the new owner of an estate worth ten thousand a year—had drawn

lots which of them was first to dance with him; and had told
all their friends on which of them the lot had fallen; then,
again, many of the country people inquired, from time to
time, of the chagrined little Mayor and Mayoress, when " Mr.
Ticklemouse," " Mr. Tipmouse," " Mr. Tipplebattle," or
" whatever his name might be," was coming; full of real
curiosity, much tinctured, however, with disgust and contempt, to see the stranger, who had suddenly acquired so commanding a station in the county, having so strong a claim to
their sympathy and respect.

Then, again, there was a very great lion there, exhibiting
for a short time only, who also wished to see the little lion,
and expressed keen regrets that it was not there according to
appointment. The great lion was Mr. Quicksilver, who had
stepped in for about half an hour, merely to show himself;
and when he heard of the expected arrival of his little client,
it occurred to Mr. Quicksilver, who could see several inches
beyond by no means a short nose, that Mr. Titmouse had
gained a verdict that would very soon make him *patron of the
borough of Yatton*—that he probably would not think of sitting for the borough himself, and that a little public civility
bestowed upon Mr. Titmouse by the great Mr. Quicksilver,
one of the counsel to whose splendid exertions he was indebted
for his all, might be, as it were, *bread thrown upon the waters,
to be found after many days*. It was true that Mr. Quicksilver, in a bitter stream of eloquent invective, had repeatedly denounced the system of close and rotten boroughs; but his heart,
all the while, secretly rebelled; and he knew that a snug
borough was a thing on every account not to be sneezed at.
He sat for one himself, though he had also contested several
counties; but that was expensive and harassing work; and the
borough for which he at present sat, he had paid far too high
a price for. He had no objection to the existence of close
boroughs; but only to so many of them being in the hands of
the opposite party; and the legislature hath since recognized
the distinction, and acted upon it. Here, however, was the
case of a borough which was going to change hands and pass
from Tory to Whig, and could Mr. Quicksilver fail to watch it
with interest. Was he, therefore, to neglect this opportunity
of slipping in for Yatton—and the *straw moving*, too, in town
—a general election looked for? So Mr. Quicksilver really regretted the absence of his little friend and client, Mr Titmouse.

Thus, and by such persons, and on such grounds, was
lamented the absence of Mr. Titmouse from the ball of the

Lady Mayoress of York; none, however, knowing the cause which kept him from so select and distinguished an assembly. As soon as Mr. Gammon had seen him properly attended to, and expressed an anxious sympathy for him, he set out for a walk—a quiet solitary walk round the ancient walls of York. If on a fine night you look up into the sky, and see it gleaming with innumerable stars, and then fix your eye intently, *without wavering*, upon some one star however vivid and brilliant may be those in its immediate vicinity, they will disappear utterly, and that on which your eye is fixed will seem alone in its glory—sole star in the firmament. Something of this kind happened with Mr. Gammon when on the walls of York—now slowly, then rapidly walking, now standing, then sitting; all the objects which generally occupied his thoughts faded away, before one on which his mind's eye was then fixed with unwavering intensity—the visage of Miss Aubrey. The golden fruit that was on the eve of dropping into the hands of the firm—ten thousand pounds—the indefinite and varied advantages to himself, personally, to which their recent successes might be turned, all vanished. What would he not undergo, what would he not sacrifice, to secure the favor of Miss Aubrey? Beautiful being—all innocence, elegance, refinement; —to possess her would elevate him in the scale of being; it would purify his feelings, it would ennoble his nature. What was too arduous or desperate to be undertaken to secure a prize so glorious as this? He fell into a long reverie, till, roused by a chill gust of night air, he rose from his seat upon one of the niches in the walls;—how lonely, how solitary he felt! He walked on rapidly, at a pace that suited the heated and rapid current of thoughts that passed through his mind.

"No, I have not a chance—not a chance!" at length he thought to himself—"That girl will be prouder in her poverty than ever she would have been in her wealth and splendor. Who am I?—a partner in the firm of Quirk, Gammon and Snap; a firm in bad odor with the profession; looking for practice from polluted sources, with a host of miscreants for clients—faugh! faugh! I feel contaminated and degraded! My name even is against me; it is growing into a by-word!—We must push our advantage—they must be driven from Yatton—he, she—all of them; yes, all." He paused for a long time, and a sort of pang passed through his mind. "They are to make way for—Titmouse!—for Titmouse!! And he, too, loves her—*bah!*" He involuntarily uttered this sound fiercely and aloud. "But stay—he really is in love with Miss Aubrey—that I know;—ah! I can turn it to good purpose

it will give me, by the way, a hold upon the little fool; I will
make him believe that through my means he may obtain Miss
Aubrey! Misery may make her accessible; I can easily bring
myself into contact with them, in their distress; for there are
the mesne profits—*the mesne profits!* Heavens! how glorious,
but how dreadful an engine are *they!* They will help to bat-
ter down the high wall of pride that surrounds *them* and *her;*
but it will require infinite care and tact in the use of such an
engine! I will be all delicacy—gentleness—generosity; I will
appear friendly to her and to her brother; and, if needs must
be, why he must be *crushed.* There is no help for it. He
looks decidedly by the way—a man of intellect. I wonder how
he bears it—how they all bear it—how *she* bears it! *Beggared
beauty*—there's something touching in the very sound! How
little they think of the power that is at this moment in my
hands!" Here a long interval elapsed, during which his
thoughts had wandered toward more practical matters. " If
they don't get a rule *nisi* next term, we shall be in a position
to ask them what course they intend to pursue; gad, they
may, if so disposed, hold out for— How very cold it is!"—he
buttoned his coat—" and, what have I been thinking of?
Really, I have been dreaming; or am I as great a fool as Tittlebat?" Within a few minutes' time he had quitted the walls,
and descended, through one of the turreted gate-ways, into the
town.

CHAPTER XV.

WHEN, about seven o'clock on the morning after the delivery of the verdict, which, if sustained, consigned the Aubreys to beggary, they met to partake of a slight and hearty
breakfast before setting off for Yatton, the countenances of
each bore the traces of great suffering, and also of the efforts
made to conceal it. They saluted each other with fervent
affection, each attempting a smile—but a smile, how wan and
forced! " The moment has arrived, dear Agnes and Kate,"
said her brother, with a fond air but a firm voice, as his sister
was preparing tea, in silence, fearful of looking at either her
brother or sister-in-law; " the moment has arrived that is to
try what stuff we are made of. If we have any strength, this
is the time to show it!"
  " I'm sure I thought of you both almost all night long!"
replied Miss Aubrey, tremulously. " You have a lion's heart,
dear Charles; and yet you are so gentle with us—"
  " I should be a poor creature indeed, Kate, to give way just

when I ought to play the man. Come, dear Kate, I will re
mind you of a noble passage from our glorious Shakespeare.
It braces one's nerves to hear it!" Then, with a fine impressive delivery, and kindling with excitement as he went on, Aubrey began—

> " In the reproof of chance
> Lies the true proof of men. The sea being smooth
> How many shallow bauble boats dare sail
> Upon her patient breast, making their way
> With those of nobler bulk?
> But let the ruffian Boreas once enrage
> The gentle Thetis, and, anon, behold
> The strong-ribb'd bark through liquid mountains cut,
> Bounding between the two moist elements
> Like Perseus' horse; where's then the saucy boat,
> Whose weak untimber'd sides but even now
> Co-rival'd greatness? Either to harbor fled,
> Or made a toast for Neptune!—Even so,
> Doth valor show, and valor's worth divide,
> In storms of fortune."*

'Twas kindly meant of Aubrey; he thought to divert the
excited feelings of his wife and sister, and occupy their imagination with the vivid imagery and noble sentiment of the
poet. While he repeated the above lines, his sister's eye had
been fixed upon him with a radiant expression of resolution,
her heart responding to what she heard. She could not, however, speak when he had ceased. For herself she cared not;
but when she looked at her brother, and thought of him, his
wife, his children, her fortitude yielded before the moving
array, and she burst into tears.

"Come, Kate—my own sweet, good Kate!" said he, cheerfully, laying his hand upon hers, "we must keep constant
guard against our *feelings*. They will be ever arraying before
out eyes the past—the dear, delightful past—happy and beautiful, in mournful contrast with the present, and stirring up,
every moment, a thousand secret and tender associations, calculated to shake our constancy. Whenever our eyes do turn
to the past, let it be with humble gratitude to God for having
allowed us all, in this changing world, so long an interval of
happiness; such, indeed, as falls to the lot of few. *What!
shall we receive good at the hand of God, and shall we not receive evil?*"

"My own Charles!" exclaimed Mrs. Aubrey, rising and
throwing her arms round her husband, whose countenance was
calm and serene as was the tone of the sentiments he ex-

* Troilus and Cressida, i. 3.

pressed solemn and elevated. Miss Aubrey was overcome with
her stronger feelings, and buried her face in her handkerchief.
Shortly afterward the carriage drew up, and also Dr. Tatham
on horseback.

"Good-morning! good-morning, my friends," cried he,
cheerfully, as he entered, holding forth both his hands; "you
can't think how fresh and pleasant the air is! The country for
me, at all times of the year! I hate towns! Did you sleep well?
I slept like a top all night long;—no, I didn't either, by the
way. Come, come, ladies! On with your bonnets and shawls!"
Thus rattled on worthy little Dr. Tatham, in order to prevent
anything being said which might disturb those whom he came
to see, or cause his own highly charged feelings to give way.
The sight of Mrs. and Miss Aubrey, however, who greeted him
in silence as they hastily drew on their bonnets and shawls,
overcame his ill-assumed cheerfulness; and before he could
bustle back, as he presently did, to the street door, his eyes
were obstructed with tears, and he wrung the hand of Mr.
Aubrey, who stood beside him, with convulsive energy. They
soon set off, and at a rapid pace, Dr. Tatham riding along beside the carriage. Yatton was about twelve miles off. For
the first few miles they preserved a tolerable show of cheerfulness; but as they perceived themselves nearing Yatton, it became plainly more and more of an effort for any of them to
speak. Dr. Tatham, also, talked to them seldomer through
the windows. At one time he dropped considerably behind;
at another, he rode as much ahead.

"Oh, Charles, don't you dread to see Yatton?" said Miss
Aubrey suddenly, as they turned a familiar corner of the road.
Neither of them replied to her.

"When you come to the village," said Mr. Aubrey presently, to the postilion, "drive through it, right up to the Hall,
as quickly as you can." He was obeyed. As they passed
through the village, with their windows up, none of them
seemed disposed to look through, but leaned back in silence in
their seats.

"God bless you! God bless you! I shall call in the evening," exclaimed Dr. Tatham, as, having reached the vicarage,
he hastily waved his hand, and turned off. Soon they had
passed the park-gates; when had they entered it before with
such heavy hearts—with eyes so dreading to encounter every
familiar object that met them? Alas! the spacious park was
no longer theirs; not a tree, not a shrub, not a flower, not an
inch of ground; the trees all putting forth their fresh green
leaves—nothing was theirs; the fine old turreted gate-way, an

object always, hitherto, of peculiar pride and attachment, their hearts seemed to tremble as they rattled under it.

"Courage, my sweet loves! Courage! courage!" exclaimed Mr. Aubrey, grasping each of their hands, and then they burst into tears. Mr. Aubrey felt his own fortitude grievously shaken as he entered the old Hall, no longer his *home*, and reflected, moreover—bitterest thought of all—that he had been declared by the law to have been hitherto the wrongful occupant of it; that he must forthwith proceed to "set his house in order," and prepare for a dreadful reckoning with him whom the law had declared to be the true owner of Yatton.

The formal result of the trial at York was, as has been already intimated, to declare Mr. Titmouse entitled to recover possession of only that insignificant portion of the estates held by Jacob Jolter; and that, too, only in the event of the first four days of the ensuing term elapsing without any successful attempt being made to impeach, before the court, the propriety of the verdict of the jury. It is a principle of our English law that the verdict of a jury is, in general, irreversible and conclusive; but, inasmuch as that verdict may have been improperly obtained—as, for instance, either through the misdirection of the judge, or his erroneous admission or rejection of evidence; or may have no force in point of law by reason of the pleadings of the party for whom it has been given, being insufficient to warrant the court to award its final judgment upon, and according to, such verdict, or by reason of the discovery of fresh evidence subsequently to the trial; therefore the law hath given the party who failed at the trial till the end of the first four days of the term next ensuing, to show the court why the verdict obtained by his opponent ought to go for nothing, and matters remain as they were before the trial, or a new trial be had. So anxious is our law to afford the utmost scope and opportunity for ascertaining what ought to be its decision, which, when obtained, is, as hath been said, solemnly and permanently conclusive upon the subject; such the effectual and practical corrective of any error or miscarriage in the working of that noble engine—trial by jury. Thus, then, it appears that the hands of Mr. Titmouse and his advisers were at all events stayed till the first four days of Easter term should have elapsed. During the considerable interval thus afforded to the advisers of Mr. Aubrey, his case, as it appeared upon the notes of his counsel on their briefs, with the indirect assistance and corroboration derived from the short-hand writers' notes, underwent repeated and most anxious examination in all its parts and bearings by all his legal advisers. It need hardly be said that every point in the case favorable to their client had been distinctly and fully raised by the Attorney-General, assisted by his very able juniors, Mr. Sterling and Mr. Crystal; and so was it with the counsel of Mr. Titmouse, as, indeed, the result showed. On subsequent examination, none of them could discover any false step, or any advantage which had been overlooked or taken inefficiently. Independently of various astute objections taken by the Attorney-General to the reception of several important portions of the plaintiff's evidence, the leading points relied on in favor of Mr. Aubrey were—the impropriety of Lord Widdrington's rejection of the deed of confirmation on account of the erasure in it; the effect of that deed, assuming the erasure not to have warranted its rejection, and several questions arising out of the doctrine of adverse possession, by which alone, it had been contended at the trial, that the claim of the descendants of Stephen Dreddlington had been peremptorily and finally barred. Two very long consultations had been held at the Attorney-General's chambers, attended by Mr. Sterling, Mr. Crystal, Mr. Mansfield, the three partners in the firm of Runnington and Company, Mr. Parkinson, and Mr. Aubrey —who had come up to town for the purpose alone. Greatly to the surprise of all of them, he stated most distinctly and emphatically that he insisted on no ground of objection being taken against his opponent, except such as was strictly just, equitable, honorable and conscientious. Rather than defeat him on mere technicalities—rather than avail himself of mere positive rules of law, while the RIGHT, as between man and man, was substantially in favor of his opponent—Mr. Aubrey declared, however absurd or Quixotic he might be thought, that he would—if he had them—lose fifty Yattons. *Fiat justitia ruat cælum.* "You mean to say, Aubrey," interrupted the Attorney-General, mildly, after listening for some time to his friend and client with evident interest, and admiration of his pure and high-minded character—"that it would be unconscientious of you to avail yourself of a fixed and beneficial rule of law, established upon considerations of general equity and utility, such, for instance, as that of adverse possession in order to retain possession, while—"

"Pray, Mr. Attorney-General, if I had lent you five hundred pounds seven or eight years ago, would you set up the *statute of limitations* against me when I asked for repayment?"

"Excuse me, Aubrey," replied the Attorney-General, with

a faint flush upon his handsome and dignified features; "but how idle all this is! One would imagine that we were sitting in a school of casuistry! What are we met for, in the name of common sense? For what, but to prevent the rightful owner of property from being deprived of it by a trumpery accidental erasure in one of his title-deeds, which time has deprived him of the means of accounting for?" He then, in a very kind way, but with a dash of peremptoriness, requested that the case might be left in their hands, and that they might be given credit for resorting to nothing that was inconsistent with the nicest and most fastidious sense of honor. This observation put an end to so unprecedented an interference; but if Mr. Aubrey supposed that it had any effect upon the Attorney-General, he was mistaken; for of course that learned and eminent person secretly resolved to avail himself of every conceivable means, great and small, available for overturning the verdict, and securing the Aubreys in the possession of Yatton. He at the same time earnestly endeavored to moderate the expectations of his client, declaring that he was by no means sanguine as to the issue; that Lord Widdrington's rulings at *Nisi Prius* were very formidable things—in fact, rarely assailable; and then, again, the senior puisne judge of the court —Mr. Justice Grayley—had been consulted by Lord Widdrington at the trial, and concurred with him in his principal ruling, now sought to be moved against. At the close of the second consultation, on the night of the first day in Easter term (the Attorney-General intending to move on the ensuing morning), after having finally gone over the case in all its bearings, and agreed upon the exact grounds of moving—the Attorney-General called back Mr. Runnington for a moment, as he was walking away with Mr. Aubrey, and whispered to him that it would be very proper to assume at once that the motion failed, and consider the best mode of negotiating concerning the surrender of the bulk of the property, and the payment of the mesne profits.

"Oh! Mr. Aubrey has quite made up his mind to the worst, Mr. Attorney-General."

"Ah, well!" replied the Attorney-General with a sigh; and about five minutes after Mr. Runnington's departure, the Attorney-General stepped into his carriage, which had been standing for the last hour opposite his chambers. He drove down to the House of Commons, where he almost immediately after delivered a long and luminous speech on one of the most important and intricate questions that had been discussed during the session. The first four days of term are an awkward interval

equally to incompetent counsel and incompetent judges—when
such there are. The slips of both then come to light; both
have to encounter the keen and vigilant scrutiny of a learned,
acute, and independent body—the English bar. If a judge
should happen to be in any degree unequal to the exigencies of
his important station—incompetent for the due discharge of
his difficult functions at *Nisi Prius*—what a store of anxiety
and mortifications accumulates at every circuit town against
the ensuing term, where his misrulings are distinctly and boldly brought under the notice of the full court and the assembled
bar! What must be his feelings as he becomes aware that all
interested in the matter look out for a *plentiful crop of new
trials* from the circuit which he has selected to favor with his
presence.   Great causes lost, verdicts set aside, and new trials
ordered, at an enormous, often a ruinous expense, entirely on
account of his inability to seize the true points and bearings of
a case, and present them properly to a jury, to apply accurately the principles of evidence! How exquisitely painful to suspect that as soon as the name is announced, the anxious attorneys withdraw records and postpone the trials of their chief
causes, in all directions trying no more than they can possibly
help, in the hope that a more competent judge will take the
circuit after! to become, every now and then, aware that counsel boldly speculate at the trial upon his inexperience and
ignorance by impudent experiments, in flagrant violation of
elementary principles!   And then for incompetent counsel—is
not his a similar position? Set to lead a cause, before a host
of keen rivals watching his every step with bitter scrutiny—
feeling himself entirely at sea; bewildered among details; forgetting his *points*, losing his presence of mind; with no fixed
principles of law to guide him; laid prostrate by a sudden objection, of which, when too late and the mischief is done and
irretrievable, he sees, or has explained to him the fallacy, and
absurdity, and even audacity; discovering from indignant
juniors, on sitting down, he has gone to the jury on quite the
wrong tack, and in effect thrown the cause away; and at
length he creeps into court of the first four days of term, to
endeavor to retrieve the false step he took at the trial; but in
vain, and he dare not look his attorney in the face, as he is
refused his rule! These and similar thoughts may perhaps, on
such occasions, be passing through the mind of a snarling sarcastic cynic, disappointed in his search for business, distanced
in the race for promotion, as he sees the bench occupied with
graceful dignity by men of acknowledged fitness chosen from
among the flower of the bar—those most qualified by experi-

ence, learning, intellect, and moral character. I would say to an inquirer, go now into any one of the superior courts of your country—to any court of *Nisi Prius* in the kingdom; and if you are able to observe and appreciate what you shall see, you will acknowledge that in no single instance has the precious trust of administering Justice been committed to unworthy or incompetent hands, whatever may have occasionally been the case in a former day. And in like manner may we rebuke our cynic, in respect of his disparaging estimate of the leading bar.

The spectacle presented by the court in banc, to a thoughtful observer, is interesting and imposing. Here, for instance, was the Court of King's Bench, presided over by Lord Widdrington, with three puisne judges—all men of powerful understandings, of great experience, and of deep and extensive legal knowledge. Observe the dignified calmness and patience with which counsel are listened to, verbose even and tiresome as occasionally they are; the judges not deranging their thoughts, or the order in which the argument has been, with much anxiety and care, prepared for them beforehand—by incessant suggestions of crude and hasty impressions—but suspending their judgment till fully possessed of the case brought before them by one whom his client has thought fit to intrust with the conduct of his case. They never interfere but in extreme cases, when the time of the court is being plainly wasted by loose irrelevant matter. Their demeanor is characterized by grave courtesy and forbearance; and their occasional interference is received by the bar with profound respect and anxious attention. Never is to be seen in any of our courts the startling spectacle of personal collision between judge and counsel—each endeavoring to rival the other in a perverse exhibition of acuteness and ingenuity. On the contrary, a thoughtful observer of what goes on in any of our courts will believe that our judges have deeply considered the truth of that saying of Seneca—*Nil sapientiæ odiosius* ACUMINE NIMIO; and modeled themselves after the great portraiture of the judicial office drawn by the most illustrious of philosophers.

"Patience and gravity of bearing are an essential part of justice; and an overspeaking judge is no well-tuned cymbal. Judges ought to be more learned than witty; more reverend than plausible; and more advised than confident. It is no grace to a judge first to find that which he might have heard in due time from the bar; or to show quickness of conceit, in cutting off evidence or counsel too short, or to prevent infor-

mation by questions, though pertinent."* Our English judges
are indeed worthy of the affection and reverence with which,
both in public and private, they are regarded; and if any one
will consider their severe and almost uninterrupted labors—
the toil and weight of responsibility they bear, equaled by that
of no other public functionaries—he will doubly appreciate the
courtesy and forbearance which are exhibited by them, and
forget any transient glimpses of asperity or impatience on the
part of men exhausted, frequently, by both bodily and mental
labor.

But I forgot that I had brought the reader into the
Court of King's Bench, where he has been standing all this
while, watching Lord Widdrington "go through the bar," as
it is termed; namely, calling on all the counsel present, in the
order of their seniority or position, to make any little motion,
of course, before proceeding with the principal business of the
day.   One learned gentleman moved, for instance, to discharge a fraudulent debtor out of custody, so that he might
start off for the Continent and avoid a debt of £3000, because,
in the copy of the writ, the word was "sheriff," and in the
writ itself "sheriffs;" and in this motion he succeeded, greatly to the astonishment of Mr. Aubrey.   But the court said,
that a "copy" *meant* a copy; and this was not a copy; where
was the line to be drawn?   Were they to have a contest on
every occasion of a party's carelessness as to the materiality,
or immateriality, of the variance it had occasioned?   So the
rule was made absolute, with costs.   Another scamp sought
to be discharged out of custody—or rather that his bail-bond
should be delivered up to be canceled, because his name
therein was called "Smyth," whereas in the writ it was
"Smythe;" but after his counsel had cited half a dozen cases,
the court thought that the maxim of *idem sonans* applied, and
discharged the rule.   Then half a dozen young gentlemen
moved for "*judgment as in case of a nonsuit*"—some of
them with real, most of them with affected self-possession and
nonchalance; another moved for an attachment against a party
for non-payment of costs, pursuant to the Master's *allocatur;*
and the last, in the very back row of all, in a husky voice, and
with a palpitating heart, rose to move for a "*rule to compute
principle and interest on a bill of exchange.*"   Then all the
bar had been gone through, in about half an hour's time; during which the Attorney-General had come into court and
arranged all his books and papers before him; Mr. Subtle sit-

---

* Lord BACON.   *Essays*—" *Of Judicature.*'

ting next to him with a slip of paper before him to take a note
of the grounds on which he moved.

"Does any other gentleman move?" inquired Lord Widdrington, looking over the court. He received no answer.

"Mr. Attorney-General," said he; and the Attorney-General rose—

"If your Lordship pleases," commenced the Attorney-General, slowly rising and bowing—"in a case of Doe on the Demise of Titmouse against Jolter, tried before your Lordship
at the last assizes for the county of York, I have humbly to
move your lordship for *a rule to show cause why a nonsuit
should not be entered, or why the verdict entered for the
plaintiff should not be set aside, and a New Trial had.*" He
proceeded to state the facts of the case, and what had taken
place at the trial, with great clearness and brevity. In like
manner—with perfect simplicity and precision—he stated the
various points arising upon the evidence, and the general
grounds of law which have been already specified; but I am so
grateful to the reader for his patience under the infliction of so
much legal detail as was contained in the last chapter of this
history, that I shall now content myself with the above general
statement of what took place before the court. As soon as he
had sat down, the court consulted together for a minute or
two; and then—

"You may take a rule to show cause, Mr. Attorney-General," said Lord Widdrington.

"On all the grounds I have mentioned, my Lord?"

"Yes—Mr. Solicitor-General, do you move?"

Up rose thereat the Solicitor-General.

"I shall discharge your rule," whispered Mr. Subtle to the
Attorney-General.

"I'm afraid you will," whispered the Attorney-General,
leaning his head close to Mr. Subtle, and with his hand before
his mouth. Then his clerk removed the battery of books
which stood before him, together with his brief; and taking
another out of his turgid red bag, the Attorney-General was
soon deep in the details of an important shipping case, in
which he was going to move when next it came to his turn.

Thus the court had granted a "RULE NISI," as it is called
(*i. e.* it commanded a particular thing to be done—"*unless*"
sufficient "*cause*" could be thereafter shown to the court why
it should not be done), for either entering a nonsuit, or having
a new trial. Now, had this rule been obtained in the present
day, at least two years must have elapsed, owing to the immense and perhaps unavoidable arrear of business, before the

other side could have been heard in answer to it; so, at least, it has been reported to me, in this green old solitude where I am writing, pleasantly recalling long-past scenes of the bustling professional life from which I am thankful for having been able, with a moderate competence, years ago to retire. Now, had such been the state of business at the time when the Rule in *Doe* d. *Titmouse* v. *Jolter* was moved for, see the practical effect of it; had Mr. Aubrey, instead of the high-minded and conscientious man he undoubtedly was, been a rogue, he might have had the opportunity of getting in twenty thousand pounds, and setting off with it to spend upon the Continent, as soon as he found that the court had decided against him; or, if the tenants should have been served with notice not to pay their rents to any one but Mr. Titmouse—at all events not to Mr. Aubrey—how was Mr. Aubrey and his family to have subsisted during this interval?—and with the possibility that, at the end of the two years, Mr. Aubrey might be declared to be the true owner of Yatton, and consequently all the while entitled to those rents, etc., the non-payment of which might have entailed upon him the most serious embarrassments. During the same interval, poor Mr. Titmouse, heart-sick with hope deferred, might have taken to liquor, as a solace under his misery, and drunk himself to death before the rule was discharged—or brought his valuable life to a more sudden and abrupt conclusion; which affecting event would have relieved the court from deciding several troublesome points of law, and kept the Aubreys in possession of the Yatton estates. If what I am informed of as to the accumulation of arrears in the Court of King's Bench in the present day,·in spite of the anxious and unprecedented exertions of its very able and active judges, be correct, I suspect that I shall not be believed when I inform the reader that within ten or twelve days after the rule *nisi* in the present case had been moved, "cause was shown" against it by Mr. Subtle and Mr. Lynx, and very admirably shown against it too. (Mr. Quicksilver, unfortunately for the interests of Mr. Titmouse, was absent, attending a great meeting in the City, called by himself, to establish a society for the Moral and Intellectual Regeneration of Mankind on the Basis of Pure Reason.) The Attorney-General exerted himself to the utmost in support of his rule. He felt that the court—though scarcely at all interfering during his address—was against him; yet he delivered, perhaps, one of the most masterly arguments that had ever been heard in the place where he was speaking. Mr. Sterling and Mr. Crystal, wisely avoiding the ground so admirably occupied by the Attorney-General, contented themselves with strengthening those positions which appeared to them less fortified by positive authority than the others; and then the court said they would take a day or two's time to consider: "less on account," said Lord Widdrington, "of the difficulty of the case, than the magnitude of the interests which would probably be affected by their decision."

"You have them dead with you, Subtle," whispered the Attorney-General, a slight expression of chagrin stealing over his features, as he heard the observation of Lord Widdrington.

"I never doubted it," replied Mr. Subtle, with a confident air. Every day afterward, from the sitting to the rising of the court, did the anxious Aubrey attend in the King's Bench, to hear the judgment of the court delivered. At length arrived the last day of the term. Soon after the sitting of the court, Lord Widdrington pronounced judgment in two or three cases; but not seeing the Attorney-General (who was engaged before the House of Lords) in his place, delayed giving judgment in the case of Doe and Jolter. About two o'clock he made his appearance; and shortly afterward, Lord Widdrington, after disposing of the matter then before the court, said—"There was a case of Doe on the demise of Titmouse against Jolter, in which, early in the term, a rule was obtained, calling upon the lessor of the plaintiff to show cause why"—and he proceeded to state the rule, and then to deliver the written unanimous judgment of the court. A clear and elaborate statement of the facts, out of which the questions submitted to the court had arisen, and of those questions themselves, was listened to by Mr. Aubrey in breathless suspense before he could obtain the faintest intimation of the judgment which the court was about to pronounce. Lord Widdrington went on to dispose, one by one, with painful deliberation and precision, of the seven points presented for the decision of the court. One or two questions they decided in favor of the defendant; but added that it had become unnecessary to do so, in consequence of the answers given by the witnesses to other questions, at the trial, and which disposed of the doubts arising on the former questions. The documentary evidence subsequently put in got rid of another difficulty in the early part of the plaintiff's case, and rendered immaterial a question put by the plaintiff's counsel, and strenuously objected to on the part of the defendant; which question the court was of opinion, as had been Lord Widdrington at the trial, ought not to have been allowed. Then, as to the question of ADVERSE POSSESSION, on which very great stress had been laid by the defendant's counsel, the court was of opinion that none existed; since there had been a *disability*—indeed a series of disabilities*—-through infancy, coverture, and absence beyond seas, of the various parties through whom the lessor of the plaintiff claimed.   Finally, as to the question concerning the ERASURE, the court was clearly of opinion that the deed in which it occurred had been properly rejected; inasmuch as the erasure occurred in a clearly material part of the deed, and there were no recitals in the deed by which it could be helped.   That it was clearly incumbent upon those proffering the deed in evidence to account for its altered appearance, although the deed was more than thirty years old, and rebut the presumption of fraud arising therefrom.   That the erasure was a clear badge of fraud! and to hold otherwise would be to open a wide door to frauds of the most extensive and serious description.   That there had been no evidence offered to show that the deed had ever been a valid deed; the very first step failed; and, in short, in its then state, it was in contemplation of law *no deed at all;* and, consequently, had been properly rejected.   "For all these reasons, therefore, we are clearly of opinion that the verdict ought not to be disturbed, and the rule will consequently be DIS-CHARGED."   As these last words were pronounced, a mist seemed for a moment to intervene between Mr. Aubrey and the objects around him; for his thoughts had reverted to Yatton and the precious objects of his affection who were there, in sickening suspense awaiting the event which had that moment taken place, as the words yet sounding in his excited ears seemed like the sentence of expulsion from Paradise passed upon our dismayed and heart-broken first parents. Yes, in that solemn region of matter-of-fact and commonplace —that *dead sea*, as far as feeling, sentiment, incident, or excitement is concerned, the Court of King's Bench—there sat a man of exquisite sensibility—pure and high-minded—whose feelings were for a while paralyzed by the words which had fallen from the judgment-seat, uttered with a cold, business-like, indifferent air—oh! how horridly out of concert with the anxious and excited tone of him whom, with his lovely family, they consigned, in fact, to destitution!   After remaining for about a quarter of an hour, during which brief interval he resumed the control over his feelings which he had so long and successfully struggled to maintain, he rose and quitted the

---

* If the reader will refer to p. 352 he may see how the *disabilities* here alluded to arose, and affected the case.

court. It was a heavy, lowering afternoon—one which seemed to harmonize with the gloomy and desolate mood in which he slowly walked homeward. He encountered many of his friends, on foot, on horseback, and in carriages, on their way down to the Houses of Parliament; the very sight of them, in the morbid state of his feelings, gave him a pang that was indescribable. With them matters were the same as they had ever been —as they had till then been with him—and as probably they would be with them to the end of their career; but he had been forced, suddenly and forever, to quit the scene of high excitement—he heaved many heavy sighs, as he exchanged nod after nod with those he met, as he approached Charing Cross. There he encountered Lord C——, the brilliant Foreign Secretary, arm in arm with two eloquent and leading members of the Government—all of them evidently in high spirits, on their way down to the House.

"Ah!—Aubrey!—In town!—An age since we met!" exclaimed they, in a breath, shaking him cordially by the hand. —"You know, of course, that the budget comes on to-night —eh?"

"I assure you," said Lord C——, "our friends will do us great service—very essential service, by being early in their attendance!—You know that Mr. Quicksilver intends to come out against us to-night in great force?—My dear Aubrey, you are going the wrong way."

"I am not going down to the House to-night."

"Not going down?—Eh?—My dear Aubrey, you astonish me!—Have you paired off! You can't think how I lament your absence!"

"I am returning to Yorkshire almost immediately."

"But surely you can come for an hour or so to-night—eh? Come! Don't let a trifle stand in the way."

"I would *not* let a trifle stand in the way," replied Mr. Aubrey, in a tone and manner that at once arrested the attention of them whom he was addressing, and suddenly reminded them of what, in their political eagerness, they had for a moment lost sight of—namely, the perilous position of his private affairs.

"My dear Aubrey, I beg a thousand pardons for intruding such matters upon you," said Lord C——, with sudden earnestness; "but shall we have an opportunity of meeting before you leave town?"

"I fear—*not*—I set off by the mail to-morrow evening— and have in the meantime much to attend to," said Mr. Aubrey, unable to repress a sigh—and they parted. But for a

determination not to yield to a morbid sensibility, he would
have got into a hackney-coach, and so have avoided the
"troops of friends," the hosts of "old familiar faces," all
wending down to the scene in which he had begun so eminently to distinguish himself—but from which he seemed now to
be forever excluded. He therefore pursued his way on foot.
One of those on whom his troubled eye lighted was a well-
known figure on horseback—the great Duke of ——, on his
way down to the House of Lords, going very slowly, his head
inclined on one side, his iron-cast features overspread with an
expression of stern thoughtfulness. He did not observe Mr.
Aubrey—in fact, he seemed too much absorbed with his own
thoughts to observe or recognize anybody; yet he now and then
mechanically raised his finger to his hat, in acknowledgment
of the obeisances of those whom he met. Poor Aubrey sighed,
and felt as if circumstances had placed him at an immeasurable
distance from him whom, so lately, he had entertained familiarly at dinner; that there seemed suddenly to have arisen, as
it were, a great and impassable gulf between them.

On reaching his house in Grosvenor Street his heart fluttered
while he knocked and rang; and he seemed to shrink from the
accustomed obsequious voice and manner of the powdered
menial who admitted him. Having ordered a slight dinner,
he repaired to his library. The only letter which had arrived
since he had left in the morning, bore the Grilston postmark,
and was in the handwriting of Mrs. Aubrey. He opened it
with trembling eagerness. It was crossed—the dear familiar
handwriting!—from beginning to end, and full of heart-
subduing tenderness. Then it had a little inclosure, with a
strange, straggling superscription, "To my Papa;" and on
opening it he read, in similar characters—

"My dear Papa, I love you very, very much. Do come
home. Mamma sends her love. Your dutiful son,
                                    "CHARLES AUBREY.
     "P.S. Agnes sends her love; she can not write because she
is so little. Please to come home directly,
                                    "CHARLES A., Yatton."

Aubrey saw how it was—that Mrs. Aubrey had either
affected to write in her little son's name, or had actually
guided his pen. On the outside she had written in pencil—

"Charles says he hopes that you will answer his letter
directly."

Aubrey's lip quivered, and his eyes filled with tears. Putting the letters into his bosom, he rose and walked to and fro, with feelings which can not be described. The evening was very gloomy; it poured with rain incessantly. He was the only person in that spacious and elegant house, except the servants left in charge of it; and dreary and desolate enough it felt. He was but its nominal owner—their nominal master! In order to save the post he sat down to write home—(*home!* his heart sunk within him at the thought)—and informed Mrs. Aubrey and his sister of the event for which his previous letters had prepared them; adding that he should set off for Yatton by the mail of the ensuing night, and that he was perfectly well. He also wrote a line or two, in large printed characters, by way of answer to his little correspondent, his son, toward whom how his heart yearned! and having dispatched his packet, probably the last he should ever frank, he partook of a hasty and slight dinner, and then resigned himself to deep meditation upon his critical circumstances. He was perfectly aware of his precise position, in point of law, namely, that he was safe in the possession of the Yatton property (with the exception of the trifle which was occupied by Jolter, and had been the object of the action just determined) till another action should have been brought, directly seeking its recovery, and that by forcing his opponent to bring such action, he might put him to considerable risk of retaining his verdict, and thereby greatly harass him, and ward off, indefinitely, the evil day from himself. By these means he might secure them, possibly, also, favorable terms for the payment of the dreadful arrear of mesne profits, in which he stood indebted to his successor. To this effect he had received several intimations from as upright and conscientious an adviser, Mr. Runnington, as was to be found in the profession. But Mr. Aubrey had decided upon his course; he had taken his ground, and intended to maintain it. However sudden and unlooked for had been the claim set up against him, it had been deliberately and solemnly confirmed by the law of the land; and he had no idea but of yielding to a prompt and hearty obedience. He resolved, therefore, to waste no time—to fritter away no energy in feeble dalliance with trouble; but to face her boldly, and comply with all her exactions. He would, on the morrow, instruct Mr. Runnington to write to his opponent's solicitors, informing them that within three weeks' time the estates at Yatton would be delivered up to their client, Mr. Titmouse. He would also direct his own private solicitor to arrange for the quickest possible disposal of his house in Grosvenor Street.

and his wines and his furniture, both there and at Yatton.
He resolved, moreover, on the morrow, to take the necessary
steps for vacating his seat in Parliament, by applying for the
Stewardship of the Chiltern Hundreds; and having determined
on these arrangements, consequent upon the adverse decision
of the Court of King's Bench of that day, he felt the momentary relief and satisfaction of the seaman who has prepared his
vessel for the approaching storm from a dreadful pressure.

He felt, indeed, relieved for a while.

"And what, now, have I really to complain of?" said he to
himself; "why murmur presumptuously and vainly against
the dispensations of Providence?   I thank God that I am still
able to recognize His hand in what has befallen me, and to believe that *He hath done all things well;* that prosperity and
adversity are equally, from Him, means of accomplishing His
all-wise purposes!   Is it for *me,* poor insect! to question the
goodness, the wisdom, or the justice of my Maker?   I thank
God for the firm belief that I have that He *governs the world
in righteousness,* and that He has declared that He will protect
and bless them who sincerely endeavor to discover, and conform to, His will concerning them.   He it was that placed me
in my late condition of prosperity and eminence: why should
I fret, when He sees fit gently to remove me from it, and place
me in a different sphere of exertion and suffering?   If the
dark heathen could spend a life in endeavoring to steel his
heart against the sense of suffering, and to look with cheerless
indifference upon the vicissitudes of life, shall I, a Christian,
shrink with impatience and terror from the first glimpse of
adversity?   Even at the worst, how favored is my situation in
comparison of that of millions of my fellow-creatures?   Shall
I not lessen my own sufferings by the contemplation of those
which the Almighty has thought fit to inflict upon my brethren?   What if I and those whom I love were the subjects of
direful disease—of vice—of dishonor?   What if I were the object of a just and universal contempt, given up to a reprobate
mind; miserable here, and without hope hereafter?   Here
have I health, a loving family—have had the inestimable advantages of education, and even now, in the imminent approach of danger, am enabled to preserve, in some measure,
a composure of feelings, a resolution which will support me
and those who are dearer to me than life."   Here his heart
beat quickly, and he walked rapidly to and fro.   "I am confident that Providence will care for them!   As for me, even in
sight of the more serious and startling peril that menaces me—
what is it to a Christian but a trial of his constancy?   *There*

hath no temptation taken you, say the Scriptures written for our instruction, *but such as is common to man ;* but God is faithful, who will not suffer to be tempted above what ye are able, but will with the temptation, also make a way to escape that ye may be able to bear it."* This consolatory passage led Aubrey in a calm and exalted mood of mind to meditate upon that picture of submission to manifold misfortune, simple and sublime beyond all comparison or approach, drawn by the pencil of one inspired with wisdom from on high—calculated at once to solemnize, to strengthen, and elevate the heart and character of man; and which is to be found in the first and second chapters of the *Book of Job.* Oh, reader! who, brilliant as may be at this moment thy position in life, may have been heretofore, or may be hereafter, placed in circumstances of dreadful suffering and peril, suffer him whose humble labors now for a moment occupy thy attention, reverently to refer thee again and yet again to that memorable passage of Holy Writ! With danger surrounding him, with utter ruin staring him in the face, Mr. Aubrey read this glorious passage; his shaken spirit gathered from it calmness and consolation, and, retiring early to bed, he enjoyed a night of tranquil undisturbed repose.

" They are determined not to let the grass grow underneath their feet, Mr. Aubrey," said Mr. Runnington, who, the next morning, made his appearance at breakfast, pursuant to appointment; " within two hours' time of the court delivering judgment, yesterday afternoon, I received the following communication." He handed to Mr. Aubrey this letter:—

" *Saffron Hill,* 25*th April,* 18—.

" GENTLEMEN,

" *Doe* d. *Titmouse* v. *Jolter.*

" The rule for a new trial herein having been this day discharged, and the unanimous judgment of the court delivered in favor of the claims to the Yatton estate of the lessor of the plaintiff in the present action, 'we shall feel obliged by an intimation from you, at your earliest possible convenience, of the course which your client may now think fit to adopt. You are, of course, aware that we are now in a situation to attack,

---

* " (Ανθρωπινος) " signifies in this place (1st Corinth. x. 13), says a great commentator on this memorable passage of Scripture, " such as is suited to the nature and circumstances of man; such as every man may reasonably expect, if he considers the nature of his body and soul, and his situation in the present world."

successfully, the entire property at Yatton, at present in the possession of Mr. Aubrey; and that, had we thought fit, we might have sought and recovered it all in the action which has just been decided in favor of our client. It is now in our power materially to strengthen the evidence adduced at the late trial; and we beg to be informed whether it is your client's intention to put Mr. Titmouse to the enormous expense and the delay of a second trial, the issue of which can not be doubtful; or, with the promptitude and candor which are to be expected from a gentleman of the station and character of your client, at once yield to our client the substantial fruits of his verdict.

"If his reasonable wishes in this matter be disregarded, we would merely intimate that it will be for your client most seriously to weigh the consequences; to see whether such a line of conduct may not greatly prejudice his interests, and place him in a far worse position than perhaps he would otherwise have occupied. As we understand your client to be in town, we trust you will forgive us for requesting you immediately to communicate with him, and at your earliest convenience enable us to announce the result to our client. We are, gentlemen, your obedient servants,

"QUIRK, GAMMON & SNAP.

"Messrs. RUNNINGTON & CO."

"Well—I own I see nothing to find fault with in this letter," said Mr. Aubrey, calmly, but with a suppressed sigh, as soon as he had read the letter.

"Rather quick work, too—is it not, Mr. Aubrey?—within an hour or two after judgment pronounced in their favor:—but, to be sure, it's very excusable, when you consider the line of business and the sort of clients that Messrs. Quirk, Gammon and Snap are accustomed to."

"I have made up my mind as to the course I shall adopt," said Mr. Aubrey.

"Oh, of course, that is quite clear!" said Mr. Runnington, pouring out his coffee—" we shall stand another shot, and see if there's ammunition enough left for the purpose: and we'll tender a bill of exceptions, and carry the case into the Exchequer Chamber, and thence into the House of Lords—ah! we'll *work* them, I warrant them!"—and he rubbed his hands, with a little excitement in his manner.

"Why, Mr. Runnington," answered Mr. Aubrey, gravely, "would it not be wanton—most unconscientious in me to put them to the expense and anxiety of a second trial, when the whole case, on both sides, has been fairly brought before both the court and the jury?''

"Good Heavens, Mr. Aubrey! who ever heard of an estate of ten thousand a year being surrendered after one assault?''

"If it were ten thousand times ten thousand a year I would submit, after such a trial as ours.''

"How do we know what fraud and perjury may have been resorted to in order to secure the late verdict, and which we may have the means of exploding against the next trial! Ah, Mr. Aubrey, you don't know the character of Messrs. Quirk, Gammon and Snap in the profession; they learn a fresh trick from every scoundrel, swindler, and thief whose case they undertake.''

"I thought that fraud and perjury were never to be presumed, Mr. Runnington! Besides, had we not the advantage of most acute and experienced counsel? How could it escape them ?''

"I would only venture to remind you,'' said Mr. Runnington, firmly but respectfully, "of the observations of the Attorney-General at our last consultation.''

"I thought I was unanswered, Mr. Runnington, though I did not feel at liberty to press the matter,'' replied Mr. Aubrey, with a melancholy smile.

"Excuse me, but we *must* take the chance of second trial,'' said Mr. Runnington.

"I have decided upon the course I shall adopt,'' replied Mr. Aubrey, calmly and determinedly—"I shall instruct you to write this day to the gentlemen upon the other side, and inform them that within three weeks I shall be prepared to deliver up possession of Yatton.''

"My dear sir!—Do I hear aright? Deliver up possession of the estates? and within three weeks?''

"That was what I said, Mr. Runnington,'' replied Mr. Aubrey, rather peremptorily.

"I give you my honor, Mr. Aubrey, that in the whole course of my practice I never heard of such a procedure.''

"And I shall further request you to state that the last quarter's rents are in my banker's hands, and will be paid over to the order of Mr. Titmouse.''

"Good gracious, Mr. Aubrey!'' interrupted Mr. Runnington, with an air of deep concern.

"I have well considered the position in which I am placed,'' said Mr. Aubrey, with a serious air.

"It is very painful for me to mention the subject, Mr Aubrey; but have you adverted to the *mesne* profits?''

"I have. It is, indeed, a very fearful matter; and I frank ly own that I see no way open before me but to trust to the forbearance of—"

"Forbearance!—The *forbearance* of Messrs. Quirk, Gammon and Snap!! or of any one counseled by them!"

"Why, what can I do? I might as well undertake to pay off the national debt as the sum of sixty thousand pounds."

"That's just the very thing," replied Mr. Runnington, with a dismayed air.

"Whatever honorable negotiation you can effect, I leave it in your hands to do. With reference to the time that may be obtained for the liquidation of it"—Mr. Aubrey changed color, but spoke with firmness—"I must own that this is a matter that has occasioned me inexpressible anxiety, Mr. Runnington. I really do not see what length of time will enable me to discharge so fearful a sum of money, or even to make any sensible impression upon it. I am quite at their mercy."

Here both maintained a silence of several minutes' duration.

"I am far from thinking it clear that equity would not interpose to relieve against *mesne* profits, in such a case as the present—a dormant claim set up."

"I can not see, Mr. Runnington, on what principle such an interference could be supported."

"No more do I, at present," replied Mr. Runnington, "but I'll lose no time in having the best advice on the subject. Gracious me! when one thinks of it, it deprives one of—" at this moment a thundering appeal to the knocker of the door announced an arrival: and presently the servant entered and stated that Lord C—— had called, and was waiting in the library. After repeating two or three directions to Mr. Runnington, Mr. Aubrey begged to be excused, and presently entered the library, where Lord C—— was waiting to receive him. Lord C—— was a middle-aged man, tall, of elegant person, a strikingly handsome countenance, and most winning address; he was a thorough politician, possessed of eloquence, immense practical knowledge, and a very commanding intellect. He was made for eminent office, and got through the most complicated and harassing business with singular ease and celerity. He had for several years entertained a sincere regard for Mr. Aubrey, whom he considered to be a very rising man in the House of Commons, and who had on several occasions rendered him special service in debate. He had been much shocked to hear of the sudden misfortune which had befallen Mr. Aubrey; and had now come to him with a sincere desire to be of service to him: and also, not without a faint hope of prevailing upon him to come down that evening and support them in a very close division. He was as kind-hearted a man as a keen politician could be.

"I am really shocked beyond expression to hear all this," said he after Aubrey had, at his earnest request, explained the position in which he was placed; the dreadful loss he had sustained, the still more dreadful liabilities to which he was subject. "Really who can be safe? It might have happened to me—to any of us? Forgive me, my dear Aubrey," continued Lord C——, earnestly, "if I venture to express a hope that at all events Mrs. Aubrey and your family are provided for, and your very lovely sister; she, I trust, is out of the reach of inconvenience?" Mr. Aubrey's lip quivered, and he remained silent.

"Allow me a friend's freedom, Aubrey, and let me repeat my question; are your family provided for?"

"I will be frank, Lord C——," replied Mr. Aubrey, with a strong effort to preserve his composure. "The little that was made for them goes with Yatton; but for them—my wife, my children, my sister—I could have submitted to this misfortune with unshrinking fortitude; but they are, alas, involved in my ruin! My wife had nothing when I married her; and of course the settlements I made on her were out of the Yatton property; as also was the little income left my sister by my father. With Yatton all is gone—that is the plain fact; and there is no disguising it."

Lord C—— seemed much moved.

"The Duke of ——, I, and two or three other of your friends, were talking about these matters last night; we wish we could serve you. What is the sort of foreign service you would prefer, Aubrey?"

"*Foreign* service," echoed Mr. Aubrey, significantly.

"Yes; an entire change of scene would be highly serviceable in diverting your thoughts from the distressing subjects which here occupy them, and must continue to occupy them for some time to come."

"It is very kindly meant, Lord C——; but do you really think I can for a single moment entertain the idea of quitting the country to escape from pecuniary liability?"

"That's the point exactly; I decidedly think you ought to do so; that you *must*," replied Lord C——, in a matter-of-fact manner.

"Nothing upon earth shall induce me to do so," replied Mr. Aubrey, firmly. "The bare idea shocks me. It would be the meanest, most unprincipled conduct—it would reflect disgrace on the King's service."

"Poh—this is mere eccentricity—knight-errantry; I'm sure that when you are in a calmer mood you will think differently. Upon my honor, I never heard of such a thing in my life. Are you to stay at home, to have your hands tied behind your back, and be thrust into prison—to court destruction for yourself and your family?" Mr. Aubrey turned aside his head, and remained silent.

"I must plead in favor of Mrs. Aubrey—your children—your sweet lovely sister;—good God! it's quite shocking to think of what you are bringing them to."

"You torture my feelings, Lord C——," said Mr. Aubrey, tremulously and very pale; "but you do not convince my judgment. Every dictate of conscience and honor combines to assure me that I should not listen to your proposal."

"Good God! what an outrage on common sense!—But has anything been yet said on the subject of these liabilities—these *mesne* profits, as I suppose they are called?"

"Nothing; but they follow as a matter of course."

"How is it that you owe *only* sixty thousand pounds, Aubrey?"

"*Only* sixty thousand!"

"At the rate of ten thousand a year you must have had at least a hundred thousand pounds of the money belonging to your successor—"

"The statute of limitations prevents more than six years' arrears being recoverable."

"But do you intend, Aubrey, to avail yourself of such a protection against the just claims of this poor, unfortunate, ill-used gentleman? Are not the remaining forty thousand pounds justly due—money of his which you have been making away with? Will you let a mere technical rule of law outweigh the dictates of honor and conscience?"

"I really don't exactly understand your drift, Lord C——," said Mr. Aubrey, coloring visibly and rapidly.

"Your sovereign has a right to command your services; and, by obeying him and serving your country, you are enabled to prevent a malignant opponent from ruining you and your family by extorting a vast sum of money not equitably due; I protest I see no difference in principle, Aubrey, between availing yourself of the statute of limitations, and of the call of the king to foreign service;—but we must talk of this again. By the way, what is the name of your worthy opponent? Tittlemouse, or some such strange name?"

"Titmouse!—By the way, you lose a seat for Yatton," said Aubrey, with a faint smile.

Lord C—— pricked up his ears. "Ay, ay! how's that?"

"The gentleman you have named professes, I understand, Liberal principles; probably he will sit for the borough himself; at all events, he will return the member."

"He's a poor ignorant creature, isn't he? What has made him take up with Liberal principles? By taking a little notice of him early, one might—eh?—influence him;—but—of course you don't intend to vacate this session?"

"I intend this day to apply for the Chiltern Hundreds; and this evening, if you like, a new writ may be moved for the borough of Yatton."

"You *must* come down to-night, my dear Aubrey, you really must," said Lord C——, with undisguised anxiety—with more than he had shown during the interview. "The numbers will run very close; they are stirring heaven and earth—good heavens! my dear Aubrey, a vote's invaluable to-night;—gad, you sha'n't have the Chiltern Hundreds; you mustn't really apply for it—at all events, not till to-morrow."

"I shall sit no more in the House of Commons," said Mr. Aubrey, with a sad, determined air; "besides, I leave for Yatton by to-night's mail. There are those waiting for me whom you would not have me disappoint, Lord C——!"

"Not for worlds, my dear Aubrey," replied Lord C——, half absently; he was intensely disappointed at not obtaining Mr. Aubrey's vote that evening, and rose to go.

"Then I direct to Yatton, when I have occasion to write to you?" said he.

"For the next three weeks only. My movements after that period are not yet fixed."

"Adieu, Aubrey; and I entreat of you to remember me most sincerely to Mrs. Aubrey and your sister; and when you look at them, *remember*—remember our conversation of to-day."

With this Lord C—— took his departure, and left poor Aubrey much depressed. He quickly, however, roused himself, and occupied the principal part of the day making the necessary and melancholy arrangements for breaking up his establishment in Grosvenor Street, and for disposing of his wines, books, and furniture at Yatton. He also instructed a house agent to look out for two or three respectable but small houses in the outskirts of town, out of which they might choose the one which should appear most suitable to himself and Mrs.

Aubrey, on their arrival in London. About eight o'clock he got into the York mail, and his heart was heavy within him.

CHAPTER XVI.

THE result of a very long consultation between Mr. Runnington and his partners, held on the day after his last interview with Mr. Aubrey, was, that he drew up the following draft of a letter, addressed to Messrs. Quirk, Gammon and Snap:

"*Lincoln's Inn, 26th April, 18—.*

"GENTLEMEN:

"*Doe* d. *Titmouse* v. *Jolter.*

"In answer to your letter of yesterday (the 25th inst.), we beg to inform you that after the judgment in this cause pronounced yesterday in the Court of King's Bench, our client, Mr. Aubrey, does not intend to resist the claim of Mr. Titmouse to the residue of the Yatton property. We now, therefore, beg to give you notice that on the 17th of next month you will be at liberty, on behalf of your client, Mr. Titmouse, to take possession of all the property at Yatton at present in the possession of Mr. Aubrey. The whole of the last quarter's rents, due at Lady-day, have been paid into the bank of Messrs. Harley, at Grilston, and will, on the 17th of May, be placed at the disposal of your client.

"We are also instructed to request the delivery of your bill at as early a period as may suit your convenience, with a view to its immediate examination and settlement.

"We can not forbear adding, while thus implicitly following the instructions of our client, our very great surprise and regret at the course which he has thought fit to adopt; since we have the strongest reasons for believing that had he been disposed to contest your client's claim further, in accordance with advice received from a high quarter, his case would have been materially strengthened, and your difficulties greatly increased. We feel confident that the magnanimity displayed by our client will be duly appreciated by yours.

"We are, Gentlemen, Your obedient servants,

"RUNNINGTON & Co.

"Messrs. QUIRK, GAMMON & SNAP."

"Really," said Mr. Runnington, when he had read over the above to his partners, "I *must* throw in a word or two about those infernal mesne profits—yet it's a very ticklish subject, especially with such people as these."

One partner shook his head, and the other looked very thoughtful.

"We must not compromise Mr. Aubrey," said the former.

"We have had no instructions on that point," said the latter—"on the contrary, you told us yourself that your instructions were to announce an unconditional surrender."

"That may be; but in so desperate a business as this, I do think we have a discretion to exercise on behalf of himself and family, which, I must say, he seems quite incapable of exercising himself. Nay, upon my honor, I think we are bound not to forego the slightest opportunity of securing an advantage for our client."

His partners seemed struck with his observation; and Mr. Runnington, after a few moments' consideration, added the following postscript—

"P.S.—As to the *mesne profits*, by the way, of course we anticipate no difficulty in effecting an amicable arrangement satisfactory to both parties, due consideration being had for the critical position in which our client finds himself so suddenly and unexpectedly placed. Indeed it is not difficult to conceive that Mr. Aubrey, in taking the step of which we have above advised you, must have contemplated—" (here Mr. Runnington paused for a considerable time) "being met in a similar frank, liberal and equitable spirit."

It was agreed at length that the whole amount and effect of the above postscript ought to be regarded as a spontaneous suggestion of Messrs. Runnington's, not in any way implicating, or calculated in any event to annoy, Mr. Aubrey; and a fair copy of the letter and postscript having been made, it was signed by the head of the firm, and forthwith dispatched to Saffron Hill.

"Struck, by Jove, Gammon!" exclaimed Mr. Quirk, as with the above letter open in his hands, he hurried, the instant that he had read it, into the room of his wily partner, and put the letter into his hands. Gammon read it with apparent calmness, but a slight flush overspread his cheek; and, as he finished the perusal, a subdued smile of excitement and triumph stole over his countenance.

"Lord, Gammon! isn't it glorious?" quoth Mr. Quirk, heatedly, rubbing his hands together; "give us your hand, Gammon! We've fought a precious hard battle together"— and he shook his partner's hand with vehement cordiality. "This fellow Aubrey is a trump—isn't he?—Egad, if I'd been in his shoes—one way or another, I'd have stuck at Yatton for a dozen years to come—ah, ha!"

"Yes, I am sure you would if you had been able," replied Gammon, dryly, and with a smile.

"Ay, that I would," replied Mr. Quirk, with a triumphant chuckle; "but now to come to business. By next quarter-day Titmouse will have £5,000 in hard cash—half of it on the 17th of next month.—Lord! what have we done for him!" he added, with a sort of sigh.

"We've put an ape into possession of Paradise—that's all!" —said Gammon, absently and half aloud, and bitterly and contemptuously.

"By the way, Gammon, you see what's said about our Bill —eh? The sooner it's made out the better, I should say— and—ahem! hem!—while Mr. Aubrey's on the tight-rope he won't think of looking down at the particular items, will he? I should say, now's our time, and strike while the iron's hot! I've got *rather* a stiff entry, I can assure you. I must say, Snap's done his duty, and *I've* not had my eyes shut—ahem!" here Mr. Quirk winked very knowingly.

"You must not *overdo* it, Mr. Quirk—but all that I leave, as usual, to your admirable management as to that of a first-rate man of business. You know I'm a sad hand at accounts; but you and Snap are—you'll do all that should be done."

"Ay, ay—trust us!" interrupted Quirk, quickly, with a significant nod, and fancying himself and Snap already at work, plundering the poor Aubreys. "And, by the way, Gammon, there are the mesne profits—that's a mighty fine postscript of theirs, isn't it?" and, replacing his spectacles, he read over the postscript aloud. "All my eye, of course!" he added, as he laid down the letter—"but I suppose one must give 'em a little time; it *is* a little hard on him just at present; but then, to be sure, that's *his* lookout—not ours or Titmouse's. Off-hand, I should say we ought to be content with —say—twenty thousand down, and the rest in two years' time, so as to give him time to look about him a little—"

"That will be quite an after consideration," said Mr. Gammon, who, for the last few minutes, had appeared lost in thought.

"Egad—an *after* consideration? Hang me if *I* think so, Gammon! There's a certain *bond*—eh? you recollect—"

"I assure you, Mr. Quirk, that my eye is fixed quite as steadily and anxiously on that point as yours," said Gammon, gravely.

"Thank you—thank you, Gammon!" replied Quirk, with

rather a relieved air—" it couldn't possibly be in better hands.
Lud—to go wrong *there!* It would send me to my grave at
a hand gallop—it would, so help me Heaven, Gammon!—Titmouse is a queer hand to deal with, isn't he? Wasn't he
strange and bumptious the other day? Egad, it made me
quake! Need we tell him just yet," he dropped his voice,
" of the letter we've got! Couldn't we safely say only they
have sent us word that we shall have Yatton by the 17th?"

" Very great caution is necessary, Mr. Quirk, just now—"

" You *don't* think the young scamp's going to turn round
on us, and snap his fingers in our face, eh?" inquired Mr.
Quirk, apprehensively, violently twirling about his watch-key.

" If you leave him implicitly to me you shall get all you
want," replied Gammon, very gravely and very pointedly.
Quirk's color changed a little, as he felt the keen gray eye of
Gammon fixed upon him, and he involuntarily shrunk under it.

" You'll excuse me, Gammon," at length said he, with
rather a disturbed air; " but there's no fathoming you, when
you get into one of your mysterious humors; and you always
look so particularly strange whenever you get on this subject!
What can you know that I don't—or ought not?"

" Nothing—nothing, I assure you," replied Gammon, with
a gay smile.

" Well, I should have *thought* not. But coming back to
the main point, if one could but *touch* some part of that same
ten thousand pounds, I *should* be a happy man!—Consider,
Gammon, what a draught there has been on my purse for this
last sixteen months."

" Well, can you doubt being soon richly repaid, my dear
sir? Only don't be too hasty."

" I take it, Gammon, we've a lien on the rents in the
banker's hands, and to become due next quarter-day, and on
the first installment of the mesne profits, both for our bill of
costs, and in respect of that same bond?"

" Mesne profits, Mr. Quirk?" echoed Gammon, rather
quickly; " you seem to take it for granted that they are all
ready to be paid over! Even supposing Titmouse not to grow
restive, do you suppose it probable that Mr. Aubrey, after so
vast and sudden a sacrifice, can have more than a very few
thousands—probably hundreds—to keep him from immediate
want, since we have reason to believe he has got no other resources than Yatton?"

" Not got 'em—not got 'em? D—n him! then he must
look sharp and *get* 'em, that's all! You know we can't be
trifled with; we must look after the interests of—Titmouse.

And what's he to start with, if there's no mesne profits forthcoming? But, hang it! they must: I should say, a gentle
pressure, by and by, as soon as he's fairly out of Yatton, must
produce money, or *security*—he must know quantities of people of rank and substance that would rush forward, if they
once heard him squeal—"

"Ah, you're for putting the thumb-screws on at once—
eh?" inquired Gammon, with subdued energy, and a very
strange sort of smile.

"Ay—capital—that's *just* what I meant"—quoth Quirk.

"Heartless old scoundrel!" thought Gammon, almost expressing as much; but his momentary excitement passed off
unobserved by Mr. Quirk. "And, I must say, I agree with
you," he added; "we ought in justice to see you first reimbursed your very heavy outlays, Mr. Quirk."

"Well, that's honorable, Gammon.—Oh, Gammon, how I
wish you would let me make a friend of you!" suddenly added
Mr. Quirk, eying wistfully his surprised companion.

"If you have one sincere disinterested friend in the world,
Mr. Quirk, he is to be found in Oily Gammon," said that
gentleman, throwing great warmth into his manner, perceiving that Mr. Quirk was laboring with some communication of
which he wished to deliver himself.

"Gammon, Gammon, how I *wish* I could think so!" replied Quirk, looking earnestly, yet half distrustingly, at Gammon, and fumbling about his hands in his pockets. The mild
and friendly expression of Gammon's countenance, however,
invited communicativeness; and after softly opening and shutting the two doors, to ascertain that no one was trying to over-
hear what might be passing, he returned to his chair, which
he drew closer to Gammon, who noticed this air of preparation
with not a little curiosity.

"I may be wrong, Gammon," commenced Mr. Quirk, in a
low tone; "but I do believe you've always felt a kind of personal friendship toward me, and there ought to be no secrets
among friends. *Friends*, indeed? Perhaps its premature to
mention so small a matter; but at a certain silversmith's, not
a thousand miles from the Strand, there's at this moment in
hand, as a present from me to you—" [Oh, dear, dear! Mr.
Quirk! what a shocking untruth! and at your advanced period
of life, too!]—"as elegant a gold snuff-box as can be made,
with a small inscription on the lid. I hope you won't value it
the less for its being the gift of the old Caleb Quirk—" he
paused, and looked earnestly at Mr. Gammon.

"My dear Mr. Quirk, you have taken me," said he apparently with great emotion, "quite by surprise. "Value it? I will preserve it to the latest moment of my life, as a memorial of one whom the more I know of, the more I respect and admire!"

"You, Gammon, are in your prime—scarce even that—but I am growing old—" tears appeared to glisten in the old gentleman's eyes; Gammon, much moved, shook him cordially by the hand in silence, wondering what upon earth was coming next. "Yes;—old Caleb Quirk's day is drawing to a close—I feel it, Gammon, I feel it! But I shall leave behind me—a—a—child—an only daughter, Gammon;" that gentleman gazed at the speaker with an expression of respectful sympathy;—"Dora! I don't think you can have known Dora so long, Gammon, without feeling a *leetle* interest in her!" Here Gammon's color mounted rapidly, and he looked with feelings of a novel description at his senior partner. Could it be possible that old Quirk wished to bring about a match between his daughter and Gammon? His thoughts were for a moment confused. All he could do was to bow with an earnest—an anxious—a deprecating air; and Mr. Quirk, rather hurriedly, proceeded—"and when I assure you, Gammon, that it is in your power to make an old friend and his only daughter happy and proud"—Gammon began to draw very long breaths, and to look more and more apprehensively at his senior partner—"in short, my dear friend Gammon, let me out with it at once—my daughter's in love with Titmouse."

["Whew!" thought Gammon, suddenly and infinitely relieved.]

"Ah, my dear Mr. Quirk, is that all?" he exclaimed, and shook Mr. Quirk cordially by the hand—"at length you have made a friend of me, indeed. But, to tell you the truth, I have long suspected as much; I have, indeed!"

"Have you really? Well, there *is* no accounting for tastes, is there—especially among the women? Poor Dora's over head and ears—quite!—she is, so help me Heaven!" continued Quirk, energetically.

"Well, my dear sir, and why this surprise?" said Gammon, earnestly. "I consider Titmouse to be a very handsome young fellow; and that he is already rapidly acquiring very gentlemanly manners; and as to his *fortune*—really, it would be most desirable to bring it about. Indeed, the sooner his heart's fixed and his word's pledged the better—for you must of course be aware that there will be many schemers on the lookout to entrap his frank and inexperienced nature—look, for instance, at Tag-rag."

"Eugh!" exclaimed Mr. Quirk, with a sudden motion of sickening disgust—"the old beast!—I smoked him long ago! Now, *that* I call villainy, Gammon; infernal villainy! Don't you?"

"Indeed, indeed, Mr. Quirk, I do; I quite agree with you! Upon my honor, I think it is a part of even *my* duty toward our client, if possible, to protect him against such infamous designs."

"Right—right, Gammon; by Jove, you're quite right—I *quite* agree with you!" replied Quirk, earnestly, not observing the lambent smile upon the features of his calm, crafty, and sarcastic companion.

"You see," said Gammon, "we've a very delicate and difficult game to play with old Tag-rag. He's certainly a toad, ugly and venomous—but then he's got a jewel in his head—he's got money, you know, and, to serve *our* purposes, we must really give him some hopes about his daughter and Titmouse."

"Faugh! eugh! feugh! Nasty wretch! a little trollop! It makes one sick to hear of her! And by the way, now we're on that subject, Gammon, what do we want of this wretch Tag-rag, now that Titmouse has actually got the property?"

"Want of him? Money—security, my dear sir!—money!"

"But, curse me! (excuse me, Gammon) why go to Tag-rag? *That's* what I can't understand! Surely any one will advance almost any amount of money to Titmouse, with such security as he can give."

"Very possibly—probably—"

"Possibly? Why, I myself don't mind advancing him five thousand—nay, ten thousand pounds—when we've once got hold of the title-deeds."

"My dear sir," interrupted Gammon, calmly, but with a very serious air, and a slight change of color which did not happen to attract the notice of his eager companion, "there are reasons why I should dissuade you from doing so; upon my word, there are; further than that I do not think it necessary to go; but I have gone far enough, I know well, to do you real service."

Mr. Quirk listened to all this with an air of the utmost amazement—even open-mouthed amazement. "What reason, Gammon, *can* there be against my advancing money on a security worth more than a hundred times the sum borrowed?" he inquired, with visible distrust, of his companion.

"I can but assure you, that were I called upon to say whether I would advance a serious sum of money to Titmouse,

on the security of the Yatton estates, I should at all events require a more substantial *collateral* security."

"Mystery again!" exclaimed Mr. Quirk, a sigh of vexation
escaping him. "You'll excuse me, Gammon, but you'd
puzzle an angel, to say nothing of the devil! May I presume
for one moment, so far on our personal and professional relationship, as to ask what the reason is on which your advice
rests?"

"Mere caution—excessive caution—anxiety to place you out
of the way of all risk. Surely, is your borrower so soon to be
pronounced firm in the saddle?"

"If you know anything, Gammon, that I don't, it's your
bounden duty to communicate it. *Look at our articles!*"

"It is; *but do I* know anything? Prove that, Mr. Quirk,
and you need trouble yourself no more. But, in the meanwhile (without saying how much I feel hurt at your evident
distrust), I have but a word or two further to add on this
point."

When Mr. Gammon chose he could assume an expression of
feature, a tone of voice, and a manner which indicated to the
person he was addressing that he was announcing a matured
opinion, an inflexible determination—and this, moreover, in
the calmest, quietest way imaginable. Thus it was that he
now said to Mr. Quirk, "My opinion is, that you should get
some third party or parties to advance any required sum, and
prevail upon Tag-rag to join in a collateral security, without—
if possible—making him aware of the extent of liability he is
incurring. By exciting him with the ridiculous notion of an
attachment between his daughter and Titmouse, he may be
induced to give his signature, as to some complimentary
matter of form only. Now, that's my opinion, Mr. Quirk;
not lightly or hastily formed; and it rests upon a deep feeling
of personal regard toward you, and also our common interests."

Mr. Quirk had listened to this comunication in perturbed
silence, eying the speaker with a ludicrous expression of mingled chagrin, apprehension, and bewilderment. "Gammon,"
at length said he, affecting a smile, "do you remember when
you and I, and Dora, went to the play to see some German
thing or other—Foss was the name, wasn't it?"

"Faust—Faust," interrupted Gammon, curiously.

"Well; and now, what was the name of that fellow that
was always—Meth—Meph—what was it?"

"Mephistopheles," replied Gammon, unable to repress a
smile.

"Ah—yes! so it was.   That's all; I only wanted to think
of the name—I'd forgotten it.   I beg your pardon, Gammon."

This was poor Mr. Quirk's way of being very sarcastic with
his friend.   He thought that he had now cut him to the very
quick.

"If it hadn't been for what's passed between us to-day,
Gammon, I should almost begin to think that you were not
sincere in your friendship—"

"Did I ever deceive you?   Did I ever attempt to overreach
you in anything, Mr. Quirk?"

"N—o—o—," replied Mr. Quirk—but not in the readiest
manner, or most confident tone in the world—"I certainly
can't say I ever found you out—but I'll tell you what, we each
keep a precious sharp lookout after each other, too—don't
we?" he inquired, with a faint smile, which seemed for a moment reflected upon the face of Gammon.

"How long," said he, "I am to be the subject of such unkind suspicions, I do not know; but your nature is suspicious;
and as every one has his fault, that is the alloy in the otherwise pure gold of your manly, kind and straightforward
character.   Time may show how you have wronged me.   My
anxious wish is, Mr. Quirk, to see your daughter occupy a
position in which we may all be proud to see her."   Here a
smile shot across Quirk's anxious countenance, like evening
sunshine on troubled waters.

"I do really believe, Gammon," said he, eagerly, "that
Dora's just the kind of girl to suit Titmouse—"

"So, indeed, my dear sir, do I.   There's a mingled softness
and spirit in Miss Quirk—"

"She's a good girl, a good girl, Gammon!   I hope he'll use
her well if he gets her."   His voice trembled.   "She's got
very much attached to him!   Gad, she's quite altered lately;
and my sister tells me that she's always playing dismal music
when he's not there.   But we can talk over these matters at
another time.   Gad, Gammon, you can't think how it's relieved me to open my mind to you on this matter!   We quite
understand one another now, Gammon—eh?"

"Quite," replied Gammon, pointedly; and Mr. Quirk having quitted the room, the former prepared to answer Messrs.
Runnington's letter.   But first he leaned back, and reflected
on several points of their late conversation.   Of course he had
resolved that Miss Quirk should never become Mrs. Titmouse.
And what struck him as not a little singular was this, viz., that
Mr. Quirk should have made no observation on the circumstance that Gammon allowed him to risk his daughter and her

all upon chances which he pronounced too frail to warrant advancing a thousand or two of money! Yet so it was.

This was the answer he presently wrote to the letter of Messrs. Runnington:—

" Saffron Hill.

" GENTLEMEN :
" *Doe* d. *Titmouse* v. *Jolter.*

" We are favored with your letter of this day's date, and beg to assure you how very highly we appreciate the prompt and honorable course which has been taken by your client, under circumstances calculated to excite the greatest possible commiseration. Every expression of respectful sympathy, on our parts, and on that of our client, Mr. Titmouse, which you may think fit to convey to your distinguished client is his.

" We shall be prepared to receive possession of the Yatton estates on the day you mention—namely, the 17th May next, on behalf of our client, Mr. Titmouse; on whose behalf, also, we beg to thank you for your communication concerning the last quarter's rents.

" With reference to the question of the mesne profits, we can not doubt that your client will promptly pursue the same line of honorable conduct which he has hitherto adopted, and sincerely trust that a good understanding in this matter will speedily exist between our respective clients.

" As you have intimated a wish upon the subject, we beg to inform you that we have given instructions for making out and delivering our bill herein.

" We are, Gentlemen,
" Your humble servants,
" QUIRK, GAMMON & SNAP.

" Messrs. RUNNINGTON & Co."

Having finished writing the above letter, Gammon sat back in his chair, with folded arms, and entered upon a long train of thought—revolving many matters which were worthy of the profound consideration they then received.

When Gammon and Titmouse returned to town from York they were fortunate in having the inside of the coach to themselves for nearly the whole of the way—an opportunity which Gammon improved to the utmost, by deepening the impression he had already made in the mind of Titmouse of the truth of one great fact—namely, that he and his fortunes would quickly part company if Gammon should at any time so will—which never would, however, come to pass, so long as Titmouse recognized and deferred to the authority of Gammon in all things. In vain did Titmouse inquire how this could be. Gammon was impenetrable, mysterious, authoritative; and at length enjoined Titmouse to absolute secrecy concerning the existence of the fact in question, on pain of the infliction of those consequences to which I have already alluded. Gammon assured him that there were many plans and plots hatching against him (Titmouse); but that it was in his (Gammon's) power to protect him from them all. Gammon particularly enjoined him, moreover, to consult the feelings and attend to the suggestions of Mr. Quirk, wherein Mr. Gammon did not intimate to the contrary, and wound up all by telling him that, as he, Gammon, was the only person on earth—and this he really believed to be the case, as the reader may hereafter see—who knew the exact position of Titmouse, so he had devoted himself for his life to the advancing and securing the interests of Titmouse.

For about a fortnight after their return, Titmouse, at Gammon's instance, continued at his former lodgings; but at length complained so earnestly of their dismal quietude, and of their being out of the way of " *life*," that Gammon yielded to his wishes, and, together with Mr. Quirk, consented to his removing to a central spot—in fact, to the CABBAGE-STALK HOTEL, Covent Garden—a queer enough name, to be sure; but it was the family name of a great wholesale green-grocer, who owned most of the property thereabouts. It was not without considerable uneasiness and anxiety that Messrs. Quirk and Snap beheld this change effected, apprehensive that it might have the effect of estranging Titmouse from them; but since Gammon assented to it, they had nothing for it but to acquiesce, considering Titmouse's proximity to his splendid independence. They resolved, however, as far as in each of them lay, not to let themselves be forgotten by Titmouse. Pending the rule for the new trial, Mr. Quirk was so confident concerning the issue that he greatly increased the allowance of Titmouse; to an extent, indeed, which admitted of his entering into almost all the gayeties that his as yet scarce initiated heart could desire. In the first place, he constantly added to his wardrobe. Then he took lessons every other day in "the noble art of self-defense," which gave him an opportunity of forming with great ease at once an extensive and brilliant circle of acquaintance. Fencing-rooms, wrestling-rooms, shooting-galleries, places for pigeon-shooting, cock-fighting, dog-fighting, and billiard-rooms; the water and boat-racing—these were the dazzling scenes which occupied the chief portion of each day. Then, in the evenings, there were theaters, great and small, the various taverns, and other places of nocturnal resort, which are the secret pride and glory of the metropolis. In addition to this, at an advanced period of the night, or rather a very early hour in the morning, he sedulously strove to perfect himself in those higher arts and accomplishments, excelled in by one or two of the more eminent of the youthful aristocracy, viz., breaking windows, pulling bells, wrenching off knockers, extinguishing lamps, tripping up old women, watchmen and children, and spoiling their clothes;—ah, how often in his humbler days had his heart panted in noble rivalry of such feats as these, and emulation of the notoriety they earned for the glittering miscreants who excelled in them! Ah, Titmouse, Titmouse! Now is your time! *Macte norâ virtute, puer !*

That he could long frequent such scenes as these without forming an extensive and varied acquaintance would be a very unlikely thing to suppose; and there was one who would fain have joined him in his new adventures—one who, as I have already intimated, had initiated him into the scenes with which he was now becoming so familiar; I mean Snap, who had been at once his

" Guide, philosopher, and friend;"

but who now had fewer and fewer opportunities of associating with him, inasmuch as his (Snap's) nose was continually " kept at the grindstone " in Saffron Hill, to compensate for the lack of attention to the business of the office of his senior partners, owing to their incessant occupation with the affairs of Titmouse. Still, however, he now and then contrived to remind Titmouse of his (Snap's) existence, by sending him intimations of interesting trials at the Old Bailey and elsewhere, and securing him a good seat to view both the criminal and the spectators—often persons of the greatest rank, fashion and beauty; for it so happens that in this country, the more hideous the crime the more intense the curiosity of the upper classes of both sexes to witness the miscreant perpetrator; the more disgusting the details, the greater the avidity with which they are listened to by the distinguished auditors—the reason being plain, that, as they have exhausted the pleasures and excitements afforded by their own sphere, their palled and sated appetites require novel and more powerful stimulants. Hence, at length, we see " fashionables " peopling even the condemned cell—rushing, in excited groups, after the shuddering malefactor, staggering, half palsied, and with horror-laden

eye, on his way to the gallows! As soon as Old Quirk had obtained an inkling of Titmouse's taste in these matters he
afforded Titmouse many opportunities of gratifying it. Once
or twice the old gentleman succeeded even in enabling Titmouse (severe trial, however, for his exquisite sensibilities!) to
shake the cold and pinioned hands of wretches within a few
minutes' time of being led out for execution!

This is a brief and general account of the way in which Titmouse passed his time and laid the groundwork of that solid,
extensive, and practical acquaintance with men and things,
which was requisite to enable him to occupy with dignity and
advantage the splendid station to which he was on the point
of being elevated.

But let us not lose sight of our early and interesting friends,
the Tag-rags—a thing which both Quirk and Gammon resolved should not happen to Titmouse; for, on the very first
Sunday after his arrival in town from York, a handsome glass
coach might have been seen, about two o'clock in the afternoon, drawing up opposite to the gates of Satin Lodge; from
which said coach, the door having been opened, presently
descended Messrs. Quirk, Gammon and Titmouse. Now, the
Tag-rags always dined at about two o'clock on Sundays, and
on the present occasion Mr., Mrs., and Miss Tag-rag, together
with a pretty constant visitor, the Reverend Dismal Horror,
were sitting at their dinner-table discussing as nice a savory leg
of roast pork, with apple sauce, as could at once have tempted
and satisfied the most fastidious and the most indiscriminating
appetite.

"Oh, ma!" exclaimed Miss Tag-rag, faintly, changing color
as she caught sight, through the blinds, of the approaching
visitors—"if there isn't Mr. Titmouse!" and almost dropping
on the table her plate, in which, with an air of tender gallantry, Mr. Horror was in the act of depositing some greens, she
flew out of the room, darted upstairs, and in a trice was standing, with beating heart, before her glass, hastily twirling her
ringlets round her trembling fingers, and making one or two
slight alterations in her dress. Her papa and mamma started
up at the same moment, hastily wiping their mouths on the
corners of the table-cloth; and, after a hurried apology to
their reverend guest, whom they begged "to go on eating till
they came back"—they bounced into the drawing-room, just
time enough to appear as if they had been seated for some
time; but they were both rather red in the face and flustered
in their manner. Yet how abortive was their attempt to disguise the disgraceful fact of their having been at dinner when

their distinguished visitors arrived. For, firstly, the house was redolent of the odors of roast pork, sage and onion-stuffing, and greens; secondly, the red-faced servant-girl was peering round the corner of the kitchen stairs, as if watching an opportunity to whip off a small dinner.tray that stood be-tween the dining-room and drawing-room; and thirdly, they caught a glimpse of the countenance of the reverend young guest, who was holding open the dining-room door just wide enough to enable him to see who passed on to the drawing-room; for, in truth, the name which had escaped from the lips of Miss Tag-rag was one that always excited unpleasant feelings in the breast of her spiritual friend.

"Ah! Mr. and Mrs. Tag-rag! 'Pon my soul—glad to see you—and—hope you're all well?" commenced Titmouse, with an air of easy confidence and grace. Mr. Gammon calmly introduced himself and Mr. Quirk.

"We were just going to sit down to—*lunch*," said Mr. Tag-rag, hurriedly.

"You won't take a little, will you, gentlemen?" inquired Mrs. Tag-rag, faintly; and both the worthy couple felt infinite relief on being assured that their distinguished visitors had al-ready lunched. Neither Mr. nor Mrs. Tag-rag could take their eyes off Mr. Titmouse, whose easy nonchalance convinced them that he must have been keeping the society of lords. He was just inquiring—as he ran his hand through his hair, and gently smacked his slight ebony cane against his leg—after Miss Tag-rag, when, pale and agitated, and holding in her hand a pocket-handkerchief, which she had first suffused with musk and bergamot, designed to overcome so much of the vulgar odor of dinner as might be lingering about *her*—that interesting young lady entered. Titmouse rose and re-ceived her in a familiar, forward manner, she turning white and red by turns. She looked such a shriveled little ugly for-mal creature that Titmouse conceived quite a hatred of her, through recollecting that he had once thought such an inferior piece of goods superfine. Old Quirk and Tag-rag, every now and then, cast distrustful glances at each other; but Gammon kept all in a calm flow of small-talk, which at length restored those whom they had come to see to something like self-pos-session. As for Mr. Quirk, the more he looked at Miss Tag-rag, the more pride and satisfaction he felt in reflecting upon the unfavorable contrast she must present, in Titmouse's eyes, to Miss Quirk. After a little further conversation, principally concerning the brilliant success of Titmouse, Mr. Quirk came to the business of the day, and invited Mr., Mrs. and Miss

Tag-rag to dinner at Alibi House, on the ensuing Sunday, at six o'clock—apologizing for the absence of Miss Quirk, on the score of indisposition—she being at the time in the highest possible state of health. Mrs. Tag-rag was on the point of saying something deprecatory of their dining out on Sunday, as contrary to their rule; but a sudden recollection of the earthly interests she might peril by so doing, aided by a fearfully significant glance from Mr. Tag-rag, restrained her. The invitation was, therefore, accepted in a very obsequious manner; and soon afterward their great visitors took their departure, leaving Mr. and Mrs. and Miss Tag-rag in a state of considerable excitement. Goodness! could there be a doubt that there must be some very potent attraction at Satin Lodge to bring thither Titmouse, after all that had occurred? And where could reside the point of that attraction, but in Miss Tag-rag?

As soon as their visitors' glass coach had driven off—its inmates laughing heartily at the people they had just quitted—Mr., Mrs., and Miss Tag-rag returned to the dining-table, like suddenly disturbed fowl returning to their roost when the disturbance had ceased. Profuse were their apologies to Mr. Horror; not aware, however, that he had improved the opportunity afforded by their absence to recruit his exhausted energies with a couple of glasses of port wine from a decanter which stood on the sideboard—a circumstance which he did not deem important enough to mention. Vehemently suspecting, as he did, what was the state of things with reference to Mr. Titmouse and Miss Tag-rag, it was somewhat of a trial of temper to the exemplary young pastor to have to listen, for the remainder of the afternoon, to the praises of Titmouse and speculations concerning the immensity of his fortune—matters, indeed (in his pious estimation), *of the earth, earthy.* In vain did the worthy minister strive, now and then, to divert the current of conversation into a more profitable channel—*i. e.,* toward himself; all he said was evidently lost upon her for whose ear it was intended. She was in a reverie, and often sighed. The principal figures before her mind's eye were—TITTLEBAT TITMOUSE, ESQUIRE, and THE REV. DISMAL HORROR. The latter was about twenty-six (he had been called to the work of the ministry in his sixteenth year); short; his face slightly pitted with small-pox; his forehead narrow; his eyes cold and watery; no eyebrows or whiskers; high cheek-bones; his short dark hair combed primly forward over each temple, and twisted into a sort of topknot in front; he wore no shirt-collars, but had a white neck-handkerchief tied very formally, and was dressed in an ill-made suit of black. He spoke in a drawling, canting tone; and his countenance was overspread with a demure expression of—CUNNING, *trying to look religious.* Then he was always talking about himself, and the devil, and his chapel, and the bottomless pit, and the number of souls which he had saved, and the number of those whom he knew were damned, and many more who certainly would be damned, and other matters of that sort, intrusted—it would seem—to his confidential keeping. All this might be very well in its way, began to think Miss Tag-rag—but it was possible to choke a dog with pudding. Poor girl, can you wonder at her dwelling fondly upon the image of Titmouse? So splendidly dressed—so handsome—such a fashionable air— and with—ten thousand a year? When she put all these things together, it almost looked like a dream; such good fortune could never be in store for a poor simple girl like herself. Yet there was such a thing as—love at first sight! After tea they all walked down to Mr. Horror's meeting-house. It was very crowded; and it was remarked that the eloquent young preacher had never delivered a more impassioned sermon from that pulpit; it was sublime. Oh, how bitterly he denounced " worldly-mindedness!" What a vivid picture he drew of the flourishing green bay-tree of the wicked, suddenly blasted in the moment of its pride and strength; while the righteous should shine like stars in the firmament forever and ever! Who can not see here shadowed out the characters of Titmouse and of Horror respectively?—who hesitate between the two? And when at length, the sermon over, he sat down in his pulpit (the congregation also sitting and singing, which had a somewhat queer effect), and drew gracefully across his damp forehead his white pocket-handkerchief, which had been given him by Miss Tag-rag, and looked with an air of most interesting languor and exhaustion toward Mr. Tag-rag's pew, where sat that young lamb of his flock—Miss Tag-rag—her father the wealthiest man in the congregation, and she his only child —he felt a most lively and tender interest in her welfare—her spiritual welfare, and resolved to call the next morning; entertaining an humble hope of finding that his zealous labors had not been in vain! Was one fruit of them to have been looked for in the benignant temper which Tag-rag, to the amazement of his shopmen, evinced the next morning, for at least an hour? Would that the like good effects had been visible in Mrs. and Miss Tag-rag; but—alas that I should have to record it!—it was so far otherwise that they laid aside some fancy-fair work on which Mr. Horror had set them—for the whole week, which they devoted to the preparation of those

8—Part II

dresses with which they purposed the profanation of the ensu
ing Sunday.

That day at length arrived, and precisely at six o'clock a
genteel fly deposited the visitants from Satin Lodge at the
splendid entrance to Alibi House.   There was the big footman
—shoulder-knot, red breeches, and all.   Tag-rag felt a *little*
nervous.   Before they had entered the gates, the fond proud
parents had kissed their trembling daughter, and entreated her
" to keep her spirits up!"   The exhortation was needful; for
when she saw the sort of style that awaited them she became
not a little agitated.   When she entered the hall—ah! on a
chair lay a glossy new hat and a delicate ebony walking-stick;
so he had come—was then upstairs!—Miss Tag-rag trembled
in every limb.

" I don't know, my dear," whispered Mrs. Tag-rag to her
husband, with a subdued sigh, as they followed the splendid
footman upstairs— " It may be all uncommon grand; but
somehow I'm afraid we're doing wrong—It's the Lord's Day
—see if any good comes of it."

" Tut—hold your tongue!   Let's have no nonsense," sternly whispered Mr. Tag-rag to his submissive wife.

" Your name, sir?" quoth the footman, in a gentlemanly
way.

" Mr., Mrs., and Miss Tag-rag," replied Mr. Tag-rag, after
clearing his throat; and so they were announced, Miss Quirk
coming forward to receive the ladies with the most charming
affability.   There stood Titmouse, in an easy attitude, with his
hands stuck into his coat pockets and resting on his hips in
a very delicate and elegant fashion.   How completely he
seemed at his ease!

" Oh Lord!" thought Tag-rag, " that's the young fellow I
used to go on so to!"

In due time dinner was announced; and who can describe
the rapture that thrilled through the bosoms of the three Tag-
rags when Mr. Quirk requested Mr. Titmouse to take down—
Miss Tag-rag!!   Her father took down Mrs. Alias; Mr. Quirk,
Mrs. Tag-rag, and Gammon, Miss Quirk.   She really might
have been proud of her partner.   Gammon was about thirty-
six years old; above the average height; with a particularly
gentlemanly appearance and address, and an intellectual and
even handsome countenance, though occasionally it wore, to a
keen observer, a sinister expression.   He wore a blue coat, a
plain white waistcoat (not disfigured by any glistening fiddle-
faddle of pins, chains, or quizzing-glasses), black trousers, and
silk stockings.   There was at once an appearance of neatness

and carelessness; and there was such a ready smile—such bland ease and self-possession about him—as communicated itself to those whom he addressed. I hardly know, Mr. Gammon, why I have thus noticed so particularly your outward appearance; it certainly, on the occasion I am describing, struck me much; but there are such things as *whited walls* and *painted sepulchers*. Dinner went off very pleasantly, the wines soon communicating a little confidence to the flustered guests. Mrs. Tag-rag had drunk so much champagne—an unusual beverage for her—that almost as soon as she had returned to the drawing-room she sat down on the sofa and fell asleep, leaving the two young ladies to amuse each other as best they might; for Mrs. Alias was very deaf, and moreover very stiff and distant, and sat looking at them in silence. To return to the dining-room for a moment. 'Twas quite delightful to see the sort of friendship that seemed to grow up between Quirk and Tag-rag, as their heads got filled with wine; at the same time each of them drawing closer and closer to Titmouse, who sat between them—volubility itself. They soon dropped all disguise—each plainly under the impression that the other could not, or did not, observe him; and at length, impelled by their overmastering motives, they became so barefaced in their sycophancy —evidently forgetting that Gammon was present—that he could several times, with only the utmost difficulty, refrain from bursting into laughter at the earnest devotion with which these two worshipers of the little golden calf strove to attract the attention of their divinity and recommend themselves to its favor.

At length the four gentlemen repaired to the drawing-room, whence issued the sounds of music; and on entering they beheld the two lovely performers seated at the piano, engaged upon a duet. The plump, flaxen-haired Miss Quirk, in her flowing white muslin dress, her thick gold chain and massive bracelets, formed rather a strong contrast to her sallow, skinny little companion, in a span-new slate-colored silk dress, with staring scarlet sash; her long corkscrew ringlets glistening in bear's grease; and as for their performance, Miss Quirk played boldly and well through her part, a smile of contempt now and then beaming over her countenance at the ridiculous incapacity of her companion. As soon as the gentlemen made their appearance the ladies ceased and withdrew from the piano; Miss Tag-rag, with a sweet air of simplicity and conscious embarrassment, gliding toward the sofa, where sat her mamma asleep, but whom she at once awoke. Mr. Quirk exclaimed, as, evidently elevated with wine, he slapped his daughter on

her fat back, "Ah, Dora, my dove!" while Tag-rag kissed
his daughter's cheek, and squeezed her hand, and then glanced
with a proud and delighted air at Titmouse, who was lolling
at full length upon the other sofa, picking his teeth.   While
Miss Quirk was making tea, Gammon gayly conversing with
her, and in an under-tone satirizing Miss Tag-rag, the latter
young lady was gazing, with a timid air, at the various elegant
knickknacks scattered upon the tables and slabs. One of these
consisted of a pretty little box, about a foot square, with a glass
lid, through which she saw the contents; and they not a little
surprised her.   They were pieces of cord; and on looking at
one of the sides of the box, she read, with a sudden shudder
—" *With these cords were tied the hands of Arthur Grizzlegut, executed for high treason, 1st May, 18—. Presented, as a
mark of respect, to Caleb Quirk, Esq., by John Ketch.*" Poor
Miss Tag-rag recoiled from the box as if she had seen it filled
with writhing adders.   She took at an early opportunity, however, of calling her father's attention to it; and he pronounced
it a " most *interesting* object," and fetched Mrs. Tag-rag to
see it.   She agreed first with her daughter and then with her
husband.   Quietly pushing her investigations, Miss Tag-rag
by and by beheld a large and splendidly bound volume—in
fact, Miss Quirk's album; and, after turning over most of the
leaves, and glancing over the " poetical effusions " and " prose
sentiments " which few fools can abstain from depositing upon
the embossed pages, when solicited by the lovely proprietresses
of such works, behold—her heart fluttered—poor Miss Tag-rag
almost dropped the magnificent volume; for there was the
idolized name of Mr. Titmouse—no doubt his own handwriting
and composition.   She read it over eagerly again and again—

> " Tittlebat Titmouse Is My name,
> England is My Nation,
> London Is My dwelling-Place,
> And Christ Is My Salvation."

It was very—very beautiful—beautiful in its simplicity! She
looked anxiously about for writing implements! but not seeing
any, was at length obliged to trust to her memory: on which,
indeed, the exquisite composition was already inscribed in indelible characters.   Miss Quirk, who was watching her motions, guessed the true cause of her excitement, and a smile of
mingled scorn and pity for her infatuated delusion shone upon
her face; in which, however, there appeared a little anxiety
when she beheld Titmouse—not, however, perceiving that he
did so in consequence of a motion from Gammon, whose eye

governed his movements as a man's those of his spaniel—walk up to her, and converse with a great appearance of interest. At length Mr. Tag-rag's "carriage" was announced. Mr. Quirk gave his arm to Mrs. Tag-rag, and Mr. Titmouse to the daughter, who endeavored, as she went down the stairs, to direct melting glances at her handsome and distinguished companion. They evidently *told*, for she could not be mistaken; he certainly once or twice squeezed her arm—and the last fond words he uttered to her were, "'Pon my soul—it's early; devilish sorry you're going!" As the Tag-rags drove home, they were all loud in the praises of those whom they had just quitted, particularly of those whose splendid hospitality they had been enjoying. With a daughter, with whom Mr. Quirk must naturally have wished to make so splendid a match as that with Titmouse—but who was plainly engaged to Mr. Gammon—how kind and disinterested was Mr. Quirk, in affording every encouragement in his power to the passion which Titmouse had so manifestly conceived for Miss Tag-rag! And was there ever so delightful a person as Gammon? How cordially he had shaken the hands of each of them at parting! As for Miss Tag-rag, she almost felt that if her heart had not been so deeply engaged to Titmouse, she could have loved Mr. Gammon!

"I hope, Tabby," said Mr. Tag-rag, "that when you're Mrs. Titmouse, you'll bring your dear husband to hear Mr. Horror? You know we ought to be grateful to the Lord—for He has done it."

"La, ma, how can I tell?" quoth Miss Tag-rag, petulantly. "I must go where Mr. Titmouse chooses, of course; and no doubt he'll take sittings in one of the West End churches; you know, *you* go where pa goes—*I* go where Titmouse goes! But I *will* come sometimes, too—if it's only to show that I'm not above it, you know. La, what a stir there will be! The three Miss Knipps—I do so hope they'll be there! I'll have your pew, ma, lined with red velvet; it will look so genteel."

"I'm not quite so sure, Tabby, though," interrupted her father with a certain swell of manner, "that we shall, after a certain event, continue to live in these parts. There's such a thing as retiring from business, Tabby; besides, we shall naturally wish to be near you."

"He's a *love* of a man, pa, isn't he?" interrupted Miss Tag-rag with irrepressible excitement. Her father folded her in his arms. They could hardly believe that they had reached Satin Lodge. That respectable structure, somehow or other, now looked to the eyes of all of them shrunk into most con-

temptible dimensions. What was it to the spacious and splendid residence which they had quitted? And what, in all
probability, could that be to the mansion—or perhaps several
mansions—to which Mr. Titmouse would be presently entitled,
and—in his right—some one else?

CHAPTER XVII.

WHILST the brilliant success of Tittlebat Titmouse was exciting so great a sensation amongst the inmates of Satin Lodge
and Alibi House, there were also certain quarters in the upper
regions of society in which it produced a considerable com-
motion, and where it was contemplated with feelings of intense
interest; nor without reason. For indeed to you, reflective
reader, much pondering men and manners, and observing the
influence of great wealth, especially suddenly and unexpectedly acquired, upon all classes of mankind—it would appear
passing strange that so prodigious an event as that of an accession to a fortune of ten thousand a year, and a large accumulation of money besides, could be looked on with indifference
in those regions where MONEY

" Is like the air they breathe—if they have it not they die;"

in whose absence, all their "honor, love, obedience, troops of
friends," disappear like snow under sunshine; the edifice of
pomp, luxury, and magnificence that "rose like an exhala-
tion," so disappears—

" And, like an unsubstantial pageant faded,
Leaves not rack behind."

Take away money, and that which raised its delicate and pam-
pered possessors above the common condition of mankind—
that of privation and incessant labor and anxiety—into one entirely artificial, engendering totally new wants and desires, is
gone, all gone; and its occupants suddenly fall, as it were,
through a highly rarefied atmosphere, breathless and dismayed, into contact with the chilling exigencies of life, of
which till then they had only heard and read, sometimes with
a kind of morbid sympathy, as we hear and read of a foreign
country, not stirring the while from our snug homes, by whose
comfortable and luxurious firesides we read of the frightful
palsying cold of the polar regions, and for a moment sigh over
and shudder at the condition of their miserable inhabitants, as
vividly pictured to us by adventurous travelers.
If the reader had reverently cast his eye over the pages of

that glittering center of aristocratic literature, and inexhausti-
ble solace against the ennui of a wet day—I mean *Debrett's
Peerage*, his attention could not have failed to be riveted,
amongst a galaxy of brilliant but minor stars, by the radiance
of one transcendant constellation.

Behold; hush; tremble!

" AUGUSTUS MORTIMER PLANTAGENET FITZ-URSE EARL OF
DREDDLINGTON, VISCOUNT FITZ-URSE, AND BARON DREL-
INCOURT; KNIGHT OF THE GOLDEN FLEECE; G.C.B.,
D.C.L., F.C.S., F.P.S., etc., etc., etc.; Lieutenant-Genèral
in the army, Colonel of the 37th Regiment of light dragoons;
Lord Lieutenant of ——shire; elder brother of the Trinity
House; formerly Lord Steward of the Household; born the
31st March, 17—; succeeded his father, PERCY CONSTANTINE
FITZ-URSE, as fifth Earl, and twentieth in the Barony, Janu-
ary 10th, 17—; married, April 1, 17—, the Right Hon. Lady
Philippa Emmeline Blanche Macspleuchan, daughter of
Archibald, ninth Duke of Tantallon, K.T., and has issue, an
only child,
" CECILIA PHILIPPA LEOPOLDINA PLANTAGENET, born
June 10, 17—.
" Town residence, Grosvenor Square.
" Seats, Gruneaghoolaghan Castle, Galway; Tre-ardevora-
veor Manor, Cornwall; Llmryllwcrwpllglly Abbey, N. Wales;
Tullyclachanach Palace, N. Britain; Poppleton Hall, Hert-
fordshire.
" Earldom, by patent, 1667; — Barony, by writ of sum-
mons, 12th Hen. II. "

Now, as to the above tremendous list of seats and residences,
be it observed that the existence of two of them, viz., Grosvenor Square and Poppleton Hall was tolerably well ascertained by the residence of the august proprietor of them, and
the expenditure therein of his princely revenue of £5,000 a
year. The existence of the remaining ones, however, the
names of which the diligent chronicler has preserved with such
scrupulous accuracy, had become somewhat problematical since
the era of the civil wars, and the physical derangement of the
surface of the earth in those parts, which one may conceive to
have taken place* consequent upon those events; those imposing feudal residences having been originally erected in positions so carefully selected, with a view to their security against

* See Dr. Bubble's " Account of the late Landslips, and of the remains of Subterranean Castles "—Quarto edition, pp. 2000–2008.

aggression, as to have become totally inaccessible—and indeed
unknown, to the present inglorious and degenerate race, no
longer animated by the spirit of chivalry and adventure.

[I have now recovered my breath, after my bold flight into
the resplendent regions of aristocracy; but my eyes are still
dazzled.]

The reader may by this time have got an intimation that
Tittlebat Titmouse, in a madder freak of fortune that any
which her incomprehensible ladyship hath hitherto exhibited
in the pages of this history, is far on his way toward a dizzy
pitch of greatness—viz., that he has now, owing to the verdict
of the Yorkshire jury, taken the place of Mr. Aubrey, and become heir-expectant to the oldest barony in the kingdom—between it and him only one old peer and his sole child, an unmarried daughter, intervening. Behold the thing demonstrated
to your very eye, in the Pedigree on the next page, which is
only our former one* a little extended.

From this I think it will appear that on the death of Augustus, fifth earl and twentieth baron, with no other issue than
Lady Cecilia, the earldom being then extinct, the barony
would descend upon the Lady Cecilia; and that, in the event
of her dying without issue in the life-time of her father, Tittlebat Titmouse would, on the earl's death, without other lawful
issue, become LORD DRELINCOURT, twenty-*first* in the
barony; and in the event of her dying without issue, after her
father's death, TITTLEBAT TITMOUSE would become the twenty-
second LORD DRELINCOURT; one or other of which two splendid positions, but for the enterprising agency of Messrs. Quirk,
Gammon and Snap, would have been occupied by CHARLES
AUBREY, ESQ.—on considering all which, one can not but remember a saying of an ancient poet, who seems to have kept
as keen an eye upon the unaccountable frolics of the goddess
Fortune as this history shows that I have. 'Tis a passage
which any little school-boy will translate to his mother or his
sisters—

> ——" Hinc apicem rapax
> Fortuna cum stridore acuto
> Sustulit, hic posuisse gaudet."†

At the time of which I am writing, the Earl of Dreddlington was about sixty-seven years old; and he would have realized
the idea of an incarnation of the sublimest PRIDE. He was of
rather a slight make, and, though of a tolerably advanced age,
stood as straight as an arrow. His hair was glossy and white

---

* *Ante*, p. 317.   † Hor. Carm. 1. 34, *ad finem.*

Geoffry de Drelincourt
Summoned as Baron, *by writ*, 12 Hen. II.

From him | descend

Henry Dreddlington, sixteenth Baron by writ,
created Earl of Dreddlington 1667.

Charles (17th Baron and 2d Earl)

Geoffry (18th Baron and 3d Earl)

Percy (19th Baron and 4th Earl)

Augustus (20th Baron and 5th Earl)

Lady Cecilia (only child)

Percy Dreddlington, *of Yatton* (younger brother of Charles)

Harry Dreddlington

Stephen Dreddlington (eldest brother)==

Charles Dreddlington

Gabriel Tittlebat Titmouse==dr and sole heiress

Gabriel T. Titmouse

Tittlebat Titmouse (only child)

Geoffry Dreddlington (2d brother)

Aubrey== dr and sole heiress

Charles Aubrey

Charles Aubrey (eldest son and heir-at-law).

as snow; his features were of an aristocratic cast; their expression was severe and haughty; and I am compelled to say that there was scarce a trace of intellect perceptible in them. His manner and demeanor were cold, imperturbable, inaccessible; wherever he went—so to speak—he radiated cold. Comparative poverty imbittered his spirit, as his lofty birth and ancient descent generated the pride I have spoken of. With what calm and supreme self-satisfaction did he look down upon all lower in the peerage than himself! and as for a newly created peer, he looked at such a being with ineffable disdain. Amongst his few equals he was affable enough; amongst his inferiors he exhibited an insupportable appearance of condescension—one which excited a wise man's smile of pity and contempt, and a fool's anger—both, however, equally naught to the Earl of Dreddlington. If any one could have ventured upon a *post-mortem* examination of so august a structure as the Earl's carcass, his heart would probably have been found to be of the size of a pea, and his brain very soft and flabby; both, however, equal to the small occasions which, from time to time, called for the exercise of their functions. The former was occupied almost exclusively by two feelings—love of himself and of his daughter (because upon her would descend his barony); the latter exhibited its powers (supposing the brain to be the seat of the mind) in mastering the military details requisite for nominal soldiership; the game of whist; the routine of petty business in the House of Lords, and the etiquette of the court. One branch of useful knowledge, by the way he had, however, completely mastered—that which is so ably condensed in *Debrett;* and he became a sort of oracle in such matters. As for his politics, he professed Whig principles—and was, indeed, a bitter, though quiet partisan. In attendance to his senatorial duties he practiced an exemplary punctuality, was always to be found in the House at its sitting and rising, and never once, on any occasion great or small, voted against his party. He had never been heard to speak in a full House; first, because he never could muster nerve enough for the purpose; secondly, because he never had anything to say; and lastly, lest he should compromise his dignity, and destroy the *prestige* of his position, by not speaking better than any one present. His services were not, however, entirely overlooked; for, on his party coming into office for a few weeks (they knew it could be for no longer a time), they made him Lord Steward of the Household; which was thenceforward an epoch to which he referred every event of his life, great and small. The great object of his ambition ever since he had been of an age to form large and comprehensive views of action and conduct, to conceive superior designs, and to achieve distinction amongst mankind—was, to obtain a step in the peerage; for considering the antiquity of his family, and his ample, nay, *superfluous* pecuniary means—so much more than adequate to support his present double dignity of earl and baron—he thought it but a reasonable return for his eminent political services to obtain the step which he coveted. But his anxiety on this point had been recently increased a thousand-fold by one circumstance. A gentleman who held an honorable and lucrative official situation in the House, and who never had treated the Earl of Dreddlington with that profound obsequiousness which the Earl conceived to be his due—but, on the contrary, had presumed to consider himself a man and an Englishman equally with the Earl—had, a short time before, succeeded in establishing his title to an earldom that had long been dormant, and was of creation earlier than that of Dreddlington. The Earl of Dreddlington took this untoward circumstance so much to heart that for some months afterward he appeared to be in a decline, always experiencing a dreadful inward spasm whenever the Earl of Fitzwalter made his appearance in the House. For this sad state of things there was plainly but one remedy—a MARQUISATE—at which the Earl gazed with the wistful eye of an old and feeble ape at a cocoa-nut just above his reach, and which he beholds at length grasped and carried off by some nimbler and younger rival.

Amongst all the weighty cares and anxieties of this life, I must do the Earl the justice to say, that he did not neglect the concerns of hereafter—the solemn realities of that future revealed to us in the Scriptures. To his enlightened and comprehensive view of the state of things around him, it was evident that the Author of the world had decreed the existence of regular gradations of society. The following lines, quoted one night in the House by the leader of his party, had infinitely delighted the Earl—

" Oh, where DEGREE is shaken,
Which is the ladder to all high designs,
The enterprise is sick!
Take but DEGREE away—untune that string,
And, hark! what discord follows! each thing meets
In mere oppugnancy!"[*]

When the Earl discovered that this was the production of Shakespeare, he conceived a great respect for that writer, and purchased a copy of his works, and had them splendidly bound

* Troilus and Cressida, I. iii.

—never to be opened, however, except at that one place where the famous passage in question was to be found. How great was the honor thus conferred upon the plebeian poet to stand amidst a collection of royal and noble authors, to whose productions, and those in elucidation and praise of them, the Earl's splendid-looking library had till then been confined! Since, thought the Earl, such is clearly the order of Providence in this world, why should it not be so in the next? He felt certain that then there would be found corresponding differences and degrees in analogy to differences and degrees existing upon earth; and with this view had read and endeavored to comprehend a very dry but learned book—Butler's *Analogy*—lent him by a deceased kinsman—a bishop. This consolatory conclusion of the Earl's was greatly strengthened by a passage of Scripture, from which he had once heard the aforesaid bishop preach—"*In my Father's house are* MANY MANSIONS*; if it had not been so, I would have told you.*" On grounds such as these, after much conversation with several old brother peers of his own rank, he and they—those wise and good men—came to the conclusion that there was no real ground for apprehending so grievous a misfortune as the huddling together hereafter of the great and small into one miscellaneous and ill-assorted assemblage; but that the rules of precedence, in all their strictness, as being founded in the nature of things, would meet with an exact observance, so that every one should be ultimately and eternally happy in the company of his equals. The Earl of Dreddlington would have, in fact, as soon supposed, with the deluded Indian, that in his voyage to the next world—

" His faithful dog should bear him company,"

as that his lordship should be doomed to participate the same regions of heaven with any of his domestics; unless, indeed, by some, in his view, not improbable dispensation, it should form an ingredient in their cup of happiness in the next world, there to perform those offices—or analogous ones—for their old masters, which they had performed upon earth. As the Earl grew older, these just, and rational, and Scriptural views, became clearer and his faith firmer. Indeed, it might be said that he was in a manner ripening for immortality—for which his noble and lofty nature, he felt, was fitter, and more likely to be in its element, than it could possibly be in this dull, degraded and confused world. He knew that there his sufferings in this inferior stage of existence would be richly recompensed; for sufferings indeed he had, though secret, arising from the scanty means which had been allotted to him for the purpose of maintaining the exalted rank to which it had pleased God to call him. The long series of exquisite mortifications and pinching privations arising from this inadequacy of means had, however, the Earl doubted not, being designed by Providence as a trial of his constancy, and from which he would, in due time, issue like thrice-refined gold. Then also would doubtless be remembered in his favor the innumerable instances of his condescension in mingling in the most open manner with those who were unquestionably his inferiors, sacrificing his own feelings of lofty and fastidious exclusiveness, and endeavoring to advance the interests, and, as far as influence and example went, polish and refine the manners of the lower orders of society. Such is an outline—alas, how faint and imperfect!—of the character of this great and good man, the Earl of Dreddlington. As for his domestic and family circumstances, he had been a widower for some fifteen years, his countess having brought him but one child, Lady Cecilia Philippa Leopoldina Plantagenet, who was, in almost all respects, the counterpart of her illustrious father. She resembled him not a little in feature, only that she partook of the plainness of her mother. Her complexion was delicately fair; but her features had no other expression than that of a languid hauteur. Her upper eyelids drooped as if she could hardly keep them open, the upper jaw projected considerably over the under one, and her front teeth were prominent and exposed. Frigid and inanimate, she seemed to take but little interest in anything on earth. In person she was of average height, of slender and well-proportioned figure, and an erect and graceful carriage, only that she had a habit of throwing her head a little backward, that gave her a singularly disdainful appearance. She had reached her twenty-seventh year without having had an eligible offer of marriage, though she would be the possessor of a barony in her own right and £5,000 a year; a circumstance, which, it may be believed, not a little imbittered her. She inherited her father's pride in all its plenitude. You should have seen the haughty couple sitting silently side by side in the old-fashioned yellow family chariot, as they drove round the crowded park, returning the salutations of those they met in the slightest manner possible. A glimpse of them at such a moment would have given you a far more just and lively notion of their real character than the most anxious and labored description of mine.

Ever since the first Earl of Dreddlington had, through a bitter pique conceived against his eldest son, the second earl, diverted the principal family revenues to the younger branch, leaving the title to be supported by only £5,000 a year, there had been a complete arrangement between the elder and the younger—the titled and the moneyed—branches of the family. On Mr. Aubrey's attaining his majority, however, the present earl sanctioned overtures being made toward a reconciliation, being of opinion that Mr. Aubrey and Lady Cecilia might, by intermarriage, effect a happy reunion of family interests; an object, this, that had long lain nearer his heart than any other upon earth, till, in fact, it became a kind of passion. Actuated by such considerations, he had done more to conciliate Mr. Aubrey than he had ever done toward any one on earth. It was, however, in vain. Mr. Aubrey's first delinquency was, an unqualified and enthusiastic adoption of Tory principles. Now, all the Dreddlingtons, from time whereof the memory of man runneth not to the contrary, had been firm, unflinching Tories, till the distinguished father of the present earl quietly walked over one day to the other side of the House of Lords, completely fascinated by a bit of ribbon which the minister held up before him: and before he had sat in that wonder-working region, the ministerial side of the House, twenty-four hours, he discovered that the true signification of Tory was *bigot*—and of Whig *patriot :* and he stuck to that version till it transformed him into a gold stick, in which capacity he died, having repeatedly and solemnly impressed upon his son the necessity and advantage of taking the same view of public affairs, with a view to arrive at similar results. And in the *way* in which he had been *trained up*, most religiously had gone the earl; and see the result; he, also, attained to eminent and responsible office—to wit, that of Lord Steward of the Household. Now, things standing thus—how could the earl so compromise his principles, and indirectly injure his party, as by suffering his daughter to marry a Tory? Great grief and vexation of spirit did *this* matter, therefore, occasion to that excellent nobleman. But, secondly, Aubrey not only declined to marry his cousin, but clinched his refusal and sealed his final exclusion from the dawning good opinion and affections of the earl by marrying, as hath been seen, some one else—Miss St. Clair. Thenceforth there was a great gulf between the Earl of Dreddlington and the Aubreys. Whenever they happened to meet, the earl greeted him with an elaborate bow and a petrifying smile; but for the last seven years, not one syllable had passed between them. As for Mr. Aubrey, he had never been otherwise than amused at the eccentric airs of his magnificent kinsman.—Now, was it not a hard thing for the earl to bear—namely, the prospect there was that his barony and estates might devolve upon this Aubrey, or his issue? for Lady Cecilia, alas! enjoyed but precarious health, and her chances of marrying seemed daily diminishing. This was a thorn in the poor earl's flesh; a source of constant *worry* to him, sleeping and waking; and proud as he was, and with such good reason, he would have gone down on his knees and prayed to Heaven to avert so direful a calamity—to see his daughter married.

Such being the relative position of Mr. Aubrey and the Earl of Dreddlington at the time when this history opens, it is easy for the reader to imagine the lively interest with which the earl first heard of the tidings that a stranger had set up a title to the whole of the Yatton estates, and the silent but profound anxiety with which he continued to regard the progress of the affair. He obtained, from time to time, by means of confidential inquiries instituted by his solicitor, a general notion of the nature of the new claimant's pretensions; but, with a due degree of delicacy toward his unfortunate kinsman, he studiously concealed the interest he felt in so important a family question as the succession to the Yatton property. The earl and his daughter were exceedingly anxious to *see* the claimant; and when he heard that that claimant was a gentleman of " decided Whig principles "—the earl was very near setting it down as a sort of special interference of Providence in his favor, and one that, in the natural order of things, would lead to the accomplishment of the other wishes of the earl. Who knew but that, before a twelvemonth had passed over, the two branches of the family might not be in a fair way of being reunited—and thus, among other incidents, invest the earl with the virtual patronage of the borough of Yatton, and, in the event of their return to power, strengthen his claim upon his party for his long-coveted marquisate? He had gone to the Continent a few days before the trial of the ejectment at York, and did not return till a day or two after the Court of King's Bench had solemnly declared the validity of the plaintiff's title to the Yatton property, and consequently established his right of succession to the barony of Drelincourt. Of this event a lengthened account was given in one of the Yorkshire papers, which fell under the earl's eye the day after his arrival from abroad; and to the report of the decision of the question of law was appended the following paragraph:—

" In consequence of the above decision, Mr. Aubrey, we are able to state on the best authority, has given formal notice of his intention to surrender the entire of the Yatton property without further litigation; thus making the promised amends in his power to those whom he has—we can not doubt unwittingly—injured. He has also accepted the Chiltern Hundreds, and has consequently retired from Parliament; so that the borough of Yatton is now vacant. We sincerely hope that the new proprietor of Yatton will either himself sit for the borough, and announce immediately his intention of doing so, or give his prompt and decisive support to some gentleman of decided Whig principles. We say *prompt*—for the enemy is vigilant and crafty. Men at Yatton! To the rescue!!!—Mr. Titmouse is now, we believe, in London. This fortunate gentleman is not only now in possession of the fine property at Yatton, with an unincumbered rent-roll of from twelve to fifteen thousand a year, and the vast accumulation of rents to be handed over by the late possessor, but is now next but one in succession to the earldom of Dreddlington and barony of Drelincourt, with the large family estates annexed thereto. We believe this is the oldest barony in the kingdom. It must be a source of great gratification to the present earl to know that his probable successor professes the same liberal and enlightened political opinions, of which his lordship has, during his long and distinguished political life, been so able and consistent a supporter."

The Earl of Dreddlington was slightly flustered on reading the above paragraph. He perused it several times with increasing satisfaction. The time had at length arrived for him to take decisive steps; nay, duty to his newly discovered kinsman required it.

Messrs. Titmouse and Gammon were walking arm in arm down Oxford Street, on their return from some livery-stables, where they had been looking at a horse which Titmouse was thinking of purchasing, when an incident occurred which ruffled him not a little. He had been recognized and publicly accosted by a vulgar fellow, with a yard-measure in his hand and a large parcel of drapery under his arm—in fact, by our old friend Mr. Huckaback. In vain did Mr. Titmouse affect, for some time, not to see his old acquaintance, and to be earnestly engaged in conversation with Mr. Gammon.

"Ah, Titty!—Titmouse! Well, *Mister* Titmouse—how are you?—Devilish long time since we met!" Titmouse directed a look at him which he wished could have blighted him, and quickened his pace without taking any further notice of the presumptuous intruder. Huckaback's blood was up, however—roused by this ungrateful and insolent treatment from one who had been under such great obligations to him; and quickening *his* pace also, he kept alongside with Titmouse.

" Ah," continued Huckaback, " why do you cut me in this way, Titty? You *aren't* ashamed of me, surely? Many's the time you've tramped up and down Oxford Street with your bundle and yard-measure—"

" Fellow!" at length exclaimed Titmouse, indignantly. " 'Pon my life I'll give you in charge if you go on so! Be off, you low fellow!—Dem vulgar brute!" he subjoined in a lower tone, bursting into perspiration, for he had not forgotten the insolent pertinacity of Huckaback's disposition.

" Give me in charge? Come, I like that, rather —You vagabond! Pay me what you owe me! You're a swindler! You owe me fifty pounds, you do! You sent a man to rob me!"

" Will any one get a constable?" inquired Titmouse, who had grown as white as death. The little crowd that was collecting round them began to suspect, from Titmouse's agitated appearance, that there must be some foundation for the charges made against him.

" Oh, go, get a constable! Nothing I should like better! Ah, my fine gentleman—what's .the time of day, when chaps like you are wound up so high?"

Gammon's interference was in vain. Huckaback got more abusive and noisy; no constable was at hand; so, to escape the intolerable interruption and nuisance, he beckoned a coach off the stand, which was close by, and Titmouse and he stepping into it, they were soon out of sight and hearing of Mr. Huckaback. Having taken a shilling drive, they alighted, and walked toward Covent Garden. As they approached the hotel they observed a yellow chariot, at once elegant and somewhat old-fashioned, rolling away from the door.

" I wonder who that is," said Gammon; " it's an earl's coronet on the panel; and a white-haired old gentleman was sitting low down in the corner—"

" Ah—it's no doubt a fine thing to be a lord, and all that— but I'll answer for it, some of 'em's as poor as a church mouse," replied Titmouse, as they entered the hotel. At that moment the waiter, with a most profound bow, presented him with a letter and a card, which had only the moment before been left for him. The card was thus:—

THE EARL OF DREDDLINGTON.

GROSVENOR SQUARE.

---

and there was written on it, in pencil, in rather a feeble and hurried character—" for Mr. Titmouse."

"My stars, Mr. Gammon!" exclaimed Titmouse, excitedly, addressing Mr. Gammon, who also seemed greatly interested by the occurrence. They both repaired to a vacant table at the extremity of the room; and Titmouse, with not a little trepidation, hastily breaking a large seal which contained the Earl's family arms, with their crowded quarterings and grim supporters—better appreciated by Gammon, however, than by Titmouse—opened the ample envelope, and, unfolding its thick gilt-edged inclosure, read as follows:—

"The Earl of Dreddlington has the honor of waiting upon Mr. Titmouse, in whom he is very happy to have, though unexpectedly, discovered so near a kinsman. On the event which has brought this to pass, the Earl congratulates himself not less than Mr. Titmouse, and hopes for the earliest opportunity of a personal introduction.

"The Earl leaves town to-day, and will not return till Monday next, on which day he begs the favor of Mr. Titmouse's company to dinner, at six o'clock. He may depend upon its being strictly a family *reunion ;* the only person present, besides Mr. Titmouse and the Earl, being the Lady Cecilia.

"Grosvenor Square, Thursday.

"TITTLEBAT TITMOUSE, ESQ., etc. etc."

As soon as Titmouse had read the above, still holding it in his hand, he gazed at Gammon with mute apprehension and delight. Of the existence, indeed, of the magnificent personage who had just introduced himself, Titmouse had certainly heard, from time to time, since the commencement of the proceedings which had just been so successfully terminated. He had seen the brightness, to be sure, but as a sort of remote splendor, like that of a fixed star which gleamed brightly, but at too vast a distance to have any sensible influence or even to arrest his attention. After a little while Titmouse even began to chatter very volubly; but Gammon, after reading over the note once or twice, seemed not much inclined for conversation; and, had Titmouse been accustomed to observation, he might have gathered, from the eye and brow of Gammon, that that gentleman's mind was very deeply occupied by some matter or other, probably suggested by the incident which had just taken place. Titmouse, by the bye, called for pens, ink, and paper, —"the very best gilt-edged paper, mind," and prepared to reply to Lord Dreddlington's note. Gammon, however, who knew the peculiarities of his friend's style of correspondence, suggested that *he* should draw up, and Titmouse copy the following note. This was presently done;

but when Gammon observed how thickly studded it was with capital letters, the numerous flourishes with which it was garnished, and its more than questionable orthography, he prevailed on Titmouse, after some little difficulty, to allow him to transcribe the note which was to be sent to Lord Dreddlington. Here it is—

"Mr. Titmouse begs to present his compliments to the Earl of Dreddlington, and to express the high sense he entertains of the kind consideration evinced by his lordship in his call and note of to-day.

"One of the most gratifying circumstances connected with Mr. Titmouse's recent success is the distinguished alliance which his lordship has been so prompt and courteous in recognizing. Mr. Titmouse will feel the greatest pleasure in availing himself of the Earl of Dreddlington's invitation to dinner for Monday next.
"Cabbage-Stalk Hotel, Thursday.
"The Right Honble. the EARL OF DREDDLINGTON, etc. etc."

"Have you a 'Peerage' here, waiter?" inquired Gammon, as the waiter brought him a lighted taper. *Debrett* was shortly laid before him; and turning to the name of Dreddlington, he read over what has been already laid before the reader. "Humph—'*Lady Cecilia*'—here she is—his *daughter*—I thought as much—I see!" This was what passed through his mind, as—having left Titmouse, who set off to deposit a card and the above "Answer" at Lord Dreddlington's—he made his way toward the delectable regions in which their office was situated—Saffron Hill. "'Tis curious—amusing—interesting, to observe his progress"—continued Gammon to himself—
"*Tag-rag*—and his daughter;
"*Quirk*—and his daughter;
"*The Earl of Dreddlington*—and his daughter. How many more? Happy! happy! happy Titmouse."
The sun that was rising upon Titmouse was setting upon he Aubreys. Dear, delightful—now too dear, now too delightful—Yatton! the shades of evening are descending upon thee and thy virtuous but afflicted occupants, who, early on the morrow, quit thee forever. Approach silently yon conservatory. Behold in the midst of it the dark slight figure of a lady, solitary, motionless, in melancholy attitude—her hands clasped before her; it is Miss Aubrey. Her face is beautiful, but grief is in her eye, and her bosom heaves with sighs, which, gentle as they are, are yet the only sounds audible. Yes, that is the sweet and once joyous Kate Aubrey.

'Twas she, indeed, and this was her last visit to her conservatory. Many rare, delicate, and beautiful flowers were there; the air was laden with the fragrant odors which they exhaled, as it were in sighs, on account of the dreaded departure of their lovely mistress. At length she stooped down, and in stooping, a tear fell right upon the small sprig of geranium which she gently detached from its stem and placed in her bosom. "Sweet flowers," thought she, "who will tend you as I have tended you, when I am gone? Why do you look now more beautiful than ever you did before?" Her eye fell upon the spot on which, till the day before, had stood her aviary. Poor Kate had sent it, as a present, to Lady De la Zouch, and it was then at Fotheringham Castle. What a flutter there used to be among the beautiful little creatures when they perceived Kate's approach! She turned her head away. She felt oppressed, and attributed it to the closeness of the conservatory—the strength of the odors given out by the numerous flowers; but it was sorrow that oppressed her, and she was in a state at once of mental excitement and physical exhaustion. The last few weeks had been an interval of exquisite suffering. She could not be happy alone, and yet could not bear the company of her brother and her sister-in-law, nor that of their innocent children. Quitting the conservatory with a look of lingering fondness, she passed along into the house with a hurried step, and escaped, unobserved, to her chamber—the very chamber in which the reader obtained his first distant and shadowy glimpse of her, and in which, now entering it silently and suddenly, the door being only closed, not shut, she observed her faithful little maid, Harriet, sitting in tears before a melancholy heap of packages prepared for traveling on the morrow. She rose as Miss Aubrey entered, and presently exclaimed, passionately, bursting afresh into tears, "Ma'am, I *can't* leave you—indeed I can't! I know all your ways; I won't go to any one else! I shall hate service! and I know they'll hate *me*, too; for I shall cry myself to death."

"Come, come, Harriet," faltered Miss Aubrey, "this is very foolish; nay, it is unkind to distress me in this manner at the last moment."

"Oh, ma'am, if you *did* but know how I love you! How I'd go on my knees to serve you all the rest of the days of my life!"

"Don't talk in that way, Harriet; that's a good girl," said Miss Aubrey, rather faintly, and, sinking into the chair, she buried her face in her handkerchief; "you know I've had a great deal to go through, Harriet, and am in very poor spirits."

"I know it, ma'am, I do; and that's why I can't *bear* to leave you!" She sunk on her knees beside Miss Aubrey. "Oh, ma'am, if you would but let me stay with you! I've been trying, ever since you first told me, to make up my mind to part with you; and, now it's coming to the time, I can't, ma'am—indeed, I can't! If you did but know, ma'am, what my thoughts have been while I've been folding and packing up your dresses here! to think that I sha'n't be with you to unpack them; it's very hard, ma'am, that madam's maid is to go with her, and I'm not to go with *you!*"

"We must have made a choice, Harriet," said Miss Aubrey, with forced calmness.

"Yes, ma'am; but why didn't you choose us both? Because we've both always done our best; and, as for me, you've never spoke an unkind word to me in your life—"

"Harriet, Harriet," said Miss Aubrey, tremulously, "I've several times explained to you that we can not any longer afford each to have our own maid; and Mrs. Aubrey's maid is older than you, and knows how to manage children—"

"What signifies *affording*, ma'am? Neither she nor I will ever take a shilling of wages; I'd really rather serve you for nothing, ma'am, than any other lady for a hundred pounds a year! Oh, so happy as I've been in your service, ma'am!" she added, bitterly.

"Don't Harriet—you would not, if you knew the pain you give me," said Miss Aubrey, faintly. Harriet got up, poured out a glass of water, and forced her pale mistress to swallow a little, which presently revived her.

"Harriet," said she, "you have never once disobeyed me, and *now* I am certain that you won't. I assure you that we have made all our arrangements, and can not alter them. I have been very fortunate in obtaining for you so kind a mistress as Lady Stratton. Remember, Harriet, she was the oldest bosom friend of my—" Miss Aubrey's voice trembled, and she ceased speaking for a minute or two, during which she struggled against her feelings with momentary success. "Here's the prayer-book," she presently resumed, opening a drawer in her dressing-table, and taking out a small volume —"Here's the prayer-book I promised you; it is very prettily bound, and I have written your name in it, Harriet, as you desired. Take it, and keep it for my sake. Will you?"

"Oh, ma'am," replied the girl, bitterly, "I shall never bear to look at it, but I'll never part with it till I die.'

"Now leave me, Harriet, for a short time—I wish to be alone," said Miss Aubrey; and she was obeyed. She presently rose and bolted the door; and then, secure from interruption, walked slowly to and fro for some time; and a long and deep current of melancholy thoughts and feelings flowed through her mind and her heart. She had but a short time before seen her sister's sweet children put into their little beds for the last time at Yatton; and, together with their mother, had hung fondly over them, kissing and embracing them—their little fellow-wanderers—till her feelings compelled her to leave them. One by one all the dear innumerable ties that had attached her to Yatton, and everything connected with it, ever since her birth, had been severed and broken—ties, not only the strength but very existence of which she had scarce been aware of till then. She had bade—as had all of them—repeated and agonizing farewells to dear and old friends. Her very heart within her trembled as she gazed at the objects familiar to her eye, and pregnant with innumerable little softening associations, ever since her infancy. Nothing around them now belonged to *them*—but to a stranger—to one who—she shuddered with disgust. She thought of the fearful position in which her brother was placed—entirely at the mercy of, it might be, selfish and rapacious men—what indeed was to become of all of them? At length she threw herself into the large old easy-chair which stood near the window, and with a fluttering heart and hasty tremulous hand, drew an open letter from her bosom. She held it for some moments, as if dreading again to peruse it—but at length unfolded and read a portion of it. 'Twas full of fervent and at the same time delicate expressions of fondness; and after a short while, her hand dropped with the letter upon her lap, and she burst into a passionate flood of tears. After an interval of several minutes she again took up the letter—read a little further—still more and more moved by the generous and noble sentiments it contained—and, at length, utterly overcome, she again dropped her hand, and sobbed aloud long and vehemently. "It can not—can not—no it can not be," she murmured, and yielded to her feelings for a long while, her tears showering down her pallid, beautiful cheeks.

At length she came to the conclusion: and in a kind of agony she pressed the signature to her lips, and then hastily folding up the letter, replaced it whence she had taken it, and continued sobbing bitterly. Alas, what additional poignancy did this give to the agonies of her last evening at Yatton! She had, however, become somewhat calmer by the time that she heard the door hastily, but gently tapped at, and then attempted to be opened. Miss Aubrey rose and unbolted it, and Mrs. Aubrey entered, her beautiful countenance as pale and sad as that of her sister-in-law. She, however, was both wife and mother; and the various cares which these relations entailed upon her at a bitter moment like the present served, in some measure, to occupy her thoughts and prevent her from being absorbed by the heart-breaking circumstances which surrounded her. Suffering had, however, a little impaired her beauty; her cheek was very pale and her eye and brow laden with trouble.

"Kate, dear Kate," said she, rather quickly, closing the door after her, "what is to be done? Did you hear carriage-wheels a few moments ago? Who do you think have arrived? As I fancied would be the case, the De la Zouches." Miss Aubrey trembled and turned pale. "You must see—you must see—Lady De la Zouch, Kate—they have driven from Fotheringham on purpose to take—*once more*—a last farewell! 'Tis very painful, but what can be done? You know what dear, dear, good friends they are!"

"Is Lord De la Zouch come also?" inquired Miss Aubrey, apprehensively.

"I will not deceive you, dearest Kate, they are *all* come, but she only is in the house: they are gone out to look for Charles, who is walking in the park." Miss Aubrey gave a sudden shudder; and after evidently a violent struggle with her feelings, the color having entirely deserted her face, and left it of an ashy whiteness.

"I can not muster up resolution enough, Agnes," she whispered. "I know their errand."

"Care not about their errand, love! You shall not be troubled—you shall not be persecuted." Miss Aubrey shook her head, and grasped Mrs. Aubrey's hand.

"They do not, they can not persecute me. It is a cruel and harsh word to use—and—consider how noble, how disinterested is their conduct; it is that which subdues me!"

Mrs. Aubrey threw her arms around her agitated sister-in-law, and tenderly kissed her forehead.

"Oh, Agnes!" faltered Miss Aubrey, pressing her hand upon her heart to relieve the intolerable oppression she suffered—"would to Heaven that I had never seen—never thought of him!"

"Don't fear, Kate! that he will attempt to see you on so sad an occasion as this. Delamere is a man of infinite delicacy and generosity!"

"I know he is, I know he is," gasped Miss Aubrey.

"Stay, I'll tell you what to do; I'll go down and return with Lady De la Zouch; we can see her here, undisturbed and alone, for a few moments; and then nothing painful *can* occur. Shall I bring her?" she inquired, rising. Miss Aubrey did not dissent; and within a very few minutes' time, Mrs. Aubrey returned, accompanied by Lady De la Zouch, rather an elderly woman, her countenance still handsome; of very dignified carriage, of an extremely mild disposition, and passionately fond of Miss Aubrey. Hastily drawing aside her veil as she entered the room, she stepped quickly up to Miss Aubrey, kissed her, and for a few moments grasped her hands in silence.

"This is very sad work, Miss Aubrey," said she at length, hurriedly glancing at the luggage lying piled up at the other end of the room. Miss Aubrey made no answer, but shook her head. "It was useless attempting it, we could not stay at home; we have risked being charged with cruel intrusion; forgive me, dearest, will you? *They* will not come near you!" Miss Aubrey trembled. "I feel as if I were parting with a daughter, Kate," said Lady De la Zouch with sudden emotion. "How your mamma and I loved one another!" and she burst into tears.

"For mercy's sake, open the window; I feel suffocated," faltered Miss Aubrey. Mrs. Aubrey threw up the window, and the cool refreshing breeze of evening quickly diffused itself through the apartment, and revived the drooping spirits of Miss Aubrey, who walked gently to and fro about the room, supported by Lady De la Zouch and Mrs. Aubrey, and soon recovered a tolerable degree of composure. The three ladies presently stood, arm in arm, gazing through the deep bay-window at the fine and extensive prospect which it commanded. The gloom of evening was beginning to steal over the landscape.

"How beautiful!" exclaimed Miss Aubrey, faintly, with a deep sigh.

"The window in the northern tower of the castle commands a still more extensive view," said Lady De la Zouch. Miss Aubrey suddenly looked at her, and burst into tears. After standing gazing through the window for some time longer, they stepped back into the room, and were soon engaged in deep and earnest conversation.

For the last three weeks Mr. Aubrey had addressed himself with calmness and energy to the painful duties which had devolved upon him, of *setting his house in order*. Immediately

After quitting the dinner-table that day—a mere nominal meal to himself, his wife, and sister—he had retired to the library, to complete the extensive and important arrangements consequent upon his abandonment of Yatton; and after about an hour thus occupied, he went forth to take a solitary walk—a melancholy—a last walk about the property. It was a moment that severely tried his fortitude; but that fortitude stood the trial. He was a man of lively sensibilities, and appreciated, to its utmost extent, the melancholy and alarming change that had come over his fortunes. Surely even the bluntest and coarsest feelings that ever tried to disguise and dignify themselves under the name of STOICISM—to convert into bravery and fortitude a stupid, sullen insensibility—must have been not a little shaken by such scenes as Mr. Aubrey had had to pass through during the last few weeks—scenes which I do not choose to distress the reader's feelings by dwelling upon in detail. Mr. Aubrey had no mean pretensions to real philosophy; but he had still juster pretensions to an infinitely higher character—that of a CHRISTIAN. He had a firm, unwavering conviction that whatever befell him, either good or evil, was the ordination of the Almighty—infinitely wise, infinitely good;— and this was the source of his fortitude and resignation. He felt himself here standing upon ground that was immovable.

To avert the misfortune which menaced him, he had neglected no rational and conscientious means to retain the advantages of fortune and station to which he had believed himself born, he had made the most strenuous exertions consistent with a rigid sense of honor. What, indeed, could he have done that he had not done? He had caused the claims of his opponent to be subjected to as severe and skillful a scrutiny as the wit of man could suggest; *and they had stood the test.* Those claims and his own had been each of them placed in the scales of justice; those scales had been held up and poised by the pure and firm hands to which the laws of God and of the country had committed the administration of justice; on what ground could a just and reasonable man quarrel with or repine at the issue? And supposing that a perverse and subtle ingenuity in his legal advisers could have devised means for delaying his surrender of the property to him who had been solemnly declared its true owner, what real and ultimate advantage could he have obtained by such a dishonorable line of conduct? Could the spirit of the Christian religion tolerate the bare idea of it? Could such purposes or intentions consist for one instant with the consciousness that the awful eye of God was always upon every thought of his

mind, every feeling of his heart, every purpose of his will? A
thorough and lively conviction of God's moral government of
the world secured him a happy composure—a glorious and immovable resolution; it enabled him to form a true estimate of
things; it extracted the sting from grief and regret; it dispelled the gloom that would otherwise have settled portentous-
ly upon the future. Thus he had not *forgotten the exhortation which spoke unto him, as unto a child: My son, despise
not thou the chastening of the Lord, nor faint when thou art
rebuked of Him.* And if, indeed, religion had not done this
for Mr. Aubrey, what could it have done, what would it have
been worth? It would have been that indeed which dull fools
suppose it—a mere name, a melancholy delusion. What hopeless and lamentable imbecility would it not have argued to
have acknowledged the reality and influence of religion in the
hour of prosperity—and to have doubted, distrusted, or denied
it in the hour of adversity? When a child beholds the sun
obscured by the dark clouds, he may think, in his simplicity,
that it is gone forever; but a MAN knows that behind is the
sun, glorious as ever, and the next moment, the clouds having
rolled away, its glorious warmth and light are again upon the
earth. Thus is it, thought Aubrey, with humble and cheerful
confidence, with the Almighty—who hath declared Himself
the *Father of the spirits of all flesh*—

> " Behind a frowning Providence
> He hides a smiling face!
> Blind unbelief is sure to err,
>   And scan His works in vain!
> God is His own interpreter,
>   And He will make it plain!"

" Therefore, O my God!" thought Aubrey, as he gazed upon
the lovely scenes familiar to him from his birth, and from
which a few short hours were to separate him forever, " I do
acknowledge Thy hand in what has befallen me, and Thy
mercy which enables me to bear it, as from Thee." The
scene around him was tranquil and beautiful—inexpressibly
beautiful. He stood under the shadow of a mighty elm-tree,
the last of a long and noble avenue, which he had been pacing
in deep thought for upward of an hour. The ground was considerably elevated above the level of the rest of the park. No
sound disturbed the serene repose of the approaching evening,
except the distant and gradually diminishing sounds issuing
from an old rookery, and the faint low bubbling of a clear
streamlet that flowed not far from where he stood. Here and

there, under the deepening shadows cast by the lofty trees, might be seen the glancing forms of deer, the only live things visible. " Life," said Aubrey to himself, with a sigh, as he leaned against the trunk of the grand old tree under which he stood, and gazed with a fond and mournful eye on the lovely scenes stretching before him, to which the subdued radiance of the departing sunlight communicated a tone of tender pensiveness, " life is, in truth, what the Scriptures—what the voice of nature—represents it—a long journey, during which the traveler stops at many resting-places. Some of them are more, others less beautiful; from some he parts with more, from others with less regret; but part he must, and pursue his journey, though he may often turn back to gaze with lingering fondness and admiration at the scene he has last quitted. The next stage may be—*as all his journey might have been*—bleak and desolate; but through that he is only passing; he will not be condemned to stay in it, as he was not permitted to dwell in the other; he is still journeying on, along a route which he can not mistake, to the point of his destination, his journey's end—the shores of the vast, immeasurable, boundless ocean of eternity—HIS HOME!"

The deepening shadows of evening warned him to retrace his steps to the Hall. Before quitting the spot upon which he had been so long standing, he turned his head a little toward the right, to take a last view of an object which called forth tender and painful feeling—it was the old sycamore which his sister's intercession had saved from the ax. There it stood, feeble and venerable object! its leafless silvery-gray branches becoming dim and indistinct, yet contrasting touchingly with the verdant strength of those by its side. A neat strong fence had been placed around it; but how much longer would it receive such care and attention? Aubrey thought of the comparison which had been made by his sister, and sighed as he looked his last at the old tree, and then slowly walked on toward the Hall. When about half-way down the avenue, he beheld two figures apparently approaching him, but undistinguishable in the gloom and the distance. As they neared him, he recognized Lord De la Zouch and Mr. Delamere. Suspecting the object of their visit, which a little surprised him, since they had taken a final leave, and a very affecting one, the day before, he felt a little anxiety and embarrassment. Nor was he entirely mistaken. Lord De la Zouch, who advanced alone toward Aubrey—Mr. Delamere turning back—most seriously pressed his son's suit for the hand of Miss Aubrey, as he had often done before; declaring, that though undoubtedly he wished a year or two first to elapse, during which his son might complete his studies at Oxford, there was no object dearer to the heart of Lady De la Zouch and himself than to see Miss Aubrey become their daughter-in-law. "Where," said Lord De la Zouch, with much energy, " is he to look elsewhere for such a union of beauty, of accomplishments, of amiability, of high-mindedness?" After a great deal of animated conversation on this subject, during which Mr. Aubrey assured Lord De la Zouch that *he* would say everything which he honorably could to induce his sister to entertain, or at all events, not to discard the suit of Delamere; at the same time reminding him of the firmness of her character, and the hopelessness of attempting to change any determination to which she had been led by her sense of delicacy and honor. Lord De la Zouch addressed himself in a very earnest manner to matters more immediately relating to the personal interests of Mr. Aubrey; entered with lively anxiety into all his future plans and purposes; and once more pressed upon him the acceptance of most munificent offers of pecuniary assistance, which, with many fervent expressions of gratitude, Aubrey again declined. But he pledged himself to communicate freely with Lord De la Zouch, in the event of an occasion arising for such assistance as his lordship had already so generously volunteered. By this time Mr. Delamere had joined them, regarding Mr. Aubrey with infinite earnestness and apprehension. All, however, he said, was—and in a hurried manner to his father— " My mother has sent me to say that she is waiting for you in the carriage, and wishes that we should immediately return." Lord De la Zouch and his son again took leave of Mr. Aubrey.

" Remember, my dear Aubrey, remember the pledges you have repeated this evening," said the former.

" I do, I will!" replied Mr. Aubrey, as they each wrung his hands; and then, having grasped those of Lady de la Zouch, who sat within the carriage powerfully affected, the door was shut, and they were quickly borne away from the presence and the residence of their afflicted friends. While Mr. Aubrey stood gazing after them, with folded arms, in an attitude of melancholy abstraction, at the hall door, he was accosted by Dr. Tatham, who had come to him from the library, where he had been, till a short time before, busily engaged reducing into writing various matters which had been the subject of conversation between himself and Mr. Aubey during the day.

" I am afraid, my dear friend," said the Doctor, " that there is a painful but interesting scene awaiting you. You will not, I am sure, forbear to gratify, by your momentary presence in the servants' hall, a body of your tenantry, who are there assembled, having come to pay you their parting respects."

"I would really rather be spared the painful scene," said Mr. Aubrey, with emotion; "I am nearly unnerved as it is! Can not you bid them adieu, in my name, and say, God bless them?"

"You must come, my dear friend! If it *be* painful, it will be but for a moment; and the recollection of their hearty and humble expressions of affection and respect will be pleasant hereafter. Poor souls!" he added, with not a little emotion, "you should see how crowded is Mr. Griffiths's room with the presents they have each brought you, and which would surely keep your whole establishment for months—cheeses, tongues, hams, bacon, and I know not what beside!"

"Come, Doctor," said Mr. Aubrey, quickly, and with evidently a great effort, "I will see them, my humble and worthy friends! if it *be* for but a moment; but I would rather have been spared the scene." He followed Dr. Tatham into the large servants' hall, which he found nearly filled by some forty or fifty of his late tenantry, who, as he entered, rose in troubled silence to receive him. There were lights, by which a hurried glance sufficed to show him the deep sorrow visible in their countenances.

"Well, sir," commenced one of them after a moment's hesitation—he seemed to have been chosen the spokesman of those present—"we've come to tak' our leave; and a sad time it be for all of us, and it may be, sir, for you." He paused, and added, abruptly—"I thought I could have said a word or two, sir, in the name of all of us, but I've clean forgotten all; and I wish we could all forget that we were come to part with you, sir;—but we sha'n't—no, never!—we shall never see your like again, sir! God help you, sir!" Again he paused, and struggled hard to conceal his emotions. Then he tried to say something further, but his voice failed him.

"Squire, it may be law, but it be not justice, we all do think, that hath taken Yatton from you, that was born to it," said one, who stood next to him that had first spoke. "Who ever heard o' a scratch in a bit o' paper signifying the loss o' so much? It never were heard of afore, sir, an' can not be right!"

"You'll forgive me, Squire," said another, "but we shall never tak' to t' new one that's coming after you!"

"My worthy, my dear friends," commenced Mr. Aubrey, with melancholy and forced composure, as he stood beside Dr.

Tatham, "this is a sad scene—one which I had not expected.
I am quite unprepared for it. I have had lately to go through
many very painful scenes; but few more so than the present.
My dear friends, I can only say from my heart, God bless you
all! I shall never forget you, whom I have always respected,
and indeed been very proud of, as my tenantry, and whom I
now, of course, look at as my friends only. We shall *never*
forget you—"

"Lord Almighty bless you, sir, and Madam, and Miss, and
little Miss—and the little squire!" said a voice, in a vehement
manner, from amidst the throng, in tones that went to Mr.
Aubrey's heart. His lips quivered, and he ceased speaking
for some moments. At length he resumed.

"You see my feelings are a little shaken by the sufferings I
have gone through. I have only a word more to say to you.
Providence has seen fit, my friends, to deprive me of that
which I had deemed to be my birthright. God is good and
wise; and I bow, as we must all bow, to His will, with reverence and resignation. And also, my dear friends, let us always
submit cheerfully to the laws under which we live. We must
not quarrel with their decision, merely because it happens to
be adverse to our own wishes. I, from my heart—and so must
you, from yours—acknowledge a firm, unshaken allegiance to
the laws; they are ordained by God, and He demands our obedience to them!" He paused. "I have to thank you," he
presently added, in a subdued tone, "my worthy friends, for
many substantial tokens of your good-will which you have
brought with you this evening. I assure you sincerely that I
value them far more "—he paused, and it was some moments
before he could proceed—"than if they had been of the most
costly kind."

"Lord, only hearken to t' Squire!" called out a voice, as if
on an impulse of eager affection, which its rough, honest
speaker could not resist. This seemed entirely to deprive Mr.
Aubrey of the power of utterance, and he turned suddenly toward Dr. Tatham with an overflowing eye and a convulsive
quivering of the lips that showed the powerful emotions with
which he was contending. The next moment he stepped forward and shook hands with those nearest. He was quickly surrounded, and every one present grasped his hands, scarcely any
of them able to utter more than a brief but ardent " God bless
you, sir!"

"I am sure, my friends," said Dr. Tatham, almost as much
affected as any of them, "that you can not wish to prolong so
affecting, so distressing a scene. Mr. Aubrey is much ex

hausted, and has a long journey to take early in the morning
—and you had better now leave.''
    " Farewell! farewell, my kind and dear friends, farewell!—
May God bless you all, and all your families!'' said Mr. Aubrey, and, most powerfully affected, withdrew from a scene
which he was not likely ever to forget. He retired, accompanied by Dr. Tatham, to his library, where Mr. Griffiths, his
steward, was in readiness to receive his signature to various
documents. This done, the steward, after a few hurried expressions of affection and respect, withdrew; and Mr. Aubrey
had completed all the arrangements, and transacted all the
business which had required his attention before quitting Yatton, which, at an early hour in the morning, he was going to
leave and go direct to London, instead of accepting any of the
numerous offers which he had received from his friends in the
neighborhood to take up with them his abode for, at all events,
some considerable period. That, however, would have been
entirely inconsistent with the plans for his future life which
he had formed and matured. He left the whole estate in admirable order and condition. There was not a farm vacant,
not a tenant dissatisfied with the terms under which he held.
Every document, all the accounts connected with the estate,
after having been carefully examined by Mr. Parkinson, and
Mr. Aubrey, and Mr. Griffiths, was in readiness for the most
scrupulous and searching investigation on the part of Mr.
Aubrey's successor and his agents.
    Mr. Aubrey's library was already carefully packed up, and
was to follow him on the ensuing day to London by water;
as also were several portions of the furniture—the residue of
which was to be sold off within a day or two's time. How
difficult—how very difficult had it been for them to choose
which articles they would part with, and which retain! The
favorite old high-backed easy-chair, which had been worked by
Miss Aubrey herself; the beautiful ebony cabinet, which had
been given by her father to her mother, who had given it to
Kate; the little chairs of Charles and Agnes—and in which
Mr. Aubrey and Kate, and all their brothers and sisters, had
sat when children; Mrs. Aubrey's piano—these and a few
other articles had been successfully pleaded for by Mrs. Aubrey and Kate, and were to accompany, or rather follow them
to London, instead of passing, by the auctioneer's hammer,
into the hands of strangers. The two old carriage-horses,
which had drawn old Mrs. Aubrey in the family coach for
many years, were to be turned to grass for the rest of their
days at Lady Stratton's. Poor old Peggy was, in like man-

ner, to have to herself a little field belonging to Dr. Tatham.
Little Charles's pony, a beautiful animal, and most reluctantly parted with, was sent as a present, in his name, to Sir Harry
Oldfield, one of his play-fellows. Hector, the magnificent Newfoundland dog, was, at the vehement instance of Pumpkin, the
gardener, who almost went on his knees to beg for the animal,
and declared that he loved the creature like a son—as I verily
believe he did, for they were inseparable, and their attachment
was mutual—given up to him on his solemn promise to take
great care of him.   Then there was a poor animal that they
hardly knew how to dispose of.   It was a fine old favorite
stag-hound, stone-blind, quite gray about the head, and so very
feeble that it could but just crawl in and out of its commodious kennel and lie basking in the genial sunshine, wagging
his tail when any one spoke to it, and affectionately licking
the hand that patted it.   Thus had it treated Mr. Aubrey that
very morning as he stood by, and stooped down to caress it for
the last time.   It was, at his earnest request, assigned to Dr.
Tatham, kennel and all; indeed, the worthy little Doctor would
have filled his premises in a similar way, by way of having
" keepsakes " and " memorials " of his friends.   Miss Aubrey's beautiful little Marlborough spaniel, with its brilliant
black eyes and long glossy graceful ears, was to accompany her
to London.

As for the servants—the housekeeper was going to keep the
house of her brother, a widower, at Grilston, and the butler
was going to marry and quit service; and for the rest, Mr.
Parkinson had, at Mr. Aubrey's desire, written about them to
Messrs. Quirk, Gammon and Snap; and Mr. Gammon had sent
word that such of the establishment as chose might continue
at Yatton, at all events, till the pleasure of Mr. Titmouse,
upon the subject, should have been known.   All the servants
had received a quarter's wages that morning from Mr. Griffiths,
in the presence of Mr. Aubrey, who spoke kindly to each, and
earnestly recommended them to conduct themselves respectfully toward his successor.   Scarce any of them could answer
him, otherwise than by an humble bow of courtesy, accompanied by sobs and tears.   One of them did contrive to speak,
and passionately expressed a wish that the first morsel Mr.
Titmouse eat in the house might choke him—a sally which
received so very grave a rebuke from Mr. Aubrey as brought
the hasty offender to her knees begging forgiveness, which, I
need hardly say, she received, with a very kind admonition.
Many of them most vehemently entreated to be allowed to
accompany Mr. Aubrey and his family to London, and con

tinue in their service, but in vain. Mr. Aubrey had made his
selection, having taken only his own valet, and Mrs. Aubrey's
maid, and one of the nursery-maids, and declaring that on no
consideration would he think of being accompanied by any
other of the servants.

There were some twenty or thirty poor old infirm cottagers,
men and women, who had been for years weekly pensioners on
the bounty of Yatton, and respecting whom Mr. Aubrey felt a
painful anxiety. What could he do? He gave the sum of
fifty pounds to Dr. Tatham for their use, and requested him
to press their claims earnestly upon the new proprietor of Yatton. He also wrote almost as many letters as there were of
these poor people, on their behalf, to his friends and neighbors. Oh, it was a moving scene that occurred at each of their
little cottages, when their benefactors, Mr. Aubrey, his wife
and sister, severally called to bid them farewell and receive
their humble and tearful blessings! But it was the parting
with her school, which neither she nor her brother saw any
probability of being kept up longer than for a month or two
after their departure, that occasioned Kate the greatest distress. There were several reasons, which will occur to the
reader, why no application should be made about the matter
from her, or on her account, to Mr. Titmouse, even if she had
not had reason to anticipate, from what she had heard of his
character, that he was not a person to feel any interest in such
an institution. Nor had she liked to trouble or burden the
friends she left behind her with the responsibility of supporting
and superintending her little establishment. She had nothing
for it, therefore, but to prepare the mistress and her scholars
for the breaking up of the school, within a month of her departure from Yatton. She gave the worthy woman, the mistress, a present of a five-pound note, and five shillings apiece
to each of the children. She felt quite unequal to the task of
personally taking leave of them, as she had intended and
several times attempted. She, therefore, with many tears,
wrote the following lines, and gave them to Dr. Tatham to
read aloud in the school when their good and beautiful writer
should be far on her way toward London. The little Doctor
paused a good many times while he read it, and complained of
his glasses.

"My dear little girls,—You know that I have already oid
each of you good-bye; and though I tried to say something to
all of you at once, I was not able, because I was so sorry to
part with you and tell you that my little school must be given

up. So I have written these few lines to tell you that I love you all and have tried to be a good friend to you. Be sure not to forget your spelling and reading and your needle. Your mothers have promised to hear you say your catechisms; you must also be sure to say your prayers, and to read your Bibles, and to behave very seriously at church, and to be always dutiful to your parents. Then God will bless you all! I hope you will not forget us, for we shall often think of you when we are a great way off; and Dr. Tatham will now and then write and tell us how you are going on. Farewell, my dear little girls; and may God bless and preserve you all! This is the prayer of both of us—Mrs. Aubrey and

"CATHERINE AUBREY.

"*Yatton, 15th May*, 18—."

The above was not written in the uniform and beautiful hand usual with Miss Aubrey; it was, on the contrary, rather irregular, and evidently written hastily; but Dr. Tatham preserved it to the day of his death, and always thought it beautiful.

On the ensuing morning, at a very early hour, Dr. Tatham left the vicarage to pay his last visit to friends whom it almost broke his heart to part with, in all human probability forever. He started, but on a moment's reflection ceased to be surprised at the sight of Mr. Aubrey approaching him from the direction of the little church-yard. He was calm, but his countenance bore the traces of very recent emotion. They greeted each other in silence, and so walked on for some time, arm in arm, slowly toward the Hall. It was a dull, heavy morning, almost threatening rain. The air seemed full of oppression. The only sounds audible were the hoarse clamorous sounds issuing from the old rookery, at some distance on their left. They interchanged but few words as they walked along the winding pathway to the Hall. The first thing that attracted their eyes on passing under the gate-way was the large old family carriage standing opposite the Hall door, where stood some luggage, sufficient for the journey, ready to be placed upon it, the remainder having been sent on the day before to London. They were all up and dressed. The children were taking their last breakfast in the nursery; Charles making many inquiries of the weeping servants, which they could answer only by tears and kisses. In vain was the breakfast-table spread for the senior travelers. There sat poor Kate, in traveling trim, before the antique silver urn, attempting to perform, with tremulous hand, her accustomed office, but neither she nor Mrs. Aubrey was equal to the task; which, summoning the housekeeper into the room, they devolved upon her, and which she performed in perturbed silence. Mr. Aubrey and Dr. Tatham were standing there; but neither of them spoke. A short time before Mr. Aubrey had requested the servants to be summoned, as usual, to morning prayer, in the accustomed room, and requested Dr. Tatham to officiate. As soon, however, as the sorrowful little assemblage was collected before him, he whispered to Mr. Aubrey that he felt unequal to go through the duty with the composure it required; and after a pause, he said, "Let us kneel down;" and in a low voice, often interrupted by his own emotions and the sobs of those around him, he read, with touching simplicity and solemnity, the Ninety-first Psalm, adding the Lord's Prayer and a benediction.

The bitter preparations for starting at an early hour, seven o'clock, were soon afterward completed. Half smothered with the kisses and caresses of the affectionate servants, little Charles and Agnes were already seated in the carriage, on the laps of their two attendants, exclaiming, "Come, papa! come, mamma! the horses are ready to start!" Just then, poor Pumpkin the gardener, scarce able to speak, made his appearance, his arms full of nosegays, which he had been culling for the last two hours—having one apiece for every one of the travelers, servants, and children, and all. The loud angry bark of Hector was heard from time to time, little Charles calling loudly for him; but Pumpkin had fastened him up, for fear of his starting off after the carriage. At length, scarce having tasted breakfast, the travelers made their appearance at the Hall door. Kate and Mrs. Aubrey were utterly overcome at the sight of the carriage, and wept bitterly. They threw their arms passionately around and kissed their venerable friend and pastor, Dr. Tatham, who was but little less agitated than themselves. Then they tore themselves from him, and hastily got into the carriage. As he stood alone, bareheaded, on their quitting him, he lifted his hands, but could scarce utter a parting benediction. Mr. Aubrey, with a flushed cheek and a quivering lip, then grasped his hand, whispering, "Farewell, my dear and venerable friend! Farewell!" "The Lord God of thy fathers bless thee!" murmured Dr. Tatham, clasping Mr. Aubrey's hand in both of his own and looking solemnly upward. Mr. Aubrey, taking off his hat, turned toward him an unutterable look, then waving his hand to the group of agitated servants that stood within and without the door, he stepped into the carriage, the door was shut, and they rolled slowly away. Outside the park gates were collected more than a hundred people to bid them farewell—all the men, when the carriage came in sight, taking off their hats. The carriage stopped for a moment. "God bless you all! God bless you!" exclaimed Mr. Aubrey, waving his hand, while from each window was extended the white hand of Kate and Mrs. Aubrey, which was fervently kissed and shaken by those who were nearest. Again the carriage moved on; and quickening their speed, the horses soon bore them out of the village. Within less than half an hour afterward the tearful eyes of the travelers, as they passed a familiar turning of the road, had looked their last on Yatton!

CHAPTER XVIII.

NOTE.—The following paragraph, which was annexed to Part XI. of this work, in Blackwood's Magazine for September, 1840, the author ventures, for a particular reason, to retain in this the separate edition:—

Several legal topics have been touched upon in these papers, which seem to have attracted some little attention among professional readers, as at least would appear from various communications—some at considerable length, some anonymous, others not—addressed, through the publishers, to "The Author of Ten Thousand a Year, in Blackwood's Magazine." The principal matters thus discussed are, *the power of an heir, in the life-time of his ancestor* (to speak popularly, though not with legal accuracy, since *nemo est hæres viventes*), *to convey away his expectancy in fee, so as to bind himself and those claiming under him, by estoppel on the subsequent descent of the estate.* On this point have been received several communications—one of which (from a great lawyer) opposes the doctrine laid down in the text. 'Tis doubtless an important point; and where doctors differ I am not presumptuous enough to volunteer an opinion. The other which seems principally to have attracted attention is the effect given by Lord Widdrington, C.J., at the trial (in which he is represented as being subsequently confirmed by the decision of the Court of King's Bench), to the ERASURE in the deed of confirmation. From two letters I learn that one or two clients of the writers of them have conceived great alarm on this subject, and have actually directed all their title-deeds to be overhauled, and, in case of an erasure being discovered, submitted to eminent counsel! Such erasures have been discovered, it would seem, in two instances. In one the counsel differed from Lord Widdrington; in the other, agreed with him. The question, then, here is, Whether, *when an ancient deed (i. e.*, upward of thirty years old, after which period a deed is said to *prove itself*) *is produced from the proper custody in support of the rights of the party producing it, and there proves to be an erasure in it in an essential part of the deed—such deed ought to be rejected, unless the erasure can be accounted for; or admitted upon the presumption that such erasure occurred before the execution of the deed?* Upon this point I confess that I have formed a pretty strong opinion, and have referred again to the authorities; and venture upon the whole, to give in my adhesion to the opinion of Lord Widdrington and his court—although two papers sent to me—(one of them very elaborate)—contest that opinion. It is rather singular that, about a fortnight ago, Lord Brougham, in delivering the judgment of the House of Lords in three appeal cases from Scotland, each of which was a case depending upon an effect of an erasure, expressly declared the Scotch law to be to the effect laid down in these papers, and decided accordingly, admitting, at the same time, the cases to be full of grievous hardship—in one instance, a widow losing the whole of the provision which had been made for her by her deceased husband. Whether or not my notions of the existing English law on this subject are antiquated, and contrary to those now entertained by the professional, I leave for the decision of those who are competent to form an opinion.—As for several other communications of a different nature—some similarly, others differently addressed—some complimentary, some far otherwise, and insinuating allusions which are groundless, and objects which have no existence—surely, on consideration, the authors of them can not expect any answer, nor yet construe silence into discourtesy or *admission.*

London, 14th August, 1840.

Rank is very apt to attract and dazzle vulgar and feeble optics; and the knowledge that such is its effect is unspeakably gratifying to a vain and ignorant possessor of that rank. Of the truth of one part of this observation, take as an illustration the case of Tittlebat Titmouse; of the other, that of the Earl of Dreddlington. The former's dinner engagement with the latter, his august and awful kinsman, was an event of such magnitude as to absorb almost all his faculties in the contemplation of it, and also occasion him great anxiety in preparing for an effective appearance upon so signal an occa-

sion. Mr. Gammon had repeatedly, during the interval, instructed his anxious pupil, if so he might be called, as to the
manner in which he ought to behave. He was—Heaven save
the mark, poor Titmouse!—to assume an air of mingled deference, self-possession, and firmness; not to be overawed by
the greatness with which he would be brought into contact,
nor unduly elated by a sense of his own suddenly acquired importance. He was, on the other hand, to steer evenly between
the extremes of timorousness and temerity—to aim at that
happy mean, so grateful to those able to appreciate the effort
and object of those attaining to it. Titmouse was to remember that great as was the Earl of Dreddlington, he was yet *but
a man*—related, too, by consanguinity to him, the aforesaid
Titmouse, who might, moreover, before many years should
have elapsed, become himself Earl of Dreddlington, or at least
Lord Drelincourt, and by consequence equally entitled, with
the present possessor of that resplendent position, to the
homage of mankind. At the same time that the earl's advanced years gave him a natural claim to the respect and deference of his young kinsman—(whom, moreover, he was
about to introduce into the sublime regions of aristocracy, and
also of political society)—Titmouse might derive a few ingre-
dients of consolation from the reflection that his income
probably *exceeded* by a third that of the Earl of Dreddlington.
This is the sum of Mr. Gammon's *general* instructions to his
eager and excited pupil; but he also gave Titmouse many
minor hints and suggestions. He was to drink very little wine
—(whereat Titmouse demurred somewhat vehemently, and
asked " How the d—l he was to *get his steam up ?*")—and on
no account to call for beer or porter, to which plebeian bever-
ages, indeed, he might consider himself as having bid a long
and last adieu—to say " my lord " and " your lordship," in
addressing the Earl—and " your ladyship," in addressing
Lady Cecilia;—and, above all, never to appear in a hurry, but
to do and say whatever he had to do and to say calmly; for
that the nerves of aristocracy were very delicate, and could not
bear a bustle or the slightest display of energy or feeling.
Then, as to his *dress*—Gammon, feeling himself treading on
very doubtful ground, intimated merely that the essence of
true fashion was *simplicity*—but here Titmouse grew fidgety,
and his Mentor ceased.

During the night which ushered in the eventful day of Titmouse's dining with the Earl of Dreddlington, our friend got
but very little sleep. Early in the morning he engaged a most
respectable glass coach to convey him westward in something

like style; and before noon his anxieties were set at rest by the punctual arrival of various articles of dress, and decoration, and scent—for Titmouse had a great idea of scents. As for his new watch and its brilliant gold guard-chain—his eyes gloated upon them. What, he thought, should he have been without them! About half past three o'clock he retired to his bedroom, and resigned himself into the hands of the tip-top hair-dresser from the Strand, whose agreeable manipulations, and still more agreeable small-talk, occupied upward of an hour—Titmouse giving the anxious operator abundant notice of the high quarter in which his handiwork was likely soon to be scrutinized.

"Pray-a, can you tell me," quoth Titmouse, drawlingly, shortly after Twirl had commenced his operations, "how long will it take me to get from this infernal part of the town to Grosvenor Square?—*Dem* long way, isn't it, Mr. what's-your-name?"

"Grosvenor Square, sir?" said Twirl, glibly, but with a perceptible dash of deference in his tone; "why it *is* as one might say a tolerable way off, certainly; but you can't well miss your way *there*, sir, of all places in town—"

"My coachman," interrupted Titmouse, with a fine air, "of course, had I thought of it, *he* must know."

"Oh! to be sure, sir. There's none but people of the most *highest* rank lives in that quarter, sir. Excuse me, sir, but I've a brother-in-law that's valet to the Duke of Dunderwhistle there—"

"Indeed! How far off is that from Lord Dreddlington's?" inquired Titmouse, carelessly.

"Lord Dreddlington's, sir?—Well, I never! Isn't it particular strange, if that's where you're going, sir—it's next door to the Duke's—the very next door, sir!"

"'Pon my life, is it indeed? How devilish odd!"

"Know the Earl of Dreddlington, then, I presume, sir?"

"Ya-a-s, I should think so: he's my—my—relation, that's all; and devilish near, too!"

Mr. Twirl instantly conceived a kind of reverence for the gentleman upon whom he was operating.

"Well, sir," he presently added, in a still more respectful tone than before, "p'r'aps you'll think it a liberty, sir; but, do you know, I've several times had the honor of seeing his lordship in the street at a little distance—and there's a—a family likeness between you, sir—'pon my word, sir. It struck me, directly I saw you, that you was like some nob I'd seen at, the other end of the town." [Here Titmouse experienced

pleasurable sensations, similar to those of a cat when you pass
your hand down its glossy coat in the right direction.] "Will
you allow me, sir, to give your hair a good brushing, sir, before I dress it? I always like to take the *greatest* pains with
the hair of my quality customers!—Do you know, sir, that I
had the honor of dressing his Grace's hair for a whole fortnight together, once when my brother-in-law was ill! and
though p'r'aps I oughtn't to say it, his Grace expressed the
highest satisfaction at my exertions, sir."

"'Pon my life, and *I* should say you were an uncommon
good hand—I've known lots worse, I assure you; men that
would have spoiled the best head of hair going, by Jove!"

"Sir, you're very kind. I assure you, sir, that to do justice
to a *gent's* hair requires an uncommon deal of practice, and a
sort of *nat'ral* talent for it besides. Lord, sir! how much depends on a gent's hair, don't it? Of two coming into a
room, it makes all the difference, sir! Believe me, sir, it's no
use being well dressed, nay, nor good looking, if as how the
hair a'n't done what I call *correct.*"

"By Jove! I really think you're nigh about the mark," said
Titmouse.

And after a pause, during which Mr. Twirl had been brushing away at one particular part of the head with some vehemence, "Well," he exclaimed, with a sigh, ceasing for a
moment his vigorous exertions, "I'm *blest* if I can manage it,
do what I will!"

"Eh? What's that? What is it?" inquired Titmouse, a
little alarmedly.

"Why, sir, it's what we gents, in our profession, calls a
feather, which is the most *hobstinatest* thing in nature."

"What's a *feather?*" quoth Titmouse, rather faintly.

"You see, sir, 'tis when a small lot of hair on a gent's head
will stick up, do we can to try and get it down; and (excuse me, sir) *you've* got a regular rattler!" Titmouse put up
his hand to feel, Twirl guiding it to the fatal spot: there it
was, just as Twirl had described it.

"What's to be done?" murmured Titmouse.

"I'm afraid, sir, you don't use our OSTRICH GREASE and
RHINOCEROS MARROW, sir."

"Your *what?*" cried Titmouse, apprehensively, with a dismally distinct recollection of the tragedy of the Cyanochaitanthropopoion, and the Damascus Cream, and the Tetaragmenon
Abracadabra; matters which he at once mentioned to Mr.
Twirl.

"Ah, it's not *my* custom, sir?" quoth Twirl, "to run down

other gents' inventions; but my real opinion is that they're all an imposition—a rank imposition, sir. I didn't like to say it, sir; but I soon saw there had been somebody a-practicing on your hair.''

"What! is it *very* plain?" cried Titmouse, starting up and stepping to the glass.

"No, sir—not so *very* plain; only *you've* got, as I might say, *accustomed* to the sight of it; but when it's properly curled and puckered up, and frizzed about, it won't show— nor the feather neither, sir; so, by your leave, here goes, sir;" and, after about a quarter of an hour's more labor, he succeeded in parting it right down the middle of the head, bringing it out into a bold curl toward each eyebrow, and giving our friend quite a new and very fascinating appearance, even in his own eyes. And as for the color—it really was not so very marked after all; a little purple-hued and mottled, to be sure, in parts, but not to a degree to attract the eye of a casual observer. Twirl having declared, at length, his labors completed—regarding Titmouse's head with a look of proud satisfaction—Titmouse paid him half a crown, and also ordered a pot of ostrich grease and of rhinoceros marrow (the one being *suet*, the other *lard*, differently scented and colored), and was soon left at liberty to proceed with the important duties of the toilet. It took him a good while; but in the end he was supremely successful. He wore black tights (*i. e.*, pantaloons fitting closely to his legs, and tied round his ankles with black ribbons), silk stockings, and shoes with glittering silver buckles. His white neckerchief was tied with great elegance, not a wrinkle superfluous being visible in it. His shirt front of lace had two handsome diamond pins, connected together by a little delicate gold chain, glistening in the middle of it. Then he had a white waistcoat edge, next a crimson one, and lastly, a glorious sky-blue satin waistcoat, spangled all over with gold flowers inwrought—and across it hung his new gold watch-guard, and his silver guard for his eyeglass, producing an inconceivably fine effect. His coat was of a light-brown, of exquisite cut, fitting him as closely as if he had been born in it, and with burnished brass buttons, of sugar-loaf shape. 'Twas padded also with great judgment, and really took off more of his round-shouldered awkwardness of figure than any coat he had ever before had. Then he had a fine white pocket-handkerchief, soaked in lavender water, and immaculate white kid gloves. Thus habited, he stood before his glass, bowing fifty different times, and adjusting his expression to various elegant forms of address. He was particularly struck with

the combined effect of the two curls of his hair toward each
eye, and the hair underneath his chin curved upward on each
side of his mouth in complete symmetry. I have ascertained
from Mr. Titmouse himself that on this memorable occasion
of his first introduction to NOBILITY, every item of dress and
decoration was entirely new; and when at length his labors
had been completed, he felt great composure of mind and a
consciousness of the decisive effect he must produce upon those
into whose presence he was soon to be ushered. His "carriage" was presently announced; and after keeping it standing a few minutes, merely for form's sake, he gently placed
his hat upon his head, drew on one glove, took his little ebony
cane in his hand, and, with a hurried inward prayer that he
might be equal to the occasion, stepped forth from his apartments, and passed on to the glass coach. Such a brilliant little
figure, I will take upon myself to say, had never before issued
nor will perhaps ever again issue, from the Cabbage-Stalk
Hotel. The waiters whom he passed inclined toward him with
instinctive reverence. He was *very* fine, to be sure; but who
could, they justly thought, be dressed too finely that had ten
thousand a year, and was going to dine with a lord in Grosvenor Square?

Titmouse was soon on his way toward that at once desired
and dreaded region. He gazed with a look of occasional pity
and contempt as he passed along at the plebeian pedestrians
and the lines of shops on each side of the narrow streets, till
he began to perceive indications of superior modes of existence; when, however, he began to feel a little fidgety and
nervous. The streets grew wider, the squares greater, hack-
ney-coaches (unsightly objects) became fewer and fewer, giving
place to splendid vehicles, coaches, and chariots, with one,
two, and even three footmen clustering behind, with long
canes, with cockades, with shoulder-knots; crimson, yellow,
blue, green hammer-cloths, with burnished crests upon them,
and sleek coachmen with wigs and three-cornered hats, and
horses that pawed the ground with very pride; ladies, within,
glistening in satin, lace, and jewels—their lords beside them,
leaning back with countenances so stern and haughty; oh, by
all that was magnificent! Titmouse felt himself getting now
within the very vortex of greatness and fashion, and experienced a frequent fluttering and catching of the breath, and an
indefinite distressing apprehension. He was, however, now in
for it—and there was no retreat. As he neared Grosvenor
Square he heard, ever and anon, terrific thundering noises at
the doors opposite which these splendid vehicles drew up—as if

the impatient footmen were infuriated because the doors did not fly open themselves at the sound of the approaching carriage-wheels. At length he entered Grosvenor Square, that " pure empyrean " of earthly greatness. Carriages rolled haughtily past him, others dashed desperately in different directions. At each side of Lord Dreddlington's house were carriages setting down with tremendous uproar. Mr. Titmouse felt his color going, and his heart began to beat much faster than usual. 'Twas quite in vain that he " hemmed " two or three times, by way of trying to reassure himself; he felt that his hour was come; and would have been glad at the moment for any decent excuse for driving off home again and putting off the evil day a little longer. Opposite the dreaded door had now drawn up Mr. Titmouse's glass coach, and the decent coachman—whose well-worn hat, and long, clean, but threadbare blue coat and ancient-looking top-boots bespoke their wearer's thriftiness—slowly alighting, threw the reins on his quiet horses' backs, and gave a modest *rat-tat-tat-tat-tat* at the door without ringing.

" What name shall I give, sir?" said he, returning to his coach, and letting down the loud clanking steps with a noise for which Titmouse could have heartily kicked him.

" Titmouse—Mr. Titmouse," replied, he hurriedly, as the lofty door was thrown open by the corpulent porter, disclosing several footmen, with powdered heads, standing in the hall waiting for him.

" Mr. Titmouse!" exclaimed the coachman to the servants: then, addressing again his flustered fare—" When shall I come back for you, sir?"

" D— me, sir—don't bother *me*," faltered Titmouse, and the next moment was in the hands of the Philistines—the door was closed upon him. All his presence of mind had evaporated; the excellent lessons given him by Mr. Gammon had disappeared like breath upon the polished mirror. Though Lord Dreddlington's servants had never before seen in the house so strange an object as poor little Titmouse, they were of far too highly polished manners to appear to notice anything unusual. They silently motioned him upstairs with a bland courteous air, he carrying his little agate-headed cane in one hand and his new hat in the other. A gentlemanly person in a full black dress suit opened the drawing-room door for him, with an elegant inclination which Titmouse very gracefully returned. A faint mist seemed to be in the drawing-room for a second or two; quickly clearing away, however, Titmouse beheld, at the upper end, but two figures, that of an

old gentleman and a young lady—in fact, the Earl of Dreddlington and Lady Cecilia. Now, that great man had not
been a whit behindhand, in the matter of dress, with the little
creature now trembling before him; being, in truth, full as
anxious to make an effective first appearance in the eyes of
Titmouse as he in those of the Earl of Dreddlington. And
each had succeeded in his way. There was little or no substantial difference between them. The Right Honorable the
Earl Dreddlington was an old experienced fool, and Tittlebat
Titmouse a young inexperienced one. They were the same
species of plant, but grown in different soils. The one had
had to struggle through a neglected existence by the dusty
hard road-side of life; the other had had all the advantages of
hot-house cultivation—its roots striking deep into, and thriving
upon the rich manure of sycophancy and adulation!—We have
seen how anxious was our little friend to appear, as became the
occasion, before his great kinsman; who, in his turn, had
several times during the day exulted secretly in the anticipation of the impression which must be produced upon the
mind of Titmouse by the sudden display, in the Earl's person,
of the sublimest distinctions which society can bestow, short of
royalty. It had once or twice occurred to the Earl whether
he could find any fair excuse for appearing in his full general's
uniform; but on maturer reflection, governed by that simplicity and severity of taste which ever distinguished him, he
abandoned that idea, and appeared in a plain blue coat, white
waistcoat, and black knee-breeches. But on his left breast
glittered one or two foreign orders, and across his waistcoat
was the broad red ribbon of the Bath. His hair was white and
fine; his cold blue eye and haughty lip gave him an expression
of severe dignity, and he stood erect as an arrow. Lady
Cecilia reclined on the sofa, with an air of languor and ennui
that had become habitual to her, and was dressed in glistening
white satin, with a necklace of large and very beautiful pearls.
The Earl was standing in an attitude of easy grace to receive
his guest, as to whose figure and height, by the way, he was
quite in the dark—Mr. Titmouse might be a great or a little
man, and forward or bashful, and require a corresponding
demeanor and address on the part of the Earl. "Ah, my
God!" involuntarily exclaimed Lord Dreddlington to himself,
the instant his eye caught sight of Titmouse, who approached
slowly, making profound and formal obeisances. The Earl
stood rooted to the spot he had occupied when Titmouse entered. If his servants had turned an ape into the drawing-
room the Earl could scarcely have felt or exhibited greater

amazement than he now experienced for a moment. "Ah, my God!" thought he, "what a fool have we here? what creature is this?" Then it flashed across his mind; "May this be THE FUTURE LORD DRELINCOURT?" He was on the point of recoiling from his suddenly discovered kinsman in dismay (as for Lady Cecilia, she gazed at him, through the glass, in silent horror, after a faint exclamation, on his first becoming visible, of "Gracious! Papa!"), when his habitual self-command came to his assistance, and advancing very slowly a step or two toward Titmouse—who, after a hurried glance around him, saw no place to deposit his hat and cane upon except the floor, on which he accordingly dropped them—the Earl extended his hand, slightly compressed the tips of Titmouse's fingers, and bowed courteously, but with infinite concern in his features.

"I am happy, Mr. Titmouse, to make your acquaintance," said the Earl, slowly—"Sir, I have the honor to present you to my daughter, the Lady Cecilia." Titmouse, who by this time had got into a sort of cold sweat—a condition from which the Earl was really not *very* far removed—made a very profound and formal bow (he had been taking lessons from a posture-master at one of the theaters), first to the Earl, and then to Lady Cecilia, who rose about two inches from the sofa, and then sunk again upon it, without removing her eyes from the figure of Titmouse, who went on bowing, first to the one and then to the other, till the Earl had engaged him in conversation.

"It gives me pleasure, sir, to see that you are punctual in your engagements. I am so, too, sir; and owe no small portion of my success in life to it. Punctuality, sir, in small matters, leads to punctuality in great matters." This was said in a very deliberate and pompous manner.

"Oh, yes, my lord! quite so, your lordship," stammered Titmouse, suddenly recollecting a part of Gammon's instructions; "to be sure—wouldn't have been behind time, your lordship, for a minute, my lord; uncommon bad manners, if it pleases your lordship—"

"Will you be seated, sir?" interrupted the Earl, deliberately motioning him to a chair, and then sitting down beside him; after which the Earl seemed, for a second or two, to forget himself, staring in silence at Titmouse, and then in consternation at Lady Cecilia. "I—I "—said he, suddenly recollecting himself, "beg your par—sir, I mean I congratulate you upon your recent success. Sir, it must have been rather a surprise to you?"

"Oh, yes, sir—my lord, most uncommon, may it please your lordship—particular—but *right is right*—please your lordship—"

["Oh, Heavens! merciful Heavens! How horrid is all this! Am I awake or only dreaming? 'Tis an idiot—and what's worse, a *vulgar* idiot. My God! *And this thing may be Lord Drelincourt.*" This was what was passing through Lord Dreddlington's mind, while his troubled eye was fixed upon Titmouse.]

"It is, indeed, Mr. Titmouse," replied his lordship, "very true, sir; what you say is correct. Quite so; exactly." His eye was fixed on Titmouse, but his words were uttered, as it were, mechanically, and in a musing manner. It flitted for a moment across his mind whether he should ring the bell and order the servant to show out of the house the fearful imp that had just been shown into it; but at that critical moment he detected poor Titmouse's eye fixed with a kind of reverent intensity upon his lordship's glittering orders. 'Twas a lucky look that for Titmouse, for it began to melt away the ice that was getting round the little heart of his august relative. 'Twas evident that the poor young man had not been accustomed to society, thought the Earl, with an approach toward the compassionate mood. He was frightfully dressed, to be sure; and as for his speech, he was manifestly overawed by the Presence in which he found himself; [that thought melted a little more of the ice]. Yes, was it not evident that he had *some* latent power of appreciating real distinction when he beheld it? [the little heart here lost *all* the ice that had begun so suddenly to incrust it]. And again;—he has actually thrust out the intolerable Aubrey, and is now lawful owner of Yatton—of TEN THOUSAND A YEAR—

"Did you see the review to-day, sir?" inquired the Earl, rather blandly. "His Majesty was there, sir, and seemed to enjoy the scene." Titmouse, with a timid air, said that he had not seen it, as he had been upon the river; and after a few more general observations—"Will you permit me, sir? It is from A QUARTER requiring the highest—a-hem!" said the Earl as a note was brought him, which he immediately opened and read. Lady Cecilia also appearing engaged reading, Titmouse had a moment's breathing time and interval of relief. What would he have given, he thought, for some other person, or several persons, to come in and divide the attention—the intolerably oppressive attention of the two august individuals then before him! He seized the opportunity to cast a furtive glance around the room. It opened into a

second, which opened into a third: how spacious each and
lofty! And glittering glass chandeliers in each! What
chimney and pier-glasses! What rich crimson satin curtains—they must have cost twelve or fourteen shillings a yard
at least!—The carpets of the finest Brussels—and they felt like
velvet to the feet;—then the brackets, of marble and gold, with
snowy statues and vases glistening upon each; chairs so delicate, and gilded all over—he almost feared to sit down on
them. What would the Quirks and Tag-rags think of this?
Faugh—only to think for a moment of Alibi House and Satin
Lodge!—Then there was the Lady Cecilia—a lady of high
rank! How rich her dress—and how haughtily beautiful she
looked as she reclined upon the sofa! [she was in fact busy
conning over the new opera, coming out the next evening].
And the Earl of Dreddlington—there he was, reading, doubtless, some letter from the King or one of the royal family—a
man of great rank—resplendent in his decorations—all just as
he had seen in pictures, and heard and read of—what must
that red ribbon have cost? [Ay, indeed, poor Lord Dreddlington, it had cost you the labor of half a life of steadfast
sycophancy, of watchful maneuvering, and desperate exertion!
And at last, the minister tossed it to you in a moment of disgust and despair—mortally perplexed by the conflicting claims
of two sulky Dukes and a querulous old Marquis, each of
whom threatened to withdraw his "*influence and support,*"
if his real *rival's* claims were preferred!] He had never seen
any of such a breadth.—It must have been manufactured on
purpose for the Earl!—How white were his hands! And he
had an antique massive signet-ring on his forefinger, and two
glittering rings at least on each of his little fingers—positively
Titmouse at length began to regard him almost as a god:—
and yet the amazing thought occurred that this august being
was allied to him by the ties of relationship!—Such were the
thoughts and reflections passing through the mind of Titmouse,
during the time that Lord Dreddlington was engaged in reading his letter—and afterward during the brief intervals which
elapsed between the various observations addressed to him by
his lordship.

  The gentleman in black at length entered the room, and
advancing slowly and noiselessly toward the Earl, said, in a
quiet manner, " Dinner, my lord;" and retired. Into what
new scenes of splendid embarrassment was this the signal for
Mr. Titmouse's introduction? thought our friend, and trembled.

  " Mr. Titmouse, will you give your arm to the Lady Cecilia?"

said the Earl, motioning him to the sofa. Up jumped Titmouse, and approached hastily the recumbent beauty, who languidly arose, arranged her train with one hand, and with the
other, having drawn on her glove, just barely touched the
proffered arm of Titmouse, extended toward her at a very
acute angle, and at right angles with his own body—stammer-
ing, "Honor to take your ladyship—uncommon proud—this
way, my lady."—Lady Cecilia took no more notice of him
than if he had been a dumb waiter, walking beside him in
silence—the Earl following. To think that a nobleman of
high rank was walking *behind* him!

Would to Heaven, thought the embarrassed Titmouse, that
he had two fronts, one for the Earl behind, and the other to
be turned full toward Lady Cecilia! The tall servants, powdered and in light-blue liveries, stood like a guard of honor
around the dining-room door. That room was extensive and
lofty; what a solitary sort of state were they about to dine in!
Titmouse felt cold, though it was summer, and trembled as he
followed, rather than led, his haughty partner to her seat; and
then was motioned into his own by the Earl, himself sitting
down opposite a chased silver soup-tureen! A servant stood
behind Lady Cecilia and Titmouse; also on the left of the
Earl, while on his right, between his lordship and the glistening sideboard, stood a portly gentleman in black, with a bald
head and a somewhat haughty countenance. Though Titmouse had touched nothing since breakfast, he felt not the
slightest inclination to eat, and would have given the world to
have dared to say as much, and be at once relieved from a vast
deal of anxiety. Is it indeed easy to conceive of a fellow-creat-
ure in a state of more complete thralldom, at that moment,
than poor little Titmouse? A little animal under the suddenly exhausted receiver of an air-pump, or a fish just plucked
out of its own element, and flung gasping and struggling upon
the grass, may serve to assist your conceptions of the position
and sufferings of Mr. Titmouse. The Earl, who was on the
lookout for it, observed his condition with secret but complete
satisfaction; here he beheld the legitimate effect of rank and
state upon the human mind. Titmouse got through the soup
—of which about half a dozen spoonfuls only were put into his
plate—pretty fairly. Anywhere else than at Lord Dreddlington's, Titmouse would have thought it thin, watery stuff, with a
few green things chopped up and swimming in it; but now he
perceived that it had a spot of superior flavor. How some red
mullet, inclosed in paper, puzzled poor Titmouse, is best
known to himself.

"The Lady Cecilia will take wine with you, Mr. Titmouse, I dare say—" observed the Earl; and in a moment's time, but with perfect deliberation, the servants poured wine into the two glasses. "Your ladyship's health, my lady—" faltered Titmouse. She slightly bowed, and a faint smile glimmered at the corners of her mouth—but unobserved by Titmouse.* *

"I think you said, Mr. Titmouse," quoth the Earl, some time afterward, "that you had not yet taken possession of Yatton?"

"No, my lord; but I go down the day after to-morrow—quite—if I may say it, my lord—quite in style—" answered Titmouse, in a style of humble and hesitiating jocularity.

"Ha, ha!" exclaimed the Earl, gently.

"Had you any acquaintance with the Aubreys, Mr. Titmouse?" inquired the Lady Cecilia.

"No, my lady—yes, your ladyship (I beg your ladyship's pardon)—but, now I think of it, I had a slight acquaintance with Miss Aubrey." [Titmouse, Titmouse, you little wretch, how dare you say so?]

"She is considered pretty in the country, I believe," drawled Lady Cecilia, languidly.

"Oh, most uncommon lovely!—middling, only middling, my lady, I should say "—added Titmouse, suddenly; having observed, as he fancied, rather a displeased look in Lady Cecilia. He had begun his sentence with more energy than he had yet shown in the house; he finished it hastily, and colored as he spoke—feeling that he had somehow committed himself.

"Do you form a new establishment at Yatton, sir?" inquired the Earl, "or take to any part of that of your predecessor?"

"I have not, please your lordship, made up my mind yet exactly—should like to know your lordship's opinion."

"Why, sir, I should be governed by circumstances—by circumstances, sir; when you get there, sir, you will be better able to judge of the course you should pursue."

"Do you intend, Mr. Titmouse, to live in town, or in the country?" inquired Lady Cecilia.

"A little of both, my lady—but mostly in town; because, as your ladyship sees, the country is devilish dull—'pon my life, my lady—my lord—beg a thousand pardons," he added, bowing to both, and blushing violently. Here he had committed himself; but his august companions bowed to him very kindly, and he presently recovered his self-possession.

"Are you fond of hunting, Mr. Titmouse?" inquired the Earl.

"Why, my lord, can't exactly say that I am—but your lordship sees, cases alter circumstances, and when I get down there among the country gents, p'r'aps I may do as they do, my lord."

"I presume, Mr. Titmouse, you have scarcely chosen a town residence yet?" inquired Lady Cecilia.

"No, my lady—not fixed it yet—was thinking of taking Mr. Aubrey's house in Grosvenor Street, understanding it is to be sold;" then turning toward the Earl—"because, as your lordship see, I was thinking of getting into *both* the nests of the old birds, while both are warm"—he added, with a very faint smile.

"Exactly; yes—I see, sir—I understand you," replied Lord Dreddlington, sipping his wine. His manner rather discomposed Titmouse, to whom it then very naturally occurred that the Earl might be warmly attached to the Aubreys, and not relish their being spoken of so lightly; so Titmouse hastily and anxiously added—"Your lordship sees I was most *particular* sorry to make the Aubreys turn out. A most uncommon respectable gent, Mr. Aubrey; I assure your lordship I think so."

"I had not the honor of his acquaintance, sir," replied the Earl, coldly and with exceeding stiffness, which flustered Titmouse not a little; and a pause occurred in the conversation for a minute or two. Dinner had now considerably advanced, and Titmouse was beginning to grow a *little* familiar with the routine of matters. Remembering Gammon's caution concerning the wine, and also observing how very little was drunk by the Earl and Lady Cecilia, Titmouse did the same, and during the whole of dinner had scarcely three full glasses of wine.

"How long is it," inquired the Earl, addressing his daughter, "since they took that house?" Lady Cecilia could not say. "Stay—now I recollect—surely it was just before my appointment to the Household. Yes; it was about that time, I now recollect. I am alluding, Mr. Titmouse," continued the Earl, addressing him in a very gracious manner, "to an appointment under the Crown of some little distinction, which I was solicited to accept, at the personal instance of his Majesty, on the occasion of our party coming into power—I mean that of Lord Steward of the Household."

"Dear me, my lord! Indeed! Only to think, your lordship!" exclaimed Titmouse, with infinite deference in his manner, which encouraged the Earl to proceed.

"That, sir, was an office of great importance, and I had

some hesitation in undertaking its responsibility. But, sir, when I had once committed myself to my sovereign and my country, I resolved to give them my best services. I had formed plans for effecting very extensive alterations, sir, in that department of the public service, which I have no doubt would have given great satisfaction to the country as soon as the nature of my intentions became generally understood; when faction, sir, unfortunately prevailed, and we were compelled to relinquish office."

"Dear me, my lord! How particular sorry I am to hear it, my lord!" exclaimed Titmouse, as he gazed at the baffled statesman with an expression of respectful sympathy.

"Sir, it gives me sincere satisfaction," said the Earl, after a pause, "to hear that our political opinions agree—"

"Oh, yes; my lord, quite; *sure* of that—"

"I assure you, sir, that some little acquaintance with the genius and spirit of the British constitution has satisfied me that this country can never be safely or advantageously governed except on sound Whig principles."—He paused.

"Yes, my lord; it's quite true, your lordship—" interposed Titmouse, reverentially.

"That, sir, is the only way I know of by which aristocratic institutions can be brought to bear effectively upon, to blend harmoniously with, the interests of the lower orders—the people, Mr. Titmouse." Titmouse thought this wonderfully fine, and sat listening as to an oracle of political wisdom. The Earl, observing it, began to form a much higher opinion of his little kinsman. "The unfortunate gentleman, your predecessor at Yatton, sir, if he had but allowed himself to have been guided by those who had mixed in public affairs before he was born," said the Earl, with great dignity—

"'Pon my word, my lord, he was, I've heard, a d——d Tory!—Oh, my lady! my lord! humbly beg pardon," he added, turning pale; but the fatal word had been uttered, and heard by both; and he felt as if he could have sunk through the floor.

"Shall I have the honor of taking another glass of wine with you, sir?" inquired the Earl, rather gravely and severely, as if wishing Mr. Titmouse fully to appreciate the fearful breach of etiquette of which he had just been guilty. After they had bowed to each other, a very awkward pause occurred, which was at length broken by the considerate Lady Cecilia.

"Are you fond of the opera, Mr. Titmouse?"

"Very, my lady—most particular," replied Titmouse, who had been there once only.

"Do you prefer the opera, or the ballet? I mean the music
or the dancing?"

"Oh, I understand, your ladyship. 'Pon my word, my
lady, I prefer them both. The dancing is most uncommon
superior; though I must say, my lady, the lady dancers there
do most uncommonly—*rather*, I should say"—He stopped
abruptly; his face flushed, and he felt as if he had burst into a
perspiration. What the deuce was he about? It seemed as if
some devil within were urging him on, from time to time, to
commit himself. Good gracious! another word, and out would
have come his opinion as to the shocking indecency of the
ballet!

"I understand you, sir; I quite agree with you," said Lady
Cecilia, calmly; "the ballet *does* come on at a sad late hour; I
often wish they would now and then have the ballet first."

"'Pon my life, my lady," quoth Titmouse, eagerly snatching at the plank that was thrown to him; "that *is* what I
meant—nothing else, upon my soul, your ladyship."

"Do you intend taking a box there, Mr. Titmouse?" inquired her ladyship, with an appearance of interest in the expected answer.

"Why, your ladyship, they say a box there is a *precious*
long figure;—but in course, my lady, when I've got to rights
a little with my property—your ladyship understands—I shall
do the correct thing."

Here a very long pause ensued. How dismally quiet and
deliberate was everything! The very servants, how noiselessly they waited! Everything done just when it was wanted, yet
no hurry, or bustle, or noise; and they looked so composed—
so much at their ease. He fancied that they had scarce anything else to do than look at him and watch all his movements, which greatly embarrassed him, and he began to *hate*
them. He tried hard to inspirit himself with a reflection upon
his own suddenly acquired and really great personal importance: absolute master of Ten Thousand a Year, a relation of
the great man at whose table he sat, and whose hired servants
they were; but then his timorously raised eye would light, for
instance, upon the splendid *insignia* of the Earl, and he felt
as oppressed as ever. What would he not have given for a
few minutes' interval and sense of complete freedom and independence? And were these to be his feelings ever hereafter?
Was this the sort of tremulous apprehension of offense and
embarrassment as to his every move, to which he was to be
doomed in high life? Oh, that he had but been *born* to it,
like the Earl and the Lady Cecilia!

" Were you ever in the House of Lords, Mr. Titmouse?" inquired Lord Dreddlington, suddenly, after casting about for some little time for a topic on which he might converse with Titmouse.

" No, my lord, never—should most uncommon like to see it, my lord "—replied Titmouse, eagerly.

" Certainly, it is an impressive spectacle, sir, and well worth seeing."

" I suppose, my lord, your lordship goes there every day?"

" Why, sir, I believe *I am* pretty punctual in my attendance. I was there to-day, sir, till the House rose. Sir, I am of opinion that hereditary legislators—a practical anomaly in a free state like this—but one which has innumerable unperceived advantages to recommend it—Sir, our country expects at our hands, in discharge of so grave a trust—in short, if we were not to be true to—we who are in a peculiar sense the guardians of public liberty—if we were once to betray our trust—Let me trouble you, sir, for a little of that—" said the Earl, using some foreign word which Titmouse had never heard of before, and looking toward a delicately constructed fabric, as of compressed snow, that stood before Titmouse, a servant stood in a twinkling beside him with his lordship's plate. Ah, me! that I should have to relate so sad an event as presently occurred to Titmouse! He took a spoon, and, imagining the glistening fabric before him to be as solid as it looked, brought to bear upon it an adequate degree of force, even as if he had been going to scoop out a piece of Stilton cheese—and inserting his spoon at the summit of the snowy and deceitful structure, souse to the bottom went spoon, hand, coat-cuff, and all, and a very dismal noise evidenced that the dish on which the spoon had descended with so much force—was no longer a dish. It was, in fact, broken in halves, and the liquid from within ran about on the cloth * * * A cluster of servants was quickly around him. * * A mist came over his eyes, the color deserted his cheek, and he had a strange feeling, as if verily the end of all things was at hand.

" I beg you will think nothing of it—it really signifies nothing at all, Mr. Titmouse," said the earl, kindly, observing his agitation.

" Oh dear! Oh, my lord—your ladyship—what an *uncommon* stupid ass!"

" Pray, *don't* distress yourself, Mr. Titmouse," said Lady Cecilia, really feeling for his evident misery, " or you will distress *us.*"

" I beg—humbly beg pardon—please your lordship—your
ladyship. I'll replace it with the best in London the very first
thing in the morning." Here the servant beside him, who
was arranging the table-cloth, uttered a faint sound of suppressed laughter, which disconcerted Titmouse still more.

" Give yourself no concern—'tis only a *trifle*, Mr. Titmouse!
—You understand, ha, ha?" said the Earl, kindly.

" But if your lordship will only allow me—expense is no object.—I know the very best shop in Oxford Street—"

" Suppose we take a glass of champagne together, Mr. Titmouse?" said the Earl, rather peremptorily; and Titmouse had
sense enough to be aware that he was to drop the subject. It
was a good while before he recovered even the little degree of
self-possession which he had had since first entering Lord
Dreddlington's house. He had afterward no very distinct
recollection of the manner in which he got through the rest of
dinner, but a general sense of his having been treated with the
most kind and delicate forbearance—no *fuss* made. Suppose
such an accident had occurred at Satin Lodge, or even Alibi
House!

Shortly after the servants had withdrawn, Lady Cecilia rose
to retire. Titmouse, seeing the Earl approaching the bell,
anticipated him in ringing it, and then darted to the door with
the speed of a lamp-lighter to open it, as he did, just before a
servant had raised his hand to it on the outside. Then he
stood within, and the servant without, each bowing, and Lady
Cecilia passed between them with stately step, her eyes fixed
upon the ground, and her lip compressed, with the effort to
check her inclination to a smile—perhaps even laughter. Titmouse was now left alone with Lord Dreddlington; and, on
resuming his seat, most earnestly renewed his entreaties to be
allowed to replace the dish which he had broken, assuring
Lord Dreddlington that " money was no object at all." He
was encountered, however, with so stern a negative by his lordship that, with a hurried apology, he dropped the subject; the
Earl, however, good-naturedly adding, that he had perceived
the *joke* intended by Mr. Titmouse—which was certainly a
very good one! This would have set off poor Titmouse again;
but a glance at the face of his magnificent host sealed his lips.

" I have heard it said, Mr. Titmouse," presently commenced the Earl, " that you have been engaged in mercantile
pursuits during the period of your exclusion from the estates
which you have just recovered. Is it so, sir?"

" Y-e-e-e-s—sir—my lord—" replied Titmouse, hastily considering whether or not he should altogether *sink the shop*

out he dared hardly venture upon so very decisive a lie—"I was, please your lordship, in one of the greatest establishments in the mercery line in London—at the West End, my lord; most confidential, my lord; management of everything; but, somehow, my lord, I never *took to it*—your lordship understands."

"Perfectly, sir; I can quite appreciate your feelings. But, sir, the mercantile interests of this great country are not to be overlooked. Those who are concerned in them are frequently respectable persons."

"Begging pardon, my lord—no they ain't—if your lordship only knew them as well as I do, my lord. Most uncommon low people. Do anything to turn a penny, my lord; and often sell damaged goods for best."

"It is very possible, sir, that there may exist irregularities, *eccentricities*, ha! ha! of that description; but upon the whole, sir, I am disposed to think that there are many very decent persons engaged in trade. I have had the happiness, sir, to assist in passing measures that were calculated, by removing restrictions and protective duties, to secure to this country the benefits of free and universal competition. We have been proceeding, sir, for many years, on altogether a wrong principle; but, not to follow out this matter further, I must remind you, sir, that your acquaintance with the principles and leading details of mercantile transactions—undoubtedly one of the mainsprings of the national greatness—may hereafter be of use to you, sir."

"Yes, my lord, 'pon my soul—when I'm furnishing my houses in town and country, I mean to go to market myself—please your lordship, I know a trick or two of the trade, and can't be taken in, my lord. For instance, my lord, there's Tag-rag — a-hem! hem!" he paused abruptly, and looked somewhat confusedly at the Earl.

"I did not mean *that* exactly," said his lordship, unable to resist a smile. "Pray, fill your glass, Mr. Titmouse." He did so. "You are of course aware that you have the absolute patronage of the borough of Yatton, Mr. Titmouse?—It occurs to me, that as our political opinions agree, and unless I am presumptuous, sir, in so thinking—I may be regarded, in a political point of view, as the head of the family—you understand me, I hope, Mr. Titmouse?"

"Exactly, my lord—'pon my soul, it's all correct, my lord."

"Well—then, sir—the family interests, Mr. Titmouse. must be looked after—"

"Oh! in course, my lord, only too happy—certainly, my lord, we shall, I hope, make a very *interesting* family, if your lordship so please—I *can* have no objection, my lord!"

"It was a vile, a disgraceful trick, by which Ministers popped in their own man for our borough, Mr. Titmouse."

[Lord Dreddlington alluded to the circumstances of a new writ having been moved for, immediately on Mr. Aubrey's acceptance of the Chiltern Hundreds, and, before the Opposition could be prepared for such a step, sent down without delay to Yatton, and Sir Percival Pickering, Bart., of Luddington Court, an intimate friend of Mr. Aubrey's, and a keen unflinching Tory, being returned as member, before the Titmouse influence could be brought for even one moment into the field; the few and willing electors of that ancient and loyal borough being only too happy to have the opportunity of voting for a man whose principles they approved—probably the last opportunity they would have of doing so.]

"Yes, my lord—Sir what-d'ye-call-him *was* a trifle too sharp for us in that business, wasn't he?"

"It has succeeded, sir, for the moment, but "—continued his lordship, in a very significant and stately manner—" it is quite possible that their triumph may be of very short duration—Mr. Titmouse. Those who, like myself, are at headquarters—let me see you fill your glass, Mr. Titmouse—I have the honor to congratulate you, sir, on the recovery of your rights, and to wish you health and long life in the enjoyment of them," quoth the Earl, with an air of the loftiest urbanity.

"May it please your lordship, your lordship's most uncommon polite "—commenced Titmouse, rising and standing while he spoke—for he had had experience enough of society to be aware that when a gentleman's health is drunk on important occasions, it becomes him to rise and acknowledge the compliment in such language as he can command—" and am particularly proud—a—a—I beg to propose, my lord, your lordship's very *superior* good health, and many thanks." Then he sat down; each poured out another glass of claret, and Titmouse drank his off.

"It is extremely singular, sir," said the Earl, musingly, after a considerable pause, " the reverses in life that one hears of!"

[I can not help pausing, for a moment, to suggest—what must have become of the Earl and his daughter, had they been placed in the situation of the unfortunate Aubreys.]

"Yes, my lord, your lordship's quite true, 'pon my word—Most uncommon *ups* and *downs!* Lord, my lord, only to fancy *me*, a few months ago, trotting up and down Oxford Street with my yard-mea—" He stopped short, and colored violently.

"Well, sir," replied the Earl, with an expression of bland and dignified sympathy—" however humble might have been your circumstances, it is a consolation to reflect that *the Fates ordained it.* Sir, there is nothing dishonorable in being poor, when—you can not help it! Reverses of fortune, sir, have happened to some of the greatest characters in our history. You remember Alfred, sir!" Titmouse bowed assentingly; but had he been questioned, could have told, I suspect, as little about the matter—as the Earl himself.

"Allow me, sir, to ask whether you have come to any arrangement with your late opponent concerning the back-rents?" inquired the Earl, with a great appearance of interest.

"No, my lord, not yet; but my solicitors say they'll soon *have the screw on*, please your lordship—that's just what they say—their very words.

"Indeed, sir!" replied the Earl, gravely. "What is the sum to which they say you are entitled, sir?"

"Sixty thousand pounds, my lord, at least—quite set me up at starting, my lord," replied Titmouse, with great glee; but the Earl shuddered involuntarily for a moment, and sipped his wine in silence.

"By the way, Mr. Titmouse," said he, after a considerable pause—" I trust you will forgive me for suggesting whether it would not be a prudent step for you to go to one of the universities for at least a twelvemonth—"

"Humbly begging your lordship's pardon, am not I too old? I've heard they're all a pack of overgrown school-boys there—and learn nothing but a bit of some old languages that a'n't the lest use nowadays, seeing it a'n't *spoke* now, anywhere "—replied Titmouse—" Besides, I've talked the thing over with Mr. Gammon, my lord—"

"Mr. Gammon? Allow me, sir, to ask who that may be?"

"One of my solicitors, my lord; a most remarkable clever man, and an out-and-out lawyer, my lord. It was he that found out all about my case, my lord. If your lordship was only to see him for a moment, your lordship would say, What a *remarkable* clever man that is!"

"You will forgive my curiosity, sir—but it must have surely required very ample means to have carried on so arduous a lawsuit as that which has just terminated so successfully?"

"Oh, yes, my lord!—Quirk, Gammon and Snap did all that,

and, between me and your lordship, I suppose I shall have to come down a pretty long figure, all on the *nail*, as your lordship understands; but I mean them to get it all out of that respectable gent, Mr. Aubrey."—By quietly pressing his questions, the Earl got a good deal more out of Titmouse than he was aware of, concerning Messrs. Quirk, Gammon and Snap; and conceived a special dislike for Gammon. The Earl gave him some pretty decisive hints about the necessity of being on his guard with such people—and hoped that he would not commit himself to anything important without consulting his lordship, who would of course give him the advantage of his experience in the affairs of the world, and open his eyes to the designs of those whose only object was to make a prey of him. Titmouse began to feel that here, at length, he had met with a *real* friend—one whose suggestions were worthy of being received with the profoundest deference. Soon afterward, he had the good fortune to please the Earl beyond expression, by venturing timidly to express his admiration of the splendid ribbon worn by his lordship, who took the opportunity of explaining that and the other marks of distinction he wore, and others which he was entitled to wear, at great length and with much minuteness—so as that he at length caused Titmouse to believe that he, Lord Dreddlington—the august head of the family —must have rendered more signal service, somehow or other, to his country, and also done more to win the admiration and gratitude of foreign countries, than most men living. His lordship might not, perhaps, have intended it; but he went on till he almost DEIFIED himself in the estimation of his little listener.—One very natural question was perpetually trembling on the tip of Titmouse's tongue; viz., how and when he could get such things for *himself*.

"Well, Mr. Titmouse," at length observed the Earl, after looking at his watch—"shall we adjourn to the drawing-room? The fact is, sir, that Lady Cecilia and I have an evening engagement at the Duchess of Diamond's. I much regret being unable to take you with us, sir; but, as it is, shall we rejoin the Lady Cecilia?" continued his lordship, rising. Up jumped Titmouse; and the Earl and he were soon in the drawing-room, where, besides the Lady Cecilia, sat another lady, to whom he was not introduced in any way. This was Miss Macspleuchan, a distant connection of the Earl's late countess—a very poor relation, who had entered the house of the Earl of Dreddlington, in order to eat the *bitter, bitter bread of dependence*. Poor soul! you might tell, by a glance at her, that she did not thrive upon it. She was about thirty, and so thin! She was dressed in plain white muslin; and there was a manifest constraint and timidity about her motions, and a depression in her countenance, whose lineaments showed that if she could be happy she might be handsome. She had a most lady-like air; and there was thought in her brow and acuteness in her eye, which, however, as it were, habitually watched the motions of the Earl and the Lady Cecilia with deference and anxiety. Poor Miss Macspleuchan felt herself gradually sinking into a sycophant; the alternative being that or starvation. She was very accomplished, particularly in music and languages, while the Lady Cecilia really knew scarcely anything—for which reason, principally, she had long ago conceived a bitter dislike to Miss Macspleuchan, and inflicted on her a number of petty but exquisite mortifications and indignities; such, perhaps, as none but a sensitive soul could appreciate, for the Earl and his daugther were exemplary persons in the proprieties of life, and would not do such things *openly*. She was a sort of companion of Lady Cecilia, and entirely dependent upon her and the Earl for her subsistence. She was sitting on the sofa beside Lady Cecilia, when Titmouse re-entered the drawing-room; and Lady Cecilia eyed him through her glass with infinite *nonchalance*, even when he had advanced to within a few feet of her. He made her, as she rose to take her seat and prepare tea, a most obsequious bow; absurd as was the style of its performance, Miss Macspleuchan saw that there was politeness in the intention; 'twas, moreover, a courtesy toward herself, that was unusual from the Earl's guests; and these considerations served to take off the edge of the ridicule and contempt with which Lady Cecilia had been preparing her to receive their newly discovered kinsman. After standing for a second or two near the sofa, Titmouse ventured to sit himself down upon it—on the very edge only—as if afraid of disturbing Lady Cecilia, who was reclining on it with an air of languid hauteur.

"So you're going, my lady, to a dance to-night, as my lord says?" quoth Titmouse, respectfully; "hope your ladyship will enjoy yourself!"

"We regret that you do not accompany us, Mr. Titmouse," said Lady Cecilia, slightly inclining toward him, and glancing at Miss Macspleuchan with a faint and bitter smile.

"Should have been most uncommon proud to have gone, your ladyship," replied Titmouse, as a servant brought him a cup of tea. "These cups and saucers, my lady, come from abroad, I suppose? Now, I dare say, though they've *rather* a funny look, they cost a good deal."

"I really do not know, sir; we have had them a very long while."

"'Pon my life, my lady, I like them amazing!" Seeing her ladyship not disposed to talk, Titmouse became silent.

"Are you fond of music, Mr. Titmouse?" inquired the Earl, presently, observing the pause in the conversation to become embarrassing to Titmouse.

"Very, indeed, my lord; is your lordship?"

"I am rather fond of vocal music, sir—of the opera."

This the Earl said, because Miss Macspleuchan played upon the piano very brilliantly, and did not sing. Miss Macspleuchan understood him.

"Do you play upon any instrument, Mr. Titmouse?" inquired Lady Cecilia, with a smile lurking about her lips, which increased a little when Titmouse replied in the negative, that he had once begun to learn the clarionet some years ago, but could not manage the notes. "Excuse me, my lady, but what an uncommon fine piano that is!" said he. "If I may make so bold, will your ladyship give us a tune?"

"I dare say Miss Macspleuchan will play for you, Mr. Titmouse, if you wish it," replied Lady Cecilia, coldly.

Some time afterward, a servant announced to her ladyship and the Earl that the carriage was at the door; and presently they both retired to their dressing-rooms to make slight alteration in their dress—the Earl to add a foreign order or two, and Lady Cecilia to place upon her haughty brow a small tiara of brilliants. As soon as they had retired—"I shall feel great pleasure, sir, in playing for you, if you wish it?" said Miss Macspleuchan, in a voice of such mingled melancholy and kindness as must have gone to Titmouse's heart, if he had possessed one. He jumped up, and bowed profoundly. She sat down to the piano, and played with great ease and brilliancy such music as she supposed would suit her auditor—namely, waltzes and marches—till the door opened, and Lady Cecilia reappeared, drawing on her gloves, with the glittering addition which I have mentioned—followed presently by the Earl.

"Well, sir," said he, with dignified affability, "I need not repeat how highly gratified I feel at our introduction to each other. I trust you will henceforth consider yourself no stranger here—"

"Oh, 'pon my life, my lord!" exclaimed Titmouse, in a low tone, and with a sudden and profound bow.

"And that on your return from Yorkshire," continued the Earl, drawing on his gloves, "you will let us see you; we both feel great interest in your good fortunes. Sir, I have the honor to wish you a good-evening." He extended his gloved hand to Mr. Titmouse, whose hand, however, he touched with little more than the ends of his fingers.

"We exceedingly regret that we must leave you, Mr. Titmouse," said Lady Cecilia, with forced seriousness; "but as we wish to leave the duchess's early, in order to go to another ball, we must *go* early. Good-evening, sir," and having dropped him a slight formal courtesy, she quitted the drawing-room, followed by the Earl, Titmouse making four or five such bows as provoked a smile from all who witnessed them. The next moment he was alone with Miss Macspleuchan. Her unaffected, good-natured address made him feel more at home within the next five minutes than he had been since entering that frigid scene of foolish state—since being in the oppressive presence of the greatness just departed. She felt at first a contempt for him bordering upon disgust, but which very soon melted into pity. What a wretched creature was *this* to be put into such a dazzling position! He soon got pretty communicative with her, and told her about the Tag-rags, Miss Tag-rag, and Miss Quirk, both of whom were absolutely dying of love for him, and thought he was in love with them, which was not the case—far from it. Then he hinted something about a most particular uncommon lovely gal that had his heart, and he hoped to have hers as soon as he had got all to rights at Yatton. Then he told her of the great style in which he was going down to take possession of his estates. Having finished this, he told her that he had been the morning before to see a man hanged for murdering his wife; that he had been into the condemned cell, and then into the press-room, and had seen his hands and arms tied, ar.d shaken hands with him; and he was going on into such a sickening minuteness of detail, that to avoid it Miss Macspleuchan, who felt both shocked and disgusted, suddenly asked him if he was fond of heraldry, and rising from the sofa, she went into the second room, where, on an elegant and antique stand lay a huge roll of parchment, on a gilded stand, splendidly mounted and most superbly illuminated—it was about three quarters of a yard in breadth, and some ten or twenty yards in length. This was the *Pedigree of the Dreddlingtons.* She was giving him an account of Simon de Drelincourt, an early ancestor of the Earl's, who had come over with William the Conqueror, and performed stupendous feats of valor at the battle of Hastings, Titmouse listening in open-mouthed wonder, and almost trembling to think that he had broken a valuable dish, belonging to a nobleman who had such wonderful ancestors, not at the mo-

ment adverting to the circumstance that he was himself descended from the same ancestors, and had as rich blood in him
as the Earl and Lady Cecilia—when a servant entered and informed him in a whisper that "his carriage had arrived." He
considered that etiquette required him to depart immediately.

"Beg your pardon; but if ever you should come down to
my estate in the country, shall be most uncommon proud to
see your ladyship."

"I beg your pardon; you are mistaken, sir," interrupted
Miss Macspleuchan, hastily, and blushing scarlet; the fact being that Titmouse had not caught her name on its having been
once or twice pronounced by Lady Cecilia, and very naturally
concluding that she also must be a lady of rank. Titmouse
was, however, so occupied with his efforts to make a graceful
exit, that he did not catch the explanation of his mistake; and
bowing almost down to the ground, reached the landing, where
the tall servant, with a very easy grace, gave him his hat and
cane, and preceded him down-stairs. As he descended, he felt
in his pockets for some loose silver, and gave several shillings
between the servants who stood in the hall to witness his departure; after which, one of them having opened the door and
let down the steps of the glass coach, Titmouse popped into it.

"Home, sir?" inquired the servant, as he closed the door.

"The Cabbage-Stalk Hotel, Covent Garden," replied Titmouse.

That was communicated to the coachman, and off rumbled
the glass coach. As soon as Titmouse had become calm enough
to reflect upon the events of the evening, he came to the conclusion that the Earl of Dreddlington was a very great man indeed; the Lady Cecilia was very beautiful, but rather proud;
and Miss Macspleuchan (Lady Somebody, as he supposed) one
of the most interesting ladies he had ever met with, something
uncommon pleasing about her; in short, he felt a sort of grateful attachment toward her, which, how long it would have
lasted after he had heard that she was only a plain miss and
a poor relative, I leave the acute reader to conjecture.

CHAPTER XIX.

MR. GAMMON was with him about half past nine o'clock the
next morning, sufficiently anxious to hear how he had got on
overnight. He was received by Titmouse in a manner totally
different from that in which he had ever before been received
by him; and concluded for a few minutes that Lord Dreddlington had been *pumping* Titmouse, had learned from him his

position with respect to him, Gammon, in particular, and had injected distrust and suspicion into the mind of Titmouse concerning him. But Gammon, with all his acuteness, was quite mistaken. The truth was, 'twas only an attempt on the part of poor Titmouse to assume the composed demeanor, the languid elegance, which he had observed in the distinguished personages with whom he had spent the preceding evening, and which had made a very deep impression on his mind. He drawled out his words, looked as if he were half asleep, and continually addressed Gammon as "Sir," and "Mr. Gammon," just as the Earl of Dreddlington had constantly addressed him—Titmouse. Our friend was sitting at breakfast, on the present occasion, in a most gaudy dressing-gown, and with the newspaper before him; in short, his personal appearance and manner were totally different from what Gammon had ever seen before, and he looked now and then at Titmouse, as if for a moment doubting his identity. Whether or not he was now on the point of throwing overboard those who had piloted him from amidst the shoals of poverty into the open sea of affluence, shone upon by the vivid sunlight of rank and distinction, Gammon did not know; but he contracted his brow, and assumed a certain sternness and peremptoriness of tone and bearing, which were not long in reducing Titmouse to his proper dimensions; and when at length Mr. Gammon entered upon the delightful subject of the morrow's expedition, telling him that he, Gammon, had now nearly completed all the preparations for going down to and taking possession of Yatton in a style of suitable splendor, according to the wish of Titmouse—this quickly melted away the thin coating of mannerism, and Titmouse was "himself again." He immediately gave Mr. Gammon a full account of what had happened at Lord Dreddlington's, and, I fear, of a great deal more than might possibly have happened, but certainly *had* not; *e. g.*, his lordship's special laudation of Mr. Gammon as a "monstrous fine lawyer," which Titmouse swore were the very exact words of his lordship, and that "he should have been most happy to see Mr. Gammon," and a good deal to the like effect. Also that he had been "most uncommon thick" with "Lady Cicely" (so he pronounced her name); and that both she and Lord Dreddlington had "pressed him very hard" to go with them to a ball *at a duke's!*" He made no mention of the broken trifle-dish; said they had nearly a dozen servants to wait on them (only three sitting down to dinner), and twenty different sorts of wine, and no end of courses, at dinner. That the Earl wore a star and garter, and ribbons—which Gam-

mon erroneously thought as apocryphal as the rest; and had
told him that he—Titmouse—might one day wear them, and
sit in the House of Lords; and had, moreover, advised him
most strenuously to get into Parliament as soon as possible, as
the "cause of the people wanted strengthening." [As Lord
Coke somewhere says, in speaking of a spurious portion of the
text of Lyttleton, "*that arrow came never out of Lyttleton's
quiver*"—so Gammon instantly perceived that the last sentence came never out of Titmouse's own head, but was that of
a wise and able man and statesman.]

As soon as Titmouse had finished his little romance, Gammon proceeded to the chief object of his visit—their next day's
journey. He said that he much regretted to say that Mr.
Snap had expressed a very anxious wish to witness the triumph
of Mr. Titmouse; and that Mr. Titmouse, unless he had some
particular objection—" Oh, none, 'pon honor!—poor Snap!—
devilish good chap in a small way!" said Titmouse; and at
once gave his consent—Gammon informing him that Mr. Snap
would be obliged to return to town by the next day's coach.
The reader will smile when I tell him, and if a lady, will frown
when she hears, that Miss Quirk was to be of the party—a
point which her anxious father had secured some time ago.
Mrs. Alias had declared that she saw no objection, as Mr. Quirk
would be constantly with his daughter, and Gammon had appeared most ready to bring about so desirable a result. He
had also striven hard, unknown to his partners, to increase
their numbers, by the Tag-rags, who might have gone down,
all three of them, if they had chosen, by coach, and so have
returned. Gammon conceived that this step might not have
been unattended with advantage in several ways, and would,
moreover, have secured him a considerable source of amusement. Titmouse, however, would not listen to the thing for
one moment, and Gammon was forced to give up his little
scheme. Two dashing young fellows, fashionable friends of
Titmouse (who had picked them up, Heaven only knows where,
but they never deserted him), infinitely to Gammon's annoyance, were to be of the party. He had seen them but once,
when he had accompanied Titmouse to the play, where they
soon joined him. One was a truly disgusting-looking fellow—
a MR. PIMP YAHOO—a man about five-and-thirty years old,
tall, with a profusion of black hair parted down the middle of
his head, and falling down in long clustering curls from each
temple upon his coat-collar. His whiskers also were ample,
and covered two thirds of his face, and spread in disgusting
amplitude round his throat. He had also a jet-black tuft—an

imperial—depending from his under lip. He had an execrable
eye—full of insolence and sensuality; in short, his whole countenance bespoke the thorough debauchee and ruffian. He had
been, he said, in the army; and was nearly connected, according to his own account—as with fellows of this description is
generally the case—with "some of the first families in the
North." He was now a man of pleasure about town—which
contained not a better billiard-player, as the admiring Titmouse had had several opportunities of judging. He was a
great patron of the ring—knew all their secrets—all their
haunts. He always had plenty of the money of other people,
and drove about in a most elegant cab, in which Titmouse had
often had a seat; and as soon as Mr. Yahoo had extracted from
his communicative little companion all about himself, he made
it his business to conciliate his good graces by all the arts of
which he was master—and he succeeded. The other chosen
companion of Titmouse was MR. ALGERNON FITZ-SNOOKS, a
complete fool. He was the sole child of a rich tradesman—
who christened him by the sounding name give above; and
afterward added the patrician prefix to the surname, which
also you see above, in order to gratify his wife and son. The
youth never "took to business"—but was allowed to saunter
about, doing and knowing nothing, till about his twenty-
second year, when his mother died, followed a year afterward
by his father, who bequeathed to his hopeful some fifty thousand pounds—absolutely and uncontrolledly. He very judiciously thought that youth was the time to enjoy life; and before
he had reached his thirtieth year he had got through all his
fortune except about five or six thousand pounds—in return
for which he had certainly got *something*, viz., an impaired
constitution and a little experience, which *might* possibly be
useful. He had a very pretty face—regular features, and interesting eyes, his light hair curled beautifully; and he spoke
in a sort of lisp and in a low tone—and, in point of dress,
always turned out beautifully. He also had a cab, and was a
great friend of Mr. Yahoo, who had introduced him into a
great deal of high society, principally in St. James's Street,
where both he and Mr. Yahoo had passed a great deal of their
time, especially during the nights. There was no intentional
mischief in poor Fitz-Snooks; nature had made him only a fool
—his prudent parents had done the rest; and if he fell into
vice, it was only because he couldn't help it. Such were the
chosen companions of Titmouse; the one a fool, the other a
rogue—and "he *must*," he said, "have them down to the
jollifying at Yatton." A groom and a valet, both newly

5—Part II.

hired the day before, would complete the party of the morrow.
Gammon assured Titmouse that he had taken all the pains in
the world to get up a triumphant entry into Yatton; his agents
at Grilston, Messrs. Bloodsuck & Son, attorneys—the Radical
electioneering attorneys of the county—who were well versed
in the matter of processions, bands, flags, etc., etc., etc., had
by that time arranged everything, and they were to be met,
when within a mile of Yatton, by a procession. The people at
the Hall, also, were under orders from Mr. Gammon, through
Messrs. Bloodsuck and Son, to have all in readiness—and a
banquet prepared for nearly a hundred persons—in fact, all
comers were to be welcome. To all this Titmouse listened
with eyes glistening, and ears tingling with rapture; but can
any tongue describe his emotion on being apprised that the
sum of £2,500, in the banker's hands, was now at his disposal
—that it would be doubled in a few weeks—and that a check
for £500, drawn by Mr. Titmouse on the London agents of the
Grilston bankers, had been honored on the preceding afternoon? Titmouse's heart beat fast, and he felt as if he could
have worshiped Gammon. As for the matter of carriages, Mr.
Gammon said, that probably Mr. Titmouse would call that
morning on Mr. Axle, in Long Acre, and select one to his
mind—it must be one with two seats—and Mr. Gammon had
pointed out several which were, he thought, eligible, and would
be shown to Mr. Titmouse. That would be the carriage in
which Mr. Titmouse himself would travel; the second, Mr.
Gammon had taken the liberty of already selecting. With this
Mr. Gammon (just as the new valet brought in no less than
seven boxes of cigars, ordered overnight by Titmouse) shook
his hand and departed, saying that he should make his appearance at the Cabbage-Stalk the next morning, precisely at
eleven o'clock—about which time it was arranged they were
all to start. Titmouse hardly knew how to contain himself on
being left alone. About an hour or two afterward, Titmouse
made his appearance at Mr. Axle's. He carried on two busi-
nesses, one public, i. e., a coach-builder—one private, i. e., a
money-lender. He was a rich man—a very obliging and
" accommodating " person, by means of which he had amassed
a fortune of, it was believed, a hundred thousand pounds. He
never made a fuss about selling on credit, lending, taking
back, exchanging carriages of all descriptions; nor in dis-
counting the bills of his customers to any amount. He was
generally right in each case in the long run. He would supply his fashionable victim with as splendid a chariot, and funds
to keep it some time going, as he or she could desire; well

knowing that in due time, after they had taken a few turns in it about the parks, and a few streets and squares in the neighborhood, it would quietly drive up to one or two huge dingy fabrics in a different part of the town, where it would deposit its burden, and then return to its maker little the worse for wear, who took it back at about a twentieth part of its cost, and soon again disposed of it in a similar way. Mr. Axle showed Mr. Titmouse very obsequiously over his premises, pointing out (as soon as he knew who he was) the carriages which Mr. Gammon had the day before desired should be shown to him, and which Mr. Titmouse, with his glass stuck in his eye—where it was kept by the pure force of muscular contraction—examined with something like the air of a connoisseur—rapping with his agate-headed cane every now and then—now against his teeth, then against his legs. He did not seem perfectly satisfied with any of them; they looked "devilish plain and dull."

"Halloo—Mr. Axletree, or whatever your name is—what have we here? 'Pon my soul, the very thing!"—he exclaimed, as his eye caught a splendid object—the state carriage of the ex-sheriff, with its gorgeously decorated panels; which, having been vamped up for some six or seven successive shrievalities —(on each occasion heralded to the public by laudatory paragraphs in the newspapers, as entirely new and signal instances of the taste and magnificence of the sheriff-elect)—seemed now *perfunctus officio.* Mr. Axle was staggered for a moment, and scarce supposed Mr. Titmouse to be in earnest— Gammon having given him no inkling of the real character of Titmouse; but observing the earnest steadfast gaze with which he regarded the glittering object, having succeeded in choking down a sudden fit of laughter, he commenced a most tempting eulogium upon the splendid structure—remarking on the singularity of the circumstance of its happening just at that exact moment to be placed at his disposal by its former owner—a gentleman of great distinction, who had no longer any occasion for it. Mr. Axle had had numerous applications for it already; on hearing which, Titmouse got excited. The door was opened—he got in; sat on each seat—"Don't it hang beautifully?" inquired the confident proprietor, swaying about the head of the carriage as he spoke.

"Let us see, who was after it yesterday? Oh—oh, I think it was Sir Fitzbiscuit Gander; but I've not closed with him."

"What's your price, Mr. Axetree?" inquired Titmouse, rather heatedly, as he got out of the carriage.

After some little higgle-haggling he bought it!!!—for there

was nothing like closing at once where there was keen competition.   Mr. Gammon could not have seen it when he was
making his choice the day before!   For the rest of the day he
felt infinitely elated at his fortunate purchase, and excited his
imagination by pictures of the astonishment and admiration
which his equipage must call forth on the morrow.   Punctual
to his appointment, Mr. Gammon, a few minutes before the
clock struck eleven on the ensuing morning, drew up to the
Cabbage-Stalk, as near, at least, as he could get to it, in a
hackney-coach, with his portmanteau and carpet-bag.   I say
as near as he could; for round about the door stood a little
crowd, gazing with a sort of awe on a magnificent vehicle
standing there, with four horses harnessed to it.   Gammon
looked at his watch, as he entered the hotel, and asked which
of the sheriff's carriages was standing at the door.   The waiter
to whom he spoke seemed nearly splitting with laughter,
which almost disabled him for answering that it was Mr. Titmouse's carriage, ready for setting off to Yorkshire.   Mr.
Gammon opened his eyes involuntarily, turned pale, and
seemed nearly dropping an umbrella which was in hand.

" Mr. Titmouse's!" he echoed, incredulously.

" Yes, sir—been here this hour at least packing; such a
crowd all the while; everybody thinks it's the sheriff, sir," replied the waiter, scarce able to keep his countenance.   Mr.
Gammon rushed upstairs with greater impetuosity than he had
perhaps ever been known to exhibit before, and burst into Mr.
Titmouse's room.   There was that gentleman, with his hat
on, his hands stuck into his coat pockets, a cigar in his mouth,
and a tumbler of brandy and water before him.   Mr. Yahoo,
and Mr. Fitz-Snooks, and Mr. Snap were similarly occupied;
and Mr. Quirk was sitting down with his hands in his pockets
and a glass of negus before him, with anything but a joyful
expression of countenance.

" Is it possible, Mr. Titmouse—" commenced Gammon,
almost breathlessly.

" Ah, how d'ye do, Gammon?—punctual!" interrupted Titmouse, extending his hand.

" Forgive me—but can it be, that the monstrous thing now
before the door, with a crowd grinning around it, is *your carriage?*" inquired Gammon, with dismay in his face.

" I—rather—think—it *is*," replied Titmouse, slightly disconcerted, but striving to look self-possessed.

" My *dear* sir," replied Gammon, in a kind of agony, " it is
impossible?   It never can be!   Do you mean to say that you
bought it at Mr. Axle's?"

"I should rather think so," replied Titmouse, with a piqued air.

"He's been grossly imposing on you, sir!—Permit me to go at once and get you a proper vehicle."

"'Pon my life, Mr. Gammon, *I* think that it's a monstrous nice thing—a great bargain—and I've bought it and paid for it, that's more."

"Gentlemen, I appeal to *you*," confidently said Gammon, turning in an agony to Mr. Yahoo and Mr. Fitz-Snooks.

"As for *me*, sir," replied the former, coolly, at the same time knocking off the ashes from his cigar—"since you ask my opinion, I confess I rather like the idea—ha! ha! 'Twill produce a *sensation* ; that's something in this dull life!—Eh, Snooks?"

"Ay—a—I confess I was a little shocked at first, but I think I'm getting over it now," lisped Mr. Fitz-Snooks, adjusting his shirt-collar, and then sipping a little of his brandy and water. "I look upon it, now, as an excellent joke—egad, it beats Chitterfield hollow, though *he*, too, has done a trick or two lately."

"Did you purchase it as a joke, Mr. Titmouse?" inquired Gammon, with forced calmness, ready to expire with vexation and anger.

"Why—a—'pon my life—if you ask *me*—wonder you don't see it! Of course I did!—Those that don't like it may ride, you know, in the other."

"We shall be hooted at, laughed at, wherever we go," said he, vehemently.

"Exactly—that's the *novelty* I like," said Mr. Yahoo, looking at Mr. Gammon with a smile of ineffable insolence.

Mr. Gammon made him no reply, but fixed an eye upon him, under which he became plainly uneasy. He felt outdone. Talk of SCORN!—the eye of Gammon, settled at that instant upon Mr. Yahoo, was its complete and perfect representative; and from that moment he, Mr. Yahoo, felt something like *fear* of the eye of man, or of *submission* to it. When, moreover, he beheld the manner in which Titmouse obeyed Gammon's somewhat haughty summons out of the room, he resolved to make a friend of Gammon. Titmouse proved, however, inexorable for once; he had bought and paid for the carriage; it suited his taste—and where was the harm of gratifying it? Besides, it was already packed—all was prepared for starting. Gammon gave it up; and, swallowing down his rage as well and as quickly as he could, endeavored to reconcile himself to this infernal and most unexpected predicament.

It seems that Miss Quirk, however really anxious to go down to Yatton—to do anything, in short, calculated to commit Mr. Titmouse to her—was quite staggered on discovering, and shocked at seeing, the kind of persons who were to be their traveling companions. As for Mr. Yahoo, she recoiled from him with horror as soon as she had seen him. What decent female, indeed, would not have done so? She had retired to a bed-chamber soon after entering the Cabbage-Stalk, and, seeing her two unexpected fellow-travelers, presently sent a chambermaid to request Mr. Quirk to come to her.

He found her considerably agitated. She wished earnestly to return to Alibi House; and consented to proceed on her journey only on the express promise of Mr. Titmouse, that no one should be in the carriage in which she went except Mr. Quirk and Mr. Gammon—unless, indeed, Mr. Titmouse thought proper to make the fourth.

Mr. Quirk, on this, sent for Mr. Gammon, who, with a somewhat bad grace ("Confound it!" thought he, "everything seems going wrong") undertook to secure Mr. Titmouse's consent to that arrangement.

While he was thus closeted for about five or ten minutes with Mr. Quirk, one of the waiters informed Mr. Titmouse that a lad had brought a parcel for him, which he, the aforesaid lad, was himself to deliver into the hands of Mr. Titmouse. Accordingly there was presently shown into the room a little lad, in tarnished livery, in whom Titmouse recollected the boy belonging to Mr. Tag-rag's one-horse chaise, and who gave a small parcel into Mr. Titmouse's hands, " with Mrs. and Miss Tag-rag's respects."

As soon as he had quitted the room, " By Jove! What have we here?" exclaimed Titmouse, just a *little* flustered, as he cut open the string. Inside was another parcel, wrapped up in white paper and tied in a pretty bow with thin satin ribbons. This again, and another within it having been opened—behold there were three nice cambric pocket-handkerchiefs, which, on being examined, proved to be each of them marked with the initials " T. T." in *hair ;* and Mr. Yahoo, happening to unfold one of them, lo! in the center was—also done in hair— the figure of a heart transfixed with an arrow!!! Mr. Yahoo roared and Mr. Fitz-Snooks lisped, " Is she pretty, Tit? Where's her nest? Any *old* birds?—eh?"

Titmouse colored a little, then grinned, and put his finger to the side of his nose, and winked his eye, as if favoring the bright idea of Mr. Fitz-Snooks. On a sheet of gilt-edged paper, and sealed with a seal bearing the tender words, " *Forget me not*," was written the following:

" SIR,—Trusting you will excuse the liberty, I send you three best cambric pocket-handkerchiefs, which my daughter have marked with her own hair, and I beg your acceptance thereof, hoping you may be resigned to all that may befall you, which is the prayer of, dear sir, yours respectfully,
                                    " MARTHA TAG-RAG.

" P. S.—My daughter sends what you may please to wish and accept. Shall we have the great happiness to see you here again?
" *Satin Lodge*, 18*th May*, 18--."

" Oh! the naughty old woman! Fy! Fy!" exclaimed Mr. Yahoo, with his intolerable smile.

" 'Pon my soul, there's nothing in it," said Titmouse, reddening.

" Where's Satin Lodge?" inquired Mr. Fitz-Snooks.

" It is a country-house on the—the Richmond road," said Titmouse, with a little hesitation; and just then the return of Gammon, who had resumed his usual calmness of manner, relieved him from his embarrassment. Mr. Gammon succeeded in effecting the arrangement suggested by Mr. Quirk and his daughter; and within about a quarter of an hour afterward, behold the ex-sheriff's resplendent but cast-off carriage filled by Miss Quirk and Titmouse, and Mr. Quirk and Gammon—the groom and valet sitting on the coach-box; while in the other, a plain yellow carriage, covered with luggage, sat Mr. Yahoo, Mr. Fitz-Snooks, and Mr. Snap, all of them with lighted cigars—Snap never having been so happy as at that moment.

Mr. Titmouse had laid aside his cigar in compliment to Miss Quirk, who had a long black veil on, and an elegant light shawl, and looked uncommonly like a young bride setting off —oh, heavens! that it *had* been so!—on her wedding excursion. Mr. Gammon slouched his hat over his eyes and inclined his head downward, fit to expire with vexation and disgust, as he observed the grin and tittering of the crowd around; but Titmouse, who was most splendidly dressed, took off his hat on sitting down, and bowed several times to, as he supposed, the admiring crowd.

" Get on, boys!" growled Mr. Gammon; and away they went, exciting equal surprise and applause wherever they

went. No one that met them but must have taken Titmouse
and Miss Quirk for a newly married couple—probably the son
or daughter of one of the sheriffs, who had lent the state carriage to add *éclat* to the interesting occasion.

With the exception of the sensation produced at every place
where they changed horses, the only incident worth noting
that occurred during their journey was at the third stage from
London. As they came dashing up to the door of the inn,
their advent setting all the bells of the establishment ringing,
and waiters and hostlers scampering up to them like mad, they
beheld a plain and laden dusty traveling-carriage waiting for
horses—and Gammon quickly perceived it to be the carriage
of the unfortunate Aubreys! The travelers had alighted.
The graceful figure of Miss Aubrey, her face pale and wearing an expression of manifest anxiety and fatigue, was standing near the door, talking kindly to a beggar-woman, with a
cluster of half-naked children around her; while little Aubrey
was romping about with Miss Aubrey's beautiful little spaniel
Cato; Agnes, looking on and laughing merrily, and trying to
escape from the hand of her attendant. Mr. and Mrs. Aubrey
were talking together, close beside the carriage door. Gammon observed all this, and particularly that Mr. Aubrey was
scrutinizing their appearance with a sort of half smile on his
countenance, melancholy as it was.

"Horses on!" said Gammon, leaning back in the carriage.

"That's a monstrous fine woman standing at the inn door,
Titmouse—eh?" exclaimed Mr. Yahoo, who had alighted for
a moment, and stood beside the door of Titmouse's carriage,
looking with his execrable eye toward Miss Aubrey. "I wonder who and what she is? By Jove! 'tis the face—the figure of
an angel! Egad! they're *somebody ;* I'll look at their panels."

"I know who it is," said Titmouse, rather faintly; "I'll
tell you by and by."

"Now, now! my dear fellow. Our divinity is vanishing,"
whispered Mr. Yahoo, eagerly, as Miss Aubrey, having slipped
something into the beggar's hand, stepped into the carriage.
She was the last to get in; and as soon as the door was closed
they drove off.

"Who's that, Mr. Titmouse?" inquired Miss Quirk, with a
little eagerness, observing—women are very quick in detecting
such matters—that both Gammon and Titmouse looked rather
embarrassed.

"It's the—the Aubreys," replied Titmouse.

"Eh! By Jove—is it?" quickly inquired old Quirk, putting his head out of the window; "how very odd, to meet the old birds? Egad! their nest must be yet warm—ha! ha!"

"What! dear papa, are those the people you've turned out! Gracious! I thought I heard some one say that Miss Aubrey was pretty! La! I'm sure *I* thought—now what do *you* think, Mr. Titmouse?" she added, turning abruptly and looking keenly at him.

"Oh! 'pon my life, I—I—see nothing at all in her—devilish plain, I should say—infernally pale, and all that!"

They were soon on their way again. Titmouse quickly recovered his equanimity, but Gammon continued silent and thoughtful for many—many miles; and the reader would not be surprised at it, if he knew as well as I do the thoughts which the unexpected sight of that traveling-carriage of Mr. Aubrey had suggested to Mr. Gammon.

As they approached the scene of triumph and rejoicing, and ascertained that they were within about a mile of the peaceful little village of Yatton, the travelers began to look out for indications of the kind which Mr. Gammon had mentioned to Titmouse, viz., a band and procession, and an attendant crowd. But however careful and extensive might have been the arrangements of those to whom that matter had been intrusted, they were likely to be sadly interfered with by a circumstance which, happening just then, might, to a weaker and more superstitious mind than that of Mr. Titmouse, have looked a little ominous—namely, a tremendous thunder-storm. It was then about five o'clock in the afternoon. The whole day had been overcast, and the sky threatening; and just as the two carriages came to that turning in the road which gave them the first glimpse of the Hall—only, however, the tops of the great chimneys, which were visible above the surrounding trees—a fearful, long-continued flash of lightning burst from the angry heavens, followed, after an interval of but a second or two, by a peal of thunder which sounded as if a park of artillery was being repeatedly discharged immediately overhead.

"Mind your horses' heads, boys," called out Mr. Gammon; "keep a tight rein."

Miss Quirk was dreadfully alarmed, and clung to her father; Titmouse also seemed disconcerted, and looked to Gammon, who was perfectly calm, though his face was not free from anxiety. The ghastly glare of the lightning was again around them—all involuntarily hid their faces in their hands—and again rattled the thunder in a peal that lasted more than half a minute, and seemed in frightful contiguity, as it were only a

few yards about their heads. Down, then, came the long-suspended rain, pouring like a deluge, and so it continued, with
frequent returns of the thunder and lightning, for nearly a
quarter of an hour. The last turning brought them within
sight of the village, and also of some fifty or sixty persons
crowding under the hedges, on each side—these were the procession: musicians, bannermen, footmen, horsemen all drip-
ping with wet—surely a piteous spectacle to behold. Out,
however they all turned, true to their orders, as soon as they
saw the carriages, which immediately slackened their speed—
the rain also somewhat abating. The flagman tried desperately
to unroll a wet banner of considerable size, with the words—

"WELCOME TO YATTON!"

in gilded letters; while the band (consisting of a man with a
big drum, another with a serpent, a third with a trumpet, a
fourth with a bassoon, two with clarionets, and a boy with a
fife) struck up—"*See the conquering hero comes!*" They
puffed and blew lustily; bang! bang! bang! went the drum;
but the rain, the thunder, and the lightning wofully interfered
with their harmony. 'Twould have made your heart ache to
see the wet flag clinging obstinately to the pole, in spite of all
the efforts of its burly bearer! First, on horseback, was Barnabas Bloodsuck (senior), Esq.; beside him rode his son,
Barnabas Bloodsuck (junior), Esq.; then came the Reverend
Gideon Fleshpot, solemn simpleton, the vicar of Grilston, the
only Radical clergyman in that part of the country; beside
him the Reverend Smirk Mudflint, a flippant, bitter, little
Unitarian parson, a great crony of Mr. Fleshpot, and his name
singularly enough exactly designating the qualities of his brain
and heart. Next to these, alone in his one-horse chaise (looking like a pill-box drawn by a leech), came the little fat Whig
apothecary, Gargle Glister, Esq. Following him came Going
Gone, Esq., the auctioneer—the main prop of the Liberal side,
being a most eloquent speaker—and Mr. Hic Hæc Hoc, a
learned school-master, who taught the Latin Grammar up as
far as the irregular verbs. Then there were Mr. Centipede,
the occasional editor, and Mr. Woodlouse, the publisher and
proprietor of the "YORKSHIRE STINGO," for which, also, Mr.
Mudflint wrote a great deal. These, and about a dozen others,
the flower of the "party" thereabouts, disdainful of the inclement weather, bent on displaying their attachment to the
new Whig owner of Yatton, and solacing each his patient
inner man with anticipation of the jolly cheer that awaited
them at the Hall, formed the principal part of the procession:

the rest, consisting of rather a miscellaneous assortment of scot-and-lot and potwalloper-looking people, all very wet and hungry, and ever and anon casting a look of devout expectation toward the Hall. Scarcely a villager of Yatton was to be seen stirring; nor did any of the tenants of the estate join in the procession; even had they not felt far otherwise disposed, they had luckily a complete excuse for their non-appearance in the deplorable state of the weather. Sometimes the band played; then a peal of thunder came; then a cry of " hurrah! Titmouse forever! hurrah!" then the band, and then the thunder, and rain! rain! rain! Thus they got to the park gates, where they paused, shouting, " Titmouse forever! hurrah—a—a!" Mr. Titmouse, bobbing about, now at one window, then at the other, with his hat off, in the most gracious manner. Really, it almost seemed as if the elements were conspiring to signalize, by their disfavor, Mr. Titmouse's assumption of Yatton; for, just as he was passing under the old gate-way, out flashed the lightning more vividly than it had yet appeared, and the thunder bellowed and reverberated among the woods as though it would never have ceased. The music and shouting ceased suddenly; carriages, horsemen, pedestrians quickened their pace in silence, as if anxious to get out of the storm; the horses now and then plunging and rearing violently. Titmouse was terribly frightened, in spite of his desperate efforts to appear unconcerned. He was as pale as death, and looked anxiously at Gammon, as if hoping to derive courage from the sight of his countenance. Miss Quirk trembled violently, and several times uttered a faint scream; but her father, old Mr. Quirk, did not seem to care a pinch of snuff about the whole matter: he rubbed his hands together cheerily, chucked his daughter under the chin, rallied Titmouse, and nudged and jeered Gammon, who seemed disposed to be serious and silent. Having drawn up opposite the Hall door, it was opened by Mr. Griffiths, with rather a saddened, but a most respectful look and manner; and in the same way might be characterized some six or seven servants standing behind him, in readiness to receive the new-comers. The half-drowned musicians tried to strike up " Rule Britannia," as the hero of the day, Mr. Titmouse, descended from his carriage, Mr. Griffiths holding an umbrella for him, and bounded out of the rain with a hop, step, and a jump into the Hall, where the first words he was heard to utter were—

" What a devilish rum old place!"

" God bless you! God bless you! God bless you, Titmouse!" exclaimed old Mr. Quirk, grasping him by the hand as soon as he had entered. Titmouse shook hands with Miss Quirk, who immediately followed a female servant to an apartment, being exceedingly nervous and agitated. Gammon seemed a little out of spirits, and said, simply, " You know, Titmouse, how fervently *I* congratulate you."

" Oh! my dear boy, Tit, do, for Heaven's sake, if you want the thunder and lightning to cease, order those wretched devils off—send them anywhere, but do stop their cursed noise, my dear boy!" exclaimed Mr. Yahoo, as soon as he had entered, putting his fingers to his ears.

" Mr. what's-your-name," said Titmouse, addressing Mr. Griffiths, " I'll trouble you to order off those fellows and their infernal noise. Demme! there's a precious row making up above, and surely *one at a time !*"

" Ah, ha, capital joke, by Jove! capital!" said Mr. Fitz-Snooks.

" A—Titmouse—by Jupiter!" said Mr. Yahoo, as, twirling his fingers about in his long black hair, of which he seemed very proud, he glanced about the Hall, " this a'n't so much amiss! Do you know, my dear boy, I rather like it; it's substantial, antique, and so forth."

" Who are those dem ugly old fellows up there?" presently exclaimed Titmouse, as, with his glass stuck into his right eye and his hands into his coat pockets, he stood staring at the old-fashioned pictures standing round the Hall.

" Some of them are ancestors of the Dreddlingtons, others of the Aubrey families. They are very old, sir," continued Mr. Griffiths, " and are much admired, and Mr. Aubrey desired me to say that if you should be disposed to part—"

" Oh, confound him, he may have 'em all, if that's what he wants; *I* shall soon send them packing off!" Mr. Griffiths bowed, and heaved a very deep sigh. By this time the Hall was crowded with the gentlemen who had formed part of the procession, and who came bowing and scraping to Titmouse, congratulating him and wishing him health and happiness. As soon as he could disengage himself from their flattering but somewhat troublesome civilities, his valet came and whispered, " Will you dress, sir? All is ready," and Titmouse followed him to the dressing-room which had formerly been young Mrs. Aubrey's. 'Twas the first time that Titmouse ever experienced the attentions of a valet, and he was quite nonplused at the multitudinousness and elegance of the arrangements around him. Such quantities of clothes of all sorts—dressing implements, combs, brushes, razors, a splendid dressing-case, scents in profusion, oils, bear's-grease, four or five different sorts of soaps, etc., etc., etc.; all this gave Titmouse a far livelier idea of his altered circumstances, of having really become a gentleman, than anything that he had up to that moment experienced. He thought his valet one of the cleverest and most obliging men in the world, only he oppressed him with his attentions, and at length Mr. Titmouse said he preferred, *this* time, dressing alone, and so dismissed his obsequious attendant. In about an hour's time, having been obliged to summon Tweedle to his assistance, after all, he had completed his toilet, and was ushered into the drawing-room, which, as well as the dining-room, was ready prepared for the banquet, forty or fifty covers being laid in the two rooms, and good substantial fare for at least as many more in the servants' hall, where operations had already commenced. On entering the drawing-room his appearance seemed to produce a great sensation, and after a little pause, the only county gentleman who was present advanced and introduced himself, his wife and daughter. This was Sir Harkaway Rotgut Wildfire, Baronet, a tall and somewhat corpulent man of about fifty, very choleric and overbearing, his countenance showing the hard life he had led, his nose being red and his forehead and mouth beset with pimples. He had been a bitter political opponent of Mr. Aubrey, and had once been a member for the county, but had so crippled his resources by hunting and horse-racing as to compel the sacrifice of their town amusements, viz., his seat in the House of Commons and Lady Wildfire's box at the opera. This had soured both of them not a little, and they had sunk, as it were, out of the county circle, in which they had once been sufficiently conspicuous. Sir Harkaway had an eye to the borough of Yatton on the happening of the next election, as soon as he had obtained an inkling that the new proprietor of Yatton was a very weak young man; and hence his patronizing presence at Yatton, in consequence of the invitation respectfully conveyed to him in Mr. Titmouse's name, through Messrs. Bloodsuck and Son. Besides Lady Wildfire and her daughter, both of whom had inquired with a sort of haughty curiosity about the lady who had accompanied Mr. Titmouse from town—a point which had been at length cleared up to their satisfaction—there were about a dozen ladies, the wives of the gentlemen who had borne so distinguished a part in the triumphal procession. They looked rather a queer set, and none of them dared to speak either to Lady Wildfire or her daughter till spoken to by them. Never had old Yatton beheld within its walls so motley a group; and had the Aubreys continued there, hospitable as they were,

accessible and charitable as they were, I leave the reader to
guess whether such creatures ever *would* have found their way
thither. By such guests, however, were the two principal
tables crowded on this joyous occasion, and about half past six
o'clock the feast commenced, and a feast it certainly was, both
elegant and substantial, nothing having been spared that money
could procure. Mr. Aubrey had a fine cellar of wines at Yatton, which, owing to some strange misunderstanding, had been
sold by private contract, not amongst his own friends in the
neighborhood, as Mr. Aubrey had intended, and imagined that
he had directed, but to Mr. Titmouse. Choice, indeed, were
these wines, and supplied on the present occasion in wanton
profusion. Champagne, burgundy, and claret, flowed like
water, and the other wines in like manner; but which last were
not, like the former class of wines, confined to the two principal rooms, but found their way into the servants' hall, and
were there drank without stint. Merriment echoed uproari-
ously from all parts of the old Hall, and Mr. Titmouse was
universally declared to be a very fine fellow, and likely to become by far the most popular man in the county. The Reverend Mr. Fleshpot said grace, and the Reverend Mr. Mudflint
returned thanks; and shortly afterward Sir Harkaway arose,
and, his eye fixed firmly on the adjoining borough, and also on
the jolly table which promised to be ever opened to him at
Yatton, he proposed the health of the distinguished proprietor
of Yatton, in certainly a somewhat fulsome strain. The toast
was received with the utmost enthusiasm; the gentlemen
shouted and jingled their glasses on the table, while the ladies
waved their handkerchiefs; indeed, the scene was one of such
overpowering excitement that Miss Quirk burst into tears,
overcome by her emotions; her papa winking very hard to
those about him, and using every exertion in his power to
point the attention of those present to the probability that a
very near and tender relationship was going to exist between
that young lady and Mr. Titmouse. Mr. Gammon, who sat
next to Titmouse, assured him that it was absolutely necessary
for him to make a speech to the company in acknowledgment
of the compliment which had just been paid him.

"I shall put my foot in it—by jingo I shall! You must
help me!" he whispered to Mr. Gammon, in an agony of
trepidation and a mist of confusion, as he rose from his chair,
being welcomed in the most enthusiastic manner by applause
of every kind, lasting for several minutes. At length, when
the noise had subsided into a fearful silence, he stammered
out, prompted incessantly by Mr. Gammon, something exceed-

ingly like the following, if, indeed, he did not use these very words:

"Mr.—I beg pardon—*Sir* Hark—away, and gentlemen—gentlemen and ladies, am most uncommon, monstrous—particular happy to—to—(eh? *what* d'ye say, Mr. Gammon?) see you all here—at this place—here—at Yatton." (*Applause.*) "Ladies and gentlemen—I say—hem!—unaccustomed as" —(*much applause*, during which Titmouse stooped and whispered to Gammon—"Curse me if I can catch a word you say!") "Happy and proud to see you all here—at Yatton—homes of my ancestry—known to you all—centuries. Enjoyed yourselves, I hope—(*great applause*)—and hope you'll often come and do the same—(*still greater applause*). Particular glad to see the ladies (*applause*)—often heard of the beauties of Yatton—never believed it—no—beg pardon, mean I now see them—(*applause*). Am fond of horses—(*applause*)—racing, hunting, and all that." (Here Sir Harkaway, extending his hand, publicly shook that of the eloquent speaker.) "Sorry to turn out the—the—old bird—but—nest not *his*—mine all the while—(*emotion*)—bear him no ill-will—(*applause*). Political principles—(*profound silence*) good old Whig principles—(*loud applause*)—rights of the people—religious liberty and all that—(*vociferous applause*)—found at my post in the hour of danger—enemy stole a march on me—(*great laughter and applause*). Won't detain you—ladies and gentlemen—drink your good healths, and many happy returns of the day." Down sat Mr. Titmouse, exhausted with his maiden speech, and quite overpowered, moreover, by the extraordinary applause with which he was greeted at its conclusion. In due course, many other toasts were drunk. "*Lady Wildfire and the married ladies.*" "*Miss Wildfire and the single ladies.*" "*Sir Harkawag Rotgut Wildfire.*" "*Religious Liberty*" (to which Mr. Mudflint responded in a very eloquent speech). "*The Liberty of the Press;*" "*Messrs. Quick Gammon and Snap, the enterprising, skillful and learned professional advisers of Mr. Titmouse.*"

Dancing was now loudly called for, and the hall was speedily prepared for it. By this time, however, it was past eleven o'clock; the free potations of all the men, and indeed of more than one of the ladies, were beginning to *tell*, and the noise and confusion were very great. Fierce confused sounds issued from the servants' hall, where it proved that a great fight was going on between Pumpkin the gardener, and a man who insisted on shouting "Titmouse forever!—down with the Tory Aubrey!" Pumpkin had much the best of it, and beat his opponent, after a severe encounter, into silence and submission. Then there were songs sung in all the rooms at once—speeches made, half a dozen at the same time; in short, never before had such scenes been witnessed, or such uproar heard within the decorous, the dignified, and venerable precincts of Yatton. Scenes ensued which really baffle description. Mr. Titmouse, of course, drank a great quantity of wine, although Mr. Gammon never left his side, and checked him fifty times when he was about to fill his glass; and the excitement produced by wine, will, I trust, in some measure, mitigate the reader's indignation at hearing of a little incident which occurred, in which Titmouse was concerned, and which, about half past three or four o'clock in the morning, served to bring that brilliant entertainment to a somewhat abrupt and rather unpleasant termination. Scarcely knowing where he was or what he was about, I am sorry to say, that while standing, as well as he could, beside Miss Wildfire, to dance for the fifth time with her—a plump, fair-faced, good-natured girl of about nineteen or twenty—he suddenly threw his arms round her and imprinted half a dozen kisses on her forehead, lips, cheek, and neck, before she could recover from the confusion into which this extraordinary assault had thrown her. Her faint shriek reached her father's ears, while he was in a distant part of the room, persecuting Miss Quirk with his drunken and profligate impertinences. Hastily approaching the quarter whence his daughter's voice had issued, he beheld her just extricated from the insolent embrace of the half-unconscious Titmouse, and greatly agitated. With flaming eye and outstretched arm, he approached his unfortunate little host and, seizing hold of his right ear, almost wrung it out of his head, Titmouse quite shrieking with the pain it occasioned. Still retaining his hold, uttering the while most fearful imprecations—he gave him three violent kicks upon the seat of honor, the last of which sent him spinning into the arms of old Mr. Quirk, who was hurrying up to his relief, and who fell flat on the floor with the violent concussion. Then Miss Quirk rushed forward and screamed; a scene of dreadful confusion ensued, and at length the infuriated and half-drunken baronet, forced away by his wife and his daughter, quitted the Hall and got into his carriage, uttering fearful threats and curses all the way home, without once adverting to the circumstance, of which also Lady Wildfire and her daughter were not aware, that he had been himself engaged in perpetrating the very same kind of misconduct which he had so severely and justly punished in poor Titmouse. As for Mr. Yahoo and Mr. Fitz-Snooks, they had been in quest of the same species of amusement the whole night; and had each of them, in pursuing their adventures in the servants' hall, very narrowly escaped much more serious indignities and injuries than had fallen to the lot of the hospitable owner of the mansion.

About half past four o'clock, the sun was shining in cloudless splendor, the air cleared and all nature seeming freshened after the storm of the preceding day, but what a scene was presented at Yatton! Two or three persons, one with his hat off, asleep; another grasping a half-empty bottle; and a third in a state of desperate indisposition, were to be seen, at considerable distances from each other, by the side of the carriage-road leading down to the park gates. Four or five horses, ready saddled and bridled, but neglected, and apparently forgotten by both servants and masters, were wandering about the fine green old court opposite the Hall door, eating the grass, and crushing with their hoofs the beautiful beds of flowers and shrubs which surrounded it. Mr. Glister's gig had got its wheels entangled with the old sun-dial—having been drawn thither by the horse, which had been put into it at least two hours before; opposite the Hall door stood the post-chaise which had brought Mr. and Mrs. Mudflint and their daughter. The latter two were sitting in it, one asleep—the other, Mrs. Mudflint, anxiously on the lookout for her husband, from time to time calling to him, but in vain; for, about half an hour before, he had quitted the room where he, Mr. Fleshpot, Mr. Going Gone, and Mr. Centipede had been playing a rubber at whist, till they almost all of them fell asleep with their cards in their hands, and made his way to the stables, where, not finding his chaise in the yard, or his horses in the stalls, he supposed his wife and daughter had gone home, whither he followed them by the footpath leading through the fields which stretched along the high-road to Grilston, and along which said fields he was, at that moment, staggering, hiccuping, not clearly understanding where he was, nor where he had last seen his wife and daughter. Candles and lamps were still burning and glimmering in some of the rooms; and in the servants' hall there were some dozen or so, who, having awoke from a deep sleep, were calling for more ale, or wine, or whatever else they could get. Some of the old family servants had fled hours ago from scenes of such unwonted riot, to their bed-rooms, and, having locked and barricaded the doors, gone to sleep. Mr. Griffiths sat in an old arm-chair in the library, the picture of misery; he had been repeatedly abused and insulted during the night, and had fled thither, unable to bear the sight of the disgusting revelry that was everywhere around going forward. In short, at every point that caught the eye were visible the evidences of the villainous debauchery that had prevailed for the last seven hours, and which, under the Titmouse dynasty, was likely to prevail at all times thereafter. As for Mr. Titmouse, half stunned with the treatment he had experienced at the hands of Sir Harkaway, he had been carried to bed—to the late bedroom of Mr. and Mrs. Aubrey—where, by his excessive, and miscellaneous, and long-continued potations, aiding the effect of the serious injuries which he had sustained, he lay sprawling on the bed, half undressed, in a truly deplorable condition. Mr. Glister, who had been summoned to his bedside upward of an hour before, sat now nodding in his chair beside his patient; and pretty nearly in a state of similar exhaustion were his valet and the housekeeper, who had, from time to time, wiped her eyes and sobbed aloud when thinking of past times and the grievous change that had come over old Yatton. Mr. Yahoo, Mr. Fitz-Snooks, Mr. Snap, Mr. Quirk, and Miss Quirk (the last having retired to her bedroom in alarm, at the time of Titmouse's mischance), were in their respective chambers, all of them probably asleep. Poor Hector, chained to his kennel, having barked himself hoarse for several hours, lay fast asleep, no one having attended to him, or given him anything to eat since Mr. Titmouse's arrival. Gammon had fled from the scene, in disgust and alarm, to his bedroom, some three hours before, but unable to sleep—not, however, with excess of wine, for he had drunk but a very few glasses—had arisen about four o'clock, and was at that moment wandering slowly, with folded arms and downcast countenance, up and down the fine avenue of elm-trees, where, it may be recollected, Mr. Aubrey had spent a portion of the last evening of his stay at Yatton.

Such is *my* account—and as fair an account as I know how to give of the matter; but it is curious to observe how very differently the same thing will strike different people. As soon as the grateful Mr. Centipede had recovered from the excitement occasioned by the part he had taken in the memorable festival above described, he set to work with the pen of a ready writer, and in the next number of the " YORKSHIRE STINGO " there appeared the following interesting account of the

" FESTIVITIES *at* YATTON HALL, *on the occasion of* POSSESSION *being taken by* TITTLEBAT TITMOUSE, ESQUIRE.

" Yesterday this interesting event came off with signal éclat. Notwithstanding the very unfavorable state of the weather,

about five o'clock in the evening an imposing cavalcade, com-
prising many of the leading gentry and yeomanry of this part
of the county, on foot and on horseback, preceded by an admirable band, and a large and splendid banner, bearing the
inscription—' Welcome to Yatton,' went out to meet the above
gentlemen, whose cortège, in two carriages, made its appearance in the village about half past five. The band immediately struck up ' See the Conquering Hero comes!' which, however, was nearly drowned in the shout which welcomed the new
proprietor of the noble estate of Yatton. His carriage was of
the most tasteful, splendid and unique description, and attracted universal admiration. Mr. Titmouse repeatedly bowed
through the carriage windows, in graceful acknowledgment of
the cordial welcome and congratulations with which he was
received. He was dressed in a light-blue surtout, with velvet
collar, full black stock, and a rich velvet waistcoat of plaid
pattern. His countenance is handsome and expressive, his eye
penetrating, and his brow strongly indicative of thought. He
appears to be little more than twenty-five years old; so that
he has before him a prospect of a long and brilliant career of
happiness and public usefulness. Tables were spread in all
the chief apartments, groaning beneath the most costly viands.
All the luxuries of the season were there; and the wines (which
we believe were those of Mr. Aubrey) were of the first description. Grace was said by the exemplary vicar of Grilston, the
Rev. Mr. Fleshpot; and the Rev. Mr. Mudflint returned
thanks. Sir Harkaway Rotgut Wildfire (whose amiable lady
and accomplished daughter were present) proposed the health
of Mr. Titmouse in a brief, but manly and cordial address; and
the manner in which Mr. Titmouse acknowledged the toast,
which was drunk with the greatest possible enthusiasm—the
simplicity, point and fervor which characterized every word he
uttered—were such as to excite lively emotion in all who heard
it, and warrant the highest expectations of his success in parliament. Nothing could be more touching than his brief
allusions to the sufferings and privations which he had undergone—nothing more delicate and forbearing than the feeling
which pervaded his momentary allusions to the late occupant
of Yatton. When, however, he distinctly avowed his political
principles as those of a strong and decided Whig—as those of
a dauntless champion of civil and religious liberty among all
classes of his Majesty's subjects—the applause was long and
enthusiastic. After dinner the great hall was cleared for dancing, which was opened by Mr. Titmouse and Miss Wildfire,
Lady Wildfire being led out by the Hon. Mr. Yahoo, an inti-

mate friend of Mr. Titmouse. We should not omit to mention
that Miss Quirk (the only daughter of Caleb Quirk, Esq., the
head of the distinguished firm of Quirk, Gammon and Snap,
of London, to whose untiring and most able exertions is owing
the happy change which has taken place in the ownership of
the Yatton property) accompanied her father, at the earnest
request of Mr. Titmouse, who danced several sets with her.
Sir Algernon Fitz-Snooks, a distinguished fashionable, also
accompanied Mr. Titmouse, and entered with great spirit into
all the gayeties of the evening. The 'light fantastic toe' was
kept 'tripping' till a late, or rather very early hour in the
morning—when the Hall was once more (for a time) surrendered to the repose and solitude from which it has been so
suddenly and joyously aroused."   [In another part of the
paper was contained an insulting paragraph, charging Mr. Aubrey with being a party to the " flagrant and iniquitous job,"
by which Sir Percival Pickering had been returned for the
borough; and intimating pretty distinctly that Mr. Aubrey
had not gone without " *a consideration* " for his share in the
nefarious transaction.]

A somewhat different account of the affair appeared in the
" York True Blue " of the same day.

" We have received one or two accounts of the orgies of
which Yatton Hall was yesterday the scene, on occasion of Mr.
Titmouse taking possession. We shall not give publicity to
the details which have been furnished us—hoping that the youth
and inexperience of the new owner of Yatton (all allowance,
also, being made for the very natural excitement of such an
occasion) will be allowed in some measure to palliate the conduct then exhibited. One fact, however, we may mention,
that a very serious *fracas* arose between Mr. Titmouse and a
certain well-known sporting Baronet, which is expected to give
employment to the gentlemen of the long robe. Nor can we
resist adverting to a circumstance, which our readers will, we
trust, credit, on being assured that we witnessed it with our
own eyes—that Mr. Titmouse positively traveled in the cast-
off state carriage of the Lord Mayor of London!!!! Nothing,
by the way, could be more absurd and contemptible than the
attempt at a 'Procession' which was got up—of which our
accounts are ludicrous in the extreme. Will our readers believe it, that the chief personages figuring on the occasion
were the editor and publisher of a certain low Radical paper
—which will no doubt, this day, favor its readers with a flaming description of this ' memorable affair.' "

Titmouse, assisted by his attentive valet, made a desperate attempt to get up and present himself the next day at dinner. Aided by a glass of pretty strong brandy and water, he at length got through the fatiguing duties of the toilet, and entered the drawing-room, where his traveling companions were awaiting his arrival—dinner being momentarily expected to be announced. He was deadly pale, his knees trembled, his eyes could not bear the light, and everything seemed in undulating motion around him, as he sunk in silent exhaustion on the sofa. After a few minutes' continuance, he was compelled to leave the room, leaning on Gammon's arm, who conducted him to his bedroom, and left him in charge of his valet, who got him again into bed, where he lay enduring much agony (Dr. Goddart being sent for), while his friends were enjoying themselves at dinner.

Snap had set off the ensuing day for town, by the first coach, pursuant to the arrangement already spoken of; but I think that old Mr. Quirk would have made up his mind to continue at Yatton until something definite had been done by Titmouse, in two matters which absorbed all the thoughts of the old gentleman—his daughter and the *Ten Thousand Pounds* bond. Miss Quirk, however, intense as was her anxiety to become the affianced bride of Titmouse, and as much the mistress of the delightful domain where at present she dwelt only as a guest, and in a very embarrassing position—was not so blind to all perception of womanly delicacy as to prolong her stay at Yatton; and at length prevailed upon her father to take their departure on the day but one after that on which they had arrived. Mr. Quirk was perfectly wretched; he vehemently distrusted Titmouse—he feared and detested Gammon. As for the former gentleman, he had not made any definite advances whatever toward Miss Quirk. He had not afforded to any one the slightest evidence of a promise of marriage, either expressed or implied. He chattered to Miss Quirk an infinite deal of civil nonsense—but that was all, in spite of the innumerable opportunities afforded him by the lady. Was Titmouse acting under the secret advice of that deceitful devil Gammon? —thought Mr. Quirk, in an ecstasy of perplexity and apprehension. Then as to the other matter—but there Gammon had almost as deep a stake in proportion as Quirk himself. On the morning of his departure, he and Gammon had a very long interview, in which they several times came to high words; but in the end Gammon vanquished his opponent as usual, allayed all his apprehensions, accounted for Titmouse's conduct in the most natural way in the world—look at his position just now, the excitement, the novelty, the bewilderment, the in-disposition he was experiencing; surely, surely *that* was not a moment to bring him to book! In short, Gammon at length brought Quirk, who had received the first intimation of the matter with a sudden *grunt* of surprise and anger, to acknowl-edge the propriety of Gammon's remaining behind, to protect Titmouse from the designing Yahoo that had got hold of him; and solemnly pledged himself, as in the sight of Heaven, to use his utmost efforts to bring about as speedily as possible the two grand objects of Mr. Quirk's wishes. With this the old gentleman was fain to be satisfied; but entered the chaise which was to convey Miss Quirk and himself to Grilston with as rueful a countenance as he had ever exhibited in his life. Mr. Titmouse was sufficiently recovered to be present at the departure of Miss Quirk, who regarded his interesting and languid looks with an eye of melting sympathy and affection. With half a smile and half a tear, she slipped into his hand, as he led her to the chaise, a little sprig of heart's-ease, which he at once stuck into the button-hole of his coat.

" 'Pon my soul—must you go? Devilish sorry you can't stay to have seen some fun!—The old gent (meaning her fa-ther) don't quite seem to like it—he, he!" said he in a low tone; then he handed her into the chaise, she dropping her veil to conceal the starting tear of mingled disappointment, and desire, and disgust, and they drove off, Titmouse kissing his hand to her as he stood upon the steps; and, as soon as they were out of sight, he exchanged a very significant smile with Mr. Gammon.

The next day Titmouse rose about ten o'clock, almost en-tirely recovered from his indisposition. Accompanied by Mr. Yahoo and Mr. Fitz-Snooks, with whom he was conversing as to the course he should take with reference to Sir Harkaway—whom, however, they advised him to treat with silent contempt, as he, Titmouse, was clearly in the wrong—he took a stroll about noon down the path leading to the park gates. They all three had cigars in their mouths, Titmouse walking be-tween them, as odious-looking a little puppy, sure, as man ever saw—puffing out his smoke slowly and with half-closed eye, his right hand stuck into his coat pocket and resting on his hip. These three figures—Heaven save the mark!—were the new lord of Yatton and his select friends!

" By jingo, surely here comes a parson," quoth Titmouse; " what the d—l can he want with me?"—'Twas Dr. Tatham, who slowly approached them, dressed in his Sunday suit, and leaning on his old-fashioned walking-stick, given him many, many years ago by the deceased Mrs. Aubrey.

"Let's have some sport," said Fitz-Snooks.

"We must look devilish serious—no grinning till the proper time," said Yahoo.

"Halloo—you, sir!" commenced Titmouse, "who are you?" Dr. Tatham took off his hat, bowed, and was passing on.

"*Devilish* cool, upon—my—soul—sir!" said Titmouse, stopping, and staring impudently at the worthy little Doctor, who seemed taken quite by surprise.

"My worthy old gentleman," said Yahoo, with mock respect, "are you aware who it was that asked you a question?"

"I am not, sir," replied Dr. Tatham, quietly, but resolutely.

"My name is Tittlebat Titmouse, at your service—and you are now in my grounds," said Titmouse, approaching him with an impudent air.

"*Have* I really the honor to address Mr. Titmouse?" inquired Dr. Tatham, somewhat incredulously.

"Why, 'pon my life I *think* so, unless I'm changed lately; and by Jove, sir!—*now*, who are you?"

"I am Dr. Tatham, sir, the vicar of Yatton; I *had* intended calling at the Hall to offer my compliments; but I fear I am intruding—"

"Devil a bit—no, 'pon honor, no! you're a very good old fellow, I don't doubt—is that little church outside yours?"

"It is, sir," replied Dr. Tatham, seriously and sternly; his manner completely abashing the presumptuous little coxcomb who addressed him.

"Oh—well—I—I—'pon my soul, happy to see you, sir—you'll find something to eat in the Hall, I dare say—"

"Do you preach in that same little church of yours next Sunday?" inquired Mr. Yahoo, whose gross countenance filled Dr. Tatham with unspeakable aversion.

"I preach there *every* Sunday, sir, twice," he replied, gravely and distantly.

"You see, sir," lisped Fitz-Snooks, "the prayers are so—so—*devilish* long and tiresome—if you could—eh?—shorten 'em a little?—"

Dr. Tatham slowly turned away from them, and, disregarding their calls to him, though their tone of voice was greatly altered, walked back again toward the gate, and quitted the park for the first time in his life with feelings of mortal repugnance. On reaching his little study, he sat down in his

old arm-chair, and fell into a sad reverie that lasted more than
an hour, and then he got up to go and see the old blind stag-
hound fed—and he looked at it, licking his hand, with feelings
of unusual tenderness; and the little Doctor shed a tear or
two as he patted its smooth gray old head.

On Saturday morning, Mr. Titmouse, at Mr. Gammon's instance, had fixed to go over the estate, accompanied by that
gentleman, and by Mr. Waters and Dickons, to give all the
information required of them, and point out the position and
extent of the property. To an eye capable of appreciating it,
in what admirable order was everything! but Titmouse quickly tired of it, and when about a mile from the Hall, discovered
that he had left his cigar-box behind him; at which he expressed infinite concern, and, greatly to the annoyance of Gammon and the contempt of his two bailiffs, insisted on returning home, so they re-entered the park. How beautiful it was!
Its gently undulating service, smooth as if overspread with
green velvet; trees, great and small, single and in clumps,
standing in positions so picturesque and commanding; the
broad, babbling, clear trout-stream winding through every
part of the park, with here and there a mimic fall, seen faintly flashing and glistening in the distance; herds of deer suddenly startled amid their green pastures and silent shades, and
moving off with graceful ease and rapidity; here and there a
rustic bridge over the stream; here an old stone bench placed
on an elevation commanding an extensive prospect; there a
kind of grotto, or an ivy-covered summer-house; then the
dense, extensive, and gloomy woods, forming a semicircular
sweep round the back of the Hall; all around, nearly as far as
the eye could reach, land of every kind in the highest state of
cultivation, plentifully stocked with fine cattle, and inter-
spersed with snug and substantial farms.

All this, thought Titmouse, might do very well for those
who fancied that sort of thing; but as for *him*, how the devil
could he have thought of leaving his cigars behind him!
Where, he wondered, were Yahoo and Fitz-Snooks? and
quickened his pace homeward.

On Gammon the scene they had been witnessing had made
a profound impression; and as his attention was now and then
called off from contemplating it by some ignorant and puerile
remark of the proprietor of the fine domain, he felt a momentary exasperation at himself for the part he had taken in
the expulsion of the Aubreys and the introduction of such a
creature as Titmouse. That revived certain other thoughts,
which led him into speculations of a description which would

have afforded uneasiness even to the little idiot beside him,
could he have been made aware of them.   But the cloud that
had darkened his brow was dispelled by a word or two of Titmouse.   "Mr. Gammon, 'pon my soul you're devilish dull to-
day," said he.   Gammon started; and with his winning smile
and cheerful voice, instantly replied,   ·
   "Oh, Mr. Titmouse, I was only thinking how happy you
are, and that you deserve it!"
   "Yes; 'pon my soul, it ought all to have been mine at my
birth!   Don't it tire you, Mr. Gammon, to walk in this up-
and-down, zigzag, here-and-there sort of way?   It does *me*,
'pon my life!   What would I give for a cigar at this moment!"
   The next day was the Sabbath, tranquil and beautiful; and
just as the little tinkling bell of Yatton church had ceased,
Dr. Tatham rose, in his reading-desk, and commenced the
prayers.   The church was quite full, for every one was naturally anxious to catch a glimpse of the new tenants of the
Squire's pew.   It was empty, however, till about five minutes
after the service had commenced, when a gentleman walked
slowly up to the church door, and having whispered an inquiry
of the old pew-opener which was the Squire's pew, she led him
into it—all eyes settled upon him, and all were struck with his
appearance, his calm, keen features and gentlemanly figure.
'Twas, of course, Gammon, who, with the utmost decorum
and solemnity, having stood for near a minute with his hat
covering his face, during which time he reflected that Miss
Aubrey had sat in that pew on the last occasion of his attendance at the church, turned round and behaved with the greatest seriousness and reverence throughout the service, paying
marked attention to the sermon.   Gammon was an unbe-
liever, but he thought Dr. Tatham an amiable and learned
enthusiast, but who was most probably in earnest; and he felt
disposed to admit, as his eye glanced round the attentive and
decent congregation, that this sort of thing was not without its
advantages.   Almost all present took him for Titmouse, and
watched every turn of his countenance with intense interest:
and, in their simplicity, they rejoiced that Mr. Aubrey's successor was, at all events, so grave and respectable-looking a
man; and they fancied that he frequently thought, with kindness and regret, of those whose seat he was occupying.   About
the middle of the service the door of the church being wide
open, the congregation beheld three gentlemen smoking cigars,
and laughing and talking together, approaching the porch.
They were dressed very finely indeed, and were supposed to be
some of the great friends of the new Squire.   They stopped

when within a few yards of the church, and after whispering together for a moment, one of them, having expelled a mouthful of smoke, stepped forward to the door, holding his cigar in one hand, and with the other taking off his hat. There was a faint smirk on his face (for he did not catch the stern countenance of Gammon anxiously directed toward him), till he beheld Dr. Tatham's solemn eye fixed upon him, while he made a momentary pause. Titmouse blushed scarlet, made a hesitating but most respectable bow, and stepping back a few paces, replaced his hat on his head, and lighted his cigar from that of Mr. Fitz-Snooks, within view, perhaps unconsciously, of more than half the congregation. Then the three gentlemen, after Mr. Titmouse had spoken a word or two to them, burst out into a laugh, and quitted the church-yard.

CHAPTER XX.

AUBREY's sudden plunge into the cold and deep stream of trouble had—the first shock over—served, as it were, to brace his nerves. 'Tis at such a time and on such an occasion that the temper and quality of the soul are tried; whether it be weak in seeming strength, or strong in seeming weakness. How many are there, walking with smiling, complacent confidence along the flowery bank, who, if suddenly bidden to strip and enter, would turn pale and tremble as they reluctantly prepared to obey the stern mandate; and, after a convulsive shudder, a faint shriek, a brief struggle, disappear from the surface paralyzed, never to be seen again! In such a point of view, let me hope that the situation of Aubrey, one of deepening difficulty and danger—the issue of which, hid in the darkness of the future, no earthly intelligence could predict—will excite in the thoughtful reader an anxiety not unmingled with confidence.

The enervating effects of *inactivity* upon the physical structure and energies of mankind, few can have failed to observe. Rust is more fatal to metal than wear. A thorough-bred racer, if confined in stable or paddock, or a boxer, born of the finest muscular make, if prematurely incarcerated in a jail, will, after a few years, become quite unable to compete with those vastly their inferiors in natural endowments and capabilities; however, they may, with careful training, be restored to the full enjoyment and exercise of their powers. Thus is it with the temper and intellect of man, which, secluded from the scenes of *appropriate* stimulus and exercise, become relaxed and weakened. What would have become of the glorious spirit and powers of Achilles if his days had all melted away in the tender, delicate, emasculating inactivity and indulgence of the court of Lycomedes? The language of the ancient orator concerning his art may be applied to *life* that not only its greatness, but its enjoyment, consists in action—*action*—ACTION. The feelings, for instance, may become so morbidly sensitive as to give an appearance of weakness to the whole character; and this is likely to be specially the case of one born with those of superior liveliness and delicacy, if he be destined to move only in the regions of silent and profound abstraction and contemplation—in those refined regions which may be termed a sort of paradise, where every conceivable source of enjoyment is cultivated for the fortunate and fastidious occupants to the very uttermost, and all those innumerable things which fret, worry, and harass the temper, the head, and the heart of the dwellers in the rude regions of ordinary life—most anxiously weeded out instead of entering into the throng of life, and taking part in its constant cares and conflicts—scenes which require all his energies always in exercise, to keep his place and escape being trodden underfoot. Rely upon it, that the man who feels a tendency to shrink from collision with his fellows, to run away with distaste or apprehension from the great practical business of life, does not enjoy moral or intellectual health; will quickly contract a silly conceit and fastidiousness, or sink into imbecility and misanthropy, and should devoutly thank Providence for the occasion, however momentarily startling and irritating, which stirs him out of his lethargy, his *cowardly* lethargy, and sends him among his fellows—puts him, in a manner, upon a course of training—upon an experience of comparative suffering, it may be of sorrow, requiring the exercise of powers of which he had before scarcely been conscious, and giving him presently the exhilarating consciousness that he is exhibiting himself—a MAN.

"It is probable," says a very acute and powerful writer of the present day, Mr. Foster, in his Essay on "Decision of Character"—"that the men most distinguished for decision have not, in general, possessed a large share of tenderness; and it is easy to imagine that the laws, according to which our nature is formed, will with great difficulty allow the combination of the refined sensibilities, with a hardy, never-shrinking, never-yielding constancy. Is it not almost of the essence of this constancy, to be free from even the *perception* of such impressions as cause a mind, weak through susceptibility, to relax, or to waver?—No doubt this firmness consists partly in overcoming feeling—but it may consist partly, too, in not having them." The case I am contemplating is perhaps the difficult, though by no means, I am persuaded, uncommon one—of a person possessing these delicate sensibilities, these lively feelings; yet with a native strength of character, beneath which, when the occasion for its display has arisen—when it is placed in a scene of constant and compulsory action, will fully evince and vindicate itself. It is then "that another essential principle of decision of character," to quote from another part of the same essay, "will be displayed; namely, a total incapability of surrendering to indifference or delay the serious determinations of the mind. A strenuous WILL accompanies the conclusions of thought, and constantly urges the utmost efforts for their practical accomplishment. The intellect is invested, as it were, with a glowing atmosphere of passion, under the influence of which the cold dictates of reason take fire, and spring into active powers."

There is, indeed, nothing like throwing a man of the description we are considering upon his own resources, and compelling him to exertion. Listen, ye languid and often gifted victims of indolence and ennui, to the noble language of one blessed with as great powers as perhaps were ever vouchsafed to man—Edmund Burke!

"DIFFICULTY is a severe instructor, set over us by the Supreme ordinance of a parental guardian and legislator, who knows us better than we know ourselves, as He loves us better, too. *Pater ipse colendi, haud facilem vesse vian oluit.* He that wrestles with us strengthens our nerves and sharpens our skill; our antagonist is our helper. This amicable contest with difficulty obliges us to an intimate acquaintance with our object, and compels us to consider it in all its relations; it will not suffer us to be superficial."

The man, moreover, whose disposition is one of sterling excellence, despite the few foibles which it may have contracted in comparative solitude and inactivity, when he is compelled to mix indiscriminately with the great family of man, oh, how patient and tolerant becomes he of the weakness and errors of others, when thus constantly reminded of and made to feel his own! Oh, how pitiful! how very pitiful is he!—how his heart yearns and overflows with love, and mercy, and charity toward his species, *individually*—whose eye looks oft on their grievous privations, their often incurable distress and misery!—and who in the spirit of a heavenly philanthropy penetrates even to those deserted quarters—

> " Where hopeless anguish pours her moan,
> And lonely want retires to die!"

It may be that some of the preceding observations are applicable to many individuals of the purest and most amiable characters and powerful and cultivated intellects, in the higher classes of society, whose affluence exempts them from the necessity of actively intermingling with the concerns of life, and feeling the consciousness of individual responsibility, of having a personal necessity for anxious care and exertion. A position of real precariousness and danger is that which is requisite for developing the energies of a man of high moral and intellectual character, as it will expose to destruction one of a contrary description.

I have endeavored, in previous portions of this history, to delineate faithfully the character of Mr. Aubrey—one (how idle and childish would have been the attempt!) by no means *perfect*, yet with very high qualities, a noble simplicity; a man, generous, confiding, sincere, affectionate—possessing a profound sense of religion, *really influencing his conduct in life;* an intellect of a superior order, of a practical turn, of a masculine strength—as had been evidenced by his successful academical career, his thorough mastery of some of the most important and difficult branches of human knowledge, and by his superior aptitude for public business. He was at the same time possessed of a sensibility that was certainly excessive. He had a morbid tendency to pensiveness, if not melancholy, which, with a feeble *physical* constitution, was partly derived from his mother, and partly accounted for by the species of life which he had led. From his early youth he had been addicted to close and severe study, which had given permanence and strength to his naturally contemplative turn. He had not, moreover, with too many possessed of his means and station, entered, just at the dawn and bloom of manhood, upon that course of dissipation which is a sure and speedy means of destroying "the freshness of thought and of feeling," and inducing a *lowered tone* of feeling, and a callousness which some seem to consider necessary to enable them to pass through life easily and agreeably. He, on the contrary, had stepped out of the gloom and solitude of the cloister into the pure and peaceful region of domestic life, with all its hallowed and unutterable tendernesses, where the affections grew luxuriantly; in the constant society of such women as his mother, his sister, his wife, and latterly his lovely children. Then he was possessed, all this while, of a fine fortune—one which placed him far beyond the necessity for anxiety or exertion. With such tastes as these, such a temperament as his, and leading such a life as his, is it surprising that the tone of his

feelings should have become relaxed? The three or four years
which he had spent in Parliament, when he plunged into its
fierce and absorbing excitement with characteristic ardor and
determination, though calculated to sharpen the faculties, and
draw forth the resources of his intellect, subjected him to
those alternations of excitement and depression, those extremes
of action and reaction, which were not calculated to *correct* his
morbid tendencies.

Therefore came there up to him a messenger from heaven,
with trouble and affliction in his countenance, telling him to
descend from the happy solitude of his high mountain, into
the dismal hubbub and conflict in the plain beneath. He
came down with humility and awe, and with reverent resignation; and was—instantly surrounded!—

A weak man would have been confused and stunned, and so
sunk helpless into the leaden arms of despair. But it was not
so with Aubrey. There was that dormant energy within,
which, when appealed to, quickly shook off the weakness contracted by inaction, and told him to *be up and doing ;* and
that not with the fitful energy of mere impulse, but the constant strength of a well-regulated mind, conscious of its critical
position; and also of a calm, inflexible determination to van-
quish difficulty, and if possible escape the imminent danger,
however long and doubtful might prove the conflict. Above
all, he was consoled and blessed by the conviction that nothing could befall him that was not the ordination of Providence,

> ——" supremely wise,
> Alike in what it gives and what denies;"

that His was the ordering of the sunshine and the gloom, the
tempest and the calm of life. This was to Aubrey—this is—
as the humble writer of these pages (who has had in his time
his measure of anxiety and affliction) has in his soul a profound and intimate persuasion and conviction of—the only
source of real fortitude and resignation, amidst the perplex-
ities, and afflictions and dangers of life. Depend upon it, that
a secret and scarce-acknowledged disbelief, or at least doubt
and distrust of the very existence of God, and of His government of the world—HIS REAL PRESENCE AND INTERFERENCE
with the men and the things of the world—lies at the bottom
of almost all impatience and despair under adverse circumstances. How can he be impatient, or despairing, who be-
lieves not only the existence of God and His moral government
of the world, but that He has mercifully vouchsafed to reveal
and declare expressly that the infliction of suffering and sorrow

is directly from Himself and designed solely for the advantage of His creatures? *If ye endure chastening, God dealeth with you as with sons ; for what son is he whom the father chasteneth not ? We have had fathers of our flesh which corrected us, and we gave them reverence ; shall we not much rather be in subjection unto the Father of spirits, and live ? For they verily for a few days chastened us after their own pleasure ; but He for our profit, that we might be partakers of his holiness. Now, no chastening for the present seemeth to be joyous, but grievous : nevertheless afterwards it yieldeth the peaceable fruit of righteousness unto them which are exercised thereby. Wherefore lift up the hands which hang down, and the feeble knees.* While thus benignantly teacheth the voice of God, thought Aubrey, shall I rather incline mine ear to the blighting whisper of the Evil One—*a liar, and the father of a lie*, who would fain that I should become *a fool, saying within my heart there is no God*—or, if I can not but believe that there is one, provoking me to *charge Him foolishly, to curse Him and die ?* Not so, however, had Aubrey read the Scriptures—not so had he learned the Christian religion.

The last time that we caught a glimpse of the ruined family they had arrived nearly at the end of their long and melancholy journey from Yatton to the metropolis. When before had such been the character of their journey to town? Had they not even looked forward with pleasure toward the brilliant gayeties of the season; their re-entrance into an extensive and splendid circle of friends—and he into the delightful excitement of political life—the opening of the parliamentary campaign? Alas, how changed now all this! how gloomy and threatening the aspect of the metropolis, whose dusky outskirts they were entering! With what feelings of oppression— of vague, indefinite apprehension—did they now approach it; their spirits heavy, their hearts bleeding with their recent severance from Yatton! Now, distress, desertion, dismay, seemed associated with the formidable name of " London." They had now no place of their own awaiting, thoroughly prepared for them, their welcome arrival—but must drive to some quiet and inexpensive family hotel for temporary shelter. As their eyes caught familiar point after point in their route through the suburbs—now passed at a moderate pace, with a modest pair of horses; formerly dashed past by them in their carriage and four—there were very few words spoken by those within the carriage. Both the children were fast asleep. Poor Kate, as they entered Piccadilly, burst into tears; her pent-up feelings suddenly gave way, and she cried

heartily; Mrs. Aubrey also shedding tears. Mr. Aubrey was
calm, but evidently oppressed with profound anxiety. Still he
affectionately grasped their hands, and, in something designed
for a cheerful tone and manner, besought them to restrain
their feelings and thank Heaven that, so far, they had got on
safely.

"I shall be better presently, Charles," said Miss Aubrey,
passionately, burying her face in her handkerchief, "but I feel
quite *afraid* of London!"

Over the pavement they rattled, meeting carriages rolling in
all directions—for it was about the dinner hour and in the
height of the season; and it was the casual but vivid evidence
thus afforded of their desolate position, this sudden glimpse of
old familiar scenes, which had momentarily overcome the fortitude of Miss Aubrey.   They drove to a quiet family hotel in a
retired street running parallel with Piccadilly; they were all
wearied, both in mind and body, and, after a very slight repast and much anxious and desponding conversation, they
bade each other affectionate adieus and retired to rest.   They
rose in the morning refreshed with repose, and in a much more
tranquil mood of mind than could have been expected.

"Now, we enter," said Aubrey, with a cheerful smile,
"upon the real business of life; so we must discard sentiment
—we must not think of the past, but the future."

At their request, they shortly after breakfast accompanied
him to the house agent, who had been commissioned by Mr.
Runnington to look out two or three residences such as, on
their arrival in town, they might easily select from.   One was
particularly recommended to them; and after due inquiry,
within three days after their arrival in town, they engaged it.
'Twas a small, but convenient, airy and comfortable house,
within five minutes' walk of Hyde Park, and situated in Vivian
Street—a recent street—and as quiet and retired as they could
have wished.   The rent, too, was moderate—fifty pounds a
year.   Though none of the houses in the street were large,
they were all strictly private residences, and had an air of
thorough respectability.   Mr. Aubrey's house had but one
window to the dining-room, and two to the drawing-room.
The passage and staircase were sufficiently commodious, as
were the rooms.   At the back of the house was a small garden,
about twenty yards in length, and about ten yards in width,
with several lilacs, laburnums, and shrubs; and a considerable
portion of the wall was covered with ivy.   Was not this a delightful place for the children to play about in?   The back
parlor, a somewhat small room certainly, looked into this

garden; and that room was at once appropriated to a study for Mr. Aubrey. Within a week's time all their luggage, furniture, etc., had arrived in town from Yatton; and they had quite sufficient to furnish their little residence out of the wreck of the furniture and equipments of the old Hall— adapted, as it was, under the tasteful superintendence of Mrs. and Miss Aubrey, with equal regard to elegance, simplicity, and economy. How busy were they all for a fortnight! Many and many an irrepressible sigh and rebellious tear would the sight of these old familiar objects, in their new situation, occasion there! Some half dozen family pictures hung upon the wall. Over the mantel-piece was suspended a piece of beautiful embroidery—by poor old Mrs. Aubrey, many years before —of the arms of the family. In the dining-room was the old high-backed chair in which she had sat for twenty years and more. In the drawing-room was Miss Aubrey's favorite cabinet and Mrs. Aubrey's piano; and in both the rooms were to be seen everywhere the delicate traces of dear, dear, graceful, and elegant *woman*—touching nothing that she adorns not! What with the silk curtains, and a carpet of simple but tasteful pattern, and the various articles of furniture and ornaments, all possessing a kind of *old family air*—all from Yatton, I declare there was a kind of richness about the general aspect of the room; and when Mrs. Aubrey and Miss Aubrey came to fetch Mr. Aubrey out of his study to witness the completion of their labors, he gazed round him, looked at each object, and then at the two dear fond beings standing beside him, awaiting his opinion with womanly eagerness; but he could not express his feelings. He kissed each of them very tenderly and in silence, and then they were a little overcome. His study, also, though *very* small, was as snug and comfortable as a bookworm could desire. All the sides were covered with books, and in the middle were the library-table and armchair which he had used in Grosvenor Street, and which were certainly on too large a scale for the little room to which they had been removed. That they were not incessantly and very painfully reminded of the contrast afforded by their present to their former circumstances, I do not pretend to assert; but it very, very seldom formed a topic of *conversation* between any of them. When, however, the little bustle and occupation of arranging their house was over, and Mrs. Aubrey and Kate were left a good deal to themselves—Mr. Aubrey being either absent from home, or in his study engaged in matters of the last importance to them all—then they would talk together with increasing eagerness and excitement about past

times and their recent troubles and bereavements, not displaying then—sweet souls!—*quite* that degree of resignation
and fortitude which they strove to exhibit in the presence of
Mr. Aubrey.

" Some natural tears they dropt, but wiped them soon."

They passed a good deal of their time in-doors in needle-
work, *practical* family needle-work, an art in which they were
not particularly accomplished, but which they quickly acquired
from a seamstress whom they kept engaged constantly in the
house for several weeks. Then sometimes they would sit down
to the piano; at other times they would read—on all occasions,
however, frequently falling into conversation on the all-
engrossing topic of their expulsion from Yatton. Now and
then they could scarcely refrain from a melancholy smile,
when they remarked upon their shrunken personal importance.
" Really, Agnes," said one day Miss Aubrey, " I feel just as
one can fancy a few poor newly shorn sheep must feel! So
light and cold! So much *less* than they were half an hour before! Surely they must hardly know what to make of themselves!"
" Then, I suppose, mamma," said Charles, who was sitting
on a stool beside them—making believe to write on a small
slate—" I am a *little* sheep." They both looked up at the child
with silent tenderness, and presently thought of Him who
" *tempers the wind* to the shorn lamb."
Their proximity to the parks was delightful, and many a
pleasant hour did they pass there with the children; and then
returning home, would occupy themselves with writing letters
—and long ones they usually were—to early and loved friends,
especially to Dr. Tatham, with whom Miss Aubrey kept up a
constant correspondence. I ought to have mentioned before
that Mr. Aubrey, in bringing his favorite valet up to town
with him, had no other design than, with that kind thoughtfulness for which he was remarkable, to have an opportunity of
securing for him a good situation, and that he succeeded in
doing, after about a fortnight's interval; but the poor fellow
was quite confounded when he first heard that he was to quit
the services of Mr. Aubrey, and almost falling on his knees,
begged to be permitted to continue and receive no wages, and
he should be a happy man. Mr. Aubrey was, however, firm;
and on parting with him, which he did with no little emotion,
put two guineas into his hand as a present, and wished him
health and happiness. The poor fellow's deep distress at parting with the family sensibly affected them all, and reminded

them vividly of one of the latest and bitterest scenes at Yatton. On his departure their little establishment consisted but of three female servants, a cook, a house-maid, and a nursery-maid. It took them some little time to familiarize themselves with the attendance of a female servant at dinner! That was one little matter—and another was Charles's now and then complaining of being tired, and then inquiring why his mamma did not drive in the carriage as she used to do, and how he liked to go with her? which brought home to them, in a lively manner, their altered circumstances—their fallen fortunes. Many, many were the anxious calculations they made together of the probable amount of their annual expenditure—which at length, inexperienced as they were, they fixed at from £300 to £500, including everything; Mrs. Aubrey and Miss Aubrey eagerly assuring Mr. Aubrey, and each other, that as for clothes—their wardrobe would, with care, last them for three or four years to come—so that *that* was an item which might be almost altogether excluded from the account; except, by the way, the children—yes *they* should be always well dressed; that all agreed upon. Then there was their education—oh, Kate would see to that! Could they, in this manner, with rigid, systematic economy, hold on their way for a year or two? was a question they often asked one another, with beating hearts. If they could, then, they said, they should be happy; for they had *health*—they had peace of mind: their consciences were not oppressed by a sense of misconduct—and they were able to put their trust in Providence.

Mr. Aubrey resolved to live in strict privacy; and they communicated their residence to but one or two of their numerous friends, and to them only in confidence. To have acted otherwise would have seriously interfered with the arrangements which, long ago contemplated, he had now fixed upon; it would be perpetually calling their attention to the contrast between former days and scenes, and the present; it would disturb their feelings, and might, moreover, subject them to kind and generous importunities and offers, which, however delicate, would be exquisitely painful and trying to an honorable pride. But it is time that I should proceed to give a more particular account of the position, the personal feelings, and purposes and prospects of Mr. Aubrey.

From the moment when Aubrey received the first intimation of the desperate assault about to be made upon his fortunes, he felt a conviction, whether arising from weakness, or superstition, or any other cause, it concerns me not here to say—that the issue would be a disastrous one for him: and, the first

alarm and confusion over, with serious calmness, with deep
anxiety, addressed himself to the determination of his future
course of life. A man of his refined taste and feeling would
inevitably appreciate exquisitely—with a most agonizing intensity—the loss of all those superior enjoyments—the *deliciæ*
of life—to which he had been from his birth accustomed.
Semper enim delicatè ac molliter vixit. I speak not here of
the mere exterior " appliances and means " of wealth and station, but of the fastidious and sensitive condition of *feeling*
and temper, which such a state of things is calculated to en-
gender in a person of his description. He could part with the
one; but how could he divest himself of the other? Even had
he been alone in the world, and not surrounded with objects
of the tenderest regard, whose safety or ruin was involved in
his own, one of the results of his opponent's success—namely,
his claim to the mesne profits—was calculated to fetter all his
movements, to hang like a mill-stone round his neck; and
that effect, indeed, it had. Still he played the man—resolved
to act promptly, and with the best consideration he could give
his critical position. He had not yet reached the prime of life;
had a fair share of health; had been blessed with the inestimable advantages of a thorough—a first-rate education—and,
above all, had followed out his early advantages by laborious
and systematic study; and had not only made accurate, extensive, and valuable acquisitions, but learned how to use them
—to turn them to practical account. What would, he thought,
have become of him, had he—or those before him—neglected
his education? Then he had acquired a considerable familiarity with business habits in the House of Commons and had
friends and connections who might be of essential service to
him, if he could but first succeed in acquiring a position that
would enable him to avail himself of them. Surely all *these*
were cheering considerations; subject, however, always to the
dreadful drawback to which I have alluded. Had he not
even advantages superior to those possessed by many in entering upon some one of the scenes of honorable struggle for a
livelihood and for even distinction? He surveyed them all
with much deliberation. The army and navy were of course
out of the question. There was the *Church :* but no—his soul
recoiled from the degradation and guilt of entering that holy
calling from mercenary motives, merely as a means of acquiring a livelihood; and he would rather have perished than prefer the prayer of one whose lamentable case is left on record—
who *came and crouched for a piece of silver and a morsel of
bread, saying, put me, I pray thee, into one of the priest's*

offices, that I may eat a piece of bread. A personage of very high distinction in the Church—of eminent piety and learning —who was aware of the misfortunes of Aubrey, and well acquainted with his pure and exemplary character—his learning and acquirements—his fitness for the ministerial office—wrote to him, offering him every facility for taking orders, and assuring him that he need not wait long before very suitable provision would be made for him. Though he assured Mr. Aubrey that he believed himself consulting the best interests, both of Mr. Aubrey and of the Church—the scruples of Mr. Aubrey were not to be overcome; and he wrote to the kind and venerable prelate a letter declining his offers, and assigning reasons which filled him with profound respect for Mr. Aubrey. Then literature, for which—for real substantial literature—he possessed superior qualifications, was proverbially precarious. As for *teaching*—he felt quite unfit for it; he had not the least inclination for it; 'twas a cheerless scene of exertion, in which, as it were, he felt his energies *perishing in the using.* The BAR was the profession to which his tastes and inclinations, and, he hoped, his qualifications, pointed him. One of the first things he did, on reaching London, was to apply for information to one consummately qualified to guide him in the matter. He wrote to the Attorney-General, soliciting an interview at his chambers upon the subject of entering the profession; and received an immediate answer, appointing ten o'clock on Saturday, on which day the Attorney-General expected to be free from public engagements. Precisely at that hour, Mr. Aubrey entered the chambers of that distinguished person, whose arrival he anticipated. Poor Aubrey felt a little nervous and depressed as the fussy clerk showed him into the room—*as he fancied,* and only fancied—with an air of patronizing civility, as if aware of his diminished personal consequence. He stood for a minute or two very close to Mr. Aubrey, with a sort of confidence in his manner, as he rubbed his hands, and observed on the innumerable engagements of the Attorney - General, which slightly — *very slightly* — displeased Mr. Aubrey, suggesting the idea of undue familiarity. He answered the voluble clerk therefore courteously, but with an evident disinclination to prolong the conversation, and was quickly left alone. Poor Aubrey's pride had taken the alarm. Was it possible that the man had been presuming to give him a hint not to occupy much of the Attorney-General's time? Was it even possible that it had been done in consequence of an intimation from the Attorney-General himself? Oh, no— his own good sense came presently to his assistance and ban-

ished so absurd a notion. There were three tables in the
room, and each was laden with briefs, some of them of prodigious bulk. Seven or eight very recent ones were placed on
the table opposite to which his vacant chair was standing; the
very sight of all this oppressed Aubrey: how could one man's
head manage so much? He was ruminating on such matters
—and especially upon the powerful, versatile, and practiced
intellect which was requisite to get through so much, especially
amid all the harassing responsibilities and occupations of
political office—when the Attorney-General entered. He was a
tall and handsome man, about forty-five, with an extremely
graceful and gentleman-like carriage—a slight dash of negli-
gence in it, his manner fraught with cheerful composure. He
looked quite a man of the world; you would have thought that
he could have nothing to do but lounge at his club, ride round
the Park, and saunter into the House of Lords for an hour or
two. There was not a trace of anxiety or exhaustion about
him; yet he had been engaged during the whole of the preceding day conducting a great political cause, and not concluding
his reply till nine o'clock at night! There was a playful smile
about his mouth; his ample forehead seemed unfurrowed by a
wrinkle; and his bright, penetrating hazel eyes seemed never
the worse for wear with all the tens of thousands of brief sheets
on which they had traveled for the last twenty years.

" Ha—Aubrey—I'm a few minutes behind time, I'm afraid!
—How are you?" said he, with a cheerful air, grasping his
saddened visitor by the hand.

" Good-morning, Mr. Attorney—*Cum tot sustineas, et tanta
negotia, solus* "—commenced Aubrey, pointing to the piles of
briefs.

" Pho, my dear Aubrey; nonsense! They've enough of my
time, surely, without grudging me half an hour's conversation
with a friend—ah, ha!" They were both quickly seated—and
within a minute or two's time the Attorney-General had *got to
business*—the business of the visit. Aubrey perceived the
rapidity of the movement; but nothing could be *kinder* than
the manner of his companion, however distinct and decisive
his intimation that time was very precious. He approved entirely of Mr. Aubrey's coming to the bar, and strongly recommended him not to lose one day in entering upon the serious
practical study of it; informing him that, as a university
man, within three years' time he would be eligible to be called to
the bar. " I'll call you myself, Aubrey, if you will allow me,"
said he; but before that period had arrived, he had taken his
seat upon the Woolsack as Lord High Chancellor of England.

"Undoubtedly," said he, among other things, when pressed by Aubrey about the difficulties he should have to encounter, "the acquisition of the *technical* knowledge will be for some little time rather troublesome; but a twelvemonth's steady study by a man who is in earnest and accustomed to work will make a vast inroad on it. Everything you master, you see, helps to master so much more. Three years' serious application to the law by a man like you will place you far ahead of the bulk of men at the bar. Besides, 'tis not the study but the *practice* of the law that teaches law most effectually. Always have an eye to *principle*, and resolve thoroughly to understand the smallest details; and it will be a wonderful assistance in fixing them for practical use in your mind to learn as much as you can of the reasons and policy in which they originated. You'll find Reeve's History of the English Law of infinite service to you; I should read it in the evenings; 'tis full of interest in every point of view. I read every word of it, very carefully, soon after I left college; and, by the way, I'll tell you another book, by which I did the same—the State Trials: ay, by Jove! Aubrey, I read every word of them—speeches, examinations, cross-examination of witnesses, reply, and summing up. That's where I first learned how to examine and cross-examine a witness. Consider, the counsel employed were, you know, generally first-rate men, and exerted themselves, on such occasions, to the utmost. And there you learn a great deal of *constitutional* law. You ask how I get through so much? To be sure, one has enough to do, and I'm afraid I neglect a good deal; but the great secret is—*attention,* and to *one thing* at a time. The sun's rays scattered are comparatively powerless; condense them, they are irresistible; but all this you know as well as I do. Certainly, law is difficult: but its difficulty is often greatly overrated, especially by imperfectly educated and ill-disciplined, *quick, sharp* men. *You* will find it a very different matter. What is wanted is a clear head, a good memory, strong common sense, an aptitude for analysis and arrangement: before these combined, the difficulties of the law fly like the morning mist before the sun. *Tact* with the court and a jury is acquired by practice, to a considerable extent, in the absence even of natural endowments. And as for *you*, Aubrey—upon my honor, I've often listened with great satisfaction to you in the House; few ever made clearer statements of facts, or reasoned more closely and cogently than you did; with practice you would have become a formidable debater. In your new profession you will find *facts* become quite different things: flexible, elastic, accom-

modating—you may do anything with them—twist, and turn,
and combine; ha! ha! Aubrey!" [Here the Attorney-General
laughed in the plenitude of his own conscious power.] " In a
word, Aubrey, if you determine to get on at the bar, you will;
and if you can but get a bit of a start at beginning; now, for
instance, there's Runnington's house—one of the very first in
London—why if *they* would push you—your fortune's made.
But you must make up your mind to wait a little: you can't
get into a great business by a hop, step, and a jump, believe
me.   Certainly *I* have no cause to be dissatisfied; I've done
pretty well; but I can tell you that eight years passed over me
before I earned enough a year to pay my laundress! With me,
accident supplied the place of *connection :* but only suppose
how I must have worked in the meantime to be able to do
business when it came to me!   I know it's said that I was
always an idle man; but people were a good deal mistaken
about that matter, I can promise them!   What *idiots,* indeed,
to suppose such a thing!   Why, my very first start lifted me
into a business of a thousand a year; and, in the name of common sense, how could I have got through it, if I hadn't worked
beforehand?   Bah!   Now, if Runningtons' will stand by you,
I'll guarantee your making £500 your first year! and if they
won't, why, don't despair, you'll have to wait a little longer;
but it will come at last, depend on it, if you continue on the
lookout!   Besides, you can help me a little bit, eh?   It will
be a sort of introduction, you know; but we've time enough
to see about that.   I recommend you to get at once into the
chambers of some hard-working man, with a good deal of general business, particularly Pleading—let me see "—Here the
Attorney-General paused and stroked his chin for a moment
or two in a musing manner, " Ah, yes, there's WEASEL, the
very man for your purpose.   He's a good pleader, and a neat
draftsman; gets through his work very *cleanly*—ah! Weasel's
a clear-headed, painstaking man—all for law; and he's got a
good deal of it.   He's not a very polished person, Weasel, ha!
ha! but he's an honorable, right-minded man—shall I introduce you?   Well, by and by, I'll walk over with you.   As to
books? oh! why—I suppose you've looked into Blackstone?
He's a fine fellow, Blackstone, and deserves all that has been
said in his praise.   Many think that he's only to be glanced
at, at the beginning of their studies; never believe it!   He's
good to the end of the chapter!   I've a profound respect for
Blackstone; it's the only book I've read four or five times
through—ay, from cover to cover; he makes law lovely! Stick
to Blackstone by all means!   Reeves—oh! I mentioned *him,*

you know. Then I should go, I think, to Coke on Littleton; but we shall have several opportunities of talking over *these* matters. I really believe, Aubrey, that you are doing a very wise thing in coming to the bar. If you've health and the average opportunities (though I think you will have *more*), I'll undertake to say that in a few years' time you will realize an income—which *may* be a great one—but which (whatever it may be) you'll *earn*, as you did not the one you've lost; and you'll enjoy it, Aubrey, ten thousand times more! All that I can do for you, in every way, I will—command me! By the way," he added, assuming a somewhat anxious expression of countenance, and a manner very different from the free, buoyant, off-hand manner in which, for the last twenty minutes, he had been speaking (Aubrey feeling all the while the easy commanding power and simplicity of the splendid intellect with which he was communing), "I'm almost afraid to ask; but how do you come on about the—Mesne Profits?"

"I have heard nothing whatever about them, as yet," replied Aubrey, sighing, his face suddenly overshadowed with gloom. A moment's pause ensued, which was interrupted by the Attorney-General saying, in a very earnest and feeling manner:

"I hope to God you'll be able to get some favorable arrangement made! You've not seen anything of Mr. Titmouse's attorneys, I suppose?"

"Oh, no! nor heard anything from them."

"I've had very little to do with them: Quirk, Gammon and Snap — these are the people, eh?" Mr. Aubrey nodded. "Quirk is a stubborn, wooden-headed fellow—an old hedgehog! Egad! that man's compounded more felonies, the old scamp, than any man in England! I should like to have him in the witness-box for a couple of hours or so! I think I'd tickle him a little," said the Attorney-General, with a bitter smile. "They say he's a confidential adviser to a sort of Thieves' Association. But there's Gammon: I've had several things to do with *him*. He is a superior man, that Gammon; a very superior man. A keen dog! I recollect him being principal witness in a cause when I was for the plaintiff; and he completely baffled Subtle—ah, ha, how well I recollect it! —Subtle lost his temper at last, because he couldn't make Gammon lose his! Ah, how cleverly the fellow twisted and turned with Subtle for nearly an hour! ah, ha—Subtle looked so chagrined!—Have you seen Mr. Gammon?"

"No, I've had no occasion."

"He has a pleasing, gentleman-like appearance; rather a

striking face. *He's* the man you'll have to deal with in any
negotiations on the subject I've named. You must mind what
you're about with him. You mustn't think me intrusive,
Aubrey, but have they sent in their bill yet?"

Mr. Aubrey involuntarily shuddered, as he answered in the
negative.

" I'd give a trifle to know how the plague such people ever
came to be concerned in such a case. 'Tis quite out of their
way—which is in the criminal line of business!—They'll make
their client pay for it through the nose, I warrant him! By
the way, what an inconceivably ridiculous little ass that Titmouse is—I saw him in court at York. If he'd only go on
the stage, and act *naturally*, he'd make his fortune as a fool!"
—Mr. Aubrey faintly smiled at this sally; but the topics which
the Attorney-General had just before touched upon had not a
little oppressed his spirits.

" As this is comparatively an idle day with me," said the
Attorney-General, " and I've got ten minutes more at your
service—suppose I go with you at once—nothing like the present moment—to Mr. Weasel's?"

" I am greatly obliged to you," replied Aubrey—and both
rose to go. " Say I shall be back in a few minutes," said the
Attorney-General, in answer to his clerk, who reminded him,
as he passed the clerk's door, that Mr. Sergeant Squelch and
Mr. Putty would be there in a moment or two's time. As
they crossed the court—" How do you do, Mr. Putty?" said
the Attorney-General, with lofty civility, to a grinning little
confident personage who met him, exclaiming, with flippant
familiarity:

" How do you do, Mr. Attorney?—Coming to your chambers—you don't forget?—Consultation—eh?"

" I perfectly recollect it, Mr. Putty. I shall return presently"—replied the Attorney-General, somewhat stiffly, and
passed on, arm in arm with Mr. Aubrey.

" Now, that forward little imp's name, Aubrey, is PUTTY,"
whispered the Attorney-General. " He was a glazier by trade;
but just as he finished his apprenticeship, an uncle left him a
few hundred pounds, with which—would you believe it?—
nothing would suit him but decking himself in a wig and
gown, and coming to the bar—ah, ha!—The fellow's creeping,
however, into a little business, positively! They say he has a
cousin who is one of the officers to the Sheriff of Middlesex,
and puts a good many little things in his way! He's my junior
in a criminal information against a newspaper, for charging
his father-in-law—a baker, who supplies some work-house with

bread—with making it of only one third flour, one third rye, and the remainder *sawdust*—ah, ha, ha!—I dared hardly look at the judges while I moved the Rule Nisi, for fear of laughing! This is the case in which we're going to have the consultation he spoke of — but here's Mr. Weasel's.'' They mounted a narrow, dingy-looking, well-worn staircase—and on the first-floor beheld ''MR. WEASEL'' painted over the door. On the Attorney-General knocking, as soon as his clear silvery voice was heard asking for Mr. Weasel, and his dignified figure had been recognized by the clerk, who had one pen in his mouth and another behind his ear—that humble functionary suddenly bent himself almost double three or four times, and with flustered obsequiousness assured the great man that Mr. Weasel was quite at liberty. The next moment the Attorney-General and Mr. Aubrey were introduced into Mr. Weasel's room—a small, dusky room, wretchedly furnished, the walls lined with book-shelves, well filled—and the table at which he was writing, and a chair on each side of him, strewed with draft paper, which he was covering at a prodigious rate. He was, in fact, drawing a '' Declaration '' in an action for a *Breach of Promise of Marriage* (taking a hasty pinch of fiery Welsh snuff every three minutes); and his task seemed to be rendered very difficult by the strange conduct of the defendant—surely the most fickle of mankind—who, with an extraordinary inconsistency, not knowing his own mind for a day together, had promised to marry Miss McSquint, the heartbroken plaintiff, *firstly*, within a reasonable time; *secondly*, on a given day; *thirdly*, on the defendant's return from the Continent; *fourthly*, on the death of his father (both of which events were averred to have taken place); *fifthly*, when the defendant should have cut his wise teeth (which it was averred he had); and lastly, on '' *being requested* '' by the lady—which it was averred she had done, and in the most precise and positive manner, had been *ready and willing, and then* [what will the ladies say?] '' *tendered and offered herself to marry the said defendant*,'' who had then wholly neglected and refused to do any such thing. One notable peculiarity of the case was, that all these promises had been made and all these events had transpired in one particular place—and that rather an odd one, viz., in '' *the parish cf Saint Mary Le Bow, in the ward of Cheap, in the City of London.*'' * If you had been better

* It may be as well to apprise the reader that this strange mode of pleading has been lately superseded by one more reasonable and intel ligible.

acquainted with Mr. Weasel's associations and mode of doing
business, you would have discovered that, in his imagination,
almost all the occurrences of life took place at this same spot!
But to return—thus was Mr. Weasel engaged when they entered. He was a bachelor, upward of forty; was of a spare
make, of low stature, had a thin, sharp, sallow face, and short
stiff black hair; there was an appearance about the eyes as if
they were half-blinded with being incessantly directed to white
paper; he had a furrowed forehead, a small, pursed-up mouth
—one hardly knew why, but really there was something about
his look that instantly suggested to you the image of the creature whose name he bore. He was a ravenous lawyer, darting
at the point and pith of every case he was concerned in, and
sticking to it—just as would his blood-thirsty namesake at the
neck of a rabbit. In *law* he lived, moved, and had his being.
In his dreams he was everlastingly spinning out pleadings
which he never could understand, and hunting for cases which
he could not discover. In the day-time, however, he was more
successful. In fact, everything he saw, heard, or read of—
wherever he was, whatever he was doing, suggested to him
questions of law that might arise out of it. At his sister's
wedding (whither he had not gone without reluctance) he got
into a wrangle with the bridegroom, on a question started by
himself, whether an *infant* was liable for goods supplied to his
wife before marriage; at his grandmother's funeral he got into
an intricate discussion with a puzzled proctor about *bona nota-
bilia*, with reference to a pair of horn spectacles, which the
venerable deceased had left behind her in Scotland, and a
poodle in the Isle of Man; and at church, the reading of the
parable of the *Unjust Steward* set his devout, ingenious, and
fertile mind at work for the remainder of the service, as to the
modes of stating the case nowadays against the offender, and
whether it would be more advisable to proceed civilly or crim-
inally: and if the former, at law or in equity. He was a hard-
headed man; very clear and acute, and accurate in his legal
knowledge: every other sort of knowledge he despised, if, indeed, he had more than the faintest hearsay knowledge of its
existence. He was a Cambridge man; and there had read
nothing but mathematics, in which he had made a decent
figure. As soon as he had taken his degree, he migrated to
the Temple, where he had ever since continued engaged in the
study, and then the successful practice, of the law, as a special
pleader under the bar. He had a very large business, which
he got through ably and rapidly. He scarcely ever went into
society; early want of opportunity for doing so had at length

given him a want of inclination for it—to say nothing of his
want of *time*.   When, as was seldom the case, he ventured out
for a walk, he went, muttering to himself, at a postman's pace,
to get the greatest quantity of exercise in the smallest space
of time.   He was not a bad-tempered man, but had become
nervous, fidgety, and irritable.   His tone of voice was feeble,
his utterance hesitating, his manner hurried.   What a laughable contrast between him and his visitor!   The Attorney-
General coming to Mr. Weasel's chambers, suggested the idea
of a magnificent mastiff suddenly poking his head into the little kennel of a querulous pug-dog; and I suppose Mr. Aubrey
might be likened to a greyhound accompanying the aforesaid
mastiff!   On seeing his visitors, Mr. Weasel instantly got up,
with a blush of surprise and a little hurry and embarrassment
of manner.   His clerk put out a couple of chairs, and down
they sat.   The Attorney-General came to the point in about
half a minute, and the matter was very quickly settled; it
being arranged that within a day or two's time, as soon as the
forms necessary for admitting Mr. Aubrey to an Inn of Court
should have been completed, he should commence his attendance at Mr. Weasel's, from ten o'clock till five, daily.

" It's a comical-looking little animal, isn't it?" quoth the
Attorney-General, with a laugh, as soon as they had got out of
hearing.

" Certainly, I don't feel particularly prepossessed—"

" Oh, pho!   He's the very man for you—the very man.
There's no nonsense with Weasel; you may learn an infinite
deal of law from him, and that is all you want.   He's a very
inoffensive fellow; and I've no doubt you'll soon like his
chambers greatly, if you're in earnest in studying the Law.
You go or not, of course, as you choose; whatever you do is
perfectly voluntary; pay him his hundred guineas, and then,
if you like, you may get many thousand pounds' worth out of
him in the twelvemonth.   Now, I *must* bid you good-morning
—I've really not another moment to spare.   God bless you,
my dear Aubrey; and," he added, with great kindness, and a
very pointed manner, " whenever you may think it worth your
while to talk over your affairs with me, come without notice or
ceremony—wherever I may be, I shall be delighted to see
you!"   Then they parted.   Mr. Aubrey was not aware of a
certain stroke of delicacy and generosity on the part of the
Attorney-General, viz., that immediately on the *Rule* being
discharged, he had sent for Mr. Runnington, and insisted on
returning every sixpence of his fees—upward of six hundred
guineas—desiring that Mr. Aubrey should not be made ac-

quainted with it, if by any means Messrs. Runnington could conceal it from him!

A little fatigued and harassed by several important matters, which kept him engaged till a late hour in the afternoon, he reached Vivian Street in a depressed and desponding mood. Just as he turned the corner, he beheld, at about twenty yards' distance, Mrs. Aubrey and Miss Aubrey slowly walking homeward, on their return from the Park. Mrs. Aubrey held Charles by the hand, who was dancing and frisking wildly about, and Miss Aubrey's beautiful little Cato she was leading along by a slender chain. They were in half-mourning; there was such an air of elegant simplicity about them—their figures, their carriage, so easy and graceful! Aubrey, as he neared them, gazed at them with mingled feelings of pride and tenderness.

"Oh, my papa! my papa!" suddenly exclaimed Charles, who, happening to turn round, had caught sight of his father, and ran eagerly down to him: with what a thrill of love did he take in his arms the beautiful, breathless boy, and how his heart yearned toward his wife and sister, as they also turned quickly round to meet him, after a long day's absence! How inexpressibly dear were they to him—how, that day, he enjoyed their quiet little dinner-table—the romp with his children afterward—and a long evening of eager and interesting conversation, after the little ones had gone to bed, Mrs. Aubrey and Kate busy the while with some slight matter of needlework! They had received several letters from Yorkshire, which they read to him. One was from poor Dr. Tatham, who, though he concealed a good deal that would have occasioned needless pain, yet gave them a melancholy notion of the altered state of things at the Hall. Though it was rather late before they retired to rest on the evening of the ensuing Sunday, Mr. Aubrey was to be found seated in his study by half past four on Monday morning, perusing, with profound attention, stimulated by the strong observation of the Attorney-General, the second volume of Blackstone's Commentaries—a work with which he had already a very tolerable familiarity. 'Twas really a thing to be proud of, that Mr. Aubrey, with so many absorbing anxieties, such distracting apprehensions concerning the future, *could* command his attention in the way he did. To be sure, he felt that it was plainly life and death work with him; but he might have derived great encouragement from perceiving himself possessed of that faculty of concentrating the attention, which the Attorney-General had spoken of as so essential an attribute of a lawyer. The way in

which he parceled out his time was this: From the time that
he entered his study till breakfast-time, he resolved to read
law—from ten o'clock till four or five, was to spent at Mr.
Weasel's chambers—and the evenings were to be devoted to
the society of his children, his wife, and sister, and also to certain occasional literary efforts, from which he hoped to derive
some little increase to his means.   This was severe work; but
it was probably the most fortunate and salutary thing in the
world for Aubrey, that his energies should be thus occupied
and his mind kept from the corroding effects of constant reflection upon his misfortunes and dismal apprehensions concerning the future.   After he had spent a few days in Mr.
Weasel's chambers, a good deal of his prejudice against that
gentleman began to wear off.   Mr. Aubrey found him all that
the Attorney-General had described him as being—a very acute
and able lawyer, with a constant current of important, varied,
and instructive business running through his chambers, and
every disposition to render his utmost assistance to Mr.
Aubrey, whom he quickly found out to be a man of very
superior intellect, and most seriously bent upon acquiring a
knowledge of the profession.   Mr. Weasel was not blessed with
the power of formally communicating elementary knowledge;
Mr. Aubrey had, as it were, to *extract* from him what he
wanted, with something like a painful effort.   The advantages
of his position were the innumerable practical hints and suggestions as to the mode of dealing with miscellaneous business,
which he derived from a watchful attention to whatever passed
in chambers—to the mode in which Weasel hunted up and applied his law, and reduced the facts involved in litigation into
legal shape and language, in the process of pleading.   The
penetrating eye of Mr. Aubrey, thus closely fixed on everything
that came under his notice, quickly began to discover and appreciate the good sense, the practical utility of most of the
positive rules of law which he saw in operation; and at the end
of a fortnight or three weeks he began to feel interest in the
study upon which he had so vigorously entered, and in which
he felt himself making real progress.   Mr. Weasel, during
even that time, perceived the prodigious superiority of Mr.
Aubrey over another pupil, who had nearly completed his second year in Mr. Weasel's chambers after a twelvemonth spent
in a conveyancer's; not, of course, in respect of legal knowledge, but of intellectual power and aptitude for business.   Mr.
Aubrey would return to Vivian Street about six o'clock each
day, a little fatigued with a very long day's work (for he was
never later than five o'clock in entering his study in the morn-

ing); but quickly cheered and refreshed by the sight of the
fond and lovely beings whom he there rejoined, and who had
been counting the very minutes till he returned.   Every day
knit that little family together, if possible, in stronger bonds
of love; for they clung to each other with a feeling of having
been thrust out of the great gay world together, and sent, as
it were, upon a pilgrimage afar, amidst scenes of increasing
gloom, difficulty, and danger.   Every day that bore them further from their expulsion from Yatton, as it were, mellowed
their recollections of past scenes, and poured upon their
wounded feelings the soothing balm of pious resignation; and
sometimes, also, faint and trembling beams of hope concerning the future would steal across the gloomy chambers of
their hearts.   Thank God, the view of the past presented to
them no occasion for shame, for remorse, for self-condemna-
tion!   They trusted that, in their day of wealth and distinction, they had not been found wanting in the discharge of the
duties imposed upon them.   Therefore they had consolation
from a view of the past.   But the FUTURE—indeed—

> " Shadows, clouds, and darkness rested on it."

Their hearts involuntarily fluttered and shrunk within them
when they gazed upon the threatening gloom that hung over
it.   Their straitened circumstances—an honorable poverty—
had been a burden light, indeed, to bear.   They were very
happy in one another's company; their house, though small,
was convenient, and even elegantly comfortable; they had
health; Mr. Aubrey had constant exercise for an active and
vigorous mind, in the acquisition of the learning of a noble
profession, the practice of which might possibly hereafter raise
all of them to even affluence and distinction—at all events,
might secure them the substantial comforts of life.   But Mr.
Aubrey would have moments of heaviness and trepidation.
When engaged in his little study, in the profound solitude and
silence of the early morning, while he was thus straining his
faculties to their utmost, on behalf of the sweet innocent beings
—his wife—his children—his sister—sleeping above, he would
sometimes lean back in his chair, with a very deep sigh, and
sink into a reverie—oh, how sad and painful!—deepening occasionally into agony; but he would suddenly arouse himself,
and resume his studies with a powerful effort at abstraction—
with additional intensity of application.   How could he be
otherwise than momentarily *paralyzed*, when he surveyed his
alarming and tremendous pecuniary liabilities?   Bills of costs
—Heaven only knew to what amount—due to Messrs. Quirk,

Gammon and Snap: to his own attorneys, Messrs. Runnington; and to Mr. Parkinson; and then—sickening and fearful
object!—the Mesene Profits—what *was* to become of them all?
The mind that, in the presence of such disturbing forces as
these, could apply its energies so successfully as did that of
Mr. Aubrey to the acquisition of knowledge, with any degree
of calmness, must surely have been of no common order, and
have undergone no slight discipline; but, alas! alas! what
could all this have availed him, unless he had been vouchsafed
assistance from on high? When the *waters were come in unto
his soul;* when he was *sinking in deep mire, where there was
no standing;* when he was *come into deep waters, where the
floods overflowed him*—whither was he to look but to one quarter, and that ABOVE, with earnest, and faithful, and constant
supplication to the Almighty?

The constant apprehension of very great evil—*suspense*—is
a state almost as terrible and insupportable, especially to those
of lively susceptibilities, as that produced by the infliction of
the evil. Every morning when Aubrey left home he dreaded
to think of what might happen before his return; and when
he quitted the Temple he felt a sinking of the heart when he
thought of what might have transpired in his absence. In
fact, they all of them felt like those whom the ominous silence
and repose of surrounding nature—a portentous calm and
gloom overhead—filled with trembling apprehension of the
coming storm. Their fears are quickened by the occasional
falling of large spreading drops of rain through the sultry sky,
not a breath of air stirring. Upward is oft turned the pale
cheek and apprehensive eye toward the black accumulating
clouds, from which may soon flame the destructive lightning
—what, in such a case, is there to rely upon but the mercy of
Him around whose throne are clouds and darkness, and the
whirlwind and tempest His ordering?

They were sitting one morning at their usual early and simple breakfast, and Mr. Aubrey was reading aloud, for his wife
and sister's suggestions, a second article which he had commenced overnight, designed for one of the Reviews—having
about a fortnight before sent off his first effort, about which,
however, he had as yet heard nothing; and Kate was playfully
patting his cheek and telling him that, for all he might say to
the contrary, a particular expression was not, in her opinion,
" *elegant English!* "

" It *is,* you pert puss of a critic," insisted Aubrey, with a
good-natured laugh; and then, turning to Mrs. Aubrey, " What
do *you* say, Agnes?"

" Oh—why—I really like it very much as it is. "

" I sha'n't alter it," said Aubrey, laughing.

" Then I'll alter it when you're gone," quoth Kate, with affected pertness, and bringing her beautiful laughing face so near his own, with a kind of air of defiance, that he kissed her forehead, and said it should be as she chose.

Just then a knock at the door announced a visitor, who proved to be Mr. Runnington. Why it was, they hardly knew; but they all slightly changed color. He had called so early, he said, to insure seeing Mr. Aubrey before he went to the Temple! and though he had been shown into the study, Mr. Aubrey insisted on his joining the breakfast-table.

" We've very plain fare for you, however," said he, as Mr. Runnington yielded to his wishes.

Mr. Aubrey perceived, with some uneasiness, that the kind and thoughtful countenance of Mr. Runnington wore rather an anxious expression. And, indeed, so it was. When he looked at those who sat before him—lovely, elegant, yet with a plainly forced cheerfulness—reflected on the sufferings which they had passed through, and that which was in store for them —and for the first bitter installment of which he had come to prepare Mr. Aubrey—could he but feel very deep sympathy for them? As soon as he had retired with Mr. Aubrey to the study, in a low tone he informed Mr. Aubrey of his errand, which was to apprise him that, the evening before, Messrs. Quirk, Gammon and Snap's BILL had come in.

" Well, show it me, if you please," said Mr. Aubrey, calmly, extending his hand.

" My dear sir, why do you suppose I have it *with me ?*" inquired Mr. Runnington with a concerned air. " You are not accustomed to such matters—God forbid you should! It is too bulky for me to have brought with me, and lies at our office!"

" What is the *amount* of it, then?" inquired Mr. Aubrey, dreading to hear the answer; while Mr. Runnington took out of his pocket-book a slip of paper, which he handed to Mr. Aubrey, and on which the latter read—" £3,946 14s. 6d. " He gazed at it for some moments in silence, and became very pale. Mr. Runnington could hardly bear to look at him, and think of the two lovely women in the adjoining room, who were so fearfully interested in the intelligence which had so dismayed Mr. Aubrey.

" This is a very—large—amount," said he, at length, with forced calmness.

" It is a most serious affair," replied Mr. Runnington, shaking his head and sighing.

"Then there is yours—-and Mr. Parkinson's."

"Oh, Mr. Aubrey—*sufficient for the day is the evil thereof.*"

"Will you oblige me by saying what is the probable amount of *your* bill?" inquired Mr. Aubrey, with a calmness which seemed lent to him by despair.

"Oh! I assure you we have thought nothing at all about it, nor shall we for some time to come, Mr. Aubrey. We have not the slightest intention of troubling ourselves, or you, with the matter till you may be in a position to attend to it without serious inconvenience."

"But *do* favor me with something like a *notion*," pressed the unhappy Aubrey.

"Why—perhaps I am hardly doing right in mentioning it; but whenever our bill is sent in, it will be less by some six hundred and fifty pounds, by the noble generosity of the At-torney-General, who has returned all his fees—"

"Returned all his fees!" echoed Mr. Aubrey, starting, while the color rushed into his cheek, and the expression of his coun-tenance was of pride struggling with astonishment, and grati-tude, and admiration. He exquisitely appreciated the conduct of his distinguished friend, and at the same time felt a totally new and very painful sense of pecuniary obligation.

"I feel, Mr. Aubrey, that I have broken my promise to the Attorney-General, who extracted from me a solemn pledge to endeavor so to manage the matter as that you should never know it. What is it, after all—noble as it is—to the Attorney-General, with his £12,000 or £15,000 a year?"

"Oh—do not talk *so*, Mr. Runnington; I am overpowered, oppressed. Never in all my life have I experienced feelings like those with which I am now agitated!" He rose, and stood opposite the window for a few minutes—neither of them speak-ing. Then he returned to his seat.

"How much does that leave me your debtor?"

"Why—really it is hard to say, unprepared—I should im-agine that our account is reduced to some £1,500 or £1,600—about which—"

"Then there is Mr. Parkinson's," said Aubrey, in a low tone, but with a desperate air; presently adding—"Here are some £6,000 or £7,000 to start with; and *then* we come to the mesne profits—gracious, gracious God!" he suddenly added, with a visible shudder. He folded his arms convulsively, and gazed, for a second or two, at Mr. Runnington, with an eye whose expression was overpowering. In his face Mr. Running-ton beheld no longer the mild and melancholy expression to which he had been accustomed. but a sternness and power were

apparent in his features, which Mr. Runnington had not imagined them capable of exhibiting. They told of a strong soul
thoroughly roused, and excited, and in agony. At that moment a knocking was heard at the door, as of very little fingers. "Come in!" exclaimed Mr. Aubrey, with unusual
quickness and sternness. The door was gently opened, and
Charles's little face peeped into the room timidly, quite startled
by the tone in which he had been addressed. "Come in, my
child!" said Mr. Aubrey, rather tremulously, when he saw
that it was *his son*, and observed the apprehensiveness overspreading his little features. Charles immediately advanced,
with a serious submissive air, saying:

"This letter is just come—Mamma sent me with it, dear
papa—"

"Give it me, Charles," said Mr. Aubrey, extending his
hand for it, while with the other he gently placed the child
upon his lap, and kissed him. "I'm not angry with you,
Charles," said he, tenderly.

"I've not been naughty, you know, dear papa!" said he,
with innocent surprise.

"No, no, my little love." The ruined FATHER could say
no more; but putting aside the child's flowing curly locks from
his temples, as it were mechanically, he gazed on his little face
for a moment, and then folded him in his arms with unspeakable tenderness. Mr. Runnington rose, and stood for some
moments gazing through the window, unwilling that his own
emotion should be observed. When Mr. Aubrey opened the
letter, it proved to be from the publisher of the Review to
which he had sent his article, inclosing a check for forty
guineas, expressing an earnest desire that he would continue
his contributions, and assuring him that the editor considered
the article "in every way admirable." As soon as he had
glanced over the letter—"You little messenger of hope and
mercy!" he thought, again kissing his son, who sat passively
gazing at the agitated countenance of his FATHER—"I can
not, I will not despair! You have brought me, as it were, a
ray of light from heaven, piercing the fearful gloom of my
situation: 'tis a token, surely, that I am not forgotten: I feel
as though an angel, momentarily brightening the night of sorrow, had come and whispered in my ear—'COURAGE!'" His
features began to resume their natural serenity of expression.
"Take it in to your mamma," said he, kissing little Charles,
and dispatching him with the letter. Shortly afterward, as
soon as he had recovered the command of his manner sufficiently to avoid occasioning uneasiness to Mrs. and Miss

Aubrey, he proposed to Mr. Runnington that they should walk toward the Temple; and, bidding adieu to those whom he left behind him, without giving them an opportunity to ask him as to the nature of Mr. Runnington's errand, but leaving them in high spirits at the letter which he had sent in to them. he quitted the house arm in arm with Mr. Runnington. I am persuaded that if that gentleman had had no one to consult, he would have relieved Mr. Aubrey altogether from liability to *him ;* but he had four partners; their own pecuniary outlay had been considerable; and, therefore, the thing was really out of the question. As they walked along, in the course of much anxious conversation, Mr. Runnington told Mr. Aubrey that he considered Messrs. Quirk, Gammon and Snap's bill to be extortionate, and that it might, on taxation—a process which he explained to Mr. Aubrey—be reduced, probably, by at least *one half.* But he also reminded Mr. Aubrey of the power which they held in their hands, in respect of the mesne profits, and intimated his opinion, that in all probability they had made out their bill with an eye to such considerations—namely, that it should be discharged without rigorous scrutiny into its constituent items, before they would listen to any terms whatever for the payment of the mesne profits; and that Mr. Aubrey's position, with respect to Messrs. Quirk, Gammon and Snap, was one which required the greatest possible deliberation and circumspection on his part, especially in the matter of the bill just delivered in by them.

"I see! The whole," said Mr. Aubrey, "comes to this: they will relieve me from liability to Mr. Titmouse for as much of what may be due to him as they can divert into their own pockets!"

"That certainly seems very much like it," replied Mr. Runnington, shrugging his shoulders; "but you will leave all such considerations and matters to us, and rely on our honor and our discretion. At what may appear to us the exact moment for doing so with effect, depend upon our most cautious interference. We know, Mr. Aubrey, the kind of people we have to deal with. Mr. Titmouse is very likely to be merely a puppet in their hands—at least in those of Mr. Gammon, who is a very long-headed man, and with whom, I have no doubt, our negotiations will have to be carried on."

"That is just what the Attorney-General said—and he invited me, moreover, to converse with him whenever I might consider that his advice would be useful."

"Could you have a better adviser? He has a most penetrating sagacity, long exercised—in short, his qualifications are consummate, and I should not hesitate about consulting him whenever we feel at a loss."

"Why should I disguise anything from you, Mr. Runnington?"—said Aubrey—"you ought to know the exact state of my affairs. I have a little family plate, which I could not bear to part with; my books, and the remnants of the furniture at Yatton, which I have saved in order to furnish our present residence. Besides this, the outside of all that I am possessed of—and I have no expectations, nor has my wife nor my poor sister, from any quarter—is a sum of about £3,000 in the funds, and £423 at my banker's. Those are my circumstances; they appall me merely in stating them:—Why, I owe double the sum I have named, for lawyers' bills only. I have not enough, without parting with my books and plate, to discharge even Messrs. Quirk, Gammon and Snap's bill!"

"It would be cruel and absurd in me not to express at once, Mr. Aubrey, my conviction that your situation is fearfully critical, and that your sole hope is in the treatment which may be expected from Messrs. Quirk, Gammon and Snap, and their client, Mr. Titmouse. Serious as are, at present, your other liabilities—to that one, they are but as a bucket of water to the Thames. As we are talking, Mr. Aubrey, in this candid and unrestrained manner, I will tell you my chief source of apprehension on your account, with reference to Messrs. Quirk, Gammon and Snap: namely, that they may possibly speculate on your being able, if placed in real peril, to call around you, in your extremity, a host of wealthy and powerful friends—as security or otherwise—"

"They will find themselves, then, utterly mistaken. If they and their client are really capable of such shocking brutality—such wanton oppression—let them do their worst: I am resigned. Providence will find out a shelter for my wife and children, and my dear, devoted, high-spirited sister; and as for myself, rather than satiate the rapacity of such wretches, by plundering good-natured and generous friends, I will end my days in prison."

Mr. Aubrey was evidently not a little excited while he said this; but there was that in his tone of voice and in his eye which told Mr. Runnington that he meant what he said; and that, as soon as it should have come to the point of oppression and injustice, no man could resist more powerfully, or endure with a more dignified and inflexible resolution. But Mr. Runnington would fain hope that it would not come to such an issue. He consoled Mr. Aubrey with assurances that, as for their own demand, it might stand over for several years: and that so, he was sure, would it be with the far lesser demand of Mr. Parkinson; and that if, by a great effort, sufficient could be raised to discharge promptly the bill of Messrs. Quirk, Gammon and Snap, some much more favorable arrangement respecting the amount and mode of payment of the mesne profits might be effected—leaving Mr. Aubrey, in the meantime, leisure to apply himself vigorously to his studies for the bar, for which Mr. Runnington assured him that he considered him peculiarly qualified; and pledged himself to back him with all the influence he had or could command.

"Gracious Heaven, Mr. Runnington!" said Aubrey, with a little excitement, "is it not very nearly intolerable that I should pass the prime of my days in thralldom to such people as these, and be encircled by the chains of such a man as this Titmouse is represented as being? I will not call myself his foe, nor his victim; but I am the one through whose sudden destitution he has obtained a splendid fortune. I did not knowingly deprive him of it—he must be bereft of all the ordinary feelings of humanity to place me, whom he has already stripped of all, upon the rack—the rack of extortion! Oh! put me in his place, and him in mine—do you think I would not have been satisfied with what I had gained? Would *I* have alarmed and tortured him by calling for an account of what he had spent with a firm, a reasonable persuasion that it was his own? Oh, no! I could not only have forgiven him all, but endeavored to secure him from future want." He sighed. "Oh, that I were at this moment a free man! *pauper —sed in meo ære;* that I had but five hundred pounds to keep me and mine for a year or two—with a mind at ease and fit for study!—but here we are, at the Temple. When shall we meet again—or shall I hear from you?"

"Very shortly," replied Mr. Runnington, who for the last few minutes had been listening to Mr. Aubrey in respectful and sympathizing silence; and, shaking him warmly by the hand with much cordiality and fervency of manner, he pledged himself to do all in his power to promote his interests.

CHAPTER XXI.

WHEN Mr. Aubrey arrived at Mr. Weasel's chambers, he looked dejected and harassed; but with a noble effort of self-command, at once addressed himself, calmly and vigorously, to the business of the day. From time to time he peremptorily excluded the harassing thoughts and recollections arising out of his morning's interview with Mr. Runnington, and succeeded in concentrating his attention upon a case of more than usual intricacy and multifariousness of details, which Mr. Weasel, having glanced over, had laid aside for a more leisurely perusal. He handed it, however, to Mr. Aubrey soon after his arrival, with something approaching to a secret satisfaction, in the expectation of its " proving too much for him;" but he was mistaken. Mr. Aubrey left a little earlier than usual; but not before he had sent in the voluminous " case " to Mr. Weasel's room by the clerk, together with a half-sheet of draft paper, containing a brief summary of the results at which he had arrived, and which not a little surprised Mr. Weasel. The case did not happen to involve much technical knowledge; but in respect of the imperfect manner in which it was drawn up, and the confusion worse confounded of the transactions themselves out of which the questions arose, required patient, persevering attention, strength of memory, and great clearheadedness. In short, Weasel owned to himself that poor Aubrey had taken a very masterly view of the case; and how would his estimate of his pupil's ability have been enhanced by a knowledge of the situation in which he was placed—one so calculated to distract his attention, and prevent that hearty and complete devotion to legal studies, without which Mr. Weasel well knew how vain was the attempt to master them?

" Have you read Aubrey's opinion on that troublesome case —I mean the Cornish Bank?" inquired Weasel, taking a pinch of snuff, of Mr. Thoroughpace, another pupil who had just taken his seat beside Mr. Weasel, to see him " settle " [*i. e.* score out, interline, and alter] a pleading drawn by the aforesaid Thoroughpace. That gentleman replied in the negative. " He's got a head-piece of his own, I can tell you. Egad! somehow or another he always contrives to hit the nail on the head."

" I'd a sort of notion, the very first day he came, that he was a superior man," replied Thoroughpace. " He makes very few notes—seems to trust entirely to his head—"

" Ah! a man may carry that too far," interrupted Mr. Weasel, thrusting a pinch of snuff up his nose.

" Then I wish *I* could," replied Thoroughpace. " Isn't there such a thing as making the hand engross the business of the head?" Mr. Weasel—recollecting that in his library stood twelve thick folio volumes of manuscript " precedents," which he had been fool enough to copy out with his own hand during his pupilage, and the first year or two of his setting up in business—hemmed, and again applied to his snuff-box. " How do you get on with him in the pupil's room?" he inquired.

"Why, I didn't like him at first. Very reserved, and has a little *hauteur*. Even now, though very courteous, he says little, seems entirely absorbed by his studies, and yet to have something or other on his mind."

"Ah, I dare say! Law's no trifle, I warrant him. No doubt it's *teasing* him!" replied Weasel, rather complacently.

"By Jove! but I don't think it *does*. I never saw a man to whom it seemed to *yield* so easily.—He's a particularly *gentle-man-like* person, by the way; and there's something very attractive in his countenance. He seems highly connected. I've seen several notes come here for him with coronets on the seals, and several well-known—"

"Oh—why, you've heard of the great cause of *Doe* d. *Tit-mouse* v. *Jolter*, a Yorkshire ejectment case, tried only last Spring assizes? Well, he's the defendant, and has, I hear, lost everything."

"You astonish me! By Jove, but he had need work!"

"Shall *we* set to work, Mr. Thoroughpace?" said Weasel, suddenly, looking at his watch lying on his desk. "I've promised to let them have this plea by six o'clock—or the other side will be signing judgment;" and plunging his pen into his inkstand, to work he went, *more suo*, as if such a man as the pupil Mr. Aubrey had never existed. He was not at all a hard-hearted man; but I believe that if a *capias ad satis-faciendum* (*i. e.* final process to take the body into custody) against Charles Aubrey, Esquire, had come into Mr. Weasel's chambers to settle, as requiring special accuracy—after humming and hawing a bit—and taking an extra pinch of snuff, he would have settled it, marked his *seven-and-sixpence* in the corner, and sent it out with other papers, consoling himself with this just reflection, that the thing *must* be done by *some-body*, and he might as well have the *fee* as any one else!

On Mr. Aubrey's return home to dinner, he found that his sister had received another long letter from Dr. Tatham, to which was appended a postscript mentioning Mr. Gammon in such terms as suggested to Mr. Aubrey a little scheme which he resolved to carry into effect on the morrow—namely, to call himself at the office of Messrs. Quirk, Gammon and Snap, and seek an interview with Mr. Gammon, who, Dr. Tatham stated, had quitted Yatton for town only the day before the Doctor had written to Miss Aubrey. After a very restless and unhappy night, during which he was tormented with all kinds of dismal dreams, Messrs. Quirk, Gammon and Snap figuring in each as the stern and mysterious arbiters of his earthly destiny, he resolved to put an end to his present insupportable

suspense—to learn at once the extent of what he had either to
hope or to fear—by calling that very afternoon at Saffron
Hill. For that purpose, he quitted Mr. Weasel's at the early
hour of three o'clock, and straightway bent his steps through
Fetter Lane to Hatton Garden, and thence inquiring his way
to Saffron Hill. He was not long in finding the house of
which he was in quest, his eye being soon attracted by the
great, gleaming brass-plate with "QUIRK, GAMMON and
SNAP," as prominent and threatening as ever those names had
appeared to Titmouse in the day of his agony and suspense.
He had stood gazing at them with idiotic longing and vulgar apprehension, as the reader has seen. How very different a per-.
son now looked at them with feelings of intense interest and
overmastering anxiety, as at the names of those who had him
completely in their power, his fortunes, his *liberty*, his livelihood, and that of the dear beings whose interests, whose all on
earth, whose personal safety were bound up in his. Mr. Aubrey, with a jaded air, dressed in a buttoned black surtout,
and with an umbrella under his arm, entered the hall, where
were sitting and standing several strange-looking people—one
or two suffering evidently great agitation; in fact, relatives of
prisoners whose trials for capital offenses were coming on the
next day at Newgate—and made his way into a room, on the
door of which he read "Clerk's Room."

"Now, sir, your business?" said a showily dressed Jewish-
looking youth, lolling at a desk from which he did not move,
and speaking in a tone of very disagreeable assurance.

"Is Mr. Gammon within?" inquired Mr. Aubrey, taking
off his hat; and there was a certain something in his voice,
countenance and bearing that induced the personage he addressed to slip off his stool, and exhibit as courteous an air as
he could possibly assume.

"Mr. Gammon is in his room, sir, and alone. I believe he
is rather busy—I've no doubt you can see him."

The fact was, that at that moment Mr. Gammon was engaged drawing up "Instructions to prepare Declaration" in an
action of mesne profits against Mr. Aubrey! He had only the
day before returned from Yatton, where circumstances had
occurred which had quickened their intended proceeding
against Mr. Aubrey—as the first quarter to which, at Mr. Titmouse's suggestion, they were to look for a considerable supply of ready money. That morning, in the very room into
which Mr. Aubrey was to be presently shown, had taken place
a long discussion between Mr. Quirk and Mr. Gammon, on the
subject which had now brought to their office Mr. Aubrey. Mr.

Quirk was for making short work of it—for "going straight ahead "—and getting the whole £60,000, or security for the greater portion, and £20,000 down. Gammon, however, was of opinion that that was mere madness; that by attempting to proceed to extremities against so unfortunate a sufferer as Mr. Aubrey, they could not fail of drawing down on themselves and their client universal execration; and, moreover, of driving Mr. Aubrey desperate, and forcing him either to quit the country, or accept the protection of the insolvent laws. He had, at length, satisfied Mr. Quirk that their only chance was in gentleness and moderation; and the old gentleman had, as usual, agreed to adopt the plan of operations suggested by Gammon. The latter personage had quite as keen a desire and firm determination as the former, to wring out of their wretched victim the very last farthing that there was the slightest probability of obtaining; for Titmouse had pointed to that quarter for the discharge of his ten thousand pound bond to the firm, and also their bill of costs to him (which contained some three hundred items, slightly varied in language, that were also charged in their bill to Mr. Aubrey); then twenty—or at least fifteen thousand pounds, were to be handed over to himself, Titmouse; and all the rest that could be got, Mr. Gammon might appropriate to his own use. His inquiries into Mr. Aubrey's circumstances had completely convinced him that it would be impossible to extract any considerable sum from that unfortunate gentleman; and that if they could contrive to get their bill paid, perhaps substantial security for four or five thousand of the mesne profits, and his own personal security for the payment of any portion of the remainder, hereafter—they had better rest satisfied—-and look for liquidation of their own heavy claim to a mortgage upon the Yatton estates. Mr. Gammon had also proposed to himself certain other objects, in dealing with Mr. Aubrey, than the mere extraction of money from him; and, in short, prompted by considerations such as those above intimated, he had come to the determination, an hour or so before Mr. Aubrey's most unexpected visit, to be at once prepared with the necessary means for setting in motion legal proceedings for the recovery of the arrear of mesne profits.

"Have I the honor to address Mr. Gammon?" commenced Mr. Aubrey, courteously, on being shown into the room—not announced by name—where Gammon sat busily engaged writing out the "Instructions" for framing the rack on which it was designed to extend the as yet unconscious Aubrey.

"Sir, my name is Gammon," he replied, coloring a little—

rising from his chair, with an expression of very great surprise
—"I believe I have the honor of seeing Mr. Aubrey?—I beg
you will allow me to offer you a chair"—he continued, placing one as far as he could from the table, and then, getting
another, he sat down between Mr. Aubrey and the table, expecting to hear his visitor at once open the subject of their bill,
which they had so recently sent in.

"Will you suffer me, Mr. Aubrey," commenced Gammon,
with a bland and subdued air, not fulsome, but extremely
deferential, "before entering on any business which may have
brought you here, to express deep sympathy with your sufferings, and my *personal* regret at the share we have had in the
proceedings which have ended so adversely for your interests?
But our duty as professional men, Mr. Aubrey, is often as
plain as painful!"

"I feel obliged, sir, for your kind expressions of sympathy
—but I can not for a moment conceive any apology necessary.
Neither I nor my advisers ever had cause to complain of harsh
or unprofessional treatment on your part. Your proceedings
certainly came upon me—upon all of us—like a thunder-
stroke," said Mr. Aubrey, with a subdued sigh. "I trust
that you have given me credit, Mr. Gammon, for offering no
vexatious or unconscientious obstacles."

"Oh, Mr. Aubrey! on the contrary, I am at a loss for words
to express my sense of your straightforward and high-minded
conduct; and have several times intimated my sentiments on
that subject to Messrs. Runningtons"—Mr. Aubrey bowed—
"and again anxiously beg that you will give me credit for feeling the profoundest sympathy"—he paused, as if from emotion; and such might well have been excited by the appearance
of Mr. Aubrey—calm and melancholy—his face full of anxiety
and exhaustion, and his figure, naturally slender, evidently
somewhat emaciated.

["I wonder," thought Gammon, "whether he has any *in-
surances on his life.*—He certainly has *rather* a consumptive
look; how could one ascertain whether he has insured? And
where?"]

"I trust, most sincerely, Mr. Aubrey, that the mental
sufferings you must have undergone have not affected your
health?" inquired Gammon, with an air of infinite concern.

"A little, but, thank God, not materially; I never was very
robust," he replied with a faint, sad smile.

["*How like his sister!*"—thought Gammon, watching his
companion's countenance with real interest.]

"I am not quite sure, Mr. Gammon," continued Aubrey

"that I am observing etiquette in thus coming to you, on a matter which you may consider ought to have been left to my attorneys, and who know nothing of my present visit—but—"

"An honorable mind like yours, Mr. Aubrey, may surely act according to its own impulses with safety! As for etiquette, I know of no professional rule which I break in entering into a discussion with you of any topic connected with the action which has recently been determined," said Gammon, cautiosuly, and particularly on his guard, as soon as his penetrating eye had detected the acuteness which was mingled with the sincerity and simplicity of character beaming in the countenance of Mr. Aubrey.

"I dare say you can guess the occasion of my visit, Mr. Gammon?"

["There goes our bill—whew!—What now?" thought Gammon.]

Mr. Gammon bowed, with an anxious, expectant air.

"I allude to the question yet remaining between your client, Mr. Titmouse, and me—the mesne profits—"

"I feared—I expected as much! It gave me infinite anxiety, as soon as I found you were approaching the subject."

"To me it is really a matter of life and death, Mr. Gammon. It is one pressing me on almost to the very verge of madness!"

"Do not, Mr. Aubrey," said Gammon, in a tone and with a look which touched the heart of his agitated companion, "magnify the mischief. Don't—I beg—imagine your position one so hopeless! What is there to stand in the way of an amicable adjustment of these claims? If I had my way, Mr. Aubrey—and if I thought I should not be acting the part of the unjust steward in Scripture—I would write sixty thousand farthings for sixty thousand pounds!"

"You have named the sum for which I believe I am legally liable to Mr. Titmouse," said Mr. Aubrey, with forced composure; "it is a sum as completely out of my power to pay, or secure—or even a quarter of it—as to give him one of the stars."

"I am aware, Mr. Aubrey, that you must have had many calls upon you, which must have temporarily crippled your resources—"

"Temporarily!" echoed Mr. Aubrey, with a sickening smile.

"I devoutly trust that it is only temporary! For your own and family's sake," he added quickly, observing the watchfulness with which his every look and word was regarded by his companion. "Any proposal, Mr. Aubrey," he continued,

with the same apparent kindness of manner, but with serious
deliberation, "which you may think proper to make, I am
ready—eager—to receive and consider in a liberal spirit. I
repeat—If you had me only to deal with—you would leave this
room with a lightened heart; but to be plain and candid, our
client, Mr. Titmouse, is a very difficult person to deal with. I
pledge my word of honor to you—[*Oh, Gammon! Gammon!
Gammon!*]—that I have repeatedly urged upon Mr. Titmouse
to release you from all the rents received by you previously
to your receiving legal notice of the late proceedings." I
suppose Gammon felt that this declaration was not received
by Mr. Aubrey as implicitly as the former desired and expected; for with a slight stiffness, he added, "I assure you, sir,
that it is a fact. I have always been of opinion that the law
is harsh, and even faulty in principle, which in such a case as
yours—where the possessor of an estate, to which he believed
himself born, is ousted by a title of which he had no previous
knowledge, nor MEANS of knowledge"—Gammon uttered this
very pointedly, and with his eye fixed searchingly upon that of
Mr. Aubrey—"requires the ousted party to make good the
rents he had so innocently appropriated to his own use. That
is my *opinion*, though it may be wrong. I am bound to say,
however, as the law now stands—if Mr. Titmouse should, contrary to my advice, determine to stand upon his strict rights—"
Gammon paused, shook his head, shrugged his shoulders, and
looked with melancholy significance at Mr. Aubrey.

"I am entirely at his mercy! I understand. I do trust,
however, that, in the name of our common humanity, he will
have some consideration for the helpless—the miserable situation in which I am so unexpectedly placed," said Aubrey, with
mournful energy. "Never having imagined it necessary to
save money—"

"Oh, no—nor, with such an income as yours was, to resort,
I fear, to any of the ordinary modes—insurance, and so
forth?" interposed Gammon, with an easy air.

"No—no! nothing of the sort"—["Ah! the deuce you
have not!" thought Gammon]—"and I confess it was improvi-
dent of me. My situation is so deplorable and desperate, that
disguise would be absurd, even could I stoop to it; and I declare, in the presence of Heaven, Mr. Gammon, that, without
parting with the little remnant of plate I have preserved, and
my books, I am unable to make up even the amount of your
bill sent in the day before yesterday"—Gammon gazed at Aubrey earnestly, but in silence—"and if my miserable remnant

of means *be* so appropriated, we are *literally beggars* "—he paused, and his voice faltered.

"Indeed—indeed, you distress me beyond measure, Mr. Aubrey," said Gammon, in a low tone.

"If you can but secure me a merciful interval, to prepare myself for the profession which I have entered—the Bar— whatever earnings I might obtain, after saving a bare maintenance for myself and family, shall be devoted faithfully to liquidate the heavy claims upon me! For myself, Mr. Gammon, I do not care about living upon bread and water for the next ten years; but there are others "—his voice trembled. "Sir, by every consideration which a gentleman may be influenced by, I conjure you to interfere between me and utter immediate ruin!" This was the real thrilling language of the heart; but it failed to produce the least impression upon Gammon, exciting only intense chagrin and disappointment.

"Oh, that it were but in my power," said he, with great energy, "to send you out of this room a free man! If I alone were to be consulted, I would instantly absolve you from all demands—or at least give you your own time, and take no other security than your honor."

"Oh! what a happy—happy man! what a happy family should we be if only—" he could not finish the sentence, for he was greatly moved.

["Here's a kettle of fish," thought Gammon to himself, and bending down his head, he covered his eyes with his hands; "worse, far worse than I had suspected. I would take five pounds for all my residuary interest in the sixty thousand pounds! I've not the least doubt that he's speaking the truth. But the *bill* part of the business is highly unsatisfactory! I should like old Quirk to be here just now! Surely Mr. Aubrey must be able to get security! With such friends and connections as his!—If one could only get them to join him in security for ten thousand pounds—stay—that won't exactly do either; I must have my thumb upon him."]

"I am so profoundly affected by the situation in which you are placed, Mr. Aubrey," said Gammon, at length appearing to have subdued his emotion, and feeling it necessary to say something, "that I think I may take upon myself to say the instructions which we have received shall not be acted upon, come what may. Those must be really monsters, not men, who could press upon one in your position; and that such should be attempted by one who has succeeded to your former advantages is inconceivably shocking. Mr. Aubrey, *you shall rot be crushed*—indeed you shall not, so long as I am a member—perhaps not the least influential one—in this firm, and have any influence with your formidable creditor, Mr. Titmouse. I can not do justice to my desire to shelter you and yours, Mr. Aubrey, from the storm you dread so justly." There was a warmth, an energy in Gammon's manner while saying all this which cheered the drooping heart of poor Mr. Aubrey. "What I am about to say, Mr. Aubrey, is in complete confidence," continued Gammon, in a low tone. Mr. Aubrey bowed, with a little anxious excitement in his manner. "May I rely upon your honor and secrecy?"

"Most implicitly, sir. What you desire me to keep within my own breast no one upon earth shall know from *me.*"

"There are serious difficulties in the way of serving you. Mr. Titmouse is a weak and inexperienced young man, naturally excited to a great pitch by his present elevation, and already embarrassed for want of ready money. You may imaigne, sir, that his liabilities to us are of considerable magnitude. You would hardly credit, Mr. Aubrey, the amount of mere money out of pocket for which he stands indebted to us; our outlay during the last two years having considerably crippled our pecuniary resources, in an extensive practice like ours, and driven us to incur liabilities which are beginning to occasion my partners and myself considerable anxiety. Of course, Mr. Aubrey, we must look to Mr. Titmouse to be speedily reimbursed; he insists upon our immediately calling upon you; and I have reason to suspect that he has at his elbow one or two very heartless advisers, who have suggested this to him; for he follows it most pertinaciously. That he can not meet the liabilities I have alluded to out of his annual income, without swallowing it up entirely for eighteen months or two years, is certain. I regret to say that Mr. Quirk and Mr. Snap encourage his disposition to press you;—do not be alarmed, my dear sir!" he continued, observing the deadly paleness of Mr. Aubrey, whose eye was riveted upon that of Gammon, "for I declare that I will stand between you and them, and it is enough for me to say that I have the power of doing so. I am the only person living who happens to possess the means of influencing Mr. Titmouse; and I am determined to avail myself of them. Now, bearing in mind that I have no legal authority from him, and am, at the same time, only one of a firm, and assuring you that I am entailing a serious responsibility upon myself in what I am doing, let me throw out for your consideration my general notion of what I think ought to be done—merely my off-hand notion."

"I perfectly understand; I listen with inexpressible anx· iety," said Mr. Aubrey.

"Had I been consulted, we should have proposed to you with reference to our bill (which I candidly acknowledge con tains a much more liberal entry than would be allowed on taxation, and which is none of *my* doing)"—Gammon knew the credit for candor which this acknowledgment of a fact of which Messrs. Runnington would quickly apprise him on looking at the bill, was likely to obtain for him with Mr. Au brey—"I say, I should have *proposed* to you, in the first in stance, the payment of our bill by installments during the next three or four years, provided you could have obtained partial security. But I am only one of three, and I know the deter mination of Mr. Quirk and Mr. Snap not to listen to any pro posal with reference to the mesne profits which is not based upon—in short, they say, *the bill must be paid at once without being looked into*—I mean," he added, quickly, "without its being subjected to the harassing and protracted scrutiny which a distrustful, an ungrateful client, has it too frequently in his power to inflict. Oh, let me disguise nothing from you, my dear sir, in a conversation of this kind between two gentle men," continued Gammon, with an admirable air of frank ness, for he perceived that Mr. Aubrey looked slightly stag gered. "I am ashamed to acknowledge that that bill does contain exorbitant entries—entries which had led to very fre quent and fierce dispute between me and my partners. But *what is to be done!* Mr. Quirk is the moneyed man of the firm; and if you were to glance at the articles of our partner ship"—Gammon shrugged his shoulders and sighed, "you would see the tyrannical extent of power over his partners which, in virtue of that circumstance, he has secured! You observe how candid I am—perhaps foolishly so."

["I've not quite mastered him—I can tell it by his eye"— thought Gammon—"is this a game of chess between us? I wonder whether, after all, Messrs. Runnington are aware of his being here—knowing and trusting to his ability—and have put him thoroughly on his guard? He is checking strong feel ings incessantly, and evidently weighing every word I utter. Misery has sharpened faculties naturally acute!"]

"Pray do not say so, Mr. Gammon; I fully appreciate your motives. I am devoured with anxiety for an intimation of the nature of the terms which you were about, so kindly, to specify."

"*Specify* is perhaps rather too strong a term—but to pro ceed. Supposing, Mr. Aubrey, the preliminary matter which

7—Part II.

I have alluded to, satisfactorily arranged, I am disposed to say that if you could find security for the payment of the sum of ten thousand pounds within a year, or a year and a half "— [Mr. Aubrey's teeth almost chattered at the mention of it]— " I—I—that is, *my* impression is—but it is only *mine* "— added Gammon, earnestly—" that the rest should be left to your own honor, giving at the same time a personal undertaking to pay, at a future—a very distant day—in the manner most convenient to yourself—the sum of ten thousand pounds more—making in all only one third of the sum due from you; and receiving an absolute release from Mr. Titmouse in respect of the remaining two thirds, namely, forty thousand pounds."

Mr. Aubrey listened to all this with his feelings and faculties strung to the utmost pitch of intensity, and when Gammon had ceased experienced a transient sense, as of the fearful mountain that had pressed so long on his heart, moving.

" Have I made myself intelligible, Mr. Aubrey?" inquired Gammon, with a kind but serious air.

" Perfectly—but I feel so oppressed and overwhelmed with the magnitude of the topics we are discussing that I scarcely at present appreciate the position in which you would place me. I must throw myself, Mr. Gammon, entirely upon your indulgence!"

Gammon looked a little disappointed.

" I can imagine your feelings, sir," said he, as he took a sheet of paper and a pencil; and while he made a few memoranda of the arrangement which he had been mentioning, he continued—" You see—the great result of what I have been hastily sketching off is—to give you ample time to pay the sums which I have named, and to relieve you at once, *absolutely*, from no less a sum than FORTY THOUSAND POUNDS," said he, with emphasis and deliberation, " for which—and with interest—you would otherwise remain liable to the day of your death;—there could be no escape—except, perhaps, into banishment, which with your feelings would be worse than death— for it would be a *dishonorable* exile, to avoid just liabilities;— and those who bear your name would, in such an—"

" Pray, sir, be silent!" exclaimed Mr. Aubrey, in a tone that electrified Gammon, who started from his chair. Mr. Aubrey's face was whitened; his eye glanced lightning at his companion. Dragon-like, Gammon had put forth his hand and touched the ark of Aubrey's honor. Gammon lost his color, and for, perhaps, the first time in his life, quailed before the majesty of man; 'twas also the majesty of suffering; for he had been torturing a noble nature. Neither of them spoke for some time—Mr. Aubrey continuing highly excited—Gammon gazing at him with unfeigned amazement. The paper which he held in his hand rustled, and he was obliged to lay it down on his lap, lest Mr. Aubrey should notice this evidence of his agitation.

"I am guilty of great weakness, sir," said at length Mr. Aubrey—his excitement only a little abated. He stood erect, and spoke with stern precision; "but you, perhaps unconsciously, provoked the display of it. Sir, I am ruined; I am a beggar; we are all ruined; we are all beggars; it is the order-ing of God, and I bow to it. But do you presume, sir, to think that at last my HONOR is in danger? and consider it necessary, as if you were warning one whom you saw about to become a criminal, to expatiate on the nature of the meditated act by which I am to disgrace myself and my family?" Here that family seemed suddenly standing around him; his lip quivered, his eyes filled, and he trembled with excessive emotion.

"This is a sally equally unexpected, Mr. Aubrey, and, per-mit me to add, unwarrantable," said Gammon, calmly, having recovered his self-possession. "You have entirely misunder-stood me; or I have ill-explained myself. Your evident excite-ment and distress touch my very soul, Mr. Aubrey." Gam-mon's voice trembled. "Suffer me to tell you that I feel an inexpressible respect and admiration for you, and am misera-ble at the thought of one word of mine having occasioned you an instant's uneasiness." When a generous nature is thus treated, it is apt to feel an excessive contrition for any fault or extravagance which it may have committed—an excessive ap-preciation of the pain it may have inflicted on another. Thus it was that by the time Gammon had done speaking, Mr. Au-brey felt ashamed and mortified at himself, and conceived an admiration of the dignified forbearance of Gammon, which quickly heightened into respect for his general character, as it appeared to Aubrey, and fervent gratitude for the disposition which he had evinced, from first to last, so disinterestedly to serve a ruined man. He seemed now to view all that Gam-mon had proposed in quite a new light—through quite an-other medium; and his excitable *feelings* were in some danger of disturbing his *judgment*.

"As I am a man of business, Mr. Aubrey," said Gammon, shortly afterward, with a very captivating smile—how frank and forgiving seemed his temper to Aubrey!—"and this is a place for business, shall we resume our conversation? With reference to the first ten thousand pounds, it can be a matter

of future arrangement as to the instruments by which its pay·
ment is to be secured; and as for the remaining ten thousand,
if I were not afraid of rendering myself liable to Mr. Titmouse
for neglecting his interests, I should be content with your verbal promise—your mere word of honor, to pay it, as and when
you conveniently could. ˙But, in justice to myself, I really
must take a *show* of security from you. Say, for instance, two
promissory notes for £5,000 each, payable to Mr. Titmouse.
You may really regard them as matters of mere form; for,
when you shall have given them to me, they will be deposited
there " (pointing to an iron safe), "and not again be heard of
until you may have inquired for them.   The influence which I
happen to have obtained over Mr. Titmouse, you may rely
upon my exercising with some energy, if ever he should be disposed to press you for payment of either of the instruments I
have mentioned.   I tell you candidly that they must be
negotiable in point of form; but I assure you, as sincerely,
that I will not permit them to be negotiated.   *Now*, may I
venture to hope we understand each other?" added Gammon,
with a cheerful air; "and that if this be an arrangement
which I shall be able to carry into effect, it is a sufficient evidence of my desire to serve you, and will have the effect of relieving you from an immense load of anxiety and liability?"

"An immense—a crushing load, indeed, sir, if Providence
shall in any manner (to me at present undiscoverable) enable
me to perform *my* part of the arrangement, and if *you* have
but power to carry your views into effect," replied Mr. Aubrey, with a sigh of anxiety and a look of gratitude.

"Leave that to *me*, Mr. Aubrey; I will undertake to do it;
I will move heaven and earth to do it—and the more eagerly
and anxiously, for that I may thereby hope to establish a kind
of set-off against the misery and loss which my professional exertions have contributed to occasion you!"

"I feel very deeply sensible of your very great—your unexpected kindness, Mr. Gammon; but still, the arrangement
suggested is one which occasions me dreadful anxiety as to my
being able to carry out my part of it."

"Never, never despair, Mr. Aubrey! Heaven helps those
who help themselves; and I really imagine I see your powerful
energies already beginning to surmount your prodigious difficulties!   When you have slept over the matter, you will feel
the full relief which this arrangement is so calculated to afford
your spirits.   Of course, too, you will lose no time in communicating to Messrs. Runnington the nature of the arrangement which I have proposed.   I can predict that they will be

not a little disposed to urge you to complete it. I can not, however, help once more reminding you, in justice to myself, Mr. Aubrey, that it is *but* a proposition, in making which I hope it will not prove that I have been carried away by my feelings much further than my duty to my client or his inter-ests—"

Mr. Aubrey was afraid to hear him finish the sentence, lest the faint dawn of hope should disappear from the dark and rough surface of the sea of trouble upon which he was being tossed. "I will consult, as you suggest, sir, my professional advisers; and am strongly inclined to believe that they will feel as you predict. I am bound to consult *them*—"

"Oh, certainly! certainly! I am very strict in the observ-ance of professional etiquette, Mr. Aubrey, I assure you; and should not think of going on with this arrangement, except with them, acting on your behalf. One thing I have to beg, Mr. Aubrey, that either you or they will communicate the re-sult of your deliberations to *me*, personally. I am very de-sirous that the suggested arrangement should be broken to them by *me*. By the way, if you would favor me with your address, I would make a point of calling at your house, either late in the evening or early in the morning."

[As if Messrs. Quirk, Gammon and Snap had not kept eagle eyes upon his every movement since quitting Yatton, with a view to any sudden application for a writ of *Ne Exeas*, which a suspicious movement of his toward the sea-coast might render necessary!]

"I am infinitely obliged to you, sir—but it would be far more convenient for both of us if you could drop me a line, or favor me with a call at Mr. Weasel's, in Pomegranate Court in the Temple."

Gammon blushed scarlet; but for this accidental mention of the name of Mr. Weasel, who was one of the pleaders occa-sionally employed by Messrs. Quirk, Gammon and Snap in heavy matters—in all probability Mr. Aubrey might, within a day or two's time, have had to exercise his faculties, if so dis-posed, upon a declaration of Trespass for Mesne Profits, in a cause of "TITMOUSE *v.* AUBREY!"

"As you like—as you like, Mr. Aubrey," replied Gammon, with difficulty concealing his feelings of pique and disappoint-ment at losing the opportunity of a personal introduction to Mr. Aubrey's family. After a few words of general conversa-tion, Gammon inquiring how Mr. Aubrey liked his new profes-sion, and assuring him, in an emphatic manner. that he might

rely upon being supported, from the moment of his being
called to the bar, by almost all the common-law business of
the firm of "Quirk, Gammon and Snap"—they parted. It
had been to Mr. Aubrey a memorable interview—and to Gammon a somewhat arduous affair, taxing to an unusual extent
his powers of self-command and of dissimulation. As soon as
he was left alone, his thoughts instantly recurred to Aubrey's
singular burst of hauteur and indignation. Gammon had a
stinging sense of submission to superior energy—and felt indignant with himself for not having resented it. Setting aside
this source of exquisite irritation to the feelings of a proud
man, he felt a depressing consciousness that he had not met
with his usual success in his recent encounter with Mr.
Aubrey, who had been throughout cautious, watchful, and
courteously distrustful. He had afforded occasional glimpses
of the unapproachable pride of his nature—and Gammon had
crouched! Was there anything in their interview—thought
he, walking thoughtfully to and fro in his room—which, when
Aubrey came to reflect upon—for instance—had Gammon disclosed too much about the extent of his influence over Titmouse? His cheek slightly flushed; a sigh of fatigue and excitement escaped him; and gathering together his papers, he
began to prepare for quitting the office for the day.

Mr. Aubrey quitted Messrs. Quirk, Gammon and Snap's
office with feelings of mingled exhaustion and despondency.
As he walked down Saffron Hill—a dismal, deplorable neighborhood!—what scenes did he witness? Poverty and profligacy
reveling on all hands in their wild and filthy excesses! *Here,*
was an Irishman, half stupefied with liquor and bathed in
blood, having just been rescued from a dreadful fight in a low
underground public-house cellar, by his squalid wife, with disheveled hair and a filthy infant in her arms—who walked beside him cursing, pinching, and striking him—reproaching him
with the knowledge that she and her seven children were lying
starving at home; presently he fell down into the gutter, and
she with her infant fell down over him!

There, was a woman—as it were a bloated mass of filth
steeped in gin—standing with a drunken smile, at an old-
clothes stall, pawning for a glass of gin a dirty little shirt,
which she had a few minutes before stripped from the back of
one of her then half-naked children!

A little further on was a noisy crowd round two men carrying a shutter, on which was strapped a bleeding body (a handkerchief spread over the face) of a poor bricklayer, fallen a
few minutes before from the top of some scaffolding in the

neighborhood, and then in the agonies of death—leaving behind him a wife and twelve children, for whom he had long
slaved from morning to night, and who were now ignorant of
the frightful fate which had befallen him, and that they were
left destitute.

There, was a skinny little terrified urchin, about eight years
old, with nothing to conceal his dirty, half-starved body, but a
tattered man's coat, pinned round him; dying with hunger,
he had stolen a villainous-looking bare bone—scarce a half-
pennyworth of meat upon it; and a brawny constable, his
knuckles fiercely dug into the poor little offender's neck (with
his tight grasp), was leading him off to the police office, followed by his shrieking mother; from the police office he would
be committed to Newgate, and thence, after two or three
months' imprisonment, and being flogged — miserable little
wretch!—by the common hangman (who had hanged the
child's father some six months before), he would be discharged
—to return several times and undergo a similar process; then
to be transported; and finally be hanged, as had been his father
before him.

These startling scenes passed before Mr. Aubrey, in the
course of a five minutes' walk down Saffron Hill—during
which period he now and then paused, and gazed around him
with feelings of pity, of astonishment, of disgust, which presently blended and deepened into one feeling of horror. These
scenes, to some so fatally familiar—*fatally,* I mean, on account of the INDIFFERENCE which their familiarity is apt to
induce—to Mr. Aubrey had on them all the frightful glare of
novelty.   He had never witnessed anything of the sort before,
and had no notion of its existence.   The people on each side
of the Hill, however, seemed perfectly familiar with such
scenes, which they seemed to view with the same stupid indifference with which a *lamb led to the slaughter* is beheld by
one that has spent his life next door to the slaughter-house.
The Jew clothesman, before whose door, arrested by the hor-
rifying spectacle of the bleeding wretch borne along to the hospital—he stood for a second or two—took the opportunity to
assail him with insolent importunity.   A fat baker and a·
greasy eating-house keeper stood each at his door, one with
folded arms, the other with his hands thrust into his pockets
—both of them gazing with a grin at two curs fighting in the
middle of the street—oh, how utterly insensible to the ravenous want that flitted incessantly past them! The pallid spec-
ters haunting the gin-palace at the corner gazed with sunken
lack-luster eye and drunken apathy at the man borne by.

What scenes were these! And what other hidden scenes did they not indicate the existence of! " Gracious mercy!" thought Aubrey, " what a world have I been living in! And this dismal aspect of it exposed to me just when I have lost all power of relieving its wretchedness!"—here a thrill of anguish passed through his heart—" but, woe, woe is me! if at this moment I had a thousand times ten thousand a year, how far would it go amid the scenes similar to this, which abound in this one city? Oh, God! what unutterable horror must be in store for those who, intrusted by Thee with an overflowing abundance, disregard the misery around them in guilty selfishness and indolence, or "—he shuddered—" expend it in sensuality and profligacy! Will Dives become sensible of his misconduct, only when he shall have entered upon his next scene of existence and punishment? Oh, merciful Creator! how is my heart wrung by the sight of such scenes as these! Awful and mysterious Author of existence, *Father of the spirits of all flesh*, are these states of being which Thou hast ordained? Are these thy children? Are these my fellow-creatures? Oh, help me! help me! my weak heart faints; my clouded understanding is confounded! I can not—insect that I am!—discern the scope and end of Thy economy, of Thy dread government of the world; yet blessed be the name of my God!—I KNOW that *Thou reignest! though clouds and darkness are around Thee! righteousness and judgment are the habitation of Thy throne! with righteousness shalt Thou judge the world*, AND THE PEOPLE WITH EQUITY!"

Like as the lesser light is lost in the greater, so, in Aubrey's case, was the lesser misery he suffered merged in his sense of the greater misery he witnessed. What, after all, was his position, in comparison with that of those now before and around him? What cause of thankfulness had he not for merciful mildness of the dispensation of Providence toward him and his? Such were his thoughts and feelings, as he stood gazing at the scenes which had called them forth, when his eye alighted on the figure of Mr. Gammon approaching him. He was threading his way, apparently lost in thought, through the scenes which had so powerfully affected Mr. Aubrey, who stood eying him with a sort of unconscious intensity, as if secure from his observation, till he was actually addressed by him.

" Mr. Aubrey!" exclaimed Gammon, courteously saluting him. Each took off his hat to the other. Though Aubrey hardly intended it, he found himself engaged in conversation with Gammon, who, in a remarkably feeling tone, and with a happy flattering deference of manner, intimated that he could guess the subject of Mr. Aubrey's thoughts, namely, the absorbing matters which they had been discussing together.

"No, it is not so," said Mr. Aubrey, with a sigh, as he walked on—Gammon keeping easily beside him—"I have been profoundly affected by scenes which I have witnessed in the immediate neighborhood of your office, since quitting it; what misery! what horror!"

"Ah, Mr. Aubrey!"—exclaimed Gammon, with a sigh, as they very slowly ascended Holborn Hill, separate, but side by side—"what a checkered scene is life! Guilt and innocence—happiness and misery—wealth and poverty—disease and health—wisdom and folly—sensuality and refinement—piety and irreligion—how strangely intermingled we behold them, wherever we look on life—how difficult to the philosopher to detect the principle—"

"Difficult? — Impossible! Impossible!" — exclaimed Mr. Aubrey, thoughtfully.

"Comparison, I have often thought," said Gammon, after a pause—"comparison of one's own misfortunes with the greater misfortunes endured by others is beneficial or prejudicial—consolatory or disheartening—according as the mind of him who makes the comparison is well or ill regulated—possessed or destitute of moral and religious principle!"

"It is so, indeed," said Mr. Aubrey; though not particularly inclined to enter into conversation, he was pleased with the tone of his companion's remark.

"As for me"—proceeded Gammon, with a slight sigh—"the absorbing anxieties of professional life; and, too, a branch of professional life which, infinitely to my distaste, brings me constantly into scenes such as you have been observing, have contributed to render me less sensible of their real character; yet can I vividly conceive the effect they must, when first seen, produce upon the mind and heart of a compassionate, an observant, a reflecting man, Mr. Aubrey!"

Gammon looked a gentleman; his address was easy and insinuating, full of delicate deference, without the slightest tendency to cant or sycophancy; his countenance was an intellectual and expressive one; his conversation that of an educated and thinking man. He was striving his utmost to produce a favorable impression on Mr. Aubrey; and, as is very little to be surprised at, he succeeded. By the time that they had got about twenty yards beyond Fetter Lane, they might have been seen walking together arm in arm. As they approached Oxford Street, they suddenly stumbled on Mr. Runnington.

"God bless me, Mr. Aubrey!" said he, surprisedly—"and

Mr. Gammon? How do you do, Mr. Gammon?"—he continued, taking off his hat with a little formality, and speaking in a corresponding tone, but he was encountered by Gammon with greatly superior ease and distance, and was not a little nettled at it; for he was so palpably foiled with his own weapons.

"Well—I shall now resign you to your legitimate adviser, Mr. Aubrey," said Gammon with a smile; then, addressing Mr. Runnington, in whose countenance pique and pride were abundantly visible—"Mr. Aubrey has favored me with a call to-day, and we have had some little discussion on a matter which he will explain to you. As for me, Mr. Aubrey, I ought to have turned off two streets ago—so I wish you good-evening."

Mr. Aubrey and he shook hands as they exchanged adieus. Mr. Runnington and he simply raised each his hat, and bowed to the other with cold politeness. As Mr. Runnington and Mr. Aubrey walked westward together, the former, who was a very cautious man, did not think fit to express the uneasiness he felt at Mr. Aubrey's having entered into anything like confidential intercourse with one whom he believed to be so subtle and dangerous a person as Mr. Gammon. He was, however, very greatly surprised when he came to hear of the proposal which had been made up by Mr. Gammon, concerning the mesne profits, which, he said, was so unaccountably reasonable and liberal, considering the parties by whom it was made, that he feared Mr. Aubrey must be lying under some mistake. He would, however, turn it anxiously over in his mind, and consult with his partners; and, in short, do whatever they conceived best for Mr. Aubrey—that he might depend upon. "And, in the meantime, my dear sir," added Mr. Runnington, with a smile designed to disguise considerable anxiety, "it may be as well for you not to have any further personal communication with these parties, whom you do not know as well as we do; but let us negotiate with them in everything!" Thus they parted; and Mr. Aubrey entered Vivian Street with a considerably lighter heart than he had ever before carried into it. A vivid recollection of the scene which he had witnessed at Saffron Hill caused him exquisitely to appreciate the comforts of his little home, and to return the welcomes and caresses he had received with a kind of trembling tenderness and energy. As he folded his still blooming but somewhat anxious wife fondly to his bosom, kissed his high-spirited and lovely sister, and fondled the prattling innocents that came clambering up upon his lap, he forgot, for awhile, the difficulties, but remembered the *lessons* of the day.

But I must return to Yatton, where some matters had transpired which are worth noticing. Though Mr. Yahoo paid
rather anxious court to Mr. Gammon, who was very far too
much for him in every way, 'twas very plain that he dreaded
and disliked, as much as he was despised by that gentleman.
Mr. Gammon easily extracted from Titmouse that Yahoo was
endeavoring, from time to time, artfully to set him against his
protector, Mr. Gammon. This was *something;* but more than
this—Yahoo, a bold, dashing scoundrel, was obtaining a growing ascendency over Titmouse, whom he was rapidly initiating
into all manner of vile habits and practices: and, in short,
completely corrupting. But, above all, Gammon ascertained
that Yahoo had already commenced, with great success, his
experiments upon the purse of Titmouse. Before they had
been a week at Yatton, down came a splendid billiard-table
with its appendages from London, accompanied by a man to
fix it—as he did—in the library, which he quickly denuded of
all traces of its former character; and here Yahoo, Titmouse,
and Fitz-Snooks would pass a good deal of their time. Then
'hey would have tables and chairs, and cards, cigars, and
brandy and water, out upon the beautiful " soft, smooth-
shaven lawn," and sit there playing *écarté,* at once pleasantly
soothed and stimulated by their cigars and brandy and water,
for half a day together. Then Yahoo got up frequent excur-
sions to Grilston, and even to York; where, together with his
two companions, he had " great sport," as the newspapers
began to intimate with growing frequency and distinctness.
Actuated by that execrable licentiousness with reference to the
female sex, by which he was peculiarly distinguished, and of
which he boasted, he had got into several curious adventures
with farmers' girls and others in the vicinity of Yatton, and
even among the female members of the establishment at the
Hall; in which latter quarter Fitz-Snooks and Titmouse began
to imitate his example. Mr. Gammon conceived a fearful, a
shuddering loathing and disgust for the miscreant leader into
these enormities, and, but for certain consequences, would
have dispatched him with as much indifference as he would
have laid arsenic in the way of a bold voracious rat, or killed a
snake. As it was, he secretly caused him to experience, on
one or two occasions, the effects of his good-will toward him.
Yahoo had offered certain atrocious indignities to the sweetheart
of a strapping young farmer; whose furious complaints coming to Mr. Gammon's ears, that gentleman, under a pledge of
secrecy, gave him two guineas to be on the lookout for
Yahoo, and give him the best taste he know how of a

pair of Yorkshire fists.   A day or two afterward, the Satyr
fell in with his unexpected enemy.   Yahoo was a strongly
built man, and an excellent bruiser; but was at first disposed
to shirk the fight, on glancing at the prodigious proportions of
Hazel, and the fury flaming in his eyes.   The instant, however, that he saw the attitude into which poor Hazel threw
himself, Yahoo smiled, stripped, and set to.   I am sorry to
say that it was a good while before Hazel could get one single
blow at his accomplished opponent; whom, however, he began
at length to wear out.   Then he gave him a miserable pom-
meling, to be sure; and finished by knocking out five of his
front teeth, viz., three in the upper and two in the under jaw
—beautifully white and regular teeth they certainly were; and
the loss of them caused him great affliction on the score of his
appearance, and also not a little inferfered with the process of
cigar-smoking, and would, besides, have debarred him from en-
listing as a soldier, inasmuch as he could not bite off the end
of his cartridge : wherefore, it would seem, that Hazel had committed the offense of *Mayhem*.   Mr. Gammon condoled heartily
with Mr. Yahoo, on hearing of the brutal attack which had
been made upon him, and as the assault had not been committed in the presence of a third party, strongly recommended him
to bring an action of trespass *vi et armis* against Hazel, which
Gammon undertook to conduct for him to—a nonsuit.   While
they were conversing in this friendly way together, it suddenly
occurred to Gammon that there was another service he could
render Mr. Yahoo, and with equally strict observance of the
injunction, *not to let his left hand know what his right hand
did ;* for he loved the character of a secret benefactor.   So he
wrote up a letter to Snap (whom he knew to have been treated
very insolently by Yahoo), desiring him to go to two or three
flash bill-brokers and money-lenders, and ascertain whether
they had any paper by them with the name of "Yahoo" on
it:—and in the event of such being discovered, he was to act
in the manner pointed out by Gammon.   Off went Snap like
a shot, on receiving this letter; and the very first gentleman
he applied to, viz., a MR. SUCK'EM DRY, proved to be possessed of an acceptance of Yahoo's for £200, for which Dry
had given only five pounds on speculation.   He readily yielded
to Snap's representation, that he would give him—Dry—a shy
at Mr. Yahoo's gratis—and put the document into the hands
of Snap; who forthwith delivered it, confidently, to Swindle
Shark, gent., etc., a little Jew attorney in Chancery Lane,
into whose office the dirty work of Quirk, Gammon and Snap
was swept—in cases where they did not choose to appear.   I

wish the mutilated Yahoo could have seen the mouthful of glittering teeth that were displayed by the hungry Jew, on receiving the above commission. His duties, though of a painful, were of a brief and simple description. 'Twas a plain case of *Indorsee* v. *Acceptor*. The affidavit of debt was sworn the same afternoon; and within an hour's time afterward, a thin slip of paper was delivered into the hand of the Under-sheriff of Yorkshire, commanding him to take the body of Pimp Yahoo, if he should be found in his bailiwick, and him safely keep—out of harm's way—to enable him to pay £200 *debt* to Suck'em Dry, and £24 6s. 10d. *costs* to Swindle Shark. Down went that little "infernal machine" to Yorkshire by that night's post.

Nothing could exceed the astonishment and concern with which Mr. Gammon, the evening but one afterward, on returning to the Hall from a ride to Grilston, heard Titmouse and Fitz-Snooks—deserted beings!—tell him how, an hour before, two big vulgar fellows, one of them with a long slip of paper in his hands, had called at the Hall, asked for the innocent, unsuspecting Yahoo, just as he had made an admirable *coup* —and insisted on his accompanying them to the house of one of the aforesaid bailiffs, and then on to York Castle. They had brought a tax-cart with them for his convenience; and into it, between his two new friends, was forced to get the astonished Yahoo—smoking, as well as he could, a cigar, with some score or two of which he had filled all his pockets, and swearing oaths enough to last the whole neighborhood for a fortnight at least. Mr. Gammon was quite shocked at the indignity which had been perpetrated, and asked why the villains had not been kept till he could have been sent for. Then, leaving the melancholy Titmouse and Fitz-Snooks to themselves for a little while, he took a solitary walk in the elm avenue, where—grief has different modes of expressing itself —he relieved his excited feelings by reiterated little bursts of gentle laughter. As soon as the *York True Blue* had, among other imitations of fashionable movements, informed the public that "*The Hon.* Pimp Yahoo" had quitted Yatton Hall for York Castle, where he intended to remain and receive a large party of friends—it was astonishing how soon they began to muster and rally round him. "*Detainers*"—so that species of visiting-cards is called—came fluttering in like snow; and, in short, there was no end of the messages of civility and congratulation which he received from those whom he had obliged with his valuable countenance and custom.

Ah me, poor Yahoo, completely done! Oft is it, in this in-

fernal world of ours, that the best concerted schemes are thus
suddenly defeated by the envious and capricious fates! Thus
were thy arms suddenly held back from behind, just as they
were encircling as pretty, plump a pigeon as ever nestled in
them with pert and playful confidence, to be plucked! Alas,
alas! And didst thou behold the danger to which it was exposed, as it fluttered upward unconsciously into the region
where thine affectionate eye detected the keen hawk in deadly
poise? Ah me! Oh, dear! What shall I do? What can I
say? How vent my grief for The Prematurely Caged?—

> " Quis desiderio sit pudor, aut mod
> Tam chari capitis?—
> Ergo *Yahoum* perpetuus *carcer*
> *Tenet?* Cui Pudor, et Justitiæ soror,
> Incorrupta Fides, nudaque Veritas,
> Quando ullum inveniet parem?
>   Multis ille bonis flebilis *abfuit!*
> Nulli flebilior quam tibi, *Tittlebat!**
> Tu frustra pius, heu! non ita creditum
> Poscis *Yahoum creditores*—
> Quem *brevi* semel horrido
> Nigro compulerit *Gammonius* gregi.
> Durum!" †

Poor Titmouse was very dull for some little time after this
sudden abduction of the bold and brilliant spirit, for whom I
have above poured out the deep sorrows of my soul, and wished
to bring an action, at the suggestion of Fitz-Snooks, against
the miscreant who had dared to set the law in motion at Yatton, under the very nose of its lord and master. As soon,
however, as Gammon intimated to him that all those who had
lent Yahoo money might now rely upon that gentleman's
honor, and whistle back their money at their leisure, Titmouse
burst out into a great rage, telling Gammon that he, Titmouse,
had only a day or two before lent Yahoo £150 of good and
lawful money of Great Britain; and that he was a " cursed
scamp," who had known when he borrowed that he could not
repay; and a Detainer, at the suit of " Tittlebat Titmouse,
Esq.," was one of the very earliest that found its way into the
Sheriff's office; this new creditor becoming one of the very bitterest and most relentless against the fallen Yahoo, except,
perhaps, Mr. Fitz-Snooks. That gentleman, having lent the
amiable Yahoo no less than thirteen hundred pounds, remained
easy all the while, under the impression that certain precious
documents called " I O U's" of the said Yahoo were as

---

* *Male. nonnulli—" Titmuscule."*   † Hor Carm. I. **xxiv.**

good as cash; and was horribly dismayed on discovering that it was otherwise; that *he* was not to be paid before all other creditors, and immediately; so he also sent a very special message in the shape of a Detainer, backed by a great number of curses.

In process of time Mr. Yahoo bethought himself of getting "*whitewashed ;*" but when he came to be inspected, it was considered that he was not properly *seasoned ;* so the operation was delayed for two years, under a very arbitrary statute, which enacted, " that if it should appear that the said prisoner had contracted any of his debts *fraudulently,* or by means of *false pretenses,* or *without having had any reasonable or probable expectation, at the time when contracted, of paying the same,*" etc., etc., etc., " or should be indebted for damages recovered in any *action for criminal conversation,* or *seduction,* or for *malicious injuries,* etc., etc., such prisoner should be discharged as to such debts and damages, so soon only as he should have been in custody at the suit of such creditors for a period or periods not exceeding two years." Such is the odious restraint upon the liberty of the subject, which at this day, in the nineteenth century, is suffered to disgrace the statute law of England; for, in order to put *other Yahoos* upon their guard against the cruel and iniquitous designs upon them, I here inform them that the laws under which Mr. Yahoo suffered his two years' incarceration (every one of his debts, etc., coming under one or other of the descriptions above-mentioned), are, *proh pudor !* re-enacted, and at this moment in force, as several most respectable gentlemen, if you could only get access to them, would tell you.

Yahoo having been thus adroitly disposed of, Mr. Gammon had the gratification of finding that mischievous simpleton, Fitz-Snooks, very soon afterward take his departure. He pined for the pleasures of the town (which he had money enough to enjoy for about three years longer, with economy; after which he might go abroad, or to *the dogs*—wherever they were to be found). 'Twas indeed monstrous dull at Yatton; the game, which Yahoo had given him a taste for, was so very *strictly preserved* there! and the birds so uncommon shy and wild, and strong on the wing! Besides, Gammon's presence was a terrible pressure upon him, overawing and benumbing him, in spite of several attempts which he had made, when charged with the requisite quantity of wine, to exhibit an impertinent familiarity, or even defiance. As soon as poor Titmouse had bade him good-bye, shaken hands with him, and lost sight of him—he was at Yatton, *alone with Gammon,* and felt as if a spell were upon him—he was completely cowed and prostrate. Yet Gammon laid himself out to the very utmost to please him and reassure his drooping spirits. Titmouse had got it into his head that the mysterious and dreadful Gammon had, in some deep way or other, been at the bottom of Yahoo's abduction and the disappearance of Fitz-Snooks, and would, by and by, do the same for *him*. He had no feeling of *ownership* of Yatton; but of being, as it were, only tenant-at-will thereof to Mr. Gammon. Whenever he tried to reassure himself, by repeating to himself that it did not signify—for Yatton was his own—and he might do as he liked, his feelings might be compared to a balloon, which, with the eye of eager and anxious thousands upon it, yet can not get inflated sufficiently to rise one inch from the ground. How was it? Mr. Gammon's manner toward him was most uncommonly respectful; what else could he wish for? Yet he would have given a thousand ¡pounds to Mr. Gammon to take himself off, and never show his nose again at Yatton! It annoyed him, too, more than he could express to perceive the deference and respect which every one at the Hall manifested toward Mr. Gammon. Titmouse would sometimes stamp his foot, when alone, with childish fury on the ground, when he thought of it. When at dinner, and sitting together afterward, Gammon would rack his invention for jokes and anecdotes to amuse Titmouse—who would certainly give a kind of laugh, exclaim, " Bravo! Ha, ha! 'Pon my life!—capital!—By Jove! Most uncommon good! you don't say so?" and go on, drinking glass after glass of wine, or brandy and water, and smoking cigar after cigar, till he felt fuddled and sick, in which condition he would retire to bed, and leave Gammon, clear and serene in head and temper, to his meditations. When, at length, Gammon broached the subject of their bill—a frightful amount it was; of the moneys advanced by Mr. Quirk, for his support for eight or nine months, on a liberal scale; and which amounted up to a sum infinitely larger than could have been supposed; and lastly, of the bond for ten thousand pounds, as the just reward to the firm for their long-continued, most anxious, and successful exertions on Titmouse's behalf—Titmouse mustered up all his resolution, as for a last desperate struggle; swore they were robbing him; and added, with a furious snap of the fingers, " they had better take the estate themselves—allow him a pound a week, and send him back to Tag-rag's." Then he burst into tears, and cried like a child, long and bitterly.

" Well, sir," said Gammon, after remaining silent for some time, looking at Titmouse calmly, but with an expression of face which frightened him out of his wits, "if this is to be really the way in which I am to be treated by you—I, the only *real disinterested* friend you have in the world (as you have had hundreds of opportunities of ascertaining), if my advice is to be spurned and my motives suspected; if your first and deliberate engagements to our firm are to be wantonly broken—"

"Ah, but, 'pon my soul, I was humbugged into making them," said Titmouse, passionately.

"Why, you little miscreant!" exclaimed Gammon, starting up in his chair, and gazing at him as if he would have scorched him with his eye, "do you DARE to say so? If you have no gratitude—have you lost your *memory?* What were you when I dug you out of your filthy hole at Closet Court? Did you not repeatedly go down on your knees to us? Did you not promise a thousand times to do infinitely more than you are now called upon to do? And is this, you insolent—despicable little insect!—is *this* the return you make us for putting you, a beggar—and very nearly, too, an idiot—"

"You're most uncommon polite," said Titmouse, suddenly and bitterly.

"Silence, sir! I am in no humor for trifling!" interrupted Gammon, sternly. "I say, is *this* the return you think of making us; not only to insult us, but refuse to pay money actually advanced by us to save you from starvation—money, and days and nights, and weeks and months, and *many* months of intense anxiety, expended in discovering how to put you in possession of a splendid fortune?—Poh! you miserable little trifler!—why should I trouble myself thus? Remember—remember, Tittlebat Titmouse," continued Gammon, in a low tone, and extending toward him threateningly his thin forefinger, "I, who made you, will in one day—one single day—unmake you—will blow you away like a bit of froth; you shall never be seen, or heard of, or thought of, except by some small draper whose unhappy shopman you may be!"

"Ah!—'pon my life! Dare say you think I'm uncommon frightened! Ah, ha! Monstrous — particular good!" said Titmouse.

Gammon perceived that he trembled in every limb; and the smile which he tried to throw into his face was so wretched that, had you seen him at that moment, and considered his position, much and justly as you now despise him, you must have pitied him. "You're always now going on in this way! —It's so very likely!" continued he. "Why, 'pon my soul, am not I to be A LORD one of these days? Can you help that?

Can you send a lord behind a draper's counter? 'Pon my soul, what do you say to that? I like that uncommon—"

"What do I say?" replied Gammon, calmly, "why, that I've a great mind to say and do something that would make you—make you—fit to jump head foremost into a sewer!"

Titmouse's heart was lying fluttering at his throat.

"Tittlebat, Tittlebat!" continued Gammon, dropping his voice, and speaking in a very kind and earnest manner, "if you did but know the extent to which an accident has placed you in my power! at this moment in my power! Really I almost tremble, myself, to think of it!" He rose, brought his chamber-candlestick out of the hall—lighted it—bade Titmouse good-night, sadly but sternly—and shook him by the hand—"I may rid you of my presence to-morrow morning, Mr. Titmouse. I shall leave you to *try to enjoy Yatton!* May you find a *truer*—a more powerful friend than you will have lost in me!" Titmouse never shrunk more helplessly under the eye of Mr. Gammon than he did at that moment.

"You—you—*won't* stop and smoke another cigar with a poor devil, will you, Mr. Gammon?" he inquired, faintly. "It's somehow—most uncommon lonely in this queer, large, old-fashioned—"

"Not to-night, thank you," replied Gammon—and withdrew, leaving Titmouse in a state of mingled alarm and anger —the former, however, predominating.

"By jingo!" he at length exclaimed, with a heavy sigh, after a reverie of about three minutes, gulping down the remainder of his brandy and water, "if that same gent, Mr. Gammon, a'n't the—the—devil—he's the very best imitation of him that ever I heard tell of!" Here he glanced furtively round the room; then he got a little flustered, rang his bell quickly for his valet, and, followed by him, retired to his dressing-room.

The next morning the storm had entirely blown over. When they met at breakfast, Titmouse, as Gammon knew would be the case, was all submission and respect; in fact, he was evidently thoroughly frightened by what Gammon had said, and infinitely more by the *manner* in which he had said what he did say overnight. Gammon, however, preserved for some little time the haughty air with which he had met him; but a few words of poor Titmouse's expressing his regret for what he had said when he had drunk too much—poor little soul!— overnight, and unqualifyingly submitting to every one of the requisitions which had been insisted on by Mr. Gammon—

quickly dispersed the cloud that was settled on Gammon's brow.

" Now, my dear sir," said he, very graciously, " you show yourself the gentleman I always took you for—and I forget, forever, all that passed between us so unpleasantly last night. I am sure it will never be so again: for now we *entirely* understand each other?"

" Oh, yes—'pon my life—quite entirely!" replied Titmouse, meekly.

Soon after breakfast they adjourned, at Gammon's request, to the billiard-room; where, though that gentleman knew how to handle a cue, and Titmouse did not, he expressed great admiration for Titmouse's play, and felt a great interest in being shown by him how to get a ball, now and then, into each pocket at one stroke, a masterly maneuver which Titmouse succeeded in two or three times, and Gammon not once, during their hour's play. 'Twas upon that occasion that they had the friendly conversation in which Titmouse made the suggestion we have already heard of, viz., that Gammon should immediately clap the screw upon Aubrey, with the view to squeezing out of him at least sufficient to pay the £10,000 bond, and their bill of costs, immediately: and Titmouse urged Gammon at once to send Aubrey packing after Yahoo to York Castle, as an inducement to an early settlement of the remainder. Gammon, however, assured Mr. Titmouse that in all probability Mr. Aubrey had not a couple of thousand pounds in the world.

" Well—that will do to begin with," said Titmouse, " and the rest *must* come sooner or later."

" Leave him to me, my dear Titmouse, or rather to Mr. Quirk—who'll *wring* him before he's done with him, I'll warrant him! But in the meanwhile, I'll work day and night, but I'll relieve you from this claim of Mr. Quirk, for, in fact, I have little or no real interest in the matter."

" You'll take a slapping slice out of the bond, eh? Aha, Mr. Gammon!—But what were you saying you'd do for me?"

" I repeat, that I am your only disinterested friend, Mr. Titmouse; I shall never see a hundred pounds of what is going into Mr. Quirk's hands, who, I must say, however, has richly earned what he's going to get by following my directions throughout. But I was saying that I had hit upon a scheme for ridding you of your difficulties. Though you have only just stepped into your property, and consequently people are very shy of advancing money on mortgage, if you'll only keep quiet and leave the affair entirely to me, I will undertake to get you a sum of possibly twenty thousand pounds."

"My eyes!" exclaimed Titmouse, excitedly; quickly, however, adding, with a sad air—"but then, what a lot of it will go to old Quirk?"

"He *is* rather a keen and hard—ahem! I own; but—"

"'Pon my life—couldn't we *do* the old gent?"

"On no consideration, Mr. Titmouse; it would be a fatal step for you—and indeed for me."

"What! and can he do anything, too? I thought it was only you."—The little fool had brought a glimpse of color into Gammon's cheek—but Titmouse's volatility quickly relieved his Prospero. "By the way—'pon my life—sha'n't I have to pay it all back again? There's a go! I hadn't thought of that."

"I shall first try to get it out of Mr. Aubrey," said Gammon, "and then out of another friend of yours. In the meanwhile we must not drop the Tag-rags just yet." They then got into a long and confidential conversation together, in the course of which, Titmouse happened to pop out a little secret of his, which till then he had managed to keep from Gammon, and which occasioned that gentleman a great and sudden inward confusion—one which it was odd that so keen an observer as Titmouse did not perceive indications of in the countenance of Gammon, viz., his—Titmouse's—fervent and disinterested love for Miss Aubrey. While he was rattling on with eager volubility upon this topic, Gammon, after casting about a little in his mind, as to how he should deal with this interesting discovery, resolved for the present to humor the notion, and got out of Titmouse a full and particular account of his original "*smite*"—the indelible impression she had made on his heart—the letter which he had addressed to her—[here Gammon's vivid fancy portrayed to him the sort of composition which must have reached Miss Aubrey, and he nearly burst into a gentle fit of laughter]—and, with a strange candor, or rather, to do him justice, with that frank simplicity which is characteristic of noble natures—he at length described his unlucky encounter with Miss Aubrey and her maid, in the winter; whereat Gammon felt a sort of sudden inward spasm, which by a sort of sympathy excited a twinging sensation in his right toe—but it passed away—'twas, after all, only a little juvenile indiscretion of Titmouse's; but Gammon, with rather a serious air, assured Titmouse that he had probably greatly endangered his prospects with Miss Aubrey.

"Eh? Why, devil take it! a'n't I going to offer to her,

though she's got nothing?" interrupted Titmouse, with astonishment.

"True!—Ah, I had lost sight of that. Well—if you will pledge yourself to address no more letters to her, nor take any steps to see her, without first communicating with me—I think I can promise—hem!" he looked archly at Titmouse.

"She's a most uncommon lovely gal!" — he simpered, sheepishly. The fact was that Gammon had conceived quite another scheme for Titmouse—wholly inconsistent with his pure, ardent, and enlightened attachment to Miss Aubrey; 'twas undoubtedly rather a bold and ambitious one, but Gammon did not despair; for he had that confidence in himself, and in his knowledge of human nature which always supported him in the most arduous and apparently hopeless undertakings.

There was a visible alteration for the better in the state of things at Yatton as soon as Messrs. Yahoo and Fitz-Snooks had been disposed of. Now and then a few of the distinguished people who had honored Mr. Titmouse by going out in procession to meet and welcome him, were invited to spend a day at Yatton; and generally quitted full of admiration of the dinner and wines they got, the unaffected good-nature and simplicity of their hospitable host, and the bland, composed, and intellectual deportment and conversation of Mr. Gammon. When rent-day arrived, Mr. Titmouse, attended by Mr. Gammon, made his appearance, from time to time, in the steward's room, and also in the hall, where, according to former custom, good substantial fare was set out for the tenants. They received him with a due respect of manner; but where was the cheerfulness, the cordiality, the rough, honest heartiness of days gone by? Few of them stayed to partake of the good things prepared for them, which greatly affected Mr. Griffiths and piqued Mr. Gammon; as for Titmouse, however, he said, with a laugh, "Curse 'em! let 'em leave it alone if they a'n't hungry!" and any faint feeling of mortification he might have experienced was dissipated by the amount of the sum paid into his banker's. Gammon was sensible that the scenes which had been exhibited at Yatton on the first night of his protégé's arrival had seriously injured him in the neighborhood and county, and was bent upon effacing, as quickly as possible, such unfavorable impressions by prevailing on Titmouse to "purge and live cleanly"—at all events for the present.

Let me pause now, for a moment, to inquire, ought not this favored young man to have felt happy? Here he was, master of a fine estate producing him a very splendid rent-roll; a de-

lightful residence, suggesting innumerable dear and dignified
associations connected with old English feeling; a luxurious
table, with the choicest liqueurs and wines in abundance;
might smoke the finest cigars that the world could produce,
from morning to night, if so disposed; had unlimited facilities
for securing a distinguished personal appearance, as far as
dress and decoration went; had all the amusements of the
county at his command; troops of servants, eager and obsequious in their attentions; horses and carriages of every description which he might have chosen to order out—had, in
short, all the "appliances and means to boot," which could
be desired or imagined by a gentleman of his station and
affluence.   Mr. Gammon was, though somewhat stern and
plain spoken, still a most sincere and powerful friend, deeply
and disinterestedly solicitous about his interests, and protecting him from villainous and designing adventurers; then he
had in prospect the brilliant mazes of fashionable life in town
—oh, in the name of everything that this world can produce,
and of the feelings it should excite, ought not Titmouse to
have enjoyed life—to have been happy?   Yet he was not; he
felt, quite independently of any constraint occasioned by the
presence of Mr. Gammon, full of deplorable ennui and wearisomeness inexpressible, and which nothing could alleviate but
the constant use of cigars and brandy and water.   On the first
Sunday after the departure of Fitz-Snooks, he was prevailed
upon to accompany the devout and exemplary Gammon to
church; where, barring a good many ill-concealed yawns and
constant fidgetiness, he conducted himself with tolerable decorum.   Yet still the style of his dress, his air, and his countenance, filled the little congregation with feelings of great astonishment when they thought that *that* was the new Squire
of Yatton, and for a melancholy moment contrasted him with
his predecessor, Mr. Aubrey.   As for the worthy vicar, Dr.
Tatham, Gammon resolved to secure his good graces, and succeeded.   He called upon him soon after having heard from
Titmouse of his, Yahoo, and Fitz-Snooks's encounter with Dr.
Tatham, and expressed profound concern on hearing of the
rude treatment he had encountered.   There was a gentleness
and affability—tempering at once and enhancing his evident
acuteness and knowledge of the world—which quite captivated
the little Doctor.   But, above all, the expressions of delicate
sympathy and regret with which he now and then alluded to
the late occupants of Yatton, and toward whom the stern requisitions of professional duty had caused him to play so odious
a part, and inquired about them, drew out almost all that was

in the little Doctor's heart concerning his departed friends. Gammon gazed with deep interest at the old blind stag-hound and feeble old Peggy, and seemed never tired of hearing the Doctor's little anecdotes concerning them. He introduced Titmouse to the vicar; and, in his presence, Gammon declared his (Titmouse's) hatred and contempt for the two fellows who were with him when first he saw Dr. Tatham; who thereupon banished from his heart all recollection of the conduct which had so deeply hurt his feelings. Gammon, on another occasion, infinitely delighted the Doctor by calling on a Monday morning, and alluding with evident interest and anxiety to certain passages in the Doctor's sermon of the day before, and which led to a very lengthened and interesting discussion. In consequence of what then transpired, the Doctor suddenly bethought himself of routing out an old sermon, which he had once preached before the judges of assize—and, during the week, he touched it up with a good deal of care for the ensuing Sunday—when he had the satisfaction of observing the marked and undeviating attention with which Mr. Gammon sat listening to him; and that candid inquirer after truth afterward stepped into the little vestry, and warmly complimented the Doctor upon his discourse. Thus it was that Doctor Tatham came to pen a postscript to one of his letters to Mrs. Aubrey, which I have formally alluded to, and of which the following is a copy:—

" P.S. By the way, the altered state of things at the Hall, I am of opinion, is entirely owing to the presence and the influence of a Mr. Gammon—one of the chief of Mr. Titmouse's solicitors, and to whom he seems very firmly attached. I have lived too long in the world to form hasty opinions, and am not apt to be deceived in my estimate of character; but I must say, I consider Mr. Gammon to be a very superior man, both in character, intellect, and acquirements. He possesses great acuteness and knowledge of the world, general information, a very calm and courteous address—and, above and beyond all, is a man of very enlightened religious feeling. He comes constantly to church, and presents a truly edifying example to all around, of decorum and attention. You would be delighted to hear the discussions we have had on points which my sermons have suggested to him. I preached one lately, specially aimed at him, which, thank God! I have every reason to believe has been attended with happy effects, and allayed some startling doubts which had been for years tormenting him. I am sure that my dear friend " (i. e. Mr. Aubrey) " would be

delighted with him. I had myself, I assure you, to overcome a
very strong prejudice against him—a thing I always love to
attempt, and have in a measure, in the present instance, succeeded. He speaks of you all frequently, with evident caution,
but, at the same time, respect and sympathy."

This postscript it was, which, as I have already intimated,
suggested to Mr. Aubrey to seek the interview with Gammon
which has been described, and during which it was frequently
present to his mind.

While, however, under the pressure of Mr. Gammon's presence and authority, Titmouse was for a brief while leading this
sober retired life at Yatton—why, he hardly knew, except that
Gammon willed it—a circumstance occurred which suddenly
placed him on the very highest pinnacle of popularity in
metropolitan society. I hardly know how to suppress my feelings of exultation, in retracing the rapid steps by which Mr.
Titmouse was transformed into a lion of the first magnitude.
Be it known that there was a MR. BLADDERY PIP, a fashionable novelist, possessed of most extraordinary versatility and
power; for he had, at the end of every nine months, during
the last nine years, produced a novel in three volumes—each
succeeding one eclipsing the splendor of its predecessor (in the
judgment of the most able and disinterested critics)—in the
" masterly structure of the plot "—the " vivid and varied delineation of character "—the " profound acquaintance with
the workings of the human heart "—" exquisite appreciation
of life in all its endless varieties "—" piercing but delicate
satire "—" bold and powerful denunciations of popular vices "
—" rich and tender domestic scenes "—" inimitable ease and
grace "—" consummate tact and judgment "—" reflection co-
extensive with observation "—" the style flowing, brilliant,
nervous, varied, picturesque," *et cetera, et cetera, et cetera.*
We have, in the present day, thank Heaven! at least a hundred such writers; but at the time about which I am writing,
Mr. Bladdery Pip was nearly alone in his glory. Such was the
man to whom it suddenly occurred, on glancing over the
newspaper report of the trial of *Doe on the demise of Titmouse*
v. *Jolter*, to make the interesting facts of the case the basis of
a new novel, on quite a new plan, and which was infinitely to
transcend all his former works, and, in fact, occasion quite a
revolution in that brilliant and instructive species of literature.
To work went Mr. Pip, within a day or two after the trial was
over, and in an incredibly short space of time had got to the
close of his labors. Practice had made him perfect, and given

him infinite facility in the production of first-rate writing. The spirited publisher (Mr. Bubble) then quickly set to work to " get the steam up " fully! ah! how secretly and skillfully! For some time there appeared numerous intimations in the daily papers that " the circles of ton " were " on the *qui vive* " with expectations of a certain, etc., etc., etc.—that " disclosures of a very extraordinary character " were being looked for—" attempts made to suppress," etc., etc.—" compromising certain distinguished," etc., and so forth; all these paragraphs being in the unquestionable *editorial* style, and *genuine* indications of a mysterious under-current of curiosity and excitement existing in those regions which were watched with reverential awe and constancy by those in the lower regions. As time advanced, more frequent and distinct became these titillations of the public palate—these intimations of what was going forward, and what might be shortly expected, from the appearance of the long-promised work. Take for instance the following, which ran the round of every newspaper, and wrought up to a high pitch the curiosity of half the fools in the country:—

" The efforts made to deprive the public of the interesting and peculiar scenes contained in the forthcoming novel, and to suppress it, have entirely failed, owing to the resolution of the gifted author, and the determination of the spirited publisher; and their only effect has been to stimulate and expedite their efforts. It will bear the exciting and *piquant* title— ' TIPPETIWINK;' and is said to be founded on the remarkable circumstances attending the recent trial of a great ejectment cause at York. More than one noble family's history is believed to be involved in some of the details which will be found in the forthcoming publication, for which, we are assured, there are already symptoms of an unprecedented demand. The ' favored few ' who have seen it predict that it will produce a prodigious sensation. The *happy audacity* with which facts are adhered to, will, we trust, not lead to the disagreeable consequences that are looked for in certain quarters with some anxiety. When we announce that the author is the gifted writer of ' THE SILVER SPOONS '—' SPINNACH '—' THE PIROUETTE '—' TITTLE-TATTLE '—' FITZ-GIBLETS '—' SQUINT,' etc., etc., etc., we trust we are violating no literary confidence. "

There was no resisting this sort of thing. In that day a skillfully directed play of puffs laid prostrate the whole reading and fashionable world, producing the excitement of which they affected to chronicle the existence. The artilleryman in

the present instance was a hack writer, hired by Mr. Bubble—
in fact, kept by him entirely—to perform services of this degrading description—and he sat from morning to night in a
back room on Mr. Bubble's premises, engaged in spinning out
these villainous and lying paragraphs concerning every work
published, or about to be published, by Mr. Bubble.   Then
he hit upon another admirable device.   He had seven hundred
copies printed off; and, allowing a hundred for a *first* edition,
he varied the title pages of the remaining six hundred by the
words— " *Second* Edition "—" *Third* Edition "—" *Fourth*
Edition " — " *Fifth* Edition " — " *Sixth* Edition " — and
" *Seventh* Edition."

By the time that the fourth edition had been announced,
there existed a real rage for the book; the circulating libraries
at the West End of the Town were besieged by applicants for
a perusal of the work; and " notices," " reviews," and " extracts " began to make their appearance with increasing frequency in the newspapers.   The idea of the work was admirable.   *Tippetiwink*, the hero, was a young gentleman of ancient family—an only child—kidnapped away in his infancy
by the malignant agency of " the demon *Mowbray*," a distant
relative, of a fierce temper and wicked character, who by these
means succeeded to the enjoyment of the estate, and would
have come, in time, to the honors and estates of the most
ancient and noble family in the kingdom, the *Earl of Frizzleton*.   Poor Tippetiwink was at length, however, discovered by
his illustrious kinsman, by mere accident, in an obscure capacity, in the employ of a benevolent linen-draper, *Black-bag*,
who was described as one of the most amiable and generous of
linen-drapers; and, after a series of wonderful adventures, in
which the hero displayed the most heroic constancy, the Earl
succeeded in reinstating his oppressed and injured kinsman in
the lofty station which he ought always to have occupied.
His daughter—a paragon of female loveliness—the *Lady
Sapphira Sigh-away*—evinced the deepest interest in the success of *Tippetiwink;* and at length—the happy result may be
guessed.   Out of these few and natural incidents, Mr. Bladdery Pip was pronounced at length, by those (*i. e.* the aforesaid newspaper scribes) who govern, if they do not indeed constitute public opinion, to have produced an imperishable record
of his genius, avoiding all the faults and combining all the
excellences of all his former productions.   The identity between Titmouse and *Tippetiwink*, Lord Dreddlington and *Lord
Frizzleton*, Lady Cecilia and *Lady Sapphira*, and Mr. Aubrey
and the " *the demon Mowbray*," was quickly established.   The

novel passed speedily into the tenth edition; an undoubted, and a very great sensation was produced; extracts descriptive of the persons, particularly that of Titmouse, and the Earl, and Lady Cecilia, figuring in the story, were given in the London papers, and thence transferred into those all over the country. The very author, Mr. Bladdery Pip, became a resuscitated lion, and dressing himself in the most exquisite style, had his portrait, looking most intensely intellectual, prefixed to the tenth edition. Then came portraits of '' Tittlebat Titmouse, Esq.'' (for which he had never sat), giving him large, melting eyes, and a very pensive face, and a most fashionable dress. The Earl of Dreddlington and Lady Cecilia became also a lion and lioness. Hundreds of opera-glasses were directed at once to their box; innumerable were the anxious salutations they received as they drove round the Park—and they drove round it three or four times as often as they had ever done before. 'Twas whispered that the King had read the book, and drank the Earl's health, under the name of Lord Frizzleton—while the Queen did the same for Lady Cecilia as Lady Sapphira. Their appearance produced a manifest sensation at both the levee and Drawing-room — Majesty looked blander than usual as they approached. Poor Lord Dreddlingon and Lady Cecilia mounted in a trice into the seventh heaven of rapturous excitement; for there was that buoyant quality about their heads which secured them a graceful and rapid upward motion. They were both unutterably happy, living in a gentle, delicious tumult of excited feelings. Irrepressible exultation glistened in the Earl's eyes; he threw an infinite deal of blandness and courtesy into his manners wherever he was and whomsoever he addressed, as if he could now easily afford it, confident in the inaccessible sublimity of his position. It was slightly laughable to observe, however, the desperate efforts he made to maintain his former frigid composure of manner—but in vain; his nervousness looked like a sudden, though gentle, accession of St. Vitus's dance. Innumerable were the inquiries made after Titmouse—his person—his manners—his character—his dress, by her friends, of Lady Cecilia. Young ladies tormented her for his autograph. 'Twas with her as if the level surface of the Dead Sea had been stirred by the freshening breeze.

When a thing of this sort is once fairly set going, where is it to end? When fashion does go mad, her madness is wonderful; and she very soon turns the world mad. Presently the young men appeared everywhere in black satin stocks, embroidered, some with flowers, and others with gold, and which went by the name of " *Titmouse Ties;*" and in hats, with high crows and rims a quarter of an inch in depth, called " *Tittle-bats.*" All the young blades about town, especially in the city, dressed themselves in the most extravagant style; an amazing impetus was given to the cigar trade—whose shops were crowded, especially at nights, and every puppy that walked the streets puffed cigar-smoke in your eyes. In short, pert and lively *Titmice* might be seen hopping about the streets in all directions. As for Tag-rag, wonders befell him. A paragraph in a paper pointed him out as the original of Black-bag, and his shop in Oxford Street as the scene of Titmouse's service. Thither quickly poured the tide of fashionable curiosity and custom. His business was soon trebled. He wore his best clothes every day, and smirked and smiled, and bustled about amidst the crowd in his shop, in a fever of excitement. He began to think of buying the adjoining premises and adding them to his own; and set his name down as a subscriber of half a guinea a year to the "Decayed Drapers' Association." These were glorious times for Mr. Tag-rag. He had to engage a dozen extra hands; there were seldom less than fifty or a hundred persons in his shop at once; strings of carriages before his door, sometimes two deep, and struggling between the coachmen for precedence; in fact, he believed that the MILLENNIUM (about which he had often heard wonders from Mr. Dismal Horror, who, it seemed, knew all about it—a fact of which he had first persuaded his congregation and then himself) was coming in earnest.

CHAPTER XXII.

THE undulations of the popular excitement in town were not long in reaching the calm retreat of Titmouse in Yorkshire. To say nothing of his having on several occasions observed artists busily engaged in sketching different views of the Hall and its surrounding scenery, and, on inquiry, discovered that they were sent from town for the express purpose of presenting to the public sketches of the "residence of Mr. Titmouse," a copy of the inimitable performance of Mr. Bladdery Pip—viz., "TIPPETIWINK" (tenth edition)—was sent down to Mr. Titmouse by Gammon; who also forwarded to him, from time to time, newspapers containing those paragraphs which identified Titmouse with the hero of the novel, and also testified the profound impression which it was making upon the thinking classes of the community. Was Titmouse's wish

to witness the ferment he had so unconsciously produced in the
metropolis unreasonable? Yatton was beginning to look
duller daily, even before the arrival of this stimulating intelligence from town; Titmouse feeling quite out of his element.
So—Gammon *non contradicente*—up came Titmouse to town.
If he had not been naturally a fool, the notice he attracted in
London must soon have made him one. He had been for coming up in a post-chaise and four; but Gammon, in a letter,
succeeded in dissuading him from incurring so useless an expense, assuring him that men of as high consideration as himself constantly availed themselves of the safe and rapid transit
afforded by the royal mail. His valet, on being appealed to,
corroborated Mr. Gammon's representations; adding, that the
late hour in the evening at which the mail arrived in town
would effectually shroud him from public observation. Giving strict and repeated orders to his valet to deposit him at
once " in a first-rate West-End hotel," the haughty lord of
Yatton, plentifully provided with cigars, stepped into the mail,
his valet perched upon the box seat. That functionary was
well acquainted with town, and resolved on his master's taking up his quarters at the Harcourt Hotel, in the immediate
vicinity of Bond Street. The mail passed the Peacock, at
Islington, about half past eight o'clock; and long before they
had reached even that point, the eager and anxious eye of Titmouse had been on the lookout for indications of his celebrity.
He was, however, compelled to own that both people and
places seemed much as usual—wearing no particular air of excitement. He was a little chagrined, till he reflected on the
vulgar ignorance of the movements of the great for which the
eastern regions of the metropolis were proverbial, and also on
the increasing duskiness of the evening, the rapid pace at which
the mail rattled along, and the circumstance of his being concealed inside. When his humble hackney-coach (its driver a
feeble old man, with a wisp of straw for a hat-band, and sitting on the rickety box like a heap of dirty old clothes, and
the flagging and limping horses looking truly miserable objects)
had rumbled slowly up to the lofty and gloomy door of the
Harcourt Hotel, it seemed to excite no notice whatever. A
tall waiter, in a plain suit of black evening dress, with his
hands stuck behind his coat-tails, continued standing in the
ample door-way, eying the plebeian vehicle which had drawn
up, with utter indifference—conjecturing, probably, that it
had come to the wrong door. With the same air of provoking
superciliousness he stood, till the valet, having jumped down
from his seat beside the driver, ran up, and in a peremptory

sort of way exclaimed, ' MR. TITMOUSE, of Yatton!'' This
stirred the waiter into something like energy.

"Here, sir!'' called out Mr. Titmouse, from within the
coach; and on the waiter's slowly approaching, he inquired, in a
sufficiently swaggering manner—"Pray, has the *Earl of Dreddlington* been inquiring for me here to-day?'' The words
seemed to operate like magic, converting the person addressed,
in a moment, into a slave—supple and obsequious.

" His lordship has not been here to-day, sir,'' he replied, in
a low tone, with a most courteous inclination, gently opening
the door and noiselessly letting down the steps. " Do you
alight, sir?''

" Why—a—have you room for me and my *fellow* there?''

" Oh, yes, sir! certainly.—Shall I show you into the coffee-
room, sir?''

" The coffee-room? Curse the coffee-room, sir! Do you
suppose I'm a commercial traveler? Show me into a private
room, sir!'' The waiter bowed low, and in silent surprise led
Mr. Titmouse to a very spacious and elegantly furnished apartment—where amidst the blaze of six wax-candles, and attended
by three waiters, he supped, an hour or two afterward, in great
state—retiring about eleven o'clock to his apartment, overcome with fatigue—and brandy and water; having fortunately
escaped the indignity of being forced to sit in the same room
where an English nobleman, one or two members of Parliament, and a couple of foreign princes, were sitting sipping
their claret, some writing letters, and others conning over the
evening papers. About noon, the next day, he called upon
the Earl of Dreddlington; and though, under ordinary circumstances, his lordship would have considered the visit rather unseasonable, he nevertheless received his fortunate and now truly
distinguished kinsman with the most urbane cordiality. At
the Earl's suggestion, and with Mr. Gammon's concurrence,
Titmouse, within about a week after his arrival in town, took
chambers in the Albany, together with the elegant furniture
which had belonged to their late tenant, a young officer of distinction, who had shortly before suddenly gone abroad upon a
diplomatic mission. Mr. Titmouse soon began to feel, in various ways, the distinction which was attached to his name—
commencing, as he did at once, the gay and brilliant life of a
man of high fashion, and under the august auspices of the
Earl of Dreddlington. Like as a cat, shod with walnut-shells
by some merry young scapegrace, doubtless feels more and
more astonished and excited at the clatter it makes in scamper-

ing up and down the bare echoing floors and staircases, so, in
some sort, was it with Titmouse, and the sudden and amazing
éclat with which all his appearances and movements were attended in the regions of fashion.   It is a matter of indifference
to a fool whether you laugh with him or at him; so as that you
do but laugh—an observation which will account for much of
the conduct both of Lord Dreddlington and Titmouse.   In
this short life and dull world, the thing is to create a *sensation*, never mind how; and every opportunity of doing so
should be gratefully seized hold of and improved to the uttermost, by those who have nothing else to do, and have an inclination to distinguish themselves from the common herd of
mankind.   Lord Dreddlington had got so inflated by the attention he excited that he set down everything he witnessed
to the score of deference and admiration.   His self-conceit
was so intense that it consumed every vestige of sense he had
about him.   He stood in solitary grandeur upon the lofty pillar
of his pride, inaccessible to ridicule, and insensible indeed of
its approach, like *vanity* " on a monument smiling at " *scorn*.
Indeed,

" His soul was like a star, and dwelt apart."

He did not conceive it possible for any one to laugh at *him*,
or anything he might choose to do or any one he might think fit
to associate with and introduce to the notice of society—which
kind office he forthwith performed for Titmouse, with whose
odd person and somewhat eccentric dress and demeanor, his
lordship (who imagined that the same operation was going on
in the minds of other people) was growing daily more familiar.
Thus that which had at first so shocked him, he got at length
thoroughly reconciled to, and began to suspect whether it was
not assumed by Titmouse, out of a daring scorn for the intrusive opinions of the world, which showed a loftiness of spirit
akin to his own.   Besides, in another point of view—suppose
the manner and appearance of Titmouse were ever so absurd,
so long as his lordship chose to tolerate them, who should venture to gainsay them?   So the Earl asked him frequently to
dinner, took him with them when his lordship and Lady
Cecilia went out in the evenings, gave him a seat in his carriage in going down to the House, and invited him to accompany him and Lady Cecilia when they either drove or rode
round the Park; as to which latter Titmouse's assiduous attention at the riding-school enabled him to appear on horseback
without being *glaringly* unequal to the management of his
horse, which, however, he once or twice contrived to give an

inclination toward backing upon those of Lady Cecilia and the
Earl. Titmouse happening to let fall, at the Earl's table, that
he had that day ordered an elegant chariot to be built for him,
his lordship intimated that a cab was the usual turn-out of a
bachelor man of fashion; whereupon Titmouse the next day
countermanded his order, and was fortunate enough to secure
a cab which had just been completed for a young nobleman
who was unable to pay for it, and whom, consequently, the
builder did not care about disappointing. He soon provided
himself with a great horse and a little tiger. What pen can
do justice to the feelings with which he first sat down in that
cab, yielding upon its well-balanced springs, took the reins
from his little tiger, and then heard him jump up behind! As
it was a trifle too early for the Park, he suddenly bethought
himself of exhibiting his splendors before the establishment of
Mr. Tag-rag; so he desired his little imp behind to run and
summon his valet, who in a trice came down; and in answer
to a question, " whether there wasn't something wanting from
a draper or hosier," was informed glibly that six dozen of best
cambric pocket-handkerchiefs, a dozen or two pair of white
kid gloves, half a dozen stocks, and various other items were
" wanting "—(*i. e.* by the valet himself, for Titmouse was
already sufficiently provided). Off, however, he drove, and
succeeded at length in reaching the Oxford Street establishment, before the door of which five or six carriages were standing. I should say that, at the moment of Mr. Titmouse's
strutting into that scene of his former miserable servitude, he
experienced a gush of delight which was sufficient to efface all
recollection of the misery, privation, and oppression endured
in his early days. There was presently an evident flutter
among the gentlemen engaged behind the counter—for,
thought they—it must be " the great Mr. Titmouse!" Tag-
rag, catching sight of him, bounced out of his little room, and
bustled up to him through the crowd of customers, bowing,
scraping, blushing, and rubbing his hands, full of pleasurable
excitement, and exhibiting the most profound obsequiousness.
" Hope you're well, sir," he commenced in a low tone, but instantly added, in a louder tone, observing that Titmouse chose
to appear to have come upon business, " what can I have the
honor to do for you, sir, this morning?" And handing him a
stool, Tag-rag, with a respectful air, received a very liberal
order from Mr. Titmouse, and minuted it down in his mem-
orandum-book.

" Dear me, sir, is that your cab?" said Tag-rag, as, having
accompanied Titmouse, bowing every step, to the door, they

both stood there for a moment. "I never saw such a beautiful turn-out in my life, sir—"

"Ya—a—s. Pretty well—pretty well; but that young rascal of mine dirtied one of his boots a little—dem him!" and he looked terrors at the tiger.

"Oh, dear!—so he has; shall I wipe it off, sir? *Do* let me—"

"No, it don't signify much. By the way, Mr. Tag-rag," added Mr. Titmouse, in a drawling way, "all well at—at— demme if I've not this moment forgot the name of your place in the country—"

"Satin Lodge, sir," said Tag-rag, meekly, but with infinite inward uneasiness.

"Oh—ay, to be sure. One sees, 'pon my soul, such a lot of places—but—all well?"

"All very well, indeed, sir; and constantly talking of you, sir."

"Ah—well! My compliments"—here he drew on his second glove, and moved toward his cab, Tag-rag accompanying him —"glad they're well. If ever I'm driving that way—good-day!" In popped Titmouse—crack went his whip—away darted the horse—Tag-rag following it with an admiring and anxious eye.

As Mr. Titmouse sat in his new vehicle, on his way to the Park, dressed in the extreme of the mode, his glossy hat perched sideways on his bushy, well-oiled, but somewhat mottled hair; his surtout lined with velvet; his full satin stock, spangled with inwrought gold flowers and with two splendid pins, connected together with delicate double gold chains; his shirt-collars turned down over his stock; his chased gold eye-glass stuck in his right eye; the stiff wristbands of his shirt turned back over his coat-cuffs; and his hands in snowy kid gloves, holding his whip and reins; when he considered the exquisite figure he must thus present to the eye of all beholders, and gave them credit for gazing at him with the same sort of feelings which similar sights had, but a few months before, excited in *his* despairing breast, his little cup of happiness was full, and even brimming over. This, though I doubt whether it was a just reflection, was still a very natural one; for he knew what his own feelings were, though not how weak and absurd they were; and of course judged of others by himself. If the Marquis of Whigborough, with his £200,000 a year, and 5,000 independent voters at his command, were on his way down to the House, absorbed with anxiety as to the effect of the final threat he was going to make to the Minister that. un-

less he had a few strawberry leaves promised him, he should
feel it his duty to reccrd his vote against the great bill for
" *Giving Every Body Every Thing*," which stood for a third
reading that evening; or if the great Duke of ——, a glance
of whose eye or a wave of whose hand would light up a
European war, and who might at that moment be balancing
in his mind the fate of millions of mankind, as depending upon
his fiat for peace or war—I say that if both or either of these
personages had passed or met Titmouse, in their cabs (which
they were mechanically urging onward, so absorbed the while
with their own thoughts, that they scarce knew whether they
were in a cab or a handbarrow, in which latter, had it been
before their gates, either of them might in his abstraction have
seated himself), Titmouse's superior acquaintance with human
nature assured him that the sight of his tip-top turn-out could
not fail of attracting their attention and nettling their pride.
Whether Milton, if cast on a desolate island, but with the
means of writing *Paradise Lost*, would have done so, had he
been certain that no human eye would ever peruse a line of it;
or whether Mr. Titmouse, had he been suddenly deposited, in
his splendid cab, in the midst of the desert of Sahara, with not
one of his species to fix an envying eye upon him, would nevertheless have experienced a great measure of satisfaction, I am
not prepared to say.   As, however, every condition of life has
its mixture of good and evil, so, if Titmouse had been placed
in the midst of the aforesaid desert at the time when he was
last before the reader, instead of dashing along Oxford Street,
he would have escaped certain difficulties and dangers which
he presently encountered.   Had an ape, not acquainted with
the science of driving, been put into Titmouse's place, he
would probably have driven much in the same style, though
he would have had greatly the advantage over his rival in respect of his simple and natural appearance; being, to the eye
of correct taste, " when unadorned, adorned the most," Mr.
Titmouse, in spite of the assistance to his sight which he derived from his neutral glass, was continually coming into
collision with the vehicles which met and passed him on his
way to Cumberland Gate.   He got into no fewer than four
distinct *rows* (to say nothing of the flying curses which he received in passing) between the point I have named and Mr.
Tag-rag's premises.   But as he was by no means destitute of
spirit, he sat in his cab, on these four occasions, cursing and
blaspheming like a little fiend, till he almost brought tears of
vexation into the eyes of one or two of his opponents (cads,
cab-drivers, watermen, hackney-coachmen, carters, stage-

coachmen, market-gardeners and draymen), who unexpectedly
found their own weapon—*i. e. slang*—wielded with such superior power and effect, for once in a way, by a swell—an aristocrat. The more manly of his opponents were filled with
secret respect for the possessor of such unsuspected powers.
Still it was unpleasant for a person of Mr. Titmouse's distinction to be engaged in these conflicts; and he would have given
the world to be able to conquer his conceit so far as to summon
his little tiger within, and surrender to him the reins. Such
a ridiculous confession of his own incapacity, however, he could
not think of, and he got into several little disturbances in the
Park; after which he drove home. The battered cab had to be
taken to the maker's, where the injuries it had sustained were
repaired for the trifling sum of forty pounds.

The eminent position secured for Titmouse by the masterly
genius of Mr. Bladdery Pip was continued to him, and
strengthened by much more substantial claims upon the respect of society, possessed by the first-named gentleman.
Rumor is a dame that always looks at objects through very
strong magnifying-glasses; and, guided by what she saw, she
soon gave out that Titmouse was patron of three boroughs,
had a clear rent-roll of thirty thousand a year, and had already
received nearly a hundred thousand pounds in hard cash from
the previous proprietor of his estates, as a compensation for
the back rents, which that usurper had been for so many years
in the receipt of. Then he was very near in succession to the
ancient and distinguished Barony of Drelincourt, and the
extensive estates thereto annexed. He was young; by no means
ill-looking; and was—unmarried. Under the mask of *naïveté*
and eccentricity, it was believed that he concealed great natural acuteness, for the purpose of ascertaining who were his
real and who only his pretended friends and well-wishers, and
that his noble relatives had given in to his little scheme for the
purpose of aiding him in the important discovery upon which
he was bent. Infinite effect was thus given to the Earl's in-
troductions. Wherever Titmouse went he found new and delightful acquaintances; and invitations to dinners, balls, routs,
soirées came showering daily into his rooms at the Albany,
where also were left innumerable cards, bearing names of very
high fashion. All who had daughters or sisters in the market
paid eager and persevering court to Mr. Titmouse, and still
more so to the Earl of Dreddlington and Lady Cecilia, his
august *sponsors;* so that—such being the will of that merry
jade Fortune—they who had once regarded him as an object
only of shuddering disgust and ineffable contempt, and had

been disposed to order their servants to show him out again
into the streets, were now, in a manner, *magnified and made
honorable* by means of their connection with him; or rather,
society, through his means, had become suddenly sensible of
the commanding qualities and pretensions of the Earl of Dreddlington and the Lady Cecilia. In the ball-room—at Almack's
even—how many young men, handsome, accomplished, and of
real consequence, applied in vain for the hand of haughty
beauty, which Mr. Titmouse had only to ask for, and have!
Whose was the opera-box into which he might not drop as a
welcome visitor, and be seen lounging in envied familiarity
with its fair and brilliant inmates? Were there not mothers
of high fashion, of stately pride, of sounding rank, who would
have humbled themselves before Titmouse, if thereby he could
have been brought a suitor to the feet of one of their daughters? But it was not over the fair sex alone that the magic of
Mr. Titmouse's name and pretensions had obtained this great
and sudden ascendency; he excited no small attention among
men of fashion—great numbers of whom quickly recognized
in him one very fit to become their butt and their dupe. What
signified it to men secure of their own position in society, that
they were seen openly associating with one so outrageously absurd in his dress—and vulgar and ignorant beyond all example?
So long as he bled freely and trotted out briskly and willingly,
his eccentricities could be not merely tolerated, but humored.
Take, for instance, the gay and popular MARQUIS GANTS-
JAUNES DE MILLEFLEURS; but he is worth a word or two of
description, because of the position he had contrived to acquire
and retain, and the influence which he managed to exercise over
a considerable portion of London society. The post he was anxious to secure was that of the leader of *ton;* and he wished it
to appear that that was the sole object of his ambition.
While, however, he affected to be entirely engrossed by such
matters as devising new and exquisite variations of dress and
equipage, he was, in reality, bent upon graver pursuits—upon
gratifying his own licentious tastes and inclinations with secrecy
and impunity. He despised folly, cultivating and practicing
only vice, in which he was, in a manner, an epicure. He was
now about his forty-second year, had been handsome, was of
bland and fascinating address, variously accomplished, of exquisite tact, of most refined taste; there was a slight fullness
and puffiness about his features, an expression in his eye which
spoke of *satiety*—and the fact was so. He was a very proud,
selfish, heartless person; but these qualities he contrived to
disguise from many of even his most intimate associates. An

object of constant anxiety to him was to ingratiate himself with the younger and weaker branches of the aristocracy, in order to secure a distinguished status in society; and he succeeded. To gain this point, he taxed all his resources; never were so exquisitely blended, as in his instance, with a view to securing his *influence,* the qualities of dictator and parasite; he always appeared the *agreeable equal* of those whom, for his life, he dared not seriously have offended. He had no fortune; no visible means of making money—did not sensibly sponge upon his friends, nor fall into conspicuous embarrassments, yet he always lived in luxury—without money, he in some inconceivable manner always contrived to be in the possession of money's worth. He had a magical power of soothing querulous tradesmen. He had a knack of always keeping himself, his clique, his sayings and doings, before the eye of the public, in such a manner as to satisfy it that he was the acknowledged leader of fashion; yet it was really no such thing; it was a false fashion, there being all the difference between him and a man of real consequence in society that there is between mock and real pearl, between paste and diamond. It was true that young men of sounding name and title were ever to be found in his train, thereby giving real countenance to one from whom they fancied that they themselves derived celebrity; thus enabling him to effect a lodgment in the outskirts of aristocracy; but he could not penetrate inland, so to speak, any more than foreign merchants can advance further than to Canton in the dominions of the Emperor of China. He was only tolerated in the regions of real aristocracy—a fact of which he had a very galling consciousness, though it did not apparently disturb his equanimity or interrupt the systematic and refined sycophancy by which alone he could secure his precarious position.

With some sad exceptions, I think that Great Britain has reason to be proud of her aristocracy. I do not speak now of those gaudy flaunting personages of either sex, who, by their excesses or eccentricities, are eternally obtruding themselves, their manners, dress and equipage upon the offended ear and eye of the public, but of those who occupy their exalted sphere in simplicity, in calmness and in unobtrusive dignity and virtue. I am no flatterer or idolater of the aristocracy. I have a profound sense of the necessity and advantage of the *institution;* but I shall ever pay its members personally an honest homage only, after a stern and keen scrutiny into their personal pretensions; thinking of them ever in the spirit of those memorable words of Scripture—" *Unto whomsoever much is given, of him shall be much required,*" and that not hereafter

only, but here also. No one would visit their faults and follies
with a more unsparing severity than I; yet, making all just
allowances for their peculiar perils and temptations, exposed
as they are, especially at the period of their entrance upon life,
to sedulous and systematic sycophancy, too often also to artful
and designing profligacy. Can, however, anything excite
greater indignation and disgust in the mind of a thoughtful
and independent observer than the instances occasionally exhibited of persons of rank presumptuously imagining that they
enjoy a sort of prescriptive immunity from the consequences
of misconduct? An insolent or profligate nobleman is a spectacle becoming every day more dangerous to exhibit in this
country; of that he may be assured.

Such are *my* sentiments—those of a contented member of
the middle classes, with whom are all his best and dearest sympathies, and who feels as stern a pride in his "Order," and
determination to "*stand by it,*" too, as ever was felt or
avowed by the haughtiest aristocrat for *his;* of one who with
very little personal acquaintance with the aristocracy, has yet
had opportunities of observing their conduct; and sincerely and
cheerfully expresses his belief that very, very many of them
are worthy of all that they enjoy—are bright patterns of honor,
generosity, loyalty and virtue; that, indeed, of by far the
greater proportion of them it may be said that they

> " Have borne their faculties so meek—have been
> So clear in their great office, that their virtues
> Will plead like angels."

And finally, I say these are the sentiments of one who, if their
order were in jeopardy, would, with the immense majority of
his brethren of the middle classes, freely shed his blood in defense of that order; for its preservation is essential to the well-
being of society, and its privileges are really ours.

To return, however, to the Marquis. The means to which,
as I have above explained, he resorted for the purpose, secured
him a certain species of permanent popularity. In matters of
dress and equipage he could really set the fashion; and being
something of a practical humorist, and desirous of frequent
exhibitions of his power, in order to enhance his pretensions
with his patrons—and also greatly applauded and indulged
by the trades-people profiting by the vagaries of fashion, he
was capricious in the exercise of his influence. He seized the
opportunity of the advent of my little hero, to display his
powers very decisively! He waved his wand over Titmouse,
and instantly transformed a little ass into a great lion. 'Twas

the Marquis, with his own hand, sketched off, from fancy, the portrait of Titmouse, causing it to be exhibited in almost every book-seller's shop window. He knew that, if he chose to make his appearance once or twice in Parks and leading streets and squares, in—for instance—the full and imposing evening costume of the clown at the theater, with painted face, capacious white inexpressibles, and tasteful cap and jacket—within a few days' time several thousands of clowns would make their appearance about town, turning it into a vast pantomime. Could a more striking instance of the Marquis's power in such matters have been exhibited, than that which had actually occurred in the case of Titmouse? Soon after the novel of Tippetiwink had rendered our friend an object of public interest, the Marquis happened, somewhere or other, to catch a glimpse of the preposterous little ape. His keen eye caught all Titmouse's personal peculiarities at a glance; and a day or two afterward appeared in public, a sort of splendid edition of Titmouse—with quizzing-glass stuck in his eye and cigar in his mouth; taper ebony cane; tight surtout, with the snowy corner of a white handkerchief peeping out of the outside breast-pocket; hat with scarce any rim, perched slantingly on his head; satin stock, bespankled with inwrought gold flowers; shirt-collar turned down; and that inimitable strut of his!—'Twas enough; the thoughtful young men about town were staggered for a moment; but their senses soon returned. The Marquis had set the thing going; and within three days' time, that bitter wag had called forth a flight of *Titmice* that would have reminded you, for a moment, of the visitation of locusts brought upon Egypt by Moses. Thus was brought about the state of things recorded toward the close of the preceding chapter of this history. As soon as the Marquis had seen a few of the leading fools about town fairly in the fashion, he resumed his former rigid simplicity of attire, and, accompanied by a friend or two in his confidence, walked about the town enjoying his triumph, witnessing his trophies — "Tittlebats" and "Titmouse ties" filling the shop windows on the week days and peopling the streets on Sundays. The Marquis was not long in obtaining an introduction to the quaint little *millionaire*, whose reputation he had, conjointly with his distinguished friend, Mr. Bladdery Pip, contributed so greatly to extend. Titmouse, who had often heard of him, looked upon him with inconceivable reverence, and accepted an invitation to one of the Marquis's *recherché* Sunday dinners, with a sort of tremulous ecstasy. Thither, on the appointed day, he went accordingly, and, by his original humor, afforded infinite amusement

to the Marquis's other guests. 'Twas lucky for Titmouse that,
getting dreadfully drunk very early in the evening, he was
quite incapacitated from accompanying his brilliant and good-
natured host to one or two scenes of fashionable entertainment,
as had been arranged, in St. James's Street.

Now, do let us pause to ask whether this poor little creature
was not to be pitied! Did he not seem to have been plucked
out of his own sphere of safe and comparatively happy obscurity, only in order to become every one's game—an object
of everybody's cupidity and cruelty? May he not be compared
to the flying-fish, who, springing out of the water to avoid his
deadly pursuer there, is instantly pounced upon by his ravenous assailants in the air? In the lower and in the upper
regions of society, was not this the condition of poor Tittlebat
Titmouse? Was not his long-coveted advancement merely a
transition from scenes of vulgar to refined rapacity? Had he,
ever since " *luck* had happened to him," had one single *friend*
to whisper in his ear one word of disinterested counsel? In
the splendid regions which he had entered, who regarded him
otherwise than as a legitimate object for plunder or ridicule,
the latter disguised by the *designing* only? Was not even his
dignified and exemplary old kinsman, the Earl of Dreddlington, Right Honorable as he was, influenced solely by considerations of paltry self-interest? Had he not his own ridiculous
and mercenary designs to accomplish, amidst all the attentions
he vouchsafed to bestow upon Titmouse? 'Twas, I think, old
Hobbes of Malmesbury, who held that the natural state of
mankind was one of war with each other. One really sees a
good deal in life, especially after tracing the progress of society,
that would seem to give some color to so strange a notion.
'Twas of course at first a matter of downright fisticuffs—of
physical strife, occasioned, in a great measure, by our natural
tendencies, according to him of Malmesbury, and aggravated
by the desire everybody had to take away from everybody else
what he had. In the progress of society we have, in a measure, dropped the physical part of the business; and instead of
punching, scratching, kicking, biting, and knocking down one
another, still true to the original principles of our nature, we
are all endeavoring to circumvent one another; everybody is
trying to take everybody in; the moment that one of us has
got together a thing or two, he is pounced upon by his neighbor, who in his turn falls a prey to another, and so on in endless succession. We can not effectually help ourselves, though
we are splitting our heads to discover devices, by way of laws,
to restrain this propensity of our nature; it will not do: we

are all overreaching, cheating, swindling, robbing one another, and, if necessary, are ready to maim and murder one another in the prosecution of our designs. So is it with nations as with individuals, and minor collections of individuals. Truly, truly, we are a precious set, whether the sage of Malmesbury be right or wrong in his speculations!—

The more that the Earl and Lady Cecilia perceived of Titmouse's popularity, the more eager were they in parading their connection with him, and openly investing him with the character of a *protégé*. In addition to this, the Lady Cecilia had begun to have now and then a glimmering notion of the objects which the Earl was contemplating. If the Earl took him down to the House of Lords, and having secured him a place at the bar, would, immediately on entering, walk up to him, and be seen for some time condescendingly pointing out to him the different peers by name, as they entered, and explaining to his intelligent auditor the period, and mode, and cause, of the creation and accession of many of them to their honors, and also the forms, ceremonies, and routine of business in the Houses; so Lady Cecilia was not remiss in availing herself, in her way, of the little opportunities which presented themselves. She invited him, for instance, one day early in the week to accompany them to church on the ensuing Sunday, and during the interval gave out among her intimate friends that they might expect to see Mr. Titmouse in her papa's pew. He accepted the invitation; and, on the arrival of the appointed hour, might have been seen in the Earl's carriage, driving to afternoon service at the Reverend MORPHINE VELVET's chapel—Rosemary Chapel, near St. James's Square. 'Twas a fashionable chapel, a chapel *of Ease ;* rightly so called, for it was a very *easy* mode of worship, discipline, and doctrine that was there practiced and inculcated. If I may not irreverently adopt the language of Scripture, but apply it very differently, I should say Mr. Morphine Velvet's yoke was very " easy," his burden very " light." He was a popular preacher; middle-aged; sleek, serene, solemn in his person and demeanor. He had a very gentleman-like appearance in the pulpit and reading-desk. There was a sort of soothing, winning, elegance and tenderness in the tone and manner in which he *prayed* and *besought* his dearly beloved brethren, as many as were there present, to accompany him, their bland and graceful pastor, to the throne of the heavenly grace. Fit leader was he of such a flock! He read the prayers remarkably well, in a quiet and subdued tone, very distinctly, and with marked emphasis and intonation, having sedulously

studied how to read the service under a crack theatrical teacher
of elocution, who had given him several " points "—in fact, a
new reading entirely of one of the clauses in the Lord's Prayer,
and which, he had the gratification of perceiving, produced a
striking, if not, indeed, a startling effect.   On the little finger
of the hand which he used most was to be observed the sparkle
of a diamond ring; and there was a sort of careless grace in
the curl of his hair, which it had taken his hair-dresser at least
half an hour, before Mr. Velvet's leaving home for his chapel,
to effect.   In the pulpit he was calm and fluent.   He rightly
considered that the pulpit ought not to be the scene for attempting intellectual display; he took care, therefore, that
there should be nothing in his sermons to arrest the understanding, or unprofitably occupy it, addressing himself entirely
to the feelings and fancy of his cultivated audience, in frequently interesting imaginative compositions.   On the occasion
I am speaking, he took for his text a fearful passage of Scripture, 2 Cor. iv. 3.—*" But if our Gospel be hid, it is hid to
them that are lost."*   If any words were calculated to startle
such a congregation as was arrayed before Mr. Velvet, out of
their guilty and fatal apathy, were not these?   Ought not their
minister to have looked round him and trembled?   So one
would have thought; but *" dear* Mr. Velvet "* knew his mission and his flock better.   He presented them with an elegant
description of heaven, with its crystal battlements, its jasper
walls, its buildings of pure gold, its foundations of precious
stones; its balmy air, its sounds of mysterious melody, its overflowing fullness of everlasting happiness—amid which friends,
parted upon earth by the cruel stroke of death, recognize and
are reunited to each other, never more to pronounce the agonizing word " adieu!"   And would his dear hearers be content to
lose all this—content to *enjoy the pleasures of sin for a season?*
Forbid it, eternal mercy!   But lest a strain like this should
disturb or distress his hearers, he took the opportunity to en-
force and illustrate the consolatory truth that—

> " Religion never was design'd
> To make our pleasures less;"

and presently resuming the thread of his discourse, went on to
speak of the really serious consequences attending persevering
indifference to religion; and proceeded to give striking instances of it in—the merchant in his counting-house, and on
'Change; the lawyer in his office; the tradesman in his shop;
the operative in the manufactory; showing how each was absorbed in his calling—*laboring for the meat which perisheth,*

till he had lost all appetite and relish for spiritual food, and
never once troubled himself about " the momentous concerns
of hereafter!'' Upon these topics he dwelt with such force and
feeling that he sent his distinguished congregation away—those
of them, at least, who could retain any recollection of what
they had heard for five minutes after entering their carriages
—fearing that there was a very black lookout, indeed, for—
the kind of persons that Mr. Velvet had mentioned—tailors,
milliners, mercers, jewelers, and so forth: and who added
graver offenses, and of a more positive character, to the misconduct which had been pointed out—in their extortion and
their rapacity! Would that some of them had been present!
—Thus was it that dear Mr. Velvet sent away his hearers overflowing with Christian sympathy; very well pleased with Mr.
Velvet, but infinitely better pleased with themselves. The
deep impression which he had made was evidenced by a note
he received that evening from the Duchess of Broadacre, most
earnestly begging permission to copy his " beautiful sermon,"·
in order to send it to her sister, Lady Belle Almacks, who
(through early dissipation) was ill of a decline at Naples.
About that time, I may as well here mention, there came out
an engraved portrait of " the Rev. Morphine Velvet, M. A.,
Minister of Rosemary Chapel, St. James's ''—a charming
picture it was, representing the aforesaid Mr. Velvet in pulpit
costume and attitude, with hands gracefully outstretched, and
his face directed upward with a heavenly expression; suggesting to you the possibility that some fine day, when his hearers
least expected it, he might gently rise out of his pulpit into
the air, like Stephen, with heaven open before him, and *be no
more seen of men !*

Four or five carriages had to set down before that containing the Earl of Dreddlington, Lady Cecilia, and Mr. Titmouse,
could draw up; by which time there had accumulated as many
in its rear, so eager were the pious aristocrats to get into this
holy retreat. As Titmouse, holding his hat and cane in one
hand, while with the other he arranged his hair, strutted up
the center aisle, following the Earl and Lady Cecilia, he could
hardly repress the exultation with which he thought of a former
visit of his to that very chapel some two years before. *Then*,
on attempting to enter the body of the chapel, the vergers had
politely but firmly repulsed him; on which, swelling with
vexation, he had ascended to the gallery, where, after being
kept standing for ten minutes at least, he had been beckoned
by the pew-opener toward, and squeezed into, the furthermost
pew, close at the back of the organ, and in which said pew

were only four footmen besides himself; and if he was disgusted with his mere contiguity, guess what must have been his
feelings when the footman nearest to him good-naturedly
forced upon him a part of his prayer-book, which Titmouse,
ready to spit in his face, held with his finger and thumb, as
though it had been the tail of a snake. *Now,* how changed
was all! He had become an aristocrat: in his veins ran some
of the richest and oldest blood in the country; his brow might
ere long be graced by the coronet which King Henry II. had
placed upon the brow of the founder of his family, some seven
hundred years before; and a tall footman, with powdered head,
glistening silver shoulder-knot, and sky-blue livery, and carrying in a bag the gilded implements of devotion, was humbly
following behind him! What a remarkable and vivid contrast
between his present and his former circumstances, was present
at that moment to his reflecting mind! As he stood, his hat
covering his face, in an attitude of devotion—" I wonder,"
thought he, " what all these nobs and swells would say if they
knew how I had worshiped here on the last time?" and again
—" 'Pon my life what would I give for—say Huckaback—to
see me just now!" What an elegant and fashionable air the
congregation wore! Surely there must be something in religion when people such as were around him came so punctually to church, and behaved so seriously! The members of
that congregation were, indeed, exemplary in their strict discharge of their public religious duties! Scarce one of them
was there that had not been at the opera till half past twelve
overnight; the dulcet notes of the singers still thrilling in their
ears, the graceful attitudes of the dancers still present to their
eyes; every previous night of the week had they been engaged
in the brilliant ball-room, and whirled in the mazes of the
voluptuous waltz, or glittering in the picturesque splendor of
fancy dress, till three, four, or five o'clock in the morning:
yet here they were in the house of God, in spite of all their exhaustion, testified by the heavy eye, the ill-suppressed yawn,
the languor and ennui visible in their countenances, prepared
to accompany their polite pastor, " with a pure heart and
humble voice, unto the throne of the heavenly grace," to acknowledge, with lively emotion, that they " had followed too
much the devices and desires of their own hearts;" praying for
" mercy upon them, miserable offenders," that God would
" restore them, being penitent," so that " they might thereafter lead a godly, righteous, and sober life." Here they
were, punctual to their time, decorous in manner, devout in
spirit, earnest and sincere in repentance and good resolutions

—knowing, nevertheless the while, how would be spent the remainder of the season—of their *lives ;* and yet resolving to attend the affectionate entreaties of Mr. Velvet, to be "*not hearers only, but doers of the word.*" Generally, I should say, that the state of mind of most, if not all of those present, was analogous to that of persons who go and sit in the pump-room to drink the Bath or Cheltenham waters. Everybody did the same thing; and each hoped that, while sitting in his pew, what he heard would, like what he drank at the pump-room in some secret mode of operation, insensibly benefit the hearer, without subjecting him to any unpleasant restraint or discipline—without requiring active exertion, or inconvenience, or sacrifice. This will give you a pretty accurate notion of Lord Dreddlington's state of mind upon the present occasion. With his gold glasses on, he followed with his eye, and also with his voice, every word of the prayers, with rigid accuracy and unwavering earnestness; but as soon as Mr. Velvet had mounted the pulpit, and risen to deliver his discourse, the Earl quietly folded his arms, closed his eyes, and in an attentive posture, dignifiedly composed himself to sleep. Lady Cecilia sat beside him perfectly motionless during the whole sermon, her eyes fixed languidly upon the preacher. As for Titmouse, he bore it pretty well for about five minutes; then he pulled his gloves off and on at least twenty times; then he twisted his handkerchief round his fingers; then he looked with a vexed air at his watch; then he stuck his glass in his eye and stared about him. By the time that Mr. Velvet had ceased, Tit-mouse had conceived a very great dislike to him, and was indeed in a fretful humor. But when the organ struck up, and they rose to go; when he mingled with the soft, crushing, flut-tering, rustling satin-clad throng—nodding to one, bowing to another, and shaking hands with a third, he felt "himself again." The only difference between him and those around him was, that they had learned to bear with calm fortitude what had so severely tried his temper. All were glad to get out: the crash of carriages at the door was music in their ears —the throng of servants delightful objects to their eyes—they were, in short, in the dear world again, and breathed as freely as ever.

Mr. Titmouse took leave of the Earl and Lady Cecilia at their carriage door, having ordered his cab to be in waiting— as it was; and entering it, he drove about leisurely till it was time to think of dressing for dinner. He had accepted an in-vitation to dine with a party of officers in the Guards, and a merry time they had on't. Titmouse in due time got blind drunk; and then one of his companions, rapidly advancing toward the same happy state, seized the opportunity, with a burned cork, to blacken poor Titmouse's face all over—who, therefore, was pronounced to bear a very close resemblance to one of the black boys belonging to the band of the regiment, and thus afforded as much fun to his friends when dead drunk as when sober. As he was quite incapable of taking care of himself, they put a servant with him into his cab (judging his little tiger to be unequal to the responsibility).

Titmouse passed a sad night, but got better toward the middle of the ensuing day; when he was sufficiently recovered to receive two visitors. One of them was young Lord Frederic Feather (accompanied by a friend), both of whom had dined in company with Titmouse overnight; and his lordship it was, who, having decorated Titmouse's countenance in the way I have described—so as to throw his valet almost into fits on seeing him brought home—imagining it might possibly come to his ears who it was that had done him such a favor, had come to acknowledge and apologize for it frankly and promptly. When, however, he perceived what a fool he had got to deal with, he suddenly changed his course—declared that Titmouse had not only done it himself, but had then presumed to act similarly toward his lordship, whose friend corroborated the charge—and they had called to receive, in private, an apology. Titmouse's breath seemed taken away on first hearing this astounding version of the affair. He swore he had done nothing of the sort, but had suffered a good deal; dropping, however, a little on observing the stern looks of his companions, he protested that " he did not recollect " anything of the sort; on which they smiled good-naturedly, and said that *that* was very possible. Then Titmouse made the requisite apology; and thus this " awkward affair " ended. Lord Frederic continued for some time with Titmouse in pleasant chat; for he foresaw that, " hard-up " as he frequently was, Mr. Titmouse was a friend who might be exceedingly serviceable. In fact, poor Lord Frederic could, on that very occasion, have almost gone on his knees for a check of Mr. Titmouse upon his bankers for three or four hundred pounds. Oh, thought that noble young spark—what would *he* have given to be in Titmouse's position, with his twenty thousand a year, and a hundred thousand pounds of hard cash! But as the reader well knows, poor Titmouse's resources, ample as they were, were upon a far less splendid scale than was supposed. Partly from inclination, and partly through a temporary sense of embarrassment, occasioned by the want of ready money, Titmouse did

not spend a tenth part of the sum which it had been everywhere supposed he could disburse freely on all hands, and this
occasioned him to be given credit for possessing all that rumor
assigned to him; and, moreover, for a disposition not to squan-
der it.   He had on several occasions been induced to try his
hand at écarté, rouge-et-noir, and hazard; and had, on the
first occasion or two, been a little hurried away through deference to his distinguished associates, and bled rather freely; but
when he found that it was a matter of business—that he must
pay—and felt his purse growing lighter, and his pocket-book,
in which he kept his bank-notes, rapidly shrinking in dimensions as the evening wore on, he experienced vivid alarm and
disgust, and an increasing disinclination to be victimized; and
his aversion to play was infinitely strengthened by the frequent
cautions of his distinguished and disinterested monitor, the
Earl of Dreddlington.

But there was one step in Mr. Titmouse's upward progress
which he presently took, and which is worthy of special mention; I mean his presentation at court by the Earl of Dreddlington.   The necessity for such a step was explained to Titmouse, by his illustrious kinsman, a day or two after the
appearance of the ordinary official announcement of the next
levee.   This momentous affair was broached by the Earl, one
day after dinner, with an air of deep anxiety and interest.   Indeed, had that stately and solemn old simpleton been instruct-
ing his gaping protégé in the minutely awful etiquettes requisite for the due discharge of his duties as an embassador sent
upon a delicate and embarrassing mission to the court of his
Sacred Majesty the King of Sulkypunctilio, he could not have
appeared more penetrated by a sense of the responsibility he
was incurring.   He commenced by giving Titmouse a very
long history of the origin and progress of such ceremonies, and
a minute account of the practical manner of their observance,
all of which, however, was to Titmouse only like breathing
upon a mirror—passing as quickly out of one ear as it had entered into the other.   When, however, the Earl came to the
point of dress, Titmouse was indeed " a thing all ear, all eye,"
his faculties being stimulated to their utmost.   The next
morning he hurried off to his tailor, to order a court-dress.
When it had been brought to his rooms, and he had put it on,
upon returning to his room in his new and imposing costume,
and glancing at his figure in the glass, his face fell; he felt infinitely disappointed.   It is to be remembered that he had not
on lace ruffles at his coat cuffs, nor on his shirt front.   After
gazing at himself for a few moments in silence, he suddenly

snapped his fingers, and exclaimed to the tailor, who, with the valet, was standing beside him, " Curse me, if I like this thing at all!''

" Not like it, sir!'' exclaimed Mr. Clipclose, with astonishment.

" No, I don't, demme! Is *this* a court-dress? It's a quaker's made into a footman's! 'Pon my soul, I look the exact image of a footman; and a devilish vulgar one, too!'' The two individuals beside him turned suddenly away from him, and from one another, and from their noses there issued the sounds of ill-suppressed laughter.

" Oh, sir—I beg a thousand pardons!''—quickly exclaimed Mr. Clipclose, " what can I have been thinking about? There's the sword—we've quite forgot it!''

" Ah—'pon my life, I thought there was *something* wrong!'' quoth Titmouse, as Mr. Clipclose, having brought the sword from the other end of the room, where he had laid it upon entering, buckled it on.

" I flatter myself that *now*, sir ''—commenced he.

" Ya—as—Quite the correct thing! 'Pon my soul, most uncommon striking!''—exclaimed Titmouse, glancing at his figure in the glass with a triumphant smile. " Isn't it odd, now, that this sword should make all the difference between me and a footman, by Jove?'' Here his two companions were seized with a simultaneous fit of coughing.

" Ah, ha—it's *so*, a'n't it?'' continued Titmouse, his eyes glued to the glass.

" Certainly, sir: it undoubtedly gives—what shall I call it? a grace—a finish—a sort of commanding—especially to a figure that becomes it ''—he continued, with cool assurance, observing that the valet understood him. " But—may I, sir, take so great a liberty? If you are not accustomed to wear a sword—as I think you said you had not been at court before— I beg to remind you that it will require particular care to manage it, and prevent it from getting between—''

" Demme, sir!'' exclaimed Titmouse, starting aside with an offended air—" d'ye think I don't know how to manage a sword? By all that's tremendous ''—and plucking the taper weapon out of its scabbard, he waved it over his head; and throwing himself into the first position—he had latterly paid a good deal of attention to fencing—and with rather an excited air, he went through several of the preliminary movements. 'Twas a subject for a painter, and exhibited a very striking spectacle—as an instance of power silently concentrated, and ready to be put forth upon an adequate occasion. The tailo and the valet, who stood separate from each other, and at a safe and respectful distance from Mr. Titmouse, gazed with silent admiration at him.

When the great day arrived—Titmouse having thought of scarce anything else in the interval, and teased every one he met with his endless questions and childish observations on the subject—he drove up, at the appointed hour, to the Earl of Dreddlington's, whose carriage, with an appearance of greater state than usual about it, was standing at the door. On alighting from his cab, he skipped so nimbly upstairs that he could not have had time to observe the amusement which his figure occasioned even to the well-disciplined servants of the Earl of Dreddlington. Much allowance ought to have been made for them. Think of Mr. Titmouse's little knee-breeches, white silks, silver shoe-buckles, shirt ruffles and frills, coat, bag, and sword; and his hair plastered up with bear's grease, parted down the middle of his head, and curling out boldly over each temple; and his open countenance irradiated with a subdued smile of triumph and excitement! On entering the drawing-room, he beheld a really striking object—the Earl in court costume, wearing his general's uniform, with all his glistening orders, standing in readiness to set off, and holding in his hand his hat, with its snowy plumes. His posture was at once easy and commanding. Had he been standing to Sir Thomas Lawrence, he could not have disposed himself more effectively. Lady Cecilia was sitting on the sofa, leaning back, and languidly talking to him; and from the start they both gave on Titmouse's entrance, it was plain that they could not have calculated upon the extraordinary transmogrification he must have undergone in assuming court costume. For a moment or two, each was as severely shocked as when his absurd figure had first presented itself in that drawing-room. "Oh, heavens!" murmured Lady Cecilia: while the Earl seemed struck dumb by the approaching figure of Titmouse. That gentleman, however, was totally changed from the Titmouse of a former day. He had now acquired a due sense of his personal importance, a just confidence in himself. Greatness had lost its former petrifying influence over him. And, as for his appearance on the present occasion, he had grown so familiar with it, as reflected in his glass, that it never occurred to him as being different with others who beheld him for the first time. At the same time that candor upon which I pride myself urges me to state, that when Titmouse beheld the military air and superb equipments of the Earl—notwithstanding that Titmouse, too, wore a sword—he felt himself *done.* He ad-

vanced, however, pretty confidently—bobbing about, first to
Lady Cecilia, and then to the Earl; and after a hasty salutation—" 'Pon my life, my lord, I hope it's no offense, but your
lordship *does* look most *particular* fine." The Earl made no
reply, but inclined toward him magnificently—not seeing the
meaning and intention of Titmouse, but affronted by his
words.

" May I ask what your lordship thinks of *me ?* First time I
ever appeared in this kind of thing, my lord—ha! ha! your
lordship sees!" As he spoke, his look and voice betrayed the
overawing effects of the Earl's splendid appearance, which was
rapidly freezing up the springs of familiarity, if not, indeed,
of flippancy, which were bubbling up within the little bosom
of Titmouse, on his entering the room. His manner became
involuntarily subdued and reverential. The Earl of Dreddlington in plain clothes, and in full court costume, were two very
different persons; though his lordship would have been mortally affronted if he had known that any one thought so.
However, he now regretted having offered to take Titmouse to
the levee, there was no escape from the calamity; so, after a
few minutes' pause, he rang the bell and announced his readiness to set off. Followed by Mr. Titmouse, his lordship slowly
descended the stairs; and when he was within two or three
steps of the hall floor, it distresses me to relate that he fell
nearly flat upon his face, and, but for his servants rushing up,
would have been seriously hurt. Poor Titmouse had been the
occasion of this disaster; for his sword getting between his
legs, down he went against the Earl, who went naturally down
upon the floor, as I have mentioned. Titmouse was not much
hurt, but terribly frightened, and went as pale as death when
he looked at the Earl, who appeared a little agitated, but, not
having been really injured, soon recovered his self-possession.
Profuse were poor Titmouse's apologies, as may be supposed;
but much as he was distressed at what had taken place, a
glance at the angry countenances with which the servants regarded him, as if inwardly cursing his stupidity and clumsi-
ness, stirred up his spirit a little and restored him to a measure of self-possession. He would have given a hundred pounds
to have been able to discharge every one of them on the spot.

" Sir—enough has been said," quote the Earl, rather coldly
and haughtily, tired of the multiplied apologies and excuses of
Titmouse. " I thank God, sir, that I am not hurt; though,
at my time of life, a fall is not a slight matter. Sir," continued the Earl bitterly, " *you* are not so much to blame as
your tailor; he should have explained to you how to wear your

sword!'' With this, having cut Titmouse to the very quick, the Earl motioned him to the door: they soon entered the carriage; the door was closed; and, with a brace of footmen behind, away rolled these two truly distinguished subjects to pay their homage to majesty—which might be well proud of such homage. They both sat in silence for some time. At length— '' Beg your lordship's pardon,'' quoth Titmouse, with some energy; '' but I wish your lordship only knew how I hate this cursed skewer that's pinned to me;'' and he looked at his sword, as if he could have snapped it into halves and thrown them through the window.

'' Sir, I can appreciate your feelings. The sword was not to blame, and *you* have my forgiveness,'' replied the still ruffled Earl.

'' Much obliged to your lordship,'' replied Titmouse, in a somewhat different tone from any in which he had ever ventured to address his august companion; for he was beginning to feel confoundedly nettled at the bitter, contemptuous manner which the Earl observed toward him. He was also not a little enraged with himself; for he knew he had been in fault, and thought of the neglected advice of his tailor. So his natural insolence, like a reptile just beginning to recover from its long torpor, made a faint struggle to show itself—but in vain; he was quite cowed and overpowered by the presence in which he was, and he wished heartily that he could have recalled even the few last words he had ventured to utter. The Earl had observed it, though without appearing to do so. He was accustomed to control his feelings; and upon the present occasion he exerted himself to do so, for fear of alienating Titmouse from him by any display of offended dignity.

'' Sir, it is a very fine day,'' he observed, in a kind manner, after a stern silence of at least five minutes.

'' Remarkable fine, my lord. I was just going to say so,'' replied Titmouse, greatly relieved; and presently they fell into their usual strain of conversation.

'' We must learn to bear these little annoyances calmly,'' said the Earl, graciously, on Titmouse's again alluding to his mishap:—'' As for me, sir, a person in the station to which it has pleased Heaven to call me, for purposes of its own, has its peculiar and very grave anxieties—substantial anx—''

He ceased suddenly. The carriage of his old rival, the Earl of Fitz-Walter, passed him; the latter waved his hand courteously; the former, with a bitter smile, was forced to do the same; and then, relapsing into silence, showed that the iron was entering his very soul, affording a striking illustration of

the truth of the observation he had been making to Titmouse.
Soon, however, they had entered the scene of splendid hubbub,
which at once occupied and excited both their minds. Without, was the eager crowd, gazing with admiration and awe at
each equipage, with its brilliant occupants, that dashed past
them:—then the life-guardsmen, in glittering and formidable
array, their long gleaming swords and polished helmets glancing and flashing in the sunlight. Within, were the tall yeo-
men of the guard, in velvet caps and scarlet uniforms, and
with ponderous partisans, lining each side of the staircase—
and who, being in the exact military costume of the time of
Henry the Eighth, forcibly recalled those days of pomp and
pageantry to the well-informed mind of Mr. Titmouse. In
short, there were all the grandeur, state, and ceremony that
fence in the dread approaches to majesty. Fortunately, Titmouse was infinitely too much bewildered and flustered by the
novel splendor around him to be aware of the ill-concealed
laughter which his appearance excited on all hands. In due
course he was borne on, and issued in due form into the presence chamber—into the immediate presence of majesty. His
heart palpitated: his dazzled eye caught a hasty glimpse of a
tall, magnificent figure standing before a throne. Advancing
—scarce aware whether on his head or his heels—he reverently
paid his homage — then rising, was promptly ushered out
through a different door; with no distinct impression of anything that he had witnessed!—'twas all a dazzling blaze of
glory—a dim vision of awe! Little was he aware, poor soul,
that the king had required him to be pointed out upon his approach, having heard of his celebrity in society; and that he
had had the distinguished honor of occasioning to majesty a
very great effort to keep its countenance. It was not till after
he had quitted the palace for some time, that he breathed freely
again. Then he began to feel as if a vast change had been
effected in him by some mysterious and awful agency—that he
was penetrated and pervaded, as it were, by the subtle essence
of royalty—like one that had experienced the sudden, strange,
thrilling, potent, influence of electricity. He imagined that
now the stamp of greatness had been impressed upon him:
that his pretensions had been ratified by the highest authority
upon earth. 'Twas as if wine had been poured into a stream,
intoxicating the *tittlebats* swimming about in it.—As for me,
however, seriously speaking, I question whether it was anything more than an imaginary change that had come over my
friend. Though I should be sorry to cite against him an
authority, couched in a language with which I have reason to

believe he was not *critically* acquainted, I can not help thinking that Horace must have had in his eye a Roman Titmouse
when he penned those bitter lines—

> " Licet superbus ambules pecuniâ
>   FORTUNA NON MUTAT GENUS
>   —Vidense Sacram metiente te Viam
>   Cum bis ter ulnarum togâ,
>   Ut ora vertat huc et huc euntium,
>   Liberrima indignatio?
>   —' Sectus flagellis hic triumviralibus
>   Præconis ad fastidium,
>   Arat Falerni mille fundi jugera,
>   Et Appiam mannis terit!'" *

While Titmouse was making this splendid figure in the
upper regions of society, and forming there every hour new
and brilliant connections and associations—in a perfect whirl
of pleasure from morning to night—he did not ungratefully
manifest a total forgetfulness of the amiable persons with
whom he had been so familiar, and from whom he had received so many good offices in his earlier days and humbler
circumstances. Had it not, however—to give the devil his due
—been for Gammon (who was ever beside him, like a mysterious pilot, secretly steering his little bark amid the strange,
splendid, but dangerous seas which it had now to navigate), I
fear that, with Titmouse, it would have been—out of sight out
of mind. But Gammon, ever watchful over the real interests
of his charge, and also delighted to become the medium of
conferring favors upon others, conveyed from time to time, to
the interesting family of the Tag-rags, special marks of Mr.
Titmouse's courtesy and gratitude. At one time a haunch of
doe venison would find its way to Mr. Tag-rag, to whom Gammon justly considered that the distinction between buck and
doe was unknown; at another, a fine work-box and a beautifully bound Bible found its way to good Mrs. Tag-rag; and
lastly, a gay guitar to Miss Tag-rag, who forthwith began
twang-twang tang-a-tanging it—from morning to night, thinking with ecstasy of its dear distinguished donor; who, together
with Mr. Gammon, had, some time afterward, the unspeakable
gratification, on occasion of their being invited to dine at Satin
Lodge, of hearing her accompany herself with her beautiful
instrument while singing the following exquisite composition,
for both the words and air of which she had been indebted to
her music-master, a youth with black mustaches, long dark

---

* Hor. Carm. V., iv.

hair parted on his head, shirt collars *à la* Byron, and eyes full of inspiration!

TO HIM I LOVE.

1.

Affettuosamente.

Ah me! I feel the smart
Of Cupid's cruel dart
Quivering in my heart,
    Heigho, ah! whew!

2.

Allegro.

With him I love
Swiftly time would move;
  With his cigar,
  And my guitar,
    We'd smoke and play
   The livelong day,
     Merrily, merrily!
      Puff—puff—puff,
    Tang-a tang, tang-a tang!

3.

Adagio, et con molto espressione.

When he's not near me,
O! of life I'm weary—
The world is dreary—
  Mystic spirits of song,
  Wreathed with cypress, come along!
  And hear me! hear me!

Teneramente.

   Singing
    Heigho, heigho—
   Tootle, tootle, too,
   A—lackaday!

Such were the tender and melting strains which this fair creature (her voice a little reedy and squeaking, to be sure) poured into the sensitive ear of Titmouse; and such are the strains by means of which many and many a Miss Tag-rag has captivated many and many a Titmouse; so that sentimental compositions of this sort have become deservedly popular, and do honor to our musical and poetical character as a nation. I said that it was on the occasion of a dinner at Satin Lodge, that Mr. Titmouse and Mr. Gammon were favored by hearing Miss Tag-rag's voice, accompanying her guitar; for when Mr. Tag-rag had sounded Mr. Gammon, and found that both he and Mr. Titmouse would be only too proud and happy to partake of his hospitality, they were invited. A very crack affair it was (though I have not time to describe it)—given on a more splendid scale than Mr. Tag-rag had ever ventured upon before. He brought a bottle of *champagne* all the way from town with his own hands, and kept it nice and cool in the kitchen cistern for three days beforehand; and there was fish, soup, roast mutton, and roast ducks, roast fowls, pease, cabbage, cauliflowers, potatoes, vegetable marrows; there was an apple-tie, a plum-pudding, custards, creams, jelly, and a man to wait, hired from the tavern at the corner of the hill. It had not occurred to them to provide themselves with champagne glasses, so they managed as well as they could with the common ones—all but Titmouse, who with a sort of fashionable recklessness, to show how little he thought of it, poured out his champagne into his tumbler, which he two thirds filled, and drank it off at a draft, Mr. Tag-rag trying to disguise the inward spasm it occasioned him by a grievous smile. He and Mrs. Tag-rag exchanged anxious looks; the whole of their sole bottle of champagne was gone already—almost as soon as it had been opened!

"I always drink champagne out of a tumbler; I do—'pon my life," said Titmouse, carelessly; "it's a devilish deal more pleasant."

"Ye-e-s—of course it is, sir," said Mr. Tag-rag, rather faintly. Shortly afterward, Titmouse offered to take a glass of champagne with Miss Tag-rag:—Her father's face flushed; and at length, with a bold effort, "Why, Mr. Titmouse," said he, trying desperately to look unconcerned—"the—fact is, I never keep more than a dozen or so in my cellar—and most unfortunately I found this afternoon that six bottles had—burst—I assure you."

"'Pon my soul, sorry to hear it," quoth Titmouse; "must send you a dozen of my own—I always keep about fifty or a hundred dozen. Oh, I'll send you half a dozen!"

Tag-rag scarcely knew, for a moment, whether he felt pleased or mortified at this stroke of delicate generosity. Thus it was that Titmouse evinced a disposition to shower marks of his favor and attachment upon the Tag-rags, in obedience to the injunctions of Gammon, who assured him that it was of very great importance for him to secure the good graces of Mr. Tag-rag. So Mr. Titmouse now drove up to Satin Lodge in his cab, and then rode thither, followed by his stylish groom; and on one occasion, artful little scamp! happening to find no one at home but Miss Tag-rag, he nevertheless alighted, and stayed for nearly ten minutes, behaving precisely in the manner of an accepted suitor, aware that he might do so with impunity since there was no witness present; a little matter which had been suggested to him by Mr. Gammon. Poor

Miss Tag-rag's cheek he kissed with every appearance of ardor, protesting that she was a monstrous lovely creature; and he left her in a state of delighted excitement, imagining herself the fated mistress of ten thousand a year, and the blooming bride of the gay and fashionable Mr. Titmouse. When her excellent parents heard of what had that day occurred between Mr. Titmouse and their daughter, they also looked upon the thing as quive settled. In the meanwhile the stream of prosperity flowed steadily in upon Mr. Tag-rag, his shop continuing crowded; his shopmen doubled in number:—in fact, he at length actually received, instead of giving payment, for allowing young men to serve a short time in so celebrated an establishment, in order that they might learn the first-rate style of doing business, and when established on their own account, write up over their doors:—" Timothy Tape, *late from Tag-rag & Co., Oxford Street.*"

Determined to make hay while the sun shone, he resorted to several little devices for that purpose, such as a shirt front with frills in the shape of a capital " T," and of which, under the name of " *Titties,*" he sold immense numbers among the inferior swells of London. At length it occurred to Gammon to suggest to Titmouse a mode of conferring upon his old friend and master a mark of permanent, public, and substantial distinction; and this was the obtaining for him, through the Earl of Dreddlington, an appointment as one of the *royal tradesmen*—namely, draper and hosier to the King. When Mr. Tag-rag's disinterested and indefatigable benefactor, Gammon, called one day in Oxford Srteet, and calling him for a moment out of the bustle of his crowded shop, mentioned the honor which Mr. Titmouse was bent upon doing his utmost, at Mr. Gammon's instance, to procure for Mr. Tag-rag, that respectable person was quite at a loss for terms in which adequately to express his gratitude. Titmouse readily consented to name the thing to the great man, and urge it in the best way he could; and he performed his promise. The Earl listened to his application with an air of anxiety. " Sir," said he, " the world is acquainted with my reluctance to ask favors of those in office. When I was in office myself, I felt the inconvenience of such applications abundantly. Besides, the appointment you have named happens to be one of considerable importance, and requiring great influence to procure it. Consider, sir, the immense number of tradesmen there are of every description, of whom drapers and hosiers (according to the last returns laid before Parliament, at the instance of my friend Lord Goose) are by far the most numerous. All of them are naturally ambitious of so high a distinction: yet, sir, observe that there is only one king and one royal family to serve. My Lord Chamberlain is, I have no doubt, harassed by applicants for such honors as you have mentioned."

Hereat Titmouse got startled at the unexpected magnitude of the favor he had applied for; and, declaring that he did not care a curse for Tag-rag, begged to withdraw his application. But the Earl, with a mighty fine air, interrupted him—"Sir, you are not in the least presuming upon your relationship with me, nor do I think you overrate the influence I may happen—in short, sir, I will make it my business to see my LORD KO-TOO this very day, and sound him upon the subject."

That same day an interview took place between the two distinguished noblemen, Lord Dreddlington and Lord Ko-too. Each approached the other upon stilts. After a display of the most delicate tact on the part of Lord Dreddlington, Lord Ko-too, who made a mighty piece of work of it, promised to consider the application.

CHAPTER XXIII.

WITHIN a day or two afterward, Mr. Tag-rag received a letter from the Lord Chamberlain's office, notifying that his Majesty had been graciously pleased to appoint him draper and hosier to his Majesty! It occasioned him feelings of tumultuous pride and pleasure, similar to those which the Earl of Dreddlington would have received tidings of his long-coveted marquisate having been conferred upon him. He started off, within a quarter of an hour after the receipt of the letter, to a carver and a gilder a few doors off, and gave orders for the immediate preparation of a first-rate cast, gilded, of the royal arms; which, in about a week's time, might be seen, a truly resplendent object, dazzling conspicuously over the central door of Mr. Tag-rag's establishment, inspiring awe into the minds of passers-by, and envy into Mr. Tag-rag's neighbors and rivals. He immediately sent off letters of gratitude to Mr. Titmouse, and to "the Right Honorable, the Most Noble the Earl of Dreddlington;" to the latter personage, at the same time, forwarding a most splendid crimson satin flowered dressing-gown, as an "humble token of his gratitude for his lordship's mark of condescension."

Both the letter and the dressing-gown gave great satisfaction to the Earl's valet (than whom they never got any further), and who, having tried on the dressing-gown, forthwith sat down and wrote a very fine reply, in his lordship's name,

to the note which had accompanied it, taking an opportunity
to satisfy his conscience by stating to the Earl the next morning that a Mr. Tag-rag had "*called*" to express his humble
thanks for his lordship's goodness. He was, moreover, so well
satisfied with this specimen of Mr. Tag-rag's articles, that he
forthwith opened an account with him, and sent a very liberal
order to start with. The same thing occurred with several of
the subordinate functionaries at the palace; and—to let my
reader, a little prematurely, however, into a secret—this was
the extent of the additional custom which Mr. Tag-rag's appointment secured him; and, even for these supplies, I never
heard of his getting paid. But it did wonders with him in the
estimation of the world. 'Twas evident that his was in a fair
way of becoming the head house in the trade. His appointment caused no little ferment in that nook of the city with
which he was connected. The worshipful Company of Squirt-
makers elected him a member; and on a vacancy suddenly occurring in the ward to which he belonged, for he had a
considerable shop in the city also, he was made a common
councilman. Mr. Tag-rag soon made a great stir as a champion of civil and religious liberty. As for church and county
rates, in particular, he demonstrated the gross injustice and
absurdity of calling upon one who had no *personal* occasion for
the use of a church, of a county bridge, a county jail, or a
lunatic asylum, to be called upon to contribute to the support
of them. A few speeches in this strain attracted so much attention to him that several leading men in the ward (a very
"liberal" one) intimated to him that he stood the best chance
of succeeding to the honor of alderman on the next vacancy;
and when he and Mrs. Tag-rag were alone together, he would
start the subject of the expenses of the mayoralty with no little
anxiety. He went to the chapel no longer on foot, but in a
stylish sort of covered gig, with a kind of coal-scuttle shaped
box screwed on behind, into which was squeezed his footboy
(who, by the way, had a thin stripe of crimson let into each
leg of his trousers, on Mr. Tag-rag's appointment to an office
under the crown); he was also a trifle later in arriving at the
chapel than he had been accustomed to be. He had a crimson
velvet cushion running along the front of his pew, and the
bibles and hymn-books were smartly gilded. He was presently advanced to the honored post of chief deacon; and on one
occasion, in the unexpected absence of the central luminary of
the system, was asked to occupy the chair at a "great meeting" of the SOCIETY FOR THE PROTECTION OF CIVIL AND
RELIGIOUS DISCORD; when he took the opportunity of declar-

ing his opinion, which was enthusiastically cheered, that the principles of free trade ought to be applied to religion; and that the voluntary system was that which was designed by God to secure the free blessings of competition. As for Satin Lodge, he stuck two little wings to it; and had one of the portraits of Tittlebat Titmouse (as Tippetiwink) hung over his drawing-room mantel-piece, splendidly framed and glazed.

Some little time after Tag-rag had obtained the royal appointment, which I have been so particular in recording, Gammon, *happening* to be passing his shop, stepped in, and observing Mr. Tag-rag, very cordially greeted him; and then, as if it had been a thought of the moment only, without taking him from the shop, intimated that he had been westward, engaged in completing the formal details of a rearrangement of the greater portion of Mr. Titmouse's estates, upon which that gentleman had recently determined, and the sight of Mr. Tag-rag's establishment had suggested to Mr. Gammon that possibly Mr. Tag-rag would feel gratified at being made a formal party to the transaction; as Mr. Gammon was sure that Mr. Titmouse would feel delighted at having associated with the Earl of Dreddlington, and one or two other persons of distinction, in the meditated arrangement, the name of so early and sincere a friend as Mr. Tag-rag; "one who, moreover"—here Gammon paused, and gave a smile of inexpressible significance, "but it was not for *him* to hint his suspicions—"

"Sir—I—I—*will* you come into my room?" interrupted Tag-rag, rather eagerly, anxious to have a more definite indication of Mr. Gammon's opinion; but that gentleman, looking at his watch, pleaded want of time, and, suddenly shaking Mr. Tag-rag by the hand, moved toward the door.

"You were talking of signing, sir— Have you got with you what you want signed? I'll sign anything!—anything for Mr. Titmouse; only too proud—it's an honor to be in any way connected with him." Gammon, on hearing this, felt in his pockets, as if he supposed that he should find there which he perfectly well knew had been lying ready, cut and dried, in his safe at Saffron Hill for months.

"I find I haven't got the little document with me," said he, carelessly; "I suppose it's lying about with other loose papers at the office, or may have been left at the Earl's"—[though Gammon's objects required him here to allude to the Earl of Dreddlington, I think it is only fair to say that he had never been, for one instant in his life, in that great man's presence].

"I'll tell you what, Mr. Gammon," said Tag-rag, considering—" Your office is at Saffron Hill? Well, I shall be passing your way to-morrow, on my way to my city establishment, about noon, and will look in and do all you wish."

"Could you arrange to meet the Earl there?—or, as his lordship's movements are—ah, ha!—not very—"

"Should be most pioud to meet his lordship, sir, to express my personal gratitude—"

"Oh, the Earl never likes to be reminded, Mr. Tag-rag, of any little courtesy or kindness he may have conferred! But if you will be with us about twelve, we can wait a little while; and if his lordship should not be punctual, we must even let you sign first, ah, ha!—and explain it to his lordship on his arrival, for I know your time's very precious, Mr. Tag-rag! Giacious! Mr. Tag-rag, what a constant stream of customers you have!—I heard it said, the other day, that you were rapidly absorbing all the leading business in your line in Oxford Street."

"You're very polite, Mr. Gammon! Certainly, I've no reason to complain. I always keep the best of everything, both here and in the city, and sell at the lowest prices, and spare no pains to please; and it's hard if—"

"Ah!—how do you do?" quoth Gammon, suddenly starting, and bowing to some one on the other side of the way, whom he did *not* see. "Well, good-day, Mr. Tag-rag—good-day! To-morrow at twelve, by the way!"

"I'm yours to command, Mr. Gammon," replied Tag-rag; and so they parted. Just about twelve o'clock the next day, the latter, in a great bustle, saying he had fifty places to call at in the city, made his appearance at Saffron Hill.

"His lordship a'n't here, I suppose?" quoth he, after shaking hands with Mr. Quirk and Mr. Gammon. The latter gentleman pulled out his watch, and, shrugging his shoulders, said with a smile, "No—we'll give him half an hour's grace."

"Half an hour, my dear sir," exclaimed Tag-rag; "I couldn't stay so long, even for the high honor of meeting his lordship. I am a man of business, he isn't; first come first served, you know, eh? All fair that!" There was a good many recently engrossed parchments and writings scattered over the table, and from among them Gammon, after tossing them about for some time, at length drew out a sheet of foolscap. It was stamped, and there was writing upon the first and second pages.

"Now, gentlemen, quick's the word—time's precious!" said Tag-rag, taking up a pen, and dipping it into the inkstand. Gammon, with an unconcerned air, placed before him the document he had been looking for. "Ah! how well I know the signature! That flourish of his—a sort of boldness about it, a'n't there?" said Tag-rag, observing the signature of Titmouse immediately above the spot on which he was going to place his own; there being written in pencil, underneath, the word "Dreddlington," evidently for the intended signature of the Earl. "I'm between two good ones, at any rate, eh?" said Tag-rag. Gammon or Quirk said something about a "term to attend the inheritance"—"trustee of an outstanding term"—"legal estate vested in the trustees"—"too great power to be put in the hands of any but those of the highest honor."

"Stay!" quoth Gammon, ringing his little hand-bell—"nothing like regularity, even in trifles." He was answered by one of the clerks, a very dashing person—"We only wish you to witness a signature," said Gammon. "Now, we shall release you, Mr. Tag-rag, in a moment. Say, 'I deliver this as my act and deed'—putting your finger on the little wafer there."

So said and so did Mr. Tag-rag as he had been directed; the clerk wrote his name under the witnessing clause "Abominable Amminadab;" and from that moment Mr. Tag-rag had unconsciously acquired an interest in the future stability of Mr. Titmouse's fortunes, to the extent of some FORTY THOUSAND POUNDS!

"Now, gentlemen, you'll make my compliments to his lordship, and if he asks how I came to sign before him, explain the hurry I was in. Time and tide wait for no man. Good-morning, gentlemen; good-morning; best regards to our friend, Mr. Titmouse." Gammon attended him to the door, cordially shaking him by the hand, and presently returned to the room he had just quitted, where he found Mr. Quirk holding in his hand the document just signed by Tag-rag; which was, in fact, a joint and several bond, conditioned in a penalty of forty thousand pounds, for the due payment by Titmouse of twenty thousand pounds and interest at five per cent, about to be advanced to him on mortgage of a portion of the Yatton property. Gammon, sitting down, gently took the instrument from Mr. Quirk, and with a bit of India-rubber calmly effaced the pencil signature of "*Dreddlington.*"

"You're a d——d clever fellow, Gammon!" exclaimed Mr. Quirk, presently, with a sort of sigh, and after, as it were, holding his breath for some time. Gammon made no reply. His face was slightly pale and wore an anxious expression. "It will do *now*," continued Mr. Quirk, rubbing his hands, and with a gleeful expression of countenance.

" That remains to be seen," replied Gammon, in a low tone.
" Eh? What? Does anything occur—eh? By Jove! no
screw loose, I hope?"

" No—but we're in *very deep water* now, Mr. Quirk—"

" Well—devil only cares, so long as *you* keep a sharp lookout, Gammon. I'll trust the helm to you."

As Gammon did not seem in a talkative mood, Quirk shortly
afterward left him.

Now, though Mr. Tag-rag is no favorite of mine, I begin to
feel a good deal of anxiety on his behalf. I wish he had not
been in so vast a " hurry," in a matter which required such
grave deliberation, as " signing, sealing, and delivering."
When a man is called on to go through so serious a ceremony,
it would be well if he could be apprised of the significance of
the formula—" *I deliver this as my act and deed.*" Thus
hath expressed himself upon this point, a great authority in
the law, old Master Plowden. 'Tis a passage somewhat quaint
in form, but not the less forcible and important in substance:—

" Words are often *spoken* unadvisedly, and pass from men
lightly and inconsiderately; but where the agreement is by
deed, there is more time for deliberation; for when a man
passes a thing by deed, first there is the determination of the
mind to do it, and upon that he causes it to be *written,* which
is one part of deliberation; and, afterward, he *puts his seal to
it,* which is another part of deliberation; and, lastly, he *de-
livers the writing as his deed,* which is the consummation of
his resolution. So that there is great deliberation used in the
making of deeds, for which reason they are received as a *lien,*
final to the party, and are adjudged to bind the party, without examination upon what cause or consideration they were
made."*

Possibly, some one now reading these pages hath had most
dismal experience in the matter above mentioned; and I hope
that such dismal experience, a due reflection will avert from
many a reader. As for Tag-rag, it may turn out that our fears
for him are groundless; nevertheless, *one hates to see men do
important things in a hurry;*—and, as we shall lose sight of
Mr. Tag-rag for some time, there can be no harm in wishing
him well out of what he has just done.

> " If 'twere *done* when 'tis done—
> *Then* 'twere well 'twere done *quickly* "—

and not otherwise.

The London season was now advancing toward its close.

* Plowden's *Commentaries*, 308, a (Sharrington *v.* Strotton).

Fine ladies were getting sated and exhausted with operas, concerts, balls, routs, soirées, assemblies, bazaars, fêtes, and the Park. Their lords were getting tired of their clubs during the day, and hurried dinners, late hours, foul air, and long speeches, at the two Houses; where, however they might doze away the time, they could seldom get the luxury of a downright nap for more than an hour or two together—always waking, and fancying themselves in the tower of Babel, and that it was on fire, so strange and startling were the lights and the hubbub! The very whippers-in were looking jaded and done —each being like a Smithfield drover's dog on a Monday night, that at length can neither bark nor bite in return for a kick or a blow, and, hoarse and wearied, falls asleep on his way home—a regular somnambulist. Where the Earl of Dreddlington and Lady Cecilia were to pass their autumn was a question which they were beginning to discuss rather anxiously. Any one glancing over their flourishing list of residences in England, Scotland, Wales, and Ireland, which were paraded in the Peerages and Court Guides, would have supposed that they had an ample choice before them; but the reader of this history knows better. The mortifying explanation—mortifying to the poor Earl—having been once given by me, I shall not again do so. Suffice it to say, that Poppleton Hall, Hertfordshire, had its disadvantages; there they must keep up a full establishment, and receive county company and other visitors—owing, as they did, much hospitality. 'Twas expensive work, also, at the watering-places; and expensive and also troublesome to go abroad at the Earl's advanced period of life. Pensively ruminating on these matters one evening, they were interrupted by a servant bringing in a note which proved to be from Titmouse—inviting them, in terms of profound courtesy and great cordiality, to honor Yatton, by making a stay there during as great a portion of the autumn as they could not better occupy. Mr. Titmouse frankly added, that he could not avoid acknowledging some little degree of selfishness in giving the invitation—namely, in expressing a hope that the Earl's presence would afford him, if so disposed, an opportunity of introducing him—Titmouse—to any of the leading members of the county who might be honored by the Earl's acquaintance; that, situated as Titmouse was, he felt an increasing anxiety on that point. He added, that he trusted the Earl and Lady Cecilia would consider Yatton, while they were there, as in all respects their own residence, and that he, Titmouse, would spare no exertion to render their stay as agreeable as possible. The humble appeal of Titmouse prevailed with

his great kinsman, who, on the next day, sent him a letter,
saying that his lordship fully recognized the claims which Mr.
Titmouse had upon him as the head of the family, and that
his lordship should feel very glad in availing himself of the
opportunity which offered itself, of placing Mr. Titmouse on a
proper footing of intercourse with the people of the county.
That, for this purpose, his lordship should decline any invitations they might receive to pass their autumn elsewhere, etc.,
etc., etc. In plain English, they jumped at the invitation. It
had emanated originally from Gammon, who, from motives of
his own, had suggested it to Titmouse, bade him act upon it,
and drew up the letter conveying it. I say, from motives of
his own, Gammon was bent upon becoming personally acquainted with the Earl, and fixing himself, if possible, thoroughly in
his lordship's confidence. He had contrived to ascertain from
Titmouse, without that gentleman's being, however, aware of
it, that the few occasions on which his (Gammon's) name
had been mentioned by the earl it had been accompanied by slighting expressions — by indications of dislike
and suspicion. Give him, however, thought he, but the opportunity, and he could very soon change the nature of the
Earl's feelings toward him. As soon, therefore, as the Earl's
acceptance of the invitation had been communicated to Gammon, he resolved to be one of the guests at Yatton during the
time of the Earl's stay—a step, into the propriety of which he
easily brought Mr. Quirk to enter, but which he did not, for
the present, communicate to Titmouse, lest he should, by
prematurely disclosing it to the Earl, raise any obstacle, arising out of an objection on the part of his lordship, who, if he
but found Gammon actually *there*, must submit to the infliction with what grace he might. In due time it was notified on
the part of the Earl, by his man of business, to Mr. Titmouse
(who had gone down to Yatton), through *his* man of business,
that the Earl and a formidable portion of his establishment
would make their appearance at Yatton by a named day. The
Earl had chosen to extend the invitation to Miss Macspleuchan,
and also to as many attendants as he thought fit to take with
him, instead of letting them consume their board wages in entire idleness in town or at Poppleton. Heavens! what accommodation was required, for the Earl, for the Lady Cecilia, each
of their personal attendants, Miss Macspleuchan, and five
servants! Then there were two other guests invited, in order
to form company and amusement for the Earl—the Marquis
Gants-Jaune de Millefleurs, and a Mr. Tuft. Accommodation
must be had for these: and, to secure it, Mr. Titmouse and

Mr. Gammon were driven to almost the extremities of the house. Four servants, in a sort of baggage-wagon, preceded the arrival of the Earl and Lady Cecilia by a day or two, in order to "arrange everything;" and, somehow or another, one of the first things that was done with this view was to install his lordship's chief servants in the quarters of Mr. Titmouse's servants, who, it was suggested, should endeavor to make themselves as comfortable as they could in some little unfurnished rooms over the stables! And, in a word, before Mr. Titmouse's grand guests had been at the Hall four-and-twenty hours, there was established there the same freezing state and solemn ceremony which prevailed in the Earl's own establishment. Down came at length, thundering through the village, the Earl's dusty traveling-carriage and four; himself, Lady Cecilia, and Miss Macspleuchan within, his valet and Lady Cecilia's maid behind; presently it wound round the park road, crashing and flashing through the gravel, and rattling under the old gate-way, and at length stood before the Hall door—the reeking horses pulled up with a sudden jerk, which almost threw them all upon their haunches. Mr. Titmouse was in readiness to receive his distinguished visitors; the carriage door was opened—down went the steps—and in a few moments' time the proud old Earl of Dreddlington and his proud daughter, having entered the Hall, had become the guests of its flustered and ambitious little proprietor. While all the guests are occupied in their dressing-rooms, recovering themselves from the cramp and fatigue of a long journey, and are preparing to make their appearance at dinner, let me take the opportunity to give you a sketch of the only one of the guests to whom you are at present a stranger: I mean Mr. Tuft—Mr. VENOM TUFT.

Oft hath an inexperienced mushroom hunter, deceived at a distance, run up to gather what seemed to be a fine cluster of mushrooms, growing under the shade of a stately tree, but which, on stooping down to gather them, he discovers with disappointment and disgust to be no mushrooms at all, but vile, unwholesome—even poisonous funguses, which, to prevent their similarly deluding others, he kicks up and crushes under foot. And is not this a type of what often happens in society? Under the "cold shade of aristocracy," how often is to be met with—THE SYCOPHANT?—Mr. Venom Tuft was one of them. His character was written in his face. Disagreeable to look at —though *he* thought far otherwise—he yet contrived to make himself pleasant to be listened to by the languid and ennuyéed fashionable. He spoke ever—

9—Part II.

> " In a *toady's* key,
> With bated breath and whispering humbleness."

His person was at once effeminate and coarse; his gesture and address were cringing—there was an intolerable calmness and gentleness about them at all times, but especially while laboring in his vocation. He had the art of administering delicate and appropriate flattery by a look only, deferential and insinuating—as well as by words. He had always at command a copious store of gossip, highly seasoned with scandal, which he collected and prepared with industry and judgment. Clever toadies are generally bitter ones. With sense enough to perceive, but not spirit enough to abandon their odious propensities, they are aware of the ignominious spectacle they exhibit before the eyes of men of the least degree of independence and discernment, and whose open contempt they have not power or manliness enough to resent. Then their smothered rage takes an inward turn; it tends to, and centers in the tongue, from which it falls in drops of scalding virus; and thus it is that the functions of sycophant and slanderer are so often found united in the same miserable individual. Does a sycophant fancy that his patron—if one may use such a term—is not aware of his degrading character and position? Would that he could but hear himself spoken of by those to whom he has last been *cottoning!* If he could but for one moment " see himself as others see him "—surely he would instantly wriggle out of the withering sight of man! But Mr. Tuft was not an every-day toady. Being a clever man, it occurred to him as calculated infinitely to enhance the value of his attention, if he could get them to be regarded as those of a man of some ability and reputation. So reasonable a wish as this to rise to eminence in the calling in life to which he had devoted himself— viz., toadyism—stimulated him to considerable exertion, which was in time rewarded by a measure of success; for he began to be looked on as *something* of a literary man. Then he would spend his mornings in reading up, in those quarters whence he might cull materials for display in society at a later period of the day; when he would watch his opportunity, or, if none presented itself, make one, by diverting the current of conversation into the channel on which was the gay and varied bordering of his very recent acquisitions. All his knowledge was of this gossiping *pro hac vice* character.—He was very skillful in administering his flattery. Did he dine with his Grace, or his Lordship, whose speech in the House appeared in that or the preeding day's newspapers? Mr. Tuft got it up carefully, and also the speech in answer to it, with a double view—to show himself at home in the question! and then to differ a little with his Grace, or his Lordship, in order to be presently set right by them and convinced by them! Or when conversation turned upon the topics which had overnight called up his Grace or his Lordship on his legs, Mr. Tuft would softly break in by observing that such and such a point had been "put in the debate with admirable point and force by *some one* of the speakers—he did not recollect whom;" and on being apprised of, and receiving a courteous bow from, the great man entitled to the undesigned compliment, look *so* surprised— almost, indeed, piqued! Carefully, however, as he managed matters, he was soon found out by *men*, and compelled to betake himself, with tenfold ardor, to the women, with whom he lasted a little longer. *They* considered him a great literary man; for he could quote and criticise a great deal of poetry, and a good many novels. He could show that what everybody else admired was full of faults; what all condemned was admirable; so that the fair creatures were forced to distrust their own judgment in proportion as they deferred to his. He would allow no one to be entitled to the praise of literary excellence except individuals of rank, and one or two men of established literary reputation, who had not thought it worth their while to repel his obsequious advances, or convenient not to do so. Then he would polish the poetry of fine ladies, touch up their little tales, and secure their insertion in fashionable periodicals. On these accounts, and of his piquant tittle-tattle, no soirée or conversazione was complete without him, any more than without tea, coffee, ice, or lemonade. All toadies hate one another; but his brethren both hated and feared Mr. Tuft; for he was not only so successful himself, but possessed and used such engines for *depressing them*. Mr. Tuft had hoped to succeed in being popped in by one of his patrons for a snug little Whig borough (for Tuft happened to be a Whig—though, for that matter, he might have been, more advantageously, a Tory); but the great man got tired of him, and turned him off, though the ladies of the family still secured him access to the dinner-table. He did not, however, make a very grateful return for such good-natured condescensions. Ugly and ungainly as he was, he yet imagined himself possessed of personal attractions for the ladies, and converted their innocent and unsuspecting familiarities, which had emanated from those confident in their purity and their greatness, into tokens of the ascendency he had gained over them, and of which, with equal cruelty, folly, and presumption, he would afterward boast pretty freely. Till this came, however, to be suspected and discovered, Mr. Tuft visited a good many leading houses in town, and spent no inconsiderable portion of each autumn at some one or other of the country mansions of his patrons— from whose "castles," "halls," "abbeys," "priories," and "seats," he took great pride in dating his letters to his friends. I must not forget to mention that he kept a book, very gorgeously bound and embellished, with silver-gilt clasps and bearing on the back the words—"Book of Autographs;" but I should have written it—"Trophies of Toadyism." This book contained autograph notes of the leading nobility, addressed familiarity to himself, thus:—

"The Duke of Walworth presents his compliments to Mr. Tuft, and feels particularly obliged by," etc.

"The Duchess of Diamond hopes Mr. Tuft will not forget to bring with him this evening," etc.

"The Marquis of M—— has the honor to assure Mr. Tuft that," etc.

"Dear Mr. Tuft,
"Why were you not at —— House last night? We were dreadfully dull without you? X—— just as stupid as you always say he *is*."

[This was from a very pretty and fashionable countess, whose initials it bore.]

"If Mr. Tuft is dead, Lady Dulcimer requests to be informed when his funeral will take place, as she, together with a host of mourners, intend to show him a last mark of respect."

"Dear Mr. Tuft,
"The poodle you brought me has got the mange, or some horrid complaint or other, which is making all his hair fall off. Do come and tell me what is to be done. Where can I send the sweet suffering angel?—Yours,

"ARABELLA D——."

[This was from the eldest and loveliest daughter of a very great duke.]

"The Lord Chancellor presents his compliments, and begs to acknowledge the receipt of Mr. Venom Tuft's obliging present of his little *Essay on Greatness*."

These are samples taken at random of the contents of Mr. Tuft's book of autographs, evidencing abundantly the satis-

factory terms of intimacy upon which he lived with the great;
and it was ecstasy to him to see this glittering record of his
triumphs glanced over by the envious, admiring eyes of those
in his own station in society.   How he delighted to be asked
about the sayings and doings of the exclusive circles!   How
confidentially would he intimate the desperate condition of a
sick peer—an expected *éclaircissement* of some fashionable folly
and crime—or a move to be made in the House that evening!
—poor Tuft little suspecting (lying so snug in his shell of self-
conceit) how frequently he fell, on these occasions, among the
Philistines—and was, unconsciously to himself, being trotted
out by a calm sarcastic hypocrite, for the amusement of the
standers-by, just as a little monkey is poked with a stick to get
up and exhibit himself and his tricks.   Such was Mr. Tuft, a
great friend and admirer of "the Marquis," through whose
influence he had procured the invitation from Titmouse, in
virtue of which he was now dressing in a nice little room at
the back of the Hall, overlooking the stables; being bent upon
improving his already tolerably familiar acquaintance with the
Earl of Dreddlington and Lady Cecilia, and also extracting
from the man whose hospitality he was enjoying, materials for
merriment among his great friends against the next season.
    When the party had collected in the drawing-room in readi-
ness for dinner, you might have seen Mr. Tuft in earnestly respectful conversation with the Lady Cecilia; Mr. Gammon
standing talking to Miss Macspleuchan, with an air of courteous ease and frankness—having observed her sitting neglected
by everybody; the Earl conversing now with the Marquis, then
with Titmouse, and anon with Tuft, with whom he appeared
to be particularly pleased.   Happening at length to be standing near Gammon—a calm, gentleman-like person, of whom he
knew nothing, nor suspected that his keen eye had taken in
his lordship's true character and capacity at a glance; nor that
he would, in a few hours' time, acquire as complete a mastery
over his said lordship as ever the present famous *hippodamist*
at Windsor, by touching a nerve in the mouth of a horse, re-
duces him to helpless docility and submission—the Earl and he
fell into casual conversation for a moment or two.   The air of
deference with which Gammon received the slight advances of
the great man was exquisite and indescribable.   It gave him
clearly to understand that his lofty pretensions were known to,
and profoundly appreciated by, the individual he was addressing.   Gammon said but little; that little, however, how significant and decisive!   He knew that the Earl would presently
inquire of Titmouse who the unknown visitor was; and that

on being told in the conceited and probably disparaging manner which Gammon knew Titmouse would adopt, if he supposed it would please the Earl, that "it was only Mr. Gammon, one of his solicitors," he would sink at once and forever
beneath the notice of the Earl. He resolved, therefore, to
anticipate—to contrive that it should ooze out easily and advantageously from himself, so that he could see the effect it
had upon the Earl, and regulate his movements accordingly.
Gammon sat down before the fortress of the Earl's pride, resolved that, for all it appeared so inaccessible and impregnable,
it should fall, however his skill and patience might be taxed in
the siege.   Till he had cast his piercing eye upon the Earl,
Gammon had felt a little of the nervousness which one may
imagine would be experienced by Van Amburgh, who, on being called into the presence of majesty to give a specimen of
his skill upon an animal concealed from him—of whose name
and qualities he was ignorant—should summon all his terrors
into his eye, and string his muscles to their highest tension;
and, on the door being opened, turn with smiling scorn—if not
indignation—from a sucking-pig, a calf, an ass, or a chicken.
Something similar were the feelings experienced by Gammon,
as soon as he had scanned the countenance and figure of the
Earl of Dreddlington. He quickly perceived that the dash of
awe which he had thrown into his manner was producing its
due effect upon that most magnificent simpleton.   Watching
his opportunity, he gently introduced the topic of the recent
change of ownership which Yatton had undergone; and in
speaking of the manner in which Mr. Titmouse had borne his
sudden prosperity—" Yes, my lord," continued Gammon, with
apparent carelessness, " I recollect making some such observation to him, and he replied, ' very true, *Mr. Gammon* ' "—
Gammon finished his sentence calmly; but he perceived that
the Earl had withdrawn himself into his earldom. He had
given a very slight start; a little color had mounted into his
cheek; a sensible hauteur had been assumed, and by the time
that Gammon had done speaking, the space between them had
been — as Lord Dreddlington imagined, unobservedly — increased by two or three inches. Gammon was a *man*—an
able and a proud man—and he felt galled; but " let it pass,"
he presently reflected—" let it pass, you pompous old idiot; I
will one day repay it with interest." The Earl separated from
him, Gammon regarding him as a gaudy craft sheering off for
a while, but doomed to be soon sunk.   Mr. Tuft (who was the
son of a respectable retired tobacconist), having ascertained
that Gammon was only Mr. Titmouse's attorney, conducted

himself for a while as though there were no such person in the
room; but being a quick observer, and catching once or twice
the faint sarcastic smile with which Gammon's eye was settled
on him, he experienced a very galling and uneasy consciousness of his presence. The Marquis's superior tact and perception of character led him to treat Gammon very differently—
with a deference and anxiety to please him, which Gammon
understood thoroughly—in fact, he and the Marquis had many
qualities in common, but Gammon was the man of *power*.
During dinner he sat beside Miss Macspleuchan, and was almost
the only person who spoke to her—in fact, he said but little to
any one else. He took wine with Titmouse with a marked but
guarded air of *confidence*. The Marquis took wine with Gammon with an air of studied courtesy. The Earl's attention
was almost entirely engrossed by Mr. Tuft, who sat next to
him, chattering in his ear like a little magpie perched upon his
shoulder. The Marquis sat next to the Lady Cecilia, for
whose amusement, as far as his cautious tact would allow him,
he from time to time drew out their little host. At length, in
answer to a question by the Marquis, the Earl let fall some
pompous observation, which the Marquis, who was getting very
tired of the vapid monotony which pervaded the table, ventured to differ from pretty decisively. Tuft instantly sided
with the Earl, and spoke with infinite fluency for some minutes; Gammon saw in a moment that he was an absurd pretender, and watching his opportunity for the first time that he
had interchanged a syllable with him, with one word exposing
a palpable historical blunder of poor Tuft's, overthrew him as
completely as a arrow from a cross-bow dislodges a tomtit from
the wall on which he is hopping about, unconscious of his danger. 'Twas a thing that there could be no mistake about
whatever.

" That's a *settler*, Tuft," said the Marquis, after a pause;
Tuft reddened violently, and gulped down a glass of wine; and
presently, with the slightly staggered Earl, became a silent
listener to the discussion into which the Marquis and Gammon
had entered. Obtuse as was the Earl, Gammon contrived to
let him see how effectually he was supporting his lordship's
opinion, which Mr. Tuft had so ridiculously failed in. The
Marquis got slightly the worst of the encounter with Gammon, whose object he saw and whose tact he admired; and
with much judgment permitted Gammon to appear to the
Earl as his successful defender, in order that he might himself
make a friend of Gammon. Moreover, he was not at all annoyed at witnessing the complete and unexpected discomfiture

of poor Tuft, whom, for all his intimacy with that gentleman,
the Marquis thoroughly despised.

However it might possibly be that his grand guests enjoyed
themselves, it was far otherwise with Mr. Titmouse, who, being
compelled to keep sober, was quite miserable.   None of those
around him were drinking men;—and the consequence was,
that he would retire early to his bedroom, and amuse himself
with brandy and water and cigars, while his guests amused
themselves with cards, billiards, or otherwise, as best they
might.   He did, indeed, "stand like a cipher in the great
account;" instead of feeling himself the Earl of Dreddlington's host, he felt himself as one of his lordship's guests,
struggling in vain against the freezing state and etiquette
which the Earl carried with him wherever he went, like a sort
of atmosphere.   In this extremity he secretly clung to Gammon, and reposed upon his powerful support and sympathy
more implicitly than ever he had done before.   As the shoot-
ing season had commenced, and game was plentiful at Yatton,
the Marquis and Tuft found full occupation during the day,
as occasionally did Mr. Gammon.   Mr. Titmouse once accompanied them; but having contrived once or twice very nearly
to blow his own hand off, and also to blow out the eyes of the
Marquis, they intimated that he had better go out alone for
the future—as he did once or twice, but soon got tired of such
solitary sport.   Besides—hares, pheasants, partridges—old and
young, cock or hen—'twas all one—none of them seemed to
care one straw for him or his gun, let him pop and blaze away
as loud and as long, as near or as far off, as he liked.   The
only thing he hit—and that plump—was one of his unfortunate dogs, which he killed on the spot; and then coming up with
it, stamped upon the poor creature's bleeding carcass, saying,
with a furious oath—"Why didn't you keep out of the way,
you brute?"

The Earl was really anxious to perform his promise of introducing, or procuring Titmouse to be introduced, to the
leading nobility and gentry of the county; but it proved a
more difficult task than his lordship had anticipated—for Titmouse's early doings at Yatton had not been forgotten; some
of the haughty Whig gentry joined with their Tory neighbors
in manifesting their open contempt and dislike for one who
could so disgrace the name and station to which he had been
elevated in the county; and the Earl had to encounter one or
two somewhat mortifying rebuffs, in the course of the efforts
which he was making for the establishment of his young kinsman.   There were some, however, whom mere political con-

sideration—some whom deference for the Earl's rank, and un-
willingness to hurt his feelings, and others from considerations
of political interest—induced to receive the new Squire of Yatton on a footing of formal intimacy and equality; so that his
lordship's numerous drives were not entirely useless.   The
whole party at the Hall attended the Earl to church on the
Sundays—entirely filling the Squire's pew and the adjoining
one; their decorous conduct presenting a very edifying spectacle to the humble congregation, and suggesting a striking
contrast between the present and the former visitors at the
Hall.   Worthy Dr. Tatham was asked several times to dinner,
at the Earl's instance, who treated him on such occasions with
great though stately courtesy.   The only persons with whom
the little Doctor felt at his ease were Mr. Gammon and Miss
Macspleuchan, who treated him with the utmost cordiality and
respect.   What became during the day of the two ladies, I
hardly know.   There was no instrument at Yatton; bagatelle-
board, and novels from a circulating library at York, frequent
rides and drives through the grounds and about the country,
and occasional visits to and from one or two families with
whom Lady Cecilia had a town acquaintance, occupied their
day; and in the evening, a rubber at whist, or écarté, with the
Earl—sometimes, too, with the Marquis and Mr. Tuft, both
of whom lost no opportunity of paying marked attention to
Lady Cecilia, with a view of dissipating as far as possible the
inevitable ennui of her situation—would while away the short
evenings, very early hours being now kept at the Hall.   'Twas
wonderful that two such men as the Marquis and Mr. Tuft
could stay so long as they did at so very dull a place, and with
such dull people.   Inwardly, they both voted the Earl an insufferable old twaddler; his daughter a piece of languid in-
sipidity; and one would have thought it daily more irksome
for them to keep up their courtly attentions.   They had, however, as may presently be seen, their objects in view.

As Gammon, a little to the Earl's surprise, continued apparently a permanent guest at the Hall, where he seemed ever engaged in superintending and getting into order the important
affairs of Mr. Titmouse, it could hardly be but that he and the
Earl should be occasionally thrown together; for as the Earl
did not shoot, and never read books, even had there been any
to read, he had little to do, when not engaged upon the ex-
peditions I have alluded to, but saunter about the house and
grounds and enter into conversation with almost any one he
met.   The assistance which Gammon had rendered the Earl
on the occasion of their first meeting at dinner had not been

forgotten by his lordship, but had served to take off the edge from his preconceived contemptuous dislike for him. Gammon steadily kept in the background, resolved that all advances should come from the Earl.   When, once or twice, his lordship inquired, with what Gammon saw to be only an affected carelessness, into the state of Mr. Titmouse's affairs, Mr. Gammon evinced a courteous readiness to give him *general* information; but with an evident caution and anxiety not unduly to expose even to the Earl, Mr. Titmouse's distinguished kinsman, the state of his property. He would, however, disclose sufficient to satisfy the Earl of Mr. Gammon's zeal and ability on behalf of Mr. Titmouse's interests, his consummate qualifications as a man of business; and from time to time perceived that his display was not lost upon the Earl.   Mr. Gammon's anxiety, in particular, to prevent the borough of Yatton from being a second time wrested out of the hands of its proprietor, and returning, by a corrupt and profligate arrangement with Ministers, a Tory to Parliament, gave the Earl peculiar satisfaction. He was led into a long conversation with Mr. Gammon upon political matters; and, at its close, was greatly struck with the soundness of his views, the strength of his liberal principles, and the vigor and acuteness with which he had throughout agreed with everything the Earl had said, and fortified every position he had taken; evincing, at the same time, a profound appreciation of his lordship's luminous exposition of political principles.   The Earl was forced to own to himself that he had never before met with a man of Mr. Gammon's strength of intellect, whose views and opinions had so intimately and entirely coincided—were, indeed, identical with his own.   'Twas delightful to listen to them upon these occasions—to observe the air of reverence and admiration with which Gammon listened to the lessons of political wisdom that fell, with increasing length and frequency, from the lips of his lordship.

"Του και απο γλωσσης μελιτος γλυκιων 'οεεν αυδη."

Nor was it only when they were alone together, that Gammon would thus sit at the feet of Gamaliel; he was not ashamed to do so openly at the dinner-table; but ah! how delicately and dexterously did he conceal from the spectators the game he was playing—more difficult to do so though it daily became—because the more willing Gammon was to receive, the more eager the Earl was to communicate instruction! If, on any of these occasions, oppressed by the multifariousness of his knowledge, and its sudden overpowering confluence, he would pause in the midst of a series of half-formed sentences, Gammon would be at hand, to glide in easily and finish what the Earl had begun, out of the Earl's own ample materials, of which Gammon had caught a glimpse, and only worked out the Earl's own, somewhat numerous, half-formed illustrations. The Marquis and Mr. Tuft began, however, at length to feel a little impatient at observing the way Gammon was making with the Earl; but of what use was it for them to interfere? Gammon was an exceedingly awkward person to meddle with; for, having once got fair play, by gaining the Earl's ear, his accuracy, readiness, extent of information upon political topics, and admirable temper told very powerfully against his two opponents, who at length interfered less and less with him; the Marquis only *feeling* pique, but Tuft also *showing* it. Had it been otherwise, indeed, with the latter gentleman, it would have been odd; for Gammon seemed to feel a peculiar pleasure in demolishing him. The Marquis, however, once resolved to show Gammon how distinctly he perceived his plan of operations, by waiting till he had accompanied the poor Earl to a climax of absurdity; and then, with his eye on Gammon, bursting into laughter. Seldom had Gammon been more ruffled than by that well-timed laugh; for he felt *found out.*

When the Earl and he were alone, he would listen with lively interest, over and over again, never wearied, to the Earl's magnificent accounts of what he had intended to do, had he only continued in office, in the important department over which he had presided, viz., the Board of Green Cloth; and more than once put his lordship into a sort of flutter of excitement by hinting at rumors which, he said, were rife—that, in the event of a change of ministers, which was looked for, his lordship was to be President of the Council. "Sir," the Earl would say, "I should not shrink from the performance of my duty to my sovereign, to whatever post he might be pleased to call me. The one you mention, sir, has its peculiar difficulties; and if I know anything of myself, sir, it is one for which—I should say—I am peculiarly qualified. Sir, the duty of presiding over the deliberations of powerful minds requires signal discretion and dignity, because, in short, especially in affairs of state—Do you comprehend me, Mr. Gammon?"

"I understand your lordship to say, that where the occasion is one of such magnitude, and the disturbing forces are upon so vast a scale, to moderate and guide conflicting interests and opinions—"

"Sir, it *is* so; *tantas componere lites, hic labor, hoc opus.*"

interrupted the Earl, with a desperate attempt to fish up a
fragment or two of his early scholarship; and his features wore
for a moment a solemn commanding expression, which satisfied Gammon of the way which his lordship would have had
when presiding at the council-board.   Gammon would also occasionally introduce the subject of heraldry, asking questions
concerning that science, and also concerning the genealogies
of leading members of the peerage, with which he safely presumed that the Earl would be, as also he proved, perfectly
familiar; and his lordship would go on for an hour at once
upon these interesting and vividly exciting subjects.

Shortly after luncheon one day, of which only Gammon, the
Earl, and the two ladies, were in the Hall to partake, Mr.
Gammon had occasion to enter the drawing-room, where he
found the Earl sitting upon the sofa, with his massive gold
spectacles on, leaning over the table, engaged in the perusal
of a portion of a work then in course of periodical publication,
which had only that day been delivered at the Hall.   The Earl
asked Gammon if he had seen it, and was answered in the
negative.

"Sir," said the Earl, rising and removing his glasses, "it
is a remarkably interesting publication, showing considerable
knowledge of a very difficult and all-important subject, and
one in respect of which the lower orders of the people—nay,
I lament to be obliged to add, the great bulk of the middle
classes also, are wofully deficient—I mean heraldry, and the
history of the origin, progress, and present state of the families
of the old nobility and gentry of this country."   The work
which had been so fortunate as thus to meet with the approbation of the Earl was the last monthly number of a History of
the County of York, and of which work, as yet, only thirty-
eight seven-and-sixpenny quarto numbers had made their appearance.   'Twas an admirable and instructive work, every
number of which had contained a glorification of some different Yorkshire family.   The discriminating patronage of Mr.
Titmouse for this inestimable performance had been secured
by a most obsequious letter from the learned editor—but more
especially by a device of his in the last number, which it would
have been strange indeed if it could have failed to catch the
eye and interest the feelings of the new aristocratical owner
of Yatton.   Opposite to the engraving of the Hall was placed
a magnificent genealogical tree, surmounted by a many-quar-
tered shield of armorial bearings, both of which purported to
be an accurate record of the ancestral glories of the house of
"TITMOUSE of YATTON!"   A minute investigation might in-

deed have detected that the recent flight of *Titmice,* which were perched on the lower branches of this imposing pedigree, bore nearly as small a proportion to the long array of chivalrous Drelincourts and Dreddlingtons which constituted the massive trunk, as did the paternal coat* (to which the pro-

* Per bend Ermine and Pean, two lions rampant combatant counterchanged, armed and languid Gules; surmounted by three bendlets under Argent, on each three fleurs-de-lis Azure; on a chief Or, three TITMICE volant proper; all within a bordure gobonated Argent and Sable.
CREST.—On a cap of maintenance a Titmous proper, ducally gorged Or, holding in his beak a wood-louse embowed Azure. Motto—"*Je le tiens.*"
Note.—The Author was favored, on the first appearance of this portion of the work, with several complimentary communications, on the subject of Sir Gorgeous Tintack's feats in heraldry; and one gentleman really eminent in that science has requested the author to annex to the separate edition in that science, as he now does, the two following very curious extracts from old heraldic writers:—the first supporting the author's ridicule of the prevalent folly of devising complicated coats of arms; and the second being a very remarkable specimen of the extent to which an enthusiast in the science was carried on its behalf.
First—"Another thing that is amiss, as I take it, and hath great neede to be reformed, is the quartering of many markes in one shield, coate, or banner; for sithence it is true that such markes serue to no other vse, but for a commander to lead by, or to be known by, it is of necessitie that the same should be *apparent, faire* and *easie to be understoode:* so that the quartering of many of them together, doth hinder the vse for which they are provided.—As how is it possible for a plaine unlearned man to discover and know a sunder, six or eight—sometimes thirty to forty several marks clustered all together in one shield or banner, nay though he had as good skill as *Robert Glower,* late Somerset that dead is, and the eies of an egle, amongst such a confusion of things, yet should he never be able to decipher the errors that are dalie committed in this one point, nor discover or know one banner or standard from an other, be the same neuer so large?—*Treatise on the True Use of Armes—by Mr. Sampson Erdswicke* [a famous antiquary in the reign of Queen Elizabeth].
[*Secondly.*—An extract from the *Book of St. Alban's,* written late in the fifteenth century, by *Dame Juliana Berners, Abbess of St. Alban's.*]—
"*Cain* and all his offspring became *churls* both by the curse of God, and his own father. *Seth* was made a *gentleman,* through his father's and mother's blessing, from whose loins issued *Noah,* a *gentleman* by kind and lineage. Of Noah's sons, *Chen* became a churl by his father's curse, on account of his gross barbarism toward his father. *Japhet* and *Shem,* Noah made gentlemen. From the offspring of gentlemanly Japhet came *Abraham, Moyses,* and the Prophets, and also the King of the right line of Mary, of whom that only absolute gentleman* Jesus

* One of our oldest dramatists, also whose name the author does not at present recollect, speaks of our Saviour as—" the first true *gentleman* that ever lived." It is to the same obliging correspondent that the author is indebted for the spirited drawing of Mr. Titmouse's crest and coat of arms which are prefixed to this edition.

found research and ingenuity of GORGEOUS TINTACK, the ——— king-at-arms, had succeeded in demonstrating the inalienable right of Tittlebat) to the interminable series of quarterings, derived from the same source, which occupied the remainder of the escutcheon. At these mysteriously significant symbols, however, Mr. Titmouse, though quite ready to believe that they indicated some just cause or other of family pride, had looked with the same appreciating intelligence which you may fancy you see a chicken displaying, while hesitatingly clapping its foot upon, and quaintly cocking its eye at, a slip of paper lying in a yard, covered over with algebraic characters and calculations. Far otherwise, however, was it with the Earl, in whose eyes the complex and recondite character of the production infinitely enhanced its value, and struck in his bosom several deep chords of genealogical feeling, as he proceeded, in answer to various anxious inquiries of Gammon, to give him a very full and minute account of the unrivaled splendor and antiquity of his lordship's ancestry. Now Gammon—while prosecuting the researches which had preceded the elevation of Mr. Titmouse to that rank and fortune of which the united voice of the fashionable world had now pronounced him so eminently worthy—had made himself pretty well acquainted with the previous history and connections of that ancient and illustrious house, of which the Earl of Dreddlington was the head; and his familiarity with this topic, though it did not *surprise* the Earl, because he conceived it to be every one's duty to acquaint himself with such momentous matters, rapidly raised him in the good opinion of the Earl, to whom, at length, it occurred to view him in quite a new light; viz., as the chosen instrument by whose means (under Providence) the perverse and self-willed Aubrey had been righteously cast down from that high place which his rebellious opposition to the wishes and political views of his liege lord had rendered him unworthy to occupy; while a more loyal branch had been raised from obscurity to his forfeited rank and estates. In fact, the Earl began to look upon Gammon as one whose just regards for his lordship's transcendent position in the aristocracy of England, had led him even to anticipate his lordship's possible wishes; and proceeded accordingly to rivet the spontaneous allegiance, by discoursing with the most condescending affability on the successive noble and princely alli-

was born: perfite God and perfite man according to his manhood, King of the land of Juda and the Jewes, and *gentleman* by his Mother Mary, princesse of coat Armor."

ances which had, during a long series of generations, refined the ancient blood of the Drelincourts into the sort of sublimated ichor which at present flowed in his own veins. Mr. Gammon marked the progress of the Earl's feelings with the greatest interest, perceiving the increasing extent to which respect for him—Gammon—was mingling with his lordship's sublime self-satisfaction; and, watching his opportunity, struck a spark into the dry tinder of his vain imagination, blew it gently—and saw that it caught and spread. Confident in his knowledge of the state of the Earl's feelings, and that his lordship had reached the highest point of credulity, Gammon intimated, in a hesitating but highly significant manner, his impression that the recent failure in the male line of the princely house of HOCH-STIFFELHAUSEN NARRENSTEIN DUMMLEINBERG* had placed his lordship, in right of the marriage of one of his ancestors, during the Thirty Years' War, with a princess of that august line, in a situation to claim, if such were his lordship's pleasure, the dormant honors and sovereign rank attached to the possession of that important principality. The Earl appeared for a few moments transfixed with awe. The bare possibility of such an event seemed too much for him to realize; but when further conversation with Gammon had familiarized his lordship with the notion, his mind's eye glanced to his old rival, the Earl of Fitz-Walter: what would *he* say to all this? How would his little honors pale beside the splendors of his Serene Highness the Prince of Hoch-Stiffelhausen Narrenstein Dummleinberg! He was not sorry when Mr. Gammon soon afterward left him to follow out unrestrainedly the swelling current of his thoughts, and yield himself up to the transporting ecstasies of anticipated sovereignty. To such a pitch did his excitement carry him that he might shortly afterward have been seen walking up and down the elm avenue, with the feelings and the air of an old KING.

Not satisfied, however, with the success of his daring experiment upon the credulity and inflammable imagination of the aspiring old nobleman—whom his suggestion had set upon instituting extensive inquiries into the position of his family with reference to the foreign alliances which it had formed in times past, and of which so dazzling an incident might really be in existence—it occurred to Mr. Gammon, on another occasion of his being left alone with the Earl, and who, he saw, was grow-

---

* I vehemently suspect myself guilty of a slight anachronism here; this ancient and illustrious monarchy having been mediatized by the Congress of Vienna in 1815—its territories now forming part of the parish of Hahnroost, in the kingdom of ——.

ing manifestly more pleased with the frequent recurrence of
them, to sink a shaft into a new mine. He therefore, on mere
speculation, introduced, as a subject of casual conversation,
the imprudence of persons of rank and large fortune devolving
the management of their pecuniary affairs so entirely upon
others—and thus leaving themselves exposed to all the serious
consequences of employing incompetent, indolent, or mercenary agents. Mr. Gammon proceeded to observe that he
had recently known an instance of a distinguished nobleman
(whose name he for very obvious reasons suppressed), who,
having occasion to raise a large sum of money by way of mortgage, left the sole negotiation of the affair to an agent, who
was afterward proved to have been in league with the lender
(the mortgagee), and permitted his employer to pay, for ten
or twelve years, an excess of interest over what he might, with
a little exertion, have obtained money for, which actually made
a difference in his income of a thousand a year. Here, looking out of the north-east corner of his eye, the placid speaker,
continuing unmoved, observed the Earl start a little, glance
somewhat anxiously at him, but in silence, and slightly quicken
the pace at which he had been walking. Gammon presently
added, in a careless sort of way, that accident had brought him
into professional intercourse with that nobleman—[Oh, Gammon! Gammon!]—whom he was ultimately instrumental in
saving from the annual robbery that was being inflicted upon
him. It was enough; Gammon saw that what he had been
saying had sunk like lead into the mind of his companion,
who, for the rest of the day, seemed burdened and oppressed
with it—or some other cause of anxiety; and, from an occasional uneasy and wistful eye which the Earl fixed upon him
at dinner, he felt conscious that not long would elapse before
he should hear something from the Earl connected with the
topic in question—and he was not mistaken. The very next
day they met in the park; and, after one or two casual observations, the Earl remarked that, by the way, with reference
to their yesterday's conversation, it "*did so happen*"—very
singularly—that the Earl had a friend who was placed in a
situation very similar to that which had been mentioned by
Mr. Gammon to the Earl; it was a very intimate friend—and
the Earl would like to hear what was Mr. Gammon's opinion
of the case. Gammon was scarcely able to refrain from a
smile, as the Earl went on, evincing every moment a more
vivid interest in behalf of his mysterious "*friend*," who at
last stood suddenly confessed as the Earl of Dreddlington; for,
in answer to a question of Mr. Gammon, his lordship unwit-

tingly spoke *in the first person!* On perceiving this, he got much confused; but Gammon passed it off very easily, and, by his earnest confidential tone and manner, soon soothed and reconciled the Earl to the vexatious disclosure he had made— vexatious only because the Earl had thought fit, so very unnecessarily, to make a mystery of an every-day matter. He rather loftily enjoined Mr. Gammon to secrecy upon the subject, to which Gammon readily pledged himself, and then they entered upon an unrestrained discussion of the matter. Suffice it to say, that in the end Gammon assured the Earl that he would without any difficulty undertake to procure a transfer of the mortgage at present existing on his lordship's property, which should lower his annual payments by at least one and a half per cent.; and which, on a rough calculation, would make a difference of very nearly five hundred a year in the Earl's favor. But Gammon explicitly informed the Earl that he was not to suppose that his interests had been in any way neglected, or he overreached, in the original transaction; that it had been conducted on his lordship's behalf, by his solicitor, Mr. Mudge, one of the most respectable men in the profession; and that a few years made all the difference in matters of this description; and before Mr. Gammon would interfere any further in the business, he requested his lordship to write to Mr. Mudge, inclosing a draft of the arrangement proposed by Mr. Gammon, and desiring Mr. Mudge to say what he thought of it. This the Earl did; and in a few days' time received an answer from Mr. Mudge, to the effect that he was happy that there was a prospect of so favorable an arrangement as that proposed, to which he could see no objection whatever, and would co-operate with Mr. Gammon in any way, and at any time, which his lordship might point out. Mr. Gammon was, in fact, rendering here a real and very important service to the Earl; being an able, acute and energetic man of business —while Mr. Mudge was very nearly superannuated—had grown rich and indolent, no longer attending to business with his pristine energy, but *pottering* and dozing over it, as it were, from day to day; unable, from his antiquated style of doing business, and the constantly narrowing circle of his connections, to avail himself of those resources which were open to younger and more energetic practitioners, with more varied resources. Thus, though money was now much more plentiful, and consequently to be got for a less sum than when, some ten years before, the Earl had been compelled to borrow a large sum upon a mortgage, old Mr. Mudge had suffered matters to remain all the while as they were, and so they would have remained but for Gammon's accidental interference; for the Earl was not a man of business—could not bear to talk to any one about the fact of his property being mortgaged—did not like even to think of it; and concluded that good old Mr. Mudge kept a sufficiently sharp eye upon his noble client's interest. The Earl gave Mr. Mudge's letter to Mr. Gammon, and requested him to lose no time in putting himself into communication with Mr. Mudge, for the purpose of effecting the suggested transfer. This Gammon undertook to do; and perceiving that he had fortunately made so strong a lodgment in the Earl's good opinion, whose interests now bound him, in a measure, to Mr. Gammon, he thought that he might safely quit Yatton and return to town, in order to attend to divers matters of pressing exigency. Before his departure, however, he had a very long interview with Titmouse, in the course of which he gave that now submissive personage a few simple, perspicuous, and decisive directions, as to the line of conduct he was to pursue, which alone could conduce to his permanent interests, and which he enjoined him to pursue, on terror of the consequences of failing to do so. The Earl of Dreddlington, in taking leave of Mr. Gammon, evinced the utmost degree of cordiality that was consistent with the stateliness of his demeanor. He felt real regret at parting with a man of such superior intellect, such a fascinating deference toward himself (the Earl), and it glanced across his mind that he would be the very fittest man that could be thought of, in respect of tact, energy and knowledge, to become prime minister to— his Serene Highness the Prince or Hoch-Stiffelhausen Narrenstein Dummleinberg!

The longer that the Earl continued at Yatton—in which he could not have more thoroughly established himself if he had in the ordinary way engaged it for the autumn—the more he was struck with its beauties; and the oftener they presented themselves to his mind's eye, the keener became his regrets at the splitting of the family interests which had so long existed, and his desire to take advantage of what seemed almost an opportunity specially afforded by Providence for reuniting them. As the Earl took his solitary walks he thought with a deep anxiety of his own advanced age and sensibly increasing feebleness. The position of his affairs was not satisfactory. Then he left behind him an only child—and that a daughter—on whom would devolve the splendid responsibility of sustaining, alone, the honors of her ancient family. Then there was his newly discovered kinsman, Mr. Titmouse, sole and unembarrassed proprietor of this fine old family property; simple

minded and confiding, with a truly reverential feeling toward
them, the heads of the family; also the undoubted, undisputed
proprietor of the borough of Yatton; who entertained and
avowed the same liberal and enlightened political opinions,
which the Earl had ever maintained with dignified consistency
and determination; and who, by a rare conjunction of personal
merit and of circumstance, had been elevated to the highest
pitch of popularity in the highest regions of society; and who
was, moreover, already next in succession, after himself and
the Lady Cecilia, to the ancient barony of Drelincourt and the
estates annexed to it. How little was there, in reality, to set
against all this? An eccentricity of manner, for which nature
only, if any one, was to blame; a tendency to extreme modish-
ness in dress, and a slight deficiency in the knowledge of the
etiquette of society—but which daily experience and intercourse were rapidly supplying; and a slight disposition toward
the pleasures of the table, which no doubt would disappear on
the instant of his having an object of permanent and elevating
attachment. Such was Titmouse. He had as yet, undoubtedly, made no advances to Lady Cecilia, nor evinced any disposition to do so; numerous and favorable had been, and continued to be, the opportunities for his doing so. Might not
this, however, be set down entirely to the score of his excessive
diffidence—distrust of his pretensions to aspire after so august
an alliance as with the Lady Cecilia? Yet there certainly was
another way of accounting for his conduct: had he got already
entangled with an attachment elsewhere?—Run after in society,
as he had been, in a manner totally unprecedented during his
very first season—had his affections been inveigled?—When the
Earl dwelt upon this dismal possibility, if it were when he was
lying awake in bed, he would be seized with a fit of intolerable
restlessness—and getting up, wrap himself in his dressing-
gown, and pace his chamber for an hour together, running
over, in his mind, the names of all the women he knew who
would be likely to lay snares for Titmouse, in order to secure
him for a daughter. Then there was the Lady Cecilia—but
she, he knew, would not run counter to his wishes, and he had,
therefore, no difficulty to apprehend on *that* score. She had
ever been calmly submissive to his will; had the same lofty
sense of family dignity that he enjoyed, and had often concurred in his deep regrets on account of the separation of the
family interests. She was still unmarried—and yet, on her
father's decease, would be a peeress in her own right, and possessed of the family estates. That fastidiousness which alone,
thought the Earl, had kept her hitherto single, would not, he

felt persuaded, be allowed by her to interfere for the purpose
of preventing so excellent a family arrangement as would be
effected by her union with Titmouse.   Once married—and he
having secured for her suitable settlements from Titmouse—if
there should prove to be any incompatibility of temper or dis-
crepancy of disposition, come the worst to the worst, there was
the shelter of a separation and separate maintenance to look
at; a thing which was becoming of daily occurrence—which
implied no reproach to either party—and left them always at
liberty to return to each other's society when so disposed. And
as for the dress and manners of Titmouse, granting them to
be a little extravagant, would not, in all probability, a word
from her suffice to *reduce* him or *elevate* him into a gentleman?   Thus thought her fond and enlightened parent, and
thus thought also she; from which it is evident, that Titmouse
once brought to the point—made sensible where his duty and
his privilege converged—it would be a straightforward, plain-
sailing business.   To bring about so desirable a state of things
as this—to give the young people an opportunity of thoroughly
knowing one another, and endearing themselves to each other,
were among the objects which the Earl had proposed to himself, in accepting the invitation to Yatton.   Time was wearing
on, however, and yet no decisive step had been taken.   Lady
Cecilia's icy coldness—her petrifying indifference of manner,
her phlegmatic temperament and lofty pride, were qualities,
all of which were calculated rather to check than encourage
the advances of a suitor, especially such a one as Titmouse;
but though the Earl did not know it, there were others whose
ardor and impatience to possess themselves of such superior
loveliness could not be similarly restrained or discouraged.
Would the reader believe that Mr. Venom Tuft, having been
long on the lookout for an aristocratic wife, had conceived it
not impossible to engage the affections of Lady Cecilia—to
fascinate her by the display of his brilliant acquirements; and
that the comparative seclusion of Yatton would afford him
the requisite opportunity for effecting his wishes?   Yet even
so it really was: intoxicated with vanity, which led him to believe himself peculiarly agreeable to women, he at length had
the inconceivable folly and presumption, on the morning after
an evening in which he fancied that he had displayed peculiar
brilliance, to intimate to her that his affections were no longer
under his own control, having been taken captive by her irresistible charms.   Vain thought! as well might a cock-sparrow
have sought to mate himself with the stately swan!   It was for
some time rather difficult for the Lady Cecilia to understand

that he was seriously making her a proposal. At length, however, he succeeded; and as much astonishment as her drooping
eyelids and languid hauteur of manner would permit the display of, she evinced. When poor Tuft found that such was
the case, his face burned like fire.

"You haven't mistaken me for Miss Macspleuchan, Mr.
Tuft, have you?" said she, with a faint smile. "You and Mr.
Titmouse, and the Marquis, I hear, sat much longer after din-
ner last night than usual!" Tuft was utterly confounded.
Was her ladyship insinuating that he was under the influence
of wine? He was speechless.

"I assure you, Lady Cecilia "—he stammered.

"Oh—now I understand!—You are rehearsing for Lady
Tawdry's private theatricals? Do you play there next month?
Well, I dare say you'll make a delicious Romeo." Here the
Earl happening to enter, Lady Cecilia, with a languid smile,
apprised him that Mr. Tuft had been rehearsing, to admiration, a love-scene which he was studying against Lady Tawdry's theatricals; on which the Earl, with a good-natured
smile, said that he should like to witness it, if not too much
trouble to Mr. Tuft. If that gentleman could have crept up
the chimney without being observed, he would have employed
the first moment of repose and security in praying that the
Lady Cecilia might bring herself to believe that he had really
been doing what at present he feared she only affected to believe. He resolved to outstay the Earl, who, indeed, withdrew in a few minutes' time, having entered only for the purpose of asking Lady Cecilia a question; and on her ladyship
and her would-be lover being again alone—

"If I have been guilty of presumption, Lady Cecilia "—he
commenced, with tremulous earnestness, looking a truly piteous
object.

"Not the least, Mr. Tuft," said she, calmly smiling; "or,
even if you *have*, I'll forgive it on one condition—"

"Your ladyship has only to intimate—"

"That you will go through it all with Miss Macspleuchan;
or, couldn't we get up a sweet scene with my maid? Annette
is a pretty little thing, and her broken English—"

"Your ladyship is pleased to be exceedingly severe; but I
feel that I deserve it. Still, knowing your ladyship's good
nature, I will venture to ask one great favor, which, if you
refuse, I will within an hour quit Yatton—that your ladyship
will, in mercy to my feelings, mention this little scene to no
one."

"If you wish it, Mr. Tuft, I will preserve your secret." she replied, in a kinder and more serious manner than he had ever witnessed in her; and, when he had escaped into solitude, he could hardly tell whom he hated most—himself or the Lady Cecilia. Several days afterward, the Marquis Gants-Jaunes de Millefleurs, purposing to quit Yatton on his way northward, sought a favorable opportunity to lay himself—the brilliant, irresistible Marquis—at the feet of the all-conquering Lady Cecilia, the future Lady Drelincourt, peeress in her own right, and mistress of the family estates. He had done the same kind of thing half a dozen times to as many women—all of them of ample fortune, and most of them also of rank. His manner was exquisitely delicate and winning; but Lady Cecilia, with a slight blush (for she was really pleased), calmly refused him. He saw it was utterly in vain; for a few moments he felt in an unutterably foolish position, but quickly recovering himself, assumed an air of delicate raillery, and put her into such good humor, that, forgetful in the moment of her promise to poor Tuft, she, in the strictest confidence in the world, communicated to the Marquis the offer which Mr. Tuft had been beforehand with him in making her! The Marquis's cheek flushed and tingled; and, without being able to analyze what passed through his mind, the result was, an intolerable feeling, as if he and Tuft were a couple of sneaking adventurers, and worse—of ridiculous and exposed adventurers. For almost the first time in his life, he felt an embarrassment amid the momentary conflict of his thoughts and feelings, which kept him silent. At length, "I presume, Lady Cecilia," said he in a low tone, with an air of distress, and a glance that did more in his behalf with Lady Cecilia than a thousand of his most flattering and eloquent speeches, "I shall, in like manner, have afforded amusement to your ladyship and Mr. Tuft?"

"Sir," said she, haughtily, and coloring—"Mr. Tuft and the Marquis Gants-Jaunes de Millefleurs are two very different persons; I am surprised, Monsieur le Marquis, that you should have made such an observation."

Hereupon he felt greatly consoled, and perfectly secure against being exposed to Tuft, as Tuft had been exposed to him. Yet he was mistaken. How can the reader forgive Lady Cecilia for her double breach of promise, when he is informed that a day or two afterward, Tuft and she being thrown together, partly out of pity to her rejected and bitterly mortified suitor, and partly from an impulse of womanly vanity, and partly from a sort of glimpse of even-handed justice, requiring such a step as a kind of reparation to Tuft for her exposure of him to the Marquis—she (in the strictest confidence, however),

informed him that his example had been followed by the Marquis, forgetful of that excellent maxim, "begin nothing of
which you have not well considered the end." It had not occurred to her ladyship as being a thing almost certain to ensue
upon her breach of faith, that Tuft would ask her whether she
had violated *his* confidence. He did so: she blushed scarlet—
and though, like her papa, she could have *equivocated* when
she could not have *lied*, here she was in a dilemma from which
nothing but a fib could possibly extricate her; and in a confident tone, but with a burning cheek, she simply told a falsehood, and had the pain of being conscious, by Mr. Tuft's look,
that he did not believe her.—Nothing could exceed the comical
air of embarrassment of the Marquis and Mr. Tuft, whenever,
after this, they were alone together! How fearful lest—how
doubtful whether—each knew as much as the other! To return, however, to the Earl of Dreddlington (who was really in
ignorance of the Marquis and Mr. Tuft's proposals to Lady
Cecilia), the difficulty which at present harassed his lordship
was, how he could, without compromising his own dignity or
injuring his darling scheme by a premature development of his
purpose, sound Titmouse upon the subject. How to break
the ice—to broach the subject—was the great problem which
the Earl turned over and over again in his mind. Now, be it
observed, that when a muddle-headed man is called upon at
length *to act*, however long beforehand he may have had notice
of it—however assured of the necessity there will be for eventually taking one course or another, and consequently enjoying
an ample opportunity for consideration, he remains confused
and irresolute up to the very *last instant*—when he acts, after
all, merely as the creature of caprice and impulse! 'Twas
thus with Lord Dreddlington. He had thought of half a dozen
different ways of commencing with Titmouse, and decided
upon adopting each; yet, when the anxiously looked for moment had arrived, he lost sight of them all, in his inward fluster and nervousness.

'Twas noon, and Titmouse, smoking a cigar, was walking
slowly up and down, his hands stuck into his surtout pockets,
and resting on his hips, in the fir-tree walk at the end of the
garden—the spot to which he seemed, during the stay of his
grand guests, to have been tacitly restricted for the enjoyment
of that luxury. When the Earl saw that Titmouse was aware
that his lordship had observed him, and tossed aside his cigar,
the Earl " begged " he would go on, and tried to calm and
steady himself, by a moment's reflection upon his overwhelming
superiority over Titmouse in every respect: but it was in vain.

Now, what anxiety and embarrassment would the Earl have been spared had he been aware of one little fact, that Mr. Gammon was unconsciously, secretly, and potently, his lordship's friend in the great matter which lay so near to his heart? For so it was, in truth. He had used all the art he was master of, and availed himself of all his mysterious power over Titmouse, to get him, at all events, to make an advance to his distinguished kinswoman. Considering, however, how necessary it was "to be off with the old love before he was on with the new," he had commenced operations by satisfying Titmouse how vain and hopeless, and, indeed, unworthy of him, was his passion for poor Miss Aubrey. Here, however, Gammon had not so much difficulty to contend with as he had anticipated; for Miss Aubrey's image had been long ago jostled out of his recollection by the innumerable brilliant and fashionable women among whom he had been latterly thrown. When, therefore, Gammon informed him that Miss Aubrey had fallen into a decline; and that, moreover, when he (Gammon) had, according to his promise to Titmouse, taken an opportunity of pressing his wishes upon her, she had scornfully scouted the bare notion of such a thing [all which was, of course, Mr. Gammon's pure invention]—

"'Pon—my soul! The—devil—she did!" said Titmouse, with an air of insolent astonishment. "The gal's a devilish pretty gal, no doubt," he presently continued, knocking the ashes off his cigar, with an indifferent air; "but—it's too good a joke—'pon my soul it is; but d'ye think, Gammon, she ever supposed I *meant* marriage? By Jove!" Here he winked his eye at Gammon, and then slowly expelled a mouthful of smoke. Gammon had grown pale with the conflict excited within by the last words of the execrable little miscreant. He controlled his feelings, however, and succeeded in preserving silence.

"Ah—well!" continued Titmouse, after another whiff or two, with an air of commiseration, "if the poor gal's *booked*— eh? it's no use; there's no harm done. Devilish poor, all of 'em, I hear! It is d——d hard, by the way, Gammon, that the prettiest gals are always the soonest picked off." As soon as Gammon had completely mastered his feelings, he proceeded to excite the pride and ambition of Titmouse, by representations of the splendor of an alliance with the last representative of so ancient and illustrious a house; in fact, when Gammon came, he said, to think of it, he found it was *too* grand a stroke, and that she would not entertain the notion for a moment; that she had refused crowds of young lords; that she would be a peeress of the realm in her own right, with an independent income of £5,000 a year; mansions, seats, and castles in each of the four quarters of the kingdom—topics such as these excited and inflated him to the full extent desired by Mr. Gammon, who, moreover—that was the great topic of his last interview with Titmouse, before leaving Yatton, as I have already apprised the reader—with great solemnity of manner, gave him distinctly to understand, that on his being able to affect an alliance with the Lady Cecilia, absolutely depended his continuance in, or expulsion from, the possession of the whole Yatton property. Thus it came to pass that Titmouse was penetrated by a far keener desire to ally himself to the Lady Cecilia than even the Earl had experienced to bring about such an auspicious event; and at the very moment of Titmouse's catching sight of the Earl, while pacing up and down the fir-tree walk, inhaling the soothing influence of his cigar—as I a short time ago presented him to the reader—he was tormenting himself with apprehensions that such a prize was too splendid for *him* to draw, and asking himself the constantly recurring question, how, in the name of all that was funny, could he set the thing a-going? When Greek met Greek, *then* came—it was said—the tug of war: and when the Earl of Dreddlington and Titmouse—a great fool and a little fool—came to encounter each other, each impelled by the same wishes, and restrained by similar apprehensions, it was like the encounter of two wily diplomatists, sitting down with the intention of outwitting each other, in obtaining an object, in respect of which their aim was, in fact, unknown to each other, precisely coincident, this hidden coincidence being the exact point which their exquisite maneuvers had succeeded in reciprocally masking: it being quite possible for Talleyrand and Pozzo di Borgo, pitted against each other, under similar circumstances, to have separated after a dozen long conferences, each having failed to secure their common object—peace.

" Well, Mr. Titmouse"—commenced the Earl, blandly, stepping at once, with graceful boldness, out of the mist, confusion and perplexity which prevailed among his lordship's ideas —"*what are you thinking about?* For you *seem* to be thinking!" and a courteous little laugh accompanied the last words.

" 'Pon—'pon my life—I—I—*beg* your lordship's pardon— but it's—monstrous odd your lordship should have known it " —stammered Titmouse; and his face suddenly grew of a scarlet color.

" Sir," replied the Earl, with greater skill than he had ever evinced in his whole life before—(such is the effect of any one's being intensely *in earnest*)—" it is not at all odd, when it happens that—the probability is—that—we are, perhaps—mind, sir, I mean possibly—thinking about the same thing!" Titmouse grew more and more confused, gazing in silence, with a simpering stare, at his noble companion, who, with his hands joined behind him, was walking slowly along with Titmouse.

" Sir," continued the Earl, in a low tone—breaking a very awkward pause—" it gives me sincere satisfaction to assure you that I can fully appreciate the delicate embarrassment which I perceive you are now—"

" My lord—your lordship's most *uncommon* polite," quoth Titmouse, suddenly taking off his hat, and bowing very low. The Earl moved his hat also, and slightly bowed, with a proudly gratified air; and again occurred a little pause, which was broken by Titmouse.

" Then your lordship thinks it will do?" he inquired, very sheepishly, but anxiously.

" Sir, I have the honor to assure you, that as far as *I* am concerned, I see no obst—"

" Yes—but excuse me, my lord — your lordship sees — I mean—my lord, your lordship sees—"

" Sir, I think—nay, I believe I *do* "—interrupted the Earl, wishing to relieve the evident embarrassment of his companion —" but—I see nothing that should—alarm you."

[How interesting to watch the mysterious process by which these two powerful minds were gradually approximating toward understanding each other! 'Twas a sort of *equation* with an unknown quantity in due course of elimination!]

" Doesn't your lordship, indeed?" inquired Titmouse, rather briskly.

" Sir, it was a saying of one of the great—I mean, sir, it is —you must often have heard, sir—in short, *nothing venture, nothing have!*"

" I'd venture a precious deal, my lord, if I only thought I could get what *I'm* after!"

" Sir?" exclaimed the Earl, condescendingly.

" If your lordship would only be so particular—so uncommon kind—as to name the thing to her ladyship—by way of—eh, my lord?—A sort of breaking the ice, and all that—"

" Sir, I feel and have a just pride in assuring you that the Lady Cecilia is a young lady of that superior delicacy of—"

" *Does* your lordship really think I've a *ghost* of a chance?" interrupted Titmouse, anxiously. " *She* must have named the thing to your lordship. no doubt—eh, my lord?"

This queer notion of the young lady's delicacy a little staggered her distinguished father for a moment or two. What
was he to say? She and he had really often named the thing
to each other; and here the question was put to him plumply.
The Earl scorned a flat lie, and never condescended to equivo-
cation except when it was absolutely necessary.

"Sir," he said, hesitatingly; "undoubtedly—if I were to
say—that now and then, when your attentions have been so
pointed—"

"'Pon my life, my lord, I never meant it; if your lordship
will only believe me," interrupted Titmouse, earnestly; " I beg
a thousand pardons—I mean no harm, my lord."

"Sir, there is no harm done," said the Earl, kindly. " Sir,
I know human nature too well, or I have lived thus long to
little purpose, not to be aware that we are not always master
of our own feelings."

"That's exactly it, my lord! Excuse me, but your lordship's hit the thing!"

"Do not imagine, Mr. Titmouse, that I think your attentions may have been *unpleasant* to the Lady Cecilia—by no
means; I can not, with truth, say any such thing!"

"Oh, my lord!" exclaimed Titmouse, taikng off his hat,
bowing, and placing his hand upon his breast, where his little
heart was palpitating with unusual force and distinctness.

"*Faint heart*, says the proverb, Mr. Titmouse, ah, ah!"
quo h the Earl with gentle gayety.

"Yes, my lord, it's enough to make one faint, indeed!
Now, if your lordship—(I'm not used to the sort of thing, my
lord!)—would just make a sort of beginning for me, my lord,
with the Lady Cicely—to set us going, my lord—the least
shove would do, my lord."

"Well, Mr. Titmouse," said the Earl, with a gracious smile,
" since your modesty is so overpowering—I'll try—to—become
your embassador to the Lady Cecilia. If, Mr. Titmouse," his
lordship presently added, in a serious tone, " you are fortunate
enough to succeed in engaging the affections of the Lady
Cecilia, you will discover that you have secured indeed an invaluable prize."

"To be sure, my lord! And consider, too, her ladyship's
uncommon high rank—it's so particular condescending.—By
the way, my lord, will she—if she and I can hit it off, so as to
marry one another—be called *Mrs. Titmouse*, or shall I be
called *Lord Titmouse?* I wonder how that will be, my lord?
'Tis only, your lordship understands, on Lady Cicely's account

I ask, because it's, in course, all one *to me* when once we're married."

The Earl was gazing at him, as he went on, with an expression of mingled surprise and concern: presently, however, he added, with calm seriousness, "Sir, it is not an unreasonable question, though I should have imagined that you could hardly have been—but—in short, the Lady Cecilia will retain her rank and become the Lady Cecilia Titmouse—that is, during my life: but, on my demise, she succeeds to the barony of Drelincourt, and then will be called, of course, Lady Drelincourt."

"And what shall *I* be then, my lord?" inquired Titmouse, eagerly.

"Sir, you will of course continue Mr. Titmouse—"

"'Pon my life, my lord—shall I indeed?" he interrupted, with a crest-fallen air, "Mr. Titmouse and Lady Drelincourt? Excuse me, my lord, but it don't sound at all like man and wife—"

"Sir, so it always has been, and will be, and so it ever ought to be," replied the Earl, gravely.

"Well but, my lord (excuse me, my lord)—but marriage is a very serious thing, my lord, your lordship knows—"

"It is, sir, indeed," replied the Earl, gloom visibly overspreading his features.

"Suppose," continued Titmouse, "Lady Cicely should die before me?"

The Earl, remaining silent, fixed on Titmouse the eye of a FATHER—a father, though a very foolish one; and, presently with a sensible tremor in his voice, replied, "Sir, these are rather singular questions—but, in such a mournful contingency as the one you have hinted at—"

"Oh, my lord! I humbly beg pardon—of course, I should be, 'pon my soul, my lord, most uncommon sorry"—interrupted Titmouse, with a little alarm in his manner.

"I was saying, sir—that in such an event, if Lady Drelincourt left no issue, you would succeed to the barony: but, should she leave issue, they will be called Honorable—"

"What!—'the Honorable Tittlebat Titmouse,' if it's a boy, and the 'Honorable Cecilia Titmouse,' if it's a girl?"

"Sir, it will be so—unless you should choose to take the name and arms of Dreddlington, on marrying the sole heiress—"

"Oh! indeed, my lord? 'Pon my life, my lord, that's worth considering—because I a'n't over and above pleased with my own name. What will it cost to change it now, my lord?"

" Sir," said the Earl, struck with the idea, " that is really a matter worth considering. In a matter of that magnitude, sir, I presume that expense would not be a matter of serious consideration."

After some further conversation, the Earl came plump upon the great pivot upon which the whole arrangement was to turn —settlements and jointures—oh, as to *them*, Titmouse, who was recovering from the shock of the discovery that his marriage, however it might degrade the Lady Cecilia, would not ennoble him—promised everything—would leave everything in the hands of his lordship. Soon afterward they separated; the Earl suggesting to him, that probably in a matter of infinite delicacy, like that on which they had been conversing, he would keep his own counsel—to which also Titmouse pledged himself. Soon afterward, and before seeing his daughter, with an anxious, but not an excited air, he ordered his horse and took a long ride, accompanied only by his groom: and if ever in his whole life he had attempted serious REFLECTION, it was on the occasion of that same long, slow, and solitary ride; then, for the first time, he forgot his peerage, and thought only of the *man*—and the father.

But to what purpose? Shortly after his return he sought Lady Cecilia, and performed his promise by preparing her to receive, probably on the ensuing day, the proposals of TITTLEBAT TITMOUSE.

The desired opportunity occurred the next day. Titmouse had slept like a top all night, after smoking in his bedroom a great many cigars, and drinking two or three tumblers of brandy and water; but Lady Cecilia had passed a very uneasy, and almost a sleepless night, and did not make her appearance at the breakfast - table. Understanding, however, that her ladyship was in the drawing-room and alone, about noon, Titmouse, who had bestowed during the interval more than usual pains upon his dress, gently opened the door, and observing that she was alone, reclining on the sofa, with a sudden beating of the heart, closed the door and approached her, bowing profoundly. Poor Lady Cecilia immediately sat up, very pale and trembling.

" Good-morning, good-morning, Lady Cicely," commenced Titmouse, taking a chair and sitting down in it, plump opposite to her. " You aren't well this morning, are you, Lady Cicely?" said he, observing how pale she looked, and that she did not seem disposed to speak.

" I am quite well," she replied, in a low tone; and then each was silent.

"It's beginning to look like winter a little, eh, Lady Cicely?" said he, after an embarrassing pause, looking through the windows. 'Twas an overcast day; and a strong wind was stripping the sere and yellow leaves in great numbers from the lofty trees which were not far distant, and which gave forth a melancholy rushing, moaning sound; and another pause ensued.

"Certainly it is getting rather cheerless," replied Lady Cecilia. Titmouse turned pale; and, twirling his fingers in his hair, fixed upon her a stupid and most embarrassing look, under which her eyes fell toward the ground, and remained looking in that direction.

"I—I—hope his lordship's been saying a good word for me, Lady Cicely?"

"My father mentioned your name to me yesterday," she replied, trembling excessively.

"'Pon my soul, monstrous kind!" said Titmouse, trying desperately to look at his ease. "Said he'd break the ice for me." Here ensued another pause. "Everybody must have a beginning, you know. 'Pon my solemn honor, all he said about me is quite true." Profoundly as was Lady Cecilia depressed, she looked up at Titmouse for a moment with evident surprise. "Now, Lady Cicely, just as between friends, didn't he tell you something *very* particular about me? Didn't he? Eh?" She made him no answer.

"I dare say, Lady Cicely, though somehow you look sad enough, you a'n't vexed to see me here? Eh? There's many and many a woman in London that would—but it's no use now. 'Pon my soul, I love you, I do, Lady Cicely;" she trembled violently, for he was drawing his chair nearer to her. She felt sick—sick almost to death.

"I know it's—it's a monstrous unpleasant piece of—I mean, it's an awkward thing to do; but I hope you love *me*, Lady Cicely, eh? a little?" Her head hung down, and a very scalding tear oozed out and trickled down her cheek. "Hope you aren't sorry, dear Lady Cicely? *I'm* most uncommon proud and happy! Come, Lady Cicely." He took the thin white hand that was nearest him, and raised it to his lips: had his perception been only a trifle keener, he could not have failed to perceive a faint thrill pervade Lady Cecilia as he performed this act of gallantry, and an expression of features which looked very much like disgust. He had seen love made on the stage frequently, and, as he had seen lovers do there, he now dropped down on one knee, still holding Lady Cecilia's hand in his, and pressing it a second time to his lips. "If your ladyship will only make me—so—happy—as to be—my wife—'pon my life, you're welcome to all I have; and you may consider this place entirely your own! Do you understand me, dearest Lady Cicely? Come! 'Pon my life—I'm quite distracted— do you love me, Lady Cicely? Only say the word." A faint —a very faint sound issued from her lips—'twas " Yes." Oh, poor Lady Cecilia! Oh, fatal—fatal falsehood. " Then, as true as God's in heaven, dear gal, I love you," said he- with ardor and energy; and rising from his knee, he sat down be-side her upon the sofa—placed an arm round her waist, and with his other hand grasped hers—and—imprinted a kiss upon the pale cheek which had been so haughtily withdrawn from the presumptuous advances of the Marquis de Millefleurs and from some half dozen others; several of whom were men of high real pretensions—elegant in person and manners—of great accomplishments—of intellect—of considerable fortune —of good family; but in her opinion, and that of the Earl her father, not of family good *enough*, nor fortune considerable enough, to entitle them to an alliance with her. " 'Pon my life, Lady Cicely, you *are* a most lovely gal," quoth Titmouse, with increasing energy—" and now you're all my own! Though I *am* only plain Mr. Titmouse, and you'll be Lady Cicely still. I'll make you a good husband!" and again he pressed her hand and kissed her cold cheek. But slow and dull as were the Lady Cecilia's feelings, they were becoming too much excited to admit of her continuing much longer in the room.

" I'm sure you'll excuse me, Mr. Titmouse," said she, ris-ing, and speaking quickly and faintly. When she had re-gained her room, she wept bitterly for upward of an hour; and Miss Macspleuchan, well aware of the cause of it, knew not how to console one who had so deliberately immolated herself before the hideous little image of Mammon; who, in degrading herself, had also—and Miss Macspleuchan shed bitter and scalding tears, and her bosom swelled with wounded pride and indignation at the thought—degraded her whole sex. In due time, however, the *Aurora*, a morning fashionable London newspaper, thus announced to the public as an auspicious event the one which I have so faithfully, feeling much pain the while, described to the reader:—

" It is rumored that Mr. Titmouse, who so lately recovered the very large estates at Yatton, in Yorkshire, and whose ap-pearance in the fashionable world has created so great a sensa-tion, and who is already connected, by consanguinity, with the ancient and noble family of Dreddlington, is about to form a closer alliance with it, and is now the accepted suitor of the lovely and accomplished Lady Cecilia Philippa Leopoldina Plantagenet, sole daughter and heiress of the Right Hon. the Earl of Dreddlington, and next in succession to the barony of Drelincourt, the most ancient, we believe, in the kingdom."

CHAPTER XXIV.

BEHOLD now, patient and reflecting reader—for in your eyes it is anxiously desired that this history may find favor—the dreadful—the desperate reverse in Mr. Aubrey's circumstances. He has suddenly fallen from a very commanding position in society: from that of a high-born English gentleman, possessed of a fine unincumbered income, and all of luxury and splendor, and of opportunity for gratifying a disposition of noble munificence, that it can secure—and whose qualifications and prospects justified him in aspiring to the highest senatorial distinction:—behold him, I say, with his beloved and helpless family, sunk—lower than into straitened circumstances—beneath even poverty—into the palsying atmosphere of *debt*—and debt, too, of a hopeless description! Seeing that no one can be so secure, but that all this, or something of the like kind, may one day or other happen to him, 'tis hoped that it will be found neither uninteresting nor uninstructive to watch carefully and closely the present condition and *conduct* of the Aubreys.

Bound hand and foot—so to speak—as Mr. Aubrey felt himself, and entirely at the mercy of Mr. Titmouse and his solicitors, Messrs. Quirk, Gammon and Snap, what could he do but submit to almost any terms on which they chose to insist? It will be recollected that Mr. Gammon's proposal * was, that Mr. Aubrey should forthwith discharge, without scrutiny, their bill of £3,946, 14s. 6d.; give sufficient security for the payment for the sum of £10,000 to Mr. Titmouse, within twelve or eighteen months' time, and two promissory notes for the sum of £5,000 each, payable at some future period, as to which he had to rely solely on the sincerity and forbearance of Mr. Gammon, and the ratification of his acts by Mr. Titmouse. This proposal was duly communicated by the unfortunate Aubrey to Messrs. Runnington, who obtained a fortnight's time in which to deliberate upon it; at the end of which period he was advised by them to accept the proposed

* *Ante*, p. 552.

terms as unquestionably fair, and, under circumstances, much
more lenient than could have been expected.   This might be
so; but yet, how dismaying and hopeless to *him* the idea of
carrying it into effect! *How, indeed, was it to be done?*
First of all, how were Messrs. Runnington's and Mr. Parkinson's bills to be got rid of—the former amounting to £1,670,
12s., the latter to £756?   And how were Mr. Aubrey and his
family to *live* in the meanwhile, and how, moreover, were to
be met the expenses of his legal education?   As was intimated
in a former part of this history, all that Mr. Aubrey had, on
settling in London, was £3,000 stock (equal to £2,640 of money)
and £423 in his banker's hands; so that all his cash in hand
was £3,063; and if he were to devote the whole of it to the discharge of the three attorneys' bills which he owed, he would
still leave a gross balance unpaid of £3,310, 12s. 6d.! And yet
for *him* to talk of *giving security* for the payment of £10,000
within eighteen months, and his own notes of hand for £10,000
more!   It was really almost maddening to sit down and contemplate all this.   But he must not fold his arms in impatience
and despair—he must look his difficulties straight in the face,
and do the best that was in his power.   He resolved to devote
every farthing he had, except £200, to the liquidation of Messrs.
Quirk, Gammon and Snap's account, and (in smaller proportion) of those also of Messrs. Runnington and Mr. Parkinson;
if necessary, he resolved, though his heart thrilled with anguish
at the thought, to sell his books and the remnant of old family plate that he had preserved.   Then he would strain every
nerve to contribute toward the support of himself and of his
family—poor oppressed soul!—by his literary exertions, in every
other moment that he could spare from his legal studies; and
practice the severest economy that was consistent with health
and preservation of a respectable exterior.   He resolved also,
though with a shudder, to commit himself to Gammon and
Titmouse's mercy, by handing to them (though a fearful farce
it seemed) his two notes of hand for £10,000—*payable on demand*—for such Gammon intimated was usual in such a case,
and would be required in the present one.   But whither was
he to look for security for the payment of £10,000 within
eighteen months' time?   This was a matter that indeed staggered him, and almost prostrated his energies whenever he
directed them to the subject; it occasioned him inexpressible
agitation and anguish.   Individuals there were, he believed—
he knew—who would cheerfully enter into the desired security
on his behalf: but what a mockery—cruel and insulting! For
them to be asked to secure *his* payment of the sum at the time

mentioned, was, in effect, palpably asking them to pay the
money for him, and in that light they could not view such an
application. The reader will easily understand the potency of
such considerations upon so sensitive and high-minded a person
as Aubrey. While revolving these distracting and harassing
topics in his mind, the name of Lord De la Zouch always presented itself to him. Had he not solemnly—repeatedly—
pledged himself to communicate with that kind, and wealthy,
and generous nobleman, in such an emergency as the present?
His lordship's income was at least eighty or a hundred thousand pounds a year; his habits were simple and unostentatious,
though he was of a truly munificent disposition; and he had
not a large and expensive family—his only child being Mr.
Delamere. He had ever professed, and, as far as he had hitherto had an opportunity, proved himself to be a devoted, a
most affectionate friend to Mr. Aubrey—did not Providence,
then, seem to point him out distinctly as one who should be
applied to, to rescue from destruction a fallen friend? And
why should Aubrey conjure up an array of imaginary obstacles, arising out of excessive and morbid fastidiousness? And
whom were such scruples reducing to destitution along with
him!—his wife, his children, his devoted and noble-minded
sister! But, alas! the thought of sweet Kate suggested another source of exquisite pain and embarrassment to Aubrey,
who well knew the ardent and inextinguishable passion for her
entertained by young Delamere. 'Twas true, that to pacify
his father, and also not to grieve or harass Miss Aubrey by the
constant attentions with which he would have otherwise followed her, he had consented to devote himself with great as-
siduity and ardor to his last year's studies at Oxford; yet was
he by no means an infrequent visitor at Vivian Street, resolutely regardless of the earnest entreaties of Miss Aubrey, and
even of her brother. Not that there was ever anything indeli-
cate or obtrusive in his attentions; how could it be? Alas!
Kate really loved him, and it required no very great acuteness
in Delamere to discover it. He was as fine, handsome a young
fellow as you could see anywhere; frank, high-spirited, accomplished, with an exceedingly elegant deportment, and simple,
winning manners—and could she but be touched with a lively
sense of the noble disinterestedness of his attachment to her!
I declare that Kate wrote him several letters in dissuasion of
his addresses, that wore such a genuine and determined air of
repulsion as would have staggered most men; but young Delamere cared not one straw for any of them: let Kate vary her
tone as she pleased, he simply told her that he had sent them

to his mother, who said they were very good letters indeed; so he would make a point of reading all she would send him, and so forth. When Kate, with too solemn an emphasis to be mistaken or encountered with raillery, assured him that nothing upon earth should prevail upon her to quit her present station in her brother's family, at all events until he had completely surmounted all his troubles, Delamere, with looks of fond admiration, would reply that it signified nothing, as he was prepared to wait her pleasure, and submit to any caprice or unkindness which her heart would let her exhibit. I must own that poor Kate was, on more than one occasion of his exhibiting traits of delicate generosity toward her brother, so moved and melted toward her lover, that she could—shall I say it?—have sunk into his arms in silent and passionate acquiescence; for her heart had, indeed, long been really his.—Now, to return, I say, that when Mr. Aubrey adverted for a moment to this state of things, was it not calculated a thousand-fold to enhance the difficulty of his applying *to the father of Delamere?* So indeed it was; and, torn with conflicting emotions and considerations of this kind, nearly the whole of the fortnight granted to him for deliberation had elapsed, before he could make up his mind to apply to Lord De la Zouch. At length, however, with a sort of calm desperation, he determined to do so; and when he had dropped into the Post-Office his letter—one in every line of which the noble and generous person to whom it was addressed might easily detect the writhings of its writer's wounded spirit—the quivering of a broken heart—he looked indeed a melancholy object. The instant that, by dropping his letter into the box, he had irrecoverably parted with all control over it, and to Lord De la Zouch it must go, Aubrey felt as if he would have given the world to recall it. Never had he heaved so many profound sighs, and felt so utterly miserable and destitute, as during his walk homeward that afternoon. There they did not know of the step he had intended to take, nor did he tell them that he had taken it. When he saw his sister he felt sick at heart; and during the whole of the evening was so oppressed and subdued that the faint, anxious raillery of Mrs. Aubrey and Kate, and the unconscious sportiveness of his children, served only to deepen the gloom that was around his spirit. He had requested Lord De la Zouch to address his answer to him at the Temple! and sure enough, by return of post, Mr. Aubrey found lying on his desk, on reaching the Temple three or four mornings afterward, a letter addressed, " Charles Aubrey, Esq., at —— Weasels, Esq., No. 3, Pome-

granate Court, Temple, London;" and franked, " DE LA
ZOUCH."

"I shall return presently," said Mr. Aubrey to the clerk,
with as much calmness as he could assume, having put the letter into his pocket, resolving to go into the Temple gardens
and there read it, where any emotion which it might excite
would be unobserved. Having at length seated himself on a
bench, under one of the old trees near the river, with a somewhat tremulous hand he took out and opened the letter, and
read as follows:—

> " *Fotheringham Castle,*
> " 18*th July,* 18—.

"MY VERY DEAR AUBREY,

"If you really value my friendship, never pain my feelings
again by expressions of distrust as to the issue of *any* application of yours to me, such as are contained in your letter now
lying before me. Has anything that has ever hitherto passed
between us justified them? For Heaven's sake, tell your attorneys not to lose a moment in procuring the necessary instruments, and forwarding them to me through Messrs. Fram-
lingham, my lawyers; I will then execute them immediately,
and return them to you by the next post or mail. If you will
but at once set about this in a business-like way, I will forgive
and forget all the absurd and *unkind* scruples with which
your letter abounds. Since you would probably make a mighty
stir about it, I shall not at present dwell upon the *inexpressible
pleasure* it would give me to be allowed to emancipate you at
once from the vulgar and grasping wretches who are now harassing you, my very dear Aubrey, and to constitute myself
your creditor instead of them. But, on further consideration,
I suppose you would distress yourself on the ground of *my restricted means* rendering it so much more difficult for me than
for them to give you time for the payment of your debt! Or
will you play the man, and act at once in the way in which, I
assure you, upon my honor, I would act by you, on a similar
solicitation, were our situations reversed? By the way, I intend to insist on being your *sole surety;* unless, indeed, your
creditors doubt my solvency, in which case I hope we shall be
able, amongst our common friends, to find a sufficient co-
surety.

"And now, dear Aubrey, how get you on with law? Does
she smile or scowl upon you? I wonder why you did not go to
the fountain-head, and become at once a pupil to your friend,
the Attorney-General. Who is the gentleman whom you are
reading with? He certainly has rather a curious name! Well,

my dear Aubrey, Heaven in its own good time crown your virtuous efforts—your unconquerable resolution—with success! Won't it be odd if, when I am dead and gone, and my son is occupying my present place on the benches, you should be sitting on the woolsack? More unlikely things than this have come to pass; look at ——!

"How are dear Mrs. Aubrey and Miss Aubrey, and your little ones? Though we are going in a fortnight's time to fill this old place (the ——s, the ——s, and the ——s, and others, are coming), we shall be till then quite deserted, and so after they are gone. Would that we could insist on all of you taking up your abode with us! Have you seen Geoffry lately? He tells me that he is working very hard indeed at Oxford; and so says his tutor. It is more than ever I did. Pray write me by return. I am ever, my dear Aubrey, yours faithfully and affectionately,

"DE LA ZOUCH.

"CHARLES AUBREY, Esq.

"P.S. On further consideration, let *your* people send the deeds, etc., at once on to me, direct from themselves;—'tis a private matter, which is of no consequence to any one but ourselves. No one, indeed, except ourselves, your own solicitors, and your opponents, need know anything about it. Neither Lady De la Zouch nor my son will have the least inkling of the matter."

No language of mine can do justice to the feelings with which Mr. Aubrey, after many pauses, occasioned by irrepressible emotion, perused the foregoing letter. Its generosity was infinitely enhanced by its delicacy; and both were most exquisitely appreciated by a man of his susceptibility and in his circumstances. His eyes—his heart overflowed with unutterable gratitude toward the Almighty and the noble instrument of his mercy. He would have flown on the wings of the wind to the dear beings in Vivian Street, with joyous face and light elastic step, to make them participators in his joy. He rose and walked to and fro by the river-side with most exhilarated spirits. The sky was cloudless; the sun shone brilliantly, and innumerable brisk and busy craft were moving to and fro upon the swelling bosom of the magnificent Thames. Gladness was in his soul. The light without was typical of that within. Several times he was on the point of starting off to Vivian Street; but, on consideration, he resolved to go to Messrs. Runnington, and set them into instant communication with Messrs. Quirk, Gammon and Snap, and matters having been set in train for the speediest possible settlement, Mr. Aubrey returned to chambers; but quitted them an hour earlier than usual, to brighten the countenances of those he loved by the joyous intelligence he bore. But he found that they also had cheering news to communicate; so that this was indeed a memorable day to them.

Old Lady Stratton, an early and bosom friend of the late Mrs. Aubrey, had, it may easily be believed, never ceased to take a lively interest in the fortunes of the unhappy Aubreys. She was now far advanced in years; and though she enjoyed an ample income, derived from the liberality of her husband, Sir Beryl Stratton, Baronet, who had died some twenty or thirty years before; yet, having no children, and seeing no necessity for saving money, she had followed the noble example of her deceased friend, Mrs. Aubrey, and bestowed annually all her surplus income in the most liberal and systematic charity. Many years before, however, she had resolved upon making a provision for Miss Aubrey, whom she loved as if she had been her mother; and the expedient she had resorted to (quite unknown to the Aubreys) was to insure her life for the sum of £15,000, the whole of which sum she had intended to bequeath to Miss Aubrey. The premiums on so large an insurance as this were heavy annual drains upon her purse; and together with her long-continued charities, and the expenditure necessary to support her station, left her but stinted means for contributing to the relief of the ruined Aubreys. With some difficulty, however, the old lady, in one way or another, principally by effecting a loan from the insurance company upon her policy, had contrived to raise a sum of £2,000; and Miss Aubrey had that morning received a letter from her, full of tenderness, begging her to present the sum in question (for which Lady Stratton had lodged a credit with her bankers in London) to her brother Mr. Aubrey, to dispose of as he pleased —trusting that it might be effectual in relieving him from the difficulties which were more immediately pressing upon him. Never had they spent so happy an evening together since they had quitted Yatton. In the excitement of the hour, even Aubrey felt for a while as if they now saw their way through all their embarrassments and dangers. Can the reader imagine what must have been the feelings of Miss Aubrey when she first heard of, and afterward reflected upon, the princely munificence of Lord De la Zouch? If he can, it is well—it is more than I am equal to describing. They kept her awake more than half the night; and when she appeared at breakfast, her brother's quick eye detected in her countenance the traces of a severe conflict of feelings. With him, also, much of the excitement occasioned by the two occurrences above mentioned had disappeared by the time that he took his seat in his little study at his usual early hour. First of all, he felt very uneasy in receiving so large a sum from Lady Stratton, whom he knew not to be rich—at all events, not rich enough to part with so considerable sum without inconvenience; and he resolved not to accept of her proffered kindness, unless she would allow him to transmit to her his bond for the amount, together with interest. Surely this was an unnecessary step; yet where is the man who, on all occasions, acts precisely as a calm and reflecting observer of his conduct, *long afterward*, could have wished him to act? One must make allowance for the feelings which prompted him—those of a highly honorable and independent and oversensitive man, who felt himself oppressed already by the weight of pecuniary obligation which he had incurred, and sought for the semblance of relief to his feelings by receiving that as a loan only which had been nobly proffered as a gift, and thus, as it were, in point of fact destroying all the grace and courtesy of the benefaction; but it is useless discussing the matter. I regret that Mr. Aubrey should have allowed himself to be influenced by such considerations; but so it was—and poor old Lady Stratton was informed by him, in a letter certainly abounding with gratitude and affection, that he had availed himself of her generous assistance, but only on the terms of his being allowed to deposit his bond for the repayment of it, with interest, with her solicitors, earnestly trusting that ere long he should be enabled to fulfill his engagements to all who had assisted him.

This seasonable assistance enabled him to make the following arrangement for liquidating the sums due on account of the tremendous attorneys' bills:—

Messrs. Quirk, Gammon and Snap's bill was . £3946 14 6
Messrs. Runnington's 1670 12 0
Mr. Parkinson's 756 0 0
                                        ————————
                                        £6373 6 6

These were his liabilities. Then his assets were:—

Money in the funds £2640
Money at the banker's 423
Advanced by Lady Stratton 2000
                                        ————
                                        £5063

As soon as he had made the foregoing statement on a slip of paper early in the morning in his study, he averted his eye from it for a moment with a sort of cold shudder.   Were he to devote every farthing of assets that he had, he still could not come within £1,310 odd of his mere attorneys' bills.   What was he to do?   The result of a long and anxious morning's calculation and scheming was to appropriate £4,000 of his assets thus—(if he could prevail upon his creditors to be for the present content with it):—

To Messrs. Quirk, Gammon and Snap . . .	£2500
Messrs. Runnington	1000
Mr. Parkinson	500
	£4000

If this arrangement could be effected, then he would be able to reserve in his own hands £1,063, and retain liabilities as under:—

Messrs. Quirk, Gammon and Snap's (balance)	£1446 14 6
Messrs. Runningtons' (ditto)	670 12 0
Mr. Parkinson's (ditto)	256 0 0
	£2373 6 6

Heavy was his heart at beholding this result of even the most favorable mode of putting his case; but he placed the memoranda in his pocket-book, and repaired to his dressing-room; and having completed his toilet, appeared at breakfast with as cheerful a countenance as he could assume.   Each of the three assembled perceived, however, that the others were *striving* to appear gay and happy.   Suffice it to say, that within a week's time, Messrs. Runnington received the necessary security from Lord De la Zouch, who had thereby bound himself in the penal sum of £20,000 that Mr. Aubrey should, on or before the 24th day of January, 18— (that is, in eighteen months' time from the date of the bond), pay the principal sum of £10,000, with interest at five per cent.; and this instrument, together with Mr. Aubrey's two promissory notes for £5,000 each, and also cash to the amount of £2,500 in part payment of their bill, having been delivered to Messrs. Quirk, Gammon and Snap—who, after a great deal of reluctance on the part of Mr. Quirk, finally consented to allow the balance of £1,146, 14s. 6d. to stand over—they delivered to him, first a receipt for so much on account of their own bill; and secondly, an instrument by which Tittlebat Titmouse, for the considerations therein expressed, did remise, release and forever quit claim, unto Charles Aubrey, his heirs, executors and administrators, all other demands whatsoever [*i. e.* other than the said sum of £20,000]. By this arrangement Mr. Aubrey was absolutely exonerated from the sum of £40,000, in which he stood indubitably indebted to Mr. Titmouse, and so far he had just cause for congratulation. But was not his situation still one calculated to depress and alarm him more and more every time that he contemplated it? Where was he to find the sum requisite to release Lord De la Zouch from any part of his dreadful liability? For with such a surety in their power as that great and opulent peer, was it likely that Messrs. Quirk, Gammon and Snap would be otherwise than peremptory and inflexible when the day of payment arrived? And if so, with what feelings must Mr. Aubrey see his noble and generous friend called upon to pay down nearly £11,000 for him? And was he not liable at any moment upon his own two notes for £5,000 each? And were they not likely to insist speedily on the discharge of their own serious balance of £1,446 odd? How likely that persons such as they and their client were represented to be, would, as soon as they decently could, proceed to extremities with him, in the confidence that the sight and the sound of his agonies would call in powerful and affluent friends to his assistance?

Still pressed, as indeed he was, his spirit had by no means lost its elasticity, supported as he was by a powerful and unconquerable WILL—and also by a devout reliance upon the protection of Providence. Though law is indeed an exhausting and absorbing study, and it was pursued by Mr. Aubrey with unflagging energy, yet he found time enough (those who choose may find time enough for everything) to contribute sensibly to the support of himself and his family by literary labors, expended principally upon compositions of a historical and political character, and which were forwarded from time to time to the distinguished Review which has been already mentioned. To produce as he produced articles of this description—of considerable length and frequency—requiring ready, extensive and accurate knowledge, and careful composition; original and vigorous in their conception and their execution, and by their intrinsic merit arresting, immediately on their appearance, the attention of the public; I say, to do all this, and only in those precious intervals which ought to have been given to the relaxation of his strained faculties and

physical powers—and under the pressure, too, of such over
powering anxieties as were his—argued surely the possession of
first-rate energies—of a perfectly indomitable resolution.   All
this while, moreover, he contrived to preserve an unruffled
temper—which, with a man of such sensibilities as his, afforded
indeed a signal instance of self-control; in short, on all these
grounds, Mr. Aubrey appears entitled to the sympathy and respect of all reflecting persons.   I spoke of his anxieties.   Suppose, thought he, health should fail him, what was to become
of him, and of those absolutely dependent upon him?   Suppose illness should invade the dear members of his family, what
was in prospect but destitution—or surrendering them up—
bitter and heart-breaking contingency! — to the precarious
charity of others?   What would avail all his exhausting labors
in the acquisition of professional knowledge, while his liberty
was entirely at the command of Mr. Titmouse, and Messrs.
Quirk, Gammon and Snap, who might, at any moment,
actuated by mercenary motives or impelled by caprice, blight
all his prospects and incarcerate him in a prison!   Yet, under this burden—to adopt the language of Sir Henry Spelman
on an analogous occasion, " *non ingentem solum, sed perpetuis
humeris sustinendum* "—Mr. Aubrey stood firmly.   He felt
that he was called upon to endure it; a blessed spirit ever, as
it were, beside him, whispering the consolatory assurance that
all this was ordered and designed by the Supreme Disposer of
events, as a *trial* of his constancy, and of his faith, and that
the *issue* was with HIM.   It is mercifully ordained, that " hope
springs eternal in the human breast," and that, too, in every
turn and variety of mortal misery.   It was so with Aubrey.
So long as he felt his health unimpaired and his mental
energies in full vigor, he looked on these blessings as a sort of
guarantee from Heaven that he should be able to carry on a
successful, though it might be a long and wearisome struggle
with adverse circumstances.   Still it cost him a very painful
effort to assume and preserve that exterior of tranquillity
which should calm and assure the beloved beings associated
with him in this hour of peril and suffering; and oftener than
they chose to let him know of it, did the keen eye of a wife's
and sister's love detect the gloom and oppression which darkened his countenance and saddened his manner.   Theirs was,
after all, with all that I have said, a happy little home.   He
was almost always punctual to his dinner-hour, to a minute,
knowing how a thousand fears on his account would otherwise
assail the fond beings who were counting the minutes till his
arrival.   When they had once thus met, they never separated

till bed-time. Sometimes Miss Aubrey would sit down to her piano, and accompany herself in some song or air, which equally, whether merry or mournful, revived innumerable touching and tender recollections of former days, and she often ceased, tremulously and in tears, in which she was not unfrequently joined by both of those who had been listening to her. Then he would betake himself to his labors for the rest of the evening (not quitting the room), they either assisting him— fair and eager amanuenses! or themselves reading, or engaged at needle-work. Oh! it was ecstasy, too, to that poor oppressed father to enter into the wild sports and gambols of his light-hearted little ones, Charles and Agnes, who always made their appearance for about a couple of hours after dinner; to tell them "stories," to listen to theirs, to show them pictures, to hear Charles read, and to join heartily in their frolics, rolling about even on the floor with them. But when he paused for a moment, and his wife and Kate succeeded him as their playmates, for a short interval, when his eye followed their movements, what sudden and sharp pangs would pass through his heart, as he thought of the future and what was to become of them!—And when their maid arrived at the appointed hour, causing all sport instantly to cease, and longing looks to be directed to papa and mamma, saying as plainly as could be said, "only a *few* minutes more," how fondly would he fold them in his arms! and when he felt their little arms clasping his neck and caressing him, and their kisses "all over" his face, feelings were excited within him which were too deep for utterance—which defy description. 'Tis said, I believe, of Robespierre, as an instance of his fearful refinement in cruelty, that a person of distinction who had become obnoxious to him he formally condemned to death, but allowed to remain in the torturing, the excruciating presence of his lovely family; he and they aware, all the while, that his doom was *irrevocable,* inevitable; and he momentarily liable to the summons to the guillotine, and which in fact came at length, when they were all seated together one day at the breakfast-table! Oh, the feelings with which that unfortunate person must have daily regarded the countenances of those around him! How applica-ble to his condition the heart-breaking strains of Medea—

Φεῦ, φεῦ, τί προσδέρκεσθέ μ' ὄμμασιν, τέκνα;
Τί προσγελᾶτε τὸν πανύστατον γέλων;
Αἰ, αἰ, τι δράσω; Καρδία γὰρ οἴχεται,
Γυναῖκες, ὄμμα φαιδρὸν ὡς εἶδον τέκνων.*

* Μήδεια, 1036-9.

The above passage was one that very frequently, on the occasions I have alluded to, occurred to the mind of Mr. Aubrey; for he felt himself indeed every moment at the mercy of those to whom he owed such tremendous sums of money, and for which he was liable to be, at any moment that might be selected by malice or rapacity, plucked from his little home and cast into prison!

Oh, happy ye, now reading these pages, "*unto whom the lines are fallen in pleasant places, yea, who have a goodly heritage;*" who live, as it were, in a "*land flowing with milk and honey;*" with whom life glides away like a tranquil and pleasant dream; who are not sternly bidden "*to eat your bread with quaking, and drink your water with trembling and with carefulness,*"* nor "*in vain to rise up early, to sit up late, to cut the bread of sorrows;*" who have, indeed, "*no thought for the morrow,*"—oh, ye who have leisure and ample means to pursue the object of an honorable ambition, undisturbed by daily fears for daily bread—by terror, lest implacable creditors should at length frustrate all your efforts, drive you from your position in society, and precipitate you and yours into ruin;—I say, oh ye! do I appeal to you in vain? Do you turn from this painful portion of my narrative with indifference, or contempt, or wearisomeness? If the mere *description*, brief though it may be, of the sufferings of the Aubreys be trying and disagreeable to you, what must have been to them the actual *endurance?* Poor Aubrey, as he walked along the crowded thoroughfares, morning and evening, between the Temple and Vivian Street, what a disheartening consciousness he felt of his personal insignificance! Which of the passengers, patrician or plebeian, that met or passed him, cared one straw for him, or would have cared a straw for him had they even known the load of misery and misfortune under which he staggered past them? Every time that he thus passed between the scene of his absorbing labors at the Temple and that green spot—his house in Vivian Street—in the world's wide desert, where only his heart was refreshed by the never-failing spring of domestic love and tenderness, he felt, as it were, but a prisoner out upon parole! It is easy to understand that when a man walks alone the streets of London, depressed in spirit, and alarmed by the consciousness of increasing pecuniary embarrassment, his temper is likely to become irritable, his deportment forbidding, his spirit stern and soured, particularly against those who appeal to his charity, which

---

* Ezek. xii. 18.

then, indeed, he might be pardoned for feeling, and bitterly—
to begin at home. It was not so, however, with Aubrey, whose
constant feeling was—*Haud ignarus mali, miseris succurrere
disco;* and though it may appear a small thing to mention, I
feel gratification in recording of him, that, desperate as were
his circumstances, infinitely enhanced to him as was the value
of money, he went seldom unprovided with the means of relieving the humbler applicants for charity whom he passed in
the streets—of dropping some small token of his love and pity
into the trembling and feeble hand of *want*—of those whose
necessities he felt to be greater even than his own. Never, indeed, did the timid eye of the most tattered, starved, and
emaciated object that is suffered to crawl along the streets
catch that of Aubrey, without making his heart acknowledge the
secret bond of misery which bound them together—that he beheld a brother in bondage, and on whom he cheerfully bestowed the humble pittance which he believed that Providence
had yet left at his disposal. Prosperity and adversity have
equally the effect upon an inferior mind and heart of gen-
erating *selfishness.* The one encourages, the other forces it.
Misery is apt to think its own sufferings greater than those of
any one else—and naturally. The eye, as it were, is filled
with the object of distress and danger—that is nearest—that is
in such fearful contiguity, obscuring from view all remoter
objects, at once scaring away presence of mind, and centering
its hopes and fears upon *self.* Not so, however, is it when a
noble nature is the sufferer—and more especially when the
nature is strengthened and brightened by the support and consolation derived from philosophy—and, above all, religion. To
many a strong spirit, destitute of such assistance, alas! how
often, under similar circumstances, have come—ghastly visitants!—*Despair* and *Madness,* with their hideous attendant,
Suicide, to do their bidding!

To Mr. Aubrey the Sabbath was indeed not only a day for
performing the public services of religion, but also a day of
real rest from the labors of life. It was not one to him of
puritanical gloom or excitement, but of sincere, cheerful,
fervent, enlightened devotion. It would have been to the
reader, I think, not an uninteresting sight to behold this unfortunate and harassed family at church. They took almost
the only pew that was vacant in the gallery—in a church not
far distant from Vivian Street—a pew just holding themselves
and little Charles, who, since their arrival in town, had begun
to accompany them to the morning service. There was something in their appearance—punctual as they were to morning

and evening service—that could hardly fail to interest any one
who observed them. Two very elegant and lovely women,
dressed in simple half-mourning—he of calm, gentlemanly
manners, an intellectual countenance, but overshadowed with
deep seriousness, if not melancholy—as, indeed, was the case
with the whole of the little group, except the beautiful child,
Charles. If their mere appearance was thus calculated to interest those around, who beheld them so punctual in their attendance, how much would that interest have been increased
had the beholder possessed an inkling of their singular and
melancholy history? Here were individuals, whose condition
was testing the reality of the consolations of religion, exhibiting humility, resignation, faith, a deep delight in attending
the house of HIM who had permitted such dreadful disasters
to befall them, and whose will it yet seemed to be that they
should pass through deeper sufferings than they had yet experienced. His temple seemed, indeed, to them a refuge and
shelter from the storm. To Mr. Aubrey every portion of the
church service was precious, for its purity, its simplicity, its
solemnity, its fervor, its truly scriptural character, its adapta-
tion to every imaginable condition of feeling and of circumstances, indeed, " to all sorts and conditions of men." There
was a little circumstance, fraught with much interest, which
occurred to them shortly after they had commenced their attendance at the church. An occasional sermon was preached
one evening by a stranger, from the words " *Though he slay
me, yet will I trust in him,*" on behalf of a neighboring dis-
pensary. Mr. Aubrey was soon struck by the unusual strength
and beauty of the sermon in point of composition. Its language was at once chaste, pointed and forcible; its illustrations
apt and vivid; its pathos genuine. As he went on, Mr. Aubrey
became more and more convinced that he had seen or heard
the preacher before; and on inquiring, afterward, his name,
his impressions proved to be correct; the preacher had been at
Oxford, at the very same college with him, and this was the
first time that they had since come within sight of each other.
Mr. Aubrey at once introduced himself, and was recognized,
and they renewed their early friendship. Mr. Neville, poor
soul, had nothing upon earth to support himself with but an
afternoon lectureship in one of the city churches, from which
he derived about £75 a year; and on this sum alone he had
contrived, for the last four or five years, to support both himself and his wife—a very amiable and fond woman. Fortunately, they had no children; but they had seen much affliction,
each of them being in but middling health, and a sad propor-

tion of his little income was, consequently, devoted to doctors' bills. He was an admirable scholar; a man of very powerful understanding, and deeply read in metaphysics and divinity. Yet this wretched pittance was all he could procure for his support; and pinching work for them, poor souls, it was indeed, to "make ends meet." They lived in very small but creditable lodgings; and amid all their privations, and with all the gloom of the future before them, they were as cheerful a little couple as the world ever saw. They dearly loved and would have sacrificed everything for each other; and so long as they could but keep their chins above water, and he realize the stern and noble feeling, " pauper, *sed in meo ære,*" they cared not for their exclusion from most of the comforts and all the elegances of life. They were, both of them, entirely resigned to the will of Heaven as to their position—nay, in all things. She generally accompanied him whithersoever he went; but on the present occasion the good little creature was lying at home in bed, enduring great suffering; and the thought of it made the preacher's heart very heavy, and his voice to falter a little, several times during his sermon. He was perfectly delighted when Mr. Aubrey introduced himself; and when the latter had heard all his friend's little history—who had indeed a child-like simplicity and frankness, and told Mr. Aubrey everything he knew about himself—Mr. Aubrey wrung his hand with great emotion, almost too great for expression. It seemed that a bishop, before whom poor Neville had accidentally preached seven years before, had sent for him, and expressed such a very high opinion of his sermon as led him reasonably to look for some little preferment at his lordship's hands, but in vain. Poor Neville had no powerful friends, and the bishop was overwhelmed with applicants for everything he had to give away; so it is not much to be wondered at that in time he totally lost sight of Mr. Neville, and of the hopes which had blossomed but to be blighted. What touched Mr. Aubrey to the soul was the unaffected cheerfulness with which poor Mr. Neville—now in his fortieth year—reconciled himself to his unpromising circumstances, the calmness with which he witnessed the door of preferment shut upon him forever. Mr. Aubrey obtained from him his address; and resolved that, though for reasons long ago mentioned he had withdrawn from almost every one of his former friends and associates, yet with this poor, this neglected but happy clergyman, he would endeavor to renew and cement firmly their early formed but long-suspended friendship. And when, on his return to Vivian Street (whither Mrs. and Miss Aubrey had proceeded alone, at

his request, while he walked on with Mr. Neville), he told
them the little history which I have above indicated to the
reader, how the hearts of all of them went forth toward one
who was in many respects a fellow-sufferer with themselves,
and, *practicing what he preached*, was really a pattern of
resignation to the will of God; of humble but hearty faith in
his mercy and loving kindness!

Mr. Aubrey was not long in paying his promised visit to Mr.
Neville, accompanied by Mrs. Aubrey. 'Twas a long and not
very agreeable walk for them toward St. George's in the East;
and on reaching a small row of neat houses, only one story
high, and being shown into Mr. Neville's very little sitting-
room, they found Mrs. Neville lying on a little rickety sofa
near the fire, looking very ill, and Mr. Neville sitting before
her, with a number of books on the table, and pen, ink, and
paper, with which he was occupied preparing his next Sunday's
sermon; but there was also a slip of paper on the table of a
different description, and which had occasioned both of them
great distress; viz., a rather peremptory note from their medical man, touching the payment of his " trifling account " of
£14 odd. Where poor Neville was to obtain such a sum,
neither he nor his wife knew; they had already almost deprived
themselves of necessary food and clothing to enable them to
discharge another account, and this new demand of an old
claim had indeed grievously disquieted them. They said nothing about it to Mr. and Mrs. Aubrey, who soon made themselves at home, and by their unaffected simplicity and cordiality
of manner, relieved their humble hosts from all anxiety. They
partook of tea, in a sufficiently homely and frugal style; and
before they rose to go they exacted a promise that, as soon as
Mrs. Neville should have recovered, they would both come and
spend a long day in Vivian Street. They soon became very
intimate; and, Mrs. Neville's health at length being such as to
preclude her from attending at all to her needle, the reader
will probably think none the less of Miss Aubrey and Mrs.
Aubrey when he hears that they insisted on taking the task
upon themselves (a matter in which they were becoming somewhat expert), and many and many an hour did these two
charming women spend, both in Vivian Street and at Mrs.
Neville's, in relieving her from her labors—particularly in
preparing their winter clothing. And now that I am on this
point, I may as well mention another not less amiable trait in
Kate; that, hearing of a girl's school about to be founded in
connection with the church which they attended, and in support of which several ladies had undertaken to prepare various

little matters, such as embroidery, lace, pictures and articles of
fancy and ornament, Kate also set to work with her pencil and
brushes. She was a very tasteful draughtswoman, and produced four or five such delicate and beautiful sketches, in
water color, of scenes in and about Yatton as made her a very
distinguished contributor to the undertaking, each of her
sketches producing upward of two guineas. She also drew a
remarkably spirited crayon sketch of the pretty little head of
Charles—who accompanied her to the place where her contributions were deposited, and delivered it in with his own hand.
—Thus, in short, were this sweet and amiable family rapidly
reconciling themselves to their altered circumstances—taking
real pleasure in the new scenes which surrounded them and
the novel duties devolving upon them; and as their feelings
became calmer, they felt how true it is that happiness in this
world depends not upon mere external circumstances, but
upon THE MIND—which, contented and well regulated, can
turn everything around it into a source of enjoyment and
thankfulness—making indeed *the wilderness to bloom and
blossom as the rose.*

They kept up—especially Kate—a constant correspondence
with good old Dr. Tatham; who, judging from the frequency and the length of his letters, which were written with
a truly old-fashioned distinctness and uniformity of character,
must have found infinite pleasure in his task. So also was it
with Kate, who, if she had even been writing to her lover—
nay, between ourselves, what would Mr. Delamere have given
to have had addressed to himself one of the long letters, crossed
down to the very postscript, full of sparkling delicacy, good
nature and good sense, which so often found their way to the
" Rev. Dr. Tatham, Yatton Vicarage, Yorkshire!" They
were thus apprised of everything of moment that transpired at
Yatton, to which their feelings clung with unalienable affection. Dr. Tatham's letters had indeed almost always a painful degree of interest attached to them. From his frequent
mention of Mr. Gammon's name—and almost equally *favorable*
as frequent—it appeared that he possessed a vast ascendency
over Mr. Titmouse, and was, whenever he was at Yatton, in a
manner its moving spirit. The Doctor represented Titmouse
as a truly wretched creature, with no more sense of religion
than a monkey; equally silly, selfish, and vulgar—unfeeling
and tyrannical whenever he had an opportunity of exhibiting
his real character.

It exquisitely pained them, moreover, to find pretty distinct
indications of a sterner and stricter rule being apparent at Yat-

ton than had ever been known there before, so far as the tenants and villagers were concerned. Rents were now required
to be paid with the utmost punctuality; many of them were
raised, and harsher terms introduced into their leases and
agreements. In Mr. Aubrey's time a distress or an action for
rent was literally a thing unheard of in any part of the estate;
but nearly a dozen had occurred since the accession of Mr. Titmouse. If this was at the instance of the ruling spirit, Mr.
Gammon had certainly got none of the odium of the proceeding, every letter announcing a resort to those extreme proceedings, being expressly authorized by Mr. Titmouse personally;
Mr. Gammon, on most of such occasions, putting in a faint
word or two in favor of the tenant, but ineffectually. The
legal proceedings were always conducted in the name of
"Bloodsuck and Son" whose town agents were "Quirk, Gammon and Snap;" but *their* names never came under the eye
of the defendants! No longer could the poor villagers, and
poorer tenants, reckon on their former assistance from the
Hall in the house of sickness and distress: cowslip wine, currant wine, elderberry wine, if made, were consumed in the
Hall. In short, there was a discontinuance of all those innumerable little endearing courtesies, and charities, and hos-
pitalities, which render a good old country mansion the very
heart of the neighborhood. The Doctor, in one of his letters,
intimated, with a sort of agony, that he had heard it mentioned by the people at the Hall, as probable that Mr. Titmouse
—the little Goth—would pull down that noble old relic, the
turreted gate-way; but that Mr. Gammon was vehemently opposed to such a measure; and that, if it were preserved, after
all, it would be entirely owing to the taste and the influence of
that gentleman. Had Dr. Tatham chosen, he could have
added a fact that would indeed have saddened his friends—
viz., that the old sycamore, which had been preserved at the
fond entreaties of Kate, and which was hallowed by so many
sad and tender associations, had been long ago removed as a
sort of eye-sore; Mr. Gammon had, in fact, directed it to be
done; but he repeatedly expressed to Dr. Tatham, confidentially, his regret at such an act on the part of Titmouse. He
could also have told them that there had been a dog-fight in
the village, at which Mr. Titmouse was present! Persons were
beginning to make their appearance in the village, of a very
different description from any that had been seen there in the
time of the Aubreys—persons, now and then, of loose, and
wild, and reckless characters. Mr. Titmouse would often get
up a fight in the village, and reward the victor with five or ten

shillings! Then the snug and quiet little "Aubrey Arms" was metamorphosed into the "Titmouse Arms;" and another set up in opposition to it, and called "The Toper's Arms;" and it was really painful to see the increasing trade driven by each of them. They were both full every night, and often during the day also; and the vigilant, and affectionate, and grieved eye of the good vicar noticed several seats in the church, which had formerly been occupied every Sunday morning and afternoon, to be—empty! In his letters, he considerably sunk the grosser features of Titmouse's conduct, which would have only uselessly grieved and disgusted his beloved correspondents. He informed them, however, from time to time of the different visitors at the Hall, particularly of the arrival and movements of their magnificent kinsfolk, the Earl of Dreddlington and Lady Cecilia, the Marquis of Gants-Jaunes de Millefleurs and Mr. Tuft—the novel state and ceremony which had been suddenly introduced there—at which they all ceased reading for a moment, and laughed, well knowing the character of Lord Dreddlington. At length, some considerable time after Mr. Titmouse's grand visitors had been at the Hall, there came a letter from Dr. Tatham, sent by a private hand, and not reaching Vivian Street till the evening, when they were sitting together, after dinner, as usual, and which contained intelligence that was received in sudden silence and with looks of astonishment; viz., *that Mr. Titmouse had become the acknowledged suitor of the Lady Cecilia!* Mr. Aubrey, after a moment's pause, laughed more heartily than they had heard him laugh for many months—getting up at the same time, and walking once or twice across the room —Mrs. Aubrey and Miss Aubrey gazed at each other for a few moments, without speaking a word; and you could not have told whether their fair countenances showed more of amusement or of disgust at the intelligence. "Well! it is as I have often told you, Kate," commenced Mr. Aubrey, after a while resuming his seat, and addressing his sister with an air of good-humored raillery; "You've lost your chance—you've held your head so high. Ah, 'tis all over now—and our fair cousin is mistress of Yatton!"

"Indeed, Charles," quoth Kate, earnestly, "I do think it's too painful a subject for a joke."

"Why, Kate!—You must bear it as well—"

"Pho, pho—nonsense, Charles! To be serious—did you ever hear anything so shocking as—"

"Do you mean to tell me, Kate," commenced her brother, assuming suddenly such a serious air as for a moment imposed

on his sister, "that to become mistress of dear old Yatton—
which was *offered* to you, you know—you would not have consented, when it came to the point, to become—Mrs. *Titmouse?*" For an instant Kate looked as if she would have
made, in the eye of the statuary, an exquisite model of beautiful disdain—provoked by the bare idea even, and put forward,
as she knew, in raillery only.

"You know, Charles," said she at length, calmly, her features relaxing into a smile, "that if such a wretch had ten
thousand Yattons, I would, rather than marry him—oh!"—
she shuddered—"spring from Dover cliff into the sea!"

"Ah, Kate, Kate!" exclaimed her brother, with a look of
infinite pride and fondness. "Even supposing for a moment
that you had no prev—"

"Come, Charles, no more nonsense," said Kate, patting his
cheek, and slightly coloring.

"I say, that even if—"

"Only fancy," interrupted Kate, "*Lady Cecilia*—TIT-
MOUSE! I see her before me now. Well, I protest it is positively insufferable; I could not have thought that there was a
woman in the whole world—why "—she paused, and added,
laughingly, "how I should like to see their correspondence!"

"What!" said Mrs. Aubrey, with a sly smile, first at her
husband, and then at Kate, "as a model for a certain *other*
correspondence that I can imagine—eh, Kate?"

"Nonsense, nonsense, Agnes!—what a provoking humor
you are both in this evening," interrupted Kate, with a slight
pettishness; "what we've heard makes *me* melancholy enough,
I assure you!"

"I suppose that about the same time that Lady Cecilia Titmouse goes to court," said her brother, "so will the Honorable Mrs. Dela—"

"If you choose to tease me, Charles, of course I can not
help it," quoth Kate, coloring still more; but it required no
very great acuteness to detect that the topic was not excessively offensive.

"Mrs. De—"

"Have done, Charles!" said she, rising; and, putting her
arm round his neck, she pressed her fair hand on his mouth;
but he pushed it aside laughingly.

"Mrs. De—Dela—Delamere," he continued.

"I will finish it for you, Charles," said Mrs. Aubrey, "the
Honorable Mr. and Mrs. Delamere—"

"What! do *you* turn against me too?" inquired Kate,
laughing very good-humoredly.

"I wonder what her stately ladyship's feelings were," said Aubrey, after a pause, "the first time that her elegant and accomplished lover *saluted* her!"

"Eugh!" exclaimed both Kate and Mrs. Aubrey, in a breath, and with a simultaneous shudder of disgust.

"I dare say poor old Lord Dreddlington's notion is that this will be a fine opportunity for bringing about his favorite scheme of *reuniting the families*—Heaven save the mark!" said Mr. Aubrey, just as the twopenny postman's knock at the door was heard; and within a few moments' time the servant brought upstairs a letter addressed to Mr. Aubrey. The very first glance at its contents expelled the color from his cheek: he turned, in fact, so pale that Mrs. Aubrey and Kate also changed color—and came and stood with beating hearts and suddenly suspended breath, one on each side of him, looking over the letter while he was reading it. As I intend presently to lay a copy of it before the reader, I shall first state a few circumstances, which will make it appear that this letter may be compared to a shell thrown into a peaceful little citadel by a skillful, though distant and unseen engineer—in short, I mean Mr. Gammon.

CHAPTER XXV.

THIS astute and determined person had long been bent upon securing one object—namely, access to Mr. Aubrey's family circle, for reasons which have been already communicated to the reader. That Mr. Aubrey was, at all events, by no means *anxious* for such a favor, had been long before abundantly manifest to Gammon, and yet not in a way to give him any legitimate or excusable grounds of offense. The Aubreys had, he acknowledged, and especially in the present circumstances, an unquestionable right to receive or reject, as they thought fit, any overtures to acquaintance. Nothing, he felt, could be more unexceptionably courteous than Mr. Aubrey's demeanor; yet had it been such as to satisfy him, that unless he resorted to some means of unusual efficacy, he never could get upon visiting terms with the Aubreys. The impression which Miss Aubrey had originally produced in his mind remained as distinct and vivid as ever. Her beauty, her grace, her elevated character (of which he had heard much on all hands), her accomplishments, her high birth — all were exquisitely appreciated by him, and conspired to constitute a prize, for the gaining of which he deemed no exertion too great, no enter-

prise too hazardous. He had, moreover, other most important
objects in view, to which a union with Miss Aubrey was in fact
essential. She was, again, the only person, the sight of whom
had in any measure given vitality to his marble heart, exciting
totally new thoughts and desires, such as stimulated him to a
fierce and inflexible determination to succeed in his purpose.
He was, in short, prepared to make almost any sacrifice, to
wait any length of time, to do or suffer anything that man
could do or suffer, whether derogatory to his personal honor or
not—in order either to secure the affections of Miss Aubrey,
or, at all events, her consent to a union with him.   Having
early discovered the spot where Mr. Aubrey had fixed his residence, Mr. Gammon had made a point of lying in wait on a
Sunday morning, for the purpose of discovering the church to
which they went; and having succeeded, he became a constant,
an impassioned, though an unseen observer of Miss Aubrey,
from whom he seldom removed his eyes during the service.
But this was to him a highly unsatisfactory state of things; he
seemed, in fact, not to have made, nor to be likely to make,
the least progress toward the accomplishment of his wishes,
though much time had already passed away. He was so deeply
engrossed with the affairs of Titmouse—which required his
presence very frequently at Yatton, and a great deal of his
attention in town—as to prevent his taking any decisive steps
for some time in the matter nearest his heart.   At length, not
having seen or heard anything of Mr. Aubrey for some weeks,
during which he—Gammon—had been in town, he resolved on
a new stroke of policy.

  " Mr. Quirk," said he one day to his excellent senior partner, " I fancy you will say that I am come to flatter you; but,
Heaven knows!—if there *is* a man on the earth with whom I
lay aside disguise, that man is my friend Mr. Quirk. Really, it
does seem, and mortifying enough it is to own it, as if events
invariably showed that you are right—and I wrong "—(Here
Mr. Quirk's appearance might have suggested the idea of a
great old tom-cat who is rubbed down the right way of the
fur, and does everything he can to testify the delight it gives
him by pressing against the person who affords him such
gratification),—" especially in financial matters—"

  " Ah, Gammon, Gammon! you're really past finding out!—
Sometimes, now, I declare I fancy you the very keenest dog
going in such matters, and at other times, eh?—not *particularly* brilliant.   When you've seen as much of this world's
villainy, Gammon, as I have, you'll find it as necessary as I
have found it, to lay aside one's—one's, I say, to lay aside all

scrup—that is—I mean—one's *fine feelings,* and so forth: you understand, Gammon?"

"Perfectly, Mr. Quirk—"

"Well—and may I ask, Gammon, what is the particular occasion of that screwed-up forehead of yours? Something in the wind?"

"Only this, Mr. Quirk—I begin to suspect that I did very wrong in recommending you to give an indefinite time to that Mr. Aubrey for payment of the heavy balance he owes us—by Heavens!—see how coldly he treats us!"

"Indeed, Gammon, I think so!—Besides—'*tis* an uncommon heavy balance to owe so long, eh?—Fifteen hundred pounds, or thereabouts?—'Gad! it's *that,* at least!"—Gammon shrugged his shoulders and bowed, as resigned to any step which Mr. Quirk might think proper to take.

"He's a villainous proud fellow, that Aubrey, eh?—Your swell debtors generally *are,* though—when they've got a bit of a hardship to harp upon—"

"Certainly we ought, when we had him in our power—"

"Ah!—D'ye recollect, Gammon? the *thumb-screw?* eh? whose fault was it that it wasn't put on? eh? Tell me that, friend Gammon! Are you coming round to old Caleb Quirk's matter-of-fact way of doing business? Depend on't, the old boy has got a trick or two left in him yet, gray as his hair's grown."

"I bow, my dear sir—I own myself worsted—and all through that absurd weakness I have, which some choose to call—"

"Oh, Lord, Gammon! Bubble, bubble and botheration—ah, ha! —Come, there's nobody here but you and me—and eh! *old Bogy* perhaps—so, why that little bit of blarney?"

"Oh! my dear Mr. Quirk, spare me that cutting irony of yours. Surely when I have made the sincere and humiliating submission to which you have been listening—but, to return to business. I assure you that I think we ought to lose not a moment in getting in our balance, or at least coming to some satisfactory and definite arrangement concerning it. Only pinch him, and he'll bleed freely, depend on it."

"Ah, ha! Pinch him, and he'll bleed! That's *my* thunder, Gammon, ah, ha, ha!—By Jove! that's it to a T!—I always thought the fellow had blood enough in him if we only squeezed him a little. So let Snap be off and have a writ out against Master Aubrey."

"Forgive me, my dear Mr. Quirk," interrupted Gammon, blandly—"we must go very cautiously to work, or we shall only injure ourselves and prejudice our most important—and *permanent* interests. We must take care not to drive him desperate, poor devil, or he may take the benefit of the act, and—"

" What a cursed scamp he would be to—"

" Certainly; but *we* should suffer more than he—"

" Surely, Gammon, they'd *remand* him! Eighteen months at the very least."

" Not an hour—not a minute, Mr. Quirk," said Gammon, very earnestly.

" The deuce they wouldn't? Well, Law's come to a pretty point! And so lenient as we've been!"

" What occurs to *me* as the best method of procedure," said Gammon, after musing for a moment—" is, for you to write a letter to him immediately—civil but peremptory—just one of those letters of yours, my dear sir, in which no man living can excel you—*suaviter in modo, fortiter in re,* Mr. Quirk."

" Gammon, you're a gentleman, every inch of you—you are, upon my soul! If there *is* one thing in which I—but *you're* a hand at a letter of that sort, too! And *you* have managed these people hitherto; why not go on to the end of the chapter?"

" Mr. Quirk, I look upon this letter as rather an important one—it ought to come from the head of the firm, and to be decisively and skillfully expressed, so as at once to—eh? but you know exactly what ought to be done."

" Well—leave it to me—leave it to me, Gammon: I think I *do* know how to draw up a teaser—egad! You can just cast your eye over it as soon as—"

" If I return in time from Clerkenwell, I will, Mr. Quirk," replied Gammon, who had, however, determined not to disable himself from saying with literal truth that he had not seen one line of the letter which might be sent! and, moreover, resolving to make his appearance at Mr. Aubrey's almost immediately after he should, in the course of the post, have received Mr. Quirk's letter—with every appearance and *expression* of distress, agitation, and even disgust; indignantly assuring Mr. Aubrey that the letter had been sent without Mr. Gammon's knowledge—against his will—and was entirely repudiated by him; and that he would take care, at all hazards to himself, to frustrate any designs on the part of his coarse and hard-hearted senior partner to harass or oppress Mr. Aubrey. With this explanation of precedent circumstances, I proceed to lay before the reader an exact copy of that old cat's-paw, Mr. Quirk's, letter to Mr. Aubrey, the arrival of which had produced the sensation I have already intimated.

" *Saffron Hill,*
" 30*th September*, 18—.

" Sir,—We trust you will excuse our reminding you of the very large balance (£1,446, 14*s.* 6*d.*, still remaining due upon our account—and which we understood, at the time when the very favorable arrangement to you, with respect to Mr. Titmouse, was made, was to have been long before this liquidated. Whatever allowances we might have felt disposed, on account of your peculiar situation, to have made (and which we *have* made), we can not but feel a little surprised at your having allowed several months to elapse without making any allusion thereto. We are satisfied, however, that you require only to be reminded thereof, to have your immediate attention directed thereto, and to act in that way that will conduce to liquidate our very heavy balance against you. We are sorry to have to press you; but being much pressed ourselves with serious outlays, we are obliged to throw ourselves (however reluctantly) upon our resources; and it gives us pleasure to anticipate that you must by this time have made those arrangements that will admit of your immediate attention to our overdue account, and that will render unnecessary our resorting to hostile and compulsory proceedings of that extremely painful description that we have always felt extremely reluctant to, particularly with those gentlemen that would feel it very disagreeable. We trust that in a week's time we shall hear from you to that effect, that will render unnecessary our proceeding to extremities against you, which would be extremely painful to us.—We remain, sir, yours most obediently,
" Quirk, Gammon & Snap.
" Charles Aubrey, Esq.

" P. S.—We should have no objection, if it would materially relieve you, to take your note of hand for the aforesaid balance (£1,446, 14*s.* 6*d.*) at two months, with interest and good security. Or say £800 down in two months, and a *warrant of attorney* for the remainder, at two months more."

As soon as all three of them had finished reading the above letter in the way I have described, Mrs. Aubrey threw her arms round her silent and oppressed husband's neck, and Kate, her bosom heaving with agitation, returned to her seat without uttering a word.

" My darling Charles!" faltered Mrs. Aubrey, and wept.

" Never mind, Charles—let us hope that we shall get through even *this*," commenced Kate; when her emotion prevented her proceeding. Mr. Aubrey appeared to cast his eye

again, but mechanically only, over the dry, civil, heart-breaking letter.

"Don't distress yourself, my Agnes," said he, tenderly,
placing her beside him, with his arm round her—"it is only
reasonable that these people should ask for what is their own;
and if their manner is a little coarse—"

"Oh, I've no patience, Charles!—It's the letter of a vulgar,
hard-hearted fellow," sobbed Mrs. Aubrey.

"Yes—they are wretches!—cruel harpies!" quoth Kate,
passionately, wiping her eyes—"they know that you have
almost beggared yourself to pay off by far the greater part of
their abominable bill, and that you are slaving day and night
to enable you to—" here her agitation was so excessive as to
prevent her uttering another word.

"I must write and tell them," said Aubrey, calmly, but
with a countenance laden with gloom—"it is all I can do—
but if they will *have patience with me, I will pay them all.*"

"Oh, they'll put you in prison, Charles, directly"—said
Kate, passionately; and rising, she threw herself into his arms,
and kissed him with a sort of frantic energy. "We're *very*
miserable, Charles—are not we? It's very hard to bear indeed," she continued, gazing with agonizing intensity on his
troubled features.   Mrs. Aubrey wept in silence.

"Are you giving way, my brave Kate, with this sudden
and momentary gust on the midnight sea of our trouble?" inquired her brother, proudly but kindly gazing at her, and with
his hand gently pushing from her pale cheeks her disordered
hair.

"Human nature, Charles, must not be tried too far—look
at Agnes, the darling little loves—"

"I am not likely to consult their interests, Kate, by yielding to unmanly emotion—am I, sweet Agnes?" She made
him no reply, but shook her head, sobbing bitterly.

"Pray what do you think, Charles, of your friend *Mr.
Gammon*, now?" inquired Kate, suddenly and scornfully.
"Oh, the smooth-tongued villain! I've always hated him!"

"I must say there's something about his eye that is anything but pleasing," said Mrs. Aubrey; "and so I thought
when I saw him at York for a moment."

"He's a hypocrite, Charles—depend upon it; and in this
letter he has thrown off the mask"—interrupted Kate.

"*Is* it *his* letter? How do we know that he has had anything to do with it?" inquired her brother, calmly—"It is
much more probable that it is the production of old Mr. Quirk
alone, for whom Mr. Gammon has, I know, a profound con-

tempt. The handwriting is Mr. Quirk's; the style is assuredly not Mr. Gammon's, and the whole tone of the letter is such as makes me confident that neither was the composition of the letter nor the idea of sending it his; besides, he has really shown on every occasion a straightforward and disinterested—"

"Oh, Charles, it is very weak of you to be so taken with such a man; he's a *horrid* fellow; I can't bear to think of him! One of these days, Charles, you'll be of my opinion!"—while she thus spoke, and while Mrs. Aubrey was, with a trembling hand, preparing tea, a double knock was heard at the street door.

"Gracious, Charles! who can that possibly be, and at this time of night?" exclaimed Kate, with alarmed energy.

"I really can not conjecture"—replied Mr. Aubrey, with no little agitation of manner, which he found it impossible to conceal—"we've certainly but very few visitors, and so late." The servant in a few minutes terminated their suspense, and occasioned them nearly equal alarm and amazement by laying down on the table a card bearing the name of MR. GAMMON.

"Mr. Gammon!" exclaimed all three in a breath, looking apprehensively at each other—"Is he *alone?*" inquired Mr. Aubrey, with forced calmness.

"Yes, sir."

"Show him into the parlor, then," replied Mr. Aubrey, "and say I will be with him in a few moments' time."

"Dear Charles, don't, dearest, think of going down," said his wife and sister, with excessive alarm and agitation: "desire him to send up his message."

"No, I shall go and see him, and at once," replied Mr. Aubrey, taking one of the candles.

"For Heaven's sake, Charles, mind what you say to the man; he will watch every word you utter. And, dearest, don't stay long; consider what tortures we shall be in!" said poor Mrs. Aubrey, accompanying him to the door.

"Rely on my prudence, and also that I shall not stop long," he replied: and descending the stairs, he entered the study. In a chair near the little book-strewn table sat his dreaded visitor, who, instantly, on seeing Mr. Aubrey, rose, with distress and agitation visible in his countenance and deportment. Mr. Aubrey, with calmness and dignity, begged him to resume his seat; and when he had done so, sat down opposite to him, with a sternly inquisitive look, awaiting his visitor's errand, who did not keep him long in suspense. For—"Oh, Mr. Aubrey!" commenced Mr. Gammon, with a somewhat tremu-

lous voice, " I perceive, from your manner, that my fears are
justified and that I am an intruder—a dishonorable and hypo-
critical one I must indeed appear; but, as one gentleman with
another, I request you to hear me. This visit appears indeed
unseasonable; but, late this afternoon, I made a discovery
which has shocked me severely, nay, I may say, disgusted me
beyond expression. Am I right, Mr. Aubrey, in supposing
that this evening you have received a letter from Mr. Quirk,
and about the balance due on our account?"

" Yes, sir," replied Mr. Aubrey, coldly.

" I thought as much," muttered Gammon with suppressed
vehemence—" execrable, heartless, sordid old—And he *knew*,"
continued Gammon, addressing Mr. Aubrey in an indignant
tone, " that my word was pledged to you that it should be long
before you were troubled about the business."

" I have nothing to complain of, sir," said Mr. Aubrey,
eying his agitated companion (who *felt* that he was) searchingly.

" But I have, Mr. Aubrey," said Gammon, haughtily.
" My senior partner has broken faith with me. Sir, you have
already paid more than will cover what is justly due to us; and
I recommend you, after this, to *have the bill taxed*. I do, sir,
and thereby you will get rid of every farthing of the balance
now demanded." Notwithstanding the air of sincerity with
which this was uttered, a cold thrill of apprehension and suspicion passed through Mr. Aubrey's heart, and he felt confident that some subtle and dangerous maneuver was being
practiced upon him—some hostile step urged upon him, for instance—which would be unsuccessful, and yet afford a pretext
to Messrs. Quirk, Gammon and Snap to treat him as one guilty
of a breach of faith, and warrant them in proceeding to extremities.

" I have no intention, sir, to do anything of the kind," said
he—" the original agreement between us was that your bill
should not be taxed. I adhere to it; and whatever course you
may feel disposed to take, I shall take no steps whatever of the
kind you mention. At the same time it is utterly impossible
for me to pay—"

" Mr. Aubrey!" interrupted Gammon, imploringly.

" And what you intend to do, for Heaven's sake, sir, do
quickly, and do not keep me in suspense."

" I perceive, Mr. Aubrey, that I am distrusted," said Gammon, with a somewhat proud and peremptory tone and manner.—" I excuse it; you are justly irritated, and have been insulted; so have I, too; and I choose to tell you, upon my sacred

word of honor as a gentleman, that I entirely disown and scout this whole procedure; that I never knew anything about it till, accidentally, I discovered lying on Mr. Quirk's desk, after his departure this evening from the office, a rough draft of a letter which I presumed you had received, especially as, on a strict inquiry of the clerks, I found that a letter had been put into the post addressed to you. Nay, more; Mr. Quirk, whose rapacity increases—I grieve to own—with his years, has been for many weeks harassing me about this detestable business, and urging me to consent, but in vain, to such an application as he has now meanly made behind my back, regardless of the injury it was calculated to do my feelings, and, indeed, the doubt it must throw over my sincerity and honor. Only a fortnight ago, he solemnly pledged himself never to mention the matter to either me or you again for at least a couple of years, unless something extraordinary should intervene. If the letter you have received is a transcript of the rough draft which I have read, it is a vulgar, unfeeling letter, and contains two or three willfully false statements. I therefore feel it due to myself to disavow all participation in this truly unworthy affair; and if you still distrust me, I can only regret it, but shall not presume to find fault with you for it. I am half disposed, on account of this and one or two other things which have happened, to close my connection with Mr. Quirk from this day—forever. He and I have nothing in common; and the kind of business which he prefers is perfectly odious to me. But if I should continue in the firm, I will undertake to supply you with one pretty conclusive evidence of my sincerity and truth in what I have been saying to you—namely, that on the faith and honor of a gentleman, you may depend upon hearing no more on this matter from any member of our firm. Let the *event*, Mr. Aubrey, speak for itself."—While Gammon was speaking with great earnestness and fervor, he had felt Mr. Aubrey's eye fixed upon him with an expression of stern incredulity—which, however, he at length perceived, with infinite inward relief and pleasure, to be giving way as he went on.

"Certainly, Mr. Gammon"—said Mr. Aubrey, when Gammon had ceased—"the letter you have mentioned has occasioned me—and my family—very great distress; for it is utterly out of my power to comply with its requisitions; and if it be intended to be really acted on and followed up"—he paused, and successfully concealed his emotion, "all my little plans are forever frustrated—and I am at your mercy—to go to prison, if you choose, and there end my days."—He paused—

his lip trembled, and his eyes were for a moment obscured with starting tears. So also was it with Mr. Gammon. "But,"— resumed Mr. Aubrey—"after the explicit and voluntary assurance which you have given me, I feel it impossible not to believe you entirely. I can imagine no motive for what would be otherwise such elaborate deception."

"*Motive*, Mr. Aubrey! The only motive I am conscious of is one resting on profound sympathy for your misfortunes— admiration of your character—and aiming at your speedy extrication from your very serious embarrassments. I am in the habit, Mr. Aubrey," he continued, in a lower tone, "of concealing and checking my feelings—but there *are* occasions"— he paused, and added, with a somewhat faltering voice—"Mr. Aubrey, it pains me inexpressibly to observe that your anxieties —your severe exertions—I trust in God I may not rightly add your *privations*—are telling on your appearance. You are certainly much thinner." It was impossible any longer to distrust the sincerity of Mr. Gammon—to withstand the arts of this consummate actor. Mr. Aubrey held out long, but at length surrendered entirely, and yielded implicit credence to all that Gammon had said — entertaining, moreover, commensurate feelings of gratitude toward one who had done so much to protect him from rapacious avarice and the ruin into which it would have precipitated him; and of respect for one who had evinced such an anxious, scrupulous, and sensitive jealousy for his own honor and reputation, and resolute determination to vindicate it against suspicion. Subsequent conversation served to strengthen his favorable disposition toward Gammon, and the same effect was also produced when he adverted to his previous and unwarrantable disgust and disbelief of that gentleman. He looked fatigued and harassed; it was growing late; he had come on his errand of courtesy and kindness, a great distance; why should not Mr. Aubrey ask him upstairs to join them at tea? To be sure, Mr. Aubrey had hitherto felt a disinclination—he scarce knew why—to have any more than mere business intercourse with Mr. Gammon, a member of such a firm as Quirk, Gammon and Snap—and, moreover, Mr. Runnington had more than once let fall expressions indicative of vehement distrust of Mr. Gammon; so had the Attorney-General; but what had Gammon's *conduct* been? Had it not practically given the lie to such insinuations and distrust, unless Mr. Aubrey was to own himself incapable of forming a judgment on a man's line of conduct, which had been so closely watched as that of Gammon by himself, Aubrey? Then Miss Aubrey had ever, and especially that very

evening—expressed a vehement dislike of Mr. Gammon—
avowed, also, her early and uniform distrust—'twould be extremely embarrassing to her suddenly to introduce into her
presence such an individual as Gammon; again, he had
promised to return quickly, in order to relieve their anxiety;
why should he not have the inexpressible gratification of letting Mr. Gammon himself, in his own pointed and impressive
manner, dispel all their fears? He would, probably, not stay
long.

"Mr. Gammon," said he, having balanced for some minutes these conflicting considerations in his mind—"there are
only Mrs. Aubrey and my sister upstairs. I am sure they will
be happy to see me return to them in time for tea, accompanied by the bearer of such agreeable tidings as yours. For
Mr. Quirk's letter, to be frank, reached me when in their presence, and we all read it together, and were dreadfully disturbed
at its contents." After a faint show of reluctance to trespass
on the ladies so suddenly, and at so late an hour, Mr. Gammon slipped off his great-coat, and, with intense but suppressed feelings of exultation at the success of his scheme, followed Mr. Aubrey upstairs. He felt not a little fluttered on
entering the room and catching a first glimpse of the two
lovely women—and one of them *Miss Aubrey*—sitting in it,
their faces turned with eager interest and anxiety toward the
door as he made his appearance. He observed that both of
them started and turned excessively pale.

"Let me introduce to you," said Mr. Aubrey, quickly, and
with a bright assuring smile, "a gentleman who has kindly
called to relieve us all from great anxiety—Mr. Gammon; Mr.
Gammon, Mrs. Aubrey—Miss Aubrey." He bowed with an
air of deep deference, but easy self-possession; his soul thrilling within him at the sight of her whose image had never been
from before his eyes since they had first seen her.

"I shall trespass on you for only a few minutes, ladies,"
said he, approaching the chair toward which he was motioned.
"I could not resist the opportunity so politely afforded me by
Mr. Aubrey of paying my compliments here, and personally
assuring you of my utter abhorrence of the mercenary and
oppressive conduct of a gentleman with whom, alas! I am
closely connected in business, and whose letter to you of this
evening I only casually became acquainted with a few moments before starting off hither. Forget it, ladies; I pledge
my honor that it shall *never be acted on!*" This he said with
a fervor of manner that could not but make an impression on
those whom he addressed.

"I'm sure we're happy to see you, Mr. Gammon, and very much obliged to you, indeed," said Mrs. Aubrey, with a sweet smile, and a face from which alarm was vanishing fast. Miss Aubrey said nothing; her brilliant eye glanced with piercing anxiety now at her brother, then at his companion. Gammon felt that he was distrusted. Nothing could be more prepossessing—more bland and insinuating, without a trace of fulsomeness, than his manner and address, as he took his seat between Mrs. Aubrey and Miss Aubrey, whose paleness rather suddenly gave way to a vivid and beautiful flush; and her eyes presently sparkled with delighted surprise on perceiving the relieved air of her brother, and the apparent cordiality and sincerity of Mr. Gammon. When she reflected, moreover, on her expressions of harshness and severity concerning him that very evening, and of which he now appeared so undeserving, it threw into her manner toward him a sort of delicate and charming embarrassment. Her ear drank in eagerly every word he uttered—so pointed, so significant, so full of earnest good-will toward her brother. His manner was that of a gentleman, his countenance and conversation that of a man of intellect;—was *this* the keen and cruel pettifogger whom she had learned at once to dread and to despise? They and he were, in a word, completely at their ease with one another, within a few minutes after he had taken his seat at the tea-table. Miss Aubrey's beauty shone that evening with even unwonted luster, and appeared as if it had not been in the least impaired by the anguish of mind which she had so long suffered. 'Tis quite impossible for me to do justice to the expression of her full beaming blue eyes—an expression of mingled passion and intellect—of blended softness and spirit, that, especially in conjunction with the rich tones of her voice, shed something like madness into the breast of Gammon. She, as well as her lovely sister-in-law, was dressed in mourning, which infinitely set off her dazzling complexion, and, simple and elegant in its drapery, displayed her exquisite proportions to the greatest possible advantage. "Oh, my God!" thought Gammon, with a momentary thrill of disgust and horror; "and this is the transcendent creature of whom that little miscreant, Titmouse, spoke to me in terms of such presumptuous and revolting license!" What would he not have given to kiss the fair and delicate white hand that passed to him his tea-cup! Then Gammon's thoughts turned for a moment inward—why, *what a scoundrel was he!* At that instant he was, as it were, reeking with his recent lie. He was there on cruel, false pretenses, which alone had secured him access into that little drawing-room and brought him into contiguity with the dazzling beauty beside him—pure and innocent as beautiful;—he was a fiend beside an angel. What an execrable hypocrite was he! He caught, on that memorable occasion, a sudden glimpse even of his own infernal SELFISHNESS—a sight that gave him a cold shudder. Then, was he not in the presence of his *victims?*— of those whom he was fast pressing on to the verge of destruction—to whom he was, at that moment, meditating profound and subtle schemes of mischief? At length they all got into animated conversation. He was infinitely struck and charmed by the unaffected simplicity and frankness of their manners, yet he felt a sad and painful consciousness of not having made the least way with them; though physically near to them, he seemed yet really at an unapproachable distance from them, and particularly from Miss Aubrey. He felt that the courtesy bestowed upon him was accidental, the result merely of his present position and of the intelligence which he had come to communicate; it was not *personal*—'twas nothing to *Gammon himself;* it would never be renewed, unless he should renew his device. There was not the faintest semblance of *sympathy* between them and him. Fallen as they were into a lower sphere, they had yet about them, so to speak, a certain atmosphere of conscious personal consequence derived from high birth and breeding—from superior feelings and associations—from a native frankness and dignity of character, which was indestructible and inalienable, which chilled and checked undue advances of any sort. They were still the Aubreys of Yatton, and he, in their presence, still Mr. Gammon, of the firm of Quirk, Gammon and Snap, of Saffron Hill—and all this on the part of the Aubreys without the least effort, the least intention, or consciousness. No, there had not been exhibited toward him the faintest indication of hauteur. On the contrary, he had been treated with perfect cordiality and frankness. Yet, dissatisfaction and vexation were, he scarce knew at the moment why, completely *flooding* him. Had he accurately analyzed his own feelings, he would have discovered the real cause to have been—*his own unreasonable, unjustifiable wishes and intentions.* They talked of Titmouse and his mode of life and conduct—of his expected alliance with the Lady Cecilia, at the mention of which Gammon's quick eye detected a passing smile of scorn on Miss Aubrey's countenance, that was death to all his own fond and ambitious hopes. After he had been sitting with them for scarcely an hour, he detected Miss Aubrey stealthily glancing at her watch, and at once arose to take his departure, with a very easy and grace-

11—Part II.

ful air, expressing an apprehension that he had trespassed upon their kindness. He was cordially assured to the contrary, but invited neither to prolong his stay nor renew his visit. Miss Aubrey made him, he thought, as he inclined toward her, *rather* a formal courtesy; and the tone of voice—soft and silvery —in which she said "Good-night, Mr. Gammon," fell on his eager ear, and sunk into his vexed heart, like music. On quitting the house, a deep sigh of disappointment escaped him. As he gazed for a moment with longing eyes at the windows of the room in which Miss Aubrey was sitting, he felt a profound depression of spirit; he had altogether *failed;* and he had a sort of cursed consciousness that he deserved to fail, on every account. Her image was before his mind's eye every moment while he was threading his way back to his chambers at Thavies' Inn; he sat for an hour or two before the remnant of his fire, lost in a reverie; and sleep came not to his eyes till a late hour in the morning. Just as his tortuous mind was losing hold of its sinister purposes in sleep, Mr. Aubrey might have been seen taking his seat in his little study, having spent a restless night. 'Twas little more than half past four o'clock when he entered, candle in hand, the scene of his early and cheerful labors, and took his seat before his table covered with loose manuscripts and books. His face was certainly overcast with anxiety, but his soul was calm and resolute. Having lighted his fire, he placed his candle on the table, and, leaning back for a moment in his chair, while the flickering increasing light of his crackling fire and candle revealed to him, with a sense of snugness, his shelves crammed with books, and the windows covered with an ample crimson curtain, effectually excluding the chill morning air—he reflected with a heavy sigh upon the precarious tenure by which he held the little comforts that were yet left to him. Oh!—thought he—if Heaven were but to relieve me from the frightful pressure of liability under which I am bound to the earth, what labor, what privation would I repine at! What gladness would not spring up in my heart! But rousing himself from vain thoughts of this kind, he began to arrange his manuscripts, when his ear caught a sound on the stairs—'twas the light step of his sister coming down to perform her promised undertaking—not an unusual one by any means—to transcribe for the press the manuscript he was about completing that morning. "My sweet Kate," said he, tenderly, as she entered with her little chamber light, which she extinguished as she entered—"I am really grieved to see you stirring so early—go back to bed." But she kissed his cheek affectionately, and refused to do any such thing; and telling him of the restless night she had passed, of which indeed her pale and depressed features bore but too legible evidence, she sat herself down in her accustomed place, nearly opposite to him, cleared away space enough for her little desk, and then opening it, was presently engaged in her delightful task—for to her it *was* indeed delightful—of copying out her brother's composition. Thus she sat, silent and industrious— scarce opening her lips, except to ask him to explain an illegible word or so, till the hour had arrived—eight o'clock—for the close of their morning toil. The reader will be pleased to hear that the article on which they had been engaged—and which was on a question of foreign politics, of great difficulty and importance—produced him a check for sixty guineas, and excited very general attention and admiration. Oh, how precious was this reward of his honorable and severe toil! How it cheered him who had earned it, and those who were, alas! entirely dependent upon his noble exertions! And how sensibly it augmented their little means! Grateful, indeed, were all of them for the success which had attended his labors!

As I do not intend to occupy the reader with any details relating to Mr. Aubrey's Temple avocations, I shall content myself with saying that the more Mr. Weasel and Mr. Aubrey came to know of each other, the more Aubrey respected his legal knowledge and ability, and he, Aubrey's intellectual energy and successful application, which, indeed, consciously brought home to Aubrey its own reward, in the daily acquisition of solid learning and increased facility in the use of it. His mind was formed for things, and was not apt to occupy itself with mere words or technicalities. He was ever in quest of the principles of the law, its reason and spirit. He quickly began to appreciate the sound practical good sense on which almost all the rules of law are founded, and the effectual manner in which they are accommodated to the innumerable and ever-varying exigencies of human affairs. The mere forms and technicalities of the law, Mr. Aubrey often compared to short-hand, whose characters to the uninitiated appear quaint and useless, but are perfectly invaluable to him who has seen the object, and patiently acquired the use of them. Whatever Mr. Aubrey's hand found to do, while studying the law, he did it, indeed, with his might—which is the grand secret of the difference in the success of different persons addressing themselves to legal studies. Great or small, easy or difficult, simple or complicated, interesting or uninteresting, he made a point of mastering it thoroughly, and, as far as possible, *by his own efforts;* which generated early a habit of self-reliance

which no one better than he knew the value of—how inestimable, how indispensable, not to the lawyer merely, but to any
one intrusted with the responsible management of affairs.   In
short, he had the success which is sure to attend the exertions
of a man of superior sense and spirit, who is in earnest in
what he is about.   He frequently surprised Mr. Weasel with
the exactness and extent of his legal information—his acuteness, clear-headedness, and tenacity in dealing with matters of
downright difficulty—and Mr. Weasel had several times, in
consultation, an opportunity of expressing his very flattering
opinion concerning Mr. Aubrey to the Attorney-General.   The
mention of that eminent person reminds me of an observation
which I intended to have made some time ago.   The reader is
not to imagine, from my silence upon the subject, that Mr.
Aubrey, in his fallen fortunes, was heartlessly forgotten or
neglected by the distinguished friends and associates of former
and more prosperous days.   It was not they that withdrew
from him, but he that withdrew from them; and that, too, of
set purpose, resolutely adhered to, on the ground that it could
not be otherwise, without seriously interfering with the due
prosecution of those plans of life on which were dependent not
only his all, and that of those connected with him—but his
fond hopes of yet extricating himself, by his own personal exertions, from the direful difficulties and dangers which at present environed him—of achieving, with his own right hand, independence.   The Attorney-General frequently called to inquire
how he was getting on; and, let me not forget here to state a
fact which I conceive infinitely to redound to poor Aubrey s
honor—viz., that he thrice refused offers made him from very
high quarters of considerable *sinecures, i. e.* handsome salaries
for purely nominal services—which he was earnestly and repeatedly reminded would at once afford him a liberal maintenance, and leave the whole of his time at his own disposal,
to follow any pursuit or profession that he chose.   Mr. Aubrey
justly considered that it was very difficult, if not indeed impossible for any honorable and high-minded man to be a sine-
curist.   He that holds a sinecure is, in my opinion, plundering
the public; and how it is more contrary to the dictates of honor
and justice, deliberately to defraud an individual, than deliberately and audaciously to defraud that collection of individuals
called the public, let casuists determine.   As for Mr. Aubrey,
he saw stretching before him the clear, straight, bright line of
honor, and he resolved to follow it, without faltering or wavering, come what, come might.   He resolved, with the blessing of
Providence, that his own exertions should procure his bread,

and, if such was the will of Heaven, lead him to distinction
among mankind. He had formed this determination, and resolved to work it out—never to pause or give way, but to die
in the struggle. Such a spirit must conquer whatever is opposed to it. What is *difficulty?* Only a word indicating the
degree of strength requisite for accomplishing particular objects; a mere notice of the necessity for exertion; a bugbear to
children and fools; only a mere stimulus to men.

Mr. Gammon felt very little difficulty in putting off Mr.
Quirk from his purpose of enforcing the payment by Mr. Aubrey of the balance of his account, in demonstrating to him
the policy of waiting a little longer. He pledged himself,
when the proper time came, to adopt measures of undoubted
efficacy—assuring his sullen senior in a low tone that since his
letter had reached Mr. Aubrey, circumstances had occurred
which would render it in the last degree dangerous to press
that gentleman upon the subject. What that was which had
happened, Mr. Gammon, as usual, refused to state. This was
a considerable source of vexation to the old gentleman; but he
had a far greater one, in the decisive and final overthrow of
his fondly cherished hopes concerning his daughter's alliance
with Titmouse. The paragraph in the *Aurora*, announcing
Mr. Titmouse's engagement to his brilliant relative, the Lady
Cecilia, had emanated from the pen of Mr. Gammon, who had
had several objects in view in giving early publicity to the
event he announced in such courtly terms. *Happening*, on
the morning on which it appeared, to be glancing over the
fascinating columns of the *Aurora* at a public office (the paper
taken in at their own establishment being the *Morning Growl*),
he made a point of purchasing that day's *Aurora;* and on returning to Saffron Hill, he inquired whether Mr. Quirk were at
home. Hearing that he was sitting alone in his room—in
rushed Mr. Gammon, breathless with surprise and haste, and
plucking the paper out of his pocket—" By heavens, Mr.
Quirk!"—he almost gasped as he doubled down the paper to
the place where stood the announcement in question, and put
it into Mr. Quirk's hands—" this young fellow's given you the
slip, after all! See! The moment that my back is turned—"

Mr. Quirk having, with a little trepidation, adjusted his
spectacles, persued the paragraph with a somewhat flushed
face. He had, in fact, for some time had grievous misgivings
on the subject of his chance of becoming the father-in-law of
his distinguished client, Mr. Titmouse; but now his faintest
glimmering of hope was suddenly and completely extinguished,
and the old gentleman felt quite desolate. He looked up, on

finishing the paragraph, and gazed rather ruefully at his indignant and sympathizing companion.

"It seems all up, Gammon, certainly—don't it?" said he,
with a flustered air.

"Indeed, my dear sir, it does! You have my sincerest—"

"Now comes t'other end of the thing, Gammon! You know
every promise of marriage has two ends—one joins the heart,
and t'other the pocket; *out* heart, *in* pocket—so have at him,
by Jove!" He rose up and rubbed his hands as he stood before the fire. "Breach of promise—thundering damages—
devilish deep purse—special jury—broken heart, and all that!
I wish he'd written her more letters! Adad, I'll have a shot
at him by next assizes—a writ on the file this very day! What
do you think on't, friend Gammon, between ourselves?"

"Why, my dear sir—to tell you the truth—aren't you really
well out of it? He's a miserable little upstart—he'd have
made a wretched husband for so superior a girl as Miss Quirk."

"Ay—ay! ay! She *is* a good girl, Gammon—there you're
right; would have made the best of wives—my eyes (between
ourselves!) how that'll go to the jury! Gad, I fancy I see 'em
—perhaps all of 'em daughters of their own."

"Looking at the thing calmly, Mr. Quirk," said Gammon,
gravely—apprehensive of Mr. Quirk's carrying too far so very
absurd an affair—"where's the *evidence* of the promise?—Because, you know, there's certainly *something* depends on that
—eh?"

"Evidence? Deuce take you, Gammon! where are your
wits? Evidence? Lots—lots of it! A'n't there? I—her
father? A'n't I a competent witness? Wait and see old
Caleb Quirk get into the box. I'll settle his hash in half a
minute."

"Yes—if you're believed, perhaps."

"*Believe* be ——! Who's to be believed, if her own father
isn't?"

"Why, you may be too much swayed by your feelings!"

"*Feelings* be ——! It's past all that; he has none—so he
must pay, for he *has* cash! He ought to be made an example
of!"

"Still, to come to the point, Mr. Quirk, I vow it quite
teases me—this matter of the evidence—"

"Evidence? Why, Lord bless my soul, Gammon," quoth
Quirk, testily, "haven't *you* had your eyes and ears open all
this while? Gad, what a crack witness you'd make? A man
of your—your intellect—serve a friend at a pinch—and in a
matter about his daughter? Ah, how often you've seen 'em

together—walking, talking, laughing, dancing, riding—writ
in her album—made her presents, and she him.   *Evidence?*
Oceans of it, and to spare! Secure Subtle—and I wouldn't
take £5,000 for my verdict!"

"Why, you see, Mr. Quirk," said Gammon, very seriously
—"though I've striven my utmost these six months to bring
it about, the artful little scamp has never given me the least
thing that I could lay hold of and *swear* to."

"Oh, you'll *recollect* enough, in due time, friend Gammon,
if you'll only turn your attention to it, and if you'll bear in
mind it's life and death to my poor girl. Oh, Lord! I must
get my sister to break it to her, and I'll send sealed instructions to Mr. —— Weasel, shall we say? or Lynx? ay, Lynx;
for he'll then have to fight for his own pleadings; and can't
turn round at the trial and say, ' this is not right,' and ' that's
wrong,' and, ' *why* didn't you have such and such evidence?'
Lynx is the man; and I'll lay the venue in Yorkshire, for Titmouse is devilish disliked down there; and a special jury will
be only too glad to give him a desperate slap in the chops!
We'll lay the damages at twenty thousand pounds! Ah! ha!
I'll teach the young villain to break the hearts of an old man
and his daughter. But, egad," he pulled out his watch, " half
past two; and Nicky Crowbar sure to be put up at three! By
Jove! it won't do to be out of the way; he's head of the gang,
and they always come down very liberally when they're in
trouble. Snap! Amminadab! halloo! who's there? Drat them
all, why don't they speak?" The old gentleman was soon,
however, attended to.

"Are they here?" he inquired, as Mr. Amminadab entered.

"Yes, sir, all three; and the coach is at the door, too.
Nicky Crowbar's to be up at three, sir—"

"I see—I know—I'm ready," replied Mr. Quirk, who was
presently seated in the coach with three gentlemen, to whom
he minutely explained the person of Mr. Nicky Crowbar, and
the place at which it was quite certain that Mr. Crowbar could
not have been at half past eleven o'clock on Tuesday night, the
9th of July, seeing that he happened at that precise time to
be elsewhere, in company with these three gentlemen—to wit,
at Chelsea, and *not at Clapham.*

Though Mr. Gammon thus sympathized with one of the
gentle beings who had been " rifled of all their sweetness," I
grieve to say that the other, Miss Tag-rag, never occupied his
thoughts for one moment. He neither knew nor cared whether
or not she was apprised of the destruction of all her fond
hopes by the paragraph which had appeared in the *Aurora.*

In fact, he felt that he had really done enough, on the part of
Mr. Titmouse, for his early friend and patron, Mr. Tag-rag,
on whom the stream of fortune had set in strong and steady;
and, in short, Mr. Gammon knew that Mr. Tag-rag had received a substantial memento of his connection with Tittlebat
Titmouse. In fact, how truly disinterested a man was Mr.
Gammon toward all with whom he came in contact! What
had he not done, as I have been saying, for the Tag-rags?
What for Mr. Titmouse? What for the Earl of Dreddlington?
What for Mr. Quirk, and even Snap? As for Mr. Quirk, had
he not been put in possession of his long-coveted bond for
£10,000? of which, by the way, he allotted £1,000 only to the
man—Mr. Gammon—by whose unwearying exertions and consummate ability he obtained so splendid a prize, and £300 to
Mr. Snap. Then, had not Mr. Quirk also been paid his bill
against Titmouse of £5,000 and upward, and £2,500 by Mr.
Aubrey? And governed by the articles of their partnership,
what a *lion's half* of this spoil had not been appropriated to
the respectable old head of the firm? Mr. Gammon did undoubtedly complain indignantly of the trifling portion allotted
to him, but he was encountered by such a desperate pertinacity
on the part of Mr. Quirk as baffled him entirely and caused
him to abandon his further claim in disgust and despair.
Thus, the £20,000 obtained by Mr. Titmouse, on mortgage of
the Yatton property, was reduced at once to the sum of £5,000;
—but out of this handsome balance had yet to come, first,
£800, with interest due to Mr. Quirk for subsistence-money
advanced to Titmouse; secondly, £500 due to Mr. Snap, for
moneys alleged to have been also lent by him to his friend Titmouse at different times, in the manner that has been already
explained to the reader—Snap's demand for repayment being
accompanied by *verbatim* copies of between forty and fifty
memoranda—many of them in pencil—notes of hand, receipts,
I O U's etc., in whose handwriting the figures representing
the sums lent, and the times when, could not be ascertained,
and did not signify; it being, in point of law, good *primâ facie*
evidence for Snap, in the event of a trial, simply to produce
the documents and prove the signature of his friend Mr. Titmouse. Titmouse discharged a volley of imprecations at
Snap's head, on receiving this unexpected claim, and referred
it to Mr. Gammon, who, after subjecting it to a *bonâ fide* and
very rigorous examination, found it in vain to attempt to resist or even diminish it; such perfect method and accuracy
had Snap observed in his accounts, that they secured him a
clear gain of £350: the difference between that sum and £500

being the amount actually and *bonâ fide* advanced by him to Titmouse. Deducting, therefore, £1,300 (the amount of the two minor demands of £800 and £500 above specified), there remained to Mr. Titmouse out of the £20,000 the sum of £3,700; and he ought to have been thankful, for he *might* have got *nothing*—or even have been brought in debt to Messrs. Quirk, Gammon and Snap. I say that Mr. Gammon would seem, from the above statement of accounts, not to have been dealt with in any degree adequately to his merits. He felt it so, but soon reconciled himself to it, occupied as he was with arduous and extensive speculations, amid all the complication of which he never for a moment lost sight of one object, viz. —*himself*. His schemes were boldly conceived, and he went about the accomplishment of them with equal patience and sagacity. Almost everything was going as he could wish. He had contrived to place himself in a very convenient fast-and-loose sort of position with reference to his fellow-partners—one which admitted of his easily disengaging himself from them, whenever the proper time arrived for taking such a step. He was absolute and paramount over Titmouse, and could always secure his instant submission, by virtue of the fearful and mysterious talisman which he occasionally flashed before his startled eyes. He had acquired great influence also over the Earl of Dreddlington—an influence which was constantly on the increase; and had seen come to pass an event which he judged to be of great importance to him—namely, the engagement between Titmouse and the Lady Cecilia. Yet was there one object which he had proposed to himself as incalculably valuable and supremely desirable—as the consummation of all his designs and wishes; I mean the obtaining the hand of Miss Aubrey—and in which he had yet a fearful misgiving of failure. But he was a man whose courage rose with every obstacle; and he fixedly resolved within himself to succeed, at any cost. 'Twas not alone his exquisite appreciation of her personal beauty—her grace, her accomplishments, her lovely temper, her lofty spirit, her high birth—objects all of them dazzling enough to a man of such a powerful and ambitious mind, and placed in such circumstances in life as Gammon. There were certain other considerations, intimately involved in all his calculations, which rendered success in this affair a matter of capital importance—nay, indispensable. Knowing, as I do, what had passed, at different times, between that proud and determined girl and her constant and enthusiastic lover, Mr. Delamere, I am as certain as a man can be of anything that has not actually happened, that, though she may possibly not be fated to become Mrs. Delamere, she will certainly NEVER become—Mrs. Gammon. Loving Kate as I do, and being thoroughly acquainted with Gammon, I feel deep interest in his movements, and am watching them with great apprehension;—she, lovely, innocent, unsuspicious; he, subtle, selfish, unscrupulous, desperate! And he has great power in his hands; is he not silently surrounding his destined prey with unperceived but inevitable meshes? God guard thee, my Kate, and reward thy noble devotion to thy brother and his fallen fortunes. Do we chide thee for clinging to them with fond tenacity in their extremity, when thou art daily importuned to enter into that station which thou wouldst so adorn?

Gammon's reception by the Aubrey's, in Vivian Street—kind and courteous though it had surely been—had ever since rankled in his heart. Their abstaining from a request to him to prolong his stay, or to renew his visit, he had noted at the time, and had ever since reflected upon with pique and discouragement. Nevertheless, he was resolved, at all hazards, to become at least an occasional visitor in Vivian Street. When a fortnight had elapsed without any further intimation to Mr. Aubrey concerning the dreaded balance due to the firm, Gammon ventured to call in, for the purpose of assuring Mr. Aubrey that it was no mere temporary lull; that he might divest his mind of all uneasiness on the subject; and of asking whether he (Gammon) had not told Mr. Aubrey truly that he both could and would restrain the hand of Mr. Quirk. Could Mr. Aubrey be otherwise than grateful for such active and manifestly disinterested kindness? Again Gammon made his appearance at Mrs. Aubrey's tea-table—and was again received with all the sweetness and frankness of manner which he had formerly experienced from her and Miss Aubrey. Again he called on some adroit pretext or another—and once heard Miss Aubrey's rich voice and exquisite performance on the piano. He became subject to emotions and impulses of a sort that he had never before experienced; yet, whenever he retired from their fascinating society, he felt an aching void, as it were, within—he perceived the absence of all sympathy toward him; he felt indignant—but that did not quench the ardor of his aspirations. 'Tis hardly necessary to say that on every occasion Gammon effectually concealed the profound and agitating feelings which the sight of Miss Aubrey called forth in him; and what a tax was this upon his powers of concealment and self-control! How he laid himself out to amuse and interest them all! With what racy humor would he describe the vulgar absurdities of Titmouse—the stately eccentricities of the Dreddlingtons! With what eager and breathless interest was he listened to! No man could make himself more unexceptionably agreeable than Gammon; and the ladies really took pleasure in his society; Kate about as far from any notion of the real state of his feelings as of what was at that moment going on at the antipodes. Her reserve toward him sensibly lessened; why, indeed, should she feel it, toward one of whom Dr. Tatham spoke so highly, and who appeared to warrant it? Moreover, Mr. Gammon took special care to speak in the most unreserved and unqualified manner of the mean and mercenary character of Mr. Quirk—of the miserable style of business in which he, Mr. Gammon, was compelled for only a short time longer, he trusted, to participate, and which was really revolting to his own feelings; in short, he did his best to cause himself to appear a sensitive and high-minded man, whose unhappy fate it had been to be yoked with those who were the reverse. Mr. Aubrey regarded him from time to time with silent anxiety and interest, as one who had it in his power, at any instant he might choose, to cause the suspended sword to fall upon him; at whose will and pleasure he continued in the enjoyment of his present domestic happiness, instead of being incarcerated in prison; but who had hitherto evinced a disposition of signal forbearance, sincere good-nature, and disinterestedness. They often used to speak of him, and compare the impression which his person and conduct had produced in their minds; and in two points they agreed—that he exhibited anxiety to render himself agreeable, and that there was a certain *something* about his eye which none of them liked. It seemed as though he had in a manner two natures, and that one of them was watching the effect of the efforts made by the other to beguile!

CHAPTER XXVI.

WHILE, however, the Fates thus seemed to frown upon the aspiring attempts of Gammon toward Miss Aubrey, they smiled benignantly enough upon Titmouse and his suit with the Lady Cecilia. The first shock over—which no lively sensibilities or strong feelings of her ladyship tended to protract, she began insensibly to get familiar with the person, manners and character of her future lord, and reconciled to her fate. " When people understand that they *must* live together," said a very great man, " they learn to soften, by mutual accommodation, that yoke which they know that they can not shake

off; they become good husbands and wives, for necessity is a
powerful master in teaching the duties which it imposes!"*
The serene intelligence of Lady Cecilia having satisfied her
that "IT WAS HER FATE" to be married to Titmouse, she
resigned herself to it tranquilly, calling in to her assistance
divers co-operative reasons for the step she had agreed to take.
She could thereby accomplish, at all events, one darling object
of her papa's—the reunion of the long and unhappily severed
family interests.   Then Yatton was certainly a delightful
estate to be mistress of—a charming residence, and one which
she might in all probability calculate on having pretty nearly
to herself.   His rent-roll was large and unincumbered, and
would admit of a handsome jointure.   On her accession to her
own independent rank, the odious name of Titmouse would
disappear in the noble one of Lady Drelincourt, peeress in her
own right, and representative of the oldest barony in the kingdom.   Her husband would then become a mere cipher—no
one would ever hear of him, or inquire after him, or think or
care about him—a mere mote in the sunbeam of her own
splendor.   But above all, thank Heaven! there were many
ways in which a *separation* might be brought about—never
mind how soon after marriage—a step which was becoming
one quite, of course, and implied nothing derogatory to the
character or lessening to the personal consequence of the lady
—who indeed was almost, as of course, recognized as an object
of sympathy, rather than of suspicion or scorn.   These were
powerful forces, all impelling her in one direction—and irre-
sistibly.   How could it be otherwise with a mere creature of
circumstances like her?   Notwithstanding all this, however,
there were occasions when Titmouse was presented to her in a
somewhat startling and sickening aspect.   It sometimes almost
choked her to see him—ridiculous object!—in the company of
gentlemen—to witness their treatment of him, and then reflect that he was about to become her—lord and master.   One
day, for instance, she accompanied the Earl in the carriage to
witness the hounds throw off, not far from Yatton, and where
a very brilliant field was expected.   There were, in fact, about
two hundred of the leading gentlemen of the county assembled
—and, dear reader, fancy the figure Titmouse must have presented among them—his quizzing-glass screwed into his eye,
and clad in his little pink and leathers!—What a seat was his!
How many significant and scornful smiles and winks and

* The late venerable and gifted Lord Stowell, in the case of *Evans* v
Evans. 1 Consistory Reports, p. 36.

shrugs of the shoulders did his appearance occasion among his bold and high-bred companions! And only about four or five minutes after they had "gone away"—this unhappy little devil was thoroughly found out by the noble animal he rode, and who equally well knew *his own business* and what he had on. In trying to take a dwarf wall, on the opposite side of an old green horse-pond by the road-side, he urged his horse with that weak and indecisive impulse which only disgusted him; so he suddenly drew back at the margin of the pond—over head and heels flew Titmouse, and descended plump on his head into the deep mud, where he remained for a moment or two, up to his shoulders, his little legs kicking about in the air—

" Who's that?" cried one—and another—and another—without stopping, any more than the Life Guards would have stopped for a sudden individual casualty in the midst of their tremendous charge at Waterloo—till the very last of them, who happened to be no less a person than Lord De la Zouch, seeing, as he came up, the desperate position of the fallen rider, reined up, dismounted, and with much effort and inconvenience aided in extricating Titmouse from his fearful yet ludicrous position—and thus fortunately preserved to society one of its brightest ornaments. As soon as he was safe—a dismal spectacle to gods and men—his preserver, not disposed, by discovering who Titmouse was, to supererogatory courtesy, mounted his horse, leaving Titmouse in the care of an old woman whose cottage was not far off, and where Titmouse, having had a good deal of the filth detached from him, remounted his horse and turned its head homeward—heartily disposed, had he but *dared*, cruelly to spur, and kick, and flog it; and in this pickle—stupid and sullen, and crest-fallen—he was overtaken and recognized by Lord Dreddlington and Lady Cecilia, returning from the field!

This was her future husband—

Then again—poor Lady Cecilia!—what thought you of the following, which was one of the letters he addressed to you?—Well might Miss Aubrey exclaim, " How I should like to see their correspondence!"

" The Albany, Picadilly, London,
" 12th Oct., 18—.

" My dear Cecilia,

" I take Up My pen To Inform you of Arriving safe Here, where Am sorry how^r· To say There is No One knows except Tradespeople Going About and so Dull on Acc^t· of Customers Out of Town, Dearest love You Are the Girl of my Heart As

I am of Your's and am particular Lonely Alone Here and wish
to be There *where she Is* how I Long to Fold My dearest girl
in My Arms hope You Don't Forget Me As soon as I am Absent do You often Think of *me* w$^{h.}$ I do indeed of *you*, and
looking Forward to The Happy Days When We are United in
the Happy bonds of Hymmen, never To part Again dearest I
Was Driving yesterday In my New Cabb In the park, where
whom Sh$^{d.}$ I Meet but That Miss Aubrey W$^{h.}$ they say (Between you And I and The post) is Truly in a Gallopping Consumption on Acc$^{t.}$ Of my Not Having Her A likely thing indeed that I ever car'd for Such an individule wh$^{h.}$ Never Did
Only of you, Dearest What shall I Send you As A Gift Shall
it Be In The cloathing Line, For there is a Wonderful Fine and
Choice Assortm$^{t.}$ of Cashmere Shawls and Most Remarkable
Handsome Cloaks, All Newly arriv'd fr. Paris, Never Think
Of The price w$^{h.}$ Betwixt Lovers Goes For Nothing.   However
Large the Figure Only Say what You Shall have and Down It
shall Come And Now dearest Girl Adieu.

        " Those Can't meet Again who Never Part."

dearest Your's to command till death
                                    " T. TITMOUSE.
    " P. T. O.—Love and Duty To My Lord (of course) who
shall Feel only Too happy to Call My Father-in-Law, the
Sooner the better."

When poor Lady Cecilia received this letter, and had read
over only half a dozen lines of it, she flung it on the floor, and
threw herself down on the sofa in her dressing-room, and remained silent and motionless for more than an hour; and when
she heard Miss Macspleuchan knock at her door for admittance,
Lady Cecilia started up, snatched the letter from the floor, and
thrust it into her dressing-case before admitting her " humble
companion."
    A succession of such letters as the above might have had the
effect upon Lady Cecilia's " *attachment* " to Titmouse, which
the repeated effusion of cold water would have upon the thermometer; but the crack-brained Fates still favored Mr. Titmouse, by presently investing him with a character, and placing him in a position calculated to give him personal dignity,
and thereby redeem and elevate him in the estimation of his
fastidious and lofty mistress—I mean that of candidate for a
seat in Parliament—for the represetnation of a borough in
which he had a commanding influence.
    After a national commotion commensurate with the magni-

tude of the boon that had been sought for, the great BILL FOR GIVING EVERYBODY EVERYTHING had passed into a law, and the people were frantic with joy. Its blooming first fruits were of a sort that satisfied the public expectation, viz., two or three Earls were turned into Marquises, and one or two Marquises into Dukes, and deservedly; for these great men had far higher titles to the gratitude and admiration of the country, in exacting this second Magna Charta from King ——, than the stern old barons in extorting the first from King John—namely, they parted with vast substantial political power for only a nominal *quid pro quo*, in the shape of a bit of ribbon or a strawberry leaf. Its next immediate effect was to cleanse the Augean stable of the House of Commons, by opening upon it the flood-gates of popular will and popular opinion; and having utterly expelled the herd of ignorant and mercenary wretches that had so long occupied and defiled it, their places were to be supplied by a band of patriots and statesmen, as gifted as disinterested—the people's own enlightened, unbiased, and deliberate choice. Once put the government of the country—the administration of affairs—into hands such as these, and the inevitable result would be, the immediate regeneration of society and the securing the greatest happiness to the greatest number. It was fearfully apparent that, under the old system, we had sunk into irredeemable contempt abroad, and were on the very verge of ruin and anarchy at home. So blessedly true is it, that when things come to the worst, they begin to mend! In short, the enlightened and enlarged constituencies began forthwith to look out for fit objects of their choice—for the best men; men of independent fortune; of deep stake in the welfare of the country; of spotless private and consistent public character; who, having had adequate leisure, opportunity, inclination, and capacity, had fitted themselves to undertake, with advantage to the country, the grave responsibilities of statesmen and legislators. Such candidates, therefore, as Mr. Tittlebat Titmouse became naturally in universal request; and the consequence was, such a prodigious flight of Titmice into the House of Commons—but whither am I wandering? I have to do with only one little borough—that of Yatton, in Yorkshire. The Great Charter operated upon it, by *first*, in a manner, *amputating* it of one of its members; *secondly*, extending its boundary—Grilston, and one or two of the adjacent places, being incorporated into the new borough; *thirdly*, by the introduction of the new qualification of voters. I have ascertained from a very high quarter—in fact from a Cabinet Minister, *since deceased*—a

curious and important fact, viz., that had Mr. Titmouse failed
in recovering the Yatton property, or been of different political opinions, in either of these cases, the little borough of Yatton was doomed to utter extinction; a circumstance which
shows the signal vigilance, the accurate and comprehensive
knowledge of local interests and capabilities evinced by those
great and good men who were remodeling the representation
of the country.   How little did my hero suspect that his political opinions, as newly installed owner of Yatton, formed a
topic of anxious discussion at more than one Cabinet meeting,
previous to the passing of the Great Bill.   Upon such considerations did it depend whether Yatton should be at once deposited in the sepulcher of " *Schedule A*," or added to the
dismal rank of surviving but *maimed* ones in " *Schedule B.*"
As its boundary was extended, so the constituency of Yatton
was, as I have said, enlarged, the invaluable elective franchise
being given to those most in need of the advantages it could
immediately procure; and the fleeting nature of whose interest naturally enhanced their desire to consult the interests of
those who had a permanent and deep stake in its welfare.
Though, however, the change effected by the new act had so
considerably added to the roll of electors, it had not given
ground for serious apprehension as to the security of the seat
of the owner of the Yatton property.   After a very long and
private interview between Gammon and Titmouse, in which
something transpired which may be referred to hereafter, it
was agreed that—(the New Writs having issued within one
week after the calmed and sobered new constituencies had been
organized—which organization, again, had been wisely effected
within a week or two after the passing of the act which created
them)—Mr. Titmouse should instantly scare away all competition, by announcing his determination to start for the borough.
As soon as this was known, a deputation from a club of the
new electors in Grilston waited upon Mr. Titmouse—to propose the pecuniary terms on which their support was to be obtained.   He hereat was somewhat startled—but Gammon saw
in it the legitimate working of the new system; and—nothing
was ever better managed!—nobody was in any mischievous
secret—neither party compromised; and yet the happy result
was—that *one hundred and nine* votes were secured in Grilston
alone for Mr. Titmouse.   Then Gammon appointed Messrs.
Bloodsuck and Son the local agents of Titmouse; for whom he
wrote an address to the electors—and, Titmouse promising to
have it printed forthwith, Mr. Gammon returned to town for
a day or two.   Nothing could have been more skillful than the

address which he had prepared—terse and comprehensive, and showy, meaning everything or nothing—(*dolosus semper versatur in generalibus*, was an observation of Lord Coke's, on which Gammon kept his eye fixed, in drawing up his " address "). Yet it came to pass, that on the evening of the day of Gammon's departure, a Mr. Phelim O'Doodle, a splendid billiard player (in fact he had commenced life in the capacity of *marker* to a billiard-table near Leicester Square), and also one of the first members returned—only a few days before —for an Irish borough in the Liberal interest, chanced to take Yatton in his way to Scotland (where he was going to officiate professionally at a grand match at billiards at the house of an early patron, Sir Archibald M'Cannon), from London; and being intimate with Mr. Titmouse, from whom (to conceal nothing from the reader) he had borrowed a little money a few months before, to enable him to present himself to his intelligent and enthusiastic constituency—they sat down to canvass the merits of the Address which the astute but *absent* Gammon had prepared for Titmouse. Mr. O'Doodle pronounced it " devilish tame and *maiger*," comparing it to toddy, with the *whisky omitted;* and availing himself of Gammon's draft as far as he approved of it, he drew up the following Address, which put Titmouse into an ecstasy; and he sent it off the very next morning for insertion in the *Yorkshire Stingo*. Here is an exact copy of that judicious and able performance—which I must own I consider quite a model in its way.

" *To the worthy and independent Electors of Yatton.*

" GENTLEMEN,—His Majesty having been pleased to dissolve the late Parliament, under very remarkable and exciting circumstances, and, in the midst of the transports of enthusiasm arising out of the passing of that second Great Charter of our Liberties, the *Act for Giving Everybody Everything*, with kindly wisdom, to call upon you to exercise immediately the high and glorious privilege of choosing your representative in the New Parliament, I beg leave to announce myself as a candidate for that distinguished honor. Gentlemen, long before I succeeded in establishing my right to reside among you in my present capacity, I felt a deep interest in the welfare of the tenants of the property, and especially of those residing in the parts adjacent, and who are now so happily introduced into the constituency of this ancient and loyal borough. I trust that the circumstance of my ancestors having resided for ages within it will not indispose you to a favorable reception of their descendant and representative. Gentlemen, my political opinions are those which led to the passing of the Great Measure I have alluded to, and which are bound up in it. Without going into details which are too multifarious for the limits of such an Address as the present, let me assure you, that though firmly resolved to uphold the agricultural interests of this great country, I am equally anxious to sustain the commercial and manufacturing interests; and whenever they are unhappily in fatal conflict with each other, I shall be found at my post, zealously supporting *both*, to the utmost of my ability. Though a sincere and firm member and friend of the Established Church, I am not insensible to the fearful abuses which at present prevail in it; particularly in its revenues, which I am disposed to lessen and equalize—devoting the surplus capital to useful purposes connected with the State, from which she derived them, as history testifies. I am bent upon securing the utmost possible latitude to every species of Dissent. In fact, I greatly doubt whether any form of religion ought to be ' *established* ' in a free country. While I am resolved to uphold the interests of Protestantism, I think I best do so by seeking to remove all restrictions from the Catholics, who, I am persuaded, will sacredly abstain from endeavoring to promote their own interests at the expense of ours. The infallible page of history establishes their humility, meekness, and moderation. Gentlemen, depend upon it, the established religion is most likely to flourish when surrounded by danger and threatened by persecution; it has an inherent vitality which will defy, in the long run, all competition. Gentlemen, I am for Peace, Retrenchment, and Reform, which are in fact the Three Polar Stars of my political conduct. I am an advocate for quarterly Parliaments, convinced that we can not too often be summoned to give an account of our stewardship —and that the frequency of elections will occasion a wholesale agitation and stimulus to trade. I am for extending the elective franchise to all, except those who are actually the inmates of a prison or a poor-house on the day of election; and for affording to electors the inviolable secrecy and protection of the Ballot. I am an uncompromising advocate of civil and religious liberty all over the globe; and, in short, of giving the greatest happiness to the greatest number. Gentlemen, before concluding, I wish to state explicitly, as the result of long and deep inquiry and reflection, that I am of opinion that every constituency is entitled, nay bound, to exact from a candidate for its suffrages the most strict and minute pledges as to his future conduct in Parliament, in every matter, great or small, that can come before it; in order to prevent his judgment being influenced and warped by the dangerous sophistries and fallacies which are broached in Parliament, and protect his integrity from the base, sinister, and corrupt influences which are invariably brought to bear on public men. I am ready, therefore, to pledge myself to anything that may be required of me by any elector who may honor me with his support. Gentlemen, such are my political principles, and I humbly hope that they will prove to be those of the electors of this ancient and loyal borough, so as to warrant the legislature in having preserved it in existence amidst the wholesale havoc which it has just made in property of this description. Though it is not probable that we shall be harassed by a contest, I shall make a point of waiting upon you all personally, and humbly answering all questions that may be put to me; and should I be returned, rely upon it, that I will never give you occasion to regret your display of so signal an evidence of your confidence in me. I have the honor to be, Gentlemen, your most obedient and humble servant,

" T. TITMOUSE.
" Yatton, 3rd December, 18—."

" Upon my soul, if that don't carry the election hollow," said Mr. O'Doodle, laying down his pen and mixing himself a fresh tumbler of half and half brandy and water, " you may call me bog-trotter to the end of my days, and be —— to me!" ! ! !

" Why—a—ya—as! 'pon my life it's quite a superior article, and no mistake "—quoth Titmouse; " but—eh? d'ye think they'll ever believe I writ it all? Egad, my fine fellow, to compose a piece of composition like that, by Jove!—requires —and besides, suppose those dem fellows begin asking me all sorts of questions and thingembobs, eh? You *couldn't* stay and go about with one a bit? Eh, Phelim?"

" Fait, Titty, an' it's mighty little awake to the way of *doing business*, that ye are! ah, ah! Murder and thieves! what does it signify what you choose to say or write them? they're only *pisintry*, and—the real point to be looked at is this—all those that you can command, of course you will, or send 'em to the right about; and those that you can't—that's the *new* blackguards round about—*buy*, if it's necessary, fait."

" It's done!—It *is*, 'pon my soul!" whispered Titmouse.

" Oh! Is it in earnest you are? Then you're M. P. for the borough; and on the strength of it I'll replenish!" and so he did, followed by Titmouse; and in a pretty state they, some hour or two afterward, were conducted to their apartments.

It is difficult to describe the rage of Gammon on seeing the address which had been substituted for that which he had prepared with so much caution and tact: but the thing was done, and he was obliged to submit. The address duly appeared in the *Yorkshire Stingo*, and was also placarded liberally all over the borough, and distributed about, and excited a good deal of interest, and also much approbation among the new electors. It was thought, however, that it was a piece of supererogation, inasmuch as there could be no possible doubt that Mr. Titmouse would *walk over the course.*

In this, however, it presently proved that the *quidnuncs* of Yatton were very greatly mistaken. A copy of the *Yorkshire Stingo*, containing the foregoing "Address," was sent, on the day of its publication, by Dr. Tatham to Mr. Aubrey, who had read it aloud, with feelings of mingled sorrow and contempt, on the evening of its arrival, in the presence of Mrs. Aubrey, Miss Aubrey, and, by no means an infrequent visitor, Mr. Delamere. The Aubreys were sad enough; and he endeavored to dissipate the gloom that hung over them by ridiculing, very bitterly and humorously, the pretensions of the would-be member for Yatton—the presumed writer (who, however, Kate protested, without giving her reasons, could never have been Mr. Titmouse) of the precious "Address." He partially succeeded. Both Aubrey and he laughed heartily as they went more deliberately over it; but Kate and Mrs. Aubrey spoke very gravely and indignantly about that part of it which related to the Established Church and the Protestant religion.

"Oh, dear! dear!" quoth Kate at length, with a sudden burst of impetuosity, after a considerable and rather melancholy pause in the conversation; "only to think that such an odious little wretch is to represent the dear old—What would I not give to see him defeated?"

"Pho, Kate," replied her brother, rather sadly, "who is there to oppose him? Pickering told me, you know, that he should not go into the House again; and even if he felt disposed to contest Yatton, what chance could he have against Mr. Titmouse's influence?"

"Oh, I'm sure all the old tenants hate the little monkey, to a man."

"That may be, Kate, but they must vote for him, or be turned out of—"

"Oh, I've no *patience*, Charles, to hear of such things!" interrupted his sister, with not a little petulance in her manner.

"Do you mean to say that you should like to see a rival start to contest your dear old borough with Mr. Titmouse?'' inquired Mr. Delamere, who had been listening to the foregoing brief colloquy in silence, his eyes fixed with eager delight on the animated and beautiful countenance of Miss Aubrey.

"*Indeed* I should, Mr. Delamere," cried Kate, eagerly; adding, however, with a sudden sigh, looking at her brother: "but—heigh-ho!—as Charles says, how absurd it is to fret one's self about it—about a thing we can't help—and—a place one's no more any concern with?" As she said this, her voice fell a little and her eyes filled with tears. But her little sally had been attended with consequences she had little dreamed of. Mr. Delamere took leave of them shortly afterward, without communicating a word of any intentions he might have conceived upon the subject to any of them. But the first place he went to, in the morning, was a great banker's, who had been appointed the principal acting executor of the Marquis of Fallowfield, a very recently deceased uncle of Delamere's, whom his lordship had left a legacy of £3,000; and 'twas to get at this same legacy that was the object of Delamere's visit to Sir Omnium Bullion's. For some time the worthy baornet—who had not then even proved the will— would not listen to the entreaties of the eager young legatee; but the moment that he heard of the purpose for which it was wanted, Sir Omnium being a very fierce Tory, and who had *lost* his own snug borough by the bill for *Giving Everybody Everything*, instantly relented. "There, my fine fellow, that's a piece of pluck I vastly admire! Sign *that*," said Sir Omnium, tossing to him an "I O U £3,000," and drawing him a check for the amount; wishing him with all imaginable and energy good speed. His eager excitement would not allow him to wait till the evening for the mail; so, within a couple of hours' time of effecting this delightful arrangement with Sir Omnium, he was seated in a post-chaise and four, rattling at top speed on his way to Yorkshire.

Sufficiently astonished were Lord and Lady De la Zouch, when he presented himself to them at Fotheringham; but infinitely more so when he named the object of his coming down, and with irresistible entreaties besought his father's sanction for the enterprise. 'Twas very hard for Lord De la Zouch to deny anything to one on whom he doted as he did upon his son. Moreover, his lordship was one of the keenest politicians living; and as for elections, he was an old campaigner, and had stood several desperate contests, and spent immense sums apon them. And here was his son, to use a well-known phrase, indeed *a chip of the old block.* Lord De la Zouch, in short, really felt a secret pleasure in contemplating the resemblance to his early self—and after a little demur he began to give way. He shook his head, however, discouragingly; spoke of Delamere's youth—barely two-and-twenty; the certainty of defeat, and the annoyance of being beaten by such a creature as Titmouse; the suddenness and lateness of the move—and so forth.

More and more impetuous, however, became his son.

"I'll tell you what, sir," said Lord De la Zouch, scarce able to speak with the gravity he wished, "it strikes me that this extraordinary and expensive and hopeless scheme of yours is all the result of—eh? I see—I understand! It's done to please—Come, now, be frank, sir! how long before you left town had you seen Miss ——."

"I pledge my word, sir," replied Delamere, emphatically, "that neither Miss Aubrey nor Mr. nor Mrs. Aubrey—whom, however, I certainly saw the very night before I started, and conversed with on the subject of Mr. Titmouse's address—has interchanged one syllable with me on the subject of my starting for the borough; and I believe them to be at this moment as ignorant of what I am about as you were the moment before you saw me here."

"It is enough," said his father, seriously, who knew that his son, equally with himself, had a rigorous regard for truth on all occasions, great and small—" and had it even been otherwise, I—I—eh? I don't think there's anything *very* monstrous in it!" He paused, and smiled kindly at his son—and added, "Well—I—I—we certainly shall be laughed at for our pains; it's really a madcap sort of business, Geoffry; but "—Lord De la Zouch had given way—" I own that I should not like to have been thwarted by *my* father on an occasion like the present; so let it be done, as you've set your heart upon it. And," he added, with a smile, "pray, Mr. Delamere, have you considered what I shall have to pay for your sport?"

"Not one penny, sir!" replied his son, with a certain swell of manner.

"Ah!" exclaimed his lordship, briskly—" How's that, sir?"

Then Delamere told him of what he had done; at which Lord De la Zouch first looked serious, and then burst into laughter at the eagerness of old Sir Omnium to aid the affair. Lord De la Zouch well knew that the old Baronet was infinitely exasperated against those who had robbed him of his borough! Never was " *Schedule A* " mentioned in his presence without a kind of spasm passing over his features! As though it were the burial-ground where lay one long and fondly loved! " No, no," said his lordship, " that must not stand; I won't have *any* risk of Sir Omnium's getting into a scrape, and shall write off to request him to annul the transaction—with many thanks for what he has done—and I'll try whether I have credit enough with my bankers—eh, Geoffry?"

" You are very kind to me, sir, but really I would rather—"

" Pho, pho—let it be as I say; and now go and dress for dinner, and, after that, the sooner you get about *your* ' Address ' the better. Let me see a draft of it as soon as it is finished. Let Mr. Parkinson be sent for immediately from Grilston, to see how the land lies; and, in short, if we *do* go into the thing, let us dash into it with spirit—I'll write off, and have down from town—a· hem!"—his lordship suddenly paused—and then added—" And hark 'ee, sir—as to that address of yours, I'll have no despicable trimming, and trying to catch votes by vague and flattering—"

" Trust me, sir!" said Delamere, with a proud smile. " Mine shall be, at all events, a contrast to that of my ' *honorable opponent.*' "

" Go straight ahead, sir," continued Lord De la Zouch, with a lofty and determined air; " nail your colors to the mast. Speak out in a plain, manly way, so that no one can misunderstand you. I'd rather a thousand times over see you beaten out of the field—lose the election like a gentleman—than win it by any sort of *trickery*, especially as far as the profession of your political sentiments and opinions is concerned. Bear yourself so, Geoffry, in this your maiden struggle, that when it is over you may be able to lay your hand on your heart, and say, ' I have *won* honorably '—' I have *lost* honorably.' So long as you can feel and say *this*, laugh at election bills—at the long faces of your friends—the exulting faces of your enemies. Will you bear all this in mind, Geoffry?" added Lord De la Zouch.

" I will, I will, sir," replied his eager son; and added, with an excited air, " Won't it come on them like—"

" Do you hear that bell, sir?" said Lord De la Zouch, laughing, and moving away. Delamere bowed, and with a brisk step, a flushed cheek, and an elated air, betook himself to his dressing-room to prepare for dinner.

Shortly after dinner, Mr. Parkinson made his appearance, and to his infinite amazement was invested instantly with the character of agent for Mr. Delamere, as candidate for the borough! After he and the Earl had heard the following Address read by Delamere, they very heartily approved of it. Mr. Parkinson took it home with him; it was in the printer's hands that very night, and by seven o'clock in the morning, was being stuck up plentifully on all the walls in Grilston, and, in fact, all over the borough:—

" *To the Independent Electors of the Borough of Yatton.*

" GENTLEMEN,—I hope you will not consider me presumptuous in venturing to offer myself to your notice as a candidate for the honor of representing you in Parliament.   In point of years, I am, I have reason to believe, even younger than the gentleman whom I have come forward to oppose. But, indeed, for the fact of his being personally a comparative stranger to you, I should have paused long before contesting with him the representation of a borough on which he has unquestionably certain legitimate claims.   The moment, however, that I had read his Address, I resolved to come forward and oppose him.   Gentlemen, the chief, if not the only ground on which I am induced to take this step, is, that I disapprove of the tone and spirit of that Address, and hold opinions entirely opposed to all those which it expresses, and which I consider to be unworthy of any one seeking so grave a trust as that of representing you in Parliament.   As for my own opinions, they are in all essential respects identical with those of the gentlemen who have, during a long series of years represented you, and especially with those of my highly honored and gifted friend Mr. Aubrey.   Gentlemen, my own family is not unknown to you, nor are the opinions and principles which for centuries they have consistently supported, and which are also mine.

" I am an affectionate and uncompromising friend of our glorious and venerable Established Church, and of its union with the State; which it is my inflexible determination to support by every means in my power, as the most effectual mode of securing civil and religious liberty.   I am disposed to resist any further concessions either to Roman Catholics or Dissenters, because I think that they can not be made safely or advantageously.   Gentlemen, there *is* a point at which toleration becomes anarchy; and I am desirous to keep as far from that point as possible.

" I earnestly deprecate putting our Agricultural or Commercial and Manufacturing interests into *competition* with each other, as needless and mischievous.   Both are essential elements in the national welfare; both should be upheld to the utmost; but if circumstances *should* unhappily bring them into inevitable conflict, I avow myself heart and soul a friend to the Agricultural interest.

"Gentlemen, I know not whether it would be more derogatory to your character, or to mine, to exact or give *pledges* as to my conduct on any particular measure, great or small, which may come before Parliament. It appears to me both absurd and ignominious, and inconsistent with every true principle of representation. One, however, I willingly give you—that I will endeavor to do my duty, by consulting your interests as a part of the general interests of the nation. I trust that I shall never be found uncourteous or inaccessible; and I am confident that none of you will entertain unreasonable expectations concerning my power to serve you individually or collectively.

"Gentlemen, having entered into this contest, I pledge myself to fight it out to the last; and if I fail, to retire with good humor. My friends and I will keep a vigilant eye on any attempts which may be made to resort to undue influence or coercion; which, however, I can not suppose will be the case.

"Gentlemen, this is the best account I can give you, within the limits of such an Address as the present, of my political opinions and of the motives which have induced me to come forward; and I shall, within a day or two, proceed to call upon you personally; and in the meanwhile I remain, Gentlemen, your faithful servant,

"GEOFFRY LOVEL DELAMERE.
"Fotheringham Castle,
"7th Dec., 18—."

Two or three days afterward, there arrived at Mr. Aubrey's, in Vivian Street, two large packets, franked "DE LA ZOUCH," and addressed to Mr. Aubrey, containing four copies of the foregoing "Address," accompanied by the following hurried note:—

"MY DEAR AUBREY,—What think you of this sudden and somewhat quixotic enterprise of my son? I fear it is quite hopeless—but there was no resisting his importunities. I must say he is going into the affair (which has already made a prodigious stir down here) in a very fine spirit. His *Address* is good, is it not? The only thing I regret is, his entering the lists with such a little creature as that fellow Titmouse—and, moreover, being *beaten* by him.—Yours ever faithfully and affectionately, DE LA ZOUCH.

"P.S.—You should only see little Dr. Tatham since he has heard of it. He spins about the village like a humming-top. I hope that, as far as his worldly interests are concerned, he is not acting imprudently. Our dear love to the ladies. (In great haste.)

"Fotheringham, 8th Dec., 18—."

The letter was read with almost suspended breath by Mr. Aubrey, and then by Mrs. and Miss Aubrey. With still greater emotion were the printed inclosures opened and read. Each was held in a trembling hand, and with color going and coming, Miss Aubrey's heart beat faster and faster; she turned very pale—but with a strong effort recovered herself. Then taking the candle, she withdrew with a hasty and excited air, taking her copy of the Address with her to her own room, and there burst into tears, and wept for some time. She felt her heart dissolving in tenderness toward Delamere; it was some time before she could summon resolution enough to return. When she did, Mrs. Aubrey made a faint effort to rally her; but each, on observing the traces of the other's recent and strong emotion, was silent, and with difficulty refrained from bursting again into tears.

Equally strong emotions, but of a very different description, were excited in the bosoms of certain persons at Yatton Hall by the appearance of Mr. Delamere's address. 'Twas Mr. Barnabas Bloodsuck (junior)—a middle-sized, square-set young man, of about thirty, with a broad face, a very flat nose, light frizzly hair, and deep-set gray eyes—a bustling, confident, hard-mouthed fellow—who, happening to be stirring in the main street of Grilston early in the morning of the 8th December, 18—, beheld a man in the act of sticking up Mr. Delamere's Address against a wall. Having prevailed on the man to part with one, Mr. Bloodsuck was within a quarter of an hour on horseback, galloping down to Yatton—almost imagining himself to be carrying with him a sort of hand grenade, which might explode in his pocket as he went on. He was ushered into the breakfast-room, where sat Mr. Gammon and Mr. Titmouse, just finishing breakfast.

"My stars—good-morning, gents—but here's a kettle of fish!" quoth Mr. Bloodsuck, with an excited air, wiping the perspiration from his forehead; and then plucking out of his pocket the damp and crumpled Address of Mr. Delamere, he handed it to Mr. Gammon, who changed color on seeing it, and read it over in silence. Mr. Titmouse looked at him with a disturbed air, and having finished his mixture of tea and brandy,

"Eh—e—eh, Gammon!—I say "—he stammered—" what's in the wind? 'Pon my soul you look—eh?"

"Nothing but a piece of good fortune, for which you are indebted to your distinguished friend, Mr. Phelim O'Something," replied Gammon, bitterly, "whose precious Address has called forth for you an opponent whom you would not otherwise have had."

" Hang Mr. O'Doodle!" exclaimed Titmouse; "I—'pon my precious soul—I always thought him a—a fool and a knave. I'll make him pay me the money he owes me!" and he strode up and down the room, with his hands thrust furiously into his pockets.

" You had perhaps better direct your powerful mind to this Address," quoth Mr. Gammon, with a blighting smile, " as it slightly concerns you;" and handing it to Titmouse, the latter sat down to try and obey him.

" That cock won't fight, though, eh?" inquired Mr. Bloodsuck, as he resumed his seat after helping himself to an enormous slice of cold beef at the side table.

" I think it *will*," replied Mr. Gammon, thoughtfully; and presently continued after a pause, with a visible effort to speak calmly, " It is useless to say anything about the haughty intolerant Toryism it displays; that is all fair; but *is* it not hard, Mr. Bloodsuck, that when I had written an Address which would have effectually—"

" Mr. Phelim O'Doodle owes me three hundred pounds, Gammon, and I hope you'll get it for me at once; 'pon my soul, he's a most cursed scamp," quoth Titmouse, furiously, looking up with an air of desperate chagrin, on hearing Gammon's last words. That gentleman, however, took no notice of him, and proceeded, addressing Mr. Bloodsuck,
" I have weighed every word in that Address; it means mischief. It has evidently been well considered; it is calm and determined —and we shall have a desperate contest, or I am grievously mistaken."

" E—e—eh? E—h? What, Gammon?" inquired Titmouse, who, though his eye appeared, in obedience to Gammon, to have been traveling over the all-important document which he held in his hand, had been listening with trembling anxiety to what was said by his companions.

" I say that we are to have a contested election for the borough; you won't walk over the course, as you might have done. Here's a dangerous opponent started."

" What? 'Pon my soul—for *my* borough? For Yatton?"

" Yes, and one who will fight you tooth and nail."

" 'Pon—my—precious soul! What a cursed scamp! What a most infernal black—Who is it?"

" No *blackguard*, sir," interrupted Gammon, very sternly; " but—a gentleman, perhaps even every way equal to yourself," he added, with a cruel smile, " the Honorable Mr. Dela-mere, the son and heir of Lord De la Zouch."

"By jingo! you don't say so! Why, he's a hundred thou-sand a year," interrupted Titmouse, turning very pale.

"Oh, *that* he has, at least," interposed Mr. Bloodsuck, who had nearly finished a disgusting breakfast; "and two such bitter Tories you never saw or heard of before—for, like fa-ther, like son."

"Egad! is it?" inquired Titmouse, completely crest-fallen. "Well! and what if—eh, Gammon? Isn't it?"

"It is a very serious business, sir, indeed," quoth Gammon, gravely.

"By Jove—isn't it a cursed piece of—impudence! What? Come into *my borough?* He might as well come into my house! Isn't one as much mine as the other? It's as bad as house-breaking — but we're beforehand with him, anyhow, with those prime chaps at Gr——." Mr. Bloodsuck's teeth chattered; he glanced toward the door; and Gammon gave Titmouse a look that almost paralyzed him, and silenced him.

"They'll bleed freely?" said Bloodsuck, by and by, with a desperate effort to look concerned—whereas he was in a secret ecstasy at the profitable work in prospect for their house.

"Lord De la Zouch would not have entered into this thing if he had not some end in view which he considers attainable— and as for money—"

"Oh, as for that," said Bloodsuck, with a matter-of-fact air, "ten thousand pounds to him is a mere drop in the bucket."

"Oh, Lord! Oh, Lord! and must *I* spend money too?" in-quired Titmouse, with a look of ludicrous alarm.

"We must talk this matter over alone, Mr. Bloodsuck," said Gammon, anxiously—"Shall we go to Grilston, or will you fetch your father hither?"

"'Pon my soul, Gammon," quoth Titmouse, desperately, and snapping his finger and thumb, "those cursed Aubreys, you may depend on't, are at the bottom of all this—"

"*That* there's not the least doubt of," quoth Bloodsuck, as he buttoned up his coat with a matter-of-fact air; but the words of Titmouse caused Mr. Gammon suddenly to dart, first at one, and then at the other of them, a keen penetrating glance; and presently his expressive countenance showed that *surprise* had been succeeded by deep chagrin, which soon set-tled into gloomy thoughtfulness.

www.ingramcontent.com/pod-product-compliance
Lightning Source LLC
Chambersburg PA
CBHW020240030726
47499CB00001B/7